SNAKESTONE AND SWORD

BOOK I OF

A CENTURION IN THE LAND OF THE FAE

J. E. Bruce

BooksForABuck.com
2011

BooksForABuck.com
October 2011
978-1-60215-160-4

This book is dedicated to the
centurions and soldiers
of Legio IX Hispana, 60CE

~Memento mori~

— I —

My name is Arrius Marcus Niger, and I am—or should I say I was Hastatus-Posterior, Centurion of the Fifth Century, First Cohort of the Ninth Legion Hispana, under the command of Quintus Petillius Cerialis.

I have seen and survived more than any decent Roman citizen and respected legionary should be required to endure. I have been to the end of the Earth and beyond and have, to my continued amazement, lived to tell the tale.

That I am still alive is, by no small measure, proof that the gods do listen—on rare occasion. Which gods, however, remain a mystery as I am left with the uncomfortable suspicion that my ultimate salvation was not the act of Mithras or even Opitulus, but rather some other equally powerful being or beings whose purpose in protecting me throughout my trials I, as a mere mortal, can only speculate.

By telling my story, my only hope is that you will heed the lessons of my experiences. You need not believe all—I know much of what I am about to retell is fantastic—and much goes against what we, as citizens of Rome, have come to accept as our role as civilizers of the world.

But understand this: there are places we should not venture; there are peoples we should not confront with our military might... and most of all, there are beings we dare not offend if we, and our Empire, is to survive.

To all who read this, I implore you—heed my warning.

I'm not sure how long I was unconscious. I wasn't even sure how I'd come to *be* unconscious but I awoke to the terrible and all too familiar sounds of battle, a blinding headache and the sudden realization that I'd been knocked out and left for dead—which is *never* an enviable position, unless of course you really *are* dead. Then it doesn't matter.

It's especially true if you're not sure who's winning and who's losing or what side of the shifting battle lines you had the fortune, or misfortune, of falling.

I've never considered myself a man favored by fortune—quite the contrary—I've earned everything I have and everything I am in the absolute hardest ways possible. I naturally presumed I was now lying helpless, but very much alive, behind the enemy line. So I began to curse—*silently*, mind you. There was nothing to be gained by alerting anyone that I was neither dead nor dying—well, to be honest I cannot vouch for the latter. I couldn't move; my breath was coming in agonizingly painful, ragged gasps and my eyes refused to stay focused—none of which boded well for my overall health, or my longevity.

But I was mad—*damned mad*. From the moment I'd enlisted as a boy of not quite sixteen and with the blessings of my wealthy patroness, I'd entertained visions of a glorious death. I'd assumed I'd take my always-worthy final opponent with me into the underworld, my youthful imagination stoked by tales of battle-scarred veterans who were always the heroes in their grandiose yarns. And to that end I'd worked—*clawed*—my way up through the ranks, never once relying on my benefactress's name to grease the wheels even though she'd urged me to do so, earning each step with blood—sometimes mine and in appallingly generous amounts, more often some other poor bastard's who was even more generous than me.

This honorable and, dare I say, *formidable* reputation proceeded me and I quickly became admired among the common soldiery as well as the officer corps as a centurion who was not one easily tempted by bribes and whom allocated work—and punishment—fairly. And while I was known to be fearless in battle, I was also recognized as being far from foolish, a centurion who did not squander the lives of his troops. My chest harness was soon thickly festooned with *phalerae*—the silvered bosses testimony to all that I was well on my way to much bigger and much better things.

That being said, perhaps my rise was just too meteoric *not* to catch the mordant gazes of the Fates.

So, instead of reaping the ultimate reward of all my hard effort, to eventually reach the highest rank a centurion could attain, that of *Primus-Pilus*, I found myself lying flat on my back in the watery edge of a bog. I was cold—chilled to the bone and my head continued to pound in painful cadence with the bash and clang of sword and armor.

As absurd as it was, I suddenly *wanted* to yell, to tell everyone to stop, to shut the hell up, that the clamor was simply more than I could bear—and I would have—except I found I couldn't speak. My tongue was firmly stuck to the roof of my mouth, wedged there, I'm sure, for safety's sake and no amount of coaxing could get it to release its death grip.

This was getting worse by the second.

I closed my eyes—it was too much effort to keep them open—and listened to the screams and bellows of men, of the near deafening clang of arms, the ominous warble of arrows in flight and the terrified wicker of horses—and entertained the cheery thought that at any moment I might be trampled underfoot by the violent ebb and flow.

Slowly, *ever so slowly*, the racket began to dim—the line had shifted some distance away; the sharp, individual sounds that made up the nonstop background clamor became blended into a constant, muffled roar by the dense baffle of trees, bog and brush.

I again opened my eyes and was intensely relieved to see large patches of pale blue sky through the fluttering canopy of bright green leaves. I could feel the warmth of the sun on me—so at least my face, chest, belly and shins were warm. My entire back was still soaking in ice-cold water. It was a very odd sensation—toasty warm on one side, freezing cold on the other.

Then again, it could have been raining. Of course, if it had been raining I wouldn't have found myself in this ugly predicament.

It *had* rained all night—buckets and buckets. Rain was the one thing this cursed land had in abundance. And if it wasn't raining, it was foggy. And if it wasn't foggy, it was sleeting. Sometimes it managed all three at the same damned time.

I'm not, by nature, a complainer. I'd learned long ago never to complain too loudly or too often about anything, lest my remarks be overheard by a superior officer who was just sadistic enough—or bored enough—to want to prove to me that things could be much, much worse. That said, I do *so* dislike being cold—even worse to be cold *and* wet. Perhaps it's true what the soldiers told me so long ago; perhaps I am still a creature of my homeland, perhaps even after all these years.

I've seen posts ranging from the hot, desolate deserts of Parthia—so reminiscent of the arid land of my birth—to the thick, heavily scented pine forests of Germania and the bitterly cold, rugged heights of the Cisalpina. This Britannia is, hands down, by far the *worst*. It's simply impossible to stay warm—or dry for that matter—just as the Greek explorer Pytheas had said. Perhaps that alone explained the equally foul nature of its inhabitants. Maybe they knew they'd been on the short end when it came to doling out territory and they'd never forgiven the slight.

Had it continued to rain, Cerialis's plans to launch a major attack would have been put on hold. It was bad enough to fight in the fog, or on soggy ground: it's utter madness to fight in the pouring rain. But the downpour tapered off towards daybreak. By mid-morning the sun had reluctantly come out, warming the cold, damp air just enough. A thick, waist-high mist quickly formed, cleverly obscuring the fact that the large meadow our scouts had reported days earlier as firm ground was in fact, at its very heart, *bog*—and now a rain-saturated bog.

The cavalry were the first to discover this. Of course, by then it was too late. The massed line of the enemy, who'd jeered and taunted us from the far side of the clearing, their true numbers hidden within the darkness of the surrounding forest, burst into laughter at the sight of our horses sinking to their bellies in the muck.

Our officers, realizing we'd been lured into a trap, drew the infantry back as the scouts desperately sought firmer ground, or a way around the bog, which meant we were forced to watch, helpless, as the panicked animals and their riders were hacked to pieces by a horde of screaming, half-naked savages—I can still hear the screams of the dying horses—a far more blood-chilling sound than anything a human throat could utter.

I cursed the sun above; I cursed the marshy ground below. But I saved my most eloquent curses for myself as I tried to roll over, to warm my cold-numb backside only to find that I couldn't feel my legs—or my arms. Actually, the more I thought about it, the more I tried to move, the more apparent it became that I couldn't feel anything below my chin and I wasn't one hundred percent sure of that, either.

Under other circumstances, this would have been very worrisome. I knew I should be scared—I'd seen with my own eyes men who'd been struck in just such a way that they never walked again.

But I *wasn't* scared. Not sure why—maybe I was just too damned cold and angry to be scared.

Then I heard an odd noise—a noise that sent a chill darting down my spine that had nothing to do with the frigid bog water I was lying in: a low, keening howl.

My wide eyes jerked towards the sound. The cheek-piece of my helmet cut off most of my side view but even so I soon spotted a blur of movement within the patchwork of shade and sun than made up the dense forest floor.

I blinked several times, hoping to clear my vision. It worked, but what I saw caused my heart to thump in brisk cadence to my labored breathing: the flash of movement solidified into a shaggy gray and black hound that slowly made its way through the carnage, the corpses—human and horse—alternately sniffing the ground, sniffing the bodies, lifting its elongated head and looking around, searching.

It was headed my way: slowly, but nevertheless unerringly.

War dogs are not uncommon—we employed them with great success in the snowy forests of Gaul and the rocky scarp of Bithynia where they were unquestionably fearsome in battle and relentless in running down enemies who'd somehow escaped our pila and swords. Unfortunately we Romans are not alone in appreciating the worth of dogs as terror weapons.

I suppose I should also confess here and now that I've harbored a private, but very justifiable fear of dogs since childhood and an even greater fear of being torn apart by a pack of them. So not unreasonably, I'd always given our war dogs—any war dogs in fact—along with their equally feral-eyed handlers, wide berth.

Now there was no choice and there was simply no point playing dead. The beast would see through my ruse, so I kept my frightened eyes on it as it came closer and closer, sniffing here and there.

Suddenly it stopped, lifted its head and fixed its gaze on me… and think me mad, but I swear it *smiled*.

My heart beat faster, *faster*.

Keeping its gaze locked with mine, it padded towards me, carefully, silently, picking its way with utmost care through the tangle of bodies, past enemy and Roman alike—all presumably dead as it paid them no mind.

It walked all the way around me, watching me, occasionally meeting my unblinking stare and all the while its nose was twitching. Seemingly satisfied, it sat down—several arm-lengths away—and stared at me with a disquieting intensity as it whined softly.

I was helpless, my injuries made it impossible for me to reach, much less wield my sword—even my dagger—and there was something *very* wrong with this dog—something within in its coppery eyes that made my already goose-pimpled skin crawl and I opened my mouth to scream.

The dog cocked its head to one side as if waiting for the ear-splitting shriek but when all I could muster was a soft gurgle, it looked… well, *disappointed*: almost but not quite sympathetic.

Then something drew the dog's interest. It rose and damned if it didn't begin wagging its feathery tail.

I reluctantly followed its intense gaze, flinching as it cut loose a single, sharp bark.

Instead of drawing a pack of its fellows, its call brought an unusually tall, heavy-set and dark-haired man out of a nearby copse of willow and into my limited view. He wore local garb and, spotting the dog, he approached, making his lumbering but determined way around the puddles of standing water that quivered, in the patchy sunlight, like pools of quicksilver.

As he stopped beside the dog, he pulled his sword from its sheath and I braced myself for the killing stroke. I would not show this barbarian fear—I refused to give him even that satisfaction and kept my gaze locked with his.

I'd been told once that as you approach the end of the Earth, seaward parts of the land spontaneously start to float, the ground spongy underfoot. Perhaps those tales were not so far off because whether I *was* truly at the geographical end of the Earth or not—and many claimed Britannia was at the end of the Earth, and beyond it, somewhere out to sea, the actual *edge* of the Earth—I was now facing the end of *my* Earth, *my* life, that this cursed bog was in fact the end of us all.

To my surprise, the man murmured something to the dog and the creature immediately bounded away.

The stranger then took a step closer and spoke directly to me.

I was surprised when I found I couldn't comprehend his gibberish; I'd quickly become fluent in the speech of those who lived in and around our garrison of Lindum, not to mention the disparate tongues of the surrounding tribes as language was a skill I was frequently called upon to put to use, but this man spoke an utterly unfamiliar dialect.

The fool repeated himself—*louder*—as if by doing so I would miraculously understand him.

I replied with an unyielding scowl and, "Kill me and be done with it!" but it was delivered in a very weak, raspy whisper, which rather diminished my attempt at bravado.

In truth he could do anything he wanted—no amount of bluster on my part could stop it. In fact I was fully prepared for what he might do, the least painful of which was to lop off my head, and my suspicions were solidified when, after repeatedly prodding me with his foot and finally coming to the conclusion that I was utterly defenseless, unable to move, he knelt beside me, placed his sword nearby—but well out of my reach even if I could have moved my arm—and looked me over, slowly, from head to toe as he shook his shaggy head.

This close up he was even bigger than I'd first thought. He was, in a word, *huge*.

I stared up at him with my vision graying around the edges as he untied the cheek-piece lacings under my chin then cautiously pried off my helmet, not an easy task with the neck guard firmly buried in the bog, painfully pulling my hair in the process. He set it aside and, grasping my forehead in a massive, gnarled hand, he very carefully turned my head this way and that.

My first thought was that it was his intent to see how much force he'd need to break my neck, how much resistance I might put up, but I quickly realized he was actually examining my skull, presumably looking for injury.

And damned if he didn't find it: he poked a spot just behind my right ear—it hurt, damned if it didn't and I grimaced. He must've have gotten the message because he promptly stopped poking, and, muttering something, released his hold. He then removed my greaves and finished by unfastening my belt.

He then *very* carefully rolled me onto my stomach—and out of the freezing water—not as a kindness to me, I had no doubt—he probably didn't want to kneel in the cold water. It would, after all, have an equally chilling effect on his intentions.

Face down in the damp, spongy earth, I heard more than felt him flip the water-swollen pteruges of my leather tunic up onto my lower back. He followed this by slicing his sword up the length of the woolen fabric that encased my left thigh. Then I heard the rest of the sodden fabric of my breeches go in a wet ripping sound.

I closed my eyes, knowing what was coming next. This was, after all, a common the fate of prisoners—the ultimate humiliation for the loser, as well as a way of releasing much of the pent up rage of the victor. It usually ended with a summary execution, sometimes during the climax of the act— *if* the prisoner was lucky.

If *I* was lucky. But, as I've already mentioned, luck was never a close friend of mine. Not even a passing acquaintance.

And I had seen with my own eyes what these people did to their war captives: hung from trees, drowned in bogs or burned alive, depending upon which of their terrible gods they wished to indulge.

I was startled out of that morose train of thought by a sudden pressure on my hip—his hand on my now bare backside—so, he was going to indulge *himself*, first.

Then I realized I'd *felt* his hand. Except for the seeping cold against my back I hadn't been able to feel anything below my neck for some time— which, under my present circumstances, is the way I would have preferred it to stay, where nothing beyond my head hurt. And if given a choice, I would have been happy even to forgo that.

My skin was ice-cold. His hand was warm—it almost felt good. *Almost.* And he was again talking to me. I thought that was *very* odd indeed—was he hoping for some friendly banter while he gratified himself at my expense?

A knee pushed its way between my legs, gently wedging them apart.

I grit my teeth and squeezed my eyes shut, while finding some small irony that I was about to die in such a manner.

I felt more pressure, against my thigh, followed by dull, throbbing ache that ran down my leg all the way to my toes—yes, I could now feel my toes. Another unhappy discovery.

Realizing he'd stopped talking, I actually managed to turn my head, just so, to look at what he was doing—even though I had a very good idea— morbid curiosity?

I was bewildered to find him not unlacing his trousers, but instead packing a bone-deep and gaping wound on my thigh with moss he was pulling from a pouch tied to his belt. I hadn't known I'd been wounded there. In fact, now that I thought about it, I wasn't sure *where* I was wounded—maybe just the leg, along with a blow to the head that had left me paralyzed. It would explain much.

He began talking again, softly.

I stared at him, annoyed that he hadn't gotten the hint that I couldn't understand him, and at the same time curious as to exactly what he was saying. Maybe he was talking to himself and not to me—I had no idea.

He snatched up my shredded, mud-soaked woolen breeches and, using his sword, cut them into several long strips, which he used to bind my leg.

Finished, he sat back on his haunches, met my gaze and smiled. He was ugly—even uglier than my tesserarius Aetius, and Aetius, as even he would admit, was *damned* ugly.

I scowled back. I was in no mood for pleasantries. *Do what you're going to do and be done with it!*

Instead, he shifted position. Grabbing my hip and shoulder, he rolled me again, onto my back and onto even firmer, dryer ground.

He snatched up a fistful of grass and used it to very gently wipe the blood and clotted mud from my face and throat, as if offering amends for what had already been done to me.

He moved on to the sticky clumps of grass and muck attached to my chest harness and underlying ring-mail shirt and in the process uncovered the shattered stub of a spear shaft. The tip was buried deeply in my flesh of my left shoulder; the splintered shaft tangled in layers of ring-mail, leather and wool.

He stared at it; so did I. We looked at each other and his expression mirrored mine: amazement that I hadn't died instantly. At the very least, I should have bled to death in short order.

Under other circumstances I might have attributed this miracle to incredible good fortune. But as it was, it wasn't—it just meant that I would live just long enough to die in another, far more creative and, most likely, *extremely* painful way.

They do say the Fates are a fickle bunch and I'd always believed it. I didn't need this kind of ironclad proof, thank you all the same.

I hoped he'd leave it be—but did he? Of course not. After some fumbling he began to carefully wiggle and tease the bits of shaft from the ring-mail loops. I won't say it hurt—it just felt... well, very odd. Almost... *ticklish*.

It took a while, but he finally freed the stub of the shaft from the ruined mail yoke then without so much as a 'by your leave', he grabbed the stub and gave it a yank hard enough that my shoulder was briefly lifted out of the muck, followed by a sickening *pop* as the tip suddenly came loose—my body weight doing most of the work. As I fell back, I reflexively clamped my teeth shut, damming up the agonized scream behind them.

He tossed the spearhead aside and stuffed his massive forefinger into the now profusely bleeding hole.

Believe it or not, he was actually doing me a favor—searching for more fragments. If there was any chance of the wound healing, any splinters had to be removed. But knowing this and experiencing it first, um, *hand,* were two *vastly* different things.

Up until that moment I'd like to think I'd managed fairly well, all things considered. But now I struggled against an overwhelming urge to vomit. I gagged then gagged again as the world around me began to spin, and the edges, which had suddenly darkened, began to close in.

He flicked the same bloody finger against my cheek, presumably to bring me back, and when that failed, he struck my face, once, twice. The blows stung, made my already abused head snap this way and that, but try as I might I just couldn't open my eyes.

He grabbed the yoke of my shirt, unintentionally grabbing the underlying and age-worn leather necklaces I always wore and again lifting my shoulders from the boggy ground, gave me a rough shake—more, I suspect, out of frustration than anything else.

I'd had a lot of close calls in my life, in my military career—a lot of *very* close calls. This time was different. This time I'd fully committed myself and there was simply no going back. Death had won the last battle—death always won and because I knew that, I'd always known that, now that it was actually happening, it was all rather, well… *anticlimactic?*

That being said, it's strange what you think about when you know your life is about to be extinguished like a guttering lamp starved of fuel. I've been told that in that last moment, when the heart stills and the lungs rest, people recall their achievements or perhaps regrets, while others remember loved ones. I had much to be proud of and equally much to regret, but loved ones I had none. So what did *I* think about? My damned necklaces— it felt as if he'd snapped the age-brittle leather cords when he shook me. Silly, really, I chided myself, to be upset about such as shortly I wouldn't care about anything.

He was talking again, but his now very angry voice was growing fainter, fainter, and finally faded out altogether and I found myself suddenly alone, surrounded by a soft-walled darkness. It wrapped itself around me and I was finally, *blessedly* warm.

So, this is death, I thought with calm detachment. *Not all that bad, really— could be worse. Much worse.*

I could be cold.

I snuggled down, making myself comfortable while I still could. I was, after all, going to be asleep for a very, *very* long time.

Perhaps it's best if I start at the very beginning in hopes that the better you know me, the more likely you'll believe me, at least in part. To that end, I will endeavor to be as accurate as possible, even if by doing so I expose to you the ugliness that has consumed most of my life.

I'm told I was born in Simitthu—although I have no proof of this—and of the most humble beginnings: the unwelcome but not altogether unexpected product of a legionary and local prostitute. Of my earliest years I have only the dimmest of memories, which is perhaps for the best. I do know that I was orphaned around age five—the result of a brawl between my mother and a customer who felt he hadn't gotten his money's worth.

Under most circumstances, this would have meant my death sentence as well. Instead the local auxiliary garrison adopted me—my mother had been very popular among the soldiery and many, upon hearing of her death, felt it was the least they could do. One, Marcellus, even made me a toy horse from scraps of cloth and told me when I was old enough, he'd teach me to ride a real horse, a simple task because as a Mauri, he assured me, I was a born horseman.

I never knew who my father was although my mother assured me he'd been a legionary; I strongly favored her, or so the soldiers said: blue-black hair and swarthy skin—although not as dark as my mother, who was almost as dark as the Nubian auxiliaries.

As a child I looked little like the soldiers my mother favored—for a woman of her trade she had always shown a remarkable weakness for the ones who were tall and light-skinned—and if they were also particularly well equipped, she was even known to offer a discount.

I always wondered if that hadn't been her downfall—that perhaps word had gotten out and her last client had felt slighted in the worst way when she demanded payment in full...

Something cold and wet touched my cheek.

Go away!

A moment later I felt it again and I very reluctantly opened my eyes.

Felix?

Instead of finding my faithful optio's face, or the worried face of one of my soldiers, looming over me, I saw wind-ruffled leafy branches.

That didn't tell me much, so I turned my head and instantly came face to muzzle with a dog—not just any dog, but the *same* damned dog. With the *same* damned-too-intelligent-for-a-dog stare. It had been curled up beside me—I have no idea for how long—sharing its warmth with me.

I immediately looked away, having no desire to show any gratitude to this creature, only to find that the sun was no longer high overhead. It was noticeably lower in the sky and its orange light streamed through the thick stand of birch and willow, low to the ground, setting the tufted marsh grass alight.

Along with this realization came another even more startling and not altogether happy one: *I'm not dead.*

I heard movement, followed by a grumbled, sleepy voice and the dog deftly leapt over me as if I was no more than a rotted log and trotted over to where its master had been napping, his back propped against the trunk of a nearby tree.

I took the opportunity to look around me; I'd been moved. Not far, but enough that I was no longer lying in the middle of a battlefield. More trees and scrub than I remembered and the surrounding clumps of grass hadn't been tramped down by hooves and feet and falling bodies.

Then I heard what sounded like a loud yawn and turned to find that the man had risen.

He stretched, gave himself a shake—like master like dog, I suppose— and trudged over to me, snatching up the neatly bound pile of my shed armor as he did so.

He gave me another slow, head to toe visual exam and motioned for me to get up. The nap had done him some small good because he now clearly grasped that I could not understand his tongue.

He motioned to me again, this time irritably, unsheathing his own sword and using it for emphasis.

It took me a moment to find my limbs: two were in good working order, two not, which was an immediate problem as the two that were able were on the same side. Nevertheless I tried to get up. I honestly did—if it had been his intention to do me immediate harm, he'd had plenty of opportunities. So I felt the least I could do was to cooperate, even if it meant I'd be walking to my own sacrificial execution. Anything was better than lying half naked on boggy ground—which was already starting to stiffen as the day grew short and the temperature dropped.

Finally, after I had made several feeble efforts just to sit up, each one failing worse than the last, he grabbed a fistful of my mailed yoke, leather tunic and woolen undertunic and jerked me to my feet.

My head swam, my vision blurred.

It had been quite some time since I'd been vertical—my body clearly preferred the horizontal, finding it far less problematic, so down I went— not all the way, mind you, just to my knees.

15

Thump!

The violent jolt reawakened every stiff joint, every bodily insult, every strained muscle. I cried out and almost passed out, again. Only my captor's firm grip on my mailed shirt kept me from falling face first back into the freezing mud.

He slipped his other hand under my uninjured arm, and again lifted me up. He was well over a foot and a half taller than me and quite burly and I suddenly wondered if he was an ogre. I'd heard about them. And he was certainly ugly, smelly and hairy enough to be one. But I'd always assumed an ogre would be even taller and much heavier.

Perhaps a stunted ogre?
Maybe the cold, wet climate has affected his growth?
And don't ogres eat people?
I guess I'll find out.

Runt or not, I was impressed with his size, not to mention his strength. I'm not a small man in any respect and right now I was dead weight, unable to stand much less walk on my own. But walk we did, despite my wounds, despite my protesting joints, despite my blurry vision and painfully pounding head, his arm around my waist, my good arm slung over his shoulder, the other bloodied and hanging uselessly at my side and the untidy bundle of my armor hanging off his back, clinking softly with each step.

If I'd entertained any thought of trying to overpower or disarm him, his cursed hound was there to remind me that escape was impossible. Even if I could run, it could outrun me; even if I could hide, it would find me.

And I swear, as it looked up at me, I sensed it was silently laughing at me, laughing at my idiocy for even entertaining such thoughts.

A part of me—the rational part—knew I was hallucinating. The dog's human-like behaviors and expression were nothing more than a fabrication of my own befuddled mind, the result of cold, blood loss and shock.

Nevertheless I felt the need to stick my tongue out at it.

The dog replied with a startled blink as if it hadn't expected me to react in such a vulgar way, and as ridiculous as it seems, that pleased me *immensely*.

It was hard going, hard enough for a fully able man, which I was not. The forest floor was dotted with large, shallow pools of ice-rimed water and what wasn't unstable, spongy bog was slippery rock covered with a lacework of vines that acted like tripwires and brambles that hooked and tore at my bare skin.

Thankfully, the ground began to rise out of the forested bog, slowly at first, then more steeply, and the trees began to thin. It was very close to twilight now and the low-angled light it made it hard to find safe footing among the loose rock and stiff bracken.

Even my captor lost his footing several times, which meant I ended up face down on the ground and close to blacking out from the pain, with him kneeling beside me, breathing hard. And each time it was more effort to rise; each time it took him several tries to get me up, to get my rubbery legs working again.

The dog had no such bother. It zigzagged endlessly among the large boulders that protruded like old bones from the sodden earth as if it was playing an obstacle game, dashing here and there after enticing scents, bounding ahead of us and disappearing into the bracken, only to reappear and return at a full gallop, its tongue lolling out of the corner of its mouth.

I despised it—I'd say I hated it, but I'd grown up in a culture where hate was reserved for only a very few and considered the purest form of respect; so, you hated Hannibal, you hated King Orodes, you hated Arminius and you *really* hated Mithridates—all worthy opponents. This creature on the other hand merited only simple, straightforward abhorrence. And I abhorred it with every fiber of my being—and it *knew* it—it *delighted* in it. I could tell because as we approached the summit of the hill we'd been climbing, it took to darting up behind me, flicking it tongue against the back of my bare thigh then flitting off again. I had no choice but to endure its teasing—*for now*. But I made a promise to myself that if I ever had the chance, I'd strangle the beast with my bare hands.

I was laboring for each breath and leaning heavily against my captor as we finally crested the hill. I had hoped we would stop—take a breather, to sit for a just a little while, maybe even lie down—I was so, so tired, and *cold*. Chilled to the very marrow of my bones.

I looked up at my captor, hoping he would understand, perhaps even take pity on me and let me take a well-earned nap. But his deep-set eyes were fixed on something else.

A knot formed in my belly as I followed his gaze: far below, tucked within a stand of oak and an outcrop of bare rock was a camp. The shifting mix of fire-glow and shadow gave the eerie impression that trees and boulders were dancing to some ghastly tune only they could hear.

And here and there, silhouetted against the orange flicker were the unmistakable forms of people.

A shiver ran down my spine.

The dog kited off down the grassy slope of the hill, barking, towards the camp, leaving no doubt in my mind that this was our destination and I abandoned all hope of rescue—no Roman had come this far, at least none voluntarily. This was the infamous Shadow Kingdom, domain of barbarians who painted their naked bodies blue, whose black-clad, wild-haired womenfolk were skilled in witchcraft and every bit as cruel and bloodthirsty as their male counterparts. It was from these hills we'd heard the echoing screams of their captives, seen the massive bonfires that lit up the night sky.

It was the point of no return.

Of course I really hadn't expected to be rescued—it had been evident, even before I was knocked senseless that our side was hugely outnumbered, that the enemy we were so damned eager to engage was just as damned eager to hand us an ignoble rout.

We were far better trained—we were Romans after all, the best-equipped, most disciplined soldiers in the world—but overwhelming numerical superiority, especially of this scope, will often tip the balance, and it had. The glorious battle we had prayed for, trained for, disintegrated in short order. If any of my troops had survived the day's slaughter, they had their own pressing problems to deal with—chasing after their missing centurion was probably not even on their to-do list. But that ever so small glimmer of hope, of reprieve from the sure and grisly fate that awaited me, no matter how unlikely that hope was, was what had kept me going.

Now even that glimmer was gone, snuffed out by grim reality: the dog loped back up the hill, followed by a dozen or so armed men carrying torches.

I began to shake—to my shame—uncontrollably. Tears rolled down my cold-numb cheeks, down my throat and under my mail, under my leather tunic and soaking the collar of my blood-stiffened undertunic. I squeezed my eyes shut and struggled to get control over myself, but I couldn't. I was too tired, too cold... and yes, I freely admit it, *too damned scared.*

I lost my tenuous command over my rubbery legs and slowly slid down the side of my captor and onto my knees.

He made no move to stop me, except to again prevent me from falling onto my face, or backwards, which would have meant a painful, if not fatal tumble down the rock-strewn slope we'd just climbed. His massive, gnarled hand grabbed the shoulder strap of my chest harness and held me there while I shivered and sobbed and my teeth chattered loudly in the cold.

Soon I was just too exhausted, just too bone-chilled to even manage that.

He gave me a gentle pat on the shoulder and murmured something to me—I have no idea what. By his tone, it sounded like he was trying to reassure me—I desperately wanted to believe he was trying to reassure me, but who knew?

So I just stared, utterly numb, as the men warily approached. I was totally undone—I knew it—worse, the men who now encircled me knew it.

One, a gaunt, black-haired man, exchanged words with my captor. I needed no translator to know I was the sole object of their discussion. Chary eyes flicked to me, back to him and again, back to me. I must have been a pitiful sight but what I saw in the torch-lit faces of that group was anything but pity.

The ogre pulled the pack of my armor from his shoulder and tossed it to the ground at the feet of the black-haired man.

Another man, with wild blond hair done up in a fancy topknot and a thick reddish beard knelt and after a moment's struggle, withdrew my helmet from the hastily bound pile and held it up for the others to see. A collective gasp followed.

Again the group turned their gazes on me as if not quite believing that a centurion's helmet, with its distinctive, transverse crest, and this pathetic, half-dead, bloodied and mud-caked creature actually came as a matched set.

Sensing he needed more evidence, the ogre stuffed his fingers down the neck slit of my tunic, grabbed the lead pendant that was my signaculum and held it up before my face for the others to see—not that any could read the identifying inscriptions on it, not that any tried. All recognized the small tablet for what it was: proof positive I was in fact a Roman soldier. These pendants were prized battle trophies among the savage races, just as barbarian torcs were among Romans. My chest harness bore two after all—and I had more, lots more secreted away back in my quarters in Lindum.

So, as they stared at it, I stared back at them and heaved for breath, each a hoarse, spasmodic gulp while I wondered who would claim the pendant as his—my bet was on the ogre.

Satisfied I was what my captor claimed, the group then turned their attention to my armor, specifically my helmet, which was passed around for closer inspection while a lengthy and heated back and forth ensued.

I reluctantly pulled my own watery gaze off the helmet and back to the argument and it slowly dawned on me that they weren't quarrelling.

They were bargaining, negotiating—to purchase *me*.

My stomach clenched. In my present state I wasn't fit to be a working slave, which left only one other logical option, and I briefly wondered if this ogre held a lucrative side job scavenging half-dead Romans for resale to the barbarians for ritual sacrifice, or if my situation was just fortunate happenstance—for the ogre.

Absurdly, as I saw a precious few coins exchange hands I felt strangely insulted. *Surely I'm worth more than that!*

The black-haired man uttered something, which, by its tone was clearly meant to be a command and motioned to me to rise as another hastily gathered up my armor.

The ogre saved me the futile effort; he scooped me into his arms as if I was a babe, heaping another humiliation onto my already wretched entrance.

I closed my eyes and prayed for the temporary refuge of unconsciousness, hoping that whatever they had planned, they would carry it out before I awoke. But I was denied even this brief escape by the repetitive bumping of my still pounding head against the ogre's knotty shoulder as he trudged down the hill, so I allowed my entire body to go limp—not to fool them, but because I was just so tired.

Finally, sensing we were no longer descending, I reluctantly reopened my eyes to find that we were now in the midst of the camp. A handful of women and children stood in silence as we passed. Some flicked me looks of hatred; others, close enough, spat on me but were quickly forced into a hasty retreat by the dog's low growls.

I was too weary to take offense at this ugly welcome, or to ponder further the dog's sudden possessiveness, except to wonder if I was to be its supper once they'd sacrificed me—ironic, when you think about it—and closed my eyes again. My aching skull was no longer being battered to a pulp and I felt the welcome tug of unconsciousness, but just as I was about to succumb to it, my captor stooped down. I instinctively tensed, fearing I was going to be dropped, then he took another step and stopped in his tracks.

Before I realized what was happening, I was placed on my feet and then held there while I was very unceremoniously—and I might add *very* painfully—separated first from my elaborate chest harness, then my ring-mail shirt and finally my leather tunic, leaving only my damp and filthy woolen undertunic to protect me from the freezing cold.

I was then frog-marched a few steps, roughly jerked to a stop and with arms held outstretched to either side, forced to my knees. The unnecessarily brutal handling made my mind spin and my left shoulder and leg throb anew.

The hands that had held me then released me and my arms fell limply to my sides. I remained motionless, barely breathing, chin on chest, eyes closed. I was very close to passing out again—actually hoped I'd pass out to be honest.

I sensed people all around me, walking around me, presumably staring at me. And there were voices—*angry* voices.

I also felt a flush of warmth, but far from feeling welcome, it burned my frozen, exposed flesh.

With great difficulty I lifted my head and opened my eyes.

At first all was a blur. Slowly, my surroundings came into fuzzy-edged focus. I was surprised to find that a copper brazier full of freshly-lit timber stood no more than a few arm-lengths away. Instead of rock and tree, heavy, woven-wool walls now surrounded me. It took my addled mind a moment to realize that I was inside of a tent with my captor and the black-haired man standing on either side of me. Three other men stood nearby, their eyes glittering in the firelight, and one, the stocky blond with the topknot eagerly fingered the grip of his sheathed sword and grinned at me.

So, I'm to be executed. Here and now—good enough.

The black-haired man said something—perhaps ordering me to get back to my feet—and gave me a painful poke in my flank with the tip of his own sword.

I shook my head—a near universal gesture of refusal. That only made my dizziness and blurry vision that much worse and now I felt intensely nauseous as well. I had a terrible urge to vomit, which I succumbed after he gave me another poke sharp enough to draw blood, in the process stepping just close enough for me to empty the remains of my last meal—presumably my *very* last meal—on his booted feet.

He leapt back with surprise and swore loudly.

Under other circumstances, I would have laughed, but at that moment all I could do is manage a small, defiant smile between dry heaves.

So it wasn't going to be the glorious death I'd long-fantasized about—at least my last act as a loyal Roman soldier was to royally piss off some gods-damned barbarian and ruin his fancy felt boots to boot.

He backed a little further away; keeping his eye on me, he knelt, grabbed one of the many fur pelts that were spread across the floor and angrily wiped his ruined footgear.

I wasn't given a chance to savor the moment. A hand lightly gripped my injured shoulder.

Flinching reflexively, I swiveled my head, expecting the ogre—or a knife at my throat—and found a red-haired girl kneeling beside me.

I met her gaze with bleak exhaustion, unable to muster up even a shred of curiosity what role she played in my upcoming execution. Maybe she was a sorceress come to reside over a sacrifice.

She looked up at my captor and said something. He muttered a reply, then I heard him trudge off. Even more surprising, she ordered the armed men—my presumed executioners—to follow, which they did unhappily, but without argument.

A moment later the cold draft that had been chilling my already thoroughly chilled backside stopped as the tent flap was tugged down.

She dropped her gaze to me and I tensed as she slipped a leather cord over my head and down, around my neck. I assumed it was a choke-cord—a garrote—but to my surprise she showed me that the thong held a pearly gray stone carved into the form of a tightly coiled snake, with the thong looped through a small hole in the center. It instantly reminded me of the sign of Amun, the ram-headed god and the talismans his followers wore. But I was not in Egypt and this amulet, I had no doubt, represented a far blacker belief.

Satisfied, she dropped the amulet against my gore-covered undertunic then picked up the signaculum, peered closely at the inscriptions on one side and then the other. Meeting my gaze with a nod, she hooked the neck slit with one finger and returned it to its proper place.

No sooner had it settled against my bare skin than I felt another tug at my neck. An instant later, my beloved bead and star necklace appeared before my watery eyes, cupped in her hand—I hadn't lost it after all and for some entirely stupid reason that gave me a shred of hope.

She fingered the small four-pointed star, the crude beads, smiled at me then as she had done with the signaculum, she carefully slipped the necklace back inside my undertunic.

"Don't be afraid," she murmured, touching my battered, blood and mud-smeared face with slim fingers, "you're with friends."

All I could muster was a slow, noncommittal blink. As far as I knew, friends didn't rough friends up, strip them nearly naked and leave them to freeze to death. At least, if mine did, I'd seriously reconsider their friendship.

She looked past me, said: "Bring some water," followed a moment later with an angry, *"Go, I said!"*

Whoever she'd been speaking to quickly exited the tent—I knew it because I felt a brief blast of cold air.

"Your wounds need tending." With that she rose and started for the brazier.

I honestly don't know what possessed me at that instant, because I did something really, I mean *really* stupid: I made a grab for her.

I missed of course and made an even bigger fool of myself by sprawling face first on hard-packed earth of the tent floor, almost tipping the fire pot over on top of me in the process—*thaaawhump!*

I heard a soft giggle and looked up to see her staring at me with an expression that was eerily reminiscent of the hound's—mocking, and yet not altogether hostile.

"I *was* going to help you lay down, but I see you've taken care of that."

I didn't even have the strength to move, so I just lay there, sprawled face down on the stony ground as the heat from the brazier burned my cold-numb skin.

Hands grasped my hip and far more carefully, my injured shoulder and rolled me onto my back, just far enough from the heat that it wasn't so painful—and in the process, I ended up on top of several thick pelts and was promptly covered with yet another fur.

"You need to warm up slowly—you're badly chilled."

I managed a sleepy murmur of agreement, but before I could fully savor the feel of the wonderfully soft pallet beneath me, the heavy fur on top of me and the smothering warmth of the fire-pot, an arm forced its way behind my neck and tipped my head forward.

A mug was pressed to my lips, followed by a terse command: "Drink!"

My eyelids fluttered and I found myself peering up at the unsmiling face of the black-haired man. *Oh… crap—*

"Drink!"

I swear he deliberately banged the mug against my teeth, in the process spilling some of the ice-cold water down my neck.

I gasped and what ended up in my mouth went down the wrong pipe and I started coughing.

"Fool!" I heard the woman's voice snap.

The supporting arm was hastily withdrawn and my head fell back against the pelts with a soft *thud.*

I was in no mood for this—not after the absolutely rotten day I'd had.

And oh, yes, I wasn't damned *thirsty,* either.

If I wasn't to be summarily executed, I wanted to sleep—couldn't they see that? Just a brief nap, *then* they could impale me on a spike or hang me from an oak—was that really so much to ask?

Obviously it was, because an arm again eeled its way under my neck to raise my head and again the mug was brought to my lips. "Drink—*come,* just a sip."

It was the woman's voice. I managed to open my eyes to find her kneeling beside me. It was her arm under me.

"You've lost a lot of blood—*come,* drink."

Something in her voice, in her encouraging smile made me not want to disappoint her—or cause her to withdraw her arm.

Fool! a part of my mind snarled. *She only wants you hale and hearty so she can drown you in a bog!*

I ignored the warning. I've always been utterly stupid around pretty women. Just like my mother had been around handsome men—a family failing.

I took a sip, promptly gagged then somehow managed to swallow it.

At her urging I took another sip. This one went down without any complaint but the whole ordeal was utterly exhausting.

"Let me sleep…" I whispered hoarsely.

And she did.

— III —

The need for small frontier garrisons ebbed and flowed along with the equally fluid borders, dependent upon forces far beyond my boyish understanding, upon politicians who'd probably never heard of, much less cared about Simitthu.

When the garrison was abandoned and the last of the soldiers left, I was orphaned yet again, left to fend for myself among townsfolk who had always despised and feared the legionaries and auxiliaries as the occupiers they were.

Now, with the soldiers gone, they turned on me.

I hid within the walls of the fort—I knew its maze of passageways better than any of the locals after all—leaving only at night to scavenge food from the scant discards of others. But there was never enough. My belly always ached, even more so when I smelled the cook fires of the nearby town. At times I was so desperate I was reduced to eating bits of plaster that had fallen from the ceiling or had peeled from the walls—anything to fill me up, even if I felt sick for days afterwards.

I cried a lot—I freely admit it. I was a child now twice deserted. I sorely missed the soldiers—even the ones who'd never known my mother and so felt no obligation to show me kindness. And one day, when I caught my own reflection in the basin I'd placed on the roof to catch rain water, I remembered what the soldiers had always told me—I looked like my mother. So I missed her terribly, too.

I was also scared—and not just of the townspeople or the pack of slat-ribbed dogs that loitered around the garbage dumps. The soldiers had spent many a night telling tales of the ghosts—the feared Lemures—who shared their barracks, of enemies who'd come back from the dead to seek their revenge. Of companions whose bodies had been left behind to rot and whose souls had been left to wander.

Now, I was alone with these angry specters—the night wind that swung doors on rusting hinges and rattled shuttered windows warned of their passage. The touch of their invisible fingers would wake me at all hours only to leave me to sob and shiver myself back into a fitful sleep.

Then one night, as I was hoping a dusty pool of brilliant moonlight would keep the ghosts at bay and trying to ignore the gripping ache in my empty belly, I came to the realization that if I remained much longer, I wouldn't have the strength to leave, much less have the strength to fight off the dogs that prowled the deserted garrison with increasing frequency, looking for an easy meal...

I awoke to the familiar and, I have to say, mouth-watering scent of roasting meat only to find the young woman leaning over me, dabbing my throat with a scrap of cloth that looked decidedly like a piece of my crimson undertunic. The last time I remembered seeing it, I was wearing it. This meant I wasn't any more, at least not all of it.

"So, you decide to rejoin us."

She didn't sound particularly happy about this and as I stared up at her, I was immediately struck by two things: first, I could understand her and had, since the moment we met and second, she was *not* speaking Latin. Not even a familiar patois.

What the hell?

I tried to open my mouth, tried to speak but my jaws were clamped tight and refused to relax. Only then did I realize I was in excruciating pain, and a heartbeat later why: my shoulder wound had just been cauterized with a hot brand.

I squeezed my eyes shut as my brain and stomach rushed to the same obvious conclusion at the exact same time: the cooked meat I smelled was my own flesh.

I wanted to vomit. I began convulsively hiccupping instead, which only made my shoulder hurt more with each violent, spasmodic jerk.

She popped her finger against my cheek. "Don't you dare pass out again—I need you to help me."

Still hiccupping violently, I reluctantly reopened my eyes.

She held a small wooden bowl in her hands. "This might hurt a bit."

Really? Can... can it hurt... hurt more than... than spit... spit roasting my... my shoulder?

She laughed. She actually *laughed.*

Startled, I squinted up at her not at all sure what she found so damned funny, unless of course she found amusement in torturing Roman soldiers, which was the prevailing consensus—

"I'm actually trying to help you—you'd prefer to slowly bleed to death?"

I managed a shake of my head. Given my druthers, I'd have opted for something quick and painless, thank you very much.

"All right. Now take a deep breath and hold it."

I didn't like the sound of this, but having little choice, I did what I was told—and let out a startled yelp as she poured the contents of the bowl onto my freshly burned shoulder. Whatever it was stung like hell and I found it hard to breathe and simply impossible to keep hiccupping.

"Here." She grabbed my left hand, pressed the wad of fabric into it and pushed my hand and the cloth against my shoulder. "Press down."

I obediently followed her direction—not sure why, as each time I did I ended up hurting even more. You'd *think* I'd learn.

After a moment or so, the burning sensation eased to a tolerably dull, throbbing ache and I actually managed to exhale.

"Better?"

Hell no! I nodded vigorously—I was sincerely afraid if I didn't, she'd do it again.

"Uh-huh." She gently pushed my hand aside and peeled the cloth away. What was left was, I assumed, her idea of a poultice. She peered at it and nodded, grabbed more of the cloth, which had been ripped into long strips, and began to bind my shoulder.

While she was busy, I glanced down at myself—or, should I say, what I could see of myself. The heavy fur covered my lower body, but my upper half was completely bare. *So much for my undertunic...*

She rocked back on her heels. "You might lose some movement in this shoulder—but at least now you shouldn't lose your arm." She wrapped her fingers around mine. "Here, squeeze my hand."

I did. Not hard. Just enough. I didn't want *her* crying out—drawing her menfolk along with some very wrong conclusions. We were doing just fine without them, thank you very much.

"Excellent."

I was pleased she was pleased—not sure why—and managed, "Thank you," in a thin, raspy voice that sounded nothing like me as she gently but determinedly pulled her hand free from mine because I didn't want to let go.

She again slipped her arm under my head and lifted it in order to tug another fur under me—a very pleasant feeling I have to admit—her arm was warm and soft and it meant she had to press herself against me. She was warm and soft too. And very, very pretty, with skin the color of the finest alabaster, flame red hair and bright green eyes.

I'd never seen eyes like this and I couldn't help but stare up at her. Even better: she didn't seem to mind me staring at her in the slightest. She smiled and wiped a lock of muck-stiffened hair from my face and I found myself desperately hoping these people would grant a condemned man one last desire.

Why men think these things at times like these I have no idea. But we do. Damned if we don't.

Her fingers slipped behind my right ear and I winced.

"There's not much we can do about this nasty bump..."

Well, for starters you could stop poking it—

"...it's no longer bleeding, but don't be surprised if you have a fierce headache for a day or two..."

I promise I won't be surprised at all—

"...and your vision might be a little blurry."

It had been, off and on, ever since I woke up in that cursed bog.

"…as for your leg—I'm afraid it's already starting to swell."

That wasn't good news.

"It needs to be drained."

That was even worse news.

"You passed out when we cauterized your shoulder—"

We? I glanced around. *Who's we?*

"—I'm afraid this might be even more painful."

My eyes darted back to hers. I couldn't help but grimace at the thought of something being more painful than what I'd just gone through. It wasn't that I was afraid of pain—fine, I am, what honest man isn't? It was the thought that I could go through what promised to be sheer and prolonged agony only to lose the leg anyway and then to be tied inside a wicker figure and set alight.

I again looked up at her suddenly no longer smiling face and realized my vision had blurred again. I blinked to clear it and felt something hot and wet roll down my cheek.

Gods, I was crying!—*me*, a highly decorated centurion! *Damn it*— "Kill me," I whispered hoarsely, "I beg you."

Using her thumb, she lightly wiped my damp cheek. "I'm not going to kill you, now, or in the future. You have my word."

Who says it's up to you? I saw a dozen or more people out there with murder on their minds.

"No one is going to harm you. You're safe with—"

There was a suddenly draft of cold air; the firelight flickered and danced.

She glanced over her shoulder and I followed her gaze. The black-haired man had returned and brought with him a grim-faced crone dressed all in black. Now *she* was *old*. Gray straggly hair, gray wrinkled face, bony hands. I'd never in my life seen someone *that* old—she looked like she'd died weeks, even months before and no one dared tell her.

The man was carrying a pitcher and mug; the decrepit hag held a fat leather bag.

The man set the pitcher and mug on the ground next to the brazier, flicked me a filthy look and without saying a word, turned on his heel and left.

The crone remained, staring at me just as a viper would size up a tasty vole.

"So, you're awake," she finally said in a voice as thin and dry and brittle as the rest of her. "Pity. It would've been easier for everyone if you'd remained unconscious. But...we'll make do, yes?"

I wasn't sure I cared to make her life easier. I seriously doubted if she cared about my life at all.

I glanced around; as far as I could tell, I was alone with the two women—neither of whom appeared armed, which seemed rather imprudent on their part. Perhaps they had no idea what a legionary was capable of doing, even a badly injured one, given the proper motivation.

The crone grinned—not a pleasant thing on such an aged hag. Her thin lips drew back, adding wrinkles to her wrinkles and exposing a mouthful of rotting teeth. Not only that, but I had the sudden and decidedly disconcerting feeling that she was looking *into* me, not just *at* me, as if her bony fingers were inside my head, poking and prodding at my brain and I instinctively recoiled. Only then did I realize that my right arm and both legs were staked to the ground, wrist and ankles bound in leather thongs that were tied securely around thick wooden pegs that in turn had been driven into the hard, rocky earth.

While I'd been thoroughly preoccupied with the crone, her young accomplice had carefully eased my free arm away from my left side and tied *it* to a peg. I was now positioned like a freshly tanned hide stretched tight and left to dry.

I kept my eyes locked with the hag as she slowly circled me, until I could turn my head no further. Every muscle in my body drew taut. My breathing quickened.

As if sensing my growing panic, the young woman filled the mug with the contents of the pitcher. "I want you to drink this—*all of it*, understood?" She again slipped her arm under me, tilted my head forward and brought the mug to my lips.

One whiff of its contents and I jerked my head away—it smelled gods-awful.

The crone, who'd knelt behind me, grabbed my head and pressed on my jaws with surprising strength, forcing my mouth open. "Drink it voluntarily—or we'll force it down your gullet."

I drank; gods know how as it tasted even worse than it smelled. But no sooner had it hit my stomach than I felt a warm glow in my belly, which rapidly spread outwards.

The woman filled the mug again, but before she brought it back to my lips, she produced a small yellow lozenge. She forced it into my mouth, past my now oddly numb lips, and followed up with the mug. "Drink."

When I hesitated, the crone slapped the side of my head and I winced. *Ow!*

"Drink, my young fool—it will help with the pain."

Now that sounded like something I could get fully behind, so I quickly emptied the mug, swallowing the very bitter-tasting lozenge in the process. I was then offered another mugful, which I obediently gulped down.

"Enough," the crone said, her voice suddenly and oddly distant.

I vehemently disagreed—I was still conscious and still in agony, although I have to admit, not quite as much agony as before. I had no desire to be awake for what I knew was coming next. *How 'bout letting me... me be the judge...*

"Let it work."

I looked around. Everything was spinning—walls, women, tent pole, the fabric roof above—slowly wheeling around me like some strange amusement.

I blinked, blinked again, but everything continued to rotate.

I heard the women talking—they sounded to my ears like they were underwater. Not only that, but my body had gone completely to jelly, even my bones felt like mush. *How... odd.*

A bony finger popped my cheek. My only response was to blink.

"He's coming along nicely... *yes.* It shouldn't take much longer."

I wondered who the crone was talking about—probably one of her equally ancient lovers. *Eeeeuuuu. Why did I think of that?* I started to giggle.

"Can you feel this?"

I continued giggling—I still had no idea what was so damned funny. Which was actually funny in itself.

"Obviously not," the crone answered. "He's ready."

The thick fur that had covered my lower body was suddenly flipped over my head. Startled, I stopped giggling and snarled, *"Hey!"*

"That wasn't nice," I overheard the young woman say.

"He's ugly. I'm tired of looking at him."

The fur was peeled back to expose my face. I stared up at the crone. *You wanna talk ugly—*

She flicked her bony finger against my cheek again. *Hard.* I could tell by the loud *pop.* But it didn't hurt in the slightest—*hah!* I stuck my tongue out at her.

She blinked—just like the dog. In fact she looked a lot like the dog, with its wiry coat of gray fur. And that set me off giggling again.

The hag shook her head and looked away. "Make sure you wash his thigh thoroughly..." Her eyes narrowed to slits. "*Just* the wound area, all right?"

I immediately shifted my amused stare from the crone to the young woman, who at least had the decency to look rather ashamed of taking liberties with my present state of numbness before she resumed her task with renewed vigor, albeit with a far more limited scope.

My body was feeling heavier and heavier with each thudding heartbeat as my giggling slowed to an occasional, spasmodic titter.

Feeling suddenly and strangely disconnected, I realized I must look like one of those peculiar wind-up mechanicals. I'd seen one once, can't remember where—Alexandria?—that was in the process of winding down, slower, slower... *slower*, and I had to wonder, again in that sense of utterly calm detachment, what would happen when I stopped completely.

The young woman murmured, "That's the best I can do."

"Then let's get started," the hag grumbled and picked up a very wicked looking blade.

That stopped my fitful tittering cold. *Where the hell'd that come from?*

I stared at the knife as she turned it over the brazier, intrigued by its peculiar transparency all the while vaguely aware that the lower half of my body was suddenly freezing.

In fact the more I thought about it, the more it made sense that I was completely naked—not that I had *anything* to be ashamed of, mind you. But it was still rather embarrassing—and *damned* chilly.

The young woman had resumed her unabashed staring and didn't seem unduly disappointed despite the cold. Then, as if sensing my attention, she very reluctantly slid her gaze back to my face. "What's your name, Centurion?"

"*I'd opt for braggart,*" the old woman muttered, briefly drawing my sidelong squint.

I'm cold, damn it!

"Mine's Sifrie."

She was clearly waiting for me to respond in kind—perhaps she was hoping to distract me from what the crone was about to be up to, or what *she* had been up to. But as I stared up at her I realized I wasn't sure. I knew I used to know it, but...

She wiped a lock of hair from my forehead then stroking my cheek murmured, "*Think.* What's your name?"

I frantically rifled through my memories, desperate to answer, desperate to please her by answering, but everything was a muddle, everything

31

seemingly just out of reach. And the harder I tried to remember, the further away everything moved.

Suddenly it wasn't just a matter of wanting to please her—I very much needed to know my name—and redoubled my efforts, snatching madly at random memories as they swirled past, hoping to shake loose the answer.

Just as I was about to panic, just as my teeth began to chatter, it came to me: "Arr... Arrius M-m-m-mar... cus... N-n-n-niger."

"That's a mouthful," the crone grumbled. "Unlike other parts of you."

The young woman scowled at her; the hag glared back. "Well it's true, isn't it?"

I watched their exchange as if it had nothing to do with me. My mind was on something else—was *somewhere* else. I could hear my mother's voice, calling to me—

"Arri?"

I flinched, startled by the oh-so familiar, oh-so angry voice.

—where in hell are you?

My eyes watered in an intense mixture of longing and fear. Tears spilled out and rolled down my face—that was the voice she used when she was going to beat me.

"Oh, *great*," the crone sighed, "*now* look what you've gone and done."

The younger woman gently wiped my cheek as her eyes flicked to the crone. "Are you sure we can't wait until we—"

"No—or we'll lose him for sure."

I didn't have a clue what she was talking about or whom she was referring to, nevertheless it didn't sound good for the unfortunate man.

The hag turned back to me with an odd look in her eye. "Ready?"

Ready? For wha—! I screamed and I kept screaming at the top of my lungs... until a wad of my own filthy tunic was stuffed into my mouth, like a cork in a bottle and with the same result damming results.

"Perhaps he wasn't *quite* ready," the crone admitted, glancing back at me. I was wide-eyed and still screaming—in my head. The gag was a very effective muffle against the gutter obscenities I was hurling at her. All that came out was a faint, wavering groan.

She returned to her gruesome work; I felt every cut she made and I struggled to free my hands and legs of the bindings but there was simply no play, no give in the tethers—I was spread-eagle and stretched tight.

Then, as I was telling myself it *couldn't* possibly get any worse, of course it *did*: I felt something *pop*—an excruciating, sudden release of pressure that left me gagging against the gag.

It was yanked from my mouth an instant before I gagged again.

When I didn't resume my screaming—hard to scream when you're alternately heaving and hyperventilating—they left the gag out, which was good, because with each spasmodic heave, each corresponding violent gasp air, what was inside of me rushed to the outside by the most expeditious means.

I was halfway between consciousness and passing out, soaked in my own urine, blood, filth and vomit, just awake enough to feel everything, hear everything, just gone enough not to be able to do a damned thing about it besides the occasional protesting whimper and sobbing moan.

I have no idea how long they worked on my leg... it seemed like an eternity—so long in fact that I started to think that perhaps I was indeed dead—*had* died on the battlefield. That *this* was death. Not some nice warm, dark place, but *this*, with Harpies tearing flesh from my body for eternity.

But then somewhere within the fog, the ceaseless agony, I heard a voice say, "I think that's the worst of it and I'm not sure he can take much more."

Sometime later, a cool hand pressed against my throat, my forehead. My eyelids fluttered in response only to find the blurry visage of the old woman leaning over me. "Go get some cold water."

I thought she was speaking to me. So I tried to get up.

She slapped the side of my head. "Not *you,* fool."

"Ow—"

She patted my arm—an almost motherly thing to do. No one had done that to me since I was a child, since my mother—

Damned if I didn't start to weep. Big, heaving sobs.

"Oh, *hell.*"

She gently lifted my head and pillowed it in her lap. It wasn't as soft as the furs, but it was strangely more comfortable. She stroked my sweat-drenched and filthy hair, my clammy cheek, tenderly, just as my mother had done after she or one of her frustrated customers had beaten me almost senseless.

"There, there... such a fuss... you're going to be all right," she murmured.

My mother used to say that, too.

My head was lifted again, and again a mug was pressed to my lips. "Drink—water this time."

I did, in between spasmodic sobs.

"Enough."

The mug was withdrawn. The heavy fur cover was replaced, covering me from toes to chin. I was warm. I felt strangely safe, cradled in my mother's lap. Safe enough, exhausted enough, that I felt myself slipping, effortlessly, into sleep.

— ii —

I awoke to find myself alone, still spread eagle, still bound and covered with a fur, my left cheek resting against another warm pelt. Only this pelt *moved* when I lifted my head to look around—and I suddenly realized the hound had been curled up beside me, just as it had done in the bog... how long ago?

It rose and stared down at me.

Then, the wiry gray fur turned into frizzy gray hair and gray wrinkled skin. With a blink, its peculiar eyes became human eyes, while the elongated face flattened and its narrow muzzle turned to a crooked nose and flop ears formed the collar of a cloak.

I blinked and blinked again, then a thought popped into my head: *you're hallucinating*—it seemed a very reasonable assumption, all things considered, only the thought strangely didn't seem to be mine. It was just *there*.

Before I could ponder that very odd feeling, the crone asked, "Are you thirsty?"

I was, desperately so, and when she held a mug of cold water to my lips I drank greedily, guzzling as much as I could without choking.

She filled it again then slipped another lozenge into my mouth—I tried to spit it out, but she held my jaws shut and brought the mug to my lips, releasing her hold as she did so. "Drink."

I emptied it in several loud wincing gulps, swallowing the bitter lozenge in the process.

"That's enough." She ran her fingers across my forehead and I felt instantly, terribly drowsy. "Now go back to sleep," she murmured as my eyelids fluttered, "you won't remember any of this."

But I did, along with the hazy recollection of being struck hard, hard enough to loosen teeth, blur vision and make my head ring, accompanied by the metallic taste of blood in my mouth—the blow to the head that almost killed me on the battlefield... and with it came a glimpse of blond hair and reddish beard accompanied by an angry voice, a voice that hissed in my ear that given the opportunity he'd gut me like he'd done so many other Romans—emphasizing the threat by running a finger across my naked belly. Then another and even more frightening threat: if I ever showed the slightest attraction to Sifrie or encouraged *her* attentions, he'd publicly castrate me—that that was the accepted punishment for slaves who dared to think, or worse, act as if a high-born woman was anything other than untouchable.

I had no reason to disbelieve the threat—it was a common and widespread form of punishment for such behavior.

And then, as if the Fates themselves felt the need to test and torment me further, Sifrie appeared before me wearing nothing more than a beguiling smile—and despite the threat, or maybe because of it, I was unable to look away, was unable to refuse her when she whispered *her* intentions in my ear. I somehow managed to satisfy both of us while she groaned and twisted beneath me, her fingers digging deeply into my flesh, drawing blood...

Of other voices curling around me like tendrils of a heavy mist, of feeling like I was floating, of something deliciously cool surrounding my pounding head. Of finally being prodded awake by an odd tickle, like being touched ever so lightly by tiny fingers.

Sifrie? I very reluctantly opened my eyes... to find myself surrounded by a teeming mass of scorpions.

They were everywhere: scuttling over the mounds of pelts, clambering up the woolen walls, crawling around the tent poles—one hung from the hair of the old crone who was kneeling beside me tending to my shoulder. Still others clung to her tattered clothing like grotesque, squirming ornaments.

These weren't the brown scorpions that I'd played with as a child, the kind that could inflict a painful but not permanent reminder to be more careful; these were the fat yellow ones, the ones that could kill a grown man with one sting—not immediately, mind you, but after days of agony.

I'd seen it happen to those careless enough not to shake out their bedding before crawling under the covers, unwise enough to go barefoot outside in the cool of twilight while not bothering to look where they stepped—or unlucky enough to have become an obstacle to someone else's ambitions.

The crone was utterly oblivious to our shared peril as she leaned over me. The scorpion in her hair was huge and its twisting grasp tenuous at best. I wanted to swat it away before it fell on me but found I couldn't move, couldn't lift my arms.

"Get away from me!"

"*Hush,* fool, I'm almost finished," she replied, heedless to the danger, her fingers brushing perilously close to the scorpion as she tucked a wispy lock behind her ear.

Its bulbous tail coiled tightly in response.

I glanced around as I heard the soft rustle and to my horror realized that my frightened cry had drawn the scorpions' collective attention and they were converging on me from every corner of the tent, boiling out from under the pelts, which rippled in response to the rushed exodus. Some had already crawled onto me, up over my flanks, up my legs, along my outstretched arms, pouring onto my chest, scraping and scratching at my flesh, their tails tightly arched, pinchers snapping: a surging yellow tide rolling towards my face from every direction.

I screamed and kept screaming until my mouth was full of them and I began to choke.

Something grabbed my jaw and a clear, unruffled voice seemed to radiate from the very center of my brain: *Listen to me—LISTEN!* The fingers gave my head a painful snap. *There aren't any scorpions!*

Still choking on the crawling, seething mass, I stared, wide-eyed up at the crone—*Are you mad?*

You're hallucinating—

LIAR!

The grip on my jaw tightened. *Listen! You're feverish—it's making you see things that aren't really there—*

I know scorpions when I see them!

Then the disembodied voice said again: *Focus on me—focus!*

I can't breathe! I'm choking—HELP ME!

Something cool pressed against my forehead, it had the feel of human flesh and with it came the almost instantaneous and terrifying sense of sliding towards darkness and I shrieked, *NO!*

I'm trying to help you...

I tried to scramble away, found my limbs useless.

Calm down—don't fight me.

I kept sliding, closer, closer to an unseen precipice, covered in a living, seething shroud of scorpions. *HELP ME!*

The scorpion was now barely clinging to a tendril of her wiry hair.

Please help me!

I'm trying... The voice was fading, now barely a whisper.

DON'T LEAVE ME!

She glanced away and the sudden, unexpected movement sent the creature flying. It hit my cheek and fell, scratching and twisting onto the pelt below my head and once righted, it instantly reacted, plunging its stinger into my neck.

Agony shot through me. My chest locked up, my back arched and my limbs cramped against the tethers to the point I was sure either the leather would snap or my bones would shatter.

Then another voice, a frightened voice... and very, very faint: *"Hanni, cut him loose—quick! He's having a convulsion..."*

Sometime later—or maybe before?—I couldn't keep track of time, events no longer fell in neat chronological order; everything was jumbled— I awoke to find my body being rocked back and forth, heard the distinctive snap and groan of harness, the clatter of wheels and hooves on pebbles.

I was on my right side, with my ankles bound together and my arms tied behind my back. My left shoulder and leg were throbbing painfully.

The last thing I was sure about was being inside a tent and being told to drink something. Clearly that was no longer the case. *So where am I?*

I tried to lift my head, look around only to find myself staring into an impenetrable darkness and I had a sudden, horrible thought—*my eyes have been gouged out!*

The realization hit my gut, my bloodstream and I tried to scream only to find my mouth gagged. So I thrashed about until a hand grabbed my shoulder—my injured shoulder—and gave it a painfully rough shake.

"Stop it or I'll disembowel you here and now and be done with it!"

The whispered threat made me struggle all the more—terrified and trussed up like some... *sacrificial animal,* unable to even see the death stroke, much less fight it off—I felt the knife slide across me and I panicked—and began writhing against the bindings, screaming against the gag—both utterly useless, which only added to my terror.

"Let go of him!" another voice, an angry female voice whispered. *"Damn you, Kyrou, you're only making it worse!"*

The fingers angrily released their grip but not before giving my shoulder one last furious shove.

An instant later the blindfold was jerked down and I found myself blinking madly at the unexpected glare and unable to catch my breath.

A blurry face loomed close.

I shrank back. *No!*

"Arri?"

The face slowly came into focus and I found myself staring up at an old woman's withered face.

I was shaking uncontrollably, every muscle twitching violently.

"You're all right, Arri—calm down." Her fingers grasped my chin. *Listen to me.*

I could barely hear the unspoken command over the rapid pounding of my heart and my labored, spasmodic gasps, much less obey.

"Calm. *Down*."

I tried. I just... couldn't. The gag made it hard to breathe, my hands were numb from the bindings, my shoulder felt as if it was on fire and I had no idea where I was, no idea who she was or why people were threatening to kill me. In all my life my memory was the only thing that had never abandoned me, even though there were times when I wished I could forget certain things—now I was completely lost and utterly alone.

She tightened her hold on my jaw, leaned close and forced me to look at her, eye to eye. *"Think! Do you remember me?"*

I didn't answer immediately but instead tried to look past her, hoping something, anything would look familiar.

Her bony fingertips dug into my cheeks, puckering my lips and drawing my wide-eyed, frightened gaze. *Listen to me.* "Think!"

I couldn't—I was just too scared, too befuddled to fix on anything.

She turned, spoke to someone else: "I was afraid of this, the fever—"

"Then he's no use to us. Slit his throat—"

"That's your answer to everything, isn't it, Kyrou? Slitting throats!"

That was the woman again, but something in her voice, the look in her eyes as she turned back to me warned me *she* was scared—of what I wasn't sure, and if she was scared, I knew I was in serious trouble, so I desperately *tried* to remember, tried to place her within the million puzzle pieces of what, at that moment, constituted my shattered self, hoping if I could just remember her—*just her*—maybe everything else would fall into place, that maybe, just maybe she'd be able to take the terrible pain and all-consuming terror away.

That maybe, just maybe, I *wasn't* insane, but each time I tried, fragments of recall that seemed close enough to grab went scattering, panicked at the lightest touch.

You're not insane, Arri, just very frightened and very, very confused. She caressed my chin, gently combed her fingers though my hair. *Listen to me. Focus on me and me alone.*

Her wordless voice rolled around inside of me, like a living thing trying to find its way out—or perhaps trying to help me find my way out of this hellish maelstrom where nothing made sense, nothing looked familiar—where I didn't even know who I was.

I stared into her eyes, my vision blurring. *Help me!*

I felt her arms encircle me, stopping me from falling into an abyss that had suddenly opened up around me, a vast, yawning darkness into which I knew, if I fell, I would never return.

I was utterly helpless, which only added to my blind panic. *HELP ME!*

I'm trying. But you must help me—you're safe, you're with me and no one's going to hurt you, I promise. Now, concentrate… imagine solid ground under you. Come, try. You simply must try.

I'm not sure how I did it, but I somehow managed to put everything I had into it and the surrounding chasm began to shrink, slowly, but perceptibly with each rapidly thumping heartbeat.

Concentrate…

The darkness vanished as abruptly as it had appeared. I felt something firm under me and with it came another revelation: *I do know you!*

Intense relief flooded into her age-bright eyes and she breathed, "Good. Now, if you stop biting down on the gag, I'll remove it, agreed?"

It took me a moment and my full attention to unlock my jaws.

"Promise not to make a sound?"

I nodded; Kyrou and his knife were nearby after all—if he couldn't slit my throat or my belly, he might satisfy himself by cutting out my tongue.

She pulled the rag from my mouth.

"There," she soothed. "Much better, yes?"

Honestly? No. I could *not* stop shaking.

She smiled as her fingers ran over my left cheek, her light touch stirring up a dull ache and I couldn't help but grimace.

Her sharp eyes darted away, came back to me. "I'm sorry we had to blindfold and gag you, but we had to pass close by a settlement not long ago. You've been running a high fever for days, it's made you see things that aren't real. I'd hoped you'd remain asleep, but…"

Days? I looked and found that I was surrounded by high, rough plank walls of what looked to be a cart. I was covered by a heavy pelt and I lying on a bed of furs and what smelled like moldy straw. Two men were seated nearby, one blond and bearded, with a bruise-red eyelid and cheek; the other with long and lank black hair. They had their backs pressed against the planks, and they were staring—*glaring* at me. Both had their unsheathed swords lying across their laps as if expecting attack at any moment—or the need for murder.

One, I had to assume, was Kyrou. I would have liked to have known which, although in truth it didn't matter. Both looked as if they were mentally reviewing how to slice and dice a Roman, *slowly*, in six easy steps.

I looked back at the old woman. *I don't—*

39

"We were afraid you might call out, reacting to something that wasn't real and they'd hear you—they're not our friends—they'd take you, we couldn't have that, now could we?"

Maybe not your friends—

"Durotriges."

Oh. I'd never met a Durotriges—but from what I'd heard, I wasn't missing much. Durotriges, much like Iceni, favored their friends medium-rare and their enemies well done.

"Thirsty?"

My tongue felt like dried leather, my lips gummy—the gag had sapped every bit of moisture from my mouth, leaving it tasting like... well, a filthy rag.

I nodded and she pressed a water skin's teat to my lips and I began sucking eagerly, frantically, gulping down as much water as my parched throat could manage.

She pulled it away before I was finished quenching my terrible thirst, quickly slipped yet another lozenge in my mouth, gave me the teat again and allowed me another gulp, just enough to swallow the lozenge but no more. "That's enough—your belly can't handle too much right now." She gave it a pat for emphasis; to my relief it felt whole, albeit extremely tender, and my eyes darted to the two men.

As tempting as it was, I decided *against* sticking out my tongue at them—I might not get it back.

She peeled a dry cloth from my forehead, pressed her bony hand to my throat and chest as she gave me a troubled look. "You're still running a high fever." She squeezed some of the water from the skin onto the strip of cloth, thoroughly soaking it and used it to dab at my face and throat, then she draped it back across my forehead as I looked up at the overcast sky.

From my limited vantage point it appeared to be mid-morning, but it might have been mid-afternoon.

"I want you to go back to sleep, all right? We've still got a long way to go before making camp."

Meaning I was being taken further and further north, or west... deep into the black heart of this demon-haunted land and I felt a lump form in my throat—escape was now unthinkable.

I flexed my arms and looked pleadingly at her, my intent clear: *untie me.*

"Later," she murmured, patting me on the arm. "Once you're more clear-headed, all right? You have my word."

I didn't believe her.

But what could I do? I closed my eyes, took a deep breath and prayed sleep would find me.

— iii —

"Arri...?"

Fingers touched my arm.

I twitched them off. *Go the hell away.*

"Arri... wake up—"

No!

Up until that moment I was perfectly happy where I was. I was comfortable; I didn't hurt, I was warm and I wasn't afraid. All was good.

I should have known it wasn't going to last. Nothing good ever does.

"Arri, *please* wake up."

When I failed to react, I was rewarded with a painful slap across my face, followed in short order by another.

I blinked myself awake and turned my baleful, albeit rheumy-eyed squint towards the voice of my tormentor.

As our gazes locked, Sifrie responded with a very worried smile.

If it was her intention to worry *me*, she succeeded—damn, this was getting old. It was if they didn't want to keep the worry to themselves, but rather share it with me at every opportunity, even if it meant rousing me from a blissfully untroubled sleep.

I tried to sit up, in the process realized I was not tied up—and strangely that worried me even more—but she none too gently shoved me back down and kept her palm pressed against my chest, pinning me with surprising and embarrassing ease.

I looked around. I was back in the tent. Was I ever outside? In a cart? You know, it's really damned scary not to know which memories are telling you the truth and which are lying to you, bald-faced. All *seemed* very real and at the same time, not. And without the ability to tell fabrication from fact you have nothing solid to grab hold of, have no way to reassemble your life in anything even close to its proper order.

Not only that, my left eye was definitely not working right—the lid felt heavy, swollen. I didn't remember it feeling this way before. It felt as if I'd been punched, hard. Maybe the blow to the head was to blame—maybe.

"Arri..."

I fixed my gaze on her. *Are you real?*

"...your leg wound... it needs to be reopened, drained and cleansed— do you understand? If we don't do something now, you're going to die."

41

I didn't like the sound of this, real or imagined—no, not the dying part. I was perfectly fine with that. It was the *'something now'* part—and that something clearly involved the ogre as he suddenly appeared, looming over me like some... well, like some damned ogre.

"Don't fight us, all right?" she continued as the ogre wiggled one massive arm under my shoulders and the other behind my knees.

"Fight...?"

"We're doing this for your good, understand?"

I understood that I was about to be picked up. "I... I can walk," I managed to say but with absolutely no conviction—male pride will make you say really, really *stupid* things like that in the presence of a woman. I don't know why, but it's a fact. Just ask any woman.

"I know you can," she replied but she clearly didn't believe it either—of course she didn't. She was just humoring me. Women do that a lot. Don't know why, but that's a fact too. "But I think it would be better this way—you can walk on the way back."

Way back... from where? I wondered as the ogre rose, not quite effortlessly, taking me with him. As I might have mentioned before, I'm not a small man.

I hadn't realized until that moment that aside from the snakestone amulet, along with the signaculum and beaded necklace, I was absolutely, positively stark naked—I'd even been stripped of the bandages. Now I was in the arms of the ogre... absolutely, positively stark naked, aside from the aforementioned necklaces, which did not provide much decorum.

This was getting more awkward by the minute.

Sifrie drew the tent flap aside and I found myself squinting into the glare of daylight.

That startled me—I'm not sure why but if I'd been asked, I'd have sworn it was night. In my delirium, night and day happily continued their eternal cycle without my consent and this slap-in-the-face reminder that I not only couldn't rely on my memory, but also had days-long holes in my life, sent a fresh surge of panic through me.

My heart began to thump wildly in response.

Oblivious to my growing distress, the ogre stepped out of the tent, into the pale yellow, angled light and gathering chill of a late afternoon and I risked a quick look around to find a campsite well hidden within an outcrop of massive boulders.

Muttered voices next drew my gaze to a knot of heavily armed men who watched us pass in hostile silence—which did nothing to ease my mind but did make me marginally less upset about being in the arms of the ogre. Aside from Sifrie, he was the only one who'd shown me any compassion—if you call rescuing me in order to sell me into slavery a kindness.

Over their voices, over the sounds of my thumping heart and gasping breath, I caught the distinctive sounds of rushing water. Looking around I spotted a goodly number of horses tethered together within a wide cleft in the rocks, two still hitched to a crudely made four-wheel cart. They all had the look of being ridden or driven hard: their coats were wet and steaming and their mouths were flecked with foam. Even I, a lifelong member of the infantry, knew better than to leave a horse like that, especially with the cold of evening fast approaching.

A soft splashing sound yanked my attention off the lathered horses and back to what should have been my chief concern: the ogre had waded into a fast moving stream that cut its way through a chasm in the rock and I had a flash of insight of what was about to happen a split second before I found myself seated on the stream-bed, up to my chest in absolutely frigid water.

I expected to scream—so did the ogre as he clapped his hand over my mouth the instant he let go of the rest of me. But... it actually felt *incredibly* good—after my shocked chest and back muscles released their death-grip on my torso and I was able to breathe.

It felt *so* good in fact that I relaxed completely—all right, so maybe I fainted—and promptly slipped under the surface.

The ogre plunged a hand in after me, grabbed my hair and pulled upwards and I broke the surface with a loud, startled splutter.

Still clutching my hair in his fist, he stared at me with a look of supreme disappointment. "I thought you Roman soldier boys could swim."

I fixed him with a watery-eyed squint. "I can swim. I just can't float."

He released his painful grip and squatted beside me. The swirling water barely came up to his hips. He stared at me for some time.

I found that rather rude, so I decided to get even: I grinned at him as I emptied my bladder. Granted, he was blithely unaware of it, but it still made me feel much better, in several ways.

"I think you're worth far more than I was paid."

I agreed with him whole-heartedly, but I also suspected that it would not be in my best long-term interest to say so. So I replied with an ambiguous, "Why so?"

"You're not bad looking, even with a black eye."

I've been told that before—many, *many* times before, and even with two black eyes, but never by an ogre while I was seated next to him naked—in fact never by an ogre, *period.*

43

"Oh." That was the only thing I could think to say. I had no desire to insult him, but neither did I want to encourage him so I figured staying noncommittal was the wisest route.

I scooped up a handful of the fast moving water and splashed it against my beard- stubbled face, then using the fingers of my right hand, vigorously scratched my scalp, careful to avoid the still very painful lump on my skull. My shoulder-length hair had been coated in dried bog muck along with clotted blood and who knows what else and the unexpected backwards dip into the swirling torrent had loosened some of it, but not all.

I leaned forward and plunged my entire head underwater and gave it a shake, followed up with another thorough, one-handed scratch. Gods... it felt *good!*

Satisfied, I lifted my head out of the water and raked my hair off my face.

What I would've given for a scraper... but as far as I'd been able to determine, the concept of bodily cleanliness was utterly alien to my captors—the ogre was certainly a hirsute and decidedly odiferous example of hygienic indifference.

So I did the next best thing: again using my right hand, I scooped handfuls of the sand from the bed of the stream and vigorously scrubbed my left forearm, my chest and neck, my uninjured leg—even my hair, and yes, lastly and *very* carefully, intimate parts of my body that were in dire need of a good wash. I even cautiously washed my injured leg—using only my fingers. That didn't feel good, not at all.

Again, I ducked under the water and gave myself a vigorous shake and the swirling water carried away not only a cloud of grit but also a lot of loosened filth.

As I broke the surface, I overheard the ogre say, "Enough?"

I assumed he was talking to me, since I was the one sitting up to my armpits in snowmelt, which suddenly didn't feel quite as refreshing as it had a few minutes before—I'd been a bit too vigorous with the sand and had rubbed my numb skin raw in spots—and it was getting damned uncomfortable. "Yes—"

"No," came the crone's stern reply, "a little longer—until he starts to shiver."

Easy for her to say—I peered around the ogre to find her standing high on the bank—on dry ground, a heavy and I suspect very warm cloak wrapped snugly around her.

I scowled at her. *Bitch.*

She stared back, unfazed.

It's very hard to fake a sustained shiver although I tried. Sadly the ogre wasn't fooled, neither did he appear to be cold or in need to rush things.

So we both sat there, staring at each other until my teeth started to chatter in earnest. I'd long since lost all feeling in my extremities, which was probably a good thing as I had a sneaking suspicion that they'd taken the bandages off prior to my frigid bath for a reason—

"Hanni."

I raised my brows.

"That's my name," the ogre said, breaking the ice, so to speak. "*Hanni.*"

"I'm—"

"Arri," he finished for me. "Sifrie told me." He grinned. "Hanni… Arri. We could be brothers."

I blinked, unable—unwilling—to follow that logic. I certainly hoped he wasn't seriously suggesting we bore even a passing resemblance, otherwise I'd been deluding myself for a very, *very* long time.

Again, it was not my desire to hurt his feelings, plus he was my ride out of this hellish glacial torrent. "Ah… w-w-well," I stuttered, "I s-s-suppose so." *In a pig's eye.* "Ha-a-anni, I… I really th-think I'm r-r-r-eady to get out n-n-n-now."

He grinned, clearly pleased I'd called him by name and rewarded me by scooping me up then trudged back up the slope with the crone leading the way and back into the tent. He placed me on a waiting pallet of straw and pelts and the crone promptly bundled me up in another fur.

I was now shivering uncontrollably and wanted to snarl, *"Satisfied?"* but I knew if I tried, it would come out as nothing more than an incomprehensible, spluttering stutter.

At that moment Sifrie entered the tent, carrying the heavily stained and now soaking wet strips of cloth that had once been, who knows when, my crimson undertunic. She knelt nearby, flashed me a dazzling smile then carefully laid the woolen strips on a ring of water-smoothed rocks that circled the brazier, which was alight, but not putting off anywhere enough heat for my liking.

To my surprise, the wool immediately began to steam. So, maybe I was wrong about the heat. Hard to judge these things when one is chilled down to the marrow of your bones.

"Feel better?" she asked, turning her full attention on me.

"Wha-t-t-t d-d-do y-you th-th-think?" I was now wide awake and freezing cold when before I'd been sleepy and toasty warm. My shoulder and leg ached to the point it made my eyes water. My butt was numb. My hands were numb. Other parts—*important parts*, at least to me—were numb. And,

if I wasn't mistaken, an ogre had just propositioned me, or had claimed me as his long lost brethren… possibly both.

But I also felt clean—*was* clean, or at least clean-*er*. I hadn't realized how filthy I felt—how filthy I'd *been* until that moment. My hair had been pressed into a sweat-stiff, itchy skullcap and my body had been coated in a crust of dried muck, blood and sweat and, well, other… *stuff* I'm loath to mention.

But I wasn't going to mention that, either, not to the crone and not to Sifrie. I was in no mood to be thankful to either of them—or the ogre—*especially* the ogre, who was still standing—or more accurately, *stooped* nearby, yet despite his hunched stance, his head still touched the top of the tent.

Now my goose-pimpled skin was a close, albeit ashen cousin to its normal tawny shade and my blue-black hair was a mass of loose, wet curls that drizzled ice water over me every time I shivered, which of course made me shiver all the more.

"Hanni," the crone said, "we need more wood for the fire—gather more than enough to last the night, yes?" She then fixed her gaze on me. "And we need to tend to your leg wound—it's gotten much worse."

I squinted at her. It was the least I could do—and, actually, the most. My jaw muscles were too busy keeping up with my chattering teeth.

With that Sifrie lifted the fur off me.

I was too damned cold to fight, too damned cold to feel anything beyond feeling damned cold. So I lay there, staring at the ceiling in very unhappy silence as Sifrie and the crone poked and prodded and whispered to each other.

Wondering what was taking so long, I looked down just in time to witness the crone place a knife against the bloated and discolored skin of my thigh.

In one quick motion, she sliced it open, almost to the knee.

I stared at her, horror-struck and unblinking, waiting for the agony to hit my brain. But it didn't. Something else did: an incredibly potent, putrid smell… and it was coming from my leg, as was a copious amount of *very* nasty looking fluid.

I again fixed my gaze on the fabric ceiling and fought down the urge to vomit—not so much at the sight, but at the smell. I knew that smell. It was the smell of rotting flesh—of a slow, agonizing death.

I felt them squeezing my leg, felt pressure, felt the *very* odd sensation of something being pulled and tugged and suddenly giving way.

I shut my eyes and clenched my teeth—not against the pain; I can honestly say I wasn't in all that much pain, which in itself was deeply worrisome. I just didn't want to watch what I knew was happening.

I must've passed out, because the next thing I knew Sifrie, who was now kneeling beside my shoulder, was crumbling something that looked like dried bird droppings into a small bowl as the hag added steaming water from a mug while stirring the concoction with a crooked finger. Then the crone poured the mixture into my now gaping thigh wound.

I wasn't quite sure I believed what I was seeing—not about the droppings, although that was certainly a bit mind boggling in itself, but that I still *had* my leg—and not just part of it—*all of it*. Or should I say I knew I had my toes because I could not only see them, but I was able, with single-minded concentration, to wiggle them, which logically meant I had to have *most* of what connected my toes to the rest of me.

Sifrie, seeing that my eyes were open and trying to follow the crone's every move, explained, "This lichen has proven medicinal properties—"

"Looks like bird shit," I mumbled.

That got a snort of laughter from the crone, and, "Indeed it does. My, I hope we haven't mixed the two up."

I stared at her, unable to think of a suitable retort. Besides, she was still holding the knife and I had no desire for her to be provoked into extending the surgery to higher parts.

Damned if she didn't wink at me.

Startled, I jerked my eyes off her and put my full concentration on the darkening patch of sky I could see through the tent's small smoke hole.

"That should hold you for now," the crone finally said, drawing my wary gaze. She motioned to my leg, which was now redressed in the strips of my undertunic.

"Now, let's have a look at that shoulder," she continued.

As she and Sifrie rose to gather more supplies, I quickly tugged the fur over my lower half. I was still shivering—and miserably cold, couldn't they see that?

The shoulder, much to my relief, did look better—if you can call a large scabbed-over burn surrounded by bruised and blistered flesh "better". At least it wasn't particularly painful to touch, which Sifrie and the hag did, a lot. Too damned much if you ask me.

They decided to rebind it without the benefit of another poultice, something I freely admit came as a huge relief—my memory of the last application was still seared into my brain. They even skipped the bird droppings. Another relief.

With that done, I was propped up on a pillow of furs, near the firepot, but not too close. According to the crone, now that they'd gotten my fever under control, and cleansed the thigh wound of most of the corrupted flesh, they weren't going to risk a relapse.

I had other ideas. The instant the hag left and Sifrie was distracted with feeding twigs to the brazier, I started wiggling closer to the source of the meager heat... until she caught me in the act.

She crossed her arms and stared down at me with a look of utter reproach. "You're not helping yourself, you know, not one bit."

I had no recourse but to look pathetic, hug myself and stutter, "I'm... I'm c-c-cold and I hurt, *all o-o-over.*"

I was actually surprised that the ploy worked: her expression immediately softened.

"Of course." She knelt beside me, rubbed my bare arms briskly then brought my cupped hands to her mouth and blew into them. "Better?"

I wanted to say no, hoping she'd keep working at it, hoping she'd find other ways to warm my hands, not to mention the rest of me, but just then the crone stepped back into the tent. She looked at me, looked at Sifrie, and clearly had the situation sized up. "I brought you something warm to drink." She offered me a bulging skin.

I grimaced, thinking it was that awful, stinky stuff they'd made me drink before, the stuff that tasted like fermented goat pee.

"Here." She held out another of those odd yellow lozenges. "Swallow this."

I hesitated. "What is it?"

"Just do as I tell you."

I had no idea what it was made of, what its purpose was, but the others I'd been forced to take hadn't done me any harm that I was aware of, so I reluctantly plucked it from her palm and once I'd placed it in my mouth she offered me the skin.

The skin was indeed warm and I clutched it tightly in my ice-cold hands, pressed it to my lips and squeezed, hard, then, as I swallowed my mouthful with a surprised wince, I looked up at her.

"Yes, it's wine—and yes, it's Roman. I thought you'd prefer it."

I had no doubt how it had been acquired and as thirsty as I was, as much as a good gulp or two of fire-warmed Roman wine sounded—all right, considering how much I'd just gone through, I could have easily drained the skin and then some—to ease the pain and thaw my insides—I was not about to stain my conscience by drinking any more of it.

"Like hell!" I hurled the skin aside for extra emphasis.

48

The crone reacted to my act of foolish defiance with an unmoved, "Suit yourself." She pulled several leather thongs from her belt. "Hold out your hands."

I had really hoped they were past doing this to me; I'd held perfectly still for their impromptu surgery after all. And we were now so far from Roman-held territory that they should be confident I wouldn't try to escape, or even if I did, I wouldn't get far—assuming I even knew which direction to flee, which I didn't, and of course I couldn't walk, much less run. And, oh yes—I was *naked*.

But there was no point in refusing. If I did, she'd just call for the men and they wouldn't be as careful. So I silently, grudgingly held out my raw and bruised wrists for her and she attached the tethers.

Sifrie repeated the process with my ankles and I was again pegged to the ground. But at least this time they left just enough slack that I could move a little. I could, if I wanted, even reach the wine skin, which, I noticed, had already disgorged most of its contents on the ground, the puddle of wine looking suspiciously like a pool of blood. Fitting, considering how it had come into my captors' possession.

Sifrie then drew several more furs over me.

I fixed my eyes on the brazier and drawing a ragged breath, tried to settle myself for another long night.

My world had been winnowed down to this: a terrible arrangement of constant pain and fear, of threats and promises, of waking up not knowing who or what or where I was. Of having to start over from scratch each time, reassembling bits and pieces that seemed to fit yet didn't and all the while struggling with this gnawing anxiety that I really *was* dead, that an afterlife of perpetual torment, something I'd been warned by certain cultists was the fate of all who failed to embrace their single god was true: that I was, in fact, in hell.

— IV —

In the lonely weeks that followed the garrison's abandonment, I kept telling myself that one of the soldiers would surely regret his decision and return for me—I even made a game out of who it might be.

I fantasized about hearing the barracks' main door grind on its rusting hinges and look up to find the familiar bearish silhouette of Gracchus standing there, to hear his gruff voice calling to me as he always had when he returned from patrol, to feel his fatherly embrace and taste the small sweet he would always produce from a pouch tied to his belt. I even hoped for the arrival of Lucullus—even if his interest in me had never been anything beyond his own carnal needs.

Lucullus had never been rough with me, never deliberately hurt me; he was usually gentle—or as gentle as possible, not at all like some of the others, not like Porsenna, who was the first to use me in that way—had, in fact made it clear that as the senior-most in the barracks it was his right to be the first. And none disputed this—not even Gracchus.

I had no reason to be afraid that day when Porsenna, sweaty from exercising, appeared in the barracks and demanded that I attend him, to the eager grins of the other soldiers. Seeing their expressions, I was eager too—I just didn't know why.

Gracchus told me to go, told me to be good, to do exactly as Porsenna said.

I'd never liked Porsenna—he was cruel and short tempered and always spoiling for a fight. But knowing Gracchus loved me and would never allow any harm to come to me, I went willingly, thinking I was going to massage Porsenna's sore back, or scrape the sweat from his skin as I had done for him and the others countless times before. Or maybe he was going to show me the weapons locker, maybe let me try on one of their helmets—perhaps even teach me how to wield a sword! It was a promise often given but never kept and Porsenna was, after all, the best swordsman in the garrison.

I was so excited by the possibilities that I hopped and skipped beside him oblivious to the tight hold he had on my wrist.

I remember him taking me into an abandoned storage room—where his intentions quickly became obvious and when I panicked and cried out for Gracchus, of him telling me that he'd been extremely patient—Gracchus had been patient—they'd all been patient, that they'd waited until I was old enough. More than old enough.

He told me that from then on, along with my regular chores, this was going to be my way of repaying him, repaying the others for their generosity, for the roof over my head and the food in my belly and if I ever refused any of them—no matter the demand—I would be thrown out, left to fend for myself.

That terrified me—terrified me more than what he was about to do, and I believed him so I submitted—not that I had any choice. I was not yet six; he was twenty-five and very strong. I still remember how much it had hurt—far more than I could have imagined and when I wouldn't stop screaming he beat me—until Lucullus intervened.

Only much later did I learn that Lucullus' timely arrival had not been providential or selfless—the others had drawn lots as to who would be next—he'd drawn the long straw and had been waiting impatiently outside.

Gracchus only rarely took me in that way. And each time I forgave him—how could I not? He said I was like a son to him.

"What are you thinking?"

I jerked my eyes off the wooden bowl I clutched tightly in my right hand and fixed them on Sifrie, who was seated beside me. I was again propped up on a mound of furs, my left hand, at least for the moment, free of its bindings, the right was on a short tether, but not my legs—my ankles were still tightly pegged down—and I was trying to convince myself to take the first bite of semi-solid food since that ill-fated morning of the battle, now, according to Sifrie, assuming she was telling the truth, over a week past.

It was not going well. My stomach rebelled at the thought of eating and I had a painfully tight knot in my throat.

"Nothing," I replied huskily. I picked up the crude wooden spoon, managed to scoop up some of the lumpy gruel and, with a very shaky hand, brought it toward my lips. I was nauseated by its smell but I needed to eat—*if* I could just get the food into my mouth. I'd worry about swallowing it once it made it that far.

She wriggled closer, now hip-to-hip, leg pressed against leg, and gently pried the spoon from my trembling fingers. "Let me help."

Her well-meaning offer pricked my pride; her closeness made me uneasy as I remembered the threat of castration—real or imagined it was a hard thing to ignore. I tried not to let my reaction show as she cupped my chin with one hand as one would a sickly child and slipped the spoon into my mouth.

The gruel was an odd mixture of greasy, gristly meat, coarsely ground meal and root vegetables all boiled to the point that the result had attained a uniform gray color, its only texture provided by the unidentifiable, chewy lumps which I made a concerted effort *not* to chew—not even a liberal splash or ten of garum would have helped this truly revolting concoction. And garum, as we all know, can make anything taste better. Well, *almost* anything.

I had no sooner swallowed with a grimace than she ladled another spoonful into my mouth. I closed my eyes and concentrated on forcing it down.

Her fingers ran through my sweat-stiffened hair, gently, combing an unruly lock from my forehead, and I gave her a wary, sidelong glance.

"You've had a *very* hard life."

"No harder than anyone else." I fixed my gaze on the bowl I still clutched in my tethered hand. My hand, fingers and forearm were lividly colored with fresh bruises and my right wrist was ringed with raw, oozing welts—the result of my feverish fights against the straps and later violent convulsions—or so the crone had told me. I wasn't sure I entirely believed her—I had vague and frightening memories of being slapped about—which might explain my black eye—of being repeatedly kicked in the stomach and groin, of the bindings being deliberately jerked so tight I lost sensation in my hands and feet and angry voices—more threats, of the familiar smacking sound of fist meeting flesh and I couldn't help but flinch.

"I think not."

I kept my eyes on the bowl, on my bruised and painfully swollen fingers and my bitter thoughts to myself. *And you think this makes it any easier?*

"Are you afraid of me?"

My eyes darted to her then back to the relative safety of the bowl. There was no point in lying. "Yes."

"Why?"

I jerked my tethered wrist against the leather binding. Answer enough. There were other reasons to be sure—

"And you believe Kyrou."

I looked at her out of the corner of my eye but said nothing.

"He's not *my* master—quite the contrary." She paused, added softly, "Would you be less afraid if I untied you?"

I hadn't expected that and replied with a blunt, albeit uneasy, "But you won't."

She again ran her fingers lightly across my forehead, sending a shiver down my spine. "You're still running a fever—you were hallucinating most of the night—in fact you've been hallucinating, off and on, since—"

"I was taken captive?" I interrupted bitterly.

"Since you were wounded," she countered as she stroked my cheek.

Now *that* sounded like truth—I had a sudden recollection of the crone shoving a wad of fabric in my mouth while telling me my frightened screams had awakened the entire camp—awakened Kyrou—and that just wouldn't do.

With a jolt that shook my entire body, I remembered why I'd been screaming: I was again locked in that abandoned storage room—just the thought set my heart thumping anew—and snakes were slithering across my legs, snakes were everywhere and with the gag I couldn't even let loose my fears by screaming.

The hag had assured me there were *no* snakes, that I *wasn't* in a storage room, but I *knew* she was lying to keep me quiet, to keep my frightened cries from waking Gracchus—*not Kyrou as she claimed*—I knew the place too well, knew its peeling plaster walls like the back of my hand, knew its moldering sacks of grain and musky stench of mouse piss—it was the place I was always taken when one of the soldiers needed his release and had no money to buy the services of a whore, or, like Lucullus, preferred me over a whore; where I was put when I'd filched some small morsel of food meant for someone else's belly; where I was left for hours, sometimes days at a time without food and water when I hadn't done *exactly* what I'd been told to do.

The room had always had its share of snakes, drawn to the mice. I'd spent many hours in the airless dark, jumping at the briefest touch of a flicking tongue, or the occasional rub of cool scales gliding past bare skin as I waited for the inevitable muffled squeak—the signal that the accursed room had claimed yet another victim. I came to identify with the mice, suspecting the snakes were in league with the soldiers and given the chance might follow their example.

In truth the snakes never bothered me—scared me, certainly, but they'd otherwise left me alone, preferring much smaller prey. But this time they were all over me, I could *feel* them gliding over my legs, my belly, eeling across my throat, coiling and slithering under the threadbare blanket and beneath me, through moldy straw that served as a bed—the soldiers' only concession to my physical needs which also served theirs—where the crone wouldn't see them.

I was terrified she was going to leave me like that, bound and gagged, helpless and spread-eagle atop the writhing mass, but she didn't. She stayed with me, talking to me—at one point I think she even sang softly as a mother would do for her frightened child—until the snakes left and I was so exhausted I fell deeply asleep.

She was still there when I awoke, and massaged my limbs, which had become stiff from being tied in one position for far too long. She stayed with me until Sifrie came with the gruel.

"The bindings are to keep you from hurting yourself—"

I snorted in disbelief.

"—or us."

I stared down at the bowl for a moment then looked at her out of the corner of my eye. "Are you afraid of me?"

She picked up the forgotten spoon and gave the now congealed gruel a stir, as if that would somehow make it more appetizing. "I'm afraid of what you're capable of, yes, but of you? No—should I be?"

I shrugged, exhaled. I was so damned tired. I couldn't even remember what it felt like *not* to be this tired. At times even taking the next breath seemed to be a labor worthy of Hercules and yet I could not stop breathing as much as I wished it.

She pressed the spoon to my lips. "Here. You need to eat."

I turned my head away and whispered, *"Why?"*

"If you don't your wounds will never heal, you'll never regain your strength."

"So I'll make a more fitting sacrifice to your gods?"

She tossed the spoon into the bowl, snatched the bowl from my hand, got back to her feet and stalked out of the tent.

I stared after her, taken aback. It seemed like a perfectly reasonable question—*she* had no right to be angry.

I did.

So I got mad. I tried to untie my right hand but the fingers of my left hand were so stiff and swollen they didn't work right. I tried to reach my ankles as they were held by what looked like simple loops. But with the right hand on a short tether, the left just could not reach that far.

Furious and now more than a little frantic, I fought the bindings, cursing loudly. I only succeeded in rubbing my already raw wrist and ankles until they bled and made my painfully sore joints ache all the more. So I satisfied myself by repeatedly punching the fur pallet beneath me until I completely exhausted myself, which, I readily admit didn't take very long.

A week before I'd been able to march twenty miles with full kit, bellowing orders the entire way and still have more than enough strength left to fight if ordered to do so and continue fighting until ordered to stop.

A week before I was able bodied; a week before I was a free man.

Now I was neither.

I gasped for breath as I stared up at the fabric roof of the tent. *Fool*, I thought as tears welled up in my eyes and trickled down my face. *Damned fool!* I squeezed my eyes shut.

I felt a cool draft on my damp cheek. My eyes snapped open and I squinted into the painfully bright glare. For an instant a shadowy form was haloed against the daylight before the tent flap was released, plunging the interior into pitch darkness.

My heart hammered against my ribs. Surely it was Kyrou, or one of the other men, come to mete out just punishment for daring to offend the high-born, untouchable Sifrie. I desperately glanced about, trying to spot my attacker as my eyes readjusted to the faint glow of the brazier.

In doing so, I caught a glimpse of long, flame red hair.

Sifrie. But realizing it was her—and *not* Kyrou—did not slow my heart's rapid beat. I *was* scared of her—in truth far more than I was of Kyrou.

She added some twigs to the brazier and the fire crackled and briefly flared, her flowing hair suddenly alight with the glow, looking like a curtain of wind-blown embers.

"I understand why you believe your fate is to be sacrificed."

Her calm offense effectively reclaimed my earlier anger and squelched my fears and I replied bitterly, "That's what I was *purchased* for, right?" I *was* property, owned—but by whom? Sifrie? The crone? The black-haired man?—he had, after all, been the one doing the bargaining.

She turned to face me. "I won't deny that coins exchanged hands, but it wasn't what you think—"

"Meaning you know I was *there*, so there's no point lying?"

"I wasn't planning on lying to you. Have I once lied to you?"

I stared at her but said nothing. I no longer trusted my memory—a fact that panicked me far more than I'd anticipated—I no longer trusted *anything* or *anyone*, even myself.

"I also understand that you will not believe me when I tell you that we *rescued* you—*you*, specifically *you* for a purpose far greater than any ritual sacrifice."

As she spoke, I suddenly recalled the day in the forest, of watching the dog approach—and again experienced that very eerie sense that the memory was not entirely my own and had appeared without my bidding—just like the dog as it searched... for something—

"You see, we'd been observing you for some time—until Turan was convinced you that were the one—waiting for the right moment to seize you, with luck unharmed..."

—no, not *something*—it had been searching for *me*. I knew that now. I knew it with a dead certainty and a shiver ran down my spine as I realized that I'd *seen* that hound several times before—long before the day of the battle. Why hadn't I remembered this? I'd taken serious blows to the head before, lots of times, blows that had knocked me out and for days afterwards left me dizzy, nauseated and seeing double. But I'd never had memory lapses—at least none that I could remember, I told myself, desperate to find some small scrap of humor in the situation I found myself in. There was not one shred of humor about this. None at all.

"…but as we quickly discovered," she smiled, "you're not an easy man to catch unawares or for that matter, alone."

I remembered now that I'd seen it pacing our column for several days on end, and once I caught a glimpse of it coursing through the high grass as I led a foraging party—I'd assumed it was chasing hare. A day or so later, while a group of us risked a bracing bath in a stream, it appeared on the far bank, a gray ghost among the winter-burnt rushes and cattails. It sat and peered out at us from its reed bastion until one of the soldiers—Pictor—who'd been standing guard over us, started throwing rocks at it, believing it to be a wolf.

Then, a fortnight before the battle, as I sat down for my evening meal, I happened to see its eyes glowing in the darkness, just beyond the ring of firelight—I never once thought it was a wolf, I *knew* it was the dog, which now, as I thought about it, seemed rather curious as wolves were a constant threat to the unwary.

At the time I'd assumed it was hungry, looking for scraps, nothing more. I was no dog lover, far from it, but I knew that look—I knew what it was like to be *that* hungry and to be alone, knew what it meant for someone to show just a little kindness, perhaps the small difference between life and death, so I rose with my bowl and started towards it—until Felix called after me, warning me not to stray beyond the firelight.

I stopped in my tracks, startled, and yes, embarrassed by my dangerous lapse in judgment: even a raw recruit knew better. I quickly tossed my leftovers into the darkness and as I cautiously backed away I heard the beast eagerly gulping down the free meal.

My companions, equally troubled by my abnormal behavior—I was not a man known for his kindness to animals—whispered to each other that I was a fool, that I'd just encouraged it, that next time it might not be so timid, the next time it might not settle for scraps.

They were right, it had been an incredibly stupid thing to do. I tried to rationalize to myself that since my life had been spared a number of times by the impulsive and foolishly kindhearted acts of others, it was nothing more than a reflexive response to a creature in similar need. Still, it disturbed me, disturbed my sleep that night.

The following day the dog was gone and did not return and I promptly forgot about it.

Until now.

"…but things didn't exactly turn out as we'd planned," Sifrie continued. "Then again, we never thought your officers would be so reckless as to launch such an inadequately considered attack." She shook her head, continued, "And we had no reason to believe *you'd* survived when your entire cohort had been slaughtered—"

I winced. While I'd made career out of attaching myself to officers who were willing to take risks, calculated risks, as that was the quickest path to advancement, Cerialis had made me very uneasy from the get-go. He had that rare deportment so prized by Roman society in their military leaders: a haughty bearing, a shrewd mind and a lethal glamour all rolled into a very charming, very masculine package. He must've looked every bit the shining hero, decked out in his burnished parade finery, to the wild cheers of the crowds that lined the streets of Rome, wishing him farewell as he departed to expand the shining light of civilization.

To the common soldiery Cerialis had a well-earned reputation for unbridled recklessness. I was not alone in my fears that he'd lead the rest of us to ruin while searching for his rightful and illustrious place in history. He seemed far too hasty, too willing to throw everything he had in at once. He refused to differentiate between subjects and allies, treating all non-Romans with the same sneering contempt, and was unwilling or perhaps too stubborn to listen to his officers, to his centurions like myself whom had far more experience with the local tribes than he.

But ultimately we all shared the same blind spot: an unyielding and fatal belief in our military superiority. The bog wasn't our undoing. It was our own supreme arrogance, plain and simple.

I knew the battle was going to be a rout, had seen defeat coming long before I was ordered to take a small hillock—a strategic gamble for dryer ground—but I ended up mired in that boggy glade along with several dozen of my century, cut off from the rest and beyond any hope of reinforcements. But I'd hoped, I'd prayed—

"—if it hadn't been for Turan and Hanni, you too would've died where you fell."

I was oblivious to her words. My mind was still entrenched in those last terrible minutes of the bloody skirmish, the startling impact of the Iceni's spear thrust, followed by the burning slice of a sword across my thigh, of falling to my knees, forcing the spear deep into me, seeing my men being hacked to pieces and not being able to do a damned thing to help them—a flash of movement, an instant of blinding pain behind my eyes...

Darkness.

My expression must have mirrored my thoughts; she paused long enough for me to realize she'd stopped talking, to collect myself as best I could.

I looked at her, unable to catch my breath.

"We *saved* you—"

"Why?" I managed to force out between labored gasps.

"You wouldn't understand if I told you now."

I jerked my watery gaze off her and fixed them on the far wall as I struggled to get my panicky breathing back under control. "I... I don't believe... you! I don't... believe any... any of you!"

"We need you, Arri—"

"Don't... call me that!"

"What would you prefer I call you?"

I refused to look at her, refused to answer. The muscles of my throat had tightened into an excruciating knot as fresh tears rolled down my face, my throat.

"We're in desperate need of your skills—"

"If you... you think you... can convince me," I croaked, "bewitch me... into fighting against my... my own, think again! Do... do what you will to me, I'll not—"

"Nothing of the sort, I assure you."

I scowled balefully at her. *"Then why?"*

"Because you're an incredibly smart, highly successful soldier..."

So, she had resorted to flattering me. I felt insulted that she would think me so easily distracted, so vain.

"...and neither am I trying to appeal to your male conceit."

That set me back. This was not the first time she'd replied to my unspoken thoughts and I asked half-joking, half-annoyed, "Can you hear my thoughts?"

"In a manner of speaking, yes—not all the time, not like Turan, but enough."

I didn't believe her—I thought perhaps she was using my weaknesses against me, playing games with my feverish mind. So I decided to test her. I thought about having sex with her, all right, I admit it—*and Kyrou be damned*—I'd thought of having sex with her *a lot*, from the moment I laid eyes on her and almost every minute I was semi-clear headed and she was nearby—and even some times when I wasn't at all clear headed and I had no idea if she was near or not. I thought I'd *had* sex with her, but now I wasn't sure—perhaps it had been just another hallucination.

Perhaps I was still hallucinating—*but what the hell.*

I thought *very* specifically of what I'd want to do—what I'd want *her* to do to me.

Her eyes widened. Her full lips parted in an intrigued smile and she murmured, "I'm willing if you are."

I blinked, stunned. And, all right, now that I thought more about it, more than a little interested, in fact a *lot* interested. She *was* beautiful, with her long red hair and milky white complexion—the antithesis of my dusky complexion.

She knelt beside me, her face no more than a hand-width from mine; I felt her warm breath on my skin. "If I do this for you, will you make an equal effort to trust me?"

I wasn't sure how to answer that. If I refused, she very well might withdraw the offer, and I had no reason to trust anyone, least of all her— but I suddenly wanted this woman in the absolute worst way and I wondered if she *was* bewitching me—that I'd stupidly walked right into her trap, eagerly led by parts of my body that, given half a chance, always got me into trouble. Serious trouble.

"I admit I find you *incredibly* attractive," she whispered in my ear.

That cinched it.

She grinned and rocked back on her heels and as I watched, she began unlacing her bodice.

I shifted against the bindings, desperately wanting to help, desperately wanting to touch.

She rose, stepped out of her clothing and allowed me a good, long look at her naked body and I, naturally, took full advantage. She was barely more than a girl, with small breasts and slim hips, but as I ran my eyes over her, I felt my body react, felt my pulse gather speed as my breathing came in short, sharp gulps.

Pleased with the result, she slipped under the fur covers and curled up against me, draping her leg across my hips, almost but not *quite* straddling me.

I tried to shift, to nudge her the rest of the way on top of me as she nuzzled my ear.

I was now breathing hard and I'd broken out in a sweat that for once had nothing to do with my wounds. "Take the bindings off," I whispered desperately as she lightly ran her fingers over my stomach.

She glanced up at me and grinned wickedly. "No—this is far more fun."

And suddenly it was no longer a game to me. She could do anything she wanted—I couldn't stop her. But this wasn't the same sense of helplessness I'd felt in the bog with the ogre, or as a child. I'd never been this helpless, this vulnerable with a woman and I was suddenly very, very scared—

Her fingers instantly stopped their delicate tracery over my naked body. "Is that what you think I'm going to do? *Rape you?*"

"I… I don't know… what—what you're… you're going to do."

"You had a *very* clear idea of what you *wanted* me to do a few minutes ago—"

"I… I did—I… I mean I *do*," I stammered. I squeezed my eyes shut, steadied my breathing. "*Please.* Untie me—I won't try to escape, I give you my word. You said you wanted me to trust you, you need to trust me too."

Instead of answering, she ducked her head under the fur covers.

I flinched and fixed my wide eyes on the ceiling as I felt her hands—her lips, her tongue, her warm mouth—

Gods…! My free hand clenched the furs beneath me, my tethered hand balled into a fist as I strained against the bindings, gasping and groaning.

If there had been any doubt in my mind or hers that I was up to the task, I quickly disproved it—*too quickly.*

She immerged from under the covers, wiping her chin, her mouth then she smiled and wrapped herself around me, bare skin to bare skin. "As good as you'd hoped?"

I couldn't speak. I couldn't think. And I was still more than a little scared.

She levered herself up onto her elbow, brows wrinkled in concern. "Did I hurt you?"

"*Nnnn… nno.*"

She kissed me on the lips and smiling, combed her fingers through my sweaty hair as she stared down at me. "You are *so* beautiful…"

Suddenly embarrassed, I looked away, mumbled, "I'm… sorry."

"For what?" she smiled. "Being beautiful?"

"I… I couldn't stop it."

She wrapped her fingers around my chin and jerked my face back to her. "Did I complain?"

"No—"

"Then shut up." She pillowed her head on my chest and using a fingertip, lightly explored my navel.

I did, for a few minutes, until her fingers began to stray.

At first I was taken aback. Did she really think I was capable? *So soon?*

"Yes," she murmured as she began fondling me.

Damn. I need to be more careful.

And a moment later: Damn again, she's right…

— V —

On a brisk autumn dawn, with a full moon high overhead and the sun just peeking above the distant fold of mountains, I gathered up what little I could rightfully call my own, bid my silent farewells to the only home I'd known and started off on a journey that would, little did I know at the time, take me where no Roman had ever set foot. In truth I had no idea where I was going—I knew nothing of the world beyond the village, beyond the walls of the garrison. I had no idea how far I would have to walk. But I knew the direction the soldiers had taken when they left me behind months before.

I'd watched each of them leave, one by one, while wondering what terrible thing I'd done that could justify them abandoning me—I had, after all, done everything they had asked of me. Perhaps that's why they left—perhaps they'd finally grown bored with me—even Lucullus.

Even... Gracchus.

I'd clung desperately to him that morning, sobbing, pleading with him to take me with him.

He angrily shook himself free of my grip then as I again grabbed him, he roughly shoved me aside, this time with enough force to send me sprawling, face-first in the dirt.

I lay there for a moment, stunned, then drawing my legs tight up against my chest and hugging the now wear-tattered cloth horse I watched with streaming eyes as he marched through the open gates and into the early morning half-light without once glancing back at me, as if I didn't exist. As if I'd never existed.

I followed him with my watery gaze until he was finally no more than another moving form, anonymous within the formation; I watched the line of men, their burnished armor catching the first rays of the sunrise and looking like some monstrous centipede eeling along until it was nothing more than a flickering ribbon of gold on the horizon.

And without warning, even that faint beacon vanished, drowned by the intense dazzle of the desert sun as it rose above the distant peaks.

My surrogate father, my protector, gone, in the blink of an eye.

I peeked out from under the heavy fur cover and was somewhat startled to find the crone standing at the brazier, feeding it twigs. There was little light inside the tent—little enough I hoped she hadn't noticed the body tucked up against me.

"Sifrie was supposed to keep this fed," she said, turning her piercing eyes on me, "to keep you warm. But I see she found another way."

I felt my face burn as if I was a boy caught in the act with the neighbor's sheep and the old hag my mother.

"That being said, I *am* very relieved you're feeling better, although in my experience a man could be stone-cold dead and still be willing."

As she spoke, a slim hand slid over my hip and down and I couldn't stop myself from visibly flinching as the fingers took hold.

"Sifrie, *stop it!* You wish to kill him?"

The fingers very reluctantly released their grip—but not without first giving me the lightest tickle, damn her.

"Are you going to just lay there? It's almost midday."

I thought she was talking to Sifrie—or should I say I hoped she was talking to Sifrie as Sifrie's parting tease had had the expected result.

Sifrie clearly thought the hag was speaking to her too, so as she slipped out from under the furs and snatched up her discarded clothing, I tugged the covers back over me and snuggled back down where it was warm. The all too brief nap had done little to restore my flagging energy—

"I said get up!" With that, the furs were yanked off me, exposing my body to the chill. I tried to curl into a ball—not very successfully as both ankles and one wrist were still tied to the pegs.

I groaned pitiably but she was unmoved.

"If you're well enough for sex, you're well enough to be on your feet and I'll have no malingerers—*up!*" She cut the tethers with her knife. "Get up or I'll dump cold water on you."

She wasn't bluffing.

After several abortive attempts I got to my hands and knees, wobbling—not exactly the best position for a naked man who's freezing cold—at least I hoped she'd think it was because I was now freezing cold. Then I asked myself why I gave a damn if a decrepit old woman was less than unimpressed by the view.

Because she, regardless of her age, is still a woman, and a man, regardless of age, always wants to look impressive, that's why, a part of my mind replied. Plus, just a moment ago I was worried about having the opposite problem.

After another moment of struggle I lurched unsteadily to my feet, albeit only with the help of a tent pole and awkwardly turned to face her.

She looked me up and down, snorted, "It's not *that* cold," and turned back to the brazier.

I stared at her with the growing suspicion that it wasn't just Sifrie who could hear my thoughts.

"You're right, I can," the crone replied as she glanced over her shoulder at me, age-bright eyes sparkling. "So I thank you for being embarrassed at being naked in front of me. Granted, I've seen you naked more than once." She turned to face me, her expression softening, just a bit. "But I *am* still a woman, and in truth you have absolutely *nothing* to be embarrassed about." With that she walked around me, her hand lightly running over my suddenly goose-pimpled body as she gave me a good once over, as one would do with a prized horse... or a slave one was about to purchase.

As she came around to face me, she met my slitted gaze. "It bothers you that money was exchanged for you."

I stood my ground—not that I had much choice because if I let go of the pole I'd lose my precarious balance. "Let's change places and see if it bothers you."

She laughed, an impervious and delighted laugh. "Hanni's right—you *are* worth more than he was paid, *a lot more*—of course at the time none of us thought you'd live the night and I saw no reason to pay handsomely for a corpse, no matter *how* handsome that corpse might be."

I couldn't think of anything to say to that, so I settled for scowling at her.

She responded by fingering the necklace of crude glass, tigers-eye and faience beads and the small, four-pointed, raw silver star. "From whom did you steal this?"

"I didn't steal it. It was freely given to me."

She didn't look like she believed me. "What's the significance of the star?"

"It indicates the four corners of the Earth." I didn't feel it prudent to provide the full explanation.

"Uh-huh. And these beads... they're *slave* beads."

"Yes—"

"Ironic, don't you think?"

"I suppose so."

"They're *very* old."

"Yes, they—"

"Ever take it off?"

I thought she was going to yank the thong from my neck and I instinctively tensed, my neck muscles cording in response. "No."

"Do you wear it for luck?" she said in a baiting tone, as if only simpletons fell prey to such beliefs. "To protect you from the evil eye?"

"If it had such powers, I wouldn't be standing here with *you* staring at me, would I?"

She chuckled. "Why then?"

"I swore to the person who gave it to me that I would wear it, always, so I have. And besides, I like it."

"Then I'll permit you to keep it, for now."

I felt a flush of outrage wash over me but before I could react, she held the snakestone amulet before my eyes. "This marks you as *my* property. I warn you now, don't take it off…"

First chance I get—

"…you'll be *severely* punished if you try." She released it, let it fall back to my bare chest, then she made another slow circuit, her eyes following her hands—her touch this time not quite as light, not quite as ticklish as she followed my body's well-defined contours of bone and muscle. "I really *must* make it up to Hanni," she murmured.

I fixed my gaze on the brazier, seething at her unashamed and deliberately demeaning hands-on inspection while keenly aware that there was absolutely nothing I could do except submit.

I heard her stop behind me and had to wonder what she was looking at—my butt was far from my best attribute, at least that's what I've been told on more than one occasion by those who fancied themselves connoisseurs of male bottoms.

I started when her fingers touched a ragged scar on my right flank. "Where'd you get this?"

"Meroë."

Her fingers slid up my spine, followed by my involuntary shiver, across my shoulders, across the interlace of welts, telltale reminders of a long ago flogging that had come so very close to killing me. "These?"

"Parthia."

"Why?"

"I killed a hostage."

"Why?"

"He asked me to."

"Meaning he goaded you into it."

"I'd prefer to think that I was sparing his unfortunate family more grief at the news of his release."

"Clearly your superiors thought otherwise."

"Publicly, yes. Privately… no."

She pressed her fingertip against an ugly scar, just above my left hip. "This?"

"Oxyrhynchus."

Her finger slid down just a bit, poked at yet another old wound and I reacted by clenching my buttocks—which I suspect was actually the whole point. "And this?"

"Galetia."

As she continued her peculiar inspection, I noted an even more peculiar pattern in her interrogation: *after* she asked the origin of an old wound and *after* I'd provided a terse explanation, she'd hesitate for a moment or so, as if listening intently, but to what and for what purpose I cannot tell you—

"You don't strike me as someone who'd be so stupid as to turn his back to an enemy."

"I didn't, not… not exactly."

"So you were running away—"

"No. It was part of a well-planned, strategic draw back in the face of overwhelming opposing forces."

"And…?" she asked as she again ran her hand over the ugly scar.

"I sorely misjudged the enemy's rate of advance and didn't draw back quite quickly enough—"

"And got an arrow in your ass." With that she slapped my butt—and I jumped. It stung, just like her words.

"Better than *up* my ass," I snapped back. It had been humiliating enough at the time as I was, well, the butt of the joke for weeks afterwards. I had no desire to revisit the matter, least of all with this hag.

"It came *extremely* close though, didn't it?" she countered, to which there was no suitable rejoinder. It had come close. *Very close.*

Clicking her tongue, she came around me, searching for more scars, as if my body was a living treasure map and happily found what she was looking for: first, a series of dimples on my left forearm made more obvious by irregular hair growth.

She carefully lifted my arm for a closer inspection. As she released it she gave me a questioning look.

"Dog bite."

"Sticking your hand where it didn't belong?"

"I'm sure that's the dog's version of the story."

And higher up, several noticeable stroke lines. She again looked up at me and raised her brows.

"Bithynia."

She quickly discovered that my right arm, which was still hooked tightly around the tent pole, bore a close match of hash marks, with the addition of a bulge just below the elbow—the underlying bones hadn't reset properly but once healed hadn't hindered my ability to hurl a pilum or wield a sword, not in the slightest.

"Thracia."

Her eyes then fell to the fingers of my right hand, three of which were more than a little crooked. She examined each of the fingers closely then worked them to see if the old injury had in any way limited my ability to move them. I wiggled them for her then curled them into a tight, white-knuckled fist. Point made.

"And this?"

"Horse bite."

She replied with another twitch of a wispy brow as she ran her hand over my flank, over the scabbed over wound from that first night and—gently—over my badly bruised stomach. She then spotted the jagged line below the navel and just above the hairline, which she simply *had* to feel for herself, damn her, and another that ran the length of my right calf. "What about these?"

"Carthage… Numidia—"

"By one of your own?"

I replied with a startled stare.

"You're Mauri—specifically Massaesyli, not *fully* Roman as you would have others believe."

I continued to stare.

"Of course you are. Your parochial accent—you've worked very hard to conceal it, haven't you? But I can still hear the rolled 'r' here and there, and occasionally a slight lilt—and of course you babble into your native tongue when you're hallucinating."

I shifted uneasily, wondering what other deeply buried secrets I'd exposed while delirious.

She grinned—a decidedly sphinx-like grin as she plucked the lead signaculum from my chest. She studied both sides then met my slitted gaze. "This does not accurately describe you."

Don't ask me how, but I somehow managed to snap my fingers. "I knew there was something I forgot to do before we left Lindum! Let me go and I *promise*, the very first thing I do when I get back is to have it updated."

She smiled, then: "Fortunate you didn't die in that bog, otherwise your comrades would be hard-pressed to identify and reclaim your rotting corpse."

What she failed to mention of course was that those very same comrades *had* most likely died in that bog and were waiting for me to come identify and reclaim *them*.

She let the lead tablet go and lightly touched the heavily stained dressing that bound my shoulder. "And now you can add Britannia to your personal inventory." She looked down—stared in fact for quite some time—then ran her hand very suggestively over my bandaged thigh, following the dressing between my legs and then, no surprise, *up.*

I tried not to flinch, didn't even blink as she gave me a good feel—I'd say grope, but this didn't appear to be anything more than her assuring herself that everything was where it should be and intact.

Finally she lifted her gaze. "Your body's a veritable roadmap of the Empire—and a testament to your truly remarkable resilience—do you enjoy fighting, Centurion?"

I licked my lips then answered truthfully, "I enjoy surviving. In truth fighting isn't all it's made out to be."

"And killing?" she asked as she dropped her gaze again.

I wanted to say, 'Hey, I'm up here,' but this was all part of her game, to humiliate me. And it was working. "May I have something to wear? I'm cold—"

"No, you may not—*answer my question!*" She poked my badly bruised and tender belly for emphasis.

That hurt, and it *really* irked me—she was deliberately keeping me at a disadvantage, despite me being well over a foot and a half taller and solid muscle to her brittle bone—a blatant reminder of who was in control and who was... *property*, and I answered bitterly, "That's the whole fucking point, isn't it?"

"So, you *enjoy* killing." Again her eyes left mine and drifted downwards.

"Let's just say I've had plenty of practice—"

"Are you good at it?"

"*Very* good." *Really good at that, too,* I added, hoping she caught that thought.

She did, because it drew her arched gaze back to mine. "No doubts?"

I grinned smugly. "Absolutely none." *On either count.*

She really liked *those* answers, spoken and unspoken. I could tell because they tugged at the corners of her wrinkled, thin-lipped mouth. *Good—give me my sword and I'll happily—*

"Is that why you joined the military, so you could kill with impunity?"

I squinted at her. Truth, there were those who joined just so they could kill—they loved killing—an equally armed enemy or a defenseless woman, old man or child, it didn't matter. I despised them—they were bad for morale, *extremely* bad for discipline. I killed when I was ordered to do so, when I had no choice, when it was absolutely necessary. Legionaries were, after all, famous—and to our enemies *infamous*—for showing no mercy in battle. But I never, *ever* killed as sport.

"I was looking for someone."

"Who?"

I hesitated, suddenly feeling rather foolish and not really sure it was any of her damned business, but knew if I failed to answer, despite her being able to read my thoughts and get the information that way, I'd get another painful poke in the belly as my reward, so I replied, "My father." It wasn't *quite* a lie—she'd know that too.

"Also a legionary."

"Yes."

"Did you find him?"

I shrugged, feigning little regret when in fact the search had fully consumed most of my youth. "No... at least I don't think I did." That was true... of a sort.

The look she gave me suggested she wasn't fooled, not one bit, but was willing to go along with my deception, at least for now. And I wasn't sure why I persisted in replying with shades of the truth since it was unlikely such prevarications would garner me any favors. Still... I couldn't help myself.

"You've certainly traveled far and wide in your search—truly to the four corners of the Earth. How did you manage that, might I ask? It's rare for a common soldier to see so many foreign lands, or, should I say, *survive* so many foreign lands."

I smiled—the absolutely best haughty smile I could muster under the circumstances. "I'm no *common* soldier."

She gave me another slow, foot to face look before answering, "No, you're not. For one thing you have a truly astonishing memory for details— do you realize that, Centurion? I don't know how you do it, but you have a way of structuring what you experience in a way that retains incredibly precise recall.

"You remember people's facial tics, their inflections, the way they walk, all without conscious intent; you remember exquisite details of battles, minutiae that might seem utterly insignificant even to you, but nevertheless you internalize it, and later, when you experience a similar event, these past experiences come into play—I strongly suspect this ability is in large part responsible for your surprising longevity, not to mention the speed at which you've risen through the ranks..."

If she was trying to flatter me, she failed as I didn't really understand what she'd just said.

"...but that still doesn't answer the question as to how you came to visit so many distant and exotic lands."

Now this was a question I could answer: "I'd find myself an officer, one who was *very* ambitious, willing to take risks in order to advance his career, which often meant being sent to the very edge of the Empire, sometimes beyond—"

"So you...?"

"Made myself *very* valuable to him. I went where he went and if he was transferred to another unit or legion, so was I. And when he was killed or recalled, I'd attach myself to another, and another and then another."

"Very calculating on your part."

"I served each of them well. *Extremely* well."

"I don't doubt you did." She gave me another slow, head to toe look. "How old are you?"

"Twenty eight—or as close as I can figure."

"How long have you held the rank of centurion?"

"Not quite three years."

"Remarkable."

It *was* remarkable, *truly* remarkable, even my officers said so and if she could grasp the significance of the silvered bosses, the *phalerae*, on my chest harness—she *should* have been able to grasp the significance of the pair of torcs at the very least as these were no common barbarian's crude torcs, these were the horse-headed torcs of chieftains and made of solid silver— she'd have a much deeper understanding and appreciation of just *how* remarkable it was, how remarkable *I* was.

I'd been told once, long ago, that while honors were transitory, deeds lasted a lifetime, perhaps even longer. Now, as I stared into her eyes, I knew with cold certainty this only held true if those deeds were recognized.

Even knowing how much the awards, the honors—tangible recognition of deeds deemed extraordinary—on my chest harness meant to me, and she had to have known that—it was written on my face and was topmost in my mind—it was, to her, *irrelevant*. I was now nothing more than chattel; my past accomplishments, no matter how noteworthy, meant absolutely nothing, which meant *I* was nothing.

So I decided to toss something out, something she couldn't possibly ignore—in sheer desperation if you must know, in hopes it might spare me further rough treatment: "I can read and write—"

"Can you now?"

I ignored her condescending tone. "Latin *and* Greek. I know all the classics by heart; I can recite them verbatim. I'm also fluent in a number of barbarian tongues."

That reaped barely a quirk of her eyebrow, nothing more and I was, I freely admit, flabbergasted. These were extremely rare skills for someone of my checkered and yes, lowly background, and one that had always left people, especially women, duly impressed. Her utter lack of interest left me feeling even more lost, even more… *vulnerable.*

Nothing I'd achieved, militarily or intellectually, meant a damned thing to this decrepit hag. I was a captive, a slave, nothing more.

"Came up through the ranks?"

I looked back at her and gathering up what little remained of my self-worth, grumbled, "Yes."

"How old were you when you joined?"

"Not quite sixteen—again, as near as I can figure."

"So, raw recruit to centurion in nine years? Very remarkable indeed. Due, I'm sure, to your *remarkable* skills."

I squinted at her, deeply peeved by her mocking tone. My hard-won accomplishments became something with which she could taunt me, but they meant everything to me. "I was incredibly fortunate—"

"Not to mention very ambitious and just as willing to take substantial risks to advance *your* career."

"I see no shame in that—"

"You've always used your body to get what you want, haven't you, Centurion?"

"Don't we all, in one way or another?"

She chuckled, "Yes, I suppose we do—only you seem to have been blessed with a huge advantage over most—" She caught my stray thought and added tartly, "I didn't mean *that.*" She cupped my chin in her bony hand, tilted my head back, turned it this way and that as she closely examined my features. "I meant you have brains along with brawn, not to mention quite a fine face. Quite fine indeed." She released her hold and lightly touched a scar on my left cheek, just below my eye. "Which, aside from this, appears to have somehow escaped unscathed the sharp edge of your worldly exploits."

"A testament to Roman armor."

"Not to mention a *very* hard head. That blow alone should have killed you—granted, it left a sizable lump on your skull and a corresponding dent in your helmet, but without both helmet and hardheadedness, you surely would have died instantly."

Pity that.

She smiled. "Indeed it would have been—a terrible waste in fact."

I scowled at her. I had nothing else. But in truth my face and head hadn't escaped unscathed. I also have a scar on my temple, along with a dent in my skull—lasting mementos from Porsenna's meaty, ring-festooned fist, another scar on my chin—*that* from an unnamed Dacian who took strong exception to me punching him in the face with my shield boss before I ran him through with my sword. My thick black hair concealed the former and the latter was now camouflaged by a scraggly growth of beard.

The hag ran her bony fingers through my hair, parting it and as I turned and tipped my head to give her a better view, she quickly found what she sought. She again grasped my chin, turned my head back to face her, then, using her thumb, she rubbed my stubbled chin. "Yes, I see what you mean. Well, all in all, they're only minor flaws, one might even say they lend you character." Satisfied, she gave me yet another lingering once over. "You've certainly kept yourself in excellent shape."

"Marching in full kit, all day, very day for months on end will do that."

"With the injuries you sustained, I doubt you'd have survived a day if you weren't in top physical condition." She again wrapped her fingers around my chin, holding it in a surprisingly firm grip—

Listen to me.

The command just popped into my head—*that* got my attention. So did the strong sense that it had happened before.

"Now, answer me this—did you find Gracchus?"

The question took me completely off guard and I showed it by flinching.

"Well?"

I glared balefully. "If you asked the question, then you *know* the answer."

"Why'd you kill him?"

"You know the answer to *that*, too."

She smiled up at me and after a moment of mutual scrutiny, she released her hold. "How's the shoulder?"

Before I could answer, she poked me just below the collarbone with the tip of a sharp, bony finger.

I winced.

"Ah-hah." She again ran her hand over my bandaged thigh. "And this?"

I hoped she wasn't going to use this 'concern' as an excuse to repeat her earlier and very humiliating inspection or notice that I was actually not putting any weight on my injured leg.

She again stabbed me in the belly with her finger and replied coldly, "When *I* ask *you* a question, I *expect* an answer—I *own* you. You are now *my*

71

property—never, *ever* forget that." She again grabbed my chin before I could jerk it out of her reach.

Listen to me.

The unspoken command focused my thoughts as if she held my brain in her bony fingers and had begun to squeeze, painfully.

It made it impossible to think beyond the immediate.

"I could have you beaten into submission—there are men just outside who'd gladly do my bidding, overly eager in fact to teach a prideful legionary a lesson he wouldn't soon forget—shall I call them, *Centurion?*"

I glowered, my eyes watering, my jaw muscles bunching against her hold, against the grip she had on my mind.

"Well?" she prompted, eyes narrowing. "Answer me."

"As you just made abundantly clear," I growled through clenched teeth, "*you* own me—so that's your decision, not… mine."

She laughed, said, "Bravado will get you only so far, Centurion. *You* are ignorant, I'll grant you that as I grant you some leeway, but there will come a time when you cannot claim ignorance and such displays of willfulness will cost you dearly." She abruptly released my chin as well as my mind and I reacted by taking an unsteady step back while drawing in a deep, spasmodic gulp of air.

"I must admit, it *is* very tempting to have this insolence of yours beaten out of you, but then all I'd have is a broken man. We need you *whole*, Centurion—mind *and* man—but *never* forget who owns you—never *ever* forget that I can break you, so choose your acts of defiance very carefully. Do exactly as I tell you, serve *me* as well if not better than you served your officers and I *will* reward you with your freedom."

I unlocked my jaws and snarled, "When? *When I'm dead?*"

"That's up to you, isn't it?"

"Is it?"

"No one is truly free, Centurion—you should know that better than most. Soldiers do what they're ordered to do—or, as you clearly learned many years ago, run the risk a severe flogging or worse. *True?*"

I swallowed, hard.

"I am not an ungenerous mistress. Ask any of the men outside—"

"Before or after they've beaten me senseless?"

She stared up at me, clearly measuring me, measuring her response as she drew a long, steady breath, then: "I recognize hard work and reward loyalty handsomely. And I very much appreciate a clever mind not to mention a beautiful body—and in those respects you please me, please my eye greatly—"

"Like I give a damn—"

"You *will* yield to me, Centurion. You *will* accept that your former life is gone for good—"

I couldn't help but shiver at the absolute finality in her coldly voiced words.

"—a very difficult thing to ask I realize, especially so soon and when that life is all you've known for a very long time, but the sooner you accept me as your mistress, the sooner you resign yourself to fact that *this* is the way it will be, from here on, the easier it will be—"

"And if I *refuse* to serve you?"

My sneering words hit home. I saw a flare of anger in her eyes. *Gotcha—*

"I can cleanse your mind with a single thought, Centurion, leave you capable of one thing and one thing only, being my bed warmer—*would you like that?*"

This was all part of the process of breaking me, bit-by-bit, I knew that, but deliberate or not, true or not, this threat cut right to my heart, my gut.

"It's been a very long time since I've had a lover," she continued, seemingly oblivious for once to my reaction, or perhaps more accurately, not caring, "and never one as exotic or finely built as you. Would you enjoy having only one duty in life for the rest of your life, Centurion, able to perform only *one* task and that's to service a very old woman, *without question*, whenever I have a whim?" She gave me another long, deliberately leering ogle. "I must say, the more I think about it, the more I find the idea quite… tempting."

"I don't believe you," I whispered, my strained voice cracking. But in truth I wasn't sure, and that doubt sent another strong shiver through me.

"Defiance, Centurion. You had fair warning." She raised her hand and I stiffened, ready for a painful slap but instead she grasped the amulet and I felt a sudden stab of pain in my chest so intense I thought my heart was about to burst; I couldn't breathe, my vision blurred and my knees buckled—

—and then it was gone, vanished as abruptly as it appeared.

I inhaled spasmodically—a huge breath that left me lightheaded as I blinked and gave my head a quick shake to clear it.

"That was just a taste of what I'm capable of doing." She raised her hand again. "Need more proof?"

I instinctively flinched and shook my head again.

"And just so you know, that's exactly what will happen if you attempt to take off this snakestone—as long as you clutch it, whether it be the cord or the amulet itself, you will feel that pain and people, when they are in that much pain cannot unclench their hand—do you follow me?"

I managed a quick nod.

"Do you want to test it to see if I tell you the truth? Better now while I'm here and can pry it from your fingers while you're still alive, than when you're alone."

Another shake of the head—once was *more* than enough.

"I'd much rather you serve me willingly, Centurion. But you *will* serve me, in one capacity or another—the decision is yours to make."

I fixed my still rather blurry gaze on the floor, swallowed convulsively then answered in a husky stammer, "I... I h-h-have n-n-no choice, d-d-do I?"

She lightly touched my cheek with her fingers—I couldn't help but shy away and that, surprisingly, seemed to pain *her*, deeply. And when she spoke, her voice had lost its heat. "No, you don't. And I'm sorry—*truly* I am. All I can hope is that eventually you'll come to appreciate what I can offer and gladly serve my interests as others have done. Until then do *exactly* as I tell you and you'll be treated fairly—disobey me and... well, you know the consequences. Hear me?"

My eyes began to water anew. I squeezed them shut and bit my lip. It was a threat I was all too familiar with. And by agreeing, by... *capitulating*, I was agreeing to be used in every way imaginable and probably in ways I couldn't even imagine—

"Good," she murmured, patting my arm as one would do with a headstrong child who had finally, albeit very reluctantly, yielded to a parent's frustrated ultimatum. "Very good."

I felt suddenly overwhelmed by a force I could not comprehend and therefore had no idea how to fight, and I again wished with all my heart that I'd died in that bog alongside my soldiers. Even being the object of a ritual sacrifice would be marginally better than this—at least with that there would be a foreseeable end to my wretched existence.

Instead I was chattel, stripped not only of my armor but also my free will, of who and what I had worked so tirelessly for over two decades to become. Added to that was the truly awful realization at any moment—by any caprice—I might end up right back where I'd started, living a life and serving a function I thought I'd left far behind—only this time, if the crone was truthful in her threat and I had no reason to disbelieve her, I could be rendered even more vulnerable to the abuse of others than I had been as a child. And that absolutely, *positively* terrified me—

"Arri...?"

I very reluctantly opened my eyes.

The crone still stood in front of me, still stared up at me with a very concerned look. "I know things seem very bleak right now," she murmured as she gently wiped my damp cheeks with her bony fingers, "but things *will* get better... I promise."

I *wanted* to believe her. Gods—I *really* did as the alternative was just too dreadful to contemplate.

She gave my elbow a squeeze, smiled and promptly changed the subject: "Now, no more physical stuff—*not* until *I* tell you—not Sifrie—she has absolutely no sense when it comes to men." She flicked Sifrie a sidelong look, as did I.

Sifrie grinned and winked at me, startling me into the realization that she'd been present the entire time, had been witness to, in fact was obviously a willing participant, a co-conspirator in my awful enslavement by lying to me, using sex—perhaps she'd hoped the hag would carry out her threat, maybe that was the arrangement so she could have me too, anytime, anywhere and anyway she chose—just like Porsenna and the others...

...and I suddenly wanted to kill her, just as I'd longed to kill Porsenna and just as suddenly she *knew* it.

She stared back at me, eyes aglitter, her leering grin replaced in a heartbeat with an expression of hurt, shock, and yes, to my intense gratification, *fear.*

"Arri?"

I continued to glare murderously at Sifrie.

"Arri, *look* at me."

Look at me.

My head swiveled and my eyes locked on the crone—the response not under my control but hers.

She stared up at me for some time; I stared back, unable to move, unable to blink, unable to look away—frozen in place.

Finally she touched my face and the rage suddenly drained out of me; I began to shake uncontrollably.

"Sit down."

I dropped like a stone, sat there for a moment then looked up to find the crone speaking.

"...but for now there's still a good chance you'll lose the leg if you don't do exactly as I say."

I squinted at her.

Something had just happened. I remembered very clearly being mad at Sifrie, ferociously mad in fact, and even why. But that now seemed utterly silly. Why should I be so furious with her? She'd done nothing to harm me, in fact quite the contrary. The old woman too, while abrupt and at times unfeeling, had saved my life, she'd even mothered me when I was scared and confused and in pain.

I simply had no reason to be ungrateful to these two women—but that didn't make sense either.

Everything was muddled; I felt like I'd just been jolted awake but was still entangled in a very bad dream, unsure what was real, what was not.

I gave my head a shake, hoping to clear it.

"Arri, are you listening to me?"

I again fixed my eyes on the crone.

She sighed, clearly exasperated and muttered, "Obviously not."

"I'm sorry," I replied, but something told me I wasn't, and I shouldn't be.

She knelt in front of me, lightly grasped my chin—her signal that she wanted my undivided attention. I'd learned *that* much.

"I said you need to do exactly as I tell you, or you might still lose your leg."

That was like a slap in the face, one I hadn't seen coming. "I... I thought I was getting better."

"You are. Here—raise your left arm."

I did—hurt like fucking hell.

"See? You couldn't do that two days ago."

I scowled sidelong at her.

"It's just stiff—you've lost some movement, maybe permanent, maybe not, but I want you to start to work it—but not a lot, here, let me show you." She rose, grasped my left shoulder in one hand, my elbow in the other then very gently, very slowly began to rotate the joint.

It hurt even more, and I could feel a sickening grinding sensation; I grimaced and bit my lip, but didn't make a sound.

"Once we get home, and you get proper care, you should get most of your movement back."

I nodded.

"Do exactly what I tell you, hear?"

I had to catch myself from saying "Yes, ma'am." That's what I would've said to my mother.

She gave my cheek another pat, murmured, "Good," and rose.

I followed her with my gaze, unable to shake the persistent, niggly feeling that something had just happened. Something critically important. But what? Try as I might, I couldn't put my finger on it.

"Hungry?"

I *was* famished, and that was odd as I hadn't felt in the least bit hungry since… just before the battle, when I deliberately ate lightly—not out dread of the coming fight, I was actually looking forward to it as those damnedable Iceni had been begging to be trounced for some time—but because of a strong belief among the rank and file, probably a complete fallacy but one I too subscribed to, that said an empty stomach might save you if you suffered a sword or spear thrust to the gut.

I'd seen few men survive such a wound, empty stomach or not, but that didn't dissuade me, or my soldiers, from the practice.

I also sensed the crone was deliberately distracting me and I realized I *wanted* to be distracted from the very odd feeling that I was no longer in control of my thoughts or reactions, that the old woman was carefully choreographing everything, every thought I had, every emotion.

But somewhere, deep down inside, I was still very, very angry, *murderously angry*, I just didn't know why.

Then I remembered the gruel and I wasn't sure I could stomach another helping.

"How about some bread and cheese instead?" The hag made no effort to hide the fact that she was reading my thoughts—for all I knew, she might have put the memory in my head about the gruel just so she could offer me something marginally better… a reward of sorts, but for what? "Think you can keep that down? And maybe some roast hare and a little beer—I assume the men have left us some." She flicked Sifrie a pointed glance and Sifrie needed no urging to hurry from the tent.

As the crone turned back to me, I was struck by something she'd said. Massaging my forehead, I asked hoarsely, "What do you mean, 'Once we get home' and, 'get the proper care'?"

"Let's worry about that later, shall we? Right now I want you to eat, but *don't* overdo it—I know Sifrie helped you work up an appetite, but you haven't had anything solid in that stomach of yours for some time and you'll make yourself quite sick if you gorge yourself—*hear?* Then I want you to rest—sleep if you can—you may even keep her with you, to keep you warm—but *only* to keep you warm—agreed?"

I wanted to say that it wasn't entirely up to me—Sifrie clearly had a mind—not to mention hands, lips and a mouth—of her own. But then again, I didn't have to *say* it and by the time I remembered that, it was too late.

She chuckled, patted my shoulder, "All right—just let her do *all* the work, all right?"

Now that was finally something I could wholeheartedly agree to, anything to keep me distracted, to keep me from digging up *why* I wanted so desperately to kill Sifrie and the crone.

"But remember, you also need your rest." She gathered up the fur and wrapped it snugly around me, around my chilled shoulders. "We break camp tomorrow at first light—you don't get sea sick, do you?"

— VI —

The well-worn road that led away from the garrison, away from the village of my birth was etched in my mind—as good a map as one could ask for. In my childish naïveté, I had no doubt I'd find Gracchus—I was convinced it would only be a matter of days before I'd find myself standing before his barracks' door, knuckles poised, ready to knock.

But days turned into weeks without finding a trace of Gracchus or any of the others for that matter, as if they'd never existed—as if I'd never existed.

By now winter had thoroughly settled in as if it was an honored and welcome guest and brought with it shrieking desert winds and the stinging bite of sand storms. I resorted to begging, stealing if need be—these were the lean and barren days and few had food enough to spare, much less to share with an emaciated urchin. I often found myself fighting stray dogs for scraps—and got used to being nipped, but once I got a little too bold and was severely bitten on the forearm—it would have been worse but for a villager who happened across the attack and drove the dogs off, then proceeded to drive me away as well, hurling obscenities and stones to make sure I knew better than to return.

It took weeks for the wounds and broken bones to heal and from then on, I did what I could to avoid the animals altogether. I was just too weak, too small—and yes, potentially just too easy a meal. I was relegated to snatching eggs from under roosting chickens then running from their startled clucking while I gulped the eggs down raw, even the shells, almost vomiting in the process.

I came perilously close, once, to being caught and killed when out of sheer desperation I decided to grab a hen—I'd had my fill of raw eggs. I managed to squeeze into a chicken coop without awakening its occupants, but when I snatched a sleeping bird from its perch, its startled squawk raised the alarm and a moment later I heard angry voices and fast approaching footfalls.

I tried to shimmy my way back out, still clutching my loudly clucking prize, but my tattered clothing got snagged. The chickens' owner—he must have thought I was a jackal—started frantically stabbing through the slats of the hutch with a large knife, heedless in his rage to the carnage he was causing the hens he was trying to protect.

But when the blade sliced my calf and I screamed, he panicked, dropped the knife and ran.

So did I, as fast as I could with a badly bleeding leg… and one very angry, loudly protesting hen.

As soon as I was far enough away I felt I was safe from pursuit, I happily strangled the bird then I tore it apart and ate it, feathers, feet and all.

I opened my eyes to find the tent aglow with the deep golden light from the brazier. The air was hot and quite stuffy and smelled of wood smoke.

I yawned and blinked several times, then lifting my head, looked around only to find the crone seated nearby, watching me.

"Sleep well?"

I squeezed my eyes shut. Had my hands been free—yes, I was tied down, yet again—I would have rubbed my eyes as the smoke stung, but as it was, squeezing them was the best I could do, then I mumbled groggily: "I... I think so."

"You realize you've slept the entire the day?"

"Oh."

"I elected not to break camp, let you sleep undisturbed, since you were clearly in need. Let's hope the risk of remaining here another day was worth it—my men are unhappy on your account I'll have you know."

I wasn't sure what to say to that, so said nothing.

She rose, walked over to me then knelt beside my right shoulder. Only then did I notice the knife in her hand.

I tensed, unsure of her intentions and warily met her gaze.

"Kyrou tells me I'm a fool to even entertain the thought of ever trusting you..."

Kyrou. He was the one who offered to slit my throat just because I briefly couldn't remember who and where I was—

"...but you're extremely bright—one might even say too bright for your own good—and because of that I'm convinced you'll come 'round, once you've been told the whole truth and have had time to fully digest it." She lightly stroked my cheek with her bony knuckles. "What do you think?"

"I... I don't know."

"Honesty. I like that." With that she rose, taking the fur cover with her, leaving me completely naked... *again.*

I was getting damned tired of this—not because I'm ashamed of my body, far from it, I'm just not used to being on display every time someone entertains a notion to see a naked man, which of late always seemed to be *me*—and of course in the back of my mind, *always* now in the back of my mind, was her threat.

At least this time the air wasn't freezing cold, which meant I wasn't, either.

She slowly walked all the way around me, gazing at me before she again knelt, this time next to my right hip. "Sifrie's utterly besotted with you."

I couldn't think of anything else to say but, "I'm... sorry."

"Why? I'd thought you'd be flattered—you're infatuated with yourself and she's a very highborn woman. She's also very beautiful—but then, so are you." With that she began to caress me and I couldn't help but inhale sharply. That made her smile. "You find me hideous, yes?" She watched her fingers work for a moment, clearly savoring my body's reaction, then met my wide-eyed gaze. "You find what I'm doing to you repugnant."

I swallowed convulsively.

"Would you let me do this if you were not tied down?"

"Prob... probably n-n-not," I stammered as I began to shiver uncontrollably despite the oppressive heat, while wondering desperately if I'd somehow, unwittingly, given her reason to change her mind about what purpose I was to serve. Maybe she wanted—excuse the pun—a 'hands on' demonstration before she committed herself, one way or the other.

"Again, honesty." She continued her gentle fondling as she watched my face, my fearful expression out of the corner of her eye. "What would you do if I were to cut you loose right now?"

"I... I d-d-don't know." I shut my eyes, *squeezed* them tightly shut in fact, and tried to visualize Sifrie caressing me—but when that failed to produce what I assumed to be the desired results, I tried to joke with myself that it could be worse—it could be the ogre molesting me rather than the hag. That didn't work, either.

It was another step in the harrowing process of my enslavement—despite her claim to the contrary, this was all part of breaking me, piece-by-piece, bit-by-bit with my body a ready accomplice.

I could make it easier on myself, or harder. Either way, the end would be the same.

So I tried to come to terms with what was obviously going to be an expected and regular part of my servitude—I could do this... willingly, or she'd just wash my mind clean and have me anyway. She owned me, owned my body and she could completely control both.

You can do this.

Perhaps she had no intention of actually going through with it—perhaps it was a test.

You've done it before—done what you had to do to survive.

Perhaps all she wanted was to feel young again, to savor the response of a young man.

"Good," I heard her murmur as she continued to caress me in a way that made thinking beyond the immediate extremely difficult. *"Very, very good."*

I wanted to say the same about her, but at this point it wasn't necessary—she was very, *very* good. Damned if she wasn't—of course she'd had a century or two to perfect her technique...

My breathing quickened, my heart was now thumping madly as reflex assumed control, my body willing even though my mind was not. But before things progressed any further, I felt a quick, sharp tug against one ankle, then the other, and next my right wrist—she was cutting the tethers, one by one. It was a test—or she really intended to go through with it and perhaps didn't share Sifrie's idea of what was amusing—or perhaps she expected me to be the active partner—despite her earlier warning. Maybe this was why she'd let me sleep the day way: to rest up, rather than recuperate.

I took a shuddering breath while wondering if I could take her without breaking her bones.

"Open your eyes, Arri."

I didn't want to—as long as I could tell myself it was Sifrie, I could maintain myself, maintain the momentum, even go through with it, but…

"I said, open your eyes." Her tone was not a request, but a command.

Defiance, Centurion… you had fair warning, her words came back to me and I did as I was ordered—and started violently.

The crone was gone, replaced by a woman who appeared to be not that much older than myself, with a mane of chestnut hair and intense blue eyes.

I blinked then blinked again, wondering if the smoke was playing tricks with my eyes—or maybe I was hallucinating again.

"I'm no illusion, Arri; you're not hallucinating. This is the real me." The rich, silky voice, while no longer thin and reedy, was still recognizably that of the crone. She pointedly released her hold on me then leaned over and cut the final tether, the one that held my left wrist. "There. You can run if you want—I won't stop you." She used the knife to gesture to the flaps in the tent.

I kept my wide-eyed gaze fixed on her and replied in an unsteady voice barely above a whisper, "I… I wouldn't get far, though, would I?"

She shrugged.

I looked away, tried to get my roiling thoughts under control, my body under control, then I glanced back at her. *"What…"* I stopped, steadied my voice. "What are you?"

"I'm a woman."

I angrily raked my hair out of my eyes with my painfully stiff, swollen fingers, growled, "You're more than that—*a helluva lot more!*"

"And you're a lot more than *just* a man, *just* a common soldier, aren't you, Centurion? We're all far more than what we appear."

I managed to find the strength, the courage, to get my right elbow under me, grimacing as I did so, and then I levered myself into a seated position, to make some attempt at being on an equal level with her, if only an equal eye level. "That's not what I meant and you know it." I gave my

82

heart a moment to settle, along with my breathing. "So what are you, *really?* The woman I now see before me, the old hag... or, the hound?"

"Ah. So, you *do* remember."

"Rather hard to forget—while I've seen people act like dogs, I've never seen a dog turn into a person before."

She chuckled, nodding in grudging concession. "I'm all of them and more—"

"So you can take the form of anything you want?" I'd heard of such before, of course I had: rumors spread among the soldiery in hopes of making us rethink our battle plans, but more often the ramblings of drunken legionaries who'd failed to return to the barracks on time and were hoping to escape their centurion's wrath by blaming some shape-shifting fiend, invariably a shape-shifting *female* fiend for their tardiness—I'd never put any stock in the veracity of such tales... until now.

"I'm not that ambitious, but... yes, I suppose so."

"How's that possible?"

"People see what they want to see, I only oblige them."

"Are you a witch? A sorceress?"

She shrugged. "I'm both... and neither."

I rubbed my temples and grumbled, "I'm not good at riddles."

"Allow me." She scooted closer and as her hands slipped under mine I couldn't help but gasp and tense up.

"Shush, fool!" she chided, *"I'm not going to hurt you."* With that she began to massage my skull, her strong fingers kneading away the tension, the throbbing headache that had suddenly appeared, fully formed, behind my eyes. From there she moved on to work the taut muscles of my neck, my back, and I slowly felt my entire body relaxing.

I exhaled and closed my eyes.

"Better?"

I nodded.

"Still want to escape?"

I squinted sidelong at her. "I think you already noticed I'm not wearing a stitch and it's *freezing* outside."

"There are some clothes over there—heavy trousers, boots, leather jerkin and a thick woolen cloak. Your size—I made sure."

I followed her gaze. There was indeed a mound of clothing not far from the firepot.

"And a horse is saddled and tethered right outside."

I glanced back at her, wary. "Do you want me to escape?"

"I want you to start trusting me. If that means giving you the means and the opportunity to escape… well, I'm willing to take the risk."

"But just to make sure, Kyrou and his buddies are waiting outside, next to the horse, ready to grab me if I try to get away… or perhaps they're already mounted and ready for a little game of hare and hound?"

"I'd imagine they're in their own tent, drinking, or possibly even asleep by now—except for whomever drew sentry duty—he best not be asleep or I'll have his hide."

"Sifrie?"

"With them."

I felt an irrational twinge of jealousy and blurted out, *"With Kyrou?"*

She chuckled softly as she lightly caressed my shoulder. "There's simply no reason to be jealous—I told her I needed to spend some time alone with you, to talk to you, that's all. As you said, it's freezing outside. You'd prefer she stand out in the cold, awaiting *your* pleasure?"

I rubbed my eyes. "Of course not."

"And you might like to know that Kyrou is very angry and more than a little jealous himself right now."

I dropped my hands away from my eyes and gave her a sidelong look, wondering if she was deliberately playing the two of us off against each other.

She smiled as her resumed her gentle, one-handed, almost playful massage of my neck, as a woman would do if seducing a man and murmured, "Kyrou forgets his place and needs to be brought to heel occasionally."

Great. Like he didn't already hate me enough…

"He's not a bad sort, once you get to know him—"

"I'd rather not, if it's all the same."

"The two of you actually have a lot in common—far more than you realize." She scooted behind me and began to knead my neck, my shoulders in earnest, using both hands this time.

The massage felt good, but I still scowled, not sure what she was suggesting—by the massage or her remark.

"Kyrou did not come into my service willingly either…"

I glanced back at her, eyebrows raised.

"…but I soon realized that while he's undeniably brave, he's also reckless, too quick to—"

"Slit throats?"

"In a word, yes." She eased herself around me and began working the fingers of my left hand, fingers that were painfully swollen. It hurt, damned

84

if it didn't, but I tolerated her overdue ministrations—not that I had much choice. "And while he's not dim-witted, I wouldn't have kept him if he were, he too often lets his emotions get the better of him. Understand, he will bully you—"

I'd like to see him try.

"—seek to goad you into doing something unwise, even go so far as to rough you up if he thinks he can make it appear as if you're the instigator, but he will *not* kill you—*or,* for that matter, castrate you, unless *I* order it."

My eyes widened.

She stopped working my fingers to meet my gaze. "He made that threat, didn't he?"

"I... I don't remember." I did remember the threat; I just wasn't entirely sure it was Kyrou who'd made it.

"Just to put your mind at ease, I will *never* order your castration—I fancy everything *just* the way it is—" she glanced down, ran her tongue over her full lips, then again met my eyes, "—no alterations necessary."

If that was her idea of a joke, I didn't find it funny. My expression clearly spoke volumes because she quickly sobered.

"I'm sorry—that was a very cruel thing to say."

I fixed my slitted gaze on the brazier, jaw muscles bunching.

She ran her finger down my cheek, feather-light. *"Arri...?* I'm really am sorry."

I looked at her out of the corner of my eye, still upset, still... scared, unsure what the rules of this new game were and unwilling to yield anything, even a point of pride.

Finally I grumbled, "Why didn't you make me this offer days ago—was it because we were still close enough to Roman-held territory that if I took you up on your offer, I might actually succeed in getting away?"

"I didn't make the offer earlier because you were far too ill—you were unconscious most of the time, if you recall—"

"Actually, I *don't,* if *you* recall."

"—or hallucinating. In other words, you wouldn't have gotten very far and you would've certainly died in the process."

I couldn't help but notice the strangely translucent knife lying within easy reach—she noticed my furtive glance, but made no move. *Another test?* "What's to stop me from killing you?"

"Nothing. Absolutely nothing but my belief in you." She picked up the knife and offered it to me. "Here. Trust has to start somewhere."

I didn't touch it—I was actually afraid to touch it. Instead I fixed my eyes on the brazier as I tried to sort things out. She was offering me almost everything I could ask for... in trade for what? My trust? I didn't even know who—*what*—I was dealing with.

A shiver ran up my spine; my teeth chattered in reply.

"You're getting chilled—I'll stoke the fire." She placed the knife beside me, rose and gathered up a bundle of twigs that had been placed near the firepot then began feeding them, one by one, to the brazier.

I grasped the nearby tent pole with both hands and grimacing, managed to lurch to my feet, and I was pleased to note, not *quite* as awkwardly as before.

She glanced back at me, smiled and returned to feeding the fire.

Another test.

I walked—staggered *very* stiffly in fact, like a drunkard as I hadn't actually walked under my own power in well over a week after all—to the mound of clothes. Everything was there, just as she said. I flicked her an over-the-shoulder glance then grabbed a tent flap and jerked it aside.

I was immediately hit with a blast of icy air. But in the instant before I dropped the tent flap back down, I overheard the restive snort of a horse and caught a glimpse of dapple-gray and the flick of a tail.

"Satisfied?"

As I limped towards her I decided to test *her*, and snatched up the knife. "I think this is yours." As I offered it, elaborately carved horn handle first, I could plainly see my palm magnified through the blade and suddenly wished I hadn't touched it at all.

"Keep it if you like."

"No," I replied, making a face. *"Please*, take it."

She plucked it from my palm and as she slipped it into her boot I briskly rubbed my upper arms. "I'm cold." In fact it was the blade that had given me gooseflesh.

"Then put your clothes on."

I stepped close, wrapped my fingers around her wrist, murmured, "I have a better idea," and roughly jerked her against me. Her earlier fondling *had* put ideas in my head, ideas that needed to be addressed—*now*, before I lost my nerve.

She grinned up at me. "Are you sure?"

"Yes."

"Not afraid of breaking my bones?"

I ran my hands over her and *very* much liked what I felt—she was fuller-bodied than Sifrie but very firm—there was hard muscle under the layer of fat; she did the same, her hands eagerly exploring me.

"Not any more."

She slipped from my embrace and walked over to the mound of pelts, loosening her clothing as she went. I followed, more than happy to assist. Then I stepped back just enough to get a better look at her body.

Sifrie was young, beautiful, small boned—almost delicate—and playful with an easy giggle and sweet voice. This woman was far older than Sifrie, older than me, handsome and voluptuous—the personification of unashamed sexuality and, I freely admit, a wee bit intimidating.

"Would you feel less intimidated if I took the form of Sifrie?"

Now *that* possibility hadn't occurred to me and I had to wonder how many times I thought it was Sifrie tending to me when in fact it was this woman.

"Never."

I have to admit that was a relief. "Is Sifrie a sorceress too? Can she change shape?"

"Yes and no—she's capable, just not disciplined enough—not yet."

Oh.

"Well?"

Her question drew me back to the business at hand. "No." I shook my head. "No not at all—definitely not." Then I had another thought, an even more unsettling thought. "Are you controlling me now? Controlling my thoughts, my body's reactions?"

"No, and I never will—not when it comes to sex," she qualified. *"While at times it's necessary, in truth there's absolutely nothing sexually gratifying in controlling another's thoughts—free will, however, is intensely arousing."*

Another huge relief and I showed it by again pulling her tight against me. I nuzzled her neck and savored her soft intake of breath.

"And my name's Turan—which I *much* prefer to crone or hag... or bitch for that matter."

Point made. "Turan, then."

"Yes."

"Turan," I murmured, carefully dropping to my knees, tugging her down with me. "I do have one *small* request."

"And that is?" she breathed in my ear, sending a jolt through me.

"*Stay* like this—don't suddenly turn into the hag... or the dog or anything else at the crucial moment—it could *really* give me a complex."

— VII —

For weeks I wandered aimlessly from village to village, never overstaying my welcome, grudging as it always was; finding Gracchus was no longer foremost in my mind. Staying alive was.

Then one day a Massyli ivory and slave caravan overtook me as I trudged along a desolate, sand and wind swept road, headed north—always headed north, to the next village and the next, following the course Gracchus had to have taken so many months before.

Many others had passed me, most riding donkeys or on horseback, others on or leading camels, a few on foot, herding sheep or goats—if I was lucky they would ride or hurry by me, urging their flocks to give me wide berth. Most pointedly ignoring me, others would spit on me, a few forced me to run from them, from their threats and jeers, making a game out of my fear.

I was aware of the caravan approaching—the rhythmic tinkle of camel bells, the protesting groans of the beasts accompanied by the cadenced response of human voices gave ample warning. But I was just too tired, too weak to run this time, to even step off the road and make way—I hadn't eaten in days and I fully expected to be knocked down, perhaps even trampled. Instead the camels flowed around me, their drivers peering down at me as if I was some strange apparition, a ghost. I was surrounded in quick order and then the caravan came to a stop and camels were tapped to lie down, which they did, but not without loud complaints.

I had no choice but to stand there as a dozen or so pairs of eyes examined me in unfriendly, suspicious silence.

Massyli and Massaesyli may, in appearance, custom and language, be indistinguishable to outsiders. The Romans, who had reasons for their contempt, tended to lump us all together, mistakenly referring to Massaesyli and Massyli as 'Mauri', or worse, thinking we were all Numidian and presumably if you've met one treacherous Numidian, you've met them all—but we are not one people, far from it.

I'd been raised to fear and despise the Massyli as nothing better than hyenas. My mother's immediate family had been wiped out by a Massyli raiding party, forcing her, with no other means of support, into her brutal profession and Massyli caravan drivers, while exceedingly rare visitors to Simitthu and usually flush with rare goods—an easy enticement for a village prostitute used to far more mundane payment—were the only customers she refused on sight, even if such a rejection earned her a beating and sometimes worse. Even the Roman soldiers loathed the Massyli, in part due to their horsemen's uncanny ability to vanish into thin air after pillaging towns that were supposed to be safe under the Empire's protection: the proverbial thumb in the eye.

Many of the villages I came across were Massyli, and in order to survive, in order not to be recognized as a Massaesyli and killed on sight—most Massyli considered

Massaesyli less than human and therefore not even worth taking as slaves—I taught myself their mannerisms, their dialects. Soon I was able to pass myself off as one, even going so far as to claim I'd been orphaned by a Massaesyli raid on my village, using my scabbed over leg and poorly healed arm as proof of my own close call, which always reaped sympathetic outrage, and on rare occasion, a meal and a place to sleep by the hearth—but I always made sure I was well gone before my threadbare deception began to unravel.

So, when the caravan came upon me, I wearily cloaked myself in that disguise once more, hoping for nothing more than a curious look over before they moved on.

When asked why I was so far from home, I told them I was searching for my father—also a driver, who had gone north, leaving us only days before the raid. I sobbed openly for their benefit, telling them that the prospect of being left an orphan was what had driven me on—it was only half a lie after all.

My distress for once and to my great surprise did not fall on deaf ears—I was told that they too were headed north, for the bottomless purses of the Empire, they said— towards Gracchus, I told myself, renewing my flagging hopes—and I begged them to let me accompany them.

A few were openly skeptical—not of my story, which all seemed to accept without question, but of permitting me to come with them. I would be an extra mouth to feed, and what could I offer in return?

Fortunately one of the younger drivers, a man named Gabba, felt pity for me, said he would share his rations with me—I was so small after all, how much could I eat?—thus costing the others nothing and so all agreed.

Another, not to be outdone in the habit of most desert folk, offered me milk from one of his female slaves. She'd birthed a baby a few days before, which the drivers had promptly killed as it was of no value, and her breasts were still quite swollen. She cried softly as I eagerly suckled—I wasn't sure why because she tightly clutched me to her breast, and I was careful not to use my teeth, but it troubled me, so when I was later offered the chance again, I refused, as hungry, as thirsty as I was.

The male slaves were not so affected and every time we stopped to rest the camels and donkeys, each took his turn with her as did some of the drivers; food was food after all, and not to be wasted.

One night as the drivers sat around the campfire, I stole away to where the slaves were huddled, chained together at the very edge of the firelight, and gave the woman my tattered horse in hopes it would comfort her as it had me, in my naïveté truly believing it would adequately replace the baby she'd lost. She accepted it with a tight smile and watery eyes and offered me her breast—perhaps she thought I was proposing a trade and was clearly surprised when I refused, then she kissed me on the forehead and murmured something—I have no idea what.

I only saw her occasionally after that, as I preferred to walk at the head of the caravan with Gabba, and she and the rest of the slaves were kept towards the back. But each time I did happen to see her, she was holding the horse and that made me very happy.

As the days wore on, the going got harder as food and water began to run short. Everyone suffered, man and beast alike, but when I began to lag behind, I was offered the back of a donkey but when the animal collapsed and died, I found myself atop a camel already laden with elephant tusks. And it was upon that camel, cradled in the hollow between two massive tusks, that I finally found my way to the sea.

Even at a distance, its sparkling, rippling surface left me open-mouthed in wonder—it looked like the glistening hide of a massive, sleeping beast. We came close enough that had I wanted to, I could have run down one of the low, sandy bluffs and actually walked upon its damp shore—Gabba said he'd come with me as he too was curious, but I was too afraid. The soldiers had spun many a tale of monsters who dwelled under the sea's enticingly sparkly surface, just waiting for the unsuspecting to wander too close to their underwater lairs. The proof was in the ripples, the waves on a windless day—evidence of their hidden movement.

Instead I remained aboard the camel, and stared at the sea from the lofty security of its back.

A few days later, after turning east, we finally reached our destination: the ancient and splendid city of Carthage.

It was there, in the bustle of a sun-drenched street packed with vendors loudly hawking their wares and buyers haggling that I slipped, unnoticed, into a dark side alley just wide enough for a small boy pass, and then into the city proper, a city so large it could swallow an army whole—where a child well used to hiding would never be found.

I won't say that the Massyli had begun to get suspicious of me, despite my prolonged stay with them—they were all from the eastern most reaches of Numidia and often excused my slips of the tongue to being forced to live in such close proximity to Massaesyli. As one said with a laugh, 'If one is forced to wallow with swine, some filth is bound to stick'—but as we entered the city, I overheard Gabba and another driver whispering to each other. Three of the slaves, including the woman, had succumbed during the last days of the trek and the rest had arrived in very poor shape indeed, and it was obvious by the men's heated, albeit murmured discussion that they were looking for ways to make up their losses. Gabba even wondered aloud, assuming I couldn't hear him over the beckoning calls of vendors and the raucous, echoing brays of donkeys, how much I would fetch at market.

I had no desire to find out.

I opened one eye a crack at the sound of Turan's whispered voice. Hanni's too, as well as a male voice I did not recognize, I just knew it *wasn't* Kyrou.

I was annoyed. I had been fast asleep, dreaming… of Sifrie? It might have been Turan. Perhaps both at the same time? *Yes… it was!*

On that enjoyable thought, I snuggled back down in hopes of recapturing my dreams while they spoke in hushed voices of a delayed rendezvous, of a ship—of a storm approaching, possibly bringing snow. Turan and the stranger began to softly argue about another route to travel, one that might be safer because it kept to rocky ground, he said—but much longer, she countered, then at his anxious mutter, assured him she was taking the precaution of always making camp on ground underlain with bedrock.

I made no serious effort to listen as they then spoke of things that made no sense—of someone called *Fay-ohm-oor.*

As I felt a cold draft slip under the furs, I stirred, drew my legs up and tried to tuck the covers more tightly around me and they instantly stopped talking; I could feel their eyes on me, watching to see if I would wake completely.

Why don't you go talk somewhere else?

I settled down, took a deep, relaxing breath as I felt the familiar pull of sleep, but just as I started to slide into it, the man asked impatiently, "And what about his armor?"

That got my undivided attention—

"*I told you, we have it all,*" Turan replied in a strained, furious whisper. "*And you'll have it—*"

Wait a gods-damned minute! I shook my head free of the fur and lifting it, peered at the group standing just outside the tent with Hanni holding open the flap.

They stared back at me. I'm not sure who was more startled—me, or the person who stood next to Turan. Probably me, because what I'd assumed was a man, *wasn't,* but before I could really get a good look, the creature darted out of my sight, leaving me with a fleeting impression of tufted ears, pot belly and bowed legs.

I sat bolt upright, turned my wide-eyed gaze on Turan and stammered, "*Wha—what the hell was that?*"

She concealed her own surprise behind a broad smile. "Arach—he's a friend."

I blinked, appalled. "It looked—"

"Arach's a *he,* not an *it,* Arri. And he's deformed—born that way."

Like hell! I glanced at Hanni. He just stared back at me, no grin, no friendly, '*Arri!*', just a pained, 'please don't look at me' stare. So I didn't. I fixed my suspicious eyes on Turan, who, I suddenly realized, was not guised

91

as a crone, but rather in the visage she claimed was her real appearance, and had been, apparently, all along.

She stepped into the tent, leaving Hanni just outside and still holding the tent flap aside. "We didn't mean to wake you."

"Then you should've discussed your thievery somewhere else!"

She sighed, knelt beside me and reached for my arm. "Arri, please—"

"Don't humor me—*and don't touch me!*" I jerked my arm out of reach. "You're giving him my armor! *My* armor, not *yours!*" I tossed the fur aside with the intention of getting up but Hanni immediately stepped into the tent and the look in his eye warned me not to try.

Turan took my moment of distraction with Hanni to grab my wrist. I looked down at her hold, then at her and it suddenly occurred to me she might make good on her threat of cleansing my mind if I persisted. But without my armor, my chest harness, I was no one.

"You cannot keep it, Arri, not as long as you remain with me."

"I don't want to remain with you!"

The friendly approach vanished. "That's not your choice, remember? I own you—"

"Oh, yes, I remember *that!* How could I forget *that?* I also remember you telling me you *bought* me because of my skills as a soldier and you said you wanted me to do your bidding willingly! How can I fight for you if I'm not properly armed?"

"You will be."

"But—"

"You *will* have the finest armor available, I promise you that."

"I want my own!"

"You cannot have it—"

"IT'S MINE!"

"You are mine!" she snapped back. *"My property—which means anything of yours belongs to me and I can do with it as I please!"*

She knew all of my soft spots; her aim was flawless, perfectly executed like a master archer or swordsman—*like Porsenna*—and I felt the air knocked out of me as if I'd just been punched in the gut.

I swallowed hard, managed hoarsely, "Don't do this to me, I beg you! My armor is all I have—it's what I am, *who* I am. *Please...*"

She lifted her gaze to Hanni. "You can go now."

His eyes darted to me then back at her. "Are you sure?"

"Yes. Arri's upset—justifiably so. We need to talk, there's no need for you to remain."

"I'll wait outside then." He favored me with one last, decidedly unfriendly look, a warning not to do anything stupid as he stepped out of the tent, closing the flap behind him.

She turned back to me. "I *had* planned on telling you…"

I squeezed my eyes shut, effectively shutting her out. I was furious, blind mad and scared. It was hard enough to accept that I was now this woman's—*this sorceress'* personal possession, relegated to a plaything whenever the urge stuck her, to do with as she wished no matter how I felt about it; I'd never thought she'd take away my identity. Give it away to some… *some hideous monster.*

"It won't even fit him," I whispered, my voice cracking.

"Arach has no plans to wear it."

"What then, hang it on a wall as some grotesque trophy?" I snapped. Just the thought made me ill.

"Arri, please, you're just making this harder on yourself."

"Me? Don't you mean you?"

She touched my cheek.

I jerked my head away, out of immediate reach. "Just give me my helmet and harness—he can have the rest, even my sword—*everything*, just not those. *Please.*"

"I can't—"

"Just my harness then—*please!*"

"No."

I drew my knees up against me, dropped my head into my hands and began to sob. I knew I was making a complete fool of myself, behaving like a child, but I didn't care, I was *that* desperate, hadn't been this desperate since—

I was suddenly back in that abandoned storage room with one of the soldiers who was very drunk and in a rage over a whore's slight. I was terrified and crying, the cloth horse clutched to my chest—Porsenna, in one of *his* black moods had been extremely rough and I was still hurting inside. I hadn't been able to eat for days I hurt so badly. The soldier simply didn't care; he ripped the horse from my hands and flung it into the darkness, threw me to the floor and did what he needed to do to reclaim his own dignity, such as it was.

Afterwards I hurt even more, so much I thought I was going to die—in fact I begged every god and goddess I could think of to let me die.

When they too ignored my pleas, I went in frantic search of the horse, hoping it at least would offer me some small comfort—blind in the pitch darkness, crawling on hands and knees, sobbing, hands frenziedly

93

searching, sending snakes slithering out of my path—the horse was after all the only thing I could call my own, the only thing that had never hurt me, never abandoned me. I finally found it, but by then I was too weak, in too much pain to crawl out of the room, or even back to the moldy straw bed, so I just curled up on the cold stone floor, holding the horse tightly and shivering uncontrollably while desperately hoping Gracchus would come looking for me.

But he didn't. No one did.

So I cried myself to sleep.

I felt Turan's hand on my back, her fingers light, hesitant, as if fearful I'd shatter into a million pieces.

"I had no idea…" she whispered hoarsely and I was hit by yet another awful, humiliating realization: she'd eavesdropped on the sickening and deeply personal memory—possibly even conjured it up from some dark recess of my mind, just to leave me even more exposed, utterly defenseless. "I'm so, so sorry, Arri—"

"Please," I sobbed, refusing to look at her, knowing what I'd see in her eyes, knowing no matter what, she wasn't going to change her mind. Porsenna, even in his worst tempers had *never* been this cruel. *"Please, I'll do anything you ask, anything, I'll never argue, I'll never question you. Just my harness and I'll do anything you ask of me, I'll willing lay down my life for you—I give you my word! Please—"*

"I can't."

I reluctantly lifted my head and peered at her through streaming eyes. "You said you wanted me to do your bidding willingly—*I will!* You can't change the rules now!"

"I'm not changing the rules. I never promised I'd return your armor to you, did I?"

"You never said you wouldn't, either!"

"True."

"So you lied to me!"

"I didn't lie. I just didn't bring it up."

I stared at her in watery-eyed horror. "I'm offering you my unquestioning loyalty, *my life*—and you're turning this into… *into a game of semantics?"* I twitched her hand off my back. *"It's called lying by omission!"*

Turan sighed, a deep, heavy and frustrated sigh; she was rapidly losing patience but I didn't care—I wanted her to be every bit as angry as I was desperate—

"If I were to give you back your armor now, even your harness and helmet, you'd kill Sifrie…"

I blinked, appalled, and gasped, *"No—"*

"You'd kill me."

"I won't! I promise!"

She caressed my chin, my jaw. *Listen to me.* "Yes, you *will.*"

I bit my lip and fixed my gaze on the brazier as I recalled the flash of murderous hatred I'd felt for Sifrie—an instant of rage—and I couldn't even remember why I'd felt so. But that single moment I now realized was my ultimate undoing and I felt the certainty of my hideous fate tightening around me, around my middle, around my neck like a noose, cutting off my air and I croaked, "Wash my mind clean—*now!*"

"You're extremely upset, Arri, understandably so—"

"It's better this way—you'll know I can't hurt you, and I... *I won't care at all. Please, I beg you, do it now!*"

"Once done, it's done, there can be no second chances, no going back—"

"I don't care!"

"Yes, you do. You care very much—"

"And you just said you don't trust me at all!"

"Trust has nothing to do with it."

"You said I'd kill you, I'd kill Sifrie!"

"If I gave you your armor back, yes."

"So you only trust me when I'm tied down and naked!" And no sooner had the words come from my mouth than I had the sudden, horrible awareness that I'd had the means to kill myself all along—*the tethers are there to stop you from hurting yourself,* Sifrie had said—they hadn't kept me tied down for fear I'd escape. They'd kept me tied down so I couldn't get hold of the snakestone, couldn't kill myself!

I risked a quick glance at Turan and clamped my hand over it.

She made no move to stop me and I quickly discovered why: *nothing happened.* No excruciating pain, no spasmodic gulp of air... no sudden, all-encompassing and permanent darkness. No... *nothing.*

I turned my stunned gaze on her, my fingers still tightly clutching the amulet.

She stared back in something akin to sympathy—or pity, pity for the utter fool who'd believed her, believed her warning. Who trusted her.

"You... you lied to me!"

"You're exhausted, Arri, still very sick and not thinking clearly—"

"YOU LIED! You said if I even touched this," I gave the amulet a hard, twisting tug, my arm muscles bunching, but the cord refused to break, *"I'd DIE!"*

95

"Arri, *please*, calm down—"

"I WANT TO DIE!" I shrieked, unaware in my rage I'd also grabbed the leather thong of my beaded necklace and as I gave it another vicious yank the thong snapped and I hurled the necklace aside, sending beads and star scattering and thong flying.

Realizing what I'd done, I froze.

"Oh, Arri…"

I squeezed my eyes shut and bit my lip.

She lightly stroked my back. "I think we should talk about this later, after you've gotten some sleep."

"I *was* asleep," I replied in a barely audible whisper.

She wrapped her fingers around my jaw, turned my face towards her. I didn't resist. There was simply no point. And I was just too tired. Tired of fighting. Tired of living. Tired of *everything*. Utterly exhausted. I just wanted to fall sleep and never, *ever* wake up.

Listen to me. "I cannot give your armor back because if I do so—"

"I'll kill you," I replied flatly, refusing to open my eyes. "Yes… you told me that already."

She tightened her hold, gave my head a painful snap. I couldn't help it; I opened my blood-shot eyes.

Listen! "If I were to remain as close to you as I am now, for as long as I've been here, while you're wearing your armor, I would surely die."

"But—"

"Your armor contains an element that is a deadly poison to me, to Sifrie, poison to *all* of our kind. That's why you were stripped of it before we came anywhere near you, and that's why I cannot return it to you—*do you understand me?*"

And I suddenly wanted to, I really did. Just as much as I suddenly and desperately wanted to believe *her,* believe she *did* trust me, that she *was* telling me the truth this time—not manipulating my emotions, my thoughts, that taking my armor was not an act of astonishing cruelty, another step in breaking me, but rather an act of survival.

"Iron. Your armor, your weapons, they all contain *iron*. And iron is death to us—we can easily tolerate what's carried in your bodily fluids, but the amounts in your armor is fatal to us if we're exposed to it for more than the briefest period of time. Arach is not so affected, neither is Hanni or Kyrou or the men who took your armor from you that first night."

I stared at her and my eyes slowly widened. *The knife—*

"Yes, the knife—you're fascinated and a little afraid if it, aren't you? Visualize of having armor made of the same material."

I did. I didn't like what I saw. Not one damned bit. "Transparent armor? I don't think that would be particularly intimidating."

"Don't sell yourself, um... *short.*"

I eyed her as I wiped my eyes, my nose on the back of my hand, a very shaky hand. *Not damned funny—*

"And I promise you, once we're home, I'll have my armorer to create the most resplendent armor for you."

"I'm not a child!" I snapped as I tried to reclaim some of my earlier outrage. "My armor's my stock and trade, not... not something to play dress up!" But in truth I knew the battle was over; Turan, yet again, had won. She'd always win. Just like death—

She grasped my arm, gave it a squeeze. "I know, Arri, and I didn't mean it that way. What I meant to say is that he'll make you anything you want."

I thought about that for a moment, then asked, almost reluctantly, knowing by doing so I was handing her everything she wanted: "Can he recreate mine?"

"Yes, if that's what you want—I'll have Hanni make impressions of the bosses on your harness, that way it will be a perfect match—" she smiled, "—minus the iron of course." She wiped my still damp cheeks with her palms then cupping my face in her hands, kissed me on the lips.

My arms suddenly felt heavy as if my blood had been replaced with lead, and my thoughts were getting more and more sluggish. It was hard to think, impossible to argue. And I was just so damned *tired.*

I settled back on the furs; she didn't stop me. In fact she pulled the heavy covers over me, then began gently stroking my hair and I felt the lingering rage, the fear bleed out of me, leaving me even more drowsy, barely able to keep my eyes open.

Despite this, one thought kept drifting around my mind: *perfect match, maybe, but it wasn't the same; it would never be the same. But... what choice do I have? None. Absolutely... none...*

— VIII —

The soldiers, even Gracchus, had often spoken of Carthage; all had reason to come through it on their way to the frontier garrison, some had even served there, briefly, in a ceremonial function. Their tales of its gleaming marble baths and massive temples—each covering more ground than the garrison and taller, much, much taller—of its legendary twin harbors and its bustling docks had filled me with awe and I wasn't quite sure I entirely believed them. Even for a gullible child it all seemed just too fantastic to be true.

The city in reality did not disappoint, in fact it was more extraordinary than any of the stories I'd heard, snuggled in Gracchus' lap or kneeling near a firepot, massaging oil into one of the soldiers' sore muscles.

I was fascinated with its exotic sights and enticing smells, and yes, overwhelmed by its sheer size—the soldiers' accounts hadn't prepared me for that—how could they? It was... huge, every bit as huge as the blue-green sea that lapped calmly at its edges, its glittering fingers reaching into the city itself, as if clutching a rare jewel. I had never seen the like, could never have imagined the like.

Carthage was a city in the truest sense of the word, a sprawling metropolis and thriving seaport, with a vast but rapidly changing population of sailors, merchants and soldiers.

At first I looked to these men as sources of information on the possible whereabouts of Gracchus, but I all too quickly found that none had ever heard of him.

I then engaged in other acts with these men, ones that I am not ashamed to admit to—they kept my belly happy and often led to a warm and safe place to sleep for the night.

Roman Carthage was renowned for her painted harlots, male and female, and I soon found refuge among them. Most were kind to me, almost protective of a boy so young. Others used me, luring in clients who had come to the baths expressly to hire a prostitute and were willing to pay handsomely for something exotic, something unusual. I was both and I never failed to please.

Seasons came and went and somewhere along the line, I stopped thinking of Gracchus. Life was, while not good, at least tolerable—and for someone of my background, that was almost enough. I formed casual friendships with some of the younger prostitutes and when we weren't satisfying paying customers' needs, we enjoyed each other, teaching one another skills we'd learned from our clients and giggling at their often truly bizarre requests.

And as I grew older and more skilled I began to cultivate my own clientele, both male and female, and it didn't take long for me to claim many of the city's wealthy and powerful among my patrons and there were times when I wondered what my mother would have thought of what I'd become.

Would she be ashamed... or proud?

Fortunately for me, I never went through the gangly phase of youth. Even as a young teenager I was tall and well-muscled—despite the deprivations of my early childhood—and, according to my clients, I was extremely eye-catching—I privately gave credit where credit was due: my mother was known for her dark beauty, and she had a proclivity for tall, well-endowed men. I had every reason to assume such a man had been my father.

But this was not the life I'd envisioned when I left Simitthu. I had no desire to follow my mother into the family business. So, when one of my regular customers, a man of letters, an elderly man, a devoutly religious man, offered me a place in his school as well as in his home in trade for my exclusivity, telling me that without education I would never rise above offering my body to anyone who had a coin and a need, I agreed and left the streets behind.

I was an able and extremely willing student and just as willing to repay his kindness in any way he desired. I quickly learned to read and write, both Latin and Greek, and I learned about the world. I was enthralled by the possibilities.

Unfortunately his wife was equally enthralled with me, or perhaps just tired of her much older husband's extreme sexual eccentricities and was willing to pay me handsomely for my services—no role-playing superfluities or props required.

I naïvely believed as long as I satisfied his very peculiar requests there was nothing wrong in satisfying hers.

I was sadly mistaken.

One day he returned unexpectedly and entered her private bedroom to find me atop her. He flew into a rage and attacked me with his dagger. I tried to get it away—I had no desire to hurt him, but I also had no intention of allowing him to hurt me.

He had no such reservations and came at me with murder in his eyes.

In the scuffle the blade sliced across my belly—he was actually aiming lower but I managed to deflect the knife—before I could wrest it away from him.

He then grabbed my throat with both hands; I panicked and stabbed him in the chest—

I hadn't meant to kill him—was horrified I'd killed him. But it didn't matter; his wife began screaming and I heard servants coming at a run—

I awoke with a violent start.

"Arri?" a sleepy voice mumbled as warm fingers clutched my hip and I couldn't help but flinch. *"Arri, are you all right?"*

"It was just a nightmare," another voice replied as a hand lightly stroked my cheek. "Go back to sleep."

Too late; I was now wide awake and trying to sort out my current, rather tangled situation. It was pitch dark. But it was plainly obvious that I was sandwiched between two warm bodies—two warm *female* bodies. One was Sifrie's—I had no doubt about that, but I also had no idea when she had slipped under the covers beside me.

That meant that the other was—

"*Turan,*" she whispered in my ear. "Now go back to sleep—daybreak's still some time off."

I tried, long enough for Sifrie's breathing to slow to a deep, regular rhythm. I suspected Turan had also fallen back asleep.

I wasn't so fortunate.

I ended up staring into the smoky darkness with their arms entwined and legs wrapped around me—almost as effective as the tethers, which Turan had elected not to reinstate—*trust,* she had said, *has to start somewhere.* But this time it was *my* trust in *her* she was talking about—not hers in me. The armor had been a serious blow to that and now she was trying to rebuild. I had to give her some credit for that because in truth she didn't have to try. She could completely control me—mind and man as she said— whenever she wanted to.

And for now I wasn't uncomfortable. Having a warm, soft woman on either side, their naked bodies curled up against mine was *very* cozy in fact. I just couldn't fall asleep.

A finger lightly touched my lips, followed by a whispered, "What's the matter?" That was Turan.

"Can't sleep."

"Pain?"

"Not *that* much." And as long as I didn't move, as long as Sifrie didn't bump my thigh or shoulder, I could almost ignore the constant, dull ache.

"Still thinking about your armor?"

"No," I lied. Which was stupid, really. She knew. "All right, *yes,* but there's nothing I can do about it, is there?" That *was* bitter truth and while I was slowly becoming resigned to it, the loss still carried a terrible sting. But along with that, other things kept floating around in my mind, poking at me each time I started to drift off.

"Worried about tomorrow?"

When I didn't answer, she levered herself up and leaned over me, and her soft hair cascaded over my bare chest. "There's no need to be afraid."

"I'm not afraid," I replied with a hint of indignation even though I was.

"Good." She kissed me firmly on the lips then resting her head on my right shoulder, began toying with the beads on the necklace. They made a soft, familiar and comforting tinkling sound in the darkness, an auditory security blanket of sorts.

I'd spent many a night before a battle fingering the slave beads to conjure up old Niger's reassuring presence, counting the tigers-eyes to remind myself each denoted a close call in my life, that they'd protected me before and would do so again, and finally rubbing the star between thumb and forefinger to the point I'd rubbed off most of the faint design of dots and swirls that had once covered its surface, rubbing my signaculum too, my fingers acting as proxies for my mind's anxiety—it wasn't until a moment later that it struck me that I was again wearing them. *What—?*

"I found them, *all* of them, and restrung them, using the original thong. It's a little shorter than it was..."

"Thank you."

"As for the snakestone—"

I opened my mouth but she pressed a finger to my lips.

"—it's simply a token of your fealty to me, Arri, *not* an emblem of your enslavement and as such, you can safely remove it at any time, although it's my hope you'll continue to wear it, voluntarily. I'm truly sorry I misled you earlier..."

I took a deep, ragged breath, then exhaled, slowly and tried to relax, tried to shake my mind loose of its troubling thoughts and find some quiet, peaceful place in which to sleep. Instead I found myself rolling the beads between thumb and forefinger, recognizing each by touch alone, then the star, followed by a brief fingering of my signaculum, then back to the beads—an all too familiar ritual—while carefully avoiding the newest addition, the snakestone, altogether.

Several minutes passed; my mind, however, just would not settle. "Ever lose your place in the world?"

Turan didn't answer immediately; I thought she might have actually fallen asleep, then, out of the darkness came her thoughtful reply, "Yes. I suppose I did, once."

"This will be number four for me—doesn't get any easier, if anything it gets harder."

"But this time you're not alone."

True. I waited a little longer then asked the question that kept nagging at me: "Where are you taking me?"

"Does it matter?"

"Yes."

"Why?"

I suddenly realized I wasn't really sure—in truth there was no one I'd be leaving behind. Those few men—Felix, Rufinius and Aetius—with whom I'd formed close bonds in recent years were, no doubt, dead and had been for many, many days—or they'd written *me* off as dead.

So there was nothing to hold me, just as when I left the abandoned garrison over two decades before. And just as then, what lay ahead was a vast unknown—but I was no longer a child. I wasn't facing a very uncertain future with a child's ignorance, a child's foolish optimism. I was facing it with an adult's hard-won wisdom and an adult's very real qualms.

"I... I don't know."

She tightened her hold on me, whispered, "I'm taking you far away—"

"How far?"

"Farther than you've ever been—farther than *any* Roman has ever been."

"Farther than Parthia?"

That garnered a soft chuckle and a gentle tug on my ear. "Yes, Centurion, much, *much* farther than Parthia."

That left only one reasonable option: "To the end of the Earth?"

"Farther even than that."

I chewed on that for a moment, not at all sure I liked the sound of it—I'd been told by some that the world was a sphere, that there was no true "end", much less "edge", which had always struck me as utterly ludicrous: how could this be? Others were convinced it was flat, with a definite end, and an even more precipitous edge. While I found that idea more plausible, I didn't like the present implications. "How's that possible?"

"You'll find out, soon enough."

I realized that was about as good an answer as I was going to get. This was Turan after all—she delighted in being an enigma.

So I was going—being forcibly taken—somewhere utterly new, someplace utterly strange, leaving everything and everyone I knew and had ever known behind, presumably forever and I couldn't help but shiver at the prospect.

I exhaled, again tried to relax. Then another question, one that had been bobbing around, just under the surface, emerged from the swirl of my subconscious mind: "Why did you rescue me?" Not capture, not enslave—*rescue.* And I was comfortable with that—I *believed* it.

"To save humanity."

"Humanity...?"

"People. Meaning like you—"

"Romans then, and those from the provinces?"

"Not just Romans or those from the provinces. *Everyone.*"

"But not barbarians," I decided decisively; surely not *them.* No one in their right mind would include barbarians in anything.

She chuckled softly, replied, "Yes, Arri, *including* barbarians…"

I flicked her a sidelong look, truly appalled, even though she was invisible in the darkness. Barbarians *are* people of a sort of that I had no doubt, but they aren't… well, you know, they aren't like me, not at all. They're *barbarians* for gods' sakes!

"…along with people you've never heard of, people you'll never meet, people who haven't even been born yet. *Everyone.*"

I had to pause a moment to digest the fact that she was deadly serious. "But… *why?*" I mean, a major part of my previous job description had been to kill barbarians and with a lot of practice I'd become very good at it—one might say I excelled at it. This new task seemed rather, well, counterproductive?

"Because if you don't, all will be lost."

This didn't sound good. *"Including Rome?"*

"Yes, Arri, *including* Rome."

"You mean the city, not the empire—"

"No. I mean the empire. *All of it.*"

I tried to get my head around that. How could anything or anyone possibly threaten the entire empire? Bits and pieces? Yes. But all of it? Then something else struck me, something even more immediate: *"Me."*

"Yes."

"All by myself."

She chuckled. "Well, no, not completely."

"Why… *me?*"

"Because you're no common soldier, remember?"

This was not exactly what I'd meant when I'd said it. "Perhaps I oversold my abilities a little bit."

"You? I find *that* hard to believe."

"Maybe. I'm not saying absolutely."

She chuckled again, kissed me on the cheek then lightly combed her fingers through my hair as I stared up into the darkness, thoughts churning anew.

I'd never thought of anyone beyond myself and now I was being asked—*commanded*—to risk my life, most likely *give* my life to save people I'd never met—people who, I strongly suspected and if given half a chance, would kill me on sight? If someone had said this to me a week ago I would have thought him utterly mad. Now it seemed perfectly…*rational?* But whatever Turan said *was* rational, *was* instantly believable—I had no doubt in it, or in her.

Which, I realized, meant I *was* hers, as she said, mind *and* man. What I had long thought was an unshakable loyalty to Rome was now an unshakable loyalty to her—and I hadn't even been aware of the transfer of allegiance.

It just *was*.

You'd have thought I would have at least taken a few minutes to weigh the merits of the matter, but I hadn't, which left me with the niggly feeling that I hadn't been consulted in the matter, hadn't been given the choice. It just… *was*.

"Turan…?"

Sifrie wriggled around, mumbled something in my ear that sounded remarkably like *'shut the fuck up'*, then buried her face in my neck—carefully, to avoid reawakening the sharp pain in my injured shoulder—another not so subtle hint on her part.

I took another deep breath, in hopes of settling my thoughts, my worries, at least for the night. It wasn't like I could back out now. All of humanity was, as Turan said, depending on me. Oh yes, that's just the thing to pop up in your head when you're desperately trying to fall back asleep. No pressure. Not at all.

If ever in my life I was going to have to face down performance anxiety *this* was going to be it. And in front of all of humanity.

Even better.

But it was certainly a step up from what had previously been my goal in life, to become *Primus-Pilus*. One hell of a step up in fact. I could hope there wasn't one hell of a fall afterwards, but in my experience one usually went hand in hand with the other.

No pressure. No, none at all. *Now, go to sleep Arri…* I made a face and didn't give a damn if Turan or Sifrie sensed it.

To add to my woes, a gust of wind suddenly whistled through the gaps between the surrounding boulders. The tent's woolen walls rippled in response and the dying coals in the brazier briefly flared and crackled, sending tiny embers spiraling upwards, towards the smoke hole.

I turned my head to the right, away from Sifrie and whispered as softly as possible, *"Turan?"*

"Yes?" she replied in a sleepy murmur.

"Is it warmer there?"

"There…?"

"Where you're taking me?"

Her fingers spread over my stomach and the tips dug into the bruised flesh. *"I'm not surprised you have a chronic bellyache—it's so full of complaints."*

I grimaced in real pain and she instantly released her hold. A moment later I replied, *"I'm not a complainer, I just don't like the cold and you didn't answer my question—"*

"It can get a lot colder—there. Satisfied?"

I groaned—*softly mind you.* Fucking wonderful—

"Now, how 'bout I help you get back to sleep?"

It was a blatant attempt at changing the subject, but I wasn't adverse, to her ploy or to what she was suggesting. *"I'd like that very much."* Sifrie be damned—or, going by recent experience once she realized what was going beside her she'd happily join in, but instead of Turan doing as I'd expected, she lightly touched my forehead and I felt a sudden heaviness wash over me; my eyelids fluttered.

"Go to sleep," she murmured as she snuggled up tight against me. And I did—but it begs the question, why didn't she do this earlier? *Damn her...*

— ii —

The next morning was heralded in by a hard but mercifully brief downpour, followed by a steady drizzle. The heavy woolen tent was surprisingly lightproof, not to mention waterproof—almost as good as a goatskin tents favored by the legions, but there was that damnedable smoke hole, along the occasional gaps in the weave, spots where the natural oil of the wool had worn thin from use and of course I found myself *directly* beneath one such spot.

An icy drop hit my left eyelid and slid down my cheek. I didn't dare move, much less twitch a muscle. If I did, I risked waking Turan and Sifrie—I'd done that once already; I didn't care to make it a habit, otherwise they might not be so keen to spend the night with me, keeping me warm and relatively comfortable—with the exception of where they'd elected to place our shared bed of course.

So I turned my head, hoping the next one would miss me. A moment later, another icy drop smacked me on the left cheek and I silently cursed the weather, fate, this wretched land and my continued lack of fortune. I inched myself slightly to the right. A third drop got me square in the left ear. I couldn't help it. I flinched.

"I was wondering when you'd wake up."

I rolled over, almost on top of Turan. "Perhaps you'd like to change places?"

"I'm actually quite comfy where I am, thank you anyway."

I eased myself over her—carefully and, not intentionally, rather suggestively and I desperately hoped she wouldn't make the wrong assumption and latch hold—then I slipped from under the covers and staggered very ungracefully to my feet.

"And where are you going?"

"To relieve myself." Aside from waking me up, the rain had stirred an urge—an *intense* urge. I looked around, not sure where the tent flap was—it was pitch dark after all. "Then I'm getting dres—*ow!*" I stumbled back from the still very toasty brazier and promptly bumped into the rough-hewn tent pole. *"Ouch!"*

"Are you all right?" That was Sifrie. She didn't sound happy.

"Fine. Thank you for asking," I grumbled as I rubbed my abused backside.

I heard movement, felt someone brush past me. A moment later there was a slit of dim light as Sifrie drew the flap aside, just enough so I could see where I was going without further wounding my pride—or collapsing the tent on top of us.

"There you go." She then scampered back to the warmth of the bed.

Clutching myself, I staggered to the opening and peered out at the dim, freezing drizzle. *Gods...*

I desperately needed to pee, the sound of running water didn't help one damned bit, but the thought of actually stepping out into the frigid wet was beyond daunting. There was also the very real possibility that if I did, I wouldn't be able to do what I needed to do, leaving me soaking wet, freezing cold and *still* desperately needing to pee.

I briefly wondered if Sifrie or Turan would be terribly displeased if I urinated in a corner—Turan said we were going to break camp anyway, so...

I sidled away from the opening, then, with a glance over my shoulder, proceeded to empty my bladder against the tent wall, all the while hoping the telltale tinkling sounds would mingle with the brisk, innocent patter of raindrops.

Finished, I then stumbled back to where I last saw the pile of clothing, tripping over someone's feet in the process.

"What *are* you doing?" Turan snapped, which left me with the distinct impression her feet had been involved.

"Trying to find my clothes—sorry I stepped on you."

She sighed—a loud, decidedly annoyed sigh. "*Stay* exactly where you are. I'll get them for you."

I stood there feeling stupid, until I heard Turan stumble and fall. *Vindication!* I couldn't help but grin—it was dark after all, who'd know? "Are you all right?"

"I'm fine—and *stop* smirking."

Damn.

I found passage aboard a merchant ship, the Aequitas, *bound for Egypt that very afternoon when the tide was high and winds most favorable—three of her crew had gone missing and her captain was desperate to get his load of grain to market, desperate enough he didn't ask too many questions and what few he did ask, I answered with cautiously ambiguous lies. I was equally desperate to escape the city—I had no doubt if I was apprehended I'd meet the customary and very unpleasant end of any common criminal: as fodder for the wild animals in Carthage's famous Circus, or sold to fill the belly of an equally hungry Roman warship—a short and very brutal life lashed to an oar.*

I harbored no allusions about my wealthy patrons coming to my defense: I was a prostitute, nothing more, and easily replaced. And now I was a murderer—the murderer of a well-respected member of the elite, which might even mean I'd be singled out for a particularly gruesome end—perhaps crucified or impaled on a stake and left to die slowly and in agony next to a heavily trafficked road—a warning to anyone of the lower classes who thought they too could be so bold.

The Aequitas *had barely left the confines of the merchant harbor behind, its sails plump with the hot wind that blew from the desert, when it became blatantly obvious to everyone aboard that I was no sailor, had, in fact never even been aboard a boat, much less a ship. So when I was dragged before the now irate captain I was sure he was going to throw me overboard, which would have been a death sentence of another kind as I could not swim.*

I again tried to lie my way out of the situation, and when that failed the captain threatened to have the truth beaten out of me and then have me thrown overboard. I had nothing to lose, so I confessed what I had done. I pleaded for his mercy, for the mercy of the crew, all of whom had joined their captain and formed an impromptu judge and jury.

None had any love for the privileged of Carthage—even their fellow Romans frowned upon Carthage's hedonistic excesses—but neither were the captain and crew sympathetic to me. Whores had their place, they all agreed, but that place was not aboard a ship that was already short several crewmembers and needed each and every man aboard to pull his own weight.

The captain took my fate under consideration, leaving me tied to the mast until we were well beyond sight of land, then he had me brought to his cabin. I had little doubt that I was to be killed on the spot, or perhaps handed over to the crew to use as they pleased after the captain had gratified himself and when they were done they'd simply toss me into the sea like so much rubbish.

Instead he gave me a stern lecture on the pitfalls of my supposedly 'chosen' profession, of lying to people, especially those who had done me a good turn. I, in turn, listened to his self-righteous harangue in obedient and seemingly respectful silence while I seethed inside.

I had been the wronged one! I was the one others had taken advantage of and brutalized, not once but for my entire life! I'd never intentionally hurt anyone and had been forced into prostitution in order to survive and into murder only in self-defense!

When he finished, I steeled myself, but instead of doing as I expected—he had, after all, repeatedly told me just punishment for my crime was death—he instead placed me under the watchful eye of the ship's cook, to assist in the preparation of meals and when I was not occupied doing that, I was to mend sails—tasks that were not all that different from those I was responsible for so many years before, in the garrison, where I repaired uniforms and helped butcher the goats and pluck the chickens. But I quickly discovered that it's extremely difficult to prepare food when the very sight or smell of it sent me running for the nearest railing.

Conditions that time of year were not particularly favorable and the captain was forced to zigzag back and forth, tacking against the wind while searching for unseen currents that would transport us east. The sea, as if toying with us, was exceedingly rough for days on end—even some of the seasoned sailors succumbed to the violent and near constant pitch and sway and like me, spent a good deal of their time staring miserably at the churning water below, groaning in their pitiable suffering. Under different circumstances I might have appreciated their companionship, but I quickly realized that the last thing someone who is seasick needs is to see or hear or smell someone else retching.

Misery, in my case, did not *love company.*

A voyage that should have taken no more than a fortnight in fact took three weeks. But it was during these long, dismal days that I managed to prove my worth to the crew, prove to the captain that he'd made the right choice in sparing me: no matter the weather, whether the sun blazed down on us or we fumbled around in the rain-lashed dark of a nighttime storm, I did what anyone asked of me without complaint, even if I was so seasick I could barely stand.

If they were thirsty, I'd fetch water; if they were hungry and the cook asleep—or seasick himself, I'd hastily create something marginally edible even if the sight of it made me heave; if their muscles were sore, I'd massage them. And when one of the sailors broke his arm in a fall, I was the first to arrive and quickly and expertly set the bones and splinted his arm with wooden stays.

And no one, not one, in the entire voyage asked me or offered to pay me for sex. To them I was no longer a whore; I was now a valued member of the crew. That in turn won my admiration of them and proved to me, once and for all, that I could be more than what I had been.

I was deeply shocked and equally moved when the captain, after meeting with the crew, offered me a permanent position aboard. But I was no sailor and certainly had no love for the sea, and I still had this desperate, one might even say foolish need to find Gracchus.

So it was aboard the Aequitas *and several days out from our destination that I came to take a fully* Roman *name—at the urging of the captain, himself from a recently conquered Roman province and bearing a non-Roman name, and therefore not fully trusted by his fellows.*

My mother had told me that all she knew about my assumed father, aside from him being a legionary, was his given name: Arrius, hence the diminutive, Arri. The captain said he had always favored the name Marcus—a good, solid Roman name, derived from the war god Mars he said, a name he'd given his own recently born son and one few would question—and the cook, a dark, wiry man and freed slave originally from the distant lands of Nok, *proudly offered me his freedman's name, Niger.*

How could I refuse? And when I gladly accepted their names as mine, the captain gave me a small pouch fat with coins—to pay for my lodgings until I could find 'respectable work', which to him meant no more whoring, and the cook, not to be outdone gave me his necklace of old trade beads and a small silver amulet in the design of a four-pointed star, to which I later added beads of tigers-eye, believed by many soldiers to protect one from being wounded or killed in battle; I figured stringing a few on my necklace couldn't hurt—so to speak—and from then on, each time I survived a particularly close call, I'd add another.

Niger told me as a child he'd been bought with trade beads such as these he was giving me, and that by wearing them, he felt he always had the means to buy his freedom again if the need arose. The star was a common gift in his culture, from father to son upon reaching manhood, to symbolically give the four corners of the world, 'because,' as the tradition went, 'one cannot know where one will die.' He said he'd been too young when slavers had taken him from his family to have received one, so he later bartered for one and wore it with the intention of resuming the tradition.

But he was now an old man, he said, far too old to father a son, too feeble to work hard labor and therefore safe from the slavers, so he wanted me to wear his necklace, to protect me from harm as it had protected him, to always remember my humble beginnings—and most of all, to always help those in greater need.

As he slipped the leather thong around my neck, he told me to make the Niger name proud.

In all the years that have followed I've never forgotten that in fact I had only one name, Arri, the name my mother had given me, the name the soldiers—Gracchus—had called me. But to everyone else, from the moment I disembarked the Aequitas *in Alexandria, waving my tearful farewells to her crew, I was Arrius Marcus Niger and so I've remained all my life.*

I barely recognized myself, dressed as I was in unsophisticated local garb rather than my customary leather tunic, ring-mail shirt and chest harness, and now with a substantial growth of beard, which I have to admit, *really* itched. It was a hard blow to my vanity—then I felt another blow, even harder, one that sent me into a mild panic: I now looked just like...*them*. The enemy.

If Romans, even those who I'd considered close friends, were to come upon us, I'd be seen *as* the enemy—and maybe, just like that, I'd *become* the enemy.

It was not a pleasant thought.

Felix *might* have understood. He'd always been the most accepting of the three, often waxing philosophical about the twists and turns of fate, much to the exasperation of Rufinius who saw the world in the simplest and most straightforward of terms: good and bad, win or lose. Aetius... well, I had no doubt he would've had a good laugh at my new, less than immaculate attire as he'd never wasted a chance when it came to poking fun at my obsession about my appearance.

I closed my eyes, forced my heart and mind to settle.

Would you rather spend the rest of your life naked?

No. Vanity—and Aetius—be damned.

The clothing fit, just as Turan said—even better, it was *warm*. Downright cozy in fact, of course anything would be warm and cozy in comparison to being stark naked in this hellish place. I could only hope the woolen cloak and hood were also waterproof, because the steady drizzle had turned back into a cold, wind-blown rain.

Did I mention that I *loathe* this Britannia?

I was, admittedly, still smarting over the loss of my armor and the rain did nothing to ease my black mood.

I walked over to the open tent flap and gazed unhappily at the goings on outside. Turan's men were breaking camp, and, I observed with growing misery, they were all clearly soaked to the damned bone.

I also noted that the cart was being abandoned—no, not *just* abandoned, it was being systematically destroyed by the ogre, which he was doing very efficiently I might add, despite the pelting rain—in fact he appeared oblivious to the foul weather.

The rest of the camp appeared destined for a similar fate. What little the men had bundled up had ended up on the backs of the horses—eleven horses to be exact. That was significant, because while I wasn't absolutely positive, I was almost certain that Turan's entourage—which now included me—added up to *twelve*. Which meant, if my math was correct, we were significantly one horse short.

Aside from my beloved cloth horse—or perhaps because of it and the painful memories associated with it—I was not overly fond of the beasts, despite many a trainer, early in my military career, trying to convince me otherwise. Mauri—Romans tend to make no distinction between Massyli *and* Massaesyli—are famed horsemen, and legionaries who had the misfortune of being stationed in and around Numidia feared these mounted brigands who appeared out of nowhere—which usually meant when the legionaries were on patrol—and then vanished again, usually without a trace aside from the stripped and mutilated corpses they'd left behind as a calling card.

So one could see why my trainers, having found themselves with a Mauri recruit, immediately sought to take advantage of my assumed innate knowledge of horses in order to return the favor. Sadly for all involved, I had no such innate knowledge. The only thing I knew for certain about horses was that they could sense if someone disliked them, and in feeling the bitter sting of my disapproval, reasonably decided the loathing was mutual.

Nevertheless, I've always been privately envious of the mounted cavalry, of their resplendent armor, their haughty glances at us lowly infantry—even if we, pardon the pun, do most of the *legwork* when it comes to the actual fighting, and oh yes, most of the dying, too. Their purpose, it seemed to me, was nothing more than to dress up war and make it look simply glorious—something like putting gobs of makeup on an ancient and decrepit whore. While she might look incredibly inviting at a distance, when you get close enough to engage in the business that brought you together in the first place, you realize too late she's actually damned fucking hideous.

But I'm *not* suggesting that cavalry are the whores of the legion. *Never.* The thought never crossed my mind—*ever.*

That being said I *was* in awe of the cavalry's massed charges: lances lowered, men roaring and hooves thundering—a solid, impenetrable wall of horseflesh and armor rushing forward, seemingly unstoppable. It was particularly awe-inspiring if the cavalry in question was that of the enemy charging *me*, which unfortunately for me far too often had been the case, and more often than not while I was out and about with a small number of soldiers, innocently foraging or reconnoitering—meaning we were facing a cavalry charge without the welcome companionship and camaraderie of the rest of our legion. These unfortunate experiences explains how I became such a damned good sprinter, even wearing full kit, and to love caltrops with all my heart.

Caltrops worked almost as well on war elephants—but don't get me started about elephants. I could go on for days.

Let's stick with horses and how I came to really loathe the beasts.

Every so often I would get a notion that I simply must overcome my antipathy of the animals—out of boredom if you really must know—being a legionary isn't all easy glory and shiny expectations after all. A lot of a soldier's time is spent doing as little as humanly possible without being *caught* doing as little as humanly possible. Hard as it might be to believe, even centurions occasionally find themselves afflicted with this failing.

I always get into serious trouble when I'm bored—from the moment I was born, or so I recall my mother telling me at least once a day. And on this point I have to agree with her. Case in point: I never had a problem finding some low-ranking cavalryman malicious enough he'd happily agree to teach an infantry centurion to ride.

Perhaps a *wee* bit too happily.

I've been thrown five times, severely bitten once, stepped on at least ten times, kicked three times and knocked flat on my ass twice. Which means the score was, at last count: horses, twenty-one; Arri, *zip*. And that's not counting all the panicked horses I've had to dodge during a battle, the dying horses whose wildly flailing legs I've had to avoid while also avoiding the sword- or spear-thrusts of an enemy, and all the fresh horseshit I've had to squish through, marching at close quarters to the hindquarters of some officer's inconsiderate and very flatulent mount.

It's really hard to stay focused, to maintain discipline among the troops with a damned horse loudly passing wind every time you open your mouth to bellow an order—I swear they do it deliberately. And I could never understand how some high-ranking officer could sit there, astride his mount and look dignified while the beast emptied its bladder—I mean, it's not like he couldn't hear what was going on beneath him as it was a damned torrent. But they always looked dignified—the horse too. Damned if they didn't—

A slim arm encircled my waist, startling me out of fond memories of marching to the next battle and my likely death while watching poop tumble endlessly out of a horse's butt.

"You know how to ride of course," Sifrie said, looking up at me with trusting, worshipful eyes that gushed, 'Of course you do—you know how to do *everything!*'

There was no point in lying. "No. *I'm* infantry." That last part was said with pride, as if that explained all.

"Oh." Her face fell. "Well, you'll just have to double up with someone."

"You?" Somehow the idea of bouncing around on the back of a horse didn't seem quite as vexing if it provided me the perfect excuse to press my crotch tight against her backside and have my arms locked around her slim waist with my hands occasionally straying higher—or lower, in order to keep my balance. What could Kyrou do about that? Not damned much, that's what.

"My pony couldn't carry both of us."

Oh—well that certainly puts a crimp in things. "Why can't we take the cart?" *Aside from the fact that it's now in several large pieces—*

"Too rugged from here on," Sifrie replied. "No road."

"Too slow," Turan said as she appeared beside me and to my obvious surprise, again *not* in her visage of a crone. Seeing my arched stare, she replied, "These men are mine—I have no secrets from them."

Explanation enough.

Then I noticed she had a look in *her* eye that left me seriously worried. "So who are we running from? Iceni? Trinovantes?" Then another possibility came to me, granted a very unlikely one: *Romans...?*

She patted my arm. "Let me worry about that, all right?"

That made me mad, damned mad. "You said you rescued me for my... *expertise*, my skills. Presumably you didn't mean my skills in bed, but rather my skills at fighting."

"True, although you have absolutely no reason to be modest about the former. I consider it an unexpected and *very* pleasant bonus."

"I'll second that," Sifrie added with a grin and a vigorous nod as she not so gently groped my backside.

I scowled at Sifrie, then Turan—I was in no mood to be fondled, flattered—or sidetracked. I was suddenly in a killing mood, a *serious* killing mood and any Iceni or Trinovantes would do; I dared not consider what I'd do if the threat was posed by Romans. "Give me a sword and I'll show you what I'm really good at—"

"And you'll do as I tell you!" Turan fired back with equal heat.

I snapped my mouth shut and fixed my slitted gaze on what the ogre was doing, then, with a defiant sidelong glance at her, I pulled my cloak's hood up over my head and bracing myself as best I could, started out of the tent.

She managed to grab my arm and jerk me to a halt before I took two steps. *"Where are you going?"*

"If you believe I'm incapable of fighting, then I'll find some other way to make myself useful!" I shook off her hold and swearing loudly I limped over to where the ogre was happily breaking apart the cart's axle.

The rain was even colder than I'd feared and by the time I reached him, I was drenched to the bone and shivering.

114

I pushed the hood back. It was worthless and limited my trained legionary's renowned peripheral vision and if we were about to be set upon, I wanted to see who and what was coming, even if I'd been denied the ability to fight back.

"Can I help?" I managed without stuttering.

He looked up and to my immense relief, grinned, the matter of Arach and the evening before forgotten. "Arri!" He rose and clapped me on the back with enough force to send me staggering sideways.

I reclaimed my balance, wiped a lock of wet hair from my wet face, asked again, "What can I do to help?"

"Seriously?"

"Seriously."

"You can grab that axe—" he jerked his chin towards a nearby boulder and the axe that was leaning against it, "break the yoke for me. That should be enough—take those damned bastards at least a week to figure out what went where."

I wasn't sure which bastards he was talking about—this land was rife with them—but clearly they weren't *our* bastards, which immediately eliminated Kyrou, regrettably. I nodded and slogged off to retrieve the axe. I was wet, I was cold, my shoulder and leg were aching... but I also felt, well... not exactly good, but marginally better that I had—since the morning of that fateful battle.

Perhaps I felt just a *wee* bit too good for my own good because as I wrapped my cold, wet hands around the cold, wet handle of the heavy axe and started to lift it, my left hand, which I should have assumed was untrustworthy as I could barely bend my fingers, suddenly lost its grip. Unbalanced, I then lost my footing in the mud, slipped and fell, landing awkwardly on my injured leg.

Have you ever done something that was so far beyond stupid that you almost couldn't believe you'd actually done it? Well... then you know just how I felt at that moment. And oh yes, I was also in sheer, blinding agony.

I bit my lip against the heaving groan that had formed in my throat.

"Arri?"

I reluctantly forced my head up. Hanni was now towering over me.

"Are you all right?"

My pride wanted to say I was fine, but my expression betrayed me... and now my lip was bleeding—yes, I'd bitten it *that* hard.

He knelt and put his arm around me, in the process sheltering me from the wind-blown rain. "It's my fault—I should have known that axe was too heavy—"

115

"No... no, I simply slipped." The male mind being what it is, I would not have it known that I couldn't lift the damned thing—I'd rather it be known that I was just incredibly clumsy because that's just *so* much more manly.

I grimaced then forced out, "I think..." I wanted to say, I think I've split open my leg, but I just couldn't admit that either, not to Hanni, not when he thought it was his fault, not when I was trying to prove how useful I could be—*fool!* "I think I pulled a muscle—" I had a sudden, horrible thought and squinted in the general direction of the tent.

I could barely see it through the pouring rain, which meant Turan and Sifrie most likely couldn't see me at all and I breathed a sigh of relief, well, as much as I could while in sheer agony. It never once occurred to me that their ability to read my mind, or overhear my silent screams of agony, did not require close proximity—not until I saw two black-clad figures who looked remarkably like really, I mean *really* infuriated Furies hurrying towards me, cloaks flying.

"Uh-oh," Hanni whispered. *"Sorry, Arri, but you're on your own."* With that he got to his feet and hastily backed up.

I had no such quarter. So I just sat there in the ice-cold, gooey mud, clutching my thigh, tears mixing with the rain and blood that streaked down my face and chin, hoping Turan would cleanse my mind, right then and there—maybe it would make the terrible, burning pain stop. At least it couldn't possibly make me any stupider.

Sifrie was the first to arrive but she didn't offer any comfort, not even a reassuring hand. She just stood there, arms crossed, mouth set in a grim line, green eyes flashing.

Turan stopped beside her and in an *ominously* calm voice, said, "Get. Up."

I didn't think I could. But something warned me not to say so. So I tried—I really did, but it was futile. Turan knew it; she just wanted to rub it in, damn her.

"Hanni."

The ogre, who'd been trying to look as inconspicuous as possible, which, as you can imagine, is really difficult for an ogre, reluctantly stepped forward.

"Assist him."

He offered me his hand. I let go of my injured leg to grab his hand with my right—I was unable to lift my left arm at all—but no sooner had he jerked me to my feet than he again withdrew.

116

Turan stepped close and stared up at my bloodied and pain-contorted face. "*You* are an idiot, you know that? And not just any idiot, but a *blithering idiot!*"

I couldn't have agreed more, and I opened my mouth to say so, but before I could get a word out, she slapped me across the face, *hard*. Hard enough to snap my head back, for me to stagger a step sideways, almost losing my footing again in the process. Once I'd recovered, she stepped close again, and I braced myself for another stinging blow.

Instead she glanced over her shoulder, yelled, "*KYROU!*"

I had a very good idea what was coming next—so did several of her men who happened to be close by—they favored me with quick, sidelong glances that ranged from barely sympathetic to impatiently gleeful before they returned to their work, presumably before Turan noticed and they suddenly found themselves on her bad side as well. So I decided to make it easier for everyone: I dropped to my knees—I was about to anyway as my injured leg felt like jelly and the rest of me was not all that much more solid. I was now shivering uncontrollably, my teeth chattering but I no longer cared if anyone thought it was from fear rather than cold and excruciating pain.

I arched my head back, exposing my throat and closed my eyes against the stinging rain as I waited, listening for the squishing sound of the approaching footsteps of my executioner.

A hand gripped my shoulder. I flinched and looked up only to find it was Turan.

"What the hell are you doing?"

"Waiting for Kyrou."

"On your knees? I'm sure he'll be flattered, but—"

"I assumed he's a lot shorter than me—thought this would make it easier for him."

"Make what easier?"

"Slitting my throat?"

Her eyes darted to Sifrie, who shrugged, then as Turan looked back at me, she shook her head and sighed, "What am I to do with you?"

I stared up at her, honestly bewildered. "I… I thought you'd already decided."

She sighed again, drew me against her and wrapped her cloak protectively around me. "I have no choice but to deal with your foolishness, and your leg—not to mention your shoulder, later—"

In other words, my execution was going to be delayed. *Wonderful.*

"I wasn't planning on executing you."

117

Oh.

"Where *do* you get these ideas?"

"From you?"

That flummoxed her for a moment. Then she recovered and said, "It's open grassland and forest from here on—" She jerked her head up and looked around, then nodded curtly to one of her men, who, I noticed, unsheathed his sword before hurrying off. She then turned back to me. "We must leave, *now*, ride fast and hard—"

Oh, even better. I had no idea how I was going to manage that.

"—our only hope is to reach the *Sulaviae.*"

Before I could ponder what a sulaviae was, the answer to how I was going to reach it arrived in the form of a hooded and cloaked man astride one of the substantial carthorses—and the combination of black cloak and black horse certainly gave the impression that one of Death's disciples had just arrived. Which, when you think about it, was pretty damned accurate.

As the rider reined in the massive animal, the ogre silently reappeared beside me and again helped me—well, actually, he just lifted me back to my feet, with me having no choice in the matter.

I had never met Kyrou face to face—at least not that I could remember. I only remembered his voice, his threats. Now that oversight was about to be remedied and I sincerely hoped he *was* shorter than me. I'd at least have that.

Kyrou slipped effortlessly from a saddle made for a much smaller horse, landed lightly on his feet—

Show off.

—pushed back his hood, in the process revealing a wild mass of blond hair done up in a fancy Swabian knot—a style favored by the tribes of Germania—and a face covered in a thick reddish-blond beard and eyes that stared at me with a look of cold hatred.

And quite the charmer, too.

But he *was* a lot shorter than me, and, even better, nowhere as good looking as me. *Hah!*

I also noted with some glee that he was sporting a black eye and a large, livid bruise on his cheek and both appeared suspiciously fresh. Maybe my intuition had been right all along; maybe he *had* slapped me around.

Clearly *he'd* been recently punched and I dearly hoped I'd done it. I had no clear remembrance of fighting back, of landing a punch with enough force to leave that much bruising, so maybe someone else had been kind enough to do the honors for me.

Maybe Hanni.

I favored the ogre with a sidelong, questioning look; his mouth quirked in response.

Before we could continue our silent conversation, Turan cleared her throat.

I tried to look innocent but too late.

"You're covered in mud, your lip's bleeding profusely, who knows what you've done to your leg or your shoulder—all due to that unbelievably asinine, wildly overblown male pride of yours, and, oh yes, we've just established that you are a *blithering idiot*. I don't think now is the time cast aspersions, do you?"

Well, that certainly put me in my place and I couldn't help but glance back at Kyrou to find his expression unchanged. Then again, how can you improve on murderous hatred?

He might be short, he might not be good looking, but he *was* dangerous looking. He was a very dangerous man and I reminded myself that I'd best not forget that. *Ever.*

I turned to the horse, hoping for a more friendly response. While I'm no expert, I swear the look the beast gave me matched Kyrou's in naked hostility.

Great. Just… great. Gripping my thigh, and with the ogre's help, I slowly approached the animal while Kyrou stepped back as if I was contagious. Or maybe he was just afraid Hanni might pop him another one just for the hell of it. One could hope.

I pointedly ignored him. My attention was fully on the horse. I really hoped it wouldn't decide to step on me, or kick me, or bite me.

It was huge. Its hooves were huge. I bet its teeth were huge.

I fixed a stiff smile on my blood-streaked face, murmured, *"Nice horsey,"* and gave it a tentative pat on its rain-slick withers—I'd been told, by one of my many extremely sadistic riding instructors that horses liked that, which I quickly learned is not *entirely* true—turns out you'll occasionally come across one that really finds it annoying, which is how I got myself seriously bitten and almost lost a couple of fingers.

Luckily, this one didn't seem to care either way. It just eyed me as it tongued its bit. And oh yes, its teeth *were* huge.

"Ready?" That was Hanni as he placed his large, gnarled hands around my waist, ready to hoist me up onto its back.

I'd assumed Kyrou would remount then I'd somehow get myself up behind him, but no. Clearly the plan was for me to sit in the saddle with Kyrou, who, I'd noticed, was armed with both a sword *and* a dagger, *behind* me—just the place I'd want a man who wanted me dead but knew better than to do anything obvious. I had to assume Turan felt I'd be more stable in the saddle, less likely to take a fatal tumble—assuming of course that Kyrou didn't help by giving me a gentle nudge—*and oops!*

So, one can understand that the thought of having this man seated right behind me did not sit well with me, but I was in no position to argue the point. "Uh, I… suppose *sooooo—!*"

I was suddenly astride the horse… and it danced sideways for some damnedable reason with me wobbling this way and that, arms flailing, and looking, I would suppose, like a drunken scarecrow. A drunken, soaking wet and *terrified* scarecrow—let's not scrimp here, because while I wasn't drunk, I *was* soaking wet *and* terrified—it had been blinding agony just to slip and fall from the height of my own two legs. I didn't want to even ponder impacting the ground after being tossed from the loftiness of this behemoth.

Hanni grabbed the bridle, gave it a jerk and the horse, amazingly, froze. Clearly he had a way with the beasts. Or maybe the horse knew something I didn't—although I wouldn't have minded being let in on the secret, just in case I had a need to know, later on.

Kyrou muttered something to Turan and Sifrie and I'd wager a month's pay it was not a compliment on my remarkable horsemanship. Sifrie giggled and Turan quickly turned away, but not fast enough. I *saw* the grin.

Kyrou's expression was still the same: pure, cold hatred but now with just the hint of smugness.

Did I mention I abhor horses?

Hanni placed my cold-stiff hands on the promontory at the front of the saddle that I suddenly recalled was called a 'horn'—and for good reason. If a horse came to an unexpected stop, which they did a lot and for no discernable reason, men quickly found parts of themselves painfully impaled. "You might want to hold onto this."

I managed a sickly, rain-drenched smile. *Thanks.*

Kyrou somehow managed to scramble up behind me, scooted himself tight up against my backside—a little *too* tight for my liking, considering the man looked like murder, then he wiggled around as he got himself settled on the animal's broad, wet back.

If it had been his intention to utterly unnerve me by this blatantly suggestive maneuvering, I had one hell of a shock for him, but before I had a chance to respond with an equally blatant suggestion of my own— something told me Kyrou might be a tad more sheltered in his sexual experiences than I—he reached around me to take the reins and hissed in my ear, *"I understand you didn't heed my warning."*

I squeezed my eyes shut. *Oh... gods—*

He kicked the horse in the belly and suddenly we were galloping pell-mell through a gap in the boulders then down a very steep, slippery and rock-strewn slope.

I dared not look back to see if anyone followed. I had to put my full concentration into hanging on as the massive animal lurched and heaved beneath us.

I've been told horses don't have very good eyesight. I desperately hoped that wasn't true as we were headed at breakneck speed for a dense copse of beech at the bottom of the hill. But at least I now knew with utter certainty where the term "breakneck speed" came from—clearly it was coined by some fool on a myopic horse racing down a rain-slick hill towards a thick stand of trees.

I had to believe Kyrou knew what he was doing—or the horse knew what he was doing. I didn't care which as long as *someone* knew what the hell he was doing.

Before I could further ponder our rapidly approaching death, I heard rapidly approaching hoof beats. Kyrou seemed unconcerned, so I had to assume it was the rest of our party playing catch-up. It was.

Sifrie passed us—red hair flying and cloak flapping, her piebald pony racing by us as if we were standing still. Then came the black-haired man, his sword drawn and clutched tightly in one hand, his bay horse running flat out and blissfully ignorant of the razor sharp blade a hand's breadth from its bobbing neck.

Turan followed and drew her dapple-gray alongside just long enough to give me a quick look over, to nod to Kyrou, then off she went. Two men, both holding bows at the ready followed her and one, I was utterly astonished to realize, was riding *bareback*. I didn't have to think very hard as to what had happened to his saddle and I suddenly hoped he wouldn't blame me personally if he lost his precarious seat. But to my chagrin, he looked perfectly at home on the animal's wet back, even when the horse took to the air to leap a small, rain-swollen gully—he just leaned into its neck, man and mount briefly becoming one—and once the horse had landed safely, if awkwardly on the far side, he actually swiveled his torso around and took his time scanning our surroundings, checking to see if anyone followed.

I was duly impressed. Clearly some people were born horsemen. How else could you explain keeping astride a soaking-wet horse at full gallop while turned almost backwards, without the aid of a saddle? He could certainly teach Parthians a thing or two. I never saw one of them try this maneuver on a slippery-wet horse.

Four more riders appeared in my peripheral vision, then slowed to keep pace with us, and finally Hanni appeared, astride the other carthorse, and, like the one horseman, bareback although he did have two advantages: one, his mount still wore its harness and two, he was as big as the horse.

He grinned at me and waved, clearly enjoying the wild ride. I would have waved back, but that would have meant briefly letting go of the horn, which I was not going to do under any circumstances, and besides, waving might have left him with the impression that I shared his exuberance, which I *didn't.*

We miraculously passed through the stand of trees without mishap, and I admit, with my head bowed, hands gripping the horn and eyes tightly closed—I really didn't need to see where we were going after all—that was up to Kyrou and the horse. And I have to give Kyrou credit, as much as it sincerely pains me, he actually drew his arms tight around me, keeping me balanced and centered, which, despite of our very prickly relationship, actually made me feel a whole lot better.

I finally, reluctantly, reopened my eyes to find most party spread out and cantering down yet another grassy slope, Hanni and our four outriders—presumably our bodyguards as Kyrou literally had his hands full and would hard pressed to defend us if need be—still keeping close to us.

Far ahead, through the rain, I saw a vast sheet of white-flecked gray. *The sea...?*

I wanted to glance back at Kyrou for confirmation, but decided against it. He had more important things on his mind—like whether he was going to castrate me first, or just gut me and take his chances explaining himself to Turan.

As we reached the bottom of the hill, in the process losing sight of the ocean, Sifrie, who was still in the lead, slowed her pony's pace to a trot and then to a sedate walk, and as the rest of us caught up we did likewise, to give the horses a chance to recover and the riders time to regroup.

Turan twisted in her saddle, eyed each of her hard-faced men. "We must press on in order to reach the rendezvous point before nightfall. It'll be too risky once it gets dark and even riskier to make camp."

There was a grumble of agreement from the men as each and every one shot me an accusing glare—as if our current predicament was *my* fault.

Turan's narrowed eyes again searched the group. "Where's Harne?"

Heads swiveled around; nervous eyes searched our surroundings.

"I last saw him just as we emerged from the woods," the bareback rider said.

"He was right behind me," the black-haired man added and turned his horse's head. "I'll go back—"

"No!" Turan snapped and with a glance up at the very ominous sky, added, *"We must go, now!"* then turning back in the saddle, gave her mount a kick to the ribs and it took off at a canter.

Everyone followed suit, although I saw several of the men glance worriedly back the way we'd just come, as if hoping to spot the missing man—or perhaps to catch a glimpse of whoever or whatever was responsible for his disappearance.

The downpour tapered off and finally stopped—not that it mattered as we were all soaked to the bone—replaced by a frigid breeze that smelled of brine. Soon we were splashing along the bed of a rain-swollen stream, following it, I assumed, to the sea while also masking our trail.

Riders hunkered down, cloaks drawn tight as the horses, oblivious to the nasty weather, slogged on at a relatively good pace.

As for me, the constant jolting of the ride had compounded what I'd done when I slipped and fell. Now that I wasn't hanging on for dear life and could actually think beyond the sheer terror of the experience I realized that I was becoming more light-headed with each passing minute.

I really, I mean *really* didn't want to say anything—least of all to Kyrou—as Turan had made it clear that speed was of the essence, but as my vision began to cloud, I very reluctantly turned my head and whispered, *"Kyrou...?"*

He leaned close, his bearded chin pressed against my shoulder and growled in my ear, *"What, Roman?"*

My lips were suddenly numb, my tongue thick and unwieldy. "I thhhink... I'm going to... to passsss out..."

— X —

I'd planned on staying in Alexandria for a week or two, a month at most—it was dirty and loud and incredibly crowded, and not at all like Carthage. No polished marble temples on a hill, no impressive military harbor, no huge public baths. Carthage was like an elegant courtesan—she had her charm, her wiles... her mystique. Alexandria, on the other hand, was more a street prostitute: hard, vulgar and miserly, demanding her due and unwilling to take anything less.

I'd heard that Alexandria boasted extravagant temples and luxurious palaces that rivaled anything in the empire, that she even had a massive library, but to me these tales were unsubstantiated rumors. The Alexandria I'd come to know, the area around the port and military garrison was simply ugly—and suffocatingly hot. The only marvel I'd seen was the Pharos—at first I hadn't believed Niger when we first spotted its incandescent gaze while still far out to sea and he claimed it was no natural phenomena, but rather the work of man—a light house he called it, used to beckon ships from far and wide. Pharos was a marvel, I'll grant its builders that, even seen close up as we sailed under its watchful presence and in the less than favorable light of midday. That said, and call me prejudiced, but one light house, no matter how tall, no matter how powerful its signal fire is just not the same league as Carthage's amazing twin harbors or her opulent baths.

Alexandria was a strange city, with strange people and even stranger customs. I kept to parts frequented by the sailors and soldiery, in part due to the familiarity but also in hopes of hearing something—anything about Gracchus.

The coins eventually ran out but I had no desire to return to my earlier trade. In truth I did not want to disappoint the crew of the Aequitas *even though they'd likely never know. Instead I'd resorted to grabbing the occasional piece of unguarded food to keep my belly quiet. The best time for my relatively harmless pilfering was in the late afternoon, to take advantage of the long shadows, the dust and the sweltering heat, all of which could be my ally if someone saw me lift a piece of fruit or a loaf of bread and decided to take chase.*

It was also when the streets were most crowded, and as tempting as it was, I never resorted to cutting purses—stealing a scrap of food was, at best, a few lashes for a first timer, at worst a one-way trip to the slave market for a repeat offender. Cutting purses was a death sentence.

On this particular afternoon my chosen street was packed with Roman soldiers just back from a successful campaign in the south and out for a day and night of carousing.

I'd already arrived at my objective, a fruit vendor's small outdoor stand and was using a Roman matron and her aged slave as a cover by helping them select the best melons. Since arriving in Alexandria, I'd become quite an expert in melons as they were highly portable and could slack thirst as well as hunger. I figured the least I could do was to share my hard-won knowledge with these elderly women in trade for their unwitting involvement in my thievery.

The stall owner assumed I was the woman's grandson or, more likely, the slave's grandson as we were far more alike in coloring. The matron and the slave in turn thought I was the fruit seller's property. It was the perfect camouflage.

And as the three of us moved along the rows of fruit, I'd carefully slip a fig here and a date there into the folds of my now very grubby tunic.

All was going to plan... until several soldiers stopped, drawn to the artfully displayed rows of colorful fruit.

They were foul-mouthed, raucous and very, very drunk—the shopkeeper, afraid they would scare off the matron and her fat purse offered them exotic delectables to draw them away from his stall. Unfortunately, he lured them close to a group of local men seated at an eatery next door—men who'd been making disparaging remarks about Romans, just loud enough for the extremely inebriated soldiers to now "accidentally" overhear.

Angry words were exchanged.

Ugly and highly personal insults followed.

The shopkeeper and food seller were desperate to avoid what appeared to be inevitable: the complete and utter destruction of their stalls and everything in them. So, while the shopkeeper tried to smooth the waters, the food seller made a mad effort to gather up as much of his wares as possible and get them to safety. I would have offered to help but I'd sampled his meat pies and wasn't at all impressed. I would have been even less impressed if I'd had to pay for them, so I decided to stick to the fruit stand, which was currently untended by its owner.

I figured one couldn't ask for a better distraction to some minor larceny than a major fracas and began grabbing anything within reach. Besides, everything was going to be smashed within the next few minutes anyway, so... one could say I was actually doing the fruit seller a favor by sparing some of his better goods from such an utterly wasteful end.

I should've snatched a melon and more figs—more than I'd eaten in several days— and run. But I got greedy. The next thing I knew a soldier catapulted over me—and into the cart full of ripe melons.

Splat.

For a few precious seconds everyone stopped as if frozen. Then the cart collapsed, taking the unconscious soldier, its load of now smashed melons, and the all too brief reprieve with it.

Now it got serious.

Soldiers appeared from everywhere as locals poured out of shops and bordellos and stalls to join the fray and what started out as a minor brawl between at most ten or eleven men turned into a major street battle, with fruit, loaves of bread and the occasional rock flying this way and that.

The matron and her slave stood there in the midst of it, paralyzed and clutching each other, as bodies flew past them or landed at their feet.

A voice told me to run. Another told me I couldn't just leave the pair where they were as they were in serious danger of being injured or even killed. Perhaps because of my own upbringing, or my promise to Niger, I just could not walk away from anyone who was this vulnerable.

I dumped what I had, then dodged this way and that and managed to reach them. I grabbed their hands and somehow got them down behind an overturned cart and there the three of us stayed until cooler heads, in the form of a Roman cavalry unit, arrived and quickly broke up the brawl.

Satisfied the two women were now safe, I hastily retrieved the melon and figs and started running down a side street.

I was running so hard I didn't hear the hoof beats coming up fast behind me—

Suddenly I was lifted bodily off the ground, held by the collar of my tunic while the rest of me bounced against the withers of a cantering horse, and of course I was so startled I dropped my ill-gotten gains, which splattered across the width of the narrow street.

My captor slowed his mount to a trot and then a walk and finally came to a stop, but he didn't let go of me, so I just hung there, limp, feet dangling as the horse glanced back at me with a look of utter disdain.

I heard more hoof beats. Next thing I knew, I was back on my feet... and completely surrounded by grim-faced soldiers and white-eyed horses staring at me as they slowly circled. Now, I hadn't been in Alexandria very long, but you'd think I'd have learned, somewhere along the line, that Roman cavalry was tasked with catching petty criminals. Didn't they have more important things to do—like advancing the borders of the empire?

Looking put upon by such rough and totally unwarranted treatment, I angrily tugged my filthy tunic back into place while I waited for just the right moment—a gap in the milling wall of horseflesh—to bolt. The street sported a number of even narrower side-alleys. If I could just reach one, no rider and horse could follow, and I had no doubt I could easily outrun a soldier in armor, especially in this oppressive heat.

As if sensing my plan, the soldiers tightened their cordon; then I heard someone clear his throat and I slowly turned around, briefly came face to highly polished bronze greave and above it a bare knee then I looked up to a man wearing a very elaborate muscled cuirass, scarlet cape, feather-plumed helmet and a seriously unsympathetic expression.

He reluctantly offered me his hand, as if somehow my very lowly position in life would rub off on his very shiny armor.

There was no point in trying to run, I stood a better chance of pleading innocence to whomever he was taking me—the evidence, after all, was smashed and scattered and who was to say I hadn't tried to pay for it?—so I took his hand and he hoisted me up behind

126

him, then he turned back to the main road and the ruined stalls as the other soldiers closed in around us, just to make sure I didn't 'accidentally' slide off the horse's rump.

Rather than ponder my fate, I fixed my gaze on the back of the officer's silvered-helmet. It was spectacular, the most elaborate I'd ever seen, with its transverse crest of scarlet feathers and elaborate designs in appliqué brass that adorned the helm crown, along with the cheek pieces and neck-guard, and I briefly imagined myself someday wearing such a truly wondrous piece.

The horse jolted me out of my flight of imagination. It had come to a halt and was now clearly eager for me to get off its back. So eager in fact it was hopping from one hind hoof to the other while swatting my bare legs with its tail.

My captor, annoyed with the animal's antsy behavior, jerked its bit and the horse turned sideways, then, thankfully, stood still. I glanced around, not sure what was going to happen next. Then my gaze fell on the matron and her slave who were standing nearby, as were a dozen or so soldiers. These were not the ones involved in the brawl—those had already been marched off, possibly dragged off to where-ever Roman soldiers go when they've been really, really bad.

Like the officer and his escort, these men were spotless, their polished band-armor pristine, and they looked like they meant business.

I was then urged to dismount by a spiteful, albeit whispered command to 'get the fuck off' from my captor, so I awkwardly slid from the back of the horse and onto the ground. The horse and rider then sidestepped away, keen to put themselves at some distance from me.

I remained where I was, my heart pounding in cadence to my rapid breathing, as the matron approached. I prepared myself for her to finger me as a thief, possibly even a cutpurse but instead she wrapped her arms around me and gave me a very wet kiss on the cheek. Unlike the soldiers, she clearly had no reservations about coming into close contact with my filthy attire despite her finery.

Then, holding me at arm's length she proceeded to chastise me in front of the silent wall of soldiers and horsemen, for running away before she could thank me properly for saving her life.

I bowed my head in feigned embarrassment while my hooded eyes darted this way and that, looking for the best route to flee.

Keeping her hold on me, she lifted her gaze and thanked the officer and his men for finding me.

He said something in reply—all I heard over the rapid thudding of my heart in my ears was the honorific, 'Lady Ilissia.'

Now I was really confused. Even more so when a litter arrived and the matron insisted I come with her—not that I had a choice. The soldiers were still there, watching me with expressions that warned me that, unlike a foolish old woman, they weren't fooled, not one damned bit—they were willing to humor her, and I might seriously consider doing the same if I valued my life.

So I very reluctantly followed her into the litter and cautiously seated myself opposite her and her slave quickly settled beside me. The dust curtains were dropped, and the litter rose then began to sway back and forth as it made its way down the street.

For a moment the matron and I stared at each other in awkward silence, then she began asking me perfectly reasonable questions—was I a runaway slave?

No, I answered empathically as she furtively glanced at my wrists, my ankles, presumably looking for the marks left by shackles, which, thankfully, there were none.

Where had I come from?

I answered honestly that I'd come from Numidia then embellished that I'd been stranded here when my ship left port without me.

She asked me the name of the vessel and I answered the Aequitas—*knowing there were records that could back me up if she bothered to check.*

As she kept up her naïve, almost motherly questioning while couching it in concerns for my welfare, it slowly began to dawn on me that this matron was no more fooled than the soldiers had been and her harmless curiosity was anything but innocent—or motherly.

She knew I was a petty thief and had possibly known it all along. I flicked the slave a sidelong glance. She replied to my unspoken question with an equally knowing smile and a nod as she parted the dust curtains just enough—the clatter of hooves that had been accompanying us where not just a part of the normal flow of traffic.

We had a mounted escort, presumably the very same officer and men, and I was clearly in very deep trouble...

A hand grasped my shoulder, followed by a bellowed command that ricocheted painfully inside my skull: "Stay right where you are—don't move!"

I wanted to say there was really no need to yell because I had no plans to get up. I wanted to say I was more than willing to stay put because if I moved, I'd vomit—in fact I had a sneaking suspicion I'd *been* vomiting and this momentary quiet was a brief respite while my stomach re-marshaled its forces. My head was throbbing, my gut was cramping painfully, my mouth tasted like bile and... oh, damn, the very ground beneath me was moving—

I heaved again.

I briefly thought about opening my eyes—to see what new nightmare I found myself in, but I didn't. Not because I was afraid of what I'd see. I can honestly say at this point I'd given up being shocked at just how creative or vindictive the Fates could be—not that I wanted that to be considered a challenge, no, no, not at all! I knew they still had surprises aplenty in store for me, all very unpleasant, I'm sure. I was just too involved in my current misery to do anything but be miserable—taking on anything more at this point would be just damned selfish.

I vomited again, so violently I felt as if my stomach was being torn from its moorings.

So you can see why opening my eyes was not a priority. Neither was getting up, and if I'd been even slightly less miserable, I would have said so. Nevertheless, the voice had drawn my attention to several things: I was lying on my side, it was pouring rain, I had a sneaking suspicion I was on a boat of some sort—that would explain the vaguely familiar not to mention very unpleasant rolling motion, and lastly, I had absolutely no memory of how I came to be where ever I was—which was actually becoming the norm in what passed for my reality these days.

I was startled out of that dismal thought by a loud clatter, accompanied by the frightened whinny of horses and men yelling as the ground beneath me shuddered then tilted precariously.

My eyes reflexively snapped open and I tried to grab onto something—I was sliding across what looked like rain-slick deck with not a handhold in sight. I dug my fingernails into the wooden planking, trying to anchor myself. A moment later, the boat abruptly righted itself and I lifted my head just enough to glance around me—to my relief, what I could see appeared to be at the correct angle. I cautiously released my death grip on the deck, and just in time, too, because I needed both hands to clutch my belly as I retched again, and then again, followed by a pause and I gulped frantically for air, knowing another agonizing spasm was on its way.

A brilliant flash overhead was followed an instant later by an ear-splitting crack of thunder. More frightened whinnying, more yells—and another flash of lightning. Followed, naturally, by an even *louder* boom of thunder that seemed to lift me right off the deck.

My vomiting increased in intensity—as if my stomach felt challenged by the ferocity of the storm raging overhead—but all things must come to an end, and finally, mercifully, my heaving did too, petering out in a series of diminishingly fierce hiccups.

The storm on the other hand was picking up steam with rain coming down in buckets while the deck resuming its rolling and pitching.

This seemed a hell more appropriate for some evildoer sailor or Imperial marine—both professions known far and wide for their dissolute behavior—not a well-respected and highly-decorated *infantry* centurion who only rarely engaged in questionable activities. I thought it just my bad luck to be the victim of mistaken iniquity.

A hand grabbed my shoulder the instant I stopped hiccupping and over the roar of the downpour, someone yelled in my ear, *"Can you get up if I help you?"*

The frightened voice, as implausible as it sounds, sounded just like Kyrou's. I peered into the pelting rain just as another flash of lightning briefly lit my surroundings. It *was* Kyrou—that stupid topknot was unmistakable.

I managed to shake my head—which of course stirred up a new wave of nausea, but there was simply nothing left to vomit up, unless my kidneys or spleen were going to volunteer and thankfully they didn't seem so inclined. Instead, my belly, unwilling to capitulate, settled instead for a round of violent dry heaving. At least when you vomit, you can entertain the slim hope that the minute you've rid yourself of whatever offended your gut, everything will, eventually, settle down and your insides will sink back into their rightful places.

With dry heaving you harbor no such optimism.

So I did what anyone in my position would do: I shut my eyes, clutched my stomach and held on for dear life.

A moment later I heard: "Grab his legs—I'll take his shoulders."

I sincerely hoped Kyrou was talking about someone else. In my present state I didn't want to be touched. I certainly didn't want to be moved. I just wanted to be left completely alone in my utter wretchedness.

Was I? Of course not! I was picked up—none too gently I might add— then half carried, half dragged across the rolling deck as Kyrou and his equally uncaring accomplice staggered this way and that with each pitch of the deck and I briefly wondered if I was going to be heaved overboard. Kyrou *was* the instigator in this unwanted journey after all and what better way of disposing of a rival than to toss him into the jaws of a storm? Even better than being shoved from the back of a galloping horse as there would be no corpse, therefore no evidence of any deliberate wrongdoing and best off all, no chance the victim might survive just long enough to finger the culprit.

Then—I'm not sure how this was done without serious mishap to everyone involved—I was carried down some rain-slippery stairs and into the bowels of the boat and out of the worst of the weather.

The trip below decks had another, unintended benefit: somewhere along the line I stopped dry heaving, I think in part because my body had been alternately squashed and pulled, akin to working a bellows as Kyrou and the other man slid and stumbled across the deck. That realization was immediately replaced with another, far more unpleasant discovery: I soaking wet and aching numb with cold.

"Over here," another voice said. "Bring him over here." After a few more staggering sidesteps from my bearers, I was unceremoniously dumped on something that smelled of wet, moldy straw—but I *wasn't* complaining.

Do I *ever* complain? Never. I just suck it up, even though I always get far more than my fair share of crap—

"Arri?"

That sounded like Sifrie. I managed to force one eye open, just a crack. Almost directly above me I could make out the familiar, albeit fuzzy form of a small oil lamp. It swung wildly back and forth, dragging my unwilling eye back and forth with it, adding an unwanted visual aid to the pitching and rolling of the boat.

I squeezed my eye shut, but too late; I was feeling intensely queasy all over again and I groaned and tried to curl up into a ball.

"Arri, we need to get you out of these wet clothes—tend to your injuries."

I ignored her, just as any protest on my part would be ignored. Sifrie never listened to me, neither did Turan or Hanni or any of them. *Ever.* But having no desire to be roughly handled, I didn't fight when I was sat up and the sopping wet leather jerkin was peeled off me. I was then eased back onto the pallet and my boots were pulled off. Next I felt the trousers being tugged, but either my leg was badly swollen or the trousers had shrunk because they wouldn't budge.

A moment later I felt a knife slice up right leg of the trousers, followed by it running up the left and as quick as you can say, 'Oh, no, not again!' I was sans clothing—all in all I was stripped not just quickly but to my surprise relatively painlessly.

Then some idiot ruined it all by vigorously rubbing my cold-numb skin, clearly trying to reestablish some circulation. It *hurt.*

"S-s-*stop it,*" I mumbled, and amazingly enough, the aforementioned idiot did.

I remained absolutely still for several heartbeats, deciding whether I should act like I'd passed out, and thus, possibly, be left alone, or open my eyes and risk again being the unwanted center of attention.

I opted for the latter because I was now lying naked—of course—wet, cold and uncovered on a moldy bed of straw and if I acted like I'd passed out, I was afraid I might be left that way. But if I was awake, maybe I could convince someone to get me a damned blanket before I died of exposure. I'd already started to shiver, not that anyone seemed to notice.

I very slowly opened my eyes—faces hovered over me, their features were fuzzy, unrecognizable and try as I might I couldn't get my eyes to focus properly.

"Arri?"

That voice I was sure of. *"T-t-t-uran?"*

She leaned really close; close enough I could recognize her. Her lips were drawn back in a worried smile and she too was soaking wet, her chestnut hair, dark with rain, clung to her scalp and one lock snaked down the side of her face and throat. "Arri, I'm going to put something in your mouth—I need you to swallow it."

I managed to shake my head, a truly feeble gesture and mumbled, "C-c-can't... s-s-sick to m-m-my... stomach—"

"I know you are, but you simply *must* keep it down." She cradled my head on her arm and pushed something past my lips and onto my tongue.

It had the bitter tang of one of those lozenges. The teat of a water skin was pressed to my lips.

I drank... barely enough to get the lozenge down, heaving several times in the process.

She responded by massaging my throat, to help it on its way—or prevent it from coming back up.

"Good," she murmured when she was satisfied it was going to stay put—I wasn't so sure. She very carefully withdrew her arm, then, thankfully, pulled a woolen blanket over me followed by a thick fur. *Bliss!*

I closed my eyes for a moment, savoring the feeling of being covered and the tantalizing prospect of being warm again, maybe sometime in the next decade.

Voices intruded—urgent, whispered voices and I lifted my head and peered around and found I could make out the dim shapes of people. They were now standing just beyond the shifting pool of light cast by the oil lamp and I sensed this was by no means accidental. And as the lamp swung back and forth, I caught a telltale glimmer, like fireflies suspended in the darkness, or in this case, lamplight reflecting on ring-mail and armor.

None of the men in our party was wearing armor—at least not visibly so. And what about this teensy little issue about iron? Was that just a ploy to give my own armor away?

I fixed my now suspicious stare on Turan. "W-w-who...?"

She stroked my wet, ice-cold cheek with equally wet, ice-cold fingers and smiled. "It's all right. They're friends of mine... and now yours."

I gave my surroundings another quick sweep with my eyes. "W-w-w-where... where a-a-are we?"

She smiled. "Just like I told you."

"W-w-when?"

"Last night."

I squinted at her. "R-re-refresh m-my memory… p-p-p-ppplllleeease…"

"On our way to the end of the Earth."

— ii —

The storm that had hurried us on our way moved on some time shortly before dawn, leaving the boat eerily silent, save for the creak and groan of rigging, the soft, ever-present rush of water along its hull and the distinctive, rhythmic wheezing and rumbling grunts of people snoring. And, more muffled, what I swear sounded like a horse whinnying and another irritably answering.

The flame of the oil lamp had long since flickered out, starved of fuel. Now the only light streamed down from the open hatch to pool on the wet decking at the base of the staircase. Cradling my head on my arm I watched as it turned from faint purple to deep orange and then finally a pale, watery yellow.

I was on my right side, under a blanket, which in turn was covered by a heavy pelt. Turan sat beside me, also wrapped in a blanket, her back to the wall, her chin propped on her chest. The black-haired man I now knew was one of Turan's bodyguards was huddled beside her, his head resting on her shoulder. Another was curled up nearby, only the top of his red-haired head visible, the rest bundled up in another blanket. The ogre was sprawled in a corner—the source of the snoring. I cautiously lifted my head and spotted the rest of our party: Sifrie and Kyrou were seated opposite each other at the cabin's small wall-mounted table and benches, slumped over, heads pillowed on their folded arms and blankets draped over their shoulders. Two men sat on the deck near the table, backs against the cabin wall and leaning against each other, heads nodding, a blanket thrown across them. Another was curled up at their feet. Yet another was wedged in the hollow of a bulkhead.

They all looked exhausted; surely none would want me to wake them just to ask permission to do a little exploring, so being the kind and thoughtful person I am, I didn't. Besides, I wasn't sure my leg would support me, so why wake them when perhaps I wouldn't be able to get up, much less walk anywhere, anyway? That would be just plain inconsiderate. They'd more than earned their undisturbed sleep—a courtesy, I must mention, that none of them had *ever* shown me. Just goes to prove I'm the bigger man in all of this, right? Much, *much* bigger.

I carefully peeled back the pelt and woolen blanket, clenched my teeth at the chill, then eased myself onto my knees. My hips and legs were incredibly stiff and painful when I moved them—a result of the wild horseback ride the day before, I had no doubt, but I managed to get to my feet without making a sound—and even more importantly, managed to *stay* on my feet, despite my lightheadedness, which wasn't helped at all by the ceaseless motion of the deck beneath me.

My thigh had been redressed—I have no memory of when—it was no longer wrapped in strips of my filthy crimson undertunic but rather a once-white cloth now heavily stained with dried blood, but to my relief, nothing fresh.

I looked around once more as I gathered up the woolen blanket.

Satisfied I hadn't awakened anyone, I tied the blanket around my waist then slowly, silently, shuffled over to the stairs, carefully stepping over the sleeping men, all the while using the wall for support.

I stopped at the lowest step and looked up to find a cloud-dotted blue sky and seagulls wheeling high overhead.

I heard footsteps on the deck above, along with voices. I ducked back into the darkness and waited until I heard whoever it was directly above me walk away.

Once the footsteps faded into the background noise of the boat, I started up the stairs, not fully trusting my left leg to support me, especially in a sustained stoop.

Just short of the hatch I stopped again and listened.

If anyone was nearby, they weren't moving and they weren't talking. So I took the third to last step in a painful crouch then very slowly raised my head above the deck just enough to look around me.

My incredible, cat-like stealth had been for naught. Two men were standing nearby, arms crossed, staring at me. One, the younger and taller of the two, was grinning. The other, a portly, middle-aged and balding man was not.

I exhaled, smiled feebly, and was planning on retreating back to the cabin when the younger man motioned to me. "Please, join us."

Turan had said these people were 'friends'. And since they were her friends, they probably meant me no harm. *Probably.* So I accepted their invitation, not that I really had much choice. I grabbed the railing and came the rest of the way out of the stairwell, then stepped onto the deck.

I must have cut a very striking figure, with my scraggly beard and wild, unkempt hair, badly bruised, bound and blistered shoulder... and oh yes, a blanket tied around my waist—a filthy and *very* threadbare blanket in fact, something I hadn't noticed while down in the darkness. There was also a strong breeze, which meant the blanket kept flapping open, despite my frantic attempts to contain it.

"My name is Perus," the younger man said as he kept his eyes firmly fixed with mine.

I wanted to thank him for that. It was a small gesture, but what remained of my dignity greatly appreciated it.

His grizzled companion wasn't as considerate. What I assumed was a grim expression wasn't—he'd been biting his lip. Without warning he burst into laughter.

My first reaction was to feel deeply offended—until I looked down at myself and found myself struggling against the urge to join him. Then Perus started to laugh as well, and so did I. Why not? I looked utterly ludicrous.

Finally, the older man swallowed his laughter then managed to say, "I'm Sapor. And you, I assume, are Lady Turan's centurion?" with a relatively straight face.

I lightly smacked my clenched fist against my bare chest in formal salute. "Arrius Marcus Niger, Hastatus-Posterior, Centurion of the Fifth Century, First Cohort of the Ninth Legion Hispana, at your service," I added in my best Centurion's Voice—the Voice that until very recently could send a ripple of unease through my troops, and yes, even some of the younger Tribunes—but now promptly threw the two into another paroxysm of laughter.

Under other circumstances this would have *really* irked me, but there's something very humbling about having the wind blowing up your ass while you're acting pompous. Of course the blanket didn't help, especially when it suddenly blew up and over my head and I had to beat down like it was an attacking harpy—which of course made them laugh all the harder, to the point the one named Perus had to grab the railing to stop himself from falling to his knees.

Finally they got themselves back under control and I managed to grab the blanket and roughly pull it back down.

"We're headed into some strong, *um*, tail winds," the older man, Sapor, said, wiping his eyes.

To which Perus added, "Perhaps now would be a good time to change into more appropriate and... dare I say, *controllable* attire?"

"A most excellent idea." Sapor nodded vigorously.

Perus looked me up and down. "We look to be about the same size, Centurion, and I have a tunic and pair of trousers you can wear until Lady Turan outfits you in her livery."

"I would appreciate that very much," I replied, keeping very tight control of the blanket.

"Come with me." He motioned for me to follow and started down the length of the deck, to another open hatch.

I followed, painfully aware Sapor was staring after me and chuckling softly, leaving me with the sneaking suspicion that I was unintentionally displaying my assets.

Perus stopped and turned, waiting for me as I followed a little more slowly—I'd yet to get my 'sea legs' as they say, which was bad enough, but my left leg was utterly undependable and I was damned if I was going to stumble, or worse fall in front of these two—my pride had already taken a substantial bruising, thank you very much.

As I finally came abreast of him, I heard another whinny—from directly below me. I gave him a questioning glance.

"Your horses were brought aboard also."

"They're not *my* horses," I replied, perhaps a little touchily.

"That's right—Lady Turan said you're infantry. But you ride on occasion, certainly."

"Not if can avoid it."

He chuckled and started down the stairs, to the deck below.

I followed, cautiously. While he appeared friendly enough, I'd learned long ago never to trust appearances.

He waited for me at the base of the stairs then as I joined him, he gestured around him. I peered into the gloom and spotted a number of narrow, high-walled stalls, a horse crammed in each, including Sifrie's piebald pony and Turan's dapple gray, with a thick rope drawn through holes in the ends of the stalls to prevent the animals from backing out on their own. They barely had room to breathe in such close quarters—especially the two massive draft horses—much less move and I could only imagine what it must have been like for them to ride out the storm—no wonder I'd heard their frightened whinnying.

I felt a twinge of compassion, possibly the first time in my life I could honestly say I felt badly for a horse.

I also had to wonder, do horses get seasick? Can they even vomit? In all my years being around them, I'd never thought to ask anyone. Probably not—because if they could, I'm sure one of them would have found a scrap of a reason to vomit on *me*.

136

I'd been aboard troop ships that had carried not just troops but the officers' horses along with the mounts of the cavalry, if we were accompanied by a *turma*, and on even rarer occasions, chariots and their teams. I'd never bothered to investigate, in fact didn't give a damn how the horses were actually transported, but if this was an example, then they suffered far worse than we did. At least we could go above decks and get some fresh air. They were trapped below for the entire trip, and if the ship were to sink... well, at least those men who could swim had a chance. Which is why I learned to swim at the first opportunity.

"Over here, Centurion."

I turned to find Perus squatting beside a small, open chest, next to a rope hammock.

I limped over to him, saying, "Please, call me Arri." In truth it was suddenly very painful to be called 'Centurion'. It was something I was no longer, and never would be again. And now I had only my signaculum to prove, if just to myself, that I'd ever even *been* a Roman soldier, much less a decorated centurion.

Suddenly needing that reassurance, I reached up to clutch the flattened lead fob only to find it missing. I looked down, grabbed the other necklaces and held them before my eyes only to have my worst fears confirmed: the signaculum and its worn leather thong were gone.

I desperately dug through my memories, trying to unearth the last time I remembered wearing it—and then it came to me: that night, in the rain. My last night in Britannia, when I discovered Turan had recovered and restrung my bead and star necklace. I had it then...

...and now it was gone.

I blinked and bit my lip as my hand fell limply back to my side.

"Something wrong?"

I squeezed my eyes shut. So, my last connection with my past life had just... disappeared, gone without a trace, just like me—

"*Arri?*"

A hand alighted on my shoulder and I slowly opened my eyes to find Perus standing next to me, a very worried look in his eye.

"Are you all right?"

I blinked again, wiped my nose, my eyes with the back of my hand and managed a less than convincing nod and lied, "I'm fine... just... just suddenly a bit queasy."

He clearly didn't believe me, but decided to change the subject back to what had brought me down into this suddenly very stuffy hold in the first place: clothing. "This should fit you." He offered me the tunic, which I took from his outstretched hands.

It was butter-soft dark brown leather—I'd never felt the like—emblazoned with a dragon, all done in gold and silver thread. I ran my fingers over the elaborate design as I gave him a sidelong glance.

"The emblem of my master, Lord Taskim." He motioned to the identical, albeit far less detailed motif on his own heavy leather hauberk then he lightly tapped the snakestone amulet I wore, in the process drawing my mind back to what I wasn't wearing any more. Sensing he'd hit a very sore spot, he added quickly, "Lady Turan's is the coiled serpent," then hurriedly turned back to the chest and pulled out a pair of equally fine leather trousers along with a pair of handsomely embroidered, knee-high felt boots and a similarly embellished belt. "Here."

I raised my brows at what was clearly formal dress attire.

"I was on a diplomatic mission," he replied to my questioning look, "delivering a message from Lord Taskim to King Togidubnus of the Regni when I was informed of your legion's stunning defeat at the hands of the Iceni..." He hesitated as if expecting an explanation, if not an outright denial, but truth is truth. It *was* a stunning, if not completely unsurprising defeat.

Realizing I was just staring back at him, jaw muscles twitching, he continued. "The king is an ally of your Empire, as you know, and he was most distressed by the news, fearing it might incite other tribes to open rebellion, and knowing of Lady Turan's plans to rendezvous with the *Sulaviae*, I elected to return as well, to confer with my master as to how to proceed in light of this unexpected and dramatic turn of events."

I nodded soberly. There wasn't anything to say—we'd been beaten and beaten badly and it was now anyone's guess how far this revolt might go—or how far Rome might go to stop it. Not that I'd probably ever know as I'd think it's a pretty safe bet that current news was rather hard to come by once you're beyond the end of the Earth.

Suddenly wanting nothing more than to change the subject—get it as far away from my past life, I looked at the tunic, said, "You're very kind, but these are far too good for me—do you have something a little more—"

"Rustic?"

"I suppose that's as good a description as anything else, but now that you mention it, yes."

"No—unless you'd prefer the clothes I'm wearing."

"And you'll wear the blanket?" I began to untie the knot.

He chuckled, "I think not." He again offered me the trousers and boots. "I'd be deeply honored if you'd wear my livery—I'm sure Lady Turan would be pleased as well." He grinned. "Kyrou, on the other hand, will be quite put out."

That clinched it. I accepted the rest of the clothing.

"He's a troublemaker," Perus continued as I happily discarded the blanket, "a bully… did you give him the black eye?"

"Hanni." As I flicked him a sidelong glance, I happened to notice a mailed hauberk draped over a nearby railing. So, I hadn't imagined seeing people wearing ring-mail…

"Indeed?" He briefly followed my gaze. "That's not like Hanni."

"He might've been provoked."

He looked me over as I stepped into the trousers, his eyes briefly lingering on my scabbed over wrists and ankles, my own discolored cheek, the scattering of bruises on my stomach, flanks and arms, then asked, "Kyrou worked you over when you were tied up did he? Is that why Hanni punched him?"

I tugged up the trousers and quickly tied the lacings, feeling distinctly uncomfortable under his intense scrutiny. "I honestly don't remember—I just woke up with this," I lightly fingered my cheek, then grabbed the boots, "and some vague memories of being knocked around. That's all." I eased myself down onto the deck, carefully tugged on the left boot, wincing as I did so then I quickly pulled on the right boot.

Perus offered me his hand and pulled me back to my feet, adding, "I'm sure it was Kyrou—all fists and knees when the opponent can't fight back and all bluster and bravado when he can. None of the others who make up her personal guard are so inclined, fortunately—Jaro makes sure of it. I've warned Lady Turan before about him, so have Jaro and Hanni, on numerous occasions. Kyrou's not to be trusted, hear?"

I didn't know this man or his allegiances, didn't know if *he* could be trusted, didn't know who this Jaro was, so I answered with a simple, "Yes," as I struggled to get the tunic over my head.

Without asking, Perus stepped close and helped, quickly tugging the tunic into place, his hands touching me in ways not at all necessary for the job. I pretended not to notice, then, mumbling my thanks, I did my best to comb the tangles from my hair with my fingers while he stepped back and gave me another sidelong, but decidedly interested stare.

It wasn't that I was unaccustomed to men staring at me. Even more I wasn't unaccustomed to men staring at me with very particular ideas written on their faces, and because of that, because of my upbringing, I rarely took offense: quite the contrary, if I found the man equally attractive, or even better, if he could in some way advance my career, as many had. But something about Perus' blatantly captivated stare made me very uneasy, because he was clearly just as uncomfortable with the thoughts racing through his head.

I flashed him a deliberately naïve smile, buckled the belt and looked down at myself. The fancy tunic and trousers were a desperately needed morale boost after my unhappy discovery of the lost signaculum—and I couldn't help but grin to myself, anticipating Turan's reaction to my startling metamorphosis, not to mention Sifrie's… and yes, Kyrou's. I almost felt a pang of empathy for him—*almost*. I mean, how could he possibly compete?

"Kyrou will eat his tongue," Perus said.

"Indeed?" I replied, feigning innocence.

"I think he might have finally met his match." He gave me another quick once over. "Yes, definitely his match."

More than his match.

"How about a tour of our fine vessel?"

I looked up. Perus was now standing at the base of the stairwell.

"Oh, uh…yes, of course."

— iii —

Perus and Sapor were good company and willing guides to this somewhat familiar, albeit transitory world in which I'd found myself. Sapor, I quickly learned, was not a deckhand but the captain of the ship, the *Sulaviae,* and a Cimbri he said with a sidelong grin. I'd met a few Cimbri during my career; all had shown a marked antipathy of water, be it an ocean, river… or the puddle at the bottom of a wash basin.

He in turn was surprised and pleased that I demonstrated more than just a passing understanding of how a ship at sea works. He expressed his amazement that a Roman centurion—an *infantry* centurion no less—would be so knowledgeable, then groused amiably that it was this sort of cross-training that was the wellspring of Rome's greatness and flexibility.

I didn't have the heart to tell him that I'd been a fugitive at the time I'd learn my sea-skills and not in the service of Rome, however I still harbored some loyalty to the Empire, even if it was only to perpetuate a false impression. I figured I owed her that much since she'd been relatively lenient with my long litany of what could only be termed *minor* deceptions—starting, of course, with my name. So I heartily agreed with him then added to it by complimenting him on his remarkable insight.

"I fought you Romans you know," Sapor said in the strange camaraderie between former arch enemies only the distance of years can provide, "learned to respect your tenacity and discipline and yes, even admire much of your culture, but unlike many of my countrymen, I had no desire to become *Romanized*. Subjugation and containment, no matter how carefully applied, is still subjugation and containment." He motioned around him. "I found the open sea far more to my liking—something even Rome's mighty armies will find impossible to conquer, yes?"

Not that Rome hadn't tried—just ask all the soldiers, sailors and marines who now called the bottom of the sea their home.

He grinned and clapped me on the back, adding, "But you're one of us now, Arri, and I for one am very glad of it."

I'm not. I smiled dubiously, reluctant to offend my affable host.

"Look," Perus said, drawing my attention as he walked over to the railing. "Over here."

Sapor and I joined him. Following Perus' pointed finger, I peered into the stiff breeze and finally spotted a barely visible black line on the horizon. I then favored him with a questioning look.

"Britannia."

I again squinted at that now distant shore. Finding my eyes watering, I silently bid my armor, my beloved helmet, harness and my signaculum too, the even more distant land of my birth, and yes, most importantly my closest and likely dead friends a belated farewell. I knew with certainty I would never see any again and I felt an intense pang of something I'd never felt before—never thought I was capable of feeling: *homesickness.*

"And to our northwest is Hibernia," Sapor continued, drawing my very reluctant gaze.

I dutifully peered in the direction he pointed, but saw nothing. I'd heard of Hibernia of course. It was even closer to the end of the Earth than Britannia, or so I'd been told. So close in fact that, as rumor had it, Rome would never attempt to conquer Hibernia for fear that any legions who stepped foot on it and laden down with armor and supplies would promptly sink and drown. And according to reports the land, people and weather were more hostile than Britannia, even more inhospitable than Caledonia, which I must say I found very hard to believe.

Still, one couldn't argue with the simple fact that no emperor had ever voiced a burning desire to find out if rumor or report were true. As far as I was concerned, the empire and its emperors should have listened to

Pytheas and avoided what he called the Isle of Pretani, its hell-borne offspring and congealed seas altogether. If they had, I wouldn't be here, paying for their foolish avarice in the most personal, not mention permanent way.

"That's where we're headed."

I jerked my eyes back to him—so, I was about to find out first hand if these tales were true. Oh, joy. On the upside, I wasn't wearing armor any more...

I opened my mouth to ask if *he'd* ever stepped foot on Hibernia, but was cut off by a startled gasp, followed by Sifrie's equally started, *"Arri...?"*

I turned around to find that Sifrie, along with Turan and two of her bodyguards—the redhead and the black-haired man—had emerged from below decks. Turan was staring at me in open-mouthed surprise, which as I watched, rapidly turned into a *very* pleased smile while Sifrie giggled and gave me a good, unabashed ogle.

Then Kyrou appeared, followed by Hanni and the remaining guards; Kyrou stopped dead in his tracks as he saw me, so suddenly in fact one of the men following ran into him, nearly knocking the two to their knees.

"Told you," Perus whispered out of the side of his mouth.

"Arri!" the ogre said and breaking away from the rest, strode across the deck, arms extended.

I let him envelop me in his massive embrace—not that I had much choice in the matter, plus I was actually becoming quite fond of him—let bygones be bygones, I say, especially when those bygones include an ogre.

By the time he'd released me, Turan and Sifrie had come closer while admiring my new look.

"M'lady, I hope you don't mind me lending Centurion Niger Lord Taskim's livery?" Perus said with a nod to Turan.

"Not at all, Perus, not at all! Come, let me look at you!" She grabbed me by the shoulders—mindful of my injury—and held me at arm's length, then looked me up and down and for the first time since I came under Turan's control, I can honestly say I didn't mind the close inspection.

She met my eyes and grinned, which for some damned reason pleased me immensely.

"Oh, Arri!" Sifrie gushed, drawing everyone's gaze, *"You're... you're simply spectacular!"*

I must have instantly gone the color of her hair because Perus coughed and Sapor turned away and put his hand to his mouth. Even Hanni looked like he was going to burst into laughter at my unabashed embarrassment.

Kyrou on the other hand just stood near the stairwell, eyes fixed on something at his feet, silently bleeding inside.

Damn.

"You gave us all quite a scare," Turan scolded, oblivious to Kyrou's troubles, "waking up and finding you gone like that."

"I'm sorry," I murmured, pulling my eyes off Kyrou and back to her. "I was curious—I've never seen the end of the Earth before." In other words I wanted to see it coming, before we fell off the edge.

Perus and Sapor looked at each other, then at Turan.

She smiled, "Arri's been as far as Parthia; I told him we were going a lot farther than that."

Sapor's mouth formed a silent 'O' as Perus flashed me a rather odd smile, then he said, "I've had a hot meal prepared, Lady Turan. I assumed you'd all be quite hungry."

"Thank you, Perus," she murmured, "I'm sure my men will greatly appreciate having some hot food in their bellies—"

There was a murmur of happy agreement from her bodyguards and Hanni.

"—and you too, Arri, yes?"

I hadn't thought about eating—wasn't particularly hungry in fact, and the last thing I wanted to do was be sick on Perus' beautiful tunic. I had a feeling that might land me in the docks alongside Kyrou.

"Then come with me." Perus started for the stern.

The others turned to follow—everyone but Kyrou, who was still intently studying the deck.

"Arri?"

I pulled my eyes off Kyrou and turned to Turan.

"Coming?"

"We'll join you in a moment, all right?"

She looked at Kyrou, as if noticing him for the first time then glanced back at me and arched a brow.

I managed a tight smile.

"Well, don't be too long—or you'll risk Hanni leaving nothing for you."

As far as I was concerned, he could have it all. "Yes, we'll be along shortly," I answered, and with that Turan, Perus, Sifrie and the others walked off towards the stern while I limped slowly over to Kyrou.

He heard me coming and turned away, grabbed the port railing and peered into the stiff wind, deliberately ignoring me.

It had been my plan to have it out with him, once and for all, to stop all this nonsense, but as I stopped beside him and followed his slitted gaze, I suddenly found myself wondering if he might have had a hand in the disappearance of my signaculum. Had Turan taken it, she would have told me, of that I had no doubt, and besides, she simply had no reason to take it—she'd gone to great lengths to find and restring my slave bead necklace after all, so why then take the signaculum, which she knew meant as much to me as the bead necklace? Kyrou on the other hand might have found fiendish delight in taking it—reasonably assuming it meant more to me than the bead necklace—and he certainly had plenty of opportunity, possibly even being able to conceal the theft from Turan. Maybe she allowed him to think he'd gotten away with it—maybe this was all part of some elaborate game of hers.

It didn't matter—none of it mattered. I just wanted my damned signaculum back—not that I thought for one instant that it was going to be as simple as asking for its immediate return. Oh hell no.

So, for several minutes neither of us spoke as I politely waited for Kyrou to offer it up and spare us both a lot of unpleasantness.

Instead he kept his eyes fixed on the horizon and finally growled, "What are you doing here, Roman?"

Like he didn't know—*hardly!* "Waiting on you."

His jaw muscles bunched—at least I think they bunched. Hard to tell with all that feral facial fur.

"That's not what I meant!" he snarled under his breath as if fearful Turan would overhear and I had to wonder if he knew she was capable of reading my mind at some distance, and I had to figure the same was true of him. He wheeled on me. "I meant what are you doing with us? Why'd Turan take you? She didn't need you, we already had plenty—*none of us need you!*"

I pointedly wiped his spittle from my own bearded cheek. "That's something you'll have to ask her, and speaking of asking, I have a question for—"

He grabbed my throat in both hands. I'd actually expected that and so didn't even flinch. I had no doubt I could break his grip if need be, even with my bad shoulder. I just stared down my nose at him and that *really* seemed to annoy him. I honestly don't know why—truly I don't.

"Should I strangle you, Roman? Throw you overboard?"

I'd like to see you try, shorty. Aloud I said, "That wouldn't exactly win back Turan or Sifrie's affections, would it?"

He tightened his already painful hold, enough to make me swallow reflexively. That made him grin. At least I think he grinned—again, with the substantial beard and that remarkable black eye, it was rather hard to tell if it was a grin or a grimace.

Damn, this close he looked like a very stunted, *very* unkempt bear, fresh, so to speak, from its winter slumber. Smelled like one, too—gods. *Do you ever bathe?* "And you had plenty of chances, yesterday, or last night. Why didn't you kill me then? I couldn't have stopped you."

"Can you stop me now?" he sneered.

"Probably."

His fingertips dug deeper, his filthy, ragged-edged nails digging into my flesh.

Now that *hurt*. And it was going to leave very obvious bruises—even if I didn't put him in his place, Turan certainly would. Or Hanni. *And speaking of Hanni, I simply must ask you about that truly impressive black eye.* "Turan told me you and I are much the same—"

"We're nothing alike!"

I couldn't agree with you more, my furry little fiend... "You were taken against your will as well, taken from everything you'd known, everyone you'd known, just as I was."

That gave him pause and his fingers eased off their grip. Taking advantage I grabbed his wrists and with a determined yank, broke his stranglehold, but I didn't let go of him and he seemed so startled by the abrupt change in fortunes that he made no immediate move to free himself.

"I had absolutely *no* desire to be taken captive, Kyrou. Given a choice, I'd have willingly died alongside my soldiers—I'd still take that option if it was offered, but like you, I wasn't *given* the choice—"

"None of us were," he muttered.

I arched a brow, *"Us?"*

His eyes flicked to the stern cabin again, again, as if fearful of being overheard, then lowering his voice, sneered, "You'll find out soon enough."

"Yes, I suppose I will."

He gave me an odd look, almost a smirk and added, "Then again, maybe you won't. Maybe you'll end up just like *them."*

Like them? Who are 'them'? I squinted at him, refusing to let him distract me—it was my job to knock *him* off balance not the other way around. "Do you miss your family?"

He blinked.

Gotcha. "I *have* no family, but I surely miss my friends—perhaps Felix the most, he was always great fun to be around—I have no doubt he's dead, no doubt they're all dead, but I none the less greatly hunger for their company, hear their voices, their laughter. But this is my life now, to serve Turan, just as it's yours. Now, we can be enemies and make each other's life miserable—"

145

"What's so miserable about your life, Roman?" he snarled and began twisting against my grip. "You can bed Sifrie any time you want! She's infatuated with you, she... she thinks you're... *spectacular!*"

I almost burst into laughter, except Kyrou didn't find it at all funny even though the joke was entirely at my expense.

I let go of him—his futile struggling was making my shoulder throb painfully. He'd already given me a pounding headache. "Is that it? This is all about petty jealousy?" Of course I knew; I was just humoring him—and myself. All right, more myself, actually, as he didn't seem at all amused.

Instead he favored me with a very black expression—made all the blacker by that damnedable black eye. *"What do you think, you stupid Roman? You show up and suddenly I'm nothing!"*

I looked down at myself, at the splatter of his saliva on Perus' beautiful tunic, then giving it a disdainful wipe with my fingers I replied calmly, "And you think by repeatedly threatening to kill me, threatening to gut me, to... *publicly castrate* me, you're going to improve your standing?" I sadly shook my head. "Clearly you haven't thought this one out."

He stared up at me and I swear his blue eyes started to glisten with tears. He looked away, grabbed the railing in both hands. *"Go away!"*

"No. We're going to have it out, here and now. I'm not going to spend the rest of my life, no matter how short or how long it might be, watching you."

He refused to look at me.

"I could kill you right now—as you said, Sifrie's besotted with me, and I'd probably have no trouble convincing Turan you started it, that I'd only acted in self-defense—I'll have the bruises after all."

"Then why don't you?" he asked, his voice a husky whisper.

"Because I'd rather not. Or, let's say I'd rather know what you did with my signaculum *first.*"

He glanced up at me, baffled.

"My necklace—" I tapped myself on my chest for emphasis, "—what did you do with it?"

He glared at me. "I don't know what you're talking about."

"Of course you don't—you're as innocent as the day is long. So let's try this: how old were you when you came into Turan's service?"

He clearly hadn't seen that question coming, either. "I... I don't know—"

"How long have you been with her?"

He fixed his eyes on the horizon then answered warily, "Not as long as the others. Three... no, this will be my fourth year—what's it to you?"

"Were you always a thief?"

He jerked his eyes back to me.

I stared back, just as innocent—two can play at this game and besides, I suspect I'd had a lot more practice perfecting the look. "Where are you from?"

He hesitated, then: "Why the hell do you care?"

"Just curious. I'm from Numidia—"

"Never heard of it," he grumbled.

"I'm Mauri—well, to be totally accurate, I'm Massaesyli."

He flicked me a sidelong look and snorted, "I *supposed* to be impressed?"

"Not unless you know what a Massaesyli is, and clearly you don't or you wouldn't have stolen something from me, so I won't hold it against you—*this* time."

He gave me another quick, confused look, then again fixed his gaze on the cloud-ruffled horizon. Finally he muttered grudgingly, "Cherusci."

I wasn't sure I heard him correctly and repeated, *"Cherusci...?"*

He again looked at me. "So you *have* heard of us, well, of course you would've—how many of your legions did we completely wipe out? *Two...?"*

"Actually it was three."

He grinned smugly; of course he knew. "You're right, it *was* three. Three *entire* legions. My, that must have been a shock to your collective arrogance."

I smiled back, impervious. The slaughter had taken place well over a generation before I was born; while I'd heard about the stunning massacre—its bitter lessons were taken to heart by Rome *and* its legions, particularly by those serving in Germania—I had no personal stake in it. Of course the Cherusci and their allies hadn't fared so well afterwards, but I felt it might not be the time or the place to mention this little historical tidbit. "Is that why you disliked me on sight?"

"Doesn't everyone hate Romans?"

"Can't say. I haven't met everyone. Have you?"

He didn't answer. Instead his beard made that funny twitching motion again, which I have to assume was him clenching his teeth although it looked remarkably like a squirrel trying to stuff one more acorn in its already bulging cheeks—clearly not the ominous visage he was after.

But rather than say so, I followed his intense gaze; I thought he was actually staring at something—perhaps that fabled and floating end of the Earth. He wasn't. He was just staring, presumably waiting for my next move—or possibly trying to sort out my previous moves. Under other circumstances, I would have just waited him out, but I was getting cold and my leg and shoulder were aching. "Is that why you stole my signaculum— as a trophy?"

"I don't know what you're talking about—*I didn't steal anything!*"

I took a deep breath, exhaled slowly, letting my own rage bleed out of me before I succumbed to it and pitched the thieving little bastard overboard, thus proving to everyone, including myself, that I was no better than Kyrou. "Turan tells me you're fearless—"

"Don't flatter me!" he snarled, turning to face me, hands balling into fists.

I kept my eyes locked with his; I was actually hoping he'd take a swing—give me a good, solid reason for knocking him flat on his ass, and if he happened to slip overboard in the process… well, these things happen. "I'm not. Believe me, I have absolutely *no* desire to flatter you—I find you thoroughly repugnant if you want the truth—you threatened me when I was tied up and helpless to fight back, you repeatedly punched me when I was delirious, and oh, yes, tied up and unable to fight back—"

He blinked, startled.

Ah, so it was you.

"—those are things I find very hard to forgive, and clearly not the actions of someone who is 'fearless'—more the actions of a sniveling coward."

His eyes got very round.

"And stealing my signaculum too—it *was* you who took it. Who else could it be? Who else would have reason? So that makes you a sniveling coward, a liar *and* a gods-damned thief."

His lips began to work furiously, smothering rage.

"Moreover, Turan warned me you're a bully and you've certainly proved that and then some. *But…* " I raised a finger as he started to raise his fists, "you also saved my life, not once, but twice yesterday. You could have let me tumble from that horse, you could have let me slide off the deck and into the sea. But you didn't. Those are things I find very hard to forget." I took a deep, steadying breath. I really didn't want to say what I knew I had to say, but I said it anyway: "Truce?"

"Like hell!" He spun on his heel and stalked off.

I sighed in feigned sadness and shook my head. *I guess I'll just have to live without my signaculum—and you…*

XI

I couldn't help but smile—after a life of deprivation, of barely scraping by, never knowing where the next meal was coming from, or if there was going to be a next meal, here I was, perfumed in rare oils and attired in a crisp white linen tunic, a very expensive tunic trimmed in gold and silver and new leather sandals—I'd never owned a pair of sandals—even a badly worn pair were an extravagance beyond my means.

I wiggled my toes unused to such confinement and wanted to laugh—at the absurdity that my change in fortunes would have hinged on offering my expertise to an old woman in choosing the best ripe melon.

The Nubian slave who'd helped me bathe and dress stood back to examine his handwork and nodded, telling me I would please 'our' mistress. He then told me of her idiosyncrasies, and warned me what not to do, otherwise I risked a flogging.

I didn't have the heart to tell him I was no slave but rather a free man and could leave whenever I chose—in truth I wasn't sure either was entirely true.

He'd seen the slave beads I wore and had drawn his own conclusions and perhaps there was more truth to it than I wanted to consider. I wanted to savor being clean, being dressed in cloth that didn't stink or chafe my skin... and wearing beautiful new leather sandals.

He motioned for me to follow him.

I did, with some trepidation. The expansive, columned interior of the Lady Ilissia's seaside villa was a tasteful confection of graceful pink-stone arches and filigreed screens that provided tantalizing glimpses of the sun-baked world beyond, and gauzy curtains, unfurled to dampen the harsh glare of the midday sun, appearing to breathe, filling and emptying with each waft of warm air. It was like nothing I'd ever seen—not even in the wealthiest houses of Carthage—and I kept stopping to gawk at my surroundings, only to find my elbow being gently but insistently tugged by the slave.

Finally we arrived at our destination: a private garden that faced onto the sparkling ocean.

The mistress of the house was seated at a marble table, waiting for me and no sooner had we arrived than the Nubian was dismissed with a wave of Lady Ilissia's hand.

She addressed me as Arrius, told me to sit beside her, which I did. More servants arrived and placed platters mounded high with food, including cooked meats, before us.

She poured us each a goblet of wine and told me to eat my fill.

While I was extremely hungry and hadn't eaten meat in months, I opted for a handful of dried figs—something my stomach was used to—which I chewed and swallowed without even tasting them. I didn't touch the wine at all—I was back to being scared, and had no desire to have my wits dulled, just in case her intentions were less than benevolent.

She watched me as she sipped her wine and when it became obvious I was not going to eat more, as patently hungry as I still was, she asked me if I knew who she was.

I answered honestly that I didn't.

She then introduced herself as Ilissia Antonia—mother of Lucius Antonius Vallus, Commander of the Alexandria Garrison.

I responded in unabashed panic. I'd heard whispered stories about this man—he was known throughout the lower city for his cruelty, his ferocious and capricious temper; from what I'd been told, even his officers feared and despised him—his troops certainly did. The graffiti on the alley walls and the rumors I'd overheard were never complimentary; in fact most referred to him as the Alexandria hippopotamus, with a temper and appearance to match one of the feared water beasts. But I felt it best I not say such. Mothers, after all, rarely see the faults of their son, no matter how glaring—my mother being an exception.

She then asked if I knew why she had brought me home with her.

I mustered my courage and told her that I had no idea why she would want to entertain someone of my humble standing.

She told me she'd been looking for someone to keep her company, someone who would play dice with her, escort her when she strolled the beach, amuse her when she was weary of the day's duties—I'd proven myself to be very clever, not to mention gallant in saving her and her slave from injury—could I read? she asked, clearly expecting the answer to be no.

Yes, I replied, both Greek and Latin.

Did I know the classics?

Yes, I assured her, because I did and proved it by quoting my favorite passage from the Iliad.

That surprised and delighted her—I was clearly no common street thief and by her expression it was obvious she was revisiting the idea that I was an escaped slave, presumably from a very wealthy household.

She asked me squarely if any within her social circle would recognize me—she did not wish to be embarrassed by being accused of harboring a fugitive.

I told her no, emphatically no. I was no slave, escaped or otherwise.

She seemed satisfied, and in return for my company, she promised me the finest clothes, a private room and servants of my very own and all I could eat—all she asked in return is that I be available to her whenever she called for me and to keep myself in top physical condition as she would not tolerate indolence—she wanted me to be a source of jealousy on the part of her friends—and not to steal from her.

So, over the next two years I served that purpose, and served her well. I never stole— in truth never had reason to as anything I wanted was freely given—I was always available, kept myself in excellent form and entertained her and her friends by reading or reciting the classics to them.

She was never cruel to me, always indulgent and genuinely kind—the first person in my life who was truly caring.

No one had ever treated me in such a way without asking for something greater in return and I came to feel something for her I never thought I could feel for anyone: deep affection. I would have done anything for her. So, after months of her attentions, of making her laugh, making her feel beautiful, she finally, almost shyly asked me one evening if I'd take care of her other needs, even though she admitted she was old enough to my grandmother, but she made it clear I could refuse, I was only a boy after all, not yet fourteen.

I did so willingly, but I also did so tentatively and deliberately awkwardly, even innocently, so as not to reveal to her that I was far more experienced than she, despite our relative ages. Lady Ilissia was open minded—easily accepting me as a petty thief, a boy forced into a life of crime through desperation, into her home, but I was genuinely afraid of how she'd react if she learned that I had been a prostitute, even if I'd been forced into that profession by a far greater desperation.

Turan and the others looked up from their meal as I slowly limped into the stern cabin.

She glanced past me, saw I was alone and asked, "Everything settled?"

"Yes."

Of course she knew that, had known it as I knew it, and she didn't seem particularly upset, which in turn troubled me. Kyrou, despite his obnoxious personally and even more noxious person deserved better. Then I realized it wasn't Kyrou's welfare I was worried about. What if this was a pattern—to cast aside a lover when someone better, or at least temporarily more intriguing, more exotic, came along? Granted, I was much better looking, and I had no doubt I was vastly much better in bed, but…

I flicked her a sidelong glance only to find her staring back at me with that all-knowing smile. Her expression did nothing to quell my sudden unease.

She motioned for me to sit beside her, next to Sapor, who scooted aside to make room on the bench.

I eased myself down between them, smiled at the captain then felt Turan tug at my sleeve as the rest went back to their meal.

I leaned close and she whispered in my ear, "Kyrou was never my lover—or Sifrie's."

"Then why take him?" I replied in kind.

I heard someone clearing his throat and looked up to find Perus offering me a wooden bowl heaped with bread and a large chunk of meat.

The meat had an unfamiliar and not altogether enticing odor, and the bread was coarse and mealy and soaked in the drippings from the meat. Neither tempted me or my appetite in the slightest, far from it—in fact they instantly killed what little appetite I had.

Nevertheless, I accepted the bowl and placed it in front of me. The smell and sight of food in the enclosed space packed with unwashed bodies left me feeling queasy and my thigh and shoulder continued to throb to the point it was hard to concentrate.

"Something wrong?" a voice asked, followed by a prompting, "Arri?"

I blinked and looked up. Hanni stared at me from across the rough-hewn table, his heavy brows crinkled in genuine concern, his comment drawing everyone else's gaze.

I glanced at my bowl—I hadn't touched the food aside from rearranging its contents—then looked back at him. "No... nothing's wrong, just not hungry, that's all."

Perus, who was seated next to Hanni, looked, at least to me, a bit relieved.

"Still feeling seasick?" Turan lightly placed her hand on my belly.

"A little." I flashed her a tight smile. "Plus my leg and shoulder— they're really starting to ache. I'd like to lie down—with your permission, m'lady."

"Of course," she murmured as she tucked a lock of my hair behind my ear, then she turned to the ogre. "Hanni, if you've finished, perhaps you would assist Arri?"

It was obvious to everyone Turan's intent: he wasn't to assist me. He was to guard me. I'd seen the furtive glances to my throat. Kyrou's fingerprints must have turned bright red by now, visible through the growth of beard. By tomorrow I had no doubt they'd be a festive purple.

Hanni wasn't finished. Hanni was still hungry. But Hanni being Hanni, he grabbed a handful of meat from the platter, stuffed it in his mouth then somehow disentangled his massive frame from the table and bench without knocking those on either side to the deck.

I managed to follow suit but I have to admit, with even less grace. In the brief time I'd been seated, my left leg had turned to mush.

"Perhaps I should go too,' Sifrie suggested, rising from her seat on the other side of Sapor.

Turan clearly wasn't fooled, not one bit and neither was anyone else at the table, which in truth was rather embarrassing. Nevertheless she nodded her agreement and Sifrie wasted no time in wrapping her arm around my waist, steadying me, then together we hobbled out of the cabin and out onto the open deck, with Hanni right behind us.

Kyrou was nowhere to be seen and I briefly wondered if he'd spared me the effort and had pitched himself overboard.

"He's with the horses."

I glanced at Sifrie, startled, and not altogether sure I'd ever get over her or Turan's knack at eavesdropping on my thoughts.

She lightly touched my bruised throat. "Why did you let him choke you?"

There was no point claiming he'd taken me by surprise. "I thought it might make him feel better."

"Did it?"

"Didn't appear so, no."

She tightened her hold on my waist and growled, "Kyrou's an ass."

"A very jealous, and therefore a very dangerous ass."

She looked up at me. "You should've thrown him overboard—I would've."

"There's still time, or we could just wait until we reach the end of the Earth and drop him over the edge and wait to see how long it takes to hear the splat."

That made her laugh, Hanni too—a deep rumbling laugh that made me briefly smile, despite myself.

"Has distinct possibilities." Then just as quickly Sifrie sobered. "But if he ever even contemplates leaving another mark on you, I'll flay him alive."

Something told me she wasn't joking.

"I will have to kill him," I said, also not joking. "I see no other way."

She looked up at me, ran her finger along my bearded jaw and nodded, but her glistening eyes spoke of a deep regret, acknowledging that Kyrou was a lost, doomed soul from the start, and I, as his presumed executioner, suddenly felt very, very sad for him.

She tugged on my waist and murmured, "Come on, let's get you to bed."

Now that sounded like a most excellent idea.

We walked the last few steps and stopped at the top of the hatchway leading to the lower deck and our shared sleeping quarters. My thigh felt as if was on fire and I'd resorted to clutching it tightly as I shuffled along.

"I'll go first," Hanni said, "you stay right behind me, that way if you stumble, I'll catch you."

I nodded. In truth he wanted to go first in case Sifrie had been wrong, in case Kyrou was lurking in the dark, waiting for me. I should have tossed him overboard when I had the chance. The thought gave me no pleasure, even if it would bring me some peace of mind.

"Coming?" Hanni said, standing half way down the stairs.

I nodded and with Sifrie's assistance, began my own slow, very awkward descent.

To my relief, Kyrou was elsewhere. With the horses just as Sifrie said—as long as he wasn't here.

I released my hold on Sifrie and hobbled the last few steps to the makeshift bed then very carefully eased myself down onto the blanket-covered straw. I felt rather guilty about sleeping in Perus' beautiful tunic, but I was just too tired and knew I'd be too damned cold if I took it off, and my shoulder was so damned stiff I wasn't sure I could take it off.

Sifrie checked my leg, satisfied herself I wasn't bleeding again, or at least bleeding through the dressing and the trousers, then pulled one of those all too familiar yellow lozenges from a small leather pouch tied to her belt. "Here." She pressed it into my hand then looked around for something to wash it down.

Hanni spotted a water skin hanging from a peg and handed it to her, and she in turn offered it to me.

At my hesitation, she said, "It's for the pain—might help with the sea sickness as well."

I needed no further encouragement. I downed the lozenge in one quick loud gulp then lay back as she drew the heavy fur cover over me. I cautiously rolled onto my right side just as she slipped under the pelt and wriggled up against me.

Hanni discreetly took up guard duty at the base of the stairs.

I expected her to do what she always seemed in the mood to do, but she surprised me when she kissed me on the cheek, wrapped her arm around me then tucked her head up under my chin. "Go to sleep," she murmured.

Relieved, I closed my eyes, safe in the knowledge that even if Kyrou could get by Hanni, which was highly unlikely, he'd never make it past Sifrie.

— ii —

I awoke sometime later to find Sifrie still curled up beside me, only now her back was pressed into my chest and my arms were wrapped tightly around her.

I'd been sound asleep, so I lifted my head and peered around, wondering what had nudged me out of my comfortable slumber. Nearby sat a wooden plate with a haunch of meat, a chunk of cheese and more bread—all in a pool of congealed grease—along with a mug of something that had a very potent scent.

The thought of eating—or drinking whatever the hell was in the mug—made my stomach turn anew.

Aside from Hanni, who was now seated on the bottom stair, head nodding but by his sheer bulk making it almost impossible for anyone to pass without waking him, the cabin was empty. Watery sunlight still poured down the stairwell and washed over the slumped, sleeping form of the ogre, but the angle had changed significantly and I judged by that that it was afternoon—assuming the ship hadn't radically changed its heading—I'd managed to sleep half the day, in fact couldn't even remember falling asleep, which was remarkable in itself considering how much my leg and shoulder had been hurting. The last thing I firmly remembered was swallowing that lozenge.

Before I could ponder the matter further, I heard muffled voices, directly above me—perhaps the real reason I'd awakened in the first place, rather than the nauseating smell of the drink, so I strained to hear what was being said, and by whom.

It didn't take long to recognize Sapor's distinctive, clipped voice, along with Turan's—and, to my annoyance, Kyrou's. Exactly what they were speaking about, I couldn't tell—all but a few words here and there were swallowed up by the creak and groan of the surrounding ship.

I eased myself out from under the fur, making sure not to awaken Sifrie, staggered to my feet and shuffled over to where Hanni sat at the base of the stairs. I braced my shoulder against the cabin wall and squinted into the rectangle of light above as I distractedly combed bits of straw from my hair.

The voices had faded—the speakers were moving away from the hatch.

Finding my curiosity getting the better of me, I squeezed around Hanni without waking him either, and I have to say, about this time my faith in the vigilance of my self-appointed bodyguards was becoming seriously questioned. I'd assumed the food and drink had been delivered with their consent: now I wasn't so sure.

I crept up the stairs, slowly, silently, not wanting to alert either Hanni or those above that I was awake and on the move, but just short of revealing myself, I stopped to listen again.

"…yes, Lady Turan," Sapor was saying. "If the weather and wind holds, we should make landfall by tomorrow."

"We'd have reached it by now if you hadn't let that storm push us so far off course," Kyrou grumbled.

"So now I'm responsible for the weather?" Sapor replied sourly.

"Kyrou meant no disrespect, Sapor, did you, Kyrou?"

Turan's mollifying question was met by stony silence—which seemed like a perfect moment to make my entrance. I came up out of the stairwell and stepped onto the deck. "Ah, there you are." I smiled at Turan as I casually raked my hair out of my eyes, looking for all the world as if I was innocent of eavesdropping. She'd know of course—perhaps she'd been aware of me crouched in the stairwell—but she seemed more than willing to go along with it as it did create a needed diversion.

Sapor looked as if he was seriously contemplating throwing Kyrou overboard, and Kyrou was staring at me as if I was to blame for all his woes—big surprise there, huh?

Turan started towards me. "Feeling any better?"

"A little."

"Did you manage to eat? Jaro left some food beside you."

Instead of answering, I looked past her to Kyrou and Sapor.

She wrapped her fingers around my elbow, drawing my distracted gaze. "Arri, you must eat."

I squinted at her, suddenly irritated by her dogged persistence on the issue. "I'm not hungry—"

"Then you must force yourself—you've only eaten once in over a week."

"Just the sight of food makes me sick—no," I shook my head for emphasis. "Maybe… maybe once we're back on land…"

She gave my elbow a sharp tug, said, "Come with me," as she glanced back at the two men with an expression that was a clear warning that they were not invited.

Of course neither was I. This was no *request* that I attend her, but a command, so I obediently limped along side as she started towards the bow of the ship. Once we were well beyond earshot of either Sapor or Kyrou, she stopped, grasped the railing and fixed her narrowed gaze on the horizon.

I dutifully stood beside her, waiting, while trying not to shiver. Thick clouds were forming up to the west—and a strong, chilly breeze blew around us.

Several minutes passed—ominously chilly minutes and I'm not just talking about the weather. Turan was clearly very angry, and just as clearly she was very angry at me—so she was generously giving me the time to mull it over, maybe make my own deductions without her having to spell it out for me and offer up an apology.

But after a thorough going over of my thoughts and actions of the past day, I came up dry. So I decided on the direct approach. "What have I done—?" I bit off the obligatory 'now' as I'd somehow managed, at least up until this moment, not to do anything to make Turan this angry—the axe incident, in my humble opinion, was a far distant second. Which is unusual for me—I normally excelled at infuriating people within a short time of meeting them—women in particular, starting with my mother of course—hence the almost reflexive addition of 'now' to one of my most oft-asked questions.

"Are you deliberately starving yourself to death?"

I blinked, taken aback at the blunt accusation. I hadn't been consciously aware of it, but the charge pricked at me, as if there was some truth to it, deep down and I stammered, "I... I don't think so, no—"

"Kyrou told me you said if given a choice, you'd have opted to die with your soldiers."

"I did say that—I told you the same thing—"

"Days ago. He said you said you'd still take that choice if offered."

"Yes, I said that too, but—"

"And here I thought... I thought maybe now you'd had some time to think about it, you'd had a change of heart."

This time I had no answer, at least not one I wanted to say aloud—if she wanted to hear it, she could listen to my thoughts after all, and by her expression, she had.

She again fixed her slitted eyes on the sea. "I'd thought you'd begun to accept this new life, accept being in my service—I actually believed that at times you even wanted..." *Me'* hung on her lips, unspoken. Aloud she finished, "...to serve me." She blinked, and I realized her eyes were glistening.

Damn. I wanted to say that I did want her, but she'd know I was lying and that would be even crueler. Turan, for all of her abilities, had made a simple but critical blunder, mistaking physical intimacy for affection, for love. Had she been anyone but Turan, I might have played along, if just to spare her feelings, her pride as I'd done, I'm ashamed to admit, countless times in the past, but the rules in this game were very different.

Honesty, she'd said, *I like that.*

157

Then honesty you shall have.

"You can hear my thoughts, Turan, you and Sifrie and in truth I have no idea who else—maybe Perus? Hanni? Everyone? I have no secrets, no privacy, simply no place to retreat to, even in my own mind. And worse, I'm never even sure when my thoughts are truly my own." The last words, while spoken softly were tainted with an unexpected bitterness that surprised even me. "I may no longer be tied down but I'm shackled nonetheless—you can make me do your bidding, make me do anything you want—you've proven that and then some." Then I said what I knew I shouldn't have said a split second after I said it: "Why don't you just make me want you, make me love you?"

For a moment we stared at each other, unblinking, across a suddenly very wide abyss, then she slapped me across the face, hard.

The blow stung more than just my face and I squeezed my eyes shut, took several steadying breaths, then reopened my eyes to find her still staring up at me, her beautiful face streaked with tears and her full lips drawn taut in hurt and rage.

Her expression left me feeling as if she'd run me through with a sword—I had no doubt my words had had the same effect on her and now we were both wounded, perhaps mortally. "I'm sorry… Turan, I'm so sorry, that was a terrible thing to—"

"You're a fucking bastard, you know that?"

I nodded, because I agreed with her completely. I was a fucking bastard—literally and figuratively—a selfish, shallow bastard who cared for no one but himself.

"I'd hoped…" she looked away as she roughly wiped her face.

I lightly touched her arm, suddenly, desperately wishing everything to go back to the way it had been—simple, uncomplicated: owner and owned, each knowing their place. "You hoped what?"

"Nothing."

She turned to leave, but I grabbed her wrist. "Turan, please…"

She looked down at my hold, then up at me, eyes flashing. *"Know your place!* You're never, *ever* to touch me again without my permission, hear me?"

I let go, dipped my head and murmured hoarsely, "Yes, m'lady, I hear you."

She drew her cape tight around her and hurried away, back to Sapor and Kyrou.

I stared after her, shivering in the awful realization that I had indeed gotten my wish, too late realizing it wasn't what I wanted at all.

Sapor acted as if nothing was amiss yet pointedly avoided my helpless gaze. Kyrou, on the other hand, stared at me, clearly delighted with the unexpected turn of events and dangerously pleased with himself as if my abrupt fall from grace had all been his doing.

I met his gaze and smiled. *When I kill you, I'm going to do it very, very slowly and make sure it really, really hurts.*

XII

I soon moved into Lady Ilissia's private quarters, slept in her bed, read to her late into the night—and became a peculiar blend of ideal son and caring lover. She in turn rewarded me with tutors who taught me even more about the world, taught me about art and culture and religion. She attired me in the finest linen, saying anything less would reflect badly on her. She also took me to social functions, her arm interlaced with mine, much to the dismay of her fellow and decidedly prim and proper matrons.

I later learned that I'd set a trend of sorts, of handsome youths as escorts, as fashion accessories, to the wealthy women of Alexandria.

I saw her son, Lucius, only on rare occasions—I'd quickly come to learn that he was not particularly fond of his mother, nor she of him, and so he made an appearance only once a month, and very reluctantly, when she held her elaborate banquets which drew the rich and influential, intellectuals and politicians alike, not only of Alexandria, but of all of lower Egypt, along with their unattached daughters in search of husbands of their social rank.

Vallus was short, thickset, knock-kneed and balding, with heavy jowls and prone to sporting a muscled cuirass over his abundant belly that only accentuated his portly frame and, as far as I was concerned, made him look utterly absurd—his mother privately divulged to me that his father was much the same, with the same vices, which is what had led the elder Vallus to an early grave, leaving her an unattached and very wealthy widow at a relatively young age.

Her son assumed I was a slave, an exotic plaything, an idle fancy of his doddering mother, and disdainfully ignored me, which, as you can imagine, was just fine with me.

I was left to watch the social maneuverings and the purely political assignations in silent, straight-faced amazement as the unmarried women carefully avoided Vallus's less than subtle acquisitive gaze, preferring instead to flirt with his tribunes and, regrettably, me.

Lady Ilissia found this all very amusing; she even encouraged their attentions, and on more than one occasion farmed me out along with a private room within her villa for the purpose, temporarily forgetting that I was not her property, but rather her protégé. But she always more than made up her lapses, so I never had reason to grumble. Besides, I found that I enjoyed making women of all ages feel beautiful and desirable—not only that, I was good at it—very good.

I'd learned from the best, after all.

I reluctantly lifted my gaze to meet that of the man seated across from me at the stern cabin's table—the same man who'd given Hanni coins in exchange for me, for my armor, and shortly thereafter he'd taken part in separating me from that armor in the most deliberately painful ways possible—twice poking me with his sword for good measure, and later he was the one seated next to Kyrou in the cart... how many days ago? I'd given up trying to keep track. He was the one with the lank black hair, coal-black and suspicious eyes... and oh, yes, the very twitchy sword arm. How could I forget that?

This time he was far friendlier, or at least was trying to be—it was clearly not a habit that came easily—but he *was* slightly less obvious than the other choices for the task of watching me when he abruptly joined me.

At my not particularly welcoming nod, he eased himself down at the table and helped himself to some of the bread and cheese that had been left, using the excuse that he'd fallen asleep and like me had missed the evening meal, then stiffly joked that he was relieved to find Hanni hadn't devoured everything. He went on to tell me his name was Jaro, which solved one inconsequential mystery but generated another—why did money change hands if he and Hanni were both in the service of Turan? He then added to it by saying he was one of Turan's most trusted men, second only to Hanni in that regard.

I knew he was lying—well, all right, not the part about being most trusted; I had no proof of that, either way. I knew why he'd joined me—knew who'd sent him.

After Turan's enraged departure, I'd spent what had remained of the day seated on the open deck not far from where we'd had our heated quarrel, near the bow, my back braced against a bale of moldy straw and staring out to sea. I'd pointedly ignored the crew who occasionally strayed into my line of sight as they tended to the *Sulaviae's* needs, ignored the biting cold and the throbbing ache in my leg and shoulder. I no longer felt welcome below decks—just as I no longer welcomed anyone's company.

Despite this, I managed to briefly fall asleep, sitting up no less, and granted a very fitful sleep, as I was weary beyond measure and it allowed me a temporary escape of sorts.

And later, as the sun grew low in the overcast sky, I ignored the gathering of Turan's entourage in the stern cabin for the evening's meal, along with their laughter—Kyrou's was particularly evident—and boisterous.

Deliberately so, I thought. *Enjoy yourself while you can, you nasty little bastard—your days are numbered.*

As night settled in bringing a spatter of cold rain, with clouds scudding overhead threatening more, I reluctantly gathered myself up, lurched stiffly and painfully to my feet and having no other sheltered place to go made my slow and shuffling way to the stern cabin, only to find the small room alight but deserted—just as I'd hoped—until Jaro unexpectedly showed up, bringing with him his unwanted company and his idea of affable chit-chat.

It was all very awkward and forced.

He kept giving me these bewildered glances, clearly expecting me to fully keep up my end of the conversation, perhaps even initiate a topic. Maybe he didn't realize I remembered him. Maybe he believed all was forgiven.

Like hell.

When my unenthusiastic, monosyllabic answers tapered off to a spiteful and inflexible silence, he finally got the hint I was in no mood for small talk and stuffed his cheeks with bread—a self-imposed gag of sorts as the bread was so dry and crumbly you took your life into your hands if you tried to speak with some of it your mouth. Even silence was no guarantee it wouldn't go down your windpipe instead of your gullet, as Jaro quickly learned.

He suddenly coughed then coughed again, and hastily grabbed a mug and in between more coughs, gulped down its contents.

I stared at him, waiting to see if he needed help while debating with myself if I should offer or not—yes, I *can* be that petty. This man would have willingly murdered *me* and slept soundly that night—need I say more?

He coughed explosively several more times but as I very reluctantly started to rise, he waved me off. "I'm all right..." he rasped and wiped his streaming eyes.

Satisfied he wasn't going to keel over dead—I had no doubt Turan would blame me for his untimely demise—I resumed my seat and fixed my gaze on my own untouched plate and he quickly returned to his meal but this time he wisely stuck to the cheese.

I picked up a chunk of gristly meat and wiped it free of its congealed grease, using a piece of bread to do the honors, but I just could not bring myself to put it in my mouth. As I tossed it back on the plate, I mulled over Turan's accusation. I'd never been a picky eater—an orphan or legionary couldn't afford such luxuries. In fact I'd prided myself on being able to eat just about anything if I was hungry enough. There had been times, early in my life, when I'd wolfed down well-rotted meat and kept it down, so it wasn't the unappetizing food that had so effectively killed my hunger.

Maybe there was something to her charge—maybe I was, on some level, starving myself to death. I certainly had no appetite, and hadn't since I'd been taken captive—aside from that one night and I had a vague memory of feeling miserably sick afterwards—and I revisited my suspicion at the time that my sudden and intense hunger had been all Turan's doing.

Which of course begged the question: why hadn't she continued to compel me to eat?

And if I truly wanted to kill myself, there were certainly faster and far more immediate ways to accomplish my aim—*very* immediate. All around me in fact. And the thought of a life as someone treated no better than Kyrou—an afterthought, an object of cursory pity, the butt of a joke, or worse, having my mind wiped and used, as Turan said, as a bed warmer with only one purpose in life left me feeling utterly empty and alone. Whatever hope, whatever promises I'd believed, suddenly and without warning failed me.

I looked at the doorway—Turan and Sifrie were presumably fast asleep as was just about everyone else—at most a few deckhands would be about, but I knew they'd keep to themselves—I was free to think for myself, and, more importantly, to act on those thoughts—the first time since I'd been taken captive. This was, most likely my only chance, my last chance to take my fate into my own hands.

It was time to go, to belatedly join my friends.

I took a steadying breath and nodded to myself. *Yes.* I lifted my gaze only to find Jaro watching me covertly as he chewed on his mouthful of cheese and I was struck with his uncanny resemblance to a rodent. Not a squirrel like Kyrou—the ears were too big. Hooked nose and prominent teeth. Beady black eyes. More like a *rat*.

He wiped his thin, greasy lips and smiled at me.

"If you'll excuse me, I think I'll go find my bed." With that, I managed to rise, grimacing with the effort. He started to follow but I motioned for him to stay where he was. "Finish your meal. I can find my way below decks."

What could he say without admitting his true reason for being there? Not a damned thing, that's what. So he very grudgingly resumed his seat and I felt a twinge of guilt, wondering if *he'd* be blamed for what *I* was about to do.

I shrugged it off—just as he would have done had he put sword to my defenseless belly—and limped slowly out of the cabin and onto the open deck.

A single lit oil lamp hung suspended from a small gibbet amidships and its pale yellow flame cast shifting shadows on the deck as the *Sulaviae* gently rocked in her watery cradle. The promised rain had failed to materialize, or been blown on: the sky above was now crystal clear and full of stars and the sails hung limp, the ship becalmed.

Two sailors sat cross-legged next to the lamp, but as I'd suspected they glanced curiously at me as I shuffled past, murmured their good evenings, then returned to repairing some frayed rigging.

I limped on, back toward my aerie in the bow. Once beyond the glow of the lamp, I stopped and clutching the railing, stared out at the starlit sea. Somewhere out there was Britannia, invisible at this distance and in the darkness, and far, far beyond that, *home*.

I took a deep, aching lungful of the cold, salty air and found myself surprised that within its bracing chill I could feel the smothering warmth of long-ago summer nights, smell the earthy fragrance of barley burned brown by the desert sun mixed with the heady perfume of flowers that only bloomed in the dark to the approving chorus of frogs and crickets. And within the creak and groan of the rigging and the sparkle of the sea, I heard the laughter of my friends, saw their armor flashing and glinting as we sat around the cook fire, Aetius and Felix alternately spinning tales more fantastic than the last—often prompting the usually laconic Rufinius to add an extremely grisly, but hysterically funny detail—all of the small luxuries, the potent memories I'd savored and held close.

Would there be night-blooming flowers where we were going? Frogs? Would I find *anything* familiar? Turan had never said—a deliberate oversight I had no doubt.

So, I'd lost my way again, and this time with absolutely no hope of finding my way back.

Sky and sea blurred and I felt hot tears rolling down my cold cheeks in a painfully immediate and intense longing for everything left behind. I reached out, as if one of my friends would grasp my hand and pull me back to where I belonged.

But of course no hand gripped mine.

All my friends were *dead*.

Suddenly feeling very foolish—and yes, absurdly angry at their collective betrayal, I dropped my hand back to the railing and my watery gaze to the sea. I was alone, utterly and completely alone. Even cast aside by Turan because I did not share her feelings.

How could I? She owned me, as she reminded me at every opportunity. How could you give your heart to someone who owned your body—even more so to someone who could control your very thoughts, where every emotion, any desire would be suspect?

The water was mirror-like, the surface glistening in the starlight, and I wondered how long it would take to drown—would I struggle? I was a strong swimmer—maybe once in the frigid water instincts would take over—I've been told a man's will to survive is often greater than a want to die. But my shoulder and leg weren't what they'd been—and the water, I had no doubt, was very, very cold.

Part of me wondered if Turan would make any effort to recover my body—and I chuckled at the absurdity, the sheer vanity of it. *What difference does it make? I'll be dead—let the fish have me. I've certainly eaten plenty of them in my lifetime. High time I repaid the debt.*

My hands gripped the railing in a stranglehold as my heart suddenly began to thump faster, *faster*, and my breath came in short, sharp gasps while I twisted up my courage to actually take the plunge.

What are you waiting for?

I leaned over the railing, took another look, as if by some miracle it might look more inviting.

Everything seemed clear-cut back in the cabin, but now that I was here, my resolve slipped—the sea looked so dark, so menacing. I'd never completely weaned myself of my childhood fear of the sea, of shadowy monsters who lurked beneath its surface, appearing only as a fin cutting the surface like a knife, a sudden plume of air erupting like a geyser... or an anomalous swell. Plus I had no doubt it was damned *cold*. I found myself shivering in fearful anticipation of that intense shock.

Then something else occurred to me, something equally chilling: what if Turan had put these thoughts in my head? Suicide had always been an obvious option—it wasn't like I hadn't tried. And they'd kept me tied down at first to *stop* me from killing myself—so why leave me alone with not just the means but also the motivation? Was this all, in some unfathomable way, part of her plan? Was my newly minted allegiance to her being tested? Or was this far more basic—was her pride *that* fragile? Was this actually a murder? Was that why I hesitated?

I studied the idea for a moment, tossed it aside, but then I picked it up again and studied it more closely—*could it be true? Am I being pushed?* It was a hard thing to consider, even in the privacy of my own mind, such as that privacy was.

I shook off the disturbing thought, telling myself it didn't matter. I could not go on like this, not under these conditions, never sure which thoughts were truly mine and which weren't. It was untenable, plain and simple—a steep slope into madness and if my death salved Turan's spurned ego as well, then so be it.

Do it. I looked down at the water again, took a deep, steadying breath. *You'll never get another—*

"Arri?"

I started violently, in the process coming perilously close to losing my balance and *unintentionally* toppling overboard, then glanced over my shoulder to find Hanni standing nearby and I had to wonder how long he'd *been* standing there, sent by Turan the moment my thoughts betrayed me, watching me, perhaps even allowing me a chance to sort things out for myself and only making his presence known when it became obvious the choice I'd made. "What?"

"Lady Turan commands you attend her."

I blinked, hurriedly wiped my wet face with the back of my hand, then managed to stammer, "Tell... tell her I'll... I'll be with her shortly." I turned back to the sea, hoping he'd get the hint, or fall for my ploy, but of course he didn't.

Instead he moved closer. "Arri?"

"Let me be," I whispered hoarsely.

"You mean let you jump overboard?"

And I knew then that I'd been a complete and utter fool to think I'd been left to my own devices, even for an instant. Turan, Hanni... the lot, they must have been watching me closely all day—they hadn't gone to all this trouble of capturing me only to stand back and allow me to kill myself. Hell no.

Turan had probably put the idea in my head that I had within my grasp the means to end to things on my terms. And I'd stupidly gone along with it, never questioning the rationality of the situation because I desperately wanted to believe it.

Fool! It was just one more step in breaking me to her will.

More tears welled up in my eyes as I flicked him a sidelong, baleful look. "Yes."

"Why? Will you answer me that?"

I didn't. Instead I bit my lip and peered into the darkness, hoping I could catch just a glimpse of Britannia while sizing up my chances of taking Hanni by surprise before he could grab me and once in the water I'd just starting swimming towards it. As I said, I'm strong swimmer. Maybe I'd make it. More likely I'd drown, but at least I'd keep myself busy by having an objective, keep my mind off the grim reality that I was paddling around in the middle of an ocean in the middle of the night with absolutely no chance in hell of reaching anything solid—if you don't count the bottom of the sea.

But I'd *had* a chance—slim as it was, to jump while Hanni was far enough away he couldn't have grabbed me in time—and couldn't do it. Was that Turan's doing as well?

I squeezed my eyes shut. I tried to sort out what were really my thoughts, my true desires, and which had been imposed by Turan but found I couldn't. I *had* no firm ground on which to determine anything—so many of my thoughts of late had been suspect. Everything was shifting, sliding, turning inside out and twisting back on themselves until I wasn't even sure of who and what I really was—was I ever even a centurion? Even that seemed in serious doubt, with no tangible proof.

I opened my eyes, peered into the darkness as if hoping to find some sense of direction all the while knowing there was none to be had.

Hanni joined me at the railing—within easy grab range I noted—and now followed my gaze. "What are you looking at?"

I didn't want to tell him—suspecting he'd laugh—but when I failed to answer this time he turned his gaze on me and kept staring with his huge, worried eyes until I couldn't stand it any more.

"Britannia."

"Britannia's that way," he pointed. "Other side of the ship."

I didn't know what else to say but, *"Oh."*

For a moment neither of us spoke then he said, "I really like you, Arri, and I never thought I'd say that about *any* Roman."

"I like you, too, Hanni—even though I never thought I'd say that about an ogre, but I really *do* wish you'd left me to die in that bog."

"Now that would have been a truly terrible waste."

"No, it wouldn't—that's where I was *supposed* to die, with my men." Suddenly my throat was very tight and I forced out, "I... I deserted them, deserted my friends." It was true and finally saying it aloud—admitting it— was a relief of sorts, akin to slicing open an infected wound to let it drain.

"You didn't desert them, Arri. They were all dead."

"I left them!"

"Not your fault—"

"I led them there, led them to their deaths!"

"You were following orders—how's that your fault?"

He didn't understand. I didn't expect him to. Like him or not, and I did truly like him, he was still a barbarian and an ogre to boot. He hadn't been trained in the Roman way of seeing the world. He'd never been responsible for men under his command. He'd never been a trusted centurion, one whose soldiers followed without question, and so of course he couldn't grasp that I wasn't looking for absolution—there was none to be had, not for desertion.

I took a ragged gulp of the cold air, unwilling, unable to let go of the blame. My mind clenched painfully around it, leaving me hemorrhaging inside. "I should've done more to protect them, I should've—"

"There was *nothing* you could have done. Fault lies with your officers who fled, abandoning you and the others."

I wheeled on him, fist coming to bear, snarling, *"THAT'S NOT TRUE!"*

He made no effort to block my blow, and that alone stopped me from actually striking him. "It *is* true, Arri. You *know* it is."

I stared up at him and I *did* know it was true. I'd watched Cerialis flee the battlefield with what remained of the cavalry and a handful of his officers, leaving the rest of us to pay with our lives for his blind overconfidence.

I'd always had an excellent memory—an *extraordinary* memory for details, according to Turan—so why hadn't I remembered this before?

Now my recall was a crystal clear as the night sky, those last moments playing out before me in incredible, appalling detail and I clutched the railing to stop myself from falling to my knees.

Had Turan deliberately blocked these memories, now spoon-feeding them to me, bit by bit, as time passed and the actual events grew more distant? Or had *I* suppressed them, something I'd never been able to do before? I'd always been able to summon up with exquisitely macabre detail the horrors of my childhood, usually when I was least able to cope with them and despite my best efforts over the years to expunge them from my mind. So why had my memory utterly failed me this time, why had these specific, equally horrific and very recent memories kept themselves so thoroughly hidden until now?

But worse than coming across yet more huge lapses in my normally faultless recall was remembering the reactions of my men. They too had witnessed Cerialis' chaotic flight—he and his officers had galloped right by us in their panic—one horseman in his haste had actually knocked Aetius down and had it not been for Rufinius' quick reflexes, Aetius would have surely been trampled by those who followed—in hindsight not the welcome rescue it first appeared to be.

These were *our* officers—men who up until that moment commanded not just our loyalty but our lives and now they were bolting for theirs, leaving us behind to die for their folly without so much as a backwards glance.

I remembered the looks on my soldiers' already bloody and battered faces as they turned to me, expressions varying from stunned horror to murderous hatred. One, Duccius, screamed an obscenity and hurled his pilum after the fleeing officers, the weapon warbling through the air as it chased its prey only to impale itself harmlessly in a tree, missing its intended target by a hand's-breadth, while several others just stood there, weapons held loosely as if already dead when the barbarians set upon us and let themselves be cut to pieces. Others, Rufinius, Felix and Aetius among them, fought with a frenzy far beyond what any normal man could achieve. But the end for all was the same, and in incredibly short order.

I swallowed against the excruciatingly tight knot in my throat.

"You did everything you could," Hanni said softly, briefly drawing my sidelong, watery gaze.

I quickly turned back to the sea and gripped the railing in both hands as my mouth worked in silent rage—all those men dead—*slaughtered… for what?*

Aside from Cerialis and his tattered handful of horsemen, I was the only one to survive the massacre. *Why?* As a centurion, I should have been one of the first to die, or the last—not the lone survivor!

I flinched as I felt Hanni's massive hand grasp my shoulder—as an act of friendship or perhaps as an anchor to keep me firmly planted to the deck.

"Turan checked *everyone*, Arri. They were all dead—*I* made sure."

I gave him a sidelong look and as our eyes met, I suddenly understood what he was saying—and with that understanding came the memory of him whispering to the dog—and the animal kiting off. Now I knew what he'd said to her, and what Turan, in her hound guise, had done—what they'd *both* done once I'd passed out after Hanni's spur-of-the-moment surgery.

Fresh tears welled up in my eyes and rolled down my cheeks and I made no effort to wipe them away. *"Thank you,"* I croaked and I was truly thankful that he'd spared the others further suffering. I'd been tormented by the fear that they'd been taken by Trinovantes or Iceni or one of their equally bloodthirsty allies. Now at least I knew that was not the case—at least not for those who had fallen in that accursed boggy glade. Hanni would not lie to me. I was certain of that. As certain as I could be of anything.

He gave my shoulder a gentle tug. "Come along now."

I refused to budge. "Tell me something—tell me the truth."

"Of course."

"Why did Jaro give you money for me?"

Hanni chuckled softly and I glared at him. *"You think that's funny? I don't!"*

169

He instantly sobered. "You're right, it's not, sorry."

"Then why?" I recalled my feelings at the time—utter humiliation, sheer terror and the gut-twisting realization that I was being sold, but for what ghastly purpose I could only imagine, and even now, how many days later? I still I didn't know.

"I suppose you could say it was a feint, a ruse of sorts."

"For my benefit?"

"No," he shook his shaggy head, "the others."

"Others? What... *others?*"

"Remember the camp?"

I nodded although I only had the haziest of memories—of children, women spitting on me, others hurling insults as Hanni carried me through a gauntlet of wavering firelight and hateful faces.

"We'd taken temporary sanctuary among them, claiming that like them, we were refugees from the fighting—Turan believed the safest thing for you was to have them believe you were being purchased for later sacrifice, otherwise they might have taken you from us by force and sacrificed you in fact—and it worked. We got you out whole."

He gave my good shoulder another gentle, prodding squeeze. "Come along. It's time for bed—things will look better in the morning."

"Will they?" I asked dubiously as I roughly wiped my nose and my wind-raw cheeks with the back of my hand—careful to avoid mussing up Perus' tunic sleeve—then I was struck by the utter irrationality of the act. A few moments ago I was planning on jumping into the ocean while wearing his beautiful tunic, as if salt water was fine, while snot was not.

"We'll be on solid ground at the very least—I'm not particularly fond of water, can't swim. Now, let me help you—you don't want to keep Lady Turan waiting, do you?"

I knew Hanni wasn't going to leave without me—I doubted he'd even turn his back on me even for an instant. But the last thing I wanted to do at that moment was to face Turan. Even in a good mood she was intimidating and I harbored no doubts she was still smarting from my rebuff, and on top of that I'd lost my chance—no, not lost. I was just too cowardly to jump. I'd never thought of myself as a coward, quite the contrary. But now I knew better. And so would Turan. With her there were absolutely *no* secrets.

"Come along." He gathered up my elbow. "You're going to catch your death if you stay out here much longer."

I did as he asked, because in truth there was no other option—Hanni made sure of that. He walked beside me, matching my slow, unsteady pace, ready to tighten his hold if I stumbled—or tried to bolt. I was badly chilled, utterly numb and very shaky—a telling combination of extreme emotional exhaustion and lack of food and water, even I knew that.

When we reached the stairwell, I needed his steadying arm even more to negotiate the steps. My legs had gone to jelly and my vision was blurring.

The cabin below decks was dimly lit, just the hanging oil lamp was alight and it swung lazily, back and forth.

Turan was curled up on the straw pallet and covered with a thick fur but hearing our scraping and shuffling descent, she levered herself up onto one elbow and fixed her cold eyes on us. The others were there too—even Jaro I noticed—but asleep, or at least pretending to be asleep.

Still using Hanni for support, I approached her then stopped. "I was told to attend you," I said in a raspy voice barely above a whisper—not because I wanted to avoid waking those asleep. My voice had gone, squeezed out by the still excruciatingly painful lump in the back of my throat.

She glared up at me. "I sent Hanni for you some time ago."

"My fault, not his."

"I'm sure it is." Her sharp eyes darted him before returning to me. "Hanni knows better than to keep me waiting."

I lifted my elbow from his hold, silent permission for him to leave me to whatever Turan had planned, which he wasted no time in doing while I fixed my eyes on the deck, awaiting her orders. I was tired—extremely so. My entire body wobbled and I wouldn't have been the least bit surprised if I suddenly collapsed. In fact I wouldn't have minded passing out right about then; I suspected doing so would spare me a lot of grief. But of course when you want to pass out, you can't. It only happens when you don't and faking it wasn't an option—Turan would know.

"I'm cold. You're to keep me warm tonight—*nothing* more. Understand?"

"Yes," I murmured and started unsteadily for the bed.

Just as my fingers reached for the fur, she snapped, "Take off the tunic and boots—I'll not have you ruin Perus's livery by sleeping in it."

I managed with some effort to straighten up then I began to disrobe—painfully aware of other eyes on me—maybe Sifrie, maybe Kyrou, awakened by Turan's sharp voice. I dared not look around—it would only add to what was intended as a deliberately public humiliation.

Turan watched in flinty silence as I awkwardly undressed, first the boots, then with far, far more difficulty, the tunic, because my joints had stiffened in the cold. I forced myself not to wince or groan as I struggled to free my aching limbs, tried not to shiver as the damp chill settled on my bare skin and when I was finished—my whole body was now quivering in exhaustion—I knelt and lifted the fur then slipped in beside her.

She immediately rolled onto her side, away from me and I tucked myself up against her and cautiously wrapped my arm around her, trying to provide as much body to body contact as possible thus as much warmth as possible—although in truth she was far warmer than I *and* she was fully clothed. I hadn't realized just how cold I was until that moment and despite myself I began to shiver. Turan, for her part, responded with a soft gasp, startled by my icy embrace. Under other circumstances that would have given me some small satisfaction; as it was, it didn't.

We remained in this awkward cuddle long enough for me to stop shivering, long enough for the oil lamp to sputter and wink out, plunging the cabin into pitch darkness.

I had no idea if Turan was asleep, or just ignoring me, so I tightened my hold, hoping she would do something, say something—*anything.*

I ached all over, my belly was cramping painfully… but worst of all I couldn't shake those hellish memories of the battle.

For my entire adult life I'd prided myself on being self-reliant, never fully trusting others, always keeping a certain distance—even with my closest friends. Now all of those self-imposed and rigorously maintained barriers had been brushed aside and all I was left with was crippling self-doubt.

Turan?

When she failed to respond to my unspoken plea, I kissed her neck then whispered hoarsely in her ear, *"Turan…?"* as I ran my hand over her stomach, then more a little more boldly I gently but insistently caressed her breast. *"Please…"*

She knew what I was thinking, what I wanted—how could she not? I desperately needed reassurance, needed to know I was not a cast-off—so for a moment or two I continued my fondling while I pressed myself against her, hoping to lose myself in the familiar motions, hoping for her acknowledgement of my needs with an invitation to satisfy hers.

But she didn't even stir, didn't react in the slightest to my fingers' tender caress and by doing so, she made her point, as cruel and as degrading as it was. But then I'd hurt her deeply. This was just her way of proving to me she could do the same and then some, and at any time.

I drew in a ragged breath. *Fair enough.* My hand resumed its loose embrace on her belly, I pressed my forehead against her shoulders and closed my eyes but I was far too afraid to fall asleep—afraid I'd relive the battle in my dreams, remember other, even more appalling details, and even more afraid if I did fall asleep what I'd find—or *not* find, when I awoke.

— XIII —

In the early summer of my second year with Lady Ilissia, Lucius came to one of her banquets accompanied by his command staff and usual crop of fresh-faced tribunes, along with an older aide I'd never seen before.

The man was clearly uncomfortable with the social setting and kept to the small and relatively isolated clump of middle-aged officers, making small talk about military matters.

As usual I was arm in arm with m'lady as she made the rounds to welcome each of her guests personally. But as we passed by the group of officers, I overheard the aide mention that he was recently of the Third Augusta out of Ammaedara and my heart skipped a beat.

I'd stopped thinking about Gracchus—having found a measure of happiness in Lady Ilissia's service and in return I wanted for nothing—but the mention of the Third Augusta brought back with full force why, no matter how I tried, I never felt as if I was whole. The Simitthu Garrison had been an auxiliary detachment of the Third Augusta, and Ammaedara, I now knew, was no more than three days march almost due south of Simitthu—once you'd rounded a range of low hills—which meant I'd searched in the entirely wrong direction.

I felt a cold chill settle over my shoulders—this man, I knew with absolute certainty, was the key to finding Gracchus. I also knew with equal certainty I risked exposing myself for who I really was if I rekindled my search, yet despite the dangers, I knew I had to try or live with my regret the rest of my life.

So, as Lady Ilissia and I walked on and she murmured her greetings to her guests I kept furtively glancing back to the aide. I knew I must somehow get close to this man, to ingratiate myself, but I also knew I had to be very careful. No matter my name and connections, I was clearly not fully Roman and with several provinces in upheaval, if not open rebellion, these were nervous days. There had been assassinations, kidnappings and plots foiled—and rumors of civil war.

Turmoil in Rome itself sent waves of unease throughout the empire. Just the week before one of Vallus's tribunes—who'd foolishly taunted a hungry mob awaiting their allotments of grain—had been dragged from his horse and badly beaten before he could be rescued by his escort. After that, soldiers were confined to barracks, which of course had a ripple effect on the local economy, adding to everyone's woes, civilian and soldier alike.

But within the high walls of the villa, everything was as it should be, or at least everything appeared as it should be. Tables were piled high with elaborately designed platters of exotic foodstuffs, other tables were thickly populated with elegant vessels containing wine imported from across the empire. There was absolutely no scrimping, no second best, yet in the time I'd been a member of her household, I'd never known Lady Ilissia to employ food testers. Now she had not one, but two, and they were extremely well

174

paid—to avoid any chance someone else could entice them to look the other way. They weren't obvious of course—she was too dignified to admit it, even she felt afraid. But they were always there, in the background, surreptitiously tasting everything before it was offered to her, or to her guests.

I escorted Lady Ilissia over to a divan, where she sunk down and exhaled wearily. She enjoyed her parties, enjoyed entertaining her friends, enjoyed providing the best of the best, but the strain of acting as if nothing was amiss was clearly evident. I smiled, kissed her and blaming her fatigue on the truly oppressive afternoon heat, I told her I'd fetch her something to eat and drink and not to move.

She smiled, gave me a pat on the cheek then made herself comfortable on the pillowed couch and gazed around her, satisfied that at least her guests were enjoying themselves.

I ducked into the crowd, made my way to one of the tables and quickly heaped a plate full of her favorite sweetmeats and fruit. I moved to the wine table, filled a goblet with the best vintage then returned to her side, only to find her son seated beside her.

They were in a heated, albeit whispered conversation, so rather than intrude, I placed my offerings next to her then at her slight, dismissive nod, I melted away, into the milling guests.

Temporarily left to my devices and realizing I might not have another opportunity, I slowly, carefully wound my way back to the group of officers.

I found the aide, along with a tribune, standing at a table sampling the fare and talking, so I casually picked up a date and popped it in my mouth, then grabbed another, aware that the aide and his younger companion were now watching me, clearly unsure if I was indeed a guest or perhaps a servant who had temporarily forgotten his place.

I turned to face them, smiled, and introduced myself.

The tribune gave me a disdainful look and muttered something under his breath to the aide.

The aide, older and wiser, knew better than to risk offending his hostess—or worse, his commanding officer—by treating me with similar contempt, and responded by introducing himself as Gaius Libius Silva. He then said he'd noticed my furtive glances, which sent my already rapidly beating heart into a fully-fledged panic, and asked if there was something he could do for me—a rhetorical question on his part, I had no doubt, but an opportunity not to be missed.

As Lady Ilissia's lover I wanted for nothing, but she was middle-aged and not in the best of health. Along with this constant uncertainty was another: she'd been talking more and more of returning to Rome—prompted by the growing unease all around her—vague plans that became even more formless when it came to her plans for me, which in turn prompted me, during the dark hours of night, or when I walked alone along her private beach, to start thinking the unthinkable: being abandoned yet again.

Rather than to yet again accept whatever the Fates handed me, I'd begun to think seriously about what I wanted to do with the rest of my life, something I'd never bothered to consider before as I'd always thought in the immediate, never in terms of having a future. And when I thought these thoughts, my mind kept coming back to that fabulous armor worn by the officer who had literally plucked me from my life as a petty thief in the back alleys of Alexandria and deposited me in Lady Ilissia's villa.

I wanted to be that officer. Desperately.

Don't think me foolish—or quite that vain: I knew there was more to being in the army than an elegant uniform—I'd seen how common soldiers lived—I'd lived with them for almost three years after all, experienced their hardships as mine. But as one of Lady Ilissia's personal guards had told me, the army was where someone with ambition and a keen mind could go far. I'd never considered myself ambitious, but I knew I was very bright, and so I said what I knew I needed to say to this man: I wanted to join the army—that as a citizen and legitimate son of a citizen, it was not only my right but my obligation to serve.

Silva looked me up and down, taking in my finery, my coiffed and perfumed hair and chuckling, asked me how old I was. I lied. I told him almost eighteen. I told him I could read and write, both Greek and Latin; I knew a number of native tongues, a myriad of local customs and could pass without question for Egyptian or Mauri—Massaesyli or Massyli.

He replied with a very interested twitch of his brows.

I went on to tell him my current situation was due to incredible good fortune, not to mention Lady Ilissia's kindness. I told him my legionary father had been killed in a skirmish and my mother had died in childbirth shortly thereafter, leaving me an orphan at a very young age. I didn't have to detail the hardships a child without close family would face—death by starvation was the most common outcome, and one I almost succumbed to, followed by being sold into slavery, often as not by less than compassionate relatives.

I said I was from Carthage—I was, wasn't I?—plus it explained my coloring. I told him I'd been born 'in camp', that my father and his detachment had been briefly stationed at some distant fort, far to the south.

That clearly piqued his curiosity.

I added for good measure that it was my hope to join my father's old unit—to suggest otherwise would have piqued his curiosity on other ways—and besides, what better way to find Gracchus than serve with soldiers who'd likely served with him?

Silva dismissed the tribune, who was more than happy to return to his fellows then he asked how I'd come to be a member of Lady Ilissia's household. In his position it would have been relatively simple for him to uncover the truth for himself—so I spared him the effort. I fabricated a story of working the docks of Carthage, of eventually joining a ship's crew—the Aequitas—*of being left behind in Alexandria when the captain found he had a need to leave port in a hurry. It was not entirely unheard of for a ship to suddenly find itself unwelcome, or, more commonly with its holds full and riding low in the water needing to take advantage of a favorable tide and prevailing winds, and raise anchor without all crew being accounted for—the latter was how I managed to find a berth aboard the* Aequitas *after all.*

He listened attentively as a slave filled his goblet with wine then he motioned to a nearby bench and bade me join him. I dutifully sat, stiff and erect, unintentionally mimicking a soldier's attentive posture, my heart hammering against my chest and he eased himself down beside me.

He gestured around us, at the lush garden and abundant banquet, then asked why I would want to leave such a luxurious lifestyle for the rigors and risk of the legion—did I have any idea just how hard such a life would be, especially for someone accustomed to such comforts?

I assured him I was all too familiar to hardship—and proved it by showing him some of the terrible and clearly old scars no son of privilege, even at my presumed age, would bear. I said I had wanted to join the army my entire life, and with two goals in mind: to avenge the death of my father and serve the empire.

He seemed genuinely sympathetic to my plight, said he'd served at Sicca, as well as Ammaedara and Tripolitania and perhaps he might have crossed paths with my father, and asked his name.

I hesitated, my heart in my throat. Either this man would be the key to opening that door where I'd find Gracchus waiting for me, or he would dash my hopes for good. I'd never seriously searched for my real sire—Gracchus was, to me, my only father. For all I knew my real father never knew I existed, or if he did, he never cared about me. Gracchus had, at least for a time. But I also only knew him as Gracchus—I never knew if that was his family, clan or first name. So, bracing myself, I told him what little I knew of the man, the name my mother had called him—I figured that was the safest thing to say—and what I remembered of his appearance: tall, bearish, with a thick black beard that he kept meticulously trimmed and a large, ragged scar that ran the length of his left arm.

Silva listened attentively, but his unchanging expression left me with a sinking feeling. It had been a long shot, I told myself—a very long shot. Gracchus was a common foot soldier, one of thousands who were regularly transferred from garrison to garrison as the political climate changed. So in desperation, I began throwing out other names, names of men I'd deliberately not thought about for years, along with sketchy descriptions: Lucullus, tall and lean, with reddish brown hair; Marcellus, a short, stocky man from the vast marshes of the far eastern provinces, known equally for his cooking and his ability to train horses and who claimed to have once been a gladiator... Porsenna, with his blond hair and explosive temper—

That name clearly caught Silva's attention and my heart reacted by thumping loudly in my ears—was Porsenna here, in Alexandria? That awful possibility had never occurred to me. Might he actually make an appearance at one of Lady Ilissia's banquets and expose me for who and what I was?

I swallowed down the sudden urge to vomit.

Yes, Silva said, watching me, watching my startled reaction closely, he'd known Porsenna. He said he'd fought alongside him then he patted me on the shoulder and added gently that Porsenna had been taken captive by the Massyli years ago, his body found days later, bearing the evidence of torture and left impaled on a stake.

I must've gasped—equally stunned by this news. Porsenna, dead? And dead by a means so fitting to his crimes? It seemed too good to be true. I asked him if he was sure of this—he said he was; he'd seen the body for himself and immediately recognized Porsenna, or, as he said, what was left of him after the jackals had eaten their fill.

He took my rapidly blinking reaction for horror, rather than what it truly was. He quickly added that he knew nothing of Lucullus or Marcellus, that I mustn't think the worst for them while my mind was still trying to sort out the flood of intense and conflicting emotions, first the stomach-twisting dread that Porsenna was here followed by the equally intense gratification at the news that he was not only dead, but had died in such a gruesome and appropriate way... and finally, the truly awful realization that Porsenna had, in fact, a far greater impact on my life than Gracchus or anyone else ever had—that if it hadn't been for Porsenna, I would have died back in Simitthu. Porsenna had been, after all, the one to introduce me to a trade—as brutal as it was—a trade that had kept me alive and shaped who and what I had become.

I fixed my shock-numbed stare on the ground at my feet, only minimally aware that Silva was still talking to me, telling me he would do what he could to help me in my search for Gracchus, that he had never known his father—leaving the reason unsaid— and so understood my drive to learn all I could about the man who'd sired me, not the least of which was his fate. I overheard him say he would also take under serious consideration my request to join the legion—adding he could use an aide, especially one as resourceful as myself, but on one condition: that I first obtain Lady Ilissia's blessing.

He rose, patting me on the shoulder, in the process drawing my distracted gaze, and added that keeping one step ahead of Vallus's moods was work enough—he didn't need Vallus's mother demanding his head as well. He then made his excuses and rejoined his fellow officers.

I remained seated on the bench, my heart still beating like mad. I was unaware of the sidelong, amused glances of the officers and their quiet laughter; I was oblivious to Lady Ilissia calling to me.

All I could focus on, now that I was completely alone, was the fact that Porsenna— my tormentor, and yes, in a strange way, my savior and the object of so many dreadful nightmares—was finally, execrably dead.

"Wake up!" A hand gripped my shoulder, followed by a familiar, whispered voice: "Come on, wake up!—we've got orders to move!"

Felix?

All around me armor clanked as men scrambled to dress themselves. In the background were the bellows of other centurions, calling their men to arms, accompanied by the warbling blast of buccinas.

"Arri, damn you!" That had to be Aetius. "You want to miss out on the fight? Come on, wake up!"

I tried, but I felt as if I was at the bottom of some deep, dark pit, unable to move.

"Wake up, Arri!" Felix's worried voice came again, followed by gentle shake; this one stirred up an intense throbbing pain in my shoulder. "Arri, please... wake *UP!*"

I couldn't open my eyes.

"Let me try," came another familiar voice—Rufinius—followed by an even rougher shaking, then, "I told you we shouldn't have let him drink so much last night—"

"He didn't drink any more than the rest of us," Aetius fired back.

"Quick!" Felix hissed, "Get him on his feet—Jotia's coming!"

I felt a similar panic race through me—Jotia was a senior centurion not to trifled with; he took great exception to any weakness, any suggestion of malingering—especially by another centurion. Arms eeled under me, forced me to a seated position, then a hand slapped me across the face, and again, snapping my head from side to side. "Wake up, damn it!"

The blows stung and made my eyes water.

"Wake up!" The snarled command was followed by another, even rougher shake.

This time I somehow managed to force open my eyes only to find that it wasn't Felix or Aetius, or even Rufinius kneeling beside me, keeping my strangely limp body upright, but a rather someone else, someone who, nevertheless, looked vaguely familiar. "Where's... Felix?" I croaked.

"Who the hell's Felix?"

The voice too sounded familiar. I squinted at the face. *Hanni?* That wasn't right—what was he doing here, in camp? I tried to look around him, but everything was a dim blur. *Where's Felix?*

"Arri?"

The firm voice drew me back to the ogre, to his very anxious expression. He gave me another rough shake. "Come on, Arri, wake up!"

"Hanni...?"

He exhaled. "Damn, you're a sound sleeper, you know that?"

"What… what are you doing here?" I mumbled as I knuckle-rubbed my burning eyes.

"What do you mean, what am I doing here?"

I eyed him. "Just what I said."

"I think you're still asleep."

I wasn't about to dispute that; it still didn't explain what an ogre, a barbarian—the enemy—was doing in the middle of a Roman encampment.

"I don't know what you're doing here," I growled, trying to get my elbows under me as his supporting arm was withdrawn, "but you'd best leave before anyone sees you."

He stared at me for a moment, shook his shaggy head, muttered, "Definitely not awake." And with that, he slapped me across the face again with enough force to knock my elbows out from under me.

"OW!" I clutched my burning cheek with my hand. *"STOP IT!"*

"Then wake up!"

"I am awake!"

"I don't think so."

"Am so! Look, my eyes are open. I'm talking to you. That means I'm awake."

"Tell me where you are."

I reluctantly lifted my head and looked around, again. What I saw was not a Roman camp in the process of being roused. What I saw was a wood-paneled room, the only illumination coming from the top of a staircase.

"Well?"

I looked back up at him, smiled a little sheepishly. "I know I'm not where I thought I was."

"Where did you think you were?"

"In camp."

He shook his head. "No. You're aboard a ship, Arri—the *Sulaviae*. Remember?"

That name sounded familiar, too. Couldn't immediately place it though. And I certainly had no idea how I'd gotten here, or why I was on a ship in the first place—not to mention I had no clue as to where the ship was headed or how long I'd been aboard. But I felt I should play along, act as if I knew, lull all those pesky missing details into a false sense of security so they might come out of hiding. "What's… wrong?"

"You tell me."

"I asked you first."

He sighed. "Fine. You really worried me when you wouldn't wake up." His expression said there was more to it than just that.

I looked around me once more—my trick had worked. I knew where I was, but along with that sudden realization came all the very painful memories of what had happened the night before. No wonder I'd wanted to be somewhere else—anywhere. Even facing Jotia's foul humor and a blow or twenty from his vine-staff would have been a fair sight better than facing Turan.

I squinted up at him, suddenly very annoyed that he hadn't left me alone, left me to sleep, left me to my comfortable oblivion… left me in the company of my friends.

"We're also about to make landfall."

I was surprised to find that I no longer cared. Not one damned bit.

"And that means you need to get up."

I eyed him. I didn't want to get up. I wanted to remain where I was. Getting up meant leaving the relative warmth and comfort of the pallet; getting up meant facing Turan again, facing what new public humiliation she'd devised. "No!" I jerked the fur cover over my head and settled back.

"Come on, Arri," he grumbled and gave my shoulder another rough shake.

I cried out—the shaking really hurt—then flipping the fur back, peered up at him and snarled, "Leave me the hell alone!"

"Turan wants you up—"

"I don't give a damn what—"

"Do I have to drag you out of bed?"

Now that was extremely unappealing. Just the thought made my already aching body ache anew, so I scowled at him as I struggled to get my right elbow back under me.

"Here, let me help." He slipped his arm under my shoulders and once he'd helped me back into a sitting position, I gave my tired, gritty eyes another vigorous rub then looked around again; aside from Hanni and me, the cabin was deserted. "Where is everyone?"

"Topside—discussing their plans over the morning meal. If I help, can you get dressed?"

I managed to toss the fur cover aside. "I can dress myself, thank you."

He gave me a long, hard look and I suddenly felt very self-conscious. "You look awful."

I forced a feeble smile. "Gee, thanks."

"I mean it. You've lost a *lot* of weight, Arri—it shows in your face, your eyes—" he looked me over again, "—not to mention the rest of you."

I couldn't help but touch my now bearded but noticeably hollow cheeks. He was right—and it went beyond the obvious loss of weight. For the past day or so my vision kept blurring, my stomach without warning would cramp painfully and my hands had taken on a fine tremor—something I'd tried to conceal, even from myself. I'd seen the like before, experienced starvation many, many times and knew the danger signs. I was in serious trouble. I should have said so, should have asked Turan for help the day before, but whether it was asinine male pride or a true desire to die that stopped me, I wasn't sure.

I did have to ask Hanni to help me to my feet. He did, then maintaining a slight stoop to avoid hitting his head on the low-beamed ceiling, stepped back and as I stood there, wobbling, suddenly and intensely dizzy he looked me up and down again then shook his shaggy head.

I ignored his worried stare, but as I slowly bent over to pick up the tunic I suddenly lost my balance and fell to my knees, gasping at the pain that jolted through me and doubling over.

"I'll fetch Turan." He turned to leave.

"*No!*" I hissed through clenched teeth. All of the intense emotions, the humiliation, hurt, desperation and fear of the previous night were still moving around in my mind and had yet to find places to alight. I was *not* about to face Turan clothed only in my trousers—I wanted at least that much. "Help me up, *damn it*—I'm fine."

He hesitated.

"Please, Hanni. I'm just a little stiff, that's all."

He eyed me as he snatched up the tunic. "And I think you're a lot sicker than you're letting on."

"Fine—if it'll make you happy you can fetch her, *once* I'm dressed. I'm damned cold—and standing around half-naked isn't making me any warmer."

He nodded, reluctantly.

A few minutes later and with his help I was back in full livery. I combed my shaky fingers though my wind-tangled hair, turned to him and smiled my best smile. "See? Much better."

He wasn't fooled, not one damned bit. He crossed his arms and jerked his head towards the nearby steps. "Let's see you walk."

My smile faded, but I refused to concede the point, so I walked—shuffled very slowly actually—over to the stairs. I grit my teeth, grabbed the railing and took the first step then the next. My hips hurt, my ankles hurt. My knees hurt. Okay, okay, just about everything hurt—and the fall certainly hadn't helped. Worse, my damned vision kept blurring.

I made it to the fifth step, with another four to go, when my legs again failed me, I stumbled and fell, banging my right elbow to boot—so now I could add that to the growing list of what smarted.

He grabbed me by the collar of the tunic and irritably hoisted me back to my feet. "I'm beginning to grasp why Turan gets so aggravated with you—you absolutely refuse to recognize the blatantly obvious."

I made a feeble attempt at humor as I gingerly massaged my abused elbow. "It's one of my most endearing qualities—or so I've been told many times."

He made a low grumbling noise—it kind of reminded me of a horse with a severe case of indigestion—as he none-too-gently helped me the rest of the way up the stairs. Once we were on the deck, he released his hold and I made a cursory effort at pulling my disarranged clothing back where it belonged—then I happened to notice land. We *were* close—no more than a few hundred feet off a wide swath of beach. High above that was a wind-swept grassy bluff. But it wasn't the beach or bluff that drew my startled attention. It was the long, undulating line of armored horses and men that crowned the heights, half a hundred at the very least, lance tips held aloft, brightly colored pennants fluttering and snapping in the stiff, icy breeze.

I glanced up at Hanni. "Our welcoming committee?"

"You could say that—that's Lord Rasaben up there," he jerked his chin towards the line of soldiers, "come to escort us to Lord Taskim's Keep—"

"Oh."

"—you'll come to appreciate that Lord Rasaben has a flare for the dramatic."

I turned back to the assemblage of heavy armor and was duly impressed—by their number, their weaponry... and that they *hadn't* sunk under the combined weight of it. Then again, maybe this wasn't Hibernia. Or maybe the rumors were totally unfounded, spread in the hopes of keeping Rome's military might—not to mention *heft*—at bay.

"Think they might've brought an extra horse?" Just the thought of again sharing the same annoyingly lively mount with Kyrou sent a cold shiver down my already chilled spine. Not that I was in any shape to actually ride alone—even I knew that. I had in mind just being thrown over the saddle, like a moldy sack of grain, arms and legs dangling, something that would put Lord Rasaben's attempt at the awe-inspiring entrance to shame and spawn a thousand to epic poems.

"Doubt it."

"Oh."

He patted my shoulder. "You're riding with me. All right?"

183

Before I could thank him, I heard voices from behind us and managed to shuffle-turn just as Sapor and Turan emerged from the stern cabin. Sifrie, Perus, Jaro, Kyrou and the rest of Turan's entourage followed.

Turan favored me with one quick, frigid glance, gave Hanni a cursory nod, then turned to Sapor and continued their conversation. The rest hurried past us, some like Sifrie, Perus and Kyrou disappearing below decks to where the horses were stabled, the rest moving over to the railing to watch the goings on. No one acknowledged me: aside from Turan no one even made eye contact—not even Kyrou. I would have thought he would have taken the chance to give me a thoroughly satisfied grin at the very least, but no. I wasn't even worth that much.

I looked up at Hanni. "You should've let me jump."

"Turan's extremely angry at you—"

"Really?" I scoffed. "Are you absolutely sure, because I just don't see it."

"—the others are just following her example, with the exception of Kyrou of course: he detested you from the start."

"Of course."

"Don't worry—I've never seen her stay this furious for long."

"How long is long?"

"A week? Longest I've ever seen her this way was a month…"

I winced.

"… but that was when Kyrou 'accidentally' killed her favorite dog."

I eyed him as this seemed to be a story worth elaborating on. Any story where Kyrou had bested me in pissing off Turan sounded like something I wanted to hear in its entirety—call it a much needed morale boost. "He killed her… dog?"

"The animal didn't much like Kyrou, you see."

I felt a sudden and abiding fondness for this poor, departed and clearly wonderful and intelligent dog.

"Used to growl and snap at him any time Kyrou came near Turan, and developed a habit of relieving himself on, and sometimes *in* Kyrou's boots."

I snorted explosively then tried to pretend I'd sneezed. I rubbed my nose vigorously to cement the ruse. "I think I'm coming down with something…"

Hanni eyed me suspiciously. "Kyrou finally had had his fill, and one day while Turan and her party were hunting deer, he shot it with an arrow then claimed he thought it was a wolf."

"An easy mistake," I said, figuring there was no harm in giving Kyrou the benefit of the doubt in something he'd already been found guilty of doing.

"Ever see a bright red wolf? I haven't. The animal was almost the color of Sifrie's hair—how could you mistake that was a wolf?"

"Maybe he meant a fox."

"He said wolf."

"Maybe he's color-blind." I'd heard of that affliction. I'd even known a few soldiers who claimed to be blind to certain hues, especially when they were drunk and those hues denoted vastly superior rank. Aetius for one...

He stooped, whispered in my ear: "Just start eating, put back some of that weight you've lost," he straightened up and patted me on the shoulder, "all right? Do that and she'll come around—you'll see..."

It's not like I'm doing it deliberately, you know—

"... she's just really worried about you. So am I."

That makes three of us. "But you're not treating me like I'm a leper."

"A... what?"

"A lep—never mind." While his ignorance ruined my point, I was glad to know he didn't know what a leper was—that meant he'd never seen one, which meant I probably wouldn't see another one. Which, so far, was the only plus I'd come across in this so far very unhappy adventure. I'd seen far too many—just the thought of lepers made my largely unblemished skin crawl.

He shrugged. "Besides, Lord Taskim is always the most generous host—I'm sure you'll find something to whet your appetite once we're seated at his banquet table—otherwise... well, I'll have to do what Turan has ordered me to do."

I really shouldn't have asked what he meant by that. Of course I did. "Which is...?"

"Force feed you."

I glanced at his massive, knotty hands and couldn't help but swallow convulsively. "Oh." Still, I had to suppose there was some hope in that—Turan clearly wasn't going to let me waste away. Then again, her reason for keeping me alive might be because she hadn't run out of ways of making my life utterly miserable. Once that happened... well, who knew?

"And speaking of," he stuffed a hand into his trouser pocket, "you need to take this." He withdrew his hand, opened his massive palm to reveal another lozenge, only this one was tan rather than yellow—and a rather grubby, lint-covered tan to boot. "Don't have any water, so you'll just have to swallow it without—and swallow it whole, hear? No chewing."

185

I made a face.

"Sorry," he mumbled. After doing his best to wipe and pick the fuzz off, he offered it to me again.

I very reluctantly plucked the lozenge from his palm. Thankfully it was smaller than the others, but I wasn't at all sure I could get it down, whole, without some lubrication. At his insistent stare, I popped it my mouth. It had a very odd taste—cloyingly sweet rather than the more familiar bitter tang of the others—and did I mention it was furry? It resembled something an owl had regurgitated—minus the obvious bones. I'd say it tasted like one, too, but that would be pure speculation on my part.

I grimaced as I struggled to force it down.

He gave me a sidelong questioning look as I kept gulping while massaging my throat—the damned thing had stuck part way down and refused to budge.

Finally, with one last hard swallow, it was on its way, which was a good thing because no sooner had I got it down than I overheard a yelled, *"Take hold!"* from a sailor perched on the mast, high above.

A moment later the *Sulaviae* lurched then came to a sudden, grinding halt and if it hadn't been for Hanni's timely grab, I would have lost my already precarious balance and gone tumbling across the deck. Below, the horses whickered fearfully—and for once I was in complete agreement.

What I'd assumed was going to be a docking was actually a deliberate grounding, which was always a risky maneuver, unless of course the plan was to abandon the ship and Sapor, as he strode purposefully towards me, didn't have the look of a captain about to lose his command.

"Low tide's about to turn," he grumbled at my questioning stare. "There're no harbors along these shores you see—this is the only way to get the horses off safely."

Which meant we'd have to either wade, or ride ashore. If given a choice I'd opt for wading—I didn't care how damned frigid the water was.

Needless to say I wasn't given a choice. We rode ashore, me sitting astride Hanni's massive carthorse, the ogre seated behind me and keeping one thickset arm wrapped around me, his knees pressing my shins to the horse's barrel chest—no saddle this time. It was an unnerving experience from start to finish: being heaved aboard a very restive horse while still aboard ship with the heavy beamed ceiling of the hold barely four feet above my head once I was on its back, then clutching its coarse mane in both hands as Hanni mounted, almost jostling me off in the process and finally him directing the animal, who was clearly very eager to disembark, onto a wide, steeply angled gangplank—all done with Hanni in a crouch and me squashed between him and the horse and barely able to breathe.

And of course all of a sudden the damned beast wasn't so damned eager, despite a lot of coaxing from Hanni.

It started back-stepping up the ramp, tossing its huge head and whinnying nervously.

I couldn't really blame it—half way down, the gang plank disappeared under the foamy surface of a very rough sea and the beach, which had looked so close from the top deck, suddenly didn't look quite so near.

It finally took a viciously hard smack on its rump from the flat of Jaro's broadsword to get it to descend the ramp. Once committed, the carthorse thundered down the steep incline and plunged into the sea—which was a hell of lot deeper than the horse or I'd assumed—and as it galloped out of the pounding surf and onto dry ground the rest of our party followed, single-file, clattering down the gangplank and splashing through the breakers and onto the beach. Sifrie's pony fared the worst: the water came half way up its neck, but Sifrie herself avoided the icy bath. Jaro, aboard his bay, led, or more accurately dragged the understandably reluctant pony down the ramp while Sifrie remained high and dry, safely seated behind Kyrou as he and the other carthorse brought up the rear.

I squinted at them, then, hearing a whinny of a horse, I turned back to the bluff. A deeply cut pathway—more a very narrow ravine—wound down from the grassy heights, and no sooner had our ragtag group formed up on the beach than the armored soldiers began their descent, their heavily laden warhorses struggling in dry sand while surrounded by narrow walls of dirt, winter-dried grass and rock barely wide enough to let them and their riders pass.

Behind me Sapor bellowed orders as ropes groaned and wood clattered against wood, but my full attention—along with everyone else on the beach—was on the approaching group. Despite Hanni's assurances, these men didn't look the least bit friendly. I sincerely hoped they were because our only means of escape was being hastily withdrawn as the sailors retracted the heavy gangplank.

Once on the beach, the first five riders cantered past us, pennant-tipped lances held high, only to stop and wheel around in perfect unison, then take up a defensive stance that was utterly unnecessary and just for show as the beach was no more than a wide, crescent shaped swath squeezed in a hollow between rugged headlands that in turn thrust their rocky fingers into the roiling sea. The only way out was up that ravine, which was presently chock-a-block with soldiers.

More armored men and horses poured onto the beach and fanned out, pennants snapping loudly in the stiff breeze, then Rasaben appeared—I had no doubt it was he—a bearded, red-haired, burly, ruddy-cheeked and hard-faced man outfitted, head to toe in armor that, like the rest, appeared to glow from within. Unlike the rest, he was bareheaded.

He urged his equally brawny warhorse from the others then jerked it to a halt in front of Turan. He and his mount dwarfed Turan and hers, but if she was at all intimidated by the display of overwhelming force—or size—she failed to show it.

"Ras—how kind of you to come meet us."

"You've kept us waiting, Turi—when you missed the original rendezvous I naturally assumed the worst, but I clearly underestimated your abilities to get yourself and your escort safely back here—and all in one piece, no less."

"Not quite. We lost Harne."

"Pity." His smile faded as his eyes swept her escort. "He was a good man and a loyal servant—" His gaze stopped on me and his expression immediately brightened. "But, unless I'm mistaken, sister, you appear to have been successful in this, um, hare-brained endeavor?"

I couldn't help but glance at Turan. *Sister?* I certainly saw no resemblance. If was a joke, neither seemed particularly amused.

"Yes," Turan replied icily, glaring at him as he stared at me.

I took heart in that—here was someone she clearly detested even more than me. Of course he was her brother—assuming he really *was* her brother—and in some social circles, one would be considered sadly remiss if you didn't despise and possibly even go so far as to plot the *demise* your siblings—the Imperial family and their close kin were the most obvious example to come to mind.

He favored me with another head to toe and decidedly dubious stare. "Let's hope the cost was worth it."

I met his gaze with as much defiance as I could muster, emboldened by Hanni's closeness, all the while painfully aware that I was at the mercy of this group—and Hanni was one of them.

Rasaben grinned, as if immensely pleased by my reaction then he looked up at the sky. What had begun as a cold, clear day had turned ominous. Dark clouds boiled on the horizon and the white-capped ocean itself had begun to churn in anticipation of the approaching gale. I briefly wondered if Sapor had made a fatal miscalculation. If he had, Rasaben clearly was not of a mind to stay long enough to find out—or help out.

"Come." He motioned to his soldiers.

The four closest broke from their eerily unmoving ranks and headed back up the ravine while the rest remained, a palisade of armor that stretched from the shifting edge of the surf to the base of the bluff.

Rasaben gave his horse a kick to the belly and it followed the others. Our group fell in behind him, again, single file with Kyrou and Sifrie this time in the lead and Hanni and I taking up the rear.

As we passed the gauntlet of silent, armored horsemen, I found myself peering at each, trying to find some glimmer of expression in their tracking eyes. All I saw were helmet-framed faces remarkably identical in their dour appearance, each with an unblinking gaze that seemed to stare right through me. Shifting my attention to their armor did little to lessen my growing unease. Even close up it had this peculiar gleam, and with the sky rapidly darkening overhead, the curious effect could not be blamed on a trick of sunlight.

I glanced over my shoulder at Hanni, hoping for a more friendly response, but he looked worried too.

Great, just... great.

I tightened my hold on the horse's bristly mane as we started up the ravine and hung on for dear life as the animal lurched and heaved, grunting and snorting and slogging its way up the steep pathway, through the knee and hock-deep sand until we were well up onto the wind-swept bluff. Then I hunkered down as best I could.

I was thoroughly chilled and even more worrisome, I found that I was suddenly and extremely sleepy—my eyelids felt like lead—no amount of blinking could keep them open and my neck could no longer support my head, which promptly nodded forward.

Alarmed, afraid I might not wake up, afraid of what Turan had planned for me while I was gone, I managed to jerk my head up and drew in a sharp breath.

"Go to sleep, Arri," Hanni murmured. "I won't let you fall."

I felt my body going to jelly—I panicked and gasping, struggled feebly against his embrace, against the overwhelming urge to sleep.

"It's all right, I've got you... *easy.*" He tightened his hold on me. *"Just relax and go to—"*

"Nnnnnoooooo...!" I slurred as I felt myself slide into something akin to a dreamless sleep.

I have no idea how long I remained in this state; it might have been minutes, hours or even a full day. I was dimly aware of voices, of the snort and whinny of the horses, the jingle of harness, and once the distinctive echo of hoof beats as if we'd entered a tunnel of some sort and then immerged, the horse beneath me changing gait, breaking into a gentle canter and Hanni adjusting his hold on my limp body.

But as the rhythmic, muffled thudding of hooves on soil abruptly changed to a hollow clatter, accompanied by Hanni gently but insistently shaking my good arm and calling my name, I somehow managed to lift my head. I forced my eyes open only to find the ramparts of a massive wood and stone fortification looming over us as our party trotted up its drawbridge. Through cold-numb lips I mumbled, *"Where…?"*

"Lord Taskim's Keep… and not a moment too soon—the blizzard's almost upon us."

I blearily looked around to find that it was snowing hard, the really wet, heavy stuff that clung to anything it touched, and clearly it had been snowing hard for quite some time as the riders ahead of me—even the neck, mane and head of our carthorse—were coated in a clumpy white crust. I'd been completely unaware of it, hadn't noticed that I was too was blanketed in a similar clumpy, frozen crust.

I tried to stretch the painfully stiff muscles of my neck and back as I smacked my gummy lips. My mouth tasted of that lozenge and I still felt very groggy with the unpleasant addition of a blinding headache. It wouldn't take much to draw me back into a deep slumber.

I forcibly shook myself awake then peered into the swirl of snowflakes just in time to see Turan and Rasaben, side-by-side, disappear into the dark maw of the gateway, followed in quick order by the rest of her escort. As we passed through, I looked up at the sharp-tipped ends of the gate, which looked suspiciously like fangs of some gigantic beast, suspended only a few feet above us.

The courtyard was covered in a deep mantle of ice-crusted snow, as were the surrounding fortifications and no sooner had the last of the soldiers entered when the gate was lowered, chains rattling loudly, to land with a resounding *tha-WHUMP!*, startling the horses who whickered uneasily as they jostled each other.

The courtyard was never meant to hold this many horsemen, but somehow Rasaben managed to dismount without being crushed and his men immediately followed suit, which meant we were expected to do the same.

Kyrou, naturally, was the first of our group to slip from the saddle, deftly swinging his leg over his horse's neck and alighting on the ground in one liquid movement. Then he helped Sifrie down. Jaro followed and assisted Turan.

Hanni eased himself off our horse then beckoned for me to do the same.

I tried, but I was still so damned drowsy and so numb with cold I felt as if I was frozen in place—in fact I think I *was* frozen in place. So he wrapped his arms around me and ever so gently pried me off the carthorse's back then with equal care placed me on my feet.

Countless hours seated astride a *very* broad-backed horse—never a good position for a man under any circumstances—along with the icy cold made my knees wobble and my hips ache the instant I put weight on them and I clung to Hanni, fearing if I let go, even for an instant, my legs would give way. And oh yes, it didn't help that I couldn't feel my feet, or my hands… or my face for that matter. I was so cold I couldn't even shiver.

Then I saw something that *almost* made me smile—and I would have, had my face not been frozen solid. Thick smoke curled from a multitude of chimneys and where there was smoke, there was fire and where there was fire there was *heat*.

"*TURAN!*" a voice boomed, startling everyone and drawing every eye, human and horse alike to a tall, white-haired and elegantly dressed man who stood in the doorway of the central Keep.

Hanni leaned close, murmured, "Lord Taskim," as the man motioned expansively to the throng in the courtyard.

"*Come, come! Inside with all of you!*"

No one, not even Kyrou—not even Rasaben's grim-faced soldiers—hesitated. While a few unfortunate souls were tasked with dealing with stabling the sixty-odd horses, the rest trooped their way up the steps and into the Keep's main hallway.

If Hanni hadn't half-carried, half-walked me up the flight of stone stairs I never would have made it, despite the incredible enticement of warmth so close.

Unfortunately, as I quickly discovered, it wasn't much warmer inside, but at least we were out of the blizzard. Others took a moment to dust themselves off as best they could, stamping their feet and leaving the stone floor coated in snow. I just stood there, cold, numb and still very, *very* sleepy. I figured eventually the snow would slide off me and in my current state of muzzy-headedness, eventually was good enough—I certainly couldn't muster up enough energy to brush myself off. I couldn't even muster up enough energy to think about brushing myself off.

Rasaben's soldiers continued on, filing past us in their habitual silence, down the long hallway, their armor glittering and glimmering strangely in the wavering torchlight until, one-by-one, they disappeared from my limited view. I stared blearily after them, dimly aware that something wasn't right, but before I could focus my sluggish mind on the matter, Taskim said, "Please, into the Great Hall—I've had hot food and drink set out. Help yourselves."

At his signal, a liveried servant drew open a huge wooden door, and gestured for us to enter and as Hanni and I followed the rest of Turan's entourage into the room I felt myself suddenly bathed in an almost smothering warmth.

It felt as if I'd stepped directly from hell into heaven.

Shields, hunting trophies and curious cloth mosaics hung from the wooden walls, carpets and furs were scattered over the flagstone floor and the central table—a massive slab that almost filled the enormous room—was covered in platters of food, pitchers of drink and a dazzling array of what looked to, my startled eyes like miniature torches, were positioned down the length of the table.

But it wasn't the impressive décor or the equally impressive offering of foodstuffs that drew my full attention. It was the floor to ceiling stone fireplace that commanded the far end of the hall.

Hanni, sensing my thoughts, helped me towards it then sat me down in a high-backed chair and drew it close, but not too close to the roaring fire. He glanced desperately back the table, clearly every bit as drawn to its tantalizing contents as I was to the fire.

"I'll get you something hot to eat and drink—"

"Let me thaw out first," I mumbled through cold-numb lips. "You… eat."

"All right—I'll be back to check on you in a bit."

I nodded my thanks and snuggled down. I was largely invisible to those at the table and I sincerely hoped I'd be forgotten about—even by Hanni.

I wasn't.

Someone carefully draped a heavy and deliciously fired-warmed blanket over me.

That was quite fine by me—but I didn't stir, didn't open my eyes, and I certainly didn't acknowledge the unexpected kindness. It was just too damned much effort.

Whoever my benefactor was stared at me for a moment—I could feel their gaze on me, which I thought was rather rude—I could hear the nervous shuffle of their feet on the flagstone hearth, then finally whoever it was walked away, their curiosity, their concern, presumably satisfied.

A moment or so after they left, an unfamiliar and oddly toned, high-pitched voice said, "Hello," followed by, "You're this centurion everyone's talking about, aren't you?"

I ignored the speaker. The pull of sleep was almost overwhelming, I was just starting to thaw out and I was in no mood to engage in an animated discussion about my former vocation with *anyone*. Plus I'd begun to shiver—actually a good sign, and my teeth immediately followed suit by chattering.

A fingertip jabbed me in my injured shoulder. "I'm talking to you!"

I remained as I was, eyes closed, chin resting on chest as I stuttered, "I k-k-know you are—now p-p-please g-g-go away, you're b-b-blocking the h-h-heat from the f-f-fire."

"No. You're a guest—I don't care how special everyone says you are, that's no way for a guest to behave."

I grit my teeth, growled, "I'm *n-n-not* a g-g-guest. I'm a p-p-prisoner and I can b-b-behave anyway I d-d-damned well p-p-please, now… *l-l-leave me alone!*"

"I don't believe you—you're just being *mean.*"

I forced open my eyes… and blinked in surprise.

A little girl was standing in front of me, arms crossed. She had long red hair—every bit as red as Sifrie's and almost as long. Freckles splashed across her milk-white cheeks and pug-nose. And she had *very* green eyes. Greener even than Sifrie's.

I squinted at her. "What d-d-do you w-w-want?"

"I want you to talk to me."

"Wha-what if I d-d-don't want to t-t-talk to you?"

That set her back, but not for long. "But you *have* to."

"W-w-why?"

She placed her hands on her hips. "Because *I* say so!"

I had to wonder if she wasn't a close relative to Turan. She certainly had the same self-important, 'it's all about me' attitude, but in a *very* small package which did not bode well for any male in her life, now or in the future.

Undaunted, she asked, "What's your name?"

"Arri," I managed without stuttering.

"That sounds like a girl's name."

"It's s-s-short f-f-for Arr-rius."

"That's no better—doesn't make you sound special at all."

I scowled. "You asked my n-n-name, I t-t-told you."

"Do you *like* being called Arri?"

193

"I *liked* b-b-being called Arri by my f-f-friends—but th-th-they're all d-d-dead."

"Oh." She stuck out her lower lip in what I assumed was supposed to be a commiserating pout. "Well, I shall call you Arri—until I can think of a better, more special name. Would you like me to think of a special name? My pony's name is Mugwort."

I did not like where this discussion was going, not one damned bit. It didn't help that I overheard a rumble of laughter from the table behind me—maybe coincidence, maybe not.

I took a deep, ragged breath then tugging the blanket over my injured shoulder and eyeing her, replied in a sleepy stutter: "That's a v-v-very nice name… for a p-p-pony."

"I named him that because he likes to eat mugwort."

"Then a very p-p-practical, not to mention unusual n-n-name as well."

She beamed. "I'll start thinking about a name for you then."

"As l-l-long as it isn't Mug-g-g-wort."

"Of course it wouldn't be Mugwort, *silly*—otherwise you wouldn't know when I was talking to you or my pony."

I replied with an ever so slight nod to her impeccable logic. "I'm really v-v-very t-t-tired and c-c-cold, perhaps we can t-t-talk about t-t-this—"

"Don't you want to know what my name is? We can't be best friends if you don't know my name too."

I exhaled wearily. I had been extremely worn out before; this little girl was sapping the scant energy that remained, but I knew she'd have her feelings hurt if I didn't ask and despite her aggravating persistence I didn't have a mind to do that—and even more importantly I knew she wouldn't let me *alone* until I asked. "All r-r-right, what's your n-n-name?"

"Ainiaan."

"That's a very p-p-pretty n-n-name for a pretty little g-g-girl."

"I am *not* little!"

All right—now I was seriously annoyed and let it show. "You're s-s-shorter than m-m-me, which makes you little in my b-b-books."

She looked me up and down. "How tall *are* you? You're sitting down—it's hard to tell."

"T-t-taller than you."

She only stared at me as she chewed furiously on her lower lip.

"All right," I continued. "Let's just s-s-say you're *very* p-p-pretty and leave it at that, all r-r-right?"

She smiled, clearly pleased by the compliment then promptly changed the subject. "If you're a prisoner, why are you wearing Lord Taskim's livery? I watched you when you came in—your tunic bears his emblem."

"I'm only b-b-borrowing it."

"Well, you're not taking very good care of it—"

"I know."

"—did you borrow it from Perus? He won't be happy you've mussed it up—he's very tidy you know."

"I c-c-couldn't help it."

"So, where's *your* uniform, your armor?"

Her question stung and my voice betrayed me: "Stolen... by s-s-some 'friend' of Lady Turan's."

"That wasn't nice."

"No, it w-w-wasn't—"

"I'd liked to have seen it. I've never seen a centurion's armor. My father says it's quite grand."

I squinted at her. "Your f-f-father's right. It is—m-m-mine *was*. V-v-very g-g-grand. Now, *p-p-please*, go away."

"No." She plopped herself down on the hearth, crossed her arms and fixed those incredibly intense green eyes on me and with a very clear message in her defiant pose: 'I'm not going anywhere.'

Fine, I thought and closed my eyes then turned and wriggled deeper into the padded, high-back chair. I *was* an adult after all—I had no doubt I could wait her out and after several minutes of silence, I actually thought she'd gotten the hint and left. Plus the shivering had finally slowed to the intermittent muscle spasm, rather than the constant, body-wracking and painful tremor.

"Aren't you well?"

Damn! I *very* reluctantly opened one blood-shot eye and peered at her over the lip of the blanket. She was still seated on the hearth, but her expression was now one of genuine concern.

"You don't look at all well, if you don't mind me saying so."

"I'm just c-c-cold."

"You look... sick. Are you sick?"

"You can't c-c-catch what I have if that's what's worrying you."

"So you are sick."

"I'm not feeling p-p-particularly well, now that you mention it, n-n-no." And that was truth. I wasn't. My head still throbbed and every joint in my body ached. Even my eyeballs ached, something I'd only experienced on

195

those rare mornings after I'd drunk far, *far* too much. And my mouth still tasted of that damned furry lozenge.

She eyed my bruised and hollow cheeked face, my sunken eyes then as I raked a lock of wet hair from my eyes with a shaky and badly discolored hand, she asked, "Did someone beat you up? It looks like someone's hit you."

"No." I tugged the blanket back up around my still chilled throat. "I f-f-fell."

Her eyebrows jumped. "You must be *really* clumsy."

I couldn't help it—I chuckled feebly, my teeth chattering in response.

She grinned, surprised by my reaction. "You have a very handsome face—if you smiled more. Why don't you smile more?"

"I'm a p-p-prisoner, *remember?*"

She nodded, suddenly very solemn, then, "I bet you'd look a lot better without the beard—doesn't suit you. Makes you look mean."

I didn't know what to say but: "Thank you, I'll b-b-bear that in mind—now, I'm really v-v-very tired—"

"I'll ask my father if he can purchase you—would you like that? He's very smart—just like you, and very wealthy too."

I stared at her. I wanted to be angry, wanted to say something equally hurtful, but she hadn't meant to hurt me. Her interest was genuine, utterly without malice. "I don't think Lady Turan's interested in s-s-selling me." Now that was questionable—she might even happily part with me for free, but since I had no idea who this little girl's father was, I felt it was prudent not to mention this.

"That's too bad—I like you. No one else wants to talk to me, except you, which is good because I like you a lot—you're really nice."

I fixed my suddenly watery gaze on the crackling fire then squeezed my eyes shut and felt a tear roll down my cheek. Under other circumstances I'd have felt intensely embarrassed to be caught like this by a child. As it was, I was just too exhausted, too miserable to care.

"Why are you so sad?"

I bit my lip, hoping my voice wouldn't crack and replied in a way I thought she'd understand, "I dearly miss my friends." And I did; I missed them terribly, missed their company more than I thought possible. Their absence tore at me, leaving a huge bleeding hole and I realized if I could just have them at my side, I could face anything—it was a stupid thought, one that only made me that much more keenly aware of just how truly alone I was—

"They can come here! There are plenty of rooms and—"

196

"They're all dead—killed when I was taken prisoner."

"Oh."

I felt her small hand grasp my knee and I very reluctantly opened my eyes. She was now kneeling beside me.

"I'm really, really sorry, really I am." She gave my knee a squeeze then wiped my damp cheek with her sleeve—a child trying her very best to comfort an adult. I didn't feel very good about that, not at all. "Please don't cry, Arri."

I was a wretched excuse for a man, truly I was, broken in every way possible.

Then, a moment later, "I'll be your best friend, all right? Then you won't be sad." Her face brightened. "You can even ride Mugwort!"

I only nodded as I had visions of me sitting astride a fat little pony, my feet flat on the ground, legs bowed out on either side—a *very* impressive sight, yes indeed. *My riding instructors would be so proud,* I thought in a desperate attempt to cheer myself up.

It didn't work.

She looked past me, to the banquet table, then back at me. "Aren't you hungry? You look *really* hungry and there's plenty of food. I'll get some for you—you stay right here," she patted the arm of the chair, "next to the fire."

"I better n-n-not."

She scrambled to her feet and leaned very close—far too close for my comfort and I reacted by pressing myself back into the chair—her expression one of utter indignation. "Is it because you're a prisoner and they won't let you eat?"

"N-n-no, really—"

"Well," she huffed, "we'll see about that!"

I thought about stopping her then just as quickly decided against it, again reminding myself that I had no idea who her 'wealthy' father was, how he might react if I touched her—he might be Rasaben... or this Taskim for all I knew. I was finally starting to thaw out and I had no desire to be dragged down into some dark and icy dungeon and beaten senseless, or even worse, to thrown out into the blizzard to freeze to death. Besides, she darted off before I could even raise my cold-stiffened arm, much less slip it from under the blanket.

I exhaled wearily, snuggled back down with the fond hope she'd get distracted, or someone would distract her and she wouldn't return.

I heard music—strangely pitched, from a lyre perhaps?—along with the muffle of conversation from the table behind me but I was so weary I couldn't pick out individual speakers, much less what they were talking about—I doubted I'd be able to follow what they were discussing, anyway, so why bother? Names and places referenced meant absolutely nothing to me.

I fixed my exhausted gaze on the fire as I savored the warmth. Even my feet were finally returning to life as the sodden felt boots steamed, parboiling my toes I'm sure. In fact I was damp all over and my hair was dripping wet from the melted snow; I was just too damned tired to care.

Lulled by the intense warmth, the familiar murmur of laughter, the music and the clink of tableware, my body slowly relaxed and I began to drift off—this time I made no effort to stop my slide into oblivion—

"Here."

I flinched awake.

Ainiaan had returned, holding a plate mounded high with an assortment of roasted meat—none, I noted, looked the least bit gristly—along with an impressive array of cooked, but still brightly colored vegetables, which meant they hadn't been boiled to death, slices of various types of finely-milled bread and two cooked and shelled eggs. She'd gone to some trouble, or more likely a servant had gone to some trouble as it was all very artfully stacked and arranged.

I didn't want to hurt her feelings, so I managed, using my right elbow, to straighten myself up in the chair.

She grinned, pleased by my interest, and offered me the heavily laden plate.

I peeled back the blanket and raised my hands to accept it but they were shaking so badly, she said, "Uh, how about I help you?"

After the humiliation of the previous night, I had nothing, not even a shred of my former pride, left. I nodded at her offer.

Ainiaan knelt beside me and placed the plate on my lap. She glanced at it then up at me. "What would you like to start with?"

"What... what would you recommend?" I asked, my voice barely above a raspy whisper—but at least I was no longer stuttering.

"How about this?" She picked up a small chunk of meat. "It's roasted venison—my favorite."

I hesitated; my belly had stopped cramping—I had a suspicion it had stopped only because my insides were still frozen solid, but the spasms had been so painful I was scared they might start up again.

"It's really good," she said and pressed it against my lips. *"Please?"*

I reluctantly let her slip the food into my mouth. Whatever it was, it seemed to melt on my tongue and had a wonderful, if unfamiliar taste.

"There's plenty more where that came from and you can eat as much as you want—no one is going to tell *me* you can't."

I swallowed my mouthful, wiped my lips and chin with my fingers and murmured, "You must be very important."

"I am. Everyone says so—even Lord Rasaben—and he's not very nice, not like you." She selected another piece. "Now, try this—it's a wild bird of some sort."

I did, and managed to get it down.

"Would you like something to drink? I brought you a mug of spiced wine—I was told it's the best."

I *was* thirsty—suddenly and extremely so. "Yes, please."

She brought the mug to my lips and I took a cautious sip. It wasn't what I would've called wine, but it was clearly alcoholic and it left a warm glow in my belly, thawing me from the inside as the fire thawed me from the outside—which, in hindsight, should have been a warning to stop while I was ahead. Instead I smiled at her and she offered me another sip, which I gladly took. The drink had a hell of a kick to it.

It wasn't until I swallowed another, larger piece of venison and was about to take another that my stomach suddenly clenched tight just as if I'd been punched in the gut, *hard*.

I squeezed my eyes shut and tried to gulp down the sudden, overwhelming nausea, but it was too late.

Ainiaan had no sooner scampered back, warned by my loud gulping and agony-contorted face than I vomited, then as I struggled to throw the blanket aside—the plate and its contents thrown across the hearth in the process—to get back to my feet, I vomited again, explosively.

I was dimly aware of a sudden, ominous silence, followed by the loud squeak and scrape of chairs being hurriedly shoved back.

Unable to rise, I managed to slide from the chair, onto my knees as I overheard Ainiaan pleading for someone to do something to help me—help her *friend*.

I wanted to tell her it wasn't her fault—I should have known better than to eat anything—but I couldn't get the words out between the excruciating, spasmodic heaves. I doubled over, clutching my stomach; it felt as if my insides were unraveling.

Hanni called my name, Sifrie too. I felt hands holding onto me as I continued to heave violently, stopping me from falling onto my face.

People were yelling, calling for someone or something called Mabog and despite the agony, despite the intense spasms that made it near impossible to breathe, I found myself desperately wanting to hear Turan's voice calling to me. If she was there, if she did call my name, I didn't hear her within the all commotion as my world closed in and suddenly everything turned black and very, *very* quiet.

XIV

It took me over a week to twist up my courage to raise the idea of enlistment with Lady Ilissia, but one evening as we lay in her bed and sipped sweet wine, I cautiously broached the plan. I feared she'd consider it a rebuff, an ungrateful response to her unquestioning generosity, perhaps even a betrayal, but to my surprise and yes, I must admit with a twinge of resentment, she responded not with anger, but intense relief.

She laughed at my obviously mixed reaction, kissed me, told me she'd known from the moment she took me into her house that this day would come, knew as I approached manhood I would eventually desire to leave, to seek my own way in the world—in fact she would have thought less of me if I hadn't wanted to move on. I was not a servant or a slave, she reminded me, but a free man who could leave any time I so chose.

Feeling an odd sense of emptiness, and needing reassurance in something familiar, I made love to her and while she responded as always with soft, delighted moans I felt as if she too realized that whatever we'd had, whatever had held us together, was gone.

In the morning as we bathed, she touched me, touched my body in ways that brought tears to my eyes and hers. But there was no going back—so I dressed in a plain linen tunic and a simple pair of sandals, then went to her to bid farewell.

She told me she was not only giving me her blessing, she was going to sponsor me, make sure I would have the best equipment any new recruit could wish for. She then handed me a note, told me to show it to any who challenged my rights as a citizen as she had officially adopted me, something she had done, she told me, over a year before but had kept it to herself, awaiting the day I chose to leave of my own free will. For a moment, this left me stunned and speechless, then as I read the note and realized it was true, I began babbling, telling her I wasn't worthy of such a gift.

She kissed me on the lips, effectively silencing my protests, then smiling tightly, told me to make her proud—unlike her other son—and stepped back: her signal to go on my way. It was such a simple parting—as if we had only just met. It hurt—if she felt the same, she didn't show it outwardly.

I wiped my eyes and murmured my goodbyes then I picked up the small bundle of my belongings and walked through the shaded and flower-perfumed garden, to the villa's main gate.

The guard, at my approach, silently opened the small door within the massive main door. I avoided his curious gaze and as I stepped through and into the bustling street beyond I was hit with the intense and almost blinding summer sunshine. An instant later I heard the door's muffled thud and click as it was closed and locked behind me and I forced myself not to look back.

I took a deep, steadying breath, squared my shoulders and walked away, towards the garrison.

My timing was, for once, impeccable, as the need for soldiers had suddenly taken on a sense of urgency that verged on panic. The political turmoil in Rome, which in turn had fostered rebellion in some of the more distant provinces, had finally spread to parts of Egypt and Cyrenacia, threatening the empire's insatiable appetite for grain.

In the harbor of Alexandria, warships outnumbered merchants in a display of Imperial might that impressed even the most jaded. The city was on edge—civilian and soldier alike feared the worst. Shops were boarded up; food shortages were now a daily occurrence in the poorer districts and those who had the wherewithal planned for a hasty departure, back to the relative safety of Rome itself.

It was in this milieu of mounting unease that I learned to properly wield a sword, hurl a pilum with great accuracy, learned to swim—each lesson hammered home by rumors that circled like vultures, by the sight of deserted streets at midday, by the frightened sidelong glances of the rare passersby as we marched, exhausted from a day spent in practice skirmishes, back to our heavily fortified barracks.

I studied military history—ours and those of our enemies, learned tactics and strategy from the best of the Alexandria Garrison, learned discipline, to listen to my superiors and, most importantly, to do exactly *as they ordered even if I privately disagreed with them—all this in an incredibly short period time. It was overwhelming and exciting—from minute to minute I vacillated between apprehension and exhilaration, convinced that I'd finally found where I truly belonged and that one day, if I worked hard enough, I would be that officer, wearing the resplendent armor I had so long admired.*

I had prided myself on keeping my body fit—Lady Ilissia had insisted on it, but in truth I'd grown soft in her company. Now every muscle ached, every joint hurt and more often than not I was so exhausted at the end of the day that I would wake up the following morning having no recollection of crawling into my bed. Sometimes I didn't make it that far and awoke to find myself curled up on the floor. A handful of my fellow recruits fared worse, succumbing to the strenuous exercise, the implacable heat, the withholding of food and water and the regular beatings for minor, often fabricated infractions.

I adapted far quicker than the others—most of whom were sons of privilege, or at the very least sons of the merchant class and not accustomed to such harsh treatment. One slit his wrists—we found him the following morning lying face down on the floor of the bath in a congealed pool of blood; another who was the constant target of bullies attacked one of the more sadistic trainers and paid for it with his life—the rest of us his compulsory executioners. That night as I lay in the stifling darkness of the barracks, unable to sleep, I heard someone softly crying.

It was a bitter lesson and one I never forgot.

But this was also the time when it became obvious that I had a drive for perfection and an inborn talent to lead. The other recruits often looked to me for direction, to help them in their lessons, or sought me out as a sympathetic ear to their woes. Even the trainers took notice and frequently called on me to demonstrate a skill all were supposed to have mastered but few, in truth, had.

On one particularly sweltering late summer morning I was pulled out of my drills, handed a rolled up piece of vellum and told to report immediately to the office of the garrison commander. The other recruits stared at me, equally baffled—but also just as clearly relieved I was called and not one of them. No one, not even me, dared ask why, so I did as I was told—after I politely asked directions.

I was hot and sweaty and wearing only my underwear—not even sandals—clearly not the accepted attire for such a meeting, which only added to my growing fears and made me sweat all the more.

Vallus's office was situated deep within one of the more luxurious official buildings that encircled the parade ground, its columned, open-air passageways decorated with friezes of famous battles, its floors paved in glazed tile. The air was cool in comparison to the sun-baked surrounds and I struggled not to shiver.

I walked as quietly as possible, my eyes lowered, hoping to be ignored by the officers I happened across. A few challenged my right to be where I was, and when I offered the vellum roll as mute reply, they glanced at it, quickly re-rolled it and handing it back to me brusquely sent me on my way. Others only glanced at me as if I were some exotic creature or perhaps an apparition, rather than a half-naked, sweat-streaked and clearly terrified recruit.

I finally reached my destination, a massive cedar door with carved fretwork inlaid with ivory and bronze hinges and as I stood before it, hesitant, I wondered what horrible crime I'd committed without realizing it.

I very reluctantly reached up for the elaborate bronze doorknocker but just as my fingers touched it, a voice—a familiar voice—called to me. I turned to find Gaius Silva standing not far away. He beckoned to me then pivoted on his heel and walked down another corridor. I looked around, saw no one else and with a confused shrug, hurried after him.

He waited for me in front of yet another, smaller and far less imposing door, this one standing ajar, then he stepped inside, motioning for me to follow.

It was a small office—with two tables placed on either side of the room, facing each other and both were stacked high with rolls of vellum along with papyri. Each table had its own chair. Beyond, through another doorway, was a small courtyard and I heard the telltale splash of a fountain. The breeze that flowed around me was delightfully cool and moist and smelled of flowers.

Silva seated himself behind one of the desks and not knowing what was to happen next I placed myself before him and clasped my trembling hands behind my back while suddenly and intensely aware of my own stink.

He offered me water to drink. I thanked him, said I wasn't thirsty but in truth I was, desperately so, I was just too scared to accept, fearful I'd spill the water, or choke on it when I swallowed.

He then pointed to the other table and told me it was mine—as his personal aide I needed a desk of my own.

I stood there, as if my bare feet were welded to the tile floor, shaking, as the full impact of his words hit me. I was no longer a raw recruit, destined to become a common foot soldier. I was now an immune, *he told me, personal aide to Gaius Libius Silva, adjutant to Lucius Antonius Vallus, commander of the Alexandria Garrison—had I forgotten his remarks so many months ago in Lady Ilissia's garden?*

I had of course—completely, my full attention at the time on something more immediate and intensely personal: the death of Porsenna.

He gave me a few minutes to recover, then leaning back and crossing his arms, he gave me his first formal order: I was to return to the barracks, retrieve my belongings and report back to him within the hour—he had work piling up and no time to spare.

I replied with a speechless nod and a wobbly salute then as I turned to leave, he added that I had his permission to take a few extra minutes to bathe and dress appropriately before returning—I now represented him, after all and needed to look the part.

I managed to take his leave without tripping on my own feet, but once back in the corridor, I started to grin. I wanted to laugh, but this wasn't the time or place for that. I had my orders after all and scant little time to fulfill them.

Running was not acceptable—I knew that, so I walked as quickly as I could back to the barracks. The other recruits were still exercising and the long, bunk-lined room that had been my home for the past weeks was deserted, aside from the ever-present swarm of flies. I stripped, hurried into the baths and scraped and scrubbed myself until my skin stung. I then combed and oiled my hair, donned my dress uniform for the first time, gathered up the few personal items each recruit was allowed to keep—including my necklace of beads and star and Lady Ilissia's letter that I'd kept squirreled away—and stuffed them in my pack, which I then slung over my back.

With one last look around me, I picked up my helmet and, grinning from ear to ear, strode purposefully out of the barracks with the sudden and supreme confidence only the truly ignorant possess.

Aetius shook his head and sighed heavily, in the process drawing my sidelong stare as I continued to comb my oiled hair.

"What?"

"I thought we were going out drinking and whoring."

"We are."

"When? You've been preening for hours!"

"Can I help it if I want to look my best?"

"Whores don't care—all they want is your money and drink tastes the same, no matter what you look or smell like."

"Actually, they do care—" I wasn't about to tell him *how* I knew; my less than savory background was something I'd kept even from my closest friends, not sure how they would react, "—why do you think they always give me a discount?"

Aetius laughed. "Maybe because they feel sorry for you."

"Maybe because they appreciate the fact that I've taken the time to wash up."

He snorted. "Nope. Pity, Centurion." He grabbed his crotch, shook it suggestively. "That's all it is. Abject pity."

That tweaked my vanity, so I shifted my wounded stare to Felix, hoping for a better reception. Aetius was never one to bother with looking his best when he was paying a woman for her company—in truth Aetius didn't have much to work with to begin with; he was, to be extremely kind, a very brave soldier but an extraordinarily homely man, with a smashed nose, watery blue, bulbous eyes and dirty-brown hair that always looked as if he was standing with his back to a strong wind. Knock-knees, thickset, extremely hairy body, ruddy face and bad teeth—what few he had—didn't help.

Felix, the bastard son of a Roman senator and his favorite Greek slave, had grown up accustomed to the finer things in life and like me knew that a little extra effort could pay off handsomely. Of course Felix was also good looking, with a thick mane of pale blond hair and rosy cheeks that dimpled when he smiled—something that for some inexplicable reason drove women wild. He wasn't as handsome as me, even with the addition of the dimples, but not at all bad, not like Aetius, who had always reminded me of a rather melancholy baboon.

"Aetius is right," Felix replied, startling me as he irritably gathered up his heavy cloak, "keep this up and the whores will've died of old age. Come on, Aetius." With that he started for the door of the barracks with a decidedly smug Aetius on his heels.

I blew out my decidedly undimpled cheeks and with a shake of my head I snatched up my cloak and hurried after them.

It was a chilly autumn evening, with the pungent scent of wood smoke and cooking meat hanging heavy in the air. Lindum was a well-established garrison town, with many of the comforts of home, including a public bath and taverns that catered strictly to the soldiers' needs. Because of that, it had taken on a familiar sameness of other garrison towns throughout the empire.

We knew exactly where we were going: our favorite haunt, an establishment tucked away at the end of a narrow alley where the food and drink were cheap and plentiful and the women, while not plentiful, were cheap and willing.

As we entered the small, fire-bright and stifling hot tavern, we were greeted by a friendly, albeit very inebriated cheer from a group of soldiers, Rufinius among them, seated at a nearby table.

"Over here!" he yelled over the background din and eagerly motioned to us with a wild flailing of his arms, in the process smacking the forehead of the soldier next to him, who was too drunk to even notice. He just toppled backwards off the communal bench and onto the straw-covered floor.

The tavern was packed and most of the women were already seated amongst the customers and pretending to enjoy their rough—and decidedly intoxicated—company.

"See?" Aetius whined. "We're late! We'll be lucky if we end up with one whore between us."

"Could be interesting," Felix replied, grinning, "depending upon which end I get."

Aetius made a face.

I chuckled as I carefully stepped over the man sprawled on the floor and eased myself down on the bench beside Rufinius, then I patted him on his shoulder and tossed a handful of coins on the table. "I'm feeling generous—order what you will."

It had become a tradition among us on payday—as centurion it was my duty to look out for my men. As the highest paid, it was only reasonable that I pay for the meal, as well as a few rounds of drinks—not for my whole century, not at one time, no. Every payday it was a different bunch—with the exception of Felix, Rufinius and Aetius—and while it was a gesture that was frowned upon by my officers and openly discouraged by the other, higher-ranking centurions, my men loved it... and so, not unreasonably, they loved me.

They say the road to a man's heart is through his stomach—true, perhaps, for women. For me, that road was down his gullet, but once my coins ran out, well, it was up to whatever a man had in his purse—or was willing to spend.

A serving woman appeared, placed several large pitchers and a number of mugs on the table, then as she leaned forward to scoop up the coins she left herself wide open for a good grope, front *and* back, top *and* bottom, by a number of the men seated at our table, men who eagerly lurched forward to do the honors.

"Hands off!" I snapped in my best Centurion's Voice, "otherwise she might spit in your food."

She flashed me a quick, thankful smile, stepped out of grab range and asked, "What are you all in the mood for?"

That garnered a round of very rude suggestions.

I motioned everyone to silence then said, "Your best for everyone—whatever that happens to be."

She ducked her head and hurried away and we wasted no further time and grabbed mugs and helped ourselves to the pitchers, having worked up a thirst walking from the barracks.

The mead was potent, our stomachs empty and by the time she and another serving woman reappeared with several platters heaped with food, we were all feeling the effects. It didn't stop us from eating until we could eat no more, however, nor did it stop us from seeking other delights.

One of my favorites, a flaxen-haired girl named Oxyrhoë appeared by my elbow and as her hand slipped between my legs she whispered in my ear, "Up for some *dessert*, Centurion?"

I nodded drunkenly and with the help of Rufinius and Aetius managed to lurch unsteadily to my feet and waving my goodnights to my men, staggered after her.

— ii —

Slowly, ever, *ever* so slowly, I became aware of an odd, rhythmic and decidedly plaintive bleat, and then, fainter and almost hidden within the bleating, muffled voices.

Felix? Aetius...?

The voices and bleat echoed in my mind, swirling, twisting, turning inside out then right side out again. I tried to listen to the garble but it was too far away and too much effort to untangle it.

Clearly I'd imbibed far, *far* too much. And now, gods knows where I was—hopefully still upstairs in the tavern. Maybe back in the barracks. I had no memory of stumbling back to my bed, which suggested that the light of morning, wherever it found me, was going to be greeted by abject misery, not to mention a fierce headache, made all the worse by a stern lecture from Jotia, each word punctuated by a whack across the kidneys from his vine-staff.

Warm fingers touch me, startling me out of that dismal train of thought—*Oxyrhoë?*—followed almost immediately by the awareness of... *pain,* an intense, burning pain that ran from belly to chest, making it hard to breathe.

I tried to pull away, only to find my limbs unwilling to obey.

Then a faraway voice said, "I've been weaning him of the heavy sedatives since early this morning... can't keep him this deeply under much longer or we risk a serious case of pneumonia on top of everything else."

"So how soon will he awaken?"

I thought I knew *that* voice—a woman's voice and not Oxyrhoë—I just... couldn't place it; the other was male—and didn't sound the least bit familiar.

"An hour or so, maybe a little less." The man paused, added, "I expect him to be disoriented so I'd like you here, just in case—might help keep him calm."

"Of course."

Both voices kept fading in and out, darting this way and that in a verbal game of hare and hound, mumbled and then crystal clear as if the voices themselves were alive and on the move, making it very hard to follow what was being said, much less recognize who was speaking. And of course most of what was being said made absolutely no sense—

"There's still a better than even chance he'll not survive, all right? The internal injuries were extensive and severe and that, combined with the delay in care—"

"Yes, yes! *I admit it*—I totally missed that he had internal injuries! He was hallucinating a goodly part of the time, not to mention at times suicidal—most of his thoughts were too fragmentary, too nonsensical to sense his injuries extended beyond the obvious!"

"I wasn't accusing you—"

"Really? It certainly sounded as if you were."

"I'm just trying to tell you I can't make any promises, nothing more."

A pause, then the woman answered in a more mollified voice, "I understand—and I'm sorry I snapped, truly. I know you're doing all you can."

"Perhaps we should attempt the transfer now, just in case—"

"No. Absolutely not."

"But—"

"I said *no.* We wait until he's more stable."

"It's your decision of course," the man capitulated, clearly annoyed, "I just need to warn you of the risks."

There was another agonizingly long pause before the man spoke again, and this time as if he was speaking to himself: "Heart rate's stabilizing… good, good. Pressure's almost within acceptable norms. I think it would be prudent to give him a long acting antibiotic, now, since he might not be so agreeable when he wakes up."

There was a soft rustle, like a stiff breeze stirring winter-dried leaves.

I felt fingers grasp my shoulder and an instant later a sharp lance of pain—damn this was getting annoying and making my head throb even worse, something I would have told you a moment before was impossible.

"Anyway, as I started to say, the combination of internal injuries, delayed care—" he was interrupted by something that sounded vaguely like a bird insistently cheeping. "I best respond to this. Shouldn't be long— you'll stay with him?"

"Of course."

Footfalls faded into the background just as something warm touched my face, my injured shoulder. Fingers squeezed mine.

I wanted to respond in kind, even if I didn't know who owned those fingers—it was a simple act of kindness, of concern—I wanted it known that I appreciated it but I couldn't move, not even a fingertip. I felt as if I was drowning in honey, my body seemingly as light as feather and at the same time as heavy as lead. A very curious sensation indeed.

The passage of time was marked by that ever-present and now damned maddening *bleat… bleat… bleat* as my mind paddled around in circles, completely aimless with no references, no landmarks—I was dimly aware of the woman's continued presence only because she kept her fingers entwined with mine.

It felt as if hours—*days*—passed before I heard footsteps approaching. I steered my sluggish mind towards the sound, dimly aware these footfalls had a different gait: heavier, more purposeful.

"What are *you* doing here?" the woman asked, her voice sharp-edged as she jerked her fingers free of mine—I couldn't stop her, although by putting my full concentration in it, I did manage to curl my fingers into my palm, albeit very, *very* slowly.

Well, it was better than nothing.

"Wanted to talk to you, *alone*—told Mabog to give us a few minutes." It was a male voice, but not the *same* male voice. Deeper. More timbre. And without a doubt very, *very* angry. Suddenly just being able to curl my fingers into my palm didn't seem quite enough. I sensed I was in serious danger— never a good thing when you are utterly boneless.

"Keep your voice down!" the woman hissed.

There was a shuffle of feet as the two speakers moved some distance away and lowered their voices but not so far and not so low that I couldn't still hear them.

"Now, what do you want to talk about?"

"You *know* what—*him*."

The woman sighed, a long, weary sigh, then, "This was all a terrible idea—I never should've agreed to this—"

The man laughed, a cold laugh. "You did more than agree—this whole scheme was *your* idea, remember?"

"Yet you offered no other ideas, aside from those which have already been tried and have cost us precious time, not to mention irreplaceable lives. I only suggested we look elsewhere for our needs, to take advantage of what we'd already proved was doable; the Lords of the Assemblage were the ones who devised this... *scheme* as you call it—and I was the logical one to carry it out. No one could have foreseen what's happened."

"I would've and in fact *did*," he replied with obvious bitterness, "had anyone troubled themselves to ask the one person who's actually seen the results of this folly in action, forced to watch as Lord Vela—"

"The purpose wasn't to win, as you well know—"

"Oh, I *know*. I know all too well. And we got what we wanted."

"Did we, really?"

"We kicked a hornet's nest and got badly stung. That was always the risk—"

"With at a truly terrible cost for all involved."

"I certainly wouldn't argue *that* point."

There was another pause—a very angry pause, then the male voice continued coldly, "I tried to warn Lord Vela—he refused to listen, just as the Assemblage refused to listen—and I'm blamed for the result!"

"I've suffered too—you aren't the only one you know, and yet *you* blame *me* for the actions of the Assemblage!"

I tried to put all of my focus on that tantalizingly familiar female voice, tried to peel away the sticky cobwebs. I could almost touch the memory of who it was, even if she was no longer touching me.

"Speaking of costing us precious time," the man asked huffily but clearly wanting to move away from what was just as clearly a very touchy subject, "why did you refuse the transfer?"

"Because it would most certainly kill him."

"That was always a possibility. You even raised the idea that once we'd succeeded in the transfer there was really no reason to *keep* the subject alive, especially if he proved troublesome—isn't that right?"

"But he *hasn't* proven troublesome, at least not any more than one would expect under the circumstances."

"Indeed? Sifrie told me he tried to kill himself, not once, but twice and that he suffers from paralyzing flashbacks."

"Wouldn't you, if you'd gone through what he's just gone through..." the woman's voice abruptly trailed off, suggesting she'd stumbled upon another very touchy area, then a whispered, *"I'm sorry."*

He laughed, a cold laugh. "I don't doubt you are. The question is, sorry for what?"

There was another strained pause then the woman replied, softly, gently, "I beg you, don't punish him for the wrongs done to you."

"Why do you care if he lives or dies? He's Roman—"

"I've come to realize that he's worth far more alive than dead, especially *after* the transfer, where his abilities, his insights could continue to prove extremely useful—"

"Useful?" he snorted. "To whom? *You?*"

"To all of us—even you, assuming *you'll* listen to him."

That remark was followed by yet another awkward pause in the bickering.

"You've developed feelings for him, haven't you?" His tone made it an accusation rather than a question.

That prompted another, even longer and more uncomfortable silence, then, finally, *"Yes."*

That softly worded concession hit me like a physical blow, and with it came instant recognition: *Turan!* I wanted to cry, pull her close—

"Well, it's not too late to put an end to this mad idea, not to mention your foolhardy infatuation. It wouldn't take much to nudge him over the edge, stop his heart—"

Now wait just a damned minute!

"—no one need know but you and me."

And me, don't forget about—

There was that odd rustle again, followed the man's softly worded but nevertheless startling statement, "This'll do the trick I'd imagine—certainly looks lethal."

I woke up for this? You couldn't have done me the favor of murdering me while I slept?

"He'll likely not survive," the man continued. "Mabog's told you as much, which is why he urged the transfer, *now*, while we still have the chance to reap some small reward from this debacle, although I must say I have my doubts about even that—implanting his knowledge, his skills into

211

the others carries the risk of transferring his psychological issues as well, magnifying and multiplying them over a thousand fold—one might even say it would be a kindness to put an end to it, now, before he wakes up, just as we should have done with the others—"

I am awake, damn it! Why don't you ask me? And you could start by explaining what the hell you're talking about—

"He's not insane—"

"—we'll just have to come up with another plan—"

"First you demand to know why I refused the transfer," she fired back, "and now you say you think it's a terrible mistake?"

"*I* thought it was a terrible mistake from the very start! I'd already volunteered—"

"And was refused by the Assemblage."

"For the very same reason! They deemed *me* unfit—"

"You keep insisting that was the case, but it isn't true! They refused because they felt it was too risky—"

"For them or for me?"

"Why do you persist in this? Can't you see what it's done to you?" She hesitated, then added, "But since you feel so strongly about it, we won't implant his knowledge. Simple."

"Simple?"

"You know what I mean," she replied dismissively.

I don't! Tell me, damn it!

"You told me you'd studied him, studied the others, decided he was the very best candidate—you and the others put yourselves at tremendous personal risk to capture him alive and bring him back here, lost Harne in the process—and one can only guess the potential ramifications from that, assuming he wasn't the victim of a simple accident—and now you want to throw all that away?"

"And what you're suggesting is better? You're suggesting we throw *him* away!"

"I'm thinking of what's best, for us, and yes, believe it or not, the best for him as well. I agree it's a waste, considering, but—"

"But what?"

"But you're letting your emotions get the better of you."

"That's certainly something no one can accuse you of, Ras!"

Ras? As in… Rasaben? Well, that certainly explains—

"The only emotion you've ever felt was the love of killing!"

He chuckled, a deep, rumbling chuckle without a snippet of humor. "If that was true, we wouldn't be standing here, having this discussion, now would we?"

That gave her pause then she quickly recovered: "He's a human being, not some wounded beast that needs to be put out of its misery!"

"That's debatable." He hesitated then continued in a slightly more mollifying tone, "I'll make you a deal, Turi: we do a transfer, *now,* to a few individuals and observe the result. If they appear to have integrated his knowledge without his psychological problems, then we'll wait until he's physically stronger before we proceed with the rest."

I didn't like this sound of this, not one damned bit—I had a sudden image of my mind being chopped up into little pieces and spoon-fed to others... and it didn't take much thought to figure out the intended recipients. Just the thought gave me the shivers. But of course was anyone asking my opinion? Hell no—

"Any transfer at this point would likely kill him," Turan replied heatedly, "you know that—yes, I see why you're offering me this... *deal.* You get what you want without dirtying your hands."

He sighed again, a deep, frustrated sigh, then in a more gentle tone added, "I ask you to reconsider, *Turi*—need I remind you of Kyrou? And where's that little bit of kindness gotten you, gotten the rest of us? Accept my offer or I give him this, now, and we'll be done with the matter."

I heard her sniff back a sob. *It's all right—just say yes, and it will be over, for both of us. Please! Just a simple—*

"No."

No? What the hell do you mean, no? I was strangely furious that she'd denied me even this. *You sure picked a hell of a time not to eavesdrop on my thoughts, damn you—*

"I'm with child."

"What!?" Rasaben's startled gasp echoed my unspoken but equally horrified response.

"I *said* I'm with child."

"By... by *him?*"

Say no—please, please say no!

"Yes."

Oh... shi—

"How did this happen?" he snarled, clearly assuming the worst.

Tell him you were the instigator, not me! Go on! I'm already on your bad side—I certainly don't want to be on his. He looked to me like he could seriously hurt people if he had a mind to, and getting his sister pregnant might be considered a solid reason to want my head—and yes, either one would do, I'm sure—

"Did he force himself on you?" His voice was now a low, menacing growl.

Overhearing approaching footsteps I tried to brace myself for his enraged stranglehold. But it's hard to brace yourself when your body's no better than a puddle of jelly.

Other footfalls followed—lighter. Turan. "No, he didn't."

"Then...?"

I felt fingers touch my cheek and I would have flinched if I could have, not knowing whether those fingers belonged to Turan or Rasaben.

"Look at him, Ras. He's *beautiful*—"

"So he's pretty, too *goddamned* pretty if you ask me—"

Uh, thanks... I think.

"—but if it's pretty you desire, take your pick from my men, take as many as you want, take *all* of them if will make you see reason."

"I don't want any of your *Kellesuf*, damn you! I want *him*. A man with his mind, his intellect intact!"

Her comment was followed by another long and not happy silence.

Finally Rasaben said, "Who you take as a lover if totally up to you, sister—"

"How *magnanimous* of you, *brother.*"

"—but *who* you choose to sire your offspring is *not* just up to you—you know that. There are political ramifications and—"

"Don't you mean political *aspirations?*" Turan fired back. "I'm not a brood mare, Ras. I'm not a favor to hand out to one of your chieftains in the hope of regaining your rightful place at the table! I thought I'd made that abundantly clear—"

"—worse, he's a goddamned Roman! How do you think that news will be received? You refuse numerous offers of marriage, all from very respectable, powerful men—"

"All of whom are old enough to be our father, or in one notable case, our *great-grandfather.*"

"—and instead you get yourself with child by... *by a Roman soldier?*"

"A Roman *Centurion*," Turan corrected in a baiting tone.

And Rasaben snapped: "Oh, yes, that makes all the difference!"

"A *highly decorated* Roman Centurion if it so pleases you."

"Are you really with child?"

"Why don't you ask Mabog?"

"I will, Turi. Believe me, I will!"

I could almost feel the searing heat from his baleful stare.

"But first, Turi, answer me this," he said in a surprisingly calm, almost smug tone of his own, "does he have feelings for you?"

The question fell to the ground like lead. *Splat.*

"Well?" he prompted, clearly sensing he'd hit a chink in her armor and wanting to press his advantage.

"No," she replied softly. "No, he doesn't."

He laughed. "That should teach you not to play with men's minds, Turi—and their bodies! Is that how he got you pregnant? You *compelled* him? Well?" he prompted. *"Answer me."*

"Yes," she whispered, "I suppose I did."

You suppose you did? I thought bitterly. *What happened to free will being intensely arousing, hum?*

"You suppose…?"

"Yes, I did—no supposing about it, at first—after that, well, he seemed quite keen without any help from me—"

"To embarrass me, embarrass Taskim."

Now it was her turn to laugh. "I must tell you, Ras, that you and Taskim never *once* entered my mind."

He exhaled forcefully, then, "Does he know?"

"That he had sex with me? Yes, he knows, in fact he quite enjoyed—"

"This is no joking matter, Turi," he growled. "Does he know you are with child—*his child?*"

"No." Emphatic. That was Turan all right.

For a moment things got really, *really* quiet—aside from the damnedable background bleating which had been rapidly picking up speed—then Rasaben replied coldly, "I want it ended. *Today.* Tell Mabog."

"You're *not* my master, Ras—"

"But as long as you remain under my protection and under Taskim's roof, you *will* do as I say!" he thundered. "And I'll not have you birth some goddamned Roman's bastard offspring! I don't even want it known this creature made you pregnant, *hear?* Even that could derail our plans—"

"Our plans? You mean *your* plans. I'm quite content with things just the way they are—"

"—you know how shaky our alliance is with Lady Urme and Lord Pateke and how much Tistriya hates Romans. He could use this—"

"Tistriya hates everyone. You, most of all, brother—so much so I doubt Romans even come in a distant second—"

"I give you a choice—him or the child!"

"That's no choice!"

"You have until nightfall to make your decision—or I'll make it for you!"

"You keep offering me choices, then making it very clear I have no choice!"

"Did you ever consider the consequences before you got yourself pregnant by this... this Roman? *No!* You never think of anyone but yourself, Turi—always *you*. You say I'm cold and cruel—and so I am, I make no apologies for what I've become, or that I've done and will continue to do what I must in order to meet our obligations, daunting as they are. Whereas what you've done is without a doubt the height of selfishness, not to mention callousness!"

"You're in no position to lecture me on principles!"

"I'm only trying to make you see reason! Do you genuinely care about this man or are you just using him as you've used me, used Kyrou, used *everyone?*"

Fingers shakily combed through my hair; lips pressed against mine. I felt something wet and warm drop on my cheek, then roll down my neck—Turan's tears.

"Choose! Him or the child..."

I struggled towards consciousness, clawing my way to the surface, suddenly, desperately wanting to tell her to pick the child—*my* child. *Please... I beg you!*

Another tear rolled down my cheek—this time it was mine, followed by her unspoken, *Arri?* I groped around, blindly, desperate to have her help pull me the rest of the way to consciousness.

"...but if you choose him, I want his mind wiped clean after the transfer, hear? That way you can have your pretty boy lover. I won't deny you that, since he so pleases—"

"Hush!" she whispered as her mind reached out for mine and I desperately grabbed hold. *"He's waking up!"*

Rasaben replied with a muttered obscenity and a growled, "I'd best call Mabog."

I waited until he'd walked away, waited a little longer, then I opened my eyes to stare dully up at the blurry face that hovered over me.

"Arri?"

"Tur... Turraaaan?" I slurred, my tongue thick, my lips numb.

She smiled—a clearly forced smile—and kissed me on the forehead, then on my lips. I expected her to caress my chin, in fact I waited eagerly for her wordless command, *Listen to me.* I desperately wanted that comforting, reassuring command—something familiar to cling to, to separate dream from reality, confirmation that what I'd heard had really been said, or was in fact just a fabrication, a deeply buried need—*or fear*—made whole in my befuddled mind.

When the command failed to appear in my mind, I began to suspect I'd dreamt it all. I squinted up at her, hoping to see some indication in her eyes.

In reply she ran her hand across my forehead and I was suddenly unable to recall what I'd heard, or what I'd dreamt I'd heard—just that *something* important had been said—or perhaps I just thought something important had been said, which left me even more confused and yes, scared and I looked around, on the verge of panic.

What I could see of my surroundings looked utterly strange and sent my heart thumping anew: white walls, white *glowing* ceiling and objects on the walls that pulsed in various colors. Everything was slightly blurry and no matter how much I tried, I couldn't get my eyes to focus properly. I fixed my frightened stare on the single familiar thing I could find: Turan's very worried, albeit still very blurry face.

"Are you in pain?" a male voice asked and with a lot of effort and no small measure of reluctance I shifted my stare from Turan—fearing she might disappear as people and thoughts had a tendency to do of late—to the person who stood beside her.

While the face, like Turan's, was fuzzy, I knew it wasn't Rasaben. This man was short, balding and gaunt—one could even say he was the complete antithesis of the bearish Rasaben.

I squinted at him and finally mumbled, "Do... do I know you?"

"We haven't met, formally. Name's Mabog—I'm Taskim's personal physician."

I knew what a physician was, damned if I didn't. I'd dealt with plenty of them in my long and injury-punctuated career. Rome was renowned for the best physicians, especially the best military physicians and I was living proof of that.

I looked around again but what I saw looked like no Roman field hospital. "Where... where am I?"

"My surgery."

I squinted up at him. *Surgery...?*

He carefully peeled back the thin drape that covered my torso and lower body. "You were far more seriously injured than anyone realized—" his eyes briefly darted to Turan, then back to me, "—you'd taken a number of fierce blows to the abdomen," he placed his hand lightly on my bare belly and I couldn't help but tense up, surprised when I realized I *could* tense up, "which was exacerbated by the daylong horseback ride..."

217

As far as I was concerned, *anything* unpleasant would be exacerbated by a horseback ride, daylong or not, but before I could ponder that further, I had a sudden memory of being struck in the stomach by a pike, or maybe it was a spear or even an appropriated pilum—I wasn't looking that closely because I was a wee bit busy fighting off my attackers—struck not once, but repeatedly, prior to the ill-fated sortie to the hillock. My armor had protected me from what had clearly been intended as impaling stabs... or so I'd assumed. Goes to show that even Roman armor isn't completely infallible, just like Roman tactics.

"...it caused internal bleeding and bruising, not to mention swelling in your gut, which eventually stopped peristalsis," he snapped his fingers, "like *that.*"

I squinted at him, wondering what Perus had to do with what was clearly some damnedable Iceni's doing. "It stopped Perus doing... *what?*"

He chuckled. "Not Perus. *Peristalsis.*" He again placed his hand on my stomach. "Movement of your gut, which is why you couldn't keep anything down—had to remove what had become gangrenous along with your appendix. But don't worry. You won't notice what I took out."

I stared up at him then, as I shifted my dull gaze back to Turan in hopes she would make sense of it all, I happened to spot Rasaben. He was standing off to one side, watching me, a very odd, dare I say murderous, look in his eye and as our gazes locked, he plastered on a smile and stepped closer.

I couldn't help but feel a sense of fear and I tried to get my elbow under me, to sit up, to see what might be coming only to find my arms were held fast against whatever I was laying on. I tensed my legs and had my worst fears confirmed. The rhythmic bleating in the background sped up, matching my heart and I suddenly found it hard to catch my breath.

The man—Mabog—glanced over his shoulder, then back at me. "There's nothing to be afraid of... calm down." He placed what I assumed was supposed to be a reassuring hand on my shoulder, drawing my panicky gaze, but it was far too little, too late. "Easy, easy, you're a little disoriented—"

"*Why am I tied down?*" My eyes darted to Turan, then Mabog and back to Turan as I frantically struggled against the restraints. "*Please! Don't tie me down!*"

"The restraints are for your safety." Mabog grabbed my shoulders. "Stop—"

"*Like hell!*" I yanked and twisted futilely against the bindings, against his hold.

"Arri," Turan soothed, "hush, hush… you're safe—no one wants to hurt you—"

"UNTIE ME!" I shrieked, fighting and squirming.

"I was afraid of this." Mabog hurriedly stepped back as Rasaben took his place.

Rasaben's large, muscular hands replaced Mabog's. He pressed down on my shoulders, making it impossible to struggle, I just was too weak and he was too strong and it really, really hurt. Then I felt pressure against my right thigh, followed by a sudden, intense burning sensation—like a scorpion's sting. I winced, then stared, wide-eyed up at the faces that loomed over me: Turan, Mabog and Rasaben.

Mabog was holding something small and shiny in his hand.

"I've just given you a tranquilizer and muscle relaxant," he said as the fingers of his other hand massaged the knotted muscle of my thigh. "Can't have you fighting like that and risk more internal bleeding."

I stared up at him, terrified and helpless with Rasaben's hands perilously close to my throat. I had no idea what Mabog was talking about, all I knew was I was sliding down an all too familiar slope as my body returned to its earlier, gelatinous state.

I sobbed, great heaving sobs as I rapidly lost my tenuous hold over my limbs, my body. *"I won't fight… please… just… just untie me…!"*

I couldn't help notice the pointed look Rasaben fixed on Turan and her worried stare in reply.

"Please!" I added desperately, then, over my loud, spasmodic sobs I heard a new voice, a child's angry voice: *"What are you doing to Arri?"*

"Ainiaan," Rasaben replied, abruptly releasing his hold on me, "you shouldn't be here—how'd you get in here?"

Hands touched my arm, my face, small hands. *"What have you done to him?"*

"I gave him a tranquilizer, that's all," Mabog replied defensively. "He was extremely upset and disoriented, he could have seriously hurt himself—"

"You're mean! He's just scared! I hate you!"

"You don't mean that, Ainiaan," Turan said softly.

"Yes I do! You're all mean! You took all his friends away! You killed them! I hate all of you!" A moment later Ainiaan's anxious face loomed over me. *"Arri?"*

I blinked; tears trickled down my cheeks but I couldn't talk—I tried, but my tongue and lips were useless.

She wrapped her arm around my neck, pressed her cheek to mine. "I won't let them touch you again—all right?"

I blinked again; it was the only thing I still had conscious control over—everything else was completely numb, paralyzed.

"I won't let them do anything else to you."

I clung onto that promise—the promise of a small child as my heart rate, my breathing slowed despite my terror, which in turn left me even more terrified. I couldn't stop my eyelids from fluttering then drifting closed. In the background I heard the steady, repetitive bleat respond, perfectly mimicking, beat for bleat, the slowing *thump... thump... thump* of my heart echoing in my ears.

"The drug's kicked in." Mabog sounded clearly relieved, his hollow voice suddenly very, very far away. "Let's get him moved next door, the room's all prepared..."

A moment later I felt release from the straps that had restrained my limbs. Not that it did me a fat lot of good at this point.

"I'll stay with him," Ainiaan said, maintaining her embrace.

"He might sleep for a *very* long time," Rasaben replied—I didn't like the way he said it. Not one bit.

"I don't care—he's my friend!"

"He needs to rest, Ainiaan," Mabog said. "Lord Rasaben, if you don't mind, would you carry him?—wait, let me disconnect this line."

Fingers tugged at my arm; it hurt. That was followed by the very odd, tickly sensation of something sliding out from under my skin of my right arm.

"Ainiaan," Turan murmured, "I think it best you do as your father says—let Arri sleep—he's very, very sick and needs his rest. Your father tells me you're raising a fox kit? I'd love to see him."

I felt a brief flutter of my earlier panic—it was all I could muster as my body felt heavier and heavier. As silly as it sounded, I'd trusted into a child to defend me against three adults who, I had no doubt, meant me harm in various ways. I was terrified what might happen if Ainiaan left me—not terrified of dying, no. Terrified of being utterly helpless to stop whatever any of them might do to me.

"No!" Ainiaan snapped. *"I'm staying with him!"*

"All right, Ainiaan, all right," Mabog relented with a sighing tone of a man well used to giving into a headstrong child. "You can take the first watch, all right? When you get tired, I'll take over."

"I *won't* get tired," she fired back. "You'll see."

Good girl... I wanted to grin, despite feeling Ainiaan let go as Rasaben's burly arms none-too-gently scooped me up, but I was just so damned... drowsy.

XV

I was a quick study—I came in early and left late each day—always arriving well before and leaving long after Silva. He was impressed with my dedication, my almost instant grasp of the incredibly complex and at times mind-numbing minutia that led to the smooth running of the massive garrison. As the weeks went by, he handed over more and more of the mundane tasks to me, and soon even stopped checking my work, having come to fully trust me to do it as proficiently as he, and, he grudgingly admitted, far quicker.

I began to get a reputation among Vallus's command and soon found myself the frequent recipient of offers from officers wanting to lure me away from Silva. I was flattered by such attention, but I respected Silva as a fair-minded and even-tempered superior, which was not the case with many of Vallus's other commanders.

Over the following months my life took on a new and, I readily admit, comfortable regimentation. I knew what was expected of me and what to expect of others. To that end I was often sent on official errands, first running messages to city officials and then, as I proved myself a discreet and reliable courier, I was more often than not the one Vallus called upon to carry orders to commanders in the field—I took immense pride in the trust Silva, and yes, Vallus placed on me—in less than six months I'd gone from his mother's plaything to a fully-accepted and highly-respected member of his command staff. A truly astonishing metamorphosis by anyone's standards.

Soon my duties extended to the far-flung legionary outposts and garrison towns that had sprouted up along the banks of the Nile, carrying communiqués of the utmost urgency and confidentiality. Out of uniform I could easily pass as a native, a disguise I was called upon to don more and more frequently as tensions between upper and lower Egypt, along with neighboring Cyrenacia continued to rise.

On one of these covert missions, I was dispatched to the city of Oxyrhynchus, deep in Upper Egypt. It took me eight days by boat to reach the city—a deliberately deliberate place so as not to garner unwanted attention and I wore the guise of a merchant's trusted subordinate dispatched to cement a trade agreement with the local military commander, a trip deemed too dangerous for the merchant himself to undertake.

Oxyrhynchus was very different than Alexandria—it was steeped in the flavors of the far south, the air thick with pungent and unfamiliar spices along with the almost overpowering stink of the open sewers that carved their way down the center of each crudely paved street. Its people were predominately dark-skinned, almost blue-black, with coarse, wiry hair, reminding me of old Niger and his gall ink-black skin. Some even bore similar patterns of scars on their faces.

The men were extremely curious and talkative to the point of being bothersome and I was constantly on the alert to the very real risk of being mugged. The women were more reserved, watching me as I passed by with slitted eyes, as if sizing me up and finding me somehow lacking. The few Romans I came across as I wandered the streets in search of the local military commander's residence, even those from the provinces, stuck out like sore thumbs with their paler skins and formal manners.

Oxyrhynchus was filthy and claustrophobic, a veritable rabbit warren of narrow allies and labyrinthine streets barely wide enough for two donkey carts to pass. By the time I reached the official residence my already frayed nerves had been rubbed raw.

I'd been sent on a number of risky missions, and this one was no more so, but there was more to my discomfort than just the personal risk of being exposed as an Imperial agent. From the moment I stepped ashore I felt a sense of growing dread—as if something terrible was about to happen—I wanted to deliver my message then return to the boat and the relative safety of the Nile as quickly as possible. The river's hippos and crocodiles made far more easy company.

I approached the guards, handed one my official papers and was promptly escorted into the entry hall of the building. It was no cooler than outside, but at least I was out of the blazing sun.

A slave approached, offered me his profuse apologies—his master, the officer I'd been sent to personally deliver my message—had been called away to settle a dispute between rival tribesmen and was not expected to return until late that afternoon.

My heart sank at the news—any chance of leaving this accursed town before sunset was dashed and with no arrangements made for a place to sleep, it looked like I was in for a very long, uncomfortable night.

I was, however, offered a shady place to sit in the residence's private, high-walled garden, next to a small and rather pathetic fountain than gurgled like some dying creature and occasionally belched out a small plume of foul-smelling greenish-brown water.

The slave returned a few minutes later, carrying a bowl of dried fruit and a pitcher of wine, along with a small cup and bade me eat and drink my fill while I waited upon his master.

I sat and dutifully gulped down a cup of the wine, knowing I needed to drink even though I had no desire—my stomach had tied itself up in knots over the vague but growing sense of foreboding—then I rose, briefly touched the grip of my sword—just in case—and began to pace the garden while I fingered my bead necklace, seeking its familiar comfort. The lead pendant, a dead-giveaway that I was a Roman soldier, had been left as it always was in such missions, in Silva's safekeeping until I returned.

After several circuits of the garden, I resumed my seat, tossed back another cup of wine and some dates, then resumed my pacing. I kept up this restless pattern all day, stopping occasionally to glance up the sky and judge the time. Had Vallus and Silva not put such trust in me and had not impressed upon me the truly critical importance of this mission, I would have made my excuses and left—but as it was, I dutifully remained, watching as the sun, along with my hopes of escaping this oppressive city, sank lower and lower in the smoke-smudged sky.

By the time dusk fell and the garden was plunged into shadow, I knew every corner of that garden, every plant, even every lizard, insect and frog that dwelled within its high plaster walls. Aside from the slave returning occasionally to see if I needed anything, I had the garden to myself the entire day—plenty of time to prepare and rehearse to perfection my indignant speech protesting this blatant snub. I was hot, sweaty and tired, my stomach was upset and I had a pounding headache to boot.

I had no sooner gathered myself up with the intention of marching back into the residence and demanding a bed for the night—it was the least my absent host could do to make amends—when I heard voices from within the residence, along with the scrape and thump of footfalls and the bobbing of lamplight.

I took a wary step back into the garden's shadows, my fingers instinctively wrapping themselves around the grip of my sword, not sure who approached—hoping it was the commander yet fearing it was the slave come to offer me yet more food and drink.

It was neither. The approaching footfalls belonged to two Nubian auxiliaries. They met my startled furious stare with broad, apologetic smiles of their own. One explained that they'd been sent in lieu of their commander, who had been further delayed. The other offered to take me to nearby tavern for supper—adding that the food was marginally better than that served in the barracks.

Clearly no arrangements had been made to offer me a meal here, in the residence, and the two seemed friendly enough, so after asking some questions and assuring myself they were who they claimed to be, I agreed to accompany them, with the added hope that they would find me a bed in the barracks for the night—an expectation even a merchant's envoy could reasonably expect.

The tavern was as clean as one could expect in a town like this, and the food—a cooked mash of fish, grain and onions drizzled in garum—was good and filling. The establishment was owned, I was told, by a retired veteran, and was clearly a favorite haunt of off-duty soldiers. Surrounded by the familiarity of fellow legionaries, I found myself relaxing a bit, and finally even enjoying myself.

The three of us drank and exchanged stories—I kept myself wrapped in the guise of a merchanter: who I really was and who'd sent me was to be revealed only to the garrison's commander and his immediate staff. The taller and more outgoing of the two, whose name was Tumhabi, told me he'd been in the service of Rome all of his life—he was grizzled and scarred, middle-aged, with long, lean muscles and skin as black and glistening as Nile mud.

Pasham was my age, and by the amount of food he packed away he was clearly still growing—of course so was I. He was lighter skinned that Tumhabi, but darker than me, with an elaborate pattern of alternating scars and raised welts on his cheeks, chin and upper arms. He didn't talk much, preferring to let Tumhabi do the honors, but he listened attentively, nodding and smiling as he wolfed down his meal.

After a few hours the strain of the day began to show in my face and voice, and Tumhabi suggested I return with them and sleep in their barracks—just as I'd hoped. He warned me the bunks were hard and the barracks itself was always hot and stuffy—unless of course I preferred to spend the night in the tavern's upstairs brothel?

I eagerly accepted the offer of the barracks—saying I was too tired to enjoy even the services of a whore, which was truth—and rose to accompany them only to find our small party had ballooned to include a number of fellow soldiers who'd drunk too much and needed a steady arm or two to guide them safely to their beds.

I could feel someone's gaze on me but I didn't want whoever it was to realize I was awake until I'd had a few minutes to myself to figure out my present situation, so I remained still, kept my breathing deep and regular while I went through my mental checklist:

I was warm—a good thing.

I didn't hurt—another good thing.

I was flat on my back on something relatively soft. It wasn't my favorite sleeping position—I far preferred my stomach—but I wasn't uncomfortable.

I then fingered my right thigh, disguising the movement within a sleep-twitch, and wasn't particularly surprised to find bare skin. But I *was* covered, from toes to throat, in a warm, heavy blanket.

My last memory was of stumbling drunkenly upstairs, following Oxyrhoë to her chambers, but I didn't recall her bed, of which I'd been a frequent occupant, being this comfortable—quite the contrary. In fact I'd long held the suspicion that her pallet, like so many others, was deliberately thin and lumpy to dissuade customers from lingering after business been completed, which to me seemed rather shortsighted.

When I'd worked the trade, I'd done everything I could to keep a client from leaving my bed prior to me completely emptying his *all* of his pockets, fabric and flesh alike by all means available to me. Instead of discouraging repeat business it had the exact opposite effect, giving me the time to learn their preferences, which in turn fostered a *very* loyal, *very* well paying clientele.

I drew in a particularly deep breath, hoping that alone might give me a hint about my whereabouts and found that the air had an odd smell—not moldy straw and unwashed bodies as I'd expected, but rather an acerbic tang. And in the background was the noise that had, I realized, drawn me out of my slumber: a faint but nevertheless maddening *bleat. Bleat. Bleat.*

A muffled cough confirmed my suspicions I wasn't alone, and my heart began to beat faster. The bleating too instantly picked up its pace. Soft footfalls approached. The *bleat, bleat, bleat* came faster, *faster,* mimicking my heartbeat perfectly.

Fingers touched my shoulder—but I'd been expecting that so I didn't flinch—followed by: "Arri?"

The voice was instantly recognizable—instantly placeable—and I opened one very gritty eye. *"Ainiaan...?"* I croaked, feigning grogginess.

She grinned, "Of course."

"What... are you... doing here?"

"I've been here all the time, silly, waiting days and days for you to wake up—"

"Days...?" Don't ask me why, but I had this foolish need to keep track, to keep things in some semblance of order, to assert control over things in truth I had absolutely no control over. "Exactly how *many* days?"

"Um," she started counting, using her fingers. "Five? No," she shook her head violently, which sent her red hair flying. "Today makes six and I was told not to bother you while you were sleeping but you're awake now. You sleep a lot, do you know that?

"Father said that meant you needed to sleep, that you'd wake up when you were better. Are you better? You look better. Father said he fixed everything what was wrong with you so you won't be sick any more..."

I rubbed my eye, still focused on the fact that I'd missed out on another six days of my life. Then I swiveled that eye back to Ainiaan. "Your father...?"

"He's Lord Taskim's physician, remember?"

I did, vaguely— *"Mabog...?"*

She grinned and nodded. "And he's made you *all* better."

"Oh." As far as I was concerned, that remained to be seen.

"I've brought Badger—he's been waiting days and days to meet you."

An instant later I found myself staring at what my still sleep-sluggish brain told me was a fox, *not* a badger.

"Want to pet him?"

I squeezed my eye shut then opened it again. Yup, still a fox. And it was staring back at me with its beady black eyes, prick ears flicking this way and that, glossy black nose twitching.

She picked up my hand and placed on the fox's furry back. "See?" she said as she began stroking him with my hand. "He likes being petted."

The fox and I stared at each other, eyeball to eyeball. He didn't look like he liked being petted, not one damned bit. He looked like he was thinking seriously about sinking his needle-sharp teeth into my forearm and I jerked my hand clear just as he snapped.

"Bad, Badger!"

The fox, to my relief, was yanked away from its uncomfortably close proximity to my nose and by the soft thump, presumably dropped to the floor.

Ainiaan then plopped herself down beside me, the fox and its bad manners instantly forgotten.

I rubbed my eyes again then looked around only to find that I was in a small, wood-paneled room, illuminated by a single torch. Its door was ajar with a wall of dressed stone beyond. And in the background was that constant, faint and rhythmic, not to mention damned annoying *bleat... bleat... bleat.*

I knew I'd heard that sound before, but try as I might—I couldn't place it. I looked back at Ainiaan, curious and aggravated at the same time. "What's that... *noise...?*"

"What noise?"

"That damned bleating sound—"

"Oh. That's your heart, silly. See?" She pointed above me and I very cautiously levered myself up on an elbow and craned my neck around to look up.

Hanging on the wall just above the head of my bed was an oblong box, its glossy black surface filled with brightly colored lines and flashing lights.

As I stared, the bleating rapidly picked up its pace, accompanied by a rapidly flashing light.

Ainiaan pointed. "This is your heart... the squiggly line, here... see?"

My eyes widened.

"...and this," she pointed to another line, "is your breathing... and that—" She suddenly frowned. "Well, I don't know what that is but I'm sure it's really important."

I warily sank back down onto the bed as I fought the urge to yank the blanket over my head. Instead I gave the magical box another frightened glance. "You... mean my heart's in... in *there?*" The bleating sound was coming fast and furious now, and getting faster and more furious with each passing second.

"No, silly! It's right here," she tapped my chest with a small, freckled finger, which drew my attention to the fact that I could hear not just that damnedable bleating but also hear the rapid pounding of my heart in my ears—each perfectly cadenced with the other. I slowly, cautiously, touched my throat and could *feel* my heart hammering like mad.

All right. Now I was really scared *and* completely confused. How could my heart be in two places... *at once?* I glanced around. "Where... are we?"

"Lord Taskim's Keep—don't you remember?"

I looked up at the box and drew the blanket up around my throat, as if that and that alone could protect me from whatever magical beast dwelled inside that ominous black container.

"What's the matter?"

I tore my eyes off the box and fixed them on Ainiaan.

"You look really scared, Arri—Badger didn't mean it, really he didn't."

"Where's your father?" I asked in an urgent whisper.

"Somewhere—why?"

"I need to see him, *please."*

She gave me a worried look. "Aren't you feeling well?"

"No... *please,* I really need to see him, *now."*

"You stay right there, all right?"

I nodded. As she ran from the room did what any sane man would do: I yanked the blanket over my head and tried to ignore the speedy *bleat-bleat-bleat* just above my head.

Then I heard a new noise: the echo of rapidly approaching footfalls. *Running* footfalls.

They stopped beside me.

"Centurion?" The blanket was jerked away from my head and I found myself staring up at an equally frightened man I immediately recognized as the same gaunt, bald-headed man who'd stood over me—how many days ago? *Mabog.*

"Ainiaan said you needed me, said you were really sick." He looked at the box for a moment then dropped his very worried stare back to me. "What's wrong? Are you in pain?"

I risked a quick, furtive glance around me. *"Where's Ainiaan?"*

"I told her I needed to examine you... *alone."* He crossed his arms, his expression shading to the mildly annoyed. "Now, what's the matter?" With that he flipped the blanket back, baring my torso and I couldn't help but flinch.

"This shouldn't hurt—I need to examine your incision."

I squinted up at him, baffled. *"My what?"*

"Your belly—*remember?* Had to cut you open, stop the bleeders and remove some of your gut."

That sounded vaguely familiar, so I acted as if I fully remembered and nodded, worried if I didn't he might want to go into more graphic detail. I didn't want details. I wanted answers. Succinct and to the point answers would be even better.

As he ran his hand over my stomach, over my flanks, I looked down at myself and realized I had a new landmark to add to my body's 'treasure map': a very neatly stitched incision that ran from just below my ribcage to just above my navel. Maybe that would make Turan happy. Maybe.

"Where's... where's my heart?"

He stopped his examination and met my wide-eyed stare. "What?"

"Ainiaan..."

He straightened up, crossed his arms and exhaled. "What did Ainiaan tell you?"

"She told me my heart... is... *up there?*" My frightened eyes darted up to the box, then back to him.

He stared at me for a moment as if not quite believing his ears, as if perhaps I was quite mad—maybe I was. I mean, who wouldn't be after all I'd been through? "No. Your heart's where it should be." He patted my chest. "That box tells me a lot about how you're doing, such as how fast or slow your heart is beating and if it's working the way it should."

I wasn't sure I believed him, even though I really, I mean I really, *really* wanted to. You know how it is when someone puts an idea in your head, even a really unpleasant one, it's extremely hard to shake it loose, even when offered another that isn't as unpleasant?

"I'm very sorry she scared you. I sometimes forget that to others my machines can be very unnerving—I actually meant to put it away well before you woke up, but, sad to say, I totally forgot, assuming the sedative I gave you earlier would guarantee you'd sleep until later this evening." He tapped the side of his head and smiled. "Bit absent minded you see."

When I didn't smile back, he immediately reached up and touched something on the box and the bleating silenced.

"Has my heart stopped?" I asked, frightened anew.

"No, you're fine. I just turned off the machine, that's all. No need for it now."

I glanced up just in time to see the box seemingly vanish into the wall. I turned my stunned gaze back to Mabog and whispered, *"Where'd it go?"*

"Back where it belongs."

As if that was answer enough. *Hardly!*

He stepped back. "If I help you, can you sit on the edge of the bed?"

I knew he was trying to change the subject, get my mind off that damned disappearing box. And I was suddenly really fine with that. I nodded and as I carefully levered myself up onto my right elbow, he slipped his arm behind me and helped me the rest of the way up, then I very slowly, very carefully dropped my bare feet to the floor, tugging the blanket over my lap as I did so.

So far, so good.

Mabog kept his arm around me as he settled beside me—I didn't like his familiarity, his closeness. I hadn't figured out where he stood in the order of things and I had no one, not even Hanni to reassure me that this man wasn't trouble. The whole situation made me intensely uneasy. The only good thing was that I didn't have to listen to that damned bleating any more.

"Feeling dizzy?"

I shook my head. Now *that* made me feel dizzy, damn it. I blinked several times then rubbed my eyes.

"I need to examine the rest of you—it won't hurt—just want to see where we stand."

We? Don't you mean me?

He started to tug the blanket off my lap.

I kept my hold on it and tugged back. Point made.

He let go, smiled uneasily then ran his hand over my lower back, stopping every so often to press down as he watched my face for any reaction. "Ainiaan doesn't have any friends," he said without preamble as he moved his hand up and across my shoulders. "There are very few children here and none anywhere near her age. So she's attached herself to you."

I winced. The last thing I needed was more woman trouble.

"Painful?"

I'd learned my lesson and instead of shaking my head, I murmured, "No."

"Good." He rose, pressed his fingers against my left shoulder then grabbing my elbow, carefully worked the joint. It hurt, but not as much as I thought it would. "You have my permission to tell her to leave you alone. Of course I doubt she'll listen to you anymore than she listens to me."

Women *never* listened to me—so it wasn't like I'd find it a novel experience to be ignored, even if it was by a little girl.

"Can you sit up straight?"

I slowly did as he asked, straightening my aching back as best I could, grunting in the process then I fixed my pinched gaze on the far wall as he pressed and poked at my flanks and finally my belly. I grimaced as he touched an especially tender spot.

"Hurt?"

I eyed him. "Yes."

"Do you realize just how lucky you are?"

I stared balefully at him.

"All right, maybe lucky isn't the best description."

"No."

He smiled, briefly then touched the incision. "All in all you're healing remarkably well."

I didn't know what to say. Thank you seemed rather, well, *odd*. I mean it wasn't like I had conscious control over these things.

"We should be able to pull out the stitches in a week."

That was not going to be fun—I'd been stitched up before of course, plenty of times, and it always hurt like hell to have those lovely bits of thread tugged and torn from my flesh the moment my body was lulled into a false sense that the worst was over. It was almost as painful as being stitched up in the first place.

I had to give it to Mabog though, he was quite the seamstress—each stitch was as neat as could be, unlike some of the Roman field surgeons I'd had the misfortune to meet and whose needlecraft left a hell of a lot to be desired, looking more like the results of a drunken practical joke than a professional's proud handiwork.

"I repaired the damage to the joint," he said as he again ran his hand over my injured shoulder, "removed some bone chips and reset your collar bone—you might be a little stiff for a while, but do exactly as I tell you and you'll get back full function."

I nodded, greatly relieved.

"As for your thigh..." Mabog, having learned from his earlier gaffe, carefully drew the blanket aside, just enough. "As you can see, you've lost some muscle..."

I stared down at my leg—the wound had been stitched closed as well, the entire area mottled purple with bruises, but as I ran my hand over the incision that spiraled from top to bottom and front to back I found it didn't hurt and even more importantly it didn't feel hot—even I knew that was a good thing. I could live with what was going to be a very large, disfiguring scar if it meant I'd have a functioning leg.

"...can't do a thing about that, surgically or cosmetically for that matter. But the infection's gone and the sooner you start walking under your own power, the better—but I best warn you, Ainiaan's named herself your nurse. Can't do much about that, either." He smiled, met my sidelong gaze. "She's always bringing home orphaned animals to nurse back to health— she presently has a baby fox, sleeps with it, or did, until she adopted you—"

I dearly hoped he wasn't suggesting she'd been sleeping with me—

"—did she tell you that? Name's Badger—don't ask me why. And then there's that pony—"

"Mugwort. Yes, she told me about him."

"Damnedable creature." Mabog snorted as he resumed his seat beside me and unwrapped a small bandage that encircled my right forearm. "Keeps getting into the stuff then afterwards can barely walk—one day this past summer Hanni had to carry him home—a pony, *carried* like a baby because he was so wobbly he couldn't walk." He sighed. "Last spring it was a new-born fawn one of the hunters brought back after killing its mother. Year before that she raised six baby birds—*six!* With her mother gone these many years, and Sifrie at the age where all she's interested in is men—"

"Sifrie's her sister?" I asked, suddenly very uncomfortable with the realization that I was seated beside the father of a woman I'd had sex with—I was sure I'd had sex with her once, and maybe some of my hallucinations weren't all fabrication—a father who might not be too pleased to learn I, a damned Roman, knew his daughter on such intimate terms without any intention of making her my wife.

Then an even more unsettling thought popped into my head: can he read my thoughts, too? So I frantically tried to tamp down the memories, like I was madly stomping on a fire that refused to go out, fearing its telltale glow would draw unwanted attention.

"Yes, didn't you know that? Oh, but of course, how could you? Yes, yes, Sifrie's her older sister by eight years."

I breathed a sigh of relief, realizing he was oblivious to the naked images cavorting in my head. Then again, since he was clearly aware of his daughter's proclivities, perhaps he accepted as a forgone conclusion that Sifrie and I had been more than just a little friendly. She might have even told him—Turan might have told him, or even Kyrou, damn him. If so I could only hope it was *after* Mabog had operated on me. He was her father after all, and fathers, in my experience, frowned on such, always believing their daughters had been seduced even when all evidence suggested the contrary—

I suddenly had the strong desire to peek under the blanket, you know… just to make sure everything was still there as up to this moment I'd just assumed it was. Now I wasn't so sure.

He finished unwrapping the bandage, revealing what looked like a piece of straw, only this piece of straw had been slipped under my skin like a wood sliver, then without further ado, said, "I think we can do without this, too," and pulled it out, leaving a bead of blood on my skin, which he then wiped away with the wadded up bandage.

I arched a brow then looked at him for an explanation to this peculiar ritual—I mean, what else could it be?

Instead he continued, "I must say I haven't been the most attentive father, so I suppose it's not unexpected that Ainiaan would feel the need to mother others who, like her, have been neglected."

I found myself shifting around—the conversation was getting very awkward and I was still a little worried about what might—or might not—be under the blanket.

"I'm afraid she sees you as another stray, Centurion. She means well, please understand that. She's *very* trusting."

I knew what he was thinking, what he was most afraid of—it was a completely reasonable reaction from a father of a young child and suddenly I was back in that storage room with Porsenna... I'd gone with him willingly, because I *trusted* Gracchus. On top of that, I wasn't much older now than Porsenna had been at the time, and Ainiaan—

Before I could stop myself I reacted with a convulsive gasp.

He grabbed my arm. "Are you all right? You've gone quite pale. *Centurion...?*"

I looked at him, replied with a quick, less than convincing nod, then fixed my gaze on the floor and took several deep breaths.

I wasn't sure he'd believe any assurance I might offer up; still, I felt the need to say something. "I... I understand your concerns, sire. I'm a soldier—a Roman soldier to boot. *The enemy—*"

He opened his mouth, to protest, but I pressed on.

"Then there's a widespread and reasonably held belief that I'm not entirely in my right mind, but I'd never hurt Ainiaan, I give you my word."

He smiled, but it was clearly forced and I made a mental note to never, *ever* be alone with her. If anything happened, *anything,* he'd assume the worst. Of course if I were in his position, I'd react the same way.

"I believe you." He patted my bare knee and rose. But he didn't; I knew he didn't. "I want you to start eating—all right? Nothing fancy, spicy or too chewy at first—porridge, soup, stew, pudding and the like. See how your gut handles that."

I had no idea what 'pudding' was—in fact I didn't even like the sound of it—but soup, porridge and even stew actually sounded good as I absently ran my hand over the incision. Then I felt something brush past my heel. Startled, I looked down and spotted the tip of a tufted russet tail sticking out from under the bed. I didn't need to ask where the fox was keeping itself now that Ainiaan had adopted me—I could only hope it didn't adopt me too. Didn't care for foxes—they reminded me of jackals.

And jackals looked like dogs… and aside from Turan's dearly departed hound, I loathed dogs.

I poked the tuft with my toe and it promptly disappeared, replaced by a black nose and ginger muzzle. It cautiously sniffed my toe then quickly withdrew. Can't say I blamed it. I stank. Even I could smell myself—*never* a good thing. "Is it possible for me to wash up?"

"Of course—I'll have one of the servants prepare a bath." He grabbed a knotted rope next to the head of the bed and gave it a tug.

I blinked. *Bath?* Perhaps these people weren't quite as barbaric as I'd first assumed and I had a fleeting image of a steaming indoor pool, such as I'd enjoyed each time I found myself in any Romanized town. But just as quickly I reminded myself he might consider a basin of cold water, or a bucket drawn from an icy horse trough a bath—perhaps even the horse trough itself.

He walked over to a nearby chair, snatching up a discarded blanket that lay on the floor in the process. He then folded the blanket and placed it on the chair. "She refused to leave your side you know." He glanced over his shoulder at me.

"Ainiaan?"

He nodded. "Slept here, ate here."

"Oh." I couldn't tell by his tone if he was proud or annoyed by his daughter's devotion to her newest 'stray'. I looked down at my belly, at the neat line of stitches, suddenly and intensely uncomfortable.

"Don't worry about getting the incisions wet—they're properly sealed."

Sealed? I ran my fingers over my belly only to find that it was coated in something completely clear, like water.

"And I assume Turan would prefer you to be attired in her livery?"

"I'm sure Perus would." I left Turan's opinion to Turan—for all I knew, she might prefer I wear a rat-chewed sack. Or nothing at all. She had, after all, shown a marked proclivity for me wearing nothing but a satisfied smile—we only started to have problems when I started wearing clothes. That being said, I had no desire to run around this icebox of a fortress in the buff.

I also had no recollection of being separated from Perus's tunic, boots and trousers, but after the soaking in salt water, then snow melt… and I had a vague memory of puking all over myself too, and if the latter had truly happened, I seriously doubted Perus would offer me another change of clothes. In fact if I'd truly vomited all over his beautiful tunic, well, I wouldn't blame him in the least if he never spoke to me again—

There was a firm knock at the doorframe and I looked up as a small, ruddy-faced woman entered. "You called, sire?"

"Our young friend here wants to wash up—would you mind helping him?"

She looked at me and smiled, a shy, wary and at the same time very relieved smile. "Of course, sire." She walked over to me, scooped up the blanket from my lap without even so much as a 'by your leave', leaving me briefly exposed. "Here, young sire." She held it up. "This'll have to do until I can fetch proper clothing…"

Mabog helped me to my feet and the woman wrapped the blanket around me and as I looked down at myself I almost laughed. I looked like I was wearing a toga, only this toga was woven in a strange checkerboard design of whites, browns and reds.

"…had to burn what you were wearing—it was beyond salvage."

So I *had* puked on the tunic. I winced at the thought of that beautiful leather going up in flames—

"Come now, young sire." Her fingers latched onto my elbow with an iron-like grip. "Let's get you clean—you'll feel so much better for it."

"I'll call for hot water," Mabog said and again tugged the rope.

Hot water? I almost grinned.

"Thank you, sire, much appreciated." She wrapped her other arm around my waist then directed me towards the door.

I draped my arm around her shoulder and very slowly limped alongside her, out of the room and into the hallway. While it really hurt to walk, really hurt to use my stomach muscles to keep myself upright, I realized I actually felt better than I had in days, even if those days were who knows how many days ago.

"In here, young sire." She stopped before another door, released her hold on my elbow just long enough to open it and my eyes widened in surprise: damned if the room beyond didn't contain large stone tub, in fact the tub took up most of the small chamber. I'd seen the like in Alexandria—Lady Ilissia had one carved out of the finest white alabaster and used it daily. This one was far cruder, made from a pinkish-gray and white-flecked stone, but it was still a tub.

"Come along," she murmured and guided me over to a wooden bench next to the tub. "Rest yourself here while I'll get the supplies. The water should be here shortly."

I nodded, eased myself down on the bench and letting out a long, weary sigh, dropped my head into my hands—the short walk had been utterly exhausting—while the woman bustled around me, opening wooden cabinets and removing items while muttering, non-stop.

I ignored her: she wasn't talking to me. But when I heard the familiar slosh of water, I slowly lifted my head from its cradle to find three servants, each carrying two large steaming buckets and standing in line while a forth finished dumping his load into the tub. Then a fifth arrived, carrying a russet leather tunic, matching trousers and boots. She placed them on the bench next to me, smiled bashfully at my sidelong, questioning stare then withdrew.

I looked down at the livery—noting with some annoyance that it was almost the same color as the fox, which would, I suppose, make me even more popular with Ainiaan. *Just* what I needed.

Once the last bucket was poured into the tub—another was left full, sitting beside the tub for a final rinse—and the other servants left, closing the door behind them, the woman again wrapped her fingers around my elbow, murmured, "All's ready, young sire," and helped me back to my feet—or should I say she *pulled* me back to my feet—there was no arguing with that grip of hers.

Without further ado, she again stripped me of the blanket and tossed it onto the bench then assisted me into the tub.

I sank to my knees in the steaming hot water, then at her insistent urging sat back and stretched out. It was bliss—sheer bliss—until she started scrubbing me. I stoically endured the ordeal, and after a while it actually started feeling good. She had very strong hands, and while she washed my skin and hair with something perfumed that also foamed when mixed with the water, she also massaged my scalp, my stiff muscles and my aching joints.

"You've got a fine body, my young sire, if you don't mind me saying. *Very fine.*"

"Thank you," I mumbled. It was hard to speak any louder as she was vigorously scrubbing my back at the time and in doing so, she'd pushed me forward so my face was less than a handbreadth from the foamy and, I have to admit, now filthy surface of the water. Only my hands' slippery grip on the tub smooth rim stopped me from going face-first into that really nasty looking scum.

Then I had a thought and I glanced back at her. "You do realize I'm not light-skinned, don't you?"

"Of course, young sire. Why, did you think I thought you were *that* dirty?"

I couldn't help but chuckle.

235

She laughed, a sweet bubbly laugh. "Young Lady Ainiaan's right—you have a *very* nice smile. And you'd look so much more handsome without the beard—again, if you don't mind me saying so."

"You think so?" I ran my fingers over the veritable forest of hair on my face—how many weeks since I'd last been clean-shaven? I hadn't a clue. I'd sported a beard while stationed in Germania—much as I dislike to admit, even now, it was a grooming tip I picked up from Aetius of all people—it kept your face and throat warm, kept your helmet's cheek-pieces from freezing to your skin in the winter, but I'd never liked it, found it too fiddly to keep it looking neat, not to mention clean—two things Aetius never seemed the slightest bit worried about. And worst of all, it always itched. "Really?"

"Indeed," she nodded vigorously.

"Well, if *you* think I should shave it off, then I will…"

I mean, what was the harm? I'd desperately wanted a shave and my comment left her beaming, plus Ainiaan would be pleased as well, and the potential of making two women very happy in one quick one sweep, so to speak, well, those were the best odds I'd had in years. It might even please Turan, cause her to revisit her anger at me, although I wasn't going to hold out much hope for that. A woman's pride, in my experience, was always the hardest wound to heal.

"Would you help? My hands aren't all that steady." I lifted them for her to see and even without my conscious help they trembled.

"Of course!" She quickly wiped her hands and hurried over to another cabinet.

While she was busy, I began splashing my face with the hot, foamy, and yes, scummy water, to soften up what was, even I had to admit, a rather formidable beard—almost as formidable as Kyrou's and his beard was *damned* formidable.

She returned a moment later with one *very* wicked looking blade in her hand.

I eyed it, then her.

She grinned. "If I'd wanted to murder you, young sire, I'd have simply drowned you. Far less messy."

I couldn't argue with that, so I very carefully leaned back, my back resting against the sloping back of the tub, my neck arched over its smoothly rounded rim—my throat completely exposed. I couldn't help but swallow nervously.

"I've done this many, many times and never had anyone complain." She pressed on my forehead with the meaty palm of her other hand, forcing my head back further, stretching the skin of my throat taut.

I squeezed my eyes shut and swallowed again. *It's hard to complain with your throat slit,* I thought as my heart beat faster, faster with each quick, upward stroke of the blade. I tried very hard not to swallow again, fearful any distraction might cause the fast moving blade to slip, but you know, the harder you try not to swallow, the more you have to. Luckily my bobbing Adam's apple didn't distract her in the slightest and with one more swipe, she finished with my throat.

She swished the blade in the water then turned my head and shaved one cheek, my upper lip and then my chin. She again rinsed the blade, turned my head the other way and shaved my other cheek. After a little touch up here and there, she was done.

"There you go, my fine young sire." She stepped back, tossed the blade onto the bench then gazed at her handiwork and grinned. "A vast improvement, if I say so myself—not that you were hard to look at with the beard, not at *all.*"

I reached up, expecting to feel a nick or two, maybe even the hot trickle of blood, but my cheeks, chin and throat were completely smooth—not even a scratch and completely, blessedly hairless too. I looked up at her and smiled. "Thank you."

"Four brothers—a husband…" Her grin vanished and her voice trailed off and I realized her eyes were now glistening. Before I could say anything, she wiped her eyes, forced a smile and added huskily, "I know how to shave a man, damned if I don't." She grabbed a wet cloth, rubbed it against the block of that odd, perfumed and foamy substance then handed it to me. "Wash your face, then… you know, the other parts of you you'd rather I not scrub."

I did as she asked—yes, in case you were wondering, everything was still there. Once I was finished she helped me lurch unsteadily to my feet.

As I stood there, naked and ringed in a tide line of filthy, foamy scum and hair shavings, she washed my lower back, butt and legs, then grabbed the bench, dragged it closer to the tub, and standing on it, poured the remaining bucketful of warm water over my head, rinsing my hair, along with the rest of me. By now the room was warm and steamy and I closed my eyes and savored the feeling of being cleaner than I had in weeks. *Bliss….*

Realizing I was just standing there in the tub, I opened my eyes to find her staring at me with a look that I'm not embarrassed to say I'm all too familiar with.

I cleared my throat. She jumped, her round cheeks flushing as she realized I knew what she'd been staring at, then she helped me out of the tub. Once she'd wrapped the blanket around my shoulders, she smiled again, this time a little awkwardly. "Whenever you want a bath, or need a shave—or *anything* else," she added with a shy, averting of the eyes, "I'd be *more* than happy to oblige. Just ask for me. Name's Boian."

It was not an uncommon custom in many lands that male guests could have their pick of servants to attend to their very personal needs—it was almost expected, and in some cases a host would consider it an insult if a guest didn't oblige himself in such a way—and as Boian turned to pluck a small pot from a shelf, I eyed her definitely delectable backside, then smiled innocently as she turned back to me.

"I'll be needing to rub this on you." She opened the pot to reveal something that looked remarkably like goose grease.

I wasn't quite sure what she had in mind—honestly I didn't. And while she was middle-aged, she was not unattractive—far from it, and she was clearly *very* interested; and I have to admit, I was tempted. The hot bath, her strong hands, the relaxing massage, her large breasts, her bottom and her furtive looks… they all gave me ideas. So did the goose grease.

But I also had no idea if those same customs held true here—or if it was a good idea to engage in such demanding activity so soon after having my belly cut open and stitched closed—grease or no. How would I explain how I came to pop open? And it wasn't like I could ask Mabog if it was safe to have sex with a servant. Word might get back to Turan and then, I had every reason suspect, there'd be hell to pay.

Before I could ponder that further, she pulled the blanket from my shoulders and tossed it aside, scooped up several fingerfuls of the grease and began to rub it into my still damp skin, starting with my face and throat, gently massaging it into the still somewhat tender, freshly shaved skin, soothing it instantly. I realized with some disappointment that it was a scented balm of sorts, nothing more. On the upside, it certainly smelled better than goose grease, which meant I'd smelled better, too.

"I'll definitely keep that offer in mind, Boian."

A short time later, after covering every bit of my naked body, and I mean *every* bit—Boian was nothing but thorough—and paying particular care to my still rope-burned and scabby wrists and ankles, she looked me up and down and smiled. "A fair sight better, young sire all clean and very *smooth,*" she purred as she ran her finger down my jaw. "But I'd have taken you just as you were or anyway you please—you're such a pretty, pretty thing." With that she gave my bare, balm-buttered butt a firm and rather prolonged squeeze. This was definitely an act far above her station, unless of course she knew I was a prisoner—little better than a slave, albeit a very valuable slave otherwise no one would have gone to all the trouble of saving my life, not mention bringing me this far, which meant she, a servant, was actually above me—and besides, I didn't mind. She was kind-faced and sweet, with very, *very* skillful hands.

"We'd best get you dressed, young sire. Don't want you catching a chill." She snatched up the trousers and helped me step into them then, with a wistful sigh, she glanced up at me, and at my obliging nod, she gave me the lightest fondle before she very reluctantly tugged my trousers up around my hips and quickly laced up the front—good thing too, as I'd begun to seriously revisit my silly concerns about popping open.

She rubbed my shoulder-length hair dry with the blanket, combed out the tangles and crimped it with her hands, urging it back into its natural waviness, then stood back and briefly admired her work.

Next came the boots and then lastly, with some work, the tunic. This one bore Turan's insignia, the coiled serpent.

As she tugged it into place, she said, "You look very dashing in this, young sire. *Very* handsome indeed—you'll have all the womenfolk vying for your attention."

I managed a feeble smile as I wondered how Kyrou, not to mention Rasaben would react to that. Not well, I'd imagine.

She grinned up at me, then turned and opened the door. "Come along."

I again needed her help to walk, but I made it back down the hallway and into the room, and finally over to the bed without once stumbling.

I eased myself down and looked up at her and managed wearily, "Thank you, Boian."

She grinned. "Anytime, young sire. Day *or* night. Now, how about something to eat? I bet you're famished."

I smiled and nodded, and with that she hurried from the room, after telling me to stay exactly where I was, not to go wandering about.

I didn't. I remained exactly where I was, seated on the edge of the bed.

Good to her word, she returned a short time later with a steaming bowl of porridge topped with thick cream and honey.

She settled beside me, spread a cloth across my chest to protect the tunic and although I'd proven I could walk under my own power, albeit very slowly and shakily, she insisted on feeding me.

I allowed it, only because it clearly made her happy—I figured I owed her that much—and as I gulped down a spoonful of the porridge I told myself that I really was a pathetic excuse for a man when it came to women. For some reason they all wanted to mother me. Most, of course, also wanted to bed me. Don't ask me why, but one almost always followed the other, but not necessarily in any particular order.

"Full...?"

I looked back at Boian and realized that I was, which was a good thing because with her help I'd managed to eat every bite of the porridge. Not only that, I didn't feel the slightest bit nauseated. "Yes."

She gently wiped my lips and chin with the cloth then gathering up the bowl, rose. "I'll let Lord Mabog know how well you did, young sire—"

"Please, Boian, call me Arri."

"Thank you, young sire, but Lord Taskim's a sticker for etiquette."

"But I'm—" I hesitated, unable to actually say, 'a slave', "—not a guest."

"I know that too, sire—but you're very special, aren't you? Otherwise... well, you know."

"No, I *don't.*" I ran my fingers through my still damp hair. "I dearly wish I did."

Her smile vanished and she fixed me with a very odd look.

Sensing I'd said the wrong thing, I added quickly, "Do you know where Lady Turan is?"

She continued to look at me with that same strange look. Disappointment? Wariness? Dismay? I couldn't tell, but I'd definitely said the wrong thing.

She turned and gathered up the folded blanket from the chair—busywork, clearly—and keeping her back to me replied, "She's out hunting with Lord Taskim, but she and the others should be back well before dark—which shouldn't that long from now. Shall I let Lady Turan know you're asking about her when she returns?" She looked over her shoulder, all businesslike and aloof as she balanced the bowl on top of the blanket.

"No... no that's all right."

"Is there anything else I can get for you?"

"No, you've been most kind, thank you."

She replied with a curt nod and started out of the room.

"Boian?"

She stopped just short of the doorway and very reluctantly turned back to me. "Yes, sire?"

"What did I say?"

She looked genuinely puzzled. "Say, sire?"

"Just now—I said something that upset you."

She glanced at the open doorway, then back at me. "No sire, not at all."

I stared at her; she stared back, clearly uncomfortable, almost frightened and I realized I was only going to make things worse if I persisted.

"If that's all?" she prompted.

This time I only nodded and she hurried out of the room. I exhaled, shook my head then looked around, still wondering what the hell I'd done—or said, and now that she'd left, what was I supposed to do? Wait for Mabog to return? Sleep? I wasn't the least bit sleepy—the bath had definitely had an invigorating effect and Mabog had said the sooner I started walking around, the better.

Then again, Boian had told me *not* to go wandering about.

So I sat there for a moment or two, drumming my fingers on my thighs.

Satisfied I'd been *extremely* patient—no one could say I hadn't dutifully sat on my bed, waiting—was it my fault no one came to check on me?—I rose and limped out of the room and into the outer passageway, figuring I might as well do a little exploring. If they'd truly wanted me confined, they'd have locked the door, true?

I stood there, looking first to my left, then my right, not sure which direction to take and annoyed with myself that I hadn't thought to follow Boian. I hadn't even paid attention to which direction she'd gone when she left in such a hurry—in truth as eager as she was to part company after my mystifying gaffe. So with a shrug, I turned to my left—the way she'd taken me to the bath and began walking slowly, wary of my leg giving out.

As I came to the door that led to the bath I glanced inside hoping to find someone there, cleaning up after me, but the empty room had already been put back to rights. So I walked on.

The passageway itself was made of smooth stone—the same pinkish-gray and white-flecked stone as the tub—and covered in more of those strange cloth mosaics, the ceiling of vaulted timber and the floor of polished flagstone. Whoever this Lord Taskim was, I thought to myself, he clearly had the means to go all out. The workmanship rivaled that of Lady Ilissia's villa.

Every so often the stone walls gave way to elaborately carved wooden doors. Each was closed and I decided it probably wouldn't be a good idea to try the handles—people might take my purely innocent curiosity as curiosity taken one step too far. So I slowly, cautiously limped on with the hope that I'd eventually hear voices, or come across someone and ask

241

directions. But then I realized I had no idea where I was, much less where I wanted to go, so I wasn't sure how much help directions might be: *Sire, would you direct me back to where I belong? Yes, I'll even settle for Britannia if that's the best you can do.*

Instead the hallway took an abrupt right turn, then a few paces further ended just as abruptly with double wooden doors, one of which had been left ajar, so I peeked inside to find a relatively small, torch-lit chamber with a fireplace, stone table and a scattering of chairs.

A chair sounded like a really good idea about now as my left leg was really aching and I was back to shuffling along, barely lifting my foot off the ground. Surely no one would mind if I rested for just a moment.

So with that guiltless thought foremost, I slipped inside and looked around. To my surprise, I found that one of the walls was covered with a floor to ceiling wooden honeycomb, for lack of a better description, each cell containing what looked to my startled eyes like rolls of vellum, possibly papyri—in other words, *books!* I was in a library, smaller but still very reminiscent of Lady Ilissia's private library—a place that even after all these years and after all my experiences I still held in great regard and with much fondness. It had been a place I'd spent uncounted hours, alone, with Lady Ilissia or in the company of one of my tutors, reading or being read to. Reading for the knowledge, reading for the entertainment. Reading for the sheer joy of reading, of hearing someone else's thoughts fill my mind with images, of strange and novel ideas—granted, this had taken on a new and not altogether enjoyable twist with Turan, nevertheless...

I grinned and hurried across the room, my throbbing and wobbly leg instantly forgotten. Not thinking how Taskim—I had to assume this was Taskim's library—would react to my uninvited snooping, I carefully pulled out a roll at random.

It *was* vellum of the highest quality and tied with a bright red ribbon.

I slipped off the tie and unrolled the manuscript on the table only to find it covered in an utterly alien, fluid script instantly reminiscent of the sinuous tracks left by snakes in soft sand. I carefully ran a fingertip over the lettering, intrigued by its sheer beauty, impressed by the calligrapher's amazingly steady hand and intensely curious as from what exotic land this document had come.

Mildly frustrated, I re-rolled it, replaced the tie and placed it back in its slot, then selected another, only to find it too was a manuscript penned in another unfamiliar, but vastly different lettering—evocative of the Egyptians' bizarre picture-writing.

Snakestone and Sword

I must have gone through one entire row—twenty or so rolled up manuscripts—each written in an unknown tongue, before I finally came to one written in Latin. I found myself blinking back tears as I ran my fingers eagerly over the letters, desperate for their familiar comfort.

Realizing I was shaking, from a potent mixture of exhaustion and emotion, I took my prize over to the chair closest to the hearth—the fire was no more than a bed of glowing coals, but it put off a fair amount of heat and a nearby torch provided enough light. I eased myself down and settled back to read—a luxury, a pure joy I thought I'd never experience again.

It wasn't the expansive tome of a philosopher or poet. It wasn't even the manuscript of Pytheas, the one often cited by my tutors despite it having been lost in the fire that consumed the Royal Alexandria Library— or so the story went—where he documented his exploration of Pretani and its companion isles, presumably ending his work with a stern warning to stay the hell away which of course we Romans had failed to heed only because we hadn't known better.

No. It was in fact nothing more than a detailed manifest of a Roman slave ship, the *Venilia*, bound for Gaul—and with references to Emperor Augustus in the present-tense making it at least fifty years old.

It struck me as odd that a mundane cargo list would find a place of honor in such a library—or maybe, I realized, it wasn't a library after all. Maybe it was a records room and Taskim and his kind maintained a lucrative trade with the Empire?

I didn't care. Just to *read*, to feel my tongue form the achingly familiar sounds, speak them aloud was enough. It was, for a few precious minutes, as if I was listening to my friends again, hearing them chatter and joke amongst themselves, Aetius in his thick, distinctly Judean accent, Felix in the carefully cultured voice of the very Roman aristocracy he always claimed he despised, Rufinius in his—

"What you're doing here?"

I jerked my head up and twisted around in the chair to find a burly man standing in the doorway, arms akimbo, his bulk silhouetted against the torchlight of the passageway.

Gracchus...?

My heart began to beat faster, *faster* as fragments of memory fled by, poking and cutting me in their haste. My breathing quickened and my stomach twisted into a painfully tight knot.

It took my startled mind a moment to realize it wasn't a ghost, but Rasaben, and I was struck with the startling and horrifying similarity of

Rasaben standing as he was, framed in the doorway and my childhood fantasy of Gracchus having returned for me.

I started to rise, realized I was clutching the vellum manifest tightly in my hands and forced my fingers to release their death grip then I managed to lurch unsteadily to my feet.

He stepped into the room. "I ask again, what are you doing here?" While his deep, booming voice was not openly hostile, he was definitely not happy—again, so chillingly reminiscent of Gracchus when he'd caught me snatching a morsel of food before he and the others had eaten their fill.

So I did what I'd done so many times as a child, hoping to avoid a beating: I lied: "I… I was looking for Hanni—"

"And you believed you'd find him here?"

I stared back sober and terrified by this man—this red-haired twin of Gracchus. "I didn't—I… I mean I wasn't sure where to go—I'm very sorry, sire. I meant no harm. I simply got lost, happened across this room, and when I realized it was a library—"

"You decided to make yourself at home."

There was no point in denying his charge—I was, literally, holding the evidence and the knot in my stomach cinched even tighter. I hadn't thought to ask permission—of course there hadn't been anyone around I could have asked. Nevertheless, I'd just, as he said, made myself at home. "Yes, sire." With that I carefully rolled up the manifest, retied the tie and placed it back in its slot. That done, I didn't know what to do next, offer my apologies again and hope he would allow me to take my leave or wait for him to tell me what do to.

Like Gracchus, this man openly advertised his intent in the furrow of the brow, the dart of the eye, the twitch of the lips and Rasaben's purpose was to do me serious harm given half a chance, of that I had no doubt. It was all there—plain as his broad, bearded face as he strode across the room, his intense blue eyes fixed on me the entire time.

I struggled not to look as unnerved as I was, but he wasn't fooled, not one damned bit.

"Who gave you permission to go wandering about alone, *boy?*"

"No one, si—"

"You just took it upon yourself to go snooping." He stopped by the fireplace, grabbed a log from the small pile on the hearth and tossed it onto the coals. The fire briefly flared.

"Yes—"

"Are you feeling better?" His tone suggested he didn't give a damn.

"Yes—"

"You vomited all over the floor—do you remember that, *boy?* It certainly ruined Taskim's welcoming feast for the rest of us and caused Lady Ainiaan great distress."

I didn't know what to say—the moment of intense fear, the gut-deep recall of events long past was thankfully dwindling, replaced by a growing, and, I knew, *very* unwise sense of indignation. Fear and offended rage in any ratio had never been a combination I'd handled well—I knew that much about myself. I'd struggled for years to learn how to use both to my advantage and had never mastered the balancing act.

It wasn't like I'd asked to be kidnapped, to be hauled to the much promised, often threatened end of the Earth? For all I knew I could still be in Britannia—maybe the *Sulaviae* just sailed out to sea and then back, to give me the mistaken impression we'd actually crossed a body of water. I remembered Sapor—or was it Perus?—mentioning Hibernia as our destination, but now, in hindsight I was left to wonder if that hadn't been a deliberate deceit, to make me think that's where I was being taken.

I fixed my gaze on the floor—in what I hoped was a suitably deferential pose, knowing if I met his gaze or opened my mouth, I'd only make the situation worse—much, *much* worse. This man wasn't just built like Gracchus in his prime—heavy-set, bearded and square-faced, with massive hands and a barrel chest—he was also short-fused. Just like Gracchus.

So I found myself falling back into the same mannerisms I'd used around Gracchus, around the other soldiers of the Simitthu garrison, to avoid being beaten senseless, to avoid being the unwilling receptacle of someone's drunken frustrations. It scared me how quickly I regressed to that former me. Twenty years—a lifetime—*gone*, in a heartbeat. It didn't help that he kept referring to me as 'boy'—I was hardly a boy, but when Gracchus was angry, that's what he called me—'boy', not Arri, and I'd hated being called 'boy', as if I didn't even merit a name—

"Well, boy?" he prompted irritably, snapping me back to the present.

"I beg your forgiveness, sire."

He took a step closer. I thought he was going to strike me and I instinctively shied but didn't move. I'd learned that too—running only made it that much worse, once the soldiers caught me, and they *always* caught me… eventually, as in truth I had no place to run. I had no doubt Rasaben would catch me too—he certainly had all the advantages.

Instead he growled, "Lady Turan told me you told her you can read and write."

I hesitated, taken off guard by his abrupt change of subject; at least I could see no straight line from retching to reading. "Yes—"

"I find *that* very difficult to believe."

I grit my teeth. *I was reading a gods-damned manuscript when you interrupted me!* My legs suddenly began to shake—not from fear or rage but simply from standing and I think I must've gone quite pale as he stepped even closer, gave me a good look over and growled, "Sit down, *boy*, before you fall down and give Mabog more unwanted work."

"Thank you, sire." I reached back and found the arm of the chair by feel alone then I slowly eased myself down onto its padded seat and fixed my eyes on my knees.

"Look at me, *boy.*"

I did as he asked but kept my expression as bland as possible.

"You're *very* good at acting the part, aren't you?"

"Sire…?"

"The docile, obedient slave—you didn't rise to the rank of centurion at such a young age by being timid, soft-spoken and submissive, did you?" He snorted. *"I think not!"*

"How would you prefer I act, sire?"

He smiled, not a friendly smile, his expression an all too eerie look-alike to Gracchus's, chilling me to the marrow of my bones. The long dead Gracchus, the *murdered* Gracchus come back to life, staring out at me from Rasaben's angry, accusative blue eyes. "Given my druthers, I'd rather I'd never laid eyes on you if you want the truth, *boy*; I'd rather you were long dead and rotting in that bog along with the rest of your bloodthirsty kind. Know this: I absolutely hate what you represent and I'm not particularly fond of you, either."

I blinked, too late realizing my churning thoughts had made themselves visible—of course there was also the likelihood he could read my thoughts as easily as Turan—and since I'd committed myself, by thought and expression, I figured I might as well finish. In as calm a voice as I could muster, I replied, "Well, since we're speaking truthfully, *sire*, I'd prefer to be anywhere but here—and yes, that even includes rotting in that bog, just as you say—and as for hating what I represent, which is presumably Rome, then I make no apologies. And I don't know you well enough to have formed an opinion either way, but given a little time I'm sure I'll find more than enough reasons to loath you, too… *sire."* Damned if I won't.

He chuckled, clearly surprised, almost pleased by my response. Grabbing another chair, he drew it close and sat down. His intense blue eyes again settled on me, and for a moment he only stared, deliberately sizing me up, only to find me—no surprise here—clearly wanting. "You have no idea what our plans are for you, do you, *boy?"*

"Turan told me—"

"You mean *Lady* Turan, don't you? Remember your *place*, if nothing else—"

"I'm *not* a servant, sire. I'm a prisoner—"

"You're a *slave*, boy, bought and paid for!"

I squinted at him, visibly seething and by doing so I'd given him exactly what he wanted, short of my untimely and agonizingly painful death, that is.

He slowly eased back in his chair, crossed his arms and smiling, said, "Go on, *boy*, what did *Lady* Turan tell you?"

"She told me I was going to save humanity."

He stared at me for a moment then laughed, more a short, sharp bark, as if it had been startled out of him.

I eyed him as I wondered if perhaps Turan had told me that just to keep my mind busy, appeal to my obvious vanity and keep me distracted, and conceited fool that I was, I'd believed her.

"*You?* All by yourself? My, my. Aren't you are full—"

"*Arri...?*"

Rasaben glanced over his shoulder and I tore my gaze off him only to find Ainiaan standing in the doorway with Boian and Mabog behind her. A surge of relief washed over me.

"We've been looking all over for you!" Ainiaan hurried into the room and over to me, Mabog following, leaving Boian to remain at the doorway. Ainiaan grabbed my hand and gave it a smack. "You're very naughty leaving like that and not telling us where you were going!"

I flushed deeply at her demeaning rebuke. 'Boy' indeed—reduced to a child even in the eyes of a child.

"My apologies Lord Rasaben," Mabog began. "It's entirely my fault. I left to check on the selection of the proto—" he flicked me a sidelong look, then added hastily, "I must've lost track of time."

Rasaben shrugged off the apology. "It's quite all right, quite all right, Mabog. The young man went looking for Hanni and became lost—I was just about to escort him back to his quarters. Lady Ainiaan, since you're here, would you mind?"

Ainiaan turned to him and his cold expression instantly changed to a friendly, almost fatherly smile.

"Can I take him to Mugwort first? Mugwort's been *dying* to meet Arri."

"Of course, Lady Ainiaan, of course." Rasaben rose and looking back at me added, "we'll have plenty of time to talk later, yes?—perhaps you can even read something to me, boy?" He motioned to the wall of manuscripts. "I'm afraid I've been far too busy to master such... frivolous hobbies."

"As you wish, sire." *And if you ask really nicely, I might even write your dirge and read it aloud at your funeral—*

"Come along now." Ainiaan tugged at my hand and I lurched unsteadily to my feet. "Coming father?"

"I need to speak with Lord Rasaben—you go on, I'll meet up with you at the stable."

She interlaced her fingers with mine and guided me towards the door.

"But remember," Mabog said, following my awkward, limping progress with his concerned eyes, "Centurion Niger's still recuperating… don't wear him out, hear?"

"Yes, father," she sighed and gave my hand another impatient tug.

"And a word of caution, Centurion Niger," Rasaben added ominously, drawing my sidelong gaze along with Ainiaan's. "There are areas of this ancient Keep where one misstep could prove injurious, if not fatal for someone unfamiliar with its layout. From now on, only venture from your quarters in the company of someone who knows what pitfalls to avoid. *Understood?*"

"Understood… sire—"

"Come along." Ainiaan insistently pulled on my hand, drawing me out of the library and back into the hallway where Boian stood.

Boian, realizing just how wobbly I was, grabbed my other arm and the three of us started down the passageway—not that I was given any choice mind you—but once well away from the library, and beyond casual eavesdropping by Rasaben or Mabog, Ainiaan stopped and motioned for me to stoop down, then she whispered in my ear, "Promise me you'll stay away from Lord Rasaben. He can be very, very mean and I don't think he likes you at all."

I straightened up and glanced back the way we'd just come, then at Boian. The woman looked afraid—but not for herself. "You'd be very wise to listen to Lady Ainiaan, young sire. People Lord Rasaben dislikes have a tendency to go missing—"

"Promise?" Ainiaan interrupted angrily, jerking at my hand to draw my gaze back to her.

"Yes, m'lady, I promise."

"Good, now come along, Mugwort's very anxious to meet you."

I limped beside her, slowly, the best pace I could manage with Ainiaan's small fingers clutching mine, as Boian, her arm around my waist now, lent me more support. We walked past the room I'd spent the past six days— assuming it was six days—it could have been a month… or a year for all I knew, past more doors, then very slowly and carefully down a wide flight of stone stairs, Ainiaan leading, Boian holding tightly onto me, and then another hallway, which, I realized, looked vaguely familiar.

As we passed by a large, open doorway, a very familiar voice boomed from within: *"ARRI!"*

Startled, I turned to find Hanni rising from a large feasting table. Only then did I recognize the massive chamber beyond the doorway as the very place I'd made such a memorable first impression.

"Come, come!" He motioned to us.

I looked down at Ainiaan. "Think Mugwort would mind waiting just a little longer, m'lady?"

"I *suppose* not," she replied, clearly disappointed that the long anticipated meeting was going to be postponed, yet again.

Boian remained outside as Ainiaan and I entered the hall. Once it was obvious I was both stable enough to make it to the table and that we were in the company of an ogre and a very friendly ogre and therefore presumably in safe hands, she hurried away.

"Sit!" Hanni patted the chair next to him. *"Sit!"*

What could I do? I sat then nodded politely to the twenty or so soldiers clustered at the far end of the massive table. They wore ring-mail hauberks under their thick cloaks, and what looked like heavy leather trousers with above the knee boots. They also looked thoroughly chilled, with ruddy cheeks and hands.

The soldiers nodded civilly in return and in perfect unison, then silently returned to their meal. Not even the scrape of spoon against bowl.

Ainiaan took the seat to my right and grinned up at Hanni. "Doesn't Arri look handsome?" She startled me by touching my cheek. "So much better without all that nasty facial hair—" she glanced at the decidedly hirsute Hanni as she realized her gaffe and quickly amended, "—which looks really fine on some people, like Hanni, but it just didn't suit you."

I bit my lip.

If Hanni was offended, he certainly didn't show it. "What do you fancy?" He gestured to the well-provisioned table.

I wasn't particularly hungry, having polished off a bowl of porridge not all that long ago and my stomach was still recovering from its reaction to Rasaben's uncanny similarity to Gracchus. Rather than offend Hanni, and possibly my host—who already had a bad first impression of me I had no doubt—I looked around at the offerings.

"Maybe some rabbit stew?" Ainiaan suggested. "I heard the cooks mentioning that they were preparing some—"

"They've eaten it all," Hanni grumbled as he cast a sidelong and decidedly peeved look at the silent group at the opposite end of the table.

"Oh." Ainiaan got up and walked down the length of the table looking for another menu suggestion.

I leaned close to Hanni. "Who are they?" I whispered, my eyes darting to the men.

He grunted, *"Kellesuf."*

I raised my brows, not sure if he'd just stifled a sneeze, or... "I beg your pardon?"

*"Kellesuf—*that's what they're called. Rasaben's men." He stuffed his mouth with a haunch of meat the size of my forearm.

"Are they always so damned quiet?" I recalled their eerie silence on the beach, not to mention none had said a word upon our arrival at the Keep. The only time I'd ever seen soldiers this quiet while stuffing their faces was when said soldiers were the survivors of an ambush and now back in the safety of camp were tucking into their first decent meal in days. Having fought my way out of more than my fair share of ambushes, I can attest that such a harrowing experience has a stifling—albeit temporary—effect on conversation while leaving the appetite largely intact. "Can't they talk?"

"They can talk," he muffled through his impressive mouthful, "they just *don't.* Stay away from them, hear?"

I looked back at the soldiers and a cold shiver ran down my spine. There was something not right about them, in fact something very, *very* wrong, I just couldn't figure out what it was. And on top of this was the realization that my rapidly shrinking world was just as rapidly filling with people I was supposed to avoid at all costs and me without a serious clue as to why.

As I think I've mentioned before, I have a knack for pissing off people and in amazingly short order, but I usually know what I've done, or perhaps I might've even done something deliberately because they'd pissed me off first and I felt fair was fair, but so far, since arriving here, I hadn't done anything that I was aware of that could warrant such abhorrence—if you discount my now infamous vomit scene by the hearth, and that had been completely beyond my control. Had I been left alone as I'd hoped it never would have happened.

Noticing that Hanni was waiting for my answer, I murmured, "Of course," then I smiled feebly as Ainiaan placed a plate mounded with what looked to be slices of raw liver in front of me and was privately relieved when Hanni immediately grabbed several large, bleeding pieces.

"I brought some for *all* of us," she said with a pointed glance at him, but too late. He'd already stuffed the handful in his mouth and grabbed another, leaving only few scraps.

She glared at him and jerked the plate out of his easy reach. "Here, Arri."

I reluctantly took the smallest piece and managed to swallow it without chewing, figuring the sooner it was on its way the better. I wasn't a picky-eater, I'd just never been a fancier of liver, cooked or raw.

Fortunately, before Ainiaan could insist I take another piece, a commotion erupted in the outer hallway: loud voices, equally loud stamping of feet.

The soldiers rose as one, hands coming to rest on the grips of their sheathed swords, again in perfect unison and turned to the doorway. Watching them gave me the shivers all over again—it was as if they shared one mind.

A tall, gaunt man with a mane of white hair and a very impressive white mustache entered the Great Hall, slapping snow from his heavy, dark red cloak and fur-lined hood.

"Lord Taskim," Hanni whispered at my sidelong, questioning glance.

He was accompanied by four men and a blond woman I did not recognize, all dressed for cold weather and dusted in snow. Then Sifrie and Turan entered the hall, arm-in-arm with—of all people—Kyrou.

Kyrou chuckled out loud at something Turan said as he helped her out of her cloak then as he turned to help Sifrie, he spotted me and froze.

So, not surprisingly, Turan and Sifrie followed his startled, rapidly turning to incensed gaze. Sifrie responded with a decidedly pleased grin; Turan only stared. If she was happy to see me dressed in her livery and clearly on the mend, she did a superb job concealing it and I briefly wondered if I should have given the "in the buff" idea more thought. At the very least it would have garnered more than a grin from Sifrie and far more than an aggrieved glance from Kyrou.

Perhaps Turan was playing the role of aloof owner for the benefit of Taskim—I had no idea the social mores at play after all, and told myself it would be wise to follow her cue and go along with it—not that I had much choice. So I silently, dutifully and, admittedly rather unsteadily rose, thus acknowledging the presence of my owner and her host, while servants appeared from side doors to take the cloaks and offer mugs of warmed wine.

As Taskim accepted a steaming mug, he too happened to look my way.

I expected a cool, appraising stare—aside from Ainiaan and Boian I hadn't exactly met a warm welcome from anyone—but he surprised me when he reacted with a startled but nevertheless delighted smile.

"Lord Taskim, permit me to formally introduce you to..." Turan hesitated, as if her tongue was caught up on exactly what to call me— Prisoner? Slave? Master vomiter?

Given my druthers, I'd have opted for the last. At least it held the slim promise of better prospects.

"...to Arrius Marcus Niger, until very recently Hastatus-Posterior, Centurion of the Fifth Century, First Cohort of the Ninth Legion Hispana of the Empire of Rome."

I forced myself not to visibly react to the full and yes, utterly unnecessary recitation of my former rank and title, while out of the corner of my eye, I saw the soldiers all fix their strangely detached eyes on me as if seeing me for who I really was, and then again in perfect unison, each tipped his head to me.

If it had been their intention to show me—or at least my former rank— proper deference, they utterly failed. I was left feeling even more unsettled.

Sensing this, Ainiaan gave my hand a squeeze.

"Centurion Niger," Turan continued, her formal tone drawing my uneasy gaze off the soldiers, "this is Taskim, Chosen Guardian of the Southern Lands, First Lord of the Sidhe... *and* your host."

Host? Do prisoners or slaves have hosts? I thought captor, owner or prospective buyer were the only possible options—and oh, yes, how could I forget?—executioner.

With the short introductions over, I knew what was expected of me, or, should I say, I suspected what was expected of me as I'd never been in this exact position before, of prisoner/slave meeting lord of the Keep: I was to walk over to Taskim, drop to my right knee and bow my head, an ancient and common ritual of yielding to a greater power. I'd done it a hundred times, for the benefit of kings, queens and tribal chieftains—even superior officers I'd somehow, don't ask me how, managed to infuriate and was hoping by showing proper obsequiousness I could avoid a severe flogging—so I wasn't all that worried about walking, or even dropping to my right knee. I had those moves down pat. It was the getting back up that had me seriously concerned. It was my right knee that would be on the ground after all; meaning I was going to have to use my left leg to get myself back up and I seriously doubted it was up to the challenge.

Nevertheless I walked, albeit a bit wobbly. I knelt, I bowed my head— all perfectly executed if I say so myself—like a trained dog, I added with a sidelong glance at Turan only to find her pointedly looking the other way—whispering something to a broadly grinning Kyrou in fact.

Taskim placed his hand on my head, jerking my attention back to the business at—*ahem*—hand, saying in a voice loud enough for everyone in the hall to hear, "Welcome Centurion Niger," then, after an awkward pause, he whispered softly, *"Son, do you need help rising?"*

I lifted my gaze and smiling feebly, nodded, "Yes, sire." I was damned if I was going to try and fall flat on my ass—or worse, stumble forward and knock my host on *his* ass.

I assumed he would motion to any one of the nearby servants to assist me—or, Furies forbid, Kyrou, or even worse one of the soldiers—but instead he offered me his hand.

I grasped it and he helped me back to my feet, his grip surprisingly strong for a man of his advanced years. He kept his hold until he was certain I was stable then he gave me a friendly pat on the back. I must say this was not the reception I'd expected, which left me somewhat unbalanced in other ways.

With the formalities over, Sifrie and Kyrou made their excuses and joined the rest of the hunting party by the crackling fire. Turan however remained standing beside Taskim, sipping on her mug of wine.

I fixed her with a bewildered stare, hoping she'd do or say *something*. Her expression remained remote.

"Are you feeling better?" Taskim looked me over while voicing the same question I'd already been asked several times. He said it with what sounded like genuine concern for my welfare.

"Yes, much, thank you, my lord—and I do sincerely apologize for what happened that first day—"

"You have nothing to apologize for, Centurion," he again patted me on the shoulder. "It is I who should apologize to you. I should have had you seen by Mabog the moment you arrived."

I stared at him, taken aback by the novel experience of someone actually *apologizing* for my continued mistreatment—and, even more shocking, sounding like he actually *meant* it.

"Now, Lady Turan tells me you can read and write Greek and Latin and that you speak a number of barbarian languages fluently?"

The moment of pleased surprise vanished, replaced in a heartbeat by angry bitterness. *Like Massaesyli?* My eyes darted to Turan, hoping she'd take the hint and read my thoughts. *My, you certainly don't waste any time bragging about the surprising skills of your slave, do you? While you're at it, do you have a ball I can fetch? Prove to everyone I'm truly no better than a trained dog?*

I looked back at Taskim, replied stiffly, "Yes, sire," and braced myself for a reaction in keeping with Rasaben's—or Turan's for that matter—in other words, unabashed incredulity that a lowly Roman soldier was actually literate—unlike the *illiterate* Rasaben... and perhaps even Turan?

Come to think of it, I'd never thought to ask *her* if she could read and write. *But I will, m'lady, given the first chance—*

"Wonderful!" Taskim said, clapping me on the back. "I have this damnedable Greek manuscript, you see—I've been having a devil of a time translating it—can't make heads or tails out of most of it to be honest. Turi," he turned to her, "may I borrow him?"

"Of course, whenever you wish, sire—"

"Wonderful, wonderful!" He grabbed my arm, started towards the table, taking me with him and leaving Turan to follow and find her own place. "Come, Centurion... I want to know everything about you."

I really wanted to be angry at this man, wanted Turan to know just how angry I was at being treated like some sort of exotic curiosity—*look at the Roman who can read and write!*—like... *chattel.* But in truth there was no point being angry. I *was* an exotic curiosity. I *was* Roman—well, to be totally accurate I wasn't Roman, but rather a Roman legionary and adopted citizen—and I could read and write. And in Taskim's eyes I was at best a prisoner, a captive, at worst a slave and if you looked at it like that, he was actually treating me extremely well. So I lost the indignant attitude and replied with a self-effacing, "There's not much to tell—"

"I don't believe that for a moment! You're a centurion after all, and an extremely young one to boot—" He stopped, gave me another appraising look. "How old are you, anyway?"

I almost expected him to say, 'boy' but he didn't. "Twenty eight—"

"Twenty eight and already Hastatus-Posterior of the First Cohort?"

I started to reply, but before I could, he again started for the table with me still in his firm grip and stumbling alongside.

"Impressive—*very* impressive indeed. I understand you've been as far as Parthia? What's it like? I've heard Parthians are expert horsemen."

"Yes, they—"

"Have you ever met an Amazon? Fought them?"

"Uh... no, not that I know of—"

"I'm told they come from Scythia—you must've at least seen some, surely."

"I might have, I'm not—"

"Have you seen an elephant? I've always wanted to see one."

"Yes—"

"Really? How simply amazing!"

Actually, more like fucking terrifying.

"You must tell me all about them—what are they like in war?"

I hesitated. When I realized he was actually waiting for me to answer, I replied, "There's not much to say except they like to squash people, and they're very good at it, too." I didn't say exactly how I knew this.

He burst into laughter, which irked me. Then as everyone who'd been seated at the table rose, he released his hold on me, said, *"Sit, sit!"* and seated himself at the head of the table. The closest unoccupied seat was the one immediately to his right—an honor in any society. Having learned not to presume anything, I looked around for another empty chair.

"Do you need help?"

I glanced back at him. "Sire?"

"Do you need help sitting down?"

"No sire, I—"

"Then please sit." He pointed to the chair next to his, leaving no room for doubt.

I sat, then glanced around, expecting hostile stares from the rest as they resumed their seats. If anyone was offended, they didn't show it.

Servants arrived, placed platters of food within our reach and filled our mugs with wine.

Taskim picked up his mug, took a gulp and in between mouthfuls of food launched into another volley of questions ranging from Greek philosophers to what I thought of Sophene cavalry tactics to who made the best wine—Greeks or Romans?

"Romans, of course," I replied, adding, "but I've heard Pompeiian wine, while sweet, is said to give one a terrible hangover even in moderation."

He laughed, said he'd take my warning seriously if he ever found himself in position to test it, and then, when he discovered I'd not only been to Egypt, but had lived in Alexandria for several years, he started another round of rapid-fire questions about Egyptian culture and religion and could I read their picture-writing and had I ever seen their war chariots in action.

In case you're wondering, yes, I had. On a dare I even rode in one—briefly, until we hit an unseen bump at full speed and I went flying. Needless to say, I was drunk at the time and myself and another equally drunk legionary—Carbo was his name—had 'borrowed' the chariot and its rather flighty team from their rightful owner. Neither of us had had any experience driving a chariot, which was the rationale we used, later, to explain the extensive damages, to the chariot, not to mention to us—not that it spared us from having our pay docked to make restitution. To add insult to injury, we also had to spend several days standing guard in the blazing Egyptian sun outside a latrine and wearing unbelted tunics, suffering the suggestive remarks, leering looks and taunting whistles from our fellow legionaries.

Amazingly, despite this unfortunate incident very early in our careers, Carbo went on to be a much admired and highly decorated *ballistarii*, commanding a unit of artillery under the command of Julius Fabius Tamphilus and gleefully wreaking havoc among the Parthians, while I excelled in the infantry—also gleefully wreaking havoc among the Parthians... until they got tired of it and began wreaking havoc among our ranks by bringing out their game-changer: a half dozen or so war elephants. It wasn't until later that I learned a badly wounded and enraged elephant had stomped Carbo and most of his engine crew to death, then smashed the machine to bits before it too died in a hail of pila and arrows.

I was extremely hard pressed to keep up with Taskim's questioning as he rarely gave me a chance to finish a thought, much less chance a sip of wine to moisten my mouth before he pressed on—and it didn't take long before I began to feel decidedly lightheaded, dizzy in the smothering warmth of the nearby fire and the potent mixture of smells, of rich and unfamiliar food, and wood smoke that left my throat raw. And of course there was that damnedable liver, which felt as if it had returned to life in my stomach. My hands, which I'd folded on my lap, began to shake and I gripped my trousers, hoping to stop the tremors.

Taskim suddenly stopped talking and peered at my face. "Where's Mabog?" He looked around, fixed his eyes on a nearby servant. "Fetch Mabog!"

The man hurried away as Taskim turned back to me and firmly grasped my shoulder. "Are you in pain? Do you need something to drink or maybe to eat?" He looked up again and servants, who'd been hovering around, scampered off to grab whatever they could.

Before I could answer, Turan, who was seated directly across from me, replied dryly, "I believe you've exhausted him, my lord."

He looked back at me, startled and genuinely appalled. "Truly?"

"I'm fine, sire," I replied hoarsely, "just tired, nothing more." In truth I dearly hoped I wasn't going to pass out, not in front of Ainiaan, who had, yet again, come to my aid and now stood just behind me. I'd seriously frightened her once already; I didn't have a mind to do it again, but I was beginning to suspect I might not be in a position to make that choice: I felt clammy all over—my heart raced, and most telling of all, my vision grayed around the edges. *Oh... no, please... no.*

I blinked madly, hoping that would keep me from creating yet another unforgettable scene—I had visions of me slumping forward and falling face first into the plate of food in front of me—*splat*. Oh yes, now that would be the ticket to everlasting fame.

Taskim grasped my chin in his hand and eyed me—I fully expected to hear an unspoken, *Listen to me.* Instead he said aloud, "Yes, yes, you're clearly in need of your bed." He released my chin. "Hanni... would you mind helping our young friend here?"

"I'm going too." Ainiaan's small fingers clamped down on my shoulder as if to assert ownership, or at least conservatorship over me, along with my convalescence.

"Of course, of course." Taskim rose then murmured something in Hanni's ear, to which the ogre nodded.

Hanni helped me back to my feet then cupped my elbow in his large palm, providing discreet support while Ainiaan clutched my other hand and guided me around the table. I risked a quick sidelong look at Turan, only to find her watching the goings on as if as if nothing was amiss. Then I happened to catch Taskim looking at me and realized he'd seen my furtive, almost beseeching glance.

"Rest well, Centurion—we'll continue this discussion tomorrow, once you've had a good night's sleep."

I gave Turan one last bemused look. With Hanni and Ainiaan's help I managed to reach the doorway, and then the hallway beyond without tripping over my own suddenly leaden feet, but my vision was blurring and my knees were wobbling.

Ainiaan waited until we were out of view of those in the Great Hall then gave Hanni a nod and he immediately scooped me up in his arms, which briefly sent my mind spinning anew. Under other circumstances I would have loudly protested being carried, but as it was I just mumbled my half-hearted objections.

I closed my eyes, let my head tip forward as Hanni followed Ainiaan up the massive staircase. I assumed we were returning to the room in which I'd awakened only a few hours before, but as I felt myself being placed on soft, cool bedding, I opened my eyes and look around.

I was in a cloth mosaic-lined room, larger and far more luxurious than my previous lodgings, with a small fireplace in one corner, several chairs and a large glass-paned window—beyond a few bright stars twinkled in a cloud-smeared twilight sky. I squinted up at Hanni, who now towered over me.

"Lord Taskim's private guest quarters," he replied to my unspoken question.

"I don't think I'm supposed to be here." I tried to get up.

He pushed me back down, using one gnarled finger to do the job. "Yes. You are."

"But—"

"Can you just for once accept someone's generosity without complaint?"

I opened my mouth to reply but was cut off by a knock at the door, followed by Mabog stepping into the room. "I understand my advice was ignored."

"It wasn't Arri's fault," Ainiaan replied defensively, "Lord Taskim—"

"I know." He sat down next to my hip, pressed his palm to my forehead, felt my pulse then slipping his hand up under my tunic, gently pressed on my belly and I couldn't help but wince, more in surprise than pain.

Seemingly satisfied, he rose from the bed. "No harm done—*this* time." With that, he shook his head then walked out of the room.

Hanni shut and locked the door behind him, then he and Ainiaan each took to tugging off a boot. I was greatly relieved when they stopped there—while the room was toasty warm, I had no desire to be stripped naked in front of Ainiaan.

Instead she drew a heavy blanket over me then mimicking her father, pressed one small hand against my forehead while the other felt for a pulse in my wrist, taking her role as nursemaid to yet another stray *very* seriously. While I found it rather embarrassing to admit it, if only to myself, I found that very comforting—as comforting as Hanni's presence. "How am I doing?" I asked, my throat tight and raw from the combination of wood smoke and answering Taskim's non-stop questions.

"You're not feverish," she replied, lifting her palm from my forehead. "Pulse is a little fast, but that's to be expected—you mustn't push yourself, Arri, or you risk a serious setback."

"Yes, m'lady."

"You just need a good, solid night's sleep then you should be almost as good as new. And if you do exactly as I tell you, you should be well enough by week's end that I might—*might* even let you ride Mugwort."

I managed a feeble smile. "Something to look forward to then."

"I'm making no promises," she replied with all seriousness. "We'll have to wait and see how you progress."

"Understood," I murmured as she tucked the covers around me.

Hanni shook his head, then picked up the sturdy dressing bench at the foot of the bed, carried it over to the crackling fire and set it down next to the hearth. With a weary sigh, he dropped heavily onto it. For a second I feared the bench might collapse under his very substantial weight, but it held fast.

I felt a pang of guilt that he was always being tasked to be my protector, but at the same time, I did feel better with him nearby.

Ainiaan drew a chair close to the bed, grabbed a blanket and made herself comfortable. Then taking my hand in hers, she leaned close, kissed me on the forehead and whispered, "Now, go to sleep."

And funny thing, I didn't have to be told twice.

XVI

I didn't sleep well that night—Tumhabi was right, the barracks was uncomfortably hot and the bunk was hard, barely more than a thin pallet of straw over slat-boards and just high enough off the ground to dissuade scorpions, snakes and other nightly visitors from paying the sleeper unwelcome calls.

The next morning I bathed, dressed and after being told that the commander was expected back around mid-day, I decided rather than spend the morning pacing back and forth in the small garden, I'd return to the tavern for a morning meal and emboldened by the very uneventful evening before, perhaps even do a little exploring and be back in plenty of time to deliver my long delayed message to the officer. Tumhabi had told me the tavern served a hearty breakfast—far better than what was offered by the barracks cooks and for very little money, which, considering my very modest means, suited me just fine.

An hour later I was seated at the same table as the night before, gazing out at the passersby and waiting for my meal of unleavened bread, fish-pickle and porridge. The sense of foreboding that had dogged me the previous day had left, gone, thankfully, to worry someone else. I felt, if not completely at ease in my surroundings, then at least far less anxious.

Then I heard a voice—more a drunken bellow demanding the serving woman bring wine. My stomach heaved over then clenched tight.

It was an all too familiar voice, a voice I thought I'd never hear again and I very slowly, cautiously glanced over my shoulder to find Gracchus standing nearby. I stared at him in unabashed, wide-eyed shock.

He had aged and had grown quite fat, but it was undeniably Gracchus—his was a voice I would never forget.

I immediately looked away and as I struggled to get my panicky breathing and racing heart under control, I analyzed my startling reactions. Here was the very person I'd spent over half my life searching for, the person who, at least in part, was the reason I'd joined the army, the person I'd spent countless lonely nights fantasizing about, creating elaborate scenarios about our long-awaited reunion, of his joyous reaction at seeing me, of him wrapping his thickset arms around me in his bear-like hug and telling me how much he'd missed me, how much he'd regretted leaving me behind, that he'd had no choice in the matter.

And now, a chance meeting in a tiny tavern in a fetid quarter of a squalid backwater city had sent me into a blind panic? It was absurd!

I rationalized it was because fantasy and reality didn't quite match—I'd never pictured Gracchus as old and fat. I'd never pictured him as a balding, pot-bellied retiree, running a ramshackle tavern and cut-rate bordello that catered to the local soldiery.

That was it—I was just taken aback. I'd been silly, assuming he would always look the same, be the same—almost nine years had passed, after all. And look how much I'd changed—which meant he probably wouldn't immediately recognize me.

That alone made me rethink my earlier panic.

Take your time, I told myself. No need to rush. And finally, as my heart began to settle: savor the anticipation—you've certainly earned it.

Yes, I assured myself, nodding as the serving woman placed my meal in front of me, and with a visibly shaky hand, I managed to bring a piece of bread to my mouth.

As I chewed without tasting the food, I found myself revisiting those childhood desires. As I did so, long-forgotten memories flooded back, as clear as if they'd happened just yesterday: of Gracchus tossing me into the air only to catch me to my loud squeals of delight, of him patiently showing me how to properly polish band-armor without leaving any telltale scratches, of him lifting me up so I could pluck a ripe fig from a high branch, of him helping me pick scarce wildflowers to place on my mother's grave...

I was only minimally aware that the tavern had emptied of customers, but when the serving woman stopped to ask if there was anything else she could get for me, I reluctantly drew myself out of my memories, shook my head and handed her a coin that would more than cover my meal.

She smiled, patted me on the shoulder and, taking the hint, left me to finish undisturbed.

I took another bite, chewed and swallowed, then glanced over my shoulder to find Gracchus seated on a bench, clutching a mug in one hand. As I watched, he belched explosively, then brought the mug to his lips and loudly gulped down what remained.

While it was a far cry from the meeting that I'd envisioned as a child, all that mattered was that I'd finally found him, found my surrogate father, no matter his flaws, now or then.

I looked around. The woman was now standing out on the street, broom in hand, arguing loudly with another woman. The tavern itself was empty, save for Gracchus and myself—as good a time as any.

I took a deep breath, gathered myself, rose and walked to the back of the tavern, to where Gracchus sat then I stopped and crossing my arms, smiled down at him. "Gracchus?"

After a moment of staring dully at my sandaled feet, he slowly lifted his blood-shot gaze to meet mine and in an irritable and slurred voice, asked, "Whaaadooooyouwaaaant?"

"Remember me?"

He squinted then shook his head, "Caaaan't ssssay ah ddddoooo." He motioned dismissively with one hand, the gesture turning into a brief, albeit wild flailing as he came close to losing his balance, "Now gooooawaay—"

"Arri, remember?" I replied and waited for his startled reaction—his sudden recollection.

Instead he belched again, and brought the mug up to his lips, too late remembering it was empty. Watching him, I realized he didn't *recognize me—moreover he didn't even remember me. Me—the child, Arri, the boy he claimed he loved like a son. The child who adored him, who trusted him—*

He grunted and threw the mug aside. Then as he rose, he roughly shoved me away as if I were no one, as if I was nothing... just as he'd done that fateful morning so many years before. As I stumbled back, almost falling to my knees in the process, something inside of me snapped.

Suddenly my dagger was in my hand and before he could react, before he could scream, I stabbed him, and kept stabbing him until my arm gave out and he fell, lifeless, to the floor.

I stood there, gasping, clutching the gore-covered dagger and staring down at him, numb and shaking, then, overhearing a muffled gasp, I turned to find a young girl standing nearby, staring at me in horror, which, as I watched, rapidly turned to fury. She flew at me, scratching and screaming, her enraged cries drawing the serving woman from outside.

The woman snatched up a filthy gutting knife and lunged at me and as I stumbled back, tripping over Gracchus' body, the girl tried to wrest my dagger away from me. As we struggled the woman bring the knife up; an instant later I felt it plunge into my left side, felt pain and the warm wash of blood over my hip—it focused my mind and I jerked the dagger free of the girl's grasp then slashed out at my attackers. With a surprised grunt, the girl fell, sprawling across Gracchus, her throat laid open.

Heaving for breath, I lifted my blood-blurry gaze to the woman.

She glanced down at the girl, then at me. Then without making a sound she turned and fled. Once out onto the street she began screaming.

My only hope was to get back to the garrison—I knew there was another door as I'd seen several customers come from the back of the tavern and leave by the same route. Gripping the dagger that was still wedged in my flank, I fled.

The next thing I knew I was staggering down a narrow alley and from there I somehow managed to find my way back to the garrison, which fortunately wasn't far.

I must've looked like death as I stumbled up to the guards—one, thankfully, was Tumhabi. He didn't recognize me at first and drew his sword, then as I collapsed, he realized who I was and began yelling for help.

I awoke from a sound sleep—startled awake in fact—by loud voices—angry voices. But part of me knew I wasn't really awake, that I was dreaming—why? Because the voices were those of Felix, Rufinius and Aetius and they were arguing. Actually, it was just Felix and Aetius arguing, with Rufinius happily tossing the occasional bit of verbal kindling into what was clearly a roaring fire.

Aetius and Felix had argued a lot, mostly about politics and religion, rarely about the more prosaic matters favored by soldiers, like food—or the lack there of—sore feet, the latest 'cure' for crotch itch, the miserable weather and of course, ungrateful superior officers. They could argue for hours about some minute and, I have to say, rather inane point of philosophy, which I readily admit was lost on me, and then without pausing for breath switch to something less philosophical and more pragmatic, such as the origin of bugs—a favorite topic of debate, one they returned to time and time again, and one that often drew a crowd to listen.

Aetius had always been of the mind that bugs were the result of a drunken wager between gods as to whom could devise the most ubiquitous and annoying creature—mice, in case you were wondering, came in a distant second and snakes an even more remote third. Felix preferred the proposition that bugs were an intentional and clear-minded creation, a perpetual and humbling reminder that man was not the master of his world, as many might suppose.

Aetius was from Judea, a baker's son who had longed for something better, something more glamorous than baking bread. His father had been a legionary and he'd grown up listening to epic tales of serving the empire, just as I'd spent my early childhood listening to the soldiers' equally heroic and largely fabricated stories of daring do. He desperately wanted to be like his father, just as I wanted to be like the soldiers. And for Aetius, as a citizen and a son of a citizen, it was his obligation to serve.

He'd spent most of his early military career in some of the more exotic eastern cities of the empire, serving in his father's former unit, where he was exposed to equally exotic ideas—and, presumably, some *very* exotic bugs. One of his favorite pastimes was telling fresh-faced recruits in incredibly gruesome detail about each and every bite and sting he'd suffered, in the process putting a whole new spin on the term "green troops". And if he sensed he wasn't believed or was extremely drunk, he'd even expose some of the more shockingly disfiguring results, always good for a few astonished gasps and sympathetic winces, even from hard-bitten—so to speak—veterans like me.

He also had the look of a man who'd known great suffering: no matter how hard he tried—how hard Felix and I worked on his appearance—he always had the bruised and rumpled look of someone who'd spent far too much time scraping his hands and knees on the coarser surfaces of life.

Black-haired, black-eyed and pale-skinned Rufinius was a puzzle—a puzzle who clearly delighted in being a puzzle. No one knew for certain from where he came and he wasn't of a mind to tell anyone—not even drop a hint or two. His accent was certainly no clue, neither was his appearance as both were an amalgam of everything and everyone around him. He looked and sounded completely ordinary—*too* ordinary; any personal questions were adroitly deflected with a casual shrug or a self-effacing, albeit fleeting smile, as if his origins were simply of no importance. But if someone dared to push, they'd get a stare that could freeze the hottest blood.

Rufinius spoke very little, while his skill as an all-around soldier spoke volumes. He was in many ways the personification of the ideal Roman legionary: laconic, fierce and unyielding, willing to do what needed to be done without serious question or lingering complaint. One could not have asked for a better subordinate—he could have easily attained the rank of centurion, had he had any desire.

Of course, rumors abounded about his background. Many believed him to be an escaped slave or a former prisoner of war who'd falsified his citizenship—not an easy thing to do—reasons repeatedly put forth by others to explain his apparent lack of ambition, which in a perverse way actually bolstered the glossed over half-truths I'd created about my own background: orphaned son of a legionary and adopted brother of none other than Lucius Antonius Vallus.

No one ever doubted my tale because I, unlike Rufinius, *was* ambitious—extremely ambitious and no one with a questionable past would be so bold. And by the time I began to draw attention of those jealous of my accomplishments, anyone who could have disputed my story was well-past questioning.

So, while it was no surprise Aetius and Felix were arguing with Rufinius playing referee as well as provocateur, it was impossible. They were all dead—had been dead for weeks now. Hanni had told me, had promised me such. And not just that, but the dream, let's call it that for lack of a better description—rang hollow. I had no memory of what they were squabbling over and yet I was clearly in the midst of it—as I always seemed to be. Each in turn asked my opinion, hoping I, as their centurion, would take sides or that my response would sway one or the other.

Even more perplexing was that our surroundings were all wrong. We were clearly in Egypt—in an open-air, seaside hostelry favored by the troops of the Alexandria Garrison to be precise—celebrating my rise to the rank of Hastatus-Posterior, centurion of the fifth century, first cohort.

I'd struck up a friendship with Aetius a year or so *after* I'd left Egypt, and after I found myself in the middle of a brawl *he'd* started with some locals. When I stepped in to help a fellow legionary in trouble—it was five against one after all—I wrongly assumed he was the victim rather than the instigator. Not that it mattered once the first punch struck my jaw. No, no. No one does that to me—I don't give a damn how big or how tough he thinks he is. He's going *down* and staying there. If my notoriously wicked left hook hasn't entirely knocked the sense out of him, it would be followed by a right uppercut that has never failed to finish the job.

I soon found that Aetius was always in the thick of it, be fighting, brawling or whoring. With Aetius you were always in for a wild time not to mention a few loose teeth.

I met and quickly became fast friends with Felix while in Dacia; I was not yet a centurion, only later attaining the rank of Decimus-Hastatus-Posterior after distinguishing myself in battle and he became my *optio* as I couldn't imagine anyone better prepared to take over my century if I was killed or disabled in combat.

And it was about this time that I also named Aetius my *tesserarius* and he demonstrated great skill at the task. Rufinius joined our tight knit group much later—during my first, and thankfully only winter in Germania.

None of them had ever been to Egypt. I knew that with absolute certainty—even Rufinius had once admitted he'd never set foot there, one of the very few details of his previous and shadowy life he'd admitted to.

It's just a dream—dreams don't have to make sense.

"Who says?" Aetius replied, turning to me, thick arms akimbo, bulbous blue eyes askance.

"And who says we aren't making sense?" Felix added, favoring me with one of his arched stares. "I think we're making perfect sense." He turned to the other two and they nodded their vigorous agreement.

"You're the one who's confused, Centurion," Rufinius said irritably.

"Be quiet—you're all dead."

"Am not!" Aetius replied, suitably offended.

"Are so—now shut the hell up and let me sleep," I grumbled, knowing I was actually talking to myself, talking to ghosts, to my personal host of Lemures.

That set them off muttering softly amongst themselves, eyes darting occasionally in my general direction.

I ignored their chary looks, just as I'd done a hundred times before, by burying my face in the crook of my arm. I took a deep breath and savoring the warmth of the fire, the softness of the bedding, relaxed.

Later, much later I awoke as I felt something small alight on my left shoulder. At the time I was flat on my belly, head still cradled in the crook of my right arm, my left arm dangling off the bed, knuckles resting loosely on the floor. I waited a moment, allowing my mind to find itself then I slowly and cautiously opened my left eye.

The fire had been reduced to a glowing bed of coals and the shifting light conjured up more ghosts from the surrounding dark. For a moment I thought I was still held in the dream and fully expected to hear Felix or Aetius softly grumble some disparaging remark as one bent over me, hand on my shoulder, perhaps trying to wake me after I'd passed out from too much carousing. I wouldn't have been at all surprised to see Rufinius adding wood to the fire—like me he never liked the cold.

Then I realized that what at first I'd though was a human hand on my shoulder, the friendly grasp of one of my companions, was in fact Ainiaan's damned fox. It sat on my shoulder, staring at me, its tiny black nose no more than a few scant finger-spans from the tip of mine.

I puffed my breath into its face; it immediately jumped off the bed and ducked underneath.

I sighed and smacked my lips, stretched languidly, then settled back down, but just as I started to fall back asleep I felt it jump back onto the bed. I waited, expecting it to resume its previous perch on my shoulder, but it instead curled up between my knees. I thought seriously about kicking it off, then thought better of it and left it alone, hoping by doing so it would afford me the same courtesy.

Sometime after that I was, yet again, nudged out of sleep—this time by a soft but insistent knocking at the door.

I peered into the darkness—now the only light came from the window, and scant little of that, just enough that I could make out Hanni's shadowy bulk, still slumped by the fireplace.

I lifted my head and looked around—Ainiaan was curled up in the chair next to me and a small furry ball, which I assumed was the fox, was now at the foot of the bed.

The knock came again, a little louder.

Muttering softly about uninvited foxes, inconsiderate ghosts and who knows who else bothering me every few minutes and how was a man to get the promised good night's sleep under these conditions, I carefully eased myself out from under the blankets and dropped my bare feet to the floor. With some effort, I rose, stiffly, stretched and giving my sleep rumpled tunic and trousers a tug here and a yank there I shuffled, barefoot, over to the door.

I thought it would be one of the servants come to rekindle the fire, or Mabog, so when I unlocked and opened the door I was startled to find Turan haloed against the flickering torchlight of the passageway. I raked my hair out of my eyes, managed a sleep-hoarse, "Lady Turan...?"

She put her finger to her lips then motioned for me to step into the hallway. I did so, closing the door softly behind me.

She looked me up and down, then reached out and ran her fingers lightly over the embroidered serpent emblazoned on the tunic.

I stared down at her, not at all sure what was she was doing here, what she wanted, especially after the chilly reception I'd received the evening before. In truth I wanted nothing more than to crawl back into the warmth of my bed—I had no desire to sort out the issues I had with her and she with me at this ungodly hour. In fact, I had no desire to sort them out at *any* hour. I'd learned the hard way that it was best to keep our relationship as simple as possible: owner and owned.

She lifted her gaze, met mine. "I wanted to check on you, see if you were feeling any better."

"I was asleep." I pointedly rubbed my gritty eyes with my knuckles, but I'd no sooner dropped my hands away than she began to caress my chin. Startled, I reflexively jerked my head away.

She deftly concealed the not completely unintentional rebuff by again touching the design on my tunic. "Do you like your livery?"

"I... I hadn't given it much thought—"

She suddenly pinned me against the door, wrapped one arm around my neck and as she roughly kissed me, she also began to fondle me.

I didn't pull away, I let her do what she wanted, and quickly realizing I wasn't responding in kind she stopped and looked up at me, her eyes glistening. *"What's wrong? Why are you behaving like this?"*

I blinked, genuinely baffled, not to mention still very much half-asleep. "You must tell me ahead of time how you want me to behave, m'lady—I'm only following your last order, which was to never touch you without your permission."

She stepped back, her expression hardening. "Attend me." With that, she turned and walked away.

I squinted blearily, muttered, *"So much for returning to bed,"* and trudged sullenly after her, knuckling my gritty eyes as I did so. The flagstone floor was ice cold, it made my bare feet throb, and the hallway wasn't much warmer. By the time she stopped at another door, the cold had seeped up my legs, my hips and spine and I was shivering and was reduced to rubbing my arms vigorously to keep my teeth from chattering.

She pointedly waited for me to open the door for her, which I did. She walked past me, into the darkness and I followed.

"Shut the door."

I did as I was told. It took my eyes a moment to adjust to the faint light cast by another small fireplace then I looked around. It was another apartment—Turan's, obviously, huge and richly appointed, with double, lead-paned glass doors leading out onto a large balcony. Beyond starlight glittered on freshly fallen snow, leaving me feeling even colder.

"Come here." She sat down on the bed.

I didn't have to guess what she wanted, why she'd brought me here, so I did as she ordered and settled beside her. It was, after all, part of my expected duties, the only one, in fact, that I was certain about.

For a moment we sat there, side by side, in very awkward silence.

Finally she turned to me and said, "I've missed you terribly, Arri."

"You concealed it well."

She smiled, briefly, and combed her fingers through my sleep-disheveled hair. "I was *very* angry with you."

"Was? You mean you aren't any longer? You could've fooled me last evening."

"You would have me show my true feelings towards you in front of Lord Taskim?"

"You could have at least given me a hint." I tapped the side of my head. "Sent me a clue."

"Can you forgive me?" Not waiting for my answer—in truth not needing my forgiveness—she kissed me on the cheek then lightly grasping my chin, turned my face towards her so she could kiss me on the lips. I responded just enough she felt encouraged and she murmured, "Lie down."

Again, I did as I was told and at her insistent tugging on my thigh, I spread my legs and she eagerly caressed me.

After a few minutes, she got back to her feet and beckoned for me to do likewise. I stood and without being asked, pulled off the tunic. She ran her hands over my bare chest, my flanks and grinning, she unlaced my trousers and they fell around my ankles. She fondled me gently, and as my body reacted, her eyes searched mine, looking for passion to match hers.

It wasn't there.

It wasn't a matter of forgiving her; in truth I wasn't sure I could as her premeditated cruelty that last night on the *Sulaviae* had cut clean to the bone, and her continued spitefulness had added salt to the gaping wound, but it didn't matter. She owned me after all and could make any physical demand of me she wished and at any time—if I refused she always had the option of wiping my mind clean and having me anyway.

But I also knew what I was feeling—or, more accurately *wasn't* feeling went beyond what she'd done, far beyond... all the way back to my childhood.

I'd always separated emotional love from physical gratification—I'd never *felt* passionate love for anyone, not that that had ever stopped me from *making* passionate love. And I had no doubt I could do it again and satisfy both Turan's physical needs and yes, my own, but as I stared down at her and saw the look of intense, raw yearning in her eyes, I realized she had opened herself up to me, leaving herself vulnerable on every level, trusting me not to hurt her—something no one had ever done for me.

I searched my mind—suddenly suspicious I had company in my internal conversation, that she was manipulating my thoughts, only to find I was completely alone. With that potent realization came another: physical gratification was no longer enough. I wanted more—I wanted her to see in my eyes what I saw so clearly in hers.

I *wanted* to love her, wanted it with all my heart. I just... *couldn't*, I wasn't capable, at least not without her help. I lightly stroked her face, her hair. *"Make me love you,"* I whispered hoarsely, *"I beg you."*

Her eyes widened and she abruptly stepped back, away from my touch as if burned, reacting to my words, not the utter desperation behind them. In that instant I knew I'd just destroyed the one thing I'd frantically searched for all of my life, the one thing I hadn't known I wanted until now, when it was snatched from my grasp by my own horrible choice of words.

I fell to my knees, doubled over and clutching my arms began to shiver uncontrollably, chilled by awful realization that I was about to be abandoned *again*—why not? I was worthless. I've always been worthless and no amount of effort on my part, no single-minded drive to be the best of the best would *ever* change that. I was a whore's unwelcome and despised issue, a whore myself—something to be used by my betters then cast aside when they tired of me, just as Gracchus had done—

I flinched violently as I felt her arms around me and as she knelt and drew me close I wrapped my arms tightly around her, holding onto her as if she was life itself.

She stroked my hair, murmured, "Arri, what am I to do with you?"

I had no reply for that—all the possibilities terrified me.

"I could compel you love me—"

"Then do so—!"

269

She pressed her finger to my lips. "But deep down we'd both know your true feelings—"

"I have no feelings, don't you understand?" I pushed myself out of her embrace and rocked back on my heels. *"I can't love you—can't love anyone!"*

"Yes, you can." She ran her finger along my jaw. "It's not that you *can't* love. You can't *trust*—which, considering everything you've gone through in your life is completely understandable." She looked away briefly then again met my watery gaze. "I certainly haven't helped in that regard, have I?"

I swallowed, hard, replied huskily, "Then make me trust you."

She gently wiped my damp cheek. "I can't do that, either."

"Can't? You mean won't!"

"I stand corrected."

"You think this is a game—another game of semantics?"

"No. I'm willing to wait as long as it takes, willing to give you all the time you need in order to trust me completely—on *your* terms, not ones I impose on you."

"Why?" I was genuinely bewildered—no one had ever asked me to trust them, never told me they would give me all the time I needed to feel comfortable with trusting them—no one, not even Lady Ilissia, had ever cared enough.

"You have your answer."

I looked away and took a deep, ragged breath.

"I want you to love me, Arri, every bit as much as I love you. But I want that love to be of your own free will not because I've compelled you, even if you're the one asking me to do just that."

I squeezed my eyes shut, whispered, *"I'm sorry."*

She again drew me against her. I buried my face in her shoulder, in her soft, silky hair as she stroked my bare, goose-pimpled back. "I know you can do this."

I wanted to believe her but she was asking something of me no one had ever asked of me; she was asking something of me I'd never even dared ask myself. I couldn't help but shiver again.

"Come to bed—you're getting chilled." She released her hold, got back to her feet and offered me her hands.

I looked up at her.

"Come along now."

I grasped her hands, lurched unsteadily to my feet and with her help managed to free my ankles from my trousers.

She gave me a lingering look and I found myself incredibly pleased that she liked what she saw. I was, admittedly, a retched mess inside, but fortunately I was damned good looking on the outside.

"Indeed you are," she murmured as she lightly touched me. It sent a jolting shiver through me.

I jerked her against me and began tugging at the lacings of her nightgown.

She watched my futile struggle with an unfamiliar knot. "I think it best if we didn't—not tonight."

I looked up just long enough to say, "You mean you don't want to?" before resuming my frantic efforts.

"That's not what I said. What I meant was you don't have to—"

"I *want* to," I replied, and I did, truly, if only to lose myself in something familiar, something I knew I was capable of doing and doing very well. "How the hell does this untie?" I gave the lacing a frustrated yank.

She pushed my fingers aside. "Keep that up and we'll have to cut this gown off."

I glanced around. "Where's a knife?"

She chuckled, "Not necessary." With a gentle tug, the lacings came undone.

I stared. "How'd you do that?"

"Here," she grabbed the lacings, "Let me show you."

Now it was my turn to grab her hands and pull them away. "Not now—later. Much, *much* later."

She giggled and with my eager assistance, stepped out of her gown then as I lifted the bedcovers, she slipped underneath. I followed and as I pulled the blankets over us, she wrapped herself around me and ran her hand over my belly. "You're healing remarkably quickly—Mabog will be pleased."

"To hell with Mabog," I muttered and pushed her onto her back.

— ii —

Hearing a deafening roar, I tore my appalled gaze off the last of our fleeing officers and wheeled around only to confront a nightmare: scores of barbarians spilled from the cover of the surrounding forest, spears raised, swords slicing the air. As I stared in horror at their massed charge, I found that everything had strangely slowed to a crawl, in the process drawing out greater and greater details—horrifically gruesome details of what was going to be a wholesale slaughter of my century—possibly the entire cohort.

We were outnumbered more than ten, twenty to one. With Cerialis and his officers taking with them any chance of an organized retreat it was every man for himself as their panicked flight had scattered us across the boggy meadow, breaking our formation and leaving everyone exposed.

I bellowed orders to regroup but it was too late.

I stumbled back and felt my left foot sink deeply in the freezing muck. I desperately struggled to free myself, but before I could, I was surrounded by Iceni. They hurled jeers and taunts at me as each took his turn thrusting his spear at me while keeping well out of range of my sword.

I somehow managed to pull my foot free then I lunged at the closest, hoping to break their encircling line. The man deftly jumped aside, not weighed down with armor as I was, smashing his puny shield against me. As I tried to recover my footing, another struck me with his spear—the tip barely penetrated my ring-mail but the force of impact sent me reeling sideways, the heavy spear shaft catching on the clumps of marsh grass, unbalancing me further.

Another man, seeing his opening, slashed out with his sword—slicing though my thigh; my knee gave out and I fell, my own weight doing what the spearman had failed to do: forcing the tip deeply into my flesh, shattering my collar bone.

Groaning in agony, I struggled to pull the spear free, but it was stuck fast, the butt end now buried in the muck. I lifted my gaze, hoping for rescue, hoping one of my men could come to my aid as I had hoped to come to theirs. Instead I witnessed Duccius and several others who'd been likewise surrounded being hacked to pieces. I screamed and tried to get back to my feet but my left leg refused to support me and I fell back to my knees, driving the spear tip in even deeper.

Laboring for breath, unable to rise, unable to do anything, I was forced to watch as Aetius, snarling and swinging his fists, was buried under mass of half-naked, sword wielding bodies, his enraged voice suddenly cut off by the sickening chorus of multiple sword stabs into flesh.

Rufinius gave as good as he got, bellowing obscenities until an axe cleanly separated his helmeted head from the rest of him. Felix tried to reach drier ground, only to get mired down and impaled on a spear, his body writhing and twitching until an Iceni sword finished the job.

I opened my mouth to scream—but no sound came out; all I could hear was my awful wet breathing, my heart thudding rapidly in my ears. Then I saw a flash of movement out of the corner of my eye, saw something swinging towards my head, tried to duck and felt my head snap back accompanied by blinding pain and—

"Arri, wake up!"

My eyes snapped open. For a moment I couldn't move. My entire body was clenched tight like a fist, waiting for the agony to hit—

"Arri… it was a *dream*. You were dreaming."

I jerked my eyes towards the voice, saw a woman's face, her very worried features visible in the shifting glow of firelight.

I swallowed convulsively, managed a very husky, *"Turan…?"*

"Yes, it's me." She very cautiously placed her hand on my heaving chest. "You were having a bad dream."

I wasn't sure I believed her, even though I really, really wanted to.

She smiled, touched my cheek. "Do you know where you are?"

I glanced around. My surroundings didn't immediately look familiar, but I was definitely not in that accursed bog.

I shook my head, licked my dry lips and managed a very unsteady, *"N-nnn-no."*

"You're in my bed, in my chambers, in Lord Taskim's Keep. Remember?"

I looked around again, still heaving for breath.

"It was *just* a dream." She leaned down, kissed me on the forehead.

I grabbed her, pulled her down on top of me and held her tightly as I continued to gulp hungrily for air.

"It's all right," she soothed, "you're safe. You were just having a really bad dream."

I squeezed my eyes shut, concentrated on slowing my panicky breathing, my pounding heart. Only then did I realize I was drenched in sweat.

I took a deep breath, held it, then shivering, exhaled slowly.

"Better?"

I wasn't, damned if I was, but at least I knew I wasn't where I thought I was. I released my grip on her and she eased herself down next to me then draped her arm across my chest and her leg across my hips.

I looked to the window and was startled to find that it was still dark outside. The deep rosy glow of the coal bed bathed the room with enough light to reassure myself that I was in fact where she said I was—that I *had* been dreaming.

She lightly stroked my clammy cheek and murmured, "Who's Felix?"

I glanced at her and my heart, which had only just started to settle, started thumping wildly again. *"What?"*

"Who's Felix? You kept yelling his name."

"Were you eavesdropping on my dream?" I was suddenly angry, furious that I couldn't keep anything private, not even my dreams, as horrible as they were.

"I didn't have much choice. I was sound asleep too—until I found myself tangled up in what you were reliving—Arri, it was horrendous. *What you went through...*" She bit her lip, blinked back tears. "I kept trying to wake you." She waited a moment then prompted gently, "So who is he?"

"You mean who *was* he—he *was* a close friend," I replied tightly.

"And Aetius, Rufinius?"

"Same."

"I'm so, *so* sorry." She lightly caressed my chin. "You miss them terribly, don't you? Ainiaan said—"

"I don't want to talk about it anymore." I rolled out from under her embrace and onto my side, away from her questions and fixed my watery gaze on what lay beyond the leaded glass doors. It looked like it was snowing and I couldn't help but grimace.

"All right. We won't talk about it now."

I took another deep, ragged breath, exhaled. *We won't talk about it, ever.*

She tried to help me relax by massaging the tense muscles of my back, then she leaned close, murmured in my ear, "Do you think you can get back to sleep?"

"I'm not sure." Actually, there was no doubt. I knew I couldn't—or, should I say, I was afraid to even try. The lingering nightmare images, the dreadful sounds and nauseating stink of that now far-away battle kept prodding at me, just as the encircling Iceni had done with their spears, probing for weakness, causing my body to twitch reflexively, robbing me of any hope, any desire for sleep, knowing they would grow into things even more frightening if I relaxed my guard.

"Want me to help?"

I wasn't in the mood if it was sex she was after; however she did have the ability to send me into a deep, dreamless sleep—she'd done it before. I carefully rolled onto my back, hoping she was offering the latter, but fully aware that she could ask—could demand the former. If she did, then at least it would get my mind, at least temporarily, off the awful memories of seeing my friends die so horribly as I watched, helpless.

She levered herself up onto an elbow, looked down at me and smiling, ran her fingers across my forehead and down my cheek as she murmured, *"Go to sleep...."*

— iii —

I awoke enveloped in Turan's warm embrace, my cheek on her breast and this time with the sun well up in a thick, overcast sky. I lifted my head and peered muzzily at her.

She gave my hair a gentle tousling and murmured, "I was beginning to wonder if you'd sleep the day away."

I yawned and stretched.

"No more bad dreams?"

I stared at her, not sure what she meant, then I remembered. "No," I mumbled—at least none that I could recall, but there was this odd, tickly feeling in the back of my mind, as if someone had been there, wandering around, poking in dark corners and leaving things disturbed, searching for something—

"Good."

I shook off the sense of unease, chalking it up to the lingering effects of the dream itself, rubbed my eyes with my knuckles—and had a sudden, horrible thought: "Ainiaan—"

"Don't worry—she knows where you are."

I wasn't sure I wanted to know how she knew, so of course Turan answered my unspoken question. "When she discovered you were gone and awoke Hanni, he reasonably suspected you were with me, so they came here, first—she even thought to bring your boots."

I groaned and buried my face in the bedding.

She patted my back. "Ainiaan's a lot more worldly than you think. She's frequently walked in on Sifrie and whoever's the latest to catch her eye. I doubt seeing you naked even gave her pause—"

"She saw me naked?" I muffled, appalled, my face still pressed into the bed.

"Not completely. Just your backside." She gave it a commiserating goose.

I groaned again.

"Had I known she was just going to burst in like that, I'd have thought to cover you up but they caught me in the act of admiring the view."

I again lifted my head and squinted at her. "Is there anyone here who *hasn't* seen me naked?"

She thought about it—a wee bit too long for my comfort. "Rasaben—oh, no wait. He did."

My eyes got very round.

"Taskim. Yes," she nodded, "definitely Taskim."

"Definitely... *what?*"

"*Hasn't* seen you naked."

I dropped my face back into the bed.

She ran her hand down the length of my spine and up over the rise of my buttocks. "Why the sudden modesty?" she asked as her fingers began to explore.

"I was never asked if I wanted to be seen naked, if you remember—I just... *was.*"

"Oh, yes, quite. Well, you certainly have *nothing* to be shy about."

"That's *not* the damned point," I muttered as I rolled onto my back, careful not to pin her hand as I got an elbow under me. For once I was not in the mood to go where her fingers were headed.

"Hungry?" she replied, looking a little disappointed.

I thought about it for a moment. "A little." I rose, stretched my stiff muscles then helped her to her feet.

"I'm extremely relieved to hear it—" she looked me up and down, "—you need to start putting back the weight you've lost and Taskim makes sure his banquet table is always well stocked—has to be with Rasaben's men coming and going all hours of the day and night."

I don't know why, but suddenly an image popped into my head of me standing naked in front of a group of those eerily silent soldiers and a shiver ran down my spine. "Can I get dressed first?"

She chuckled, "That's completely up to you."

As I bent over to snatch up my discarded tunic and trousers from the flagstone floor, she took the opportunity give my unguarded backside another goosing.

When I flicked her an aggrieved, over the shoulder look as I straightened up, she shrugged as if that was apology enough.

I squinted at her then held my trousers and tunic close to the fire before I dared pull them on.

A few minutes later, and now fully attired in my livery, I turned to find Turan in the process of getting dressed, then I heard a high-pitched squeal from outside. Curious, I stepped close to the balcony's lead-paned doors and peered out at the wintry landscape and spotted Ainiaan and Hanni running around in freshly fallen snow, the two chasing what I had to assume was the infamous steed Mugwort around the courtyard below.

The pony was fatter and shorter than I could have imagined. He looked like a large brown and white dog—a *very* fat dog—in fact I would have assumed he *was* a large fat dog except he was bedecked in a bright red saddle and bridle. And lo and behold, dashing here and there between the galloping hooves and darting feet was a small reddish brown speck—Badger.

As I watched Ainiaan running after her pony, I caught myself smiling and wishing I was down there with her, sharing the fun of the chase. Then, without warning, I recalled Turan telling Rasaben that she was with child—*my child*. Which meant...

"Why did you choose me?" I asked softly, my narrowed eyes fixed on Ainiaan's every move.

Turan walked over to me and slipped her arm around my waist. "Sifrie told you—we'd watched you for days, knew you were the one—" She glanced up at my face as she realized I hadn't meant that at all. "Oh... *Arri.*" She winced and hugged me tightly.

"Why?" I asked again, hoarsely, as I kept my intense stare glued on the frantic game of chase on beyond the leaded panes, hoping by doing so, I could keep the true depth of my feelings suppressed. There was no need to add to Turan's hurt—what was done was done.

"I didn't."

I couldn't help but look down at her, unable contain my sudden rage at the thought that someone else—who else but Rasaben—had made the choice for her. *"He forced you...?"*

She tugged on my lower lip and smiled. "I'm still with child—*our* child."

I blinked. I didn't know what to say but a soft, deflated, *"Oh,"* as the rage left me just as abruptly.

"Ras never asked again—he'd overstepped himself, knew he couldn't force the issue, so wisely just let it drop."

I tentatively placed my hand on her belly. I would be the first to admit I knew very little about the inner workings of women, but somewhere along the line I'd come to believe women were never sure they were with child until they were at least a month or two along. Assuming I hadn't been misled about how much time had elapsed since that ill-fated day in the bog—and granted, that was a big assumption—I figured I'd known Turan for barely three weeks, so how—

"I'm a sorceress, remember?" she replied to my unspoken question. "I knew immediately, or should I say I was absolutely sure within an hour of conceiving."

"Oh." It wasn't the most original response, but it seemed the only suitable one.

"Are you upset? Happy? Not sure?"

I thought about it, answered honestly, "Not sure."

She ran her finger down my jaw, again tugged at my lip. "I didn't do this to entrap you, Arri."

I couldn't help but laugh at that. "Well, it's not like I can say, 'You're great in bed but now I've got you pregnant I think I'll take my leave,' never to be seen again?—you own me, remember? I don't think I'm going anywhere."

"I must correct that—as soon as I can. And I *will*, I promise you—unless of course you'd prefer to wait for Ainiaan to come of age."

I fixed her with a bewildered stare.

Turan smiled and toyed with a lock of my hair. "She told Boian and Hanni she's going to marry you the moment she's old enough."

I blinked then replied perhaps a bit too hastily, "I didn't do anything to encourage her!"

She laughed at that. "I never once thought you did. But understand, when Ainiaan sets her mind on something, it's very hard to dissuade her."

"Oh."

"I thought you'd be flattered."

"That a little girl wants to marry me?"

"Not just any little girl, but *Lady* Ainiaan."

"Yes, that makes all the difference." Then: "Does her father know?"

"That she plans on marrying you? Yes, in fact she asked him to purchase you so that he could then free you when she comes of age, so you would then be free to marry her—she even offered up Mugwort as a deposit of sorts."

"Oh." I shifted my gaze back to the goings on outside and reminded myself again never to be alone with her.

"You needn't worry," she continued, running her fingers through my hair, "Ainiaan would never falsely accuse you of anything."

In my experience a woman rebuffed is a woman capable of anything—and while I'd never been in a situation to test my theory, I felt it safe to assume the same was true of young, very headstrong girls. But the price of rebuffing a woman was still a sore point, at least with me, and, I assumed with Turan, so instead I said, "But others would." I flicked her a sidelong glance. "Chief among them, your brother—I'm sure he'd just love to concoct some story about me molesting her as justification for having me drawn and quartered."

"True. Which is why you're much safer if you remain 'my property' for now, at least as far as everyone else is concerned, which is why I told Ainiaan that you aren't—"

"For sale?" I interrupted with audible bitterness.

She sighed, nodded, then lightly grasping my arm. "But when it's just the two of us, I want no talk of owner and owned, understand? I love you—" She put her fingers to my lips, silencing me before I could speak, "—and it's my hope that eventually you'll feel the same way about me. If that never happens, then so be it, but no matter what, I won't force you to be involved with the child, understand?"

"You're saying I can sire a child by you, then have nothing to do with it?"

"If that's what you want—this was my decision, Arri, admittedly a very selfish decision."

"But why me? You must have men falling all over you, offering their hand in marriage, powerful men, men who could give you everything you could ever want in trade for an heir."

"I wanted you—the moment I saw you, that very first time, I knew you were, in more ways than one, the *one*." She lightly rapped her knuckles against the side of my head. "*Brains*, Arri—that's why. But it's more than just intelligence, more than that truly astonishing memory of yours. You think like no other man I've ever met—you see the world like no other, not in black and white, or even shades of gray, but in every imaginable color, every conceivable hue—does that make sense?"

"Not really—"

"I found myself lusting after your body that first night, filthy and delirious as you were at the time—I mean, I knew you were smart, knew you had an amazing memory—that's why we rescued you after all—and knew you had a fine face to match your mind, knew you had very nice knees," she wiggled her brows. "But your armor isn't exactly the most... um, revealing."

"You *do* understand the purpose of armor, don't you?"

"Of course," she nodded. "And your armor *is* very handsome—"

"It's supposed to *protect* the wearer," I added, mildly peeved. "Not attract the opposite sex." Granted, even I knew it did both, but that was not the point.

Undeterred, she continued, "I didn't know until that night that you had an equally fine body." She dropped her gaze, grinned, then again meeting my eyes added, "I was quite irked when I discovered that Sifrie had had you, *first*, you know—"

Another loud squeal from outside drew our gazes and I couldn't help but chuckle as Hanni made a lunge for the bolting Mugwort, the pony's stubby legs and tiny hooves surprisingly nimble in the snow. Hanni was not quite so nimble: he badly misjudged both Mugwort's speed and trajectory.

279

With no pony waiting at the end of his lunge, he drove his head and shoulders into a snow bank.

"I watched you with Ainiaan that first day," Turan continued. "We all did, saw how kind and patient you were despite how terribly sick you were—and you're surprised she's besotted with you? She has no friends her own age, only Hanni and Boian, her sister's too busy bedding every man she can find and her father... well, to be kind Mabog is not very attentive—far too preoccupied with his work. You, on the other hand, were a novelty at first, someone she could dote on—"

"Another stray you mean."

She acknowledged that with a slight shrug. *"Yes.* You, in return have been attentive and respectful—in a word, courtly. You don't dismiss her as a child, you treat her as an equal—"

"But she's not my equal—she's *Lady* Ainiaan as you said, and I'm... a—" I almost said 'prisoner', but with all this talk of owning and owned, of being purchased, first with a measly few coins and now Ainiaan offering up a grossly overweight and badly behaved pony as a down payment, it was time to face facts, *"—a slave."*

She winced. "As far as everyone else is concerned... *yes,"* she sighed. "But I don't see you as a slave and I never will."

Really? Could have fooled me. I tried to keep that sulky thought to myself by again fixing my eyes and my attention on the goings on within the courtyard; after a few minutes I found myself grinning again at Hanni's increasingly desperate attempts to capture Mugwort. The pony definitely had the edge when it came to maneuverability.

Turan seemed willing to go along, to drop the matter—or so I thought.

She suddenly tightened her embrace. "You'll be a wonderful father—"

I squeezed my eyes shut and grit my teeth.

She immediately released her hold, murmured, "I'm sorry, I shouldn't have said that," and stepped back.

I remained where I was, in front of the window. I didn't love Turan—I wasn't sure I'd ever love her. Doubted I was capable. *Trust,* she'd said. Once I learned to trust, then I'd be able to love someone—love *her.*

She deserved better than that—she certainly deserved far better than me. She'd once called me a bastard, and I was—a selfish, self-centered bastard and for most my life I was fine with that, one might even say I was proud of it, but now I was suddenly very afraid that that was all I'd ever be.

I took a deep, ragged breath and opened my eyes. Ainiaan, with Hanni's help, had finally cornered Mugwort, or maybe the pony had just tired of the game and was ready to return to the warmth of the stable.

If it was just that easy... I shook my head, unwilling to concede the similarities between my life and that of a rotund pony. I turned to an even more pressing issue: *I'm going to be a father.*

While I had no doubt I'd fathered more than a few children in my life—in fact had pointedly avoided thinking about it, not wanting to draw any unwelcome comparisons between myself and my own absent sire—I'd never been confronted with the reality. And now that I was, I found it to be such an odd, almost bizarre concept—*me*, a father, someone who had no idea what a real father was.

Silva had probably been the closest to a father figure; he was certainly the most stable male role model I'd had up to that point in my life, but even he, eventually, discarded me, like all the rest. Maybe that was it— maybe I'd been right so many, many years ago as I watched the soldiers, watched Gracchus march off without looking back. Maybe I'd been the problem all along—

"Arri...?"

I turned to find Turan now standing by the open door.

She smiled, a sweet, kind smile and I had to wonder how, with all of her abilities, how she could be so utterly blind to ugliness that lived inside of me—how she could possibly love me.

She held her hand out for me. "Didn't you say you were hungry?"

— XVII —

I remember nothing of the trip down the Nile from Oxyrhynchus to Alexandria. Tumhabi accompanied me, or so I was later told, along with Pasham and three other Nubian axillaries along with the commander's personal physician. I'd been delirious the entire time, had in fact almost died en route from the stab wound to my hip which had become badly infected.

Silva visited my sickbed every day, brought me a few simple tasks to do—make-work really, told me that Vallus himself had even visited me in the company of his mother, Lady Ilissia, but I was in the throes of a fever and didn't recognize either.

There were times I'd awaken to find Silva seated beside my bed, sound asleep, a stack of reports held loosely on his lap or scattered on the floor at his feet.

As soon as I was able to get out of bed on my own, I began to nag and plead with Silva and the garrison physicians to let me return to work. Finally they relented, albeit reluctantly, and released me to a limited work schedule with the agreement that I would return to the infirmary each night. I knew I was being extended unusual latitude in my recovery and while I should've gratefully accepted this curious privilege, I quickly came to resent it. I repeatedly pressed for a heavier workload, to be allowed to return to my bunk in the immunes's barracks. When my requests were continually denied without explanation and furious at what I perceived as pity—an affront to any decent legionary—I angrily confronted Silva.

He countered that what I saw as an insult was in fact an honor: that despite my injuries, I'd still managed to deliver the secret communiqué, and as a result a detachment of Roman soldiers—including the very military commander who'd kept me waiting—had later avoided being killed in an ambush.

I had no memory of the mission, based my assumptions on others' third-hand accounts—and I believed what I was told by one of my physicians, a Greek by the name of Iulius, that I'd been the victim of a simple but very vicious mugging. But no sooner had I satisfied everyone that I was well enough to return to a full workload not to mention my bunk in the barracks than the dreams began, conjured up from long-buried childhood memories—shaking me out of sound sleeps.

To keep the nightmares at bay I started keeping long hours—longer even than before I'd been dispatched to Oxyrhynchus—often sleeping in snatches at my desk, which soon extended to sleeping in the office. At the same time I began to pointedly avoid others, I exercised on my own, often in the full heat of midday just to guarantee my solitude and almost to the point of collapse; I sought the comforts of the baths only when I knew there was little chance of finding myself with unwanted company. I rarely spoke to others, even to Silva, and only when directly spoken to. I never smiled; I ate—when I bothered to eat—by myself, and took to talking aloud to myself, oblivious to the sidelong stares of my fellows and their worried whispers.

About a month and a half after my return to work I was startled awake by a particularly vivid and terrifying nightmare, an adult's recollection of a deeply suppressed childhood trauma: of being raped by Gracchus—an event I'd long before convinced myself never happened, or so I thought. Even as I sat there, trembling, I desperately denied it, tried to convince myself it was nothing more than a result of working too hard, not eating enough—the same excuses I'd used before, to explain away the increasingly disturbing nature of my dreams and the same reasons Iulius had voiced on the rare times I'd sought him out, or, more commonly, when he'd come to me, warned by others of my increasingly odd behavior.

But this time I was so unnerved the ready-made excuses failed utterly.

I gathered myself up with the intention of finishing some work but found the desk's lamp had burned itself empty of oil while I'd slept. It had happened before, countless times, but this time I flew into a rage, hurled the lamp at the wall then I shoved the desk, toppling it and sending its contents flying.

I stood there, shaking uncontrollably—murderously angry and at the same time terrified by appalling intensity of my fury, so I decided to go to the exercise yard, work off my temper and violent shakes by working up a sweat in the chill of the night.

I returned to the office shortly before sunrise, exhausted, sweat-soaked and shivering, only to find Silva already at his desk. Even more worrisome, he was not alone. A soldier I'd never seen before was seated at my desk—my desk!—now righted and everything back as it should be. Even the smashed lamp had been cleaned up.

I stopped, stared incensed at the interloper, then at Silva.

He rose, told me to accompany him in a tone of voice that precluded argument. Then he walked into the small courtyard. I followed, but not before flicking the man seated at my desk a deliberately murderous stare—which prompted him into a frenzy of feigned activity.

Silva strode over to the stone bench beside the fountain and sat. It was a common place to go when discretion was a must: the loud splashing of water made eavesdropping on whispered conversations difficult without detection—even Vallus's private office was rumored to be little better than the floor of the senate in Rome herself when it came to secret discussions.

At his grim-faced urging, I very reluctantly settled beside him then fixed my furious gaze on my knees, awaiting a proper apology.

Instead he said he no choice but to replace me, permanently—*my absolute worst fears realized—that I'd become careless, forgetful, that I'd fouled up several important contracts simply by failing to act on them. He said he blamed himself first and foremost. He said he should have remained steadfast in refusing my demands to return to work when I was far from fully recovered—he said he should've gone along with the physicians, Iulius chief among them, who'd recommended a longer convalescence, possibly even a permanent transfer, or worse, to be discharged as unfit.*

He said his failure to do what they'd urged was purely an act of selfishness, that he'd come to rely too heavily on me and was, in truth, as eager for me to return to work as I was.

As he spoke, as his uncompromising and painfully frank words filled my ears, the rage slowly bled out of me. There was no point arguing with him, pleading with him to give me another chance. What he'd said was true: for inexplicable reasons I was no longer able to perform even the simplest of tasks.

I heaved a sigh and looked up at the dawn sky, which was now a brilliant rosy pink streaked with pale yellow clouds only to find my gaze blurring.

He grasped my shoulder—I couldn't help but jump—squeezed it tightly and leaning close, told me he knew all about Gracchus, that he'd patched it together from the dribbles of news from Oxyrhynchus and my own feverish ramblings.

Gracchus? I asked, bewildered, unable to find any connection between Gracchus and my mission to Oxyrhynchus, and at the same time panicked by the underlying tone in his voice and the odd look in his eye.

He looked around; satisfied we were alone, he whispered that he'd patiently waited for me to voluntarily confess, to explain myself, and if I had, then he would have done what he could to help. Confess to what? I interrupted, my earlier rage resurfacing, wondering what concocted charge had been leveled against me by those jealous of my position, of my rapid rise to an immune, and yes, of my relationship with Silva, not to mention Vallus. It had happened before, but each time I'd seen it coming and was able to defend myself, or better, turn the tables on my detractors. But of late I'd been too preoccupied to notice anything, least of all a trumped-up accusation that had, in my distraction, plenty time to gain traction—

To murdering Gracchus, he replied softly.

I stared at him in open-mouthed shock. I'd murdered *Gracchus? I didn't believe it! I wouldn't believe it! Silva was wrong—Gracchus had been like a father to me; I'd spent my life searching for him—*

At that instant that it struck me like a thunderbolt: I abhorred Gracchus, abhorred him all along, abhorred him more than Porsenna, more than anyone, for his betrayal, for him handing me over to Porsenna and the others to brutalize, to brutalize himself, not once, but repeatedly, for destroying the child... for refusing to acknowledge the monster he'd created.

I hadn't been searching for him for almost a decade, I realized in that moment of absolute and astonishing clarity, I'd been hunting *him so I could finally prove to myself that despite what he'd done to me, what everyone else had done, I'd survived—instead I murdered in cold-blood a defenseless old drunkard, too intoxicated to recognize anyone...*

I looked sidelong at Silva, managed a quick nod, silent acknowledgement of my guilt and was surprised and yes, intensely relieved when he didn't ask why as I had no ready deception to explain my inexplicable actions. As far as Silva was concerned, I'd murdered my own father—by all accounts a popular and respected veteran.

I braced myself, thinking he was going to tell me I was under arrest.

Instead he told me this was as good a time as any for me to leave his employ—he warned me that one of Vallus's more cutthroat tribunes, Celsianus, a man who'd never spared the chance to make my life hell after I'd rebuffed his advances had been overheard asking questions, clearly suspicious. Silva said it was only a matter of time before Celsianus put the pieces together just as he had done and demand suitable punishment. If that happened, it could reflect very badly on Lady Ilissia. I was her adopted son, he reminded me—as if I needed reminding—and the timing couldn't be worse, he continued. She was preparing to return to Rome within the week and everyone knew that in Rome any scandal could and probably would be blown far out of proportion—I didn't want that, did I?

Of course not! I replied and meant it.

It had the potential for leaving an indelible mark on Vallus's career as well, he told me, not to mention his own, especially if anyone implied he and Vallus had known of my crime and had willingly conspired to conceal it, and he knew I wouldn't want that either, that I would never want my actions to harm those who had helped me, which was also true.

He went on to say that I was far too gifted to end my life chained to an oar or worse, and even if I was spared that, even if Celsianus' suspicions eventually came to naught, I was too bright to remain a garrison officer's clerk and so, effectively immediately, I was being transferred—that he'd arranged everything, in fact had all the paperwork approved the week before. He'd even worded it so that it appeared as if the transfer had been at my request—it was better that way, he said, less suspicious, as everyone knew I was ambitious.

He told me it would be good for me, good for my career, good for all involved—a chance to put some welcome distance between recent events and myself.

I'd heard the likes before, many times and in all manner of forms—I'd failed to please and because of my failure I was being cast aside—and as I stared at him, unable to think of anything to say in my defense, I felt that all too familiar bitter taste of abandonment well up from my gut.

Silva smiled tightly, gave my shoulder another squeeze and said he envied me because I was going to be part of an historic undertaking, that I would see wonders no Roman had ever seen before.

He then got back to his feet and told me I'd better return to the barracks to gather my belongings and to write a note to Lady Ilissia, thanking her for her kindness and her generosity, because by nightfall I, along with a large detachment of the legion would be marching our way south, to the Kingdom of Kush and the ancient city of Meroë and from there to Adulis, of the Empire of Aksum, and I should expect to be gone for at least a year, if not two.

I was stunned—I'd be leaving within a few hours? I'd be leaving everything I'd known, everyone I'd known with barely time to pack?

Such was the life of a legionary, he reminded me. Did I expect it to be different for me? He then assured me that when I returned to Alexandria, if I still wished to be his aide, he could take my request seriously.

I knew he was lying—I suspect he knew I knew it; still I managed to nod, silently accepting his decision while acknowledging his empty promise. Little did I know that I would never see Silva again, never see Alexandria or Lady Ilissia again, and that the wonders of Meroë and Adulis would pale in comparison to what followed; that his words were prophetic indeed, that I would indeed see wonders no Roman had ever seen before—and live to tell about it.

I stared down at the clean plate, startled and rather embarrassed that I'd wolfed down everything—not even a crumb was left. Beside me, Turan smiled and gave my thigh a squeeze, immensely pleased by my effort.

A servant approached, offered me more venison, more bread… more food than I'd seen in months—rich food, not the usual fare of a legionary, and I reminded myself I wasn't marching twenty miles a day with full kit anymore and if I didn't start getting some exercise, I'd get as fat as Mugwort.

Turan leaned close and whispered in my ear, "Don't worry, I'm sure we'll find ways to keep you in good form." She slipped her hand between my legs and got a firm hold.

Under other circumstances this maneuver wouldn't have particularly bothered me, in fact I might have actually encouraged what she was doing as she had very skillful hands, but we weren't alone at the end of the huge table and my startled intake of breath hardly went unnoticed.

Hanni and Ainiaan were seated directly across from us, and Sifrie, Jaro and two of Turan's men were seated on either side of them, so I had quite an audience.

I couldn't help but flush deeply at their pointed stares—clearly everyone, including Ainiaan—had a very good idea where Turan's hand was and what it was doing. Ainiaan, thankfully, didn't seem particularly put out by Turan taking such liberties with her future husband. Perhaps she was even hoping Turan would get me properly broken in prior to our nuptials…

Fortunately, Taskim chose that moment to enter the Great Hall, along with Rasaben, Perus and a number of soldiers and everyone turned their attention on them, including, I'm relieved to say, Turan.

As Taskim's met mine, he grinned and strode towards the table as I, now free of Turan's grasp, hurriedly pushed myself to my feet, relieved that a platter stacked high with bread was placed in such a way as to conceal my lower half.

"Centurion Niger! How good to see you up and about!"

I flashed him a quick smile, painfully aware that Rasaben was right behind him with a far less pleased expression on his face. I dipped my head, murmured, "Thank you, Lord Taskim."

Jaro, who by now was also on his feet, stepped back, yielding his chair to Rasaben as another gave up his seat to Perus. Taskim seated himself in his customary place at the head of the table. Rasaben's grim-faced soldiers, thankfully, found seats at the far end of the table, which seemed to be their habitual place where they could eat in their equally habitual silence.

"Please, everyone, sit." Taskim said, then, "Feeling better today, Centurion?"

As I reseated myself I looked back at him and sensed he was deliberately trying to draw my uneasy stare away from the soldiers.

"Yes sire, thank you."

He glanced down at my seemingly clean plate. "Not hungry? Come, I'm sure we can find something to tempt your palate."

Before I could reply, tell him I'd found more than enough to tempt my palate—far too much in fact—he clapped his hands and several servants came running. Then he turned back to me. "My cooks can prepare anything you desire—venison pie, perhaps? Or would you prefer hare or pheasant? I think they might even be able to produce some passable roast boar stuffed with eggs and onions."

My expression must've given me away—this had been one of Lady Ilissia's favorites and it had quickly become one of mine, not that I'd had the chance to savor such a delicacy after leaving her household—because he nodded to the nearest servant, said, "The boar—and a mug of fresh goat's milk." He looked sidelong at me, brows raised. "Yes?"

At my startled nod he motioned to the servant and the woman hurried off. "I thought you might like that—" he favored Perus with a glance, adding, "—King Togidubnus had mentioned stuffed boar was a favorite among his Roman guests."

"In other words," Turan whispered in my ear, "he had it specially prepared for you."

I wasn't sure what to say. It wasn't just the boar that was stuffed. I couldn't eat another bite, but I also didn't want to offend him by begging off, especially since he'd had the dish made just for me—*a prisoner*—and I hadn't tasted fresh goat's milk since our cohort had left Lindum on our way to teach those damnable Iceni a lesson they wouldn't soon forget. Even so I wasn't sure I could drink more than a sip or two. Fortunately for me, I was spared this awkward situation by being immediately thrust into another.

"Did he sleep well?" Taskim asked, directing his question not to Hanni or Ainiaan, but to Turan.

"Once I left him alone, yes." She flicked a challenging glance at Rasaben.

I stared at her wide-eyed as Taskim replied, "Leave it to a woman to know the perfect cure for what ails a man!" He slapped his hands on the table and roared with laughter, several others, including Hanni, Jaro, Sifrie, Perus and Turan, even Ainiaan joining in—but *not* Rasaben.

I sat there, face burning, not sure what to say or do. I mean, I'd already done it and Turan had said so. Which didn't leave much else.

The servant finally returned, accompanied by several others laden with platters of food for the new arrivals setting them on the table in front of us and providing a much-needed diversion. As I glanced up from my intense examination of the large slice of stuffed and roasted boar in front of me I noticed Rasaben staring at me as a cat would at a cornered mouse.

I did what any mouse would do: I returned to my single-minded study of the food in front of me. The cooks had gone all out; pity I had no appetite.

Taskim, Hanni and Ainiaan had fallen into an animated discussion about ponies and were blissfully oblivious to the silent exchange. Turan too seemed unaware as she turned to talk to Jaro and Perus. Rasaben, now satisfied he'd unnerved me, *again*, attacked his plate of food with a relish that left me even more unsettled.

I forced down several small pieces of the boar, followed by a deep gulp of goat's milk then began pushing what remained of the meal around the plate.

At first no one seemed to notice, then out of the corner of my eye I realized Taskim was watching me, at which point he asked: "Something wrong, Centurion? Is the boar not to your liking?"

His question drew everyone's eye, along with Rasaben's very unwelcome attention.

"No sire, it tastes wonderful—I'm just not very hungry. My apologies."

Rasaben muttered something under his breath then he promptly reached across the table and helped himself to my plate.

"We'd just finished eating when you arrived," Turan explained, eyeing her brother disapprovingly.

Taskim looked back and me. "Why didn't you say something?"

"I—"

"Perhaps later then—and don't concern yourself with the fact that Ras has taken it all," Taskim added pointedly. "There's more where that came from."

Rasaben looked up, and I swear he actually looked a little embarrassed. Then his blue eyes darted to me and the old Rasaben and his hateful stare were back. Ah, yes. I knew it was too good to last.

"Feel up to a little exercise?" Taskim said, abruptly rising from the table and motioning for me to follow his lead. "It'll do you good."

"Sire?" I asked as I stiffly got to my feet.

"It's a lovely day for a walk."

I flicked Turan a quick, sidelong look, expecting an encouraging smile and a nod, implying I should indulge the old man. Instead I found her eyes tainted with worry before she averted them.

My heart began to pound and I hesitated; clearly something was afoot. I looked to Ainiaan, but she only stared back at me, clearly just as baffled as I.

"Just the two of us, Centurion." Taskim had noticed my silent exchange with Ainiaan, which of course only added to my growing unease. With that he started for the doorway. "Come along."

I hurried to catch up, accepting a heavy cloak from a servant just as I came abreast of Taskim.

He drew his own cloak around him, as did I then together we walked out of the Keep's main doors and down the stairs and into the courtyard.

It *wasn't* a lovely day. It was a damned freezing cold day and the sky looked to be seriously considering dumping more snow on top of the slushy stuff that filled the courtyard. I tucked my bare hands inside my cloak and clenched my teeth as I limped along beside him. And as it turns out, it wasn't "just the two of us." A burly manservant followed; I had to assume he was well armed under his heavy cloak—just in case I decided to try my luck at overpowering the lord of the Keep.

Oblivious to my apprehension, not to mention my noticeable and painful hobble, Taskim strode across the yard, through an open door, up a flight of stone steps, through an arched doorway and then up a narrow flight of wooden stairs. I followed, hard pressed to keep up, while the servant silently and as discreetly as possible brought up the rear. Slogging through the deep snow had been work, and I was laboring for breath as Taskim briskly started up the wooden stairs. Refusing to concede that a man well over twice my age was in better shape—even if my leg was largely to blame—I doggedly followed.

By the time I reached the top of the staircase and stepped out onto a wooden landing, my face felt as if it had frozen solid, my throat and lungs burned from inhaling the frigid air and the muscles of my left leg quivered uncontrollably.

Taskim stopped long enough to smile at me then he walked over a door, opened it and stepped through and into what was obviously the top floor one of the Keep's two massive round towers that flanked the portcullis.

I followed while the servant remained just outside, unobtrusive, ready if needed to repel any attack—not that I was capable of mounting one even if that had been my plan I was so winded and yes, in so much pain.

Lead-paned windows regularly interrupted the room's rough-hewn, curved stone walls and provided an unparalleled view of the surrounding countryside. But the windows were shut, and without the benefit, such as it was, of a breeze, it was even colder inside than out. On top of that the air had an oppressive stuffiness to it.

I walked over to the nearest window, hoping what I'd see would not only give me some clue as to why he'd brought me here but also shake loose the sudden grip of panic that had tightened around my midriff.

What I saw was a thickly forested world held in the vise-like grip of winter with snow and wood for as far as the eye could see. I had no doubt there was snow and wood for a great deal further than that—maybe even all the way to that oft-mentioned end of the Earth as I'd been told, countless times, that the end of the Earth was a wilderness of densely packed trees, the shores of which were constantly attacked by a relentless sea... and where people, so far away from the center of civilization, behaved in the most uncivilized ways.

I leaned even closer—I knew better than to press my nose against the glass, having learned while in Germania never to touch frozen metal or icy glass with bare skin—and looked down. A narrow road eeled its way out of the Keep's maw, over an iced-over moat, then through the trees only to be quickly swallowed up by the thick, snow-covered woodland. Countless hooves and feet had chewed and churned the snow that had blanketed the road and wooden drawbridge—the only mark of man's passage in an otherwise wild and pristine white landscape.

"This is one of my favorite places." Taskim stopped beside me, his warm breath briefly visible in the still, stale air.

I briskly rubbed my arms. *"Indeed?"* If true, the man was a damned masochist.

"Can't argue with the view—"

Yes I could, most eloquently in fact, but felt it prudent to hold my tongue.

"—beautiful, isn't it?"

I looked again. Nope. Still covered in damned snow. "I'm not fond of the cold, my lord."

He placed his hand on my shoulder. "That's right, you're originally from Numidia—but it gets quite cold there, too, doesn't it?"

"Not *this* cold, sire." I was desperately trying not to shiver, because if I did, then I'd start to stutter and that just would not do. "Never saw snow, never experienced this kind of c-c-cold until I was stationed in G-G-Ger-Germania." *Damn!*

"Wait until spring—then you'll fully appreciate what I mean."

I favored him with a sidelong look. "But... it *is* s-s-spring, sire."

"Not here—we've yet to reach midwinter. Spring's still many months off."

My first reaction was absolute dismay—*more* months of this flesh-freezing weather? Then another thought came to me—how could this be? Before I could ask, he said, "Oh, but of course! I see your confusion—it *was* spring in Britannia."

"You mean it c-c-can be spring there and n-n-not even mid-winter here—*at the s-s-s-same time?*"

He nodded.

"How's th-th-that p-p-possible?"

"Didn't Turi tell you? She assured me she'd told you you were being taken beyond the end of the Earth."

"She did, b-b-but—"

His eyebrows shot up, as if he suddenly realized he was speaking to a naïve simpleton and felt decidedly hoodwinked. "And you expected the seasons to be the same?"

I hesitated. "You m-m-mean we're *not* in Hibernia?"

He smiled, not a nice smile. "You were, very briefly. But not now."

My eyes widened. "You mean we *are* b-b-b-beyond the end of the Earth?"

"Of course. *Far* beyond, Centurion."

"Farther th-th-than P-P-Parthia?" My landmark, my measurement of all things involving great distance earned the same reaction from Taskim as it had from Turan: a soft, patronizing chuckle.

"Much, *much* further, Centurion. I'd tell you exactly how far, but I'm afraid it would make absolutely no sense to you."

I didn't like anyone assuming I was too stupid to grasp something, so I replied irritably, "Try me…*s-s-sire.*"

He stared at me then with a nod and a shrug replied, "Would it make sense to you if I said you were no longer *on* Earth?"

I blinked, utterly baffled. In a literal sense I *wasn't* standing on earth any longer. Solid ground lay some distance below. But something told me that wasn't what he'd meant, which meant I wasn't sure what to say. If I agreed it made no sense, then his opinion of me as a naïve simpleton would be made fast. If I agreed it made sense, he'd know better, again, cementing his low opinion of me and adding to it that I was also a liar—and a bad liar to boot.

"Perhaps it's more accurate to say you're no longer on the Earth you knew—imagine the world as a table, with finite edges."

All right… this I *could* grasp. I nodded my understanding.

"One could say we're *underneath*, standing on the underside of that very same table."

My eyes got even rounder and my mouth popped open. I must have looked every bit the gaping, shivering imbecile—but at least I didn't do what my mind was screaming at me to do: grab something secure and hang on for dear life.

He must've seen my fingers twitch because he gave my shoulder what I assume was supposed to be a reassuring pat. "I realize it's a difficult concept to… *grasp*, so to speak, but you will, Centurion, *you will*. With time." With that he turned his full attention to what lay beyond the windows and appeared to lose himself in thought, in the process leaving me alone to confront his mind-boggling, disconcerting allusions.

On top of this—not that I needed anything else—the room had given me the shivers from the moment I'd entered, and not just because of the intense cold. It had instantly reminded me of the storeroom: a private place, seldom visited, where even screams would be hard pressed to escape… where truly ugly things could happen.

Perhaps this was why it was his favorite place. I glanced at the door—the only door— to see the servant standing there, idly picking at his fingernails as if nothing was amiss. But what if that was a ruse? He was conveniently blocking my path if I chose to bolt.

To make matters worse, I recalled Turan's apprehensive look—perhaps it *was* a trap, perhaps she knew something bad was about to happen.

Perhaps at any moment Rasaben might appear, accompanied Kyrou and Jaro, their less than friendly intentions clearly written on their faces.

I began to perspire—a very odd sensation, let me tell you. Freezing cold and shivering, and at the same time sweating. My heart and breathing, which had just started to slow, resumed their earlier rapid pace, but this time in a reflexive panic.

I felt the walls closing in. I desperately wanted out—wanted to run.

"Centurion?"

A hand squeezed my shoulder—my bad shoulder.

I flinched violently, jerking my gaze off the now very attentive servant standing in the doorway only to find Taskim staring at me, his eyes narrowed in alarm.

"*Centurion...?*"

I managed a husky whisper: "*S-s-sire?*"

"Are you all right? You've gone pale again."

"Yes, s-s-sire... j-j-just... just c-c-c-cold."

"And I've worn you out, *again*." He smiled. "You must forgive an old man his lapses."

"Of c-c-course—"

"And you're wondering why I've brought you here."

There was no point denying it. I suspect that question was written all over my now thoroughly frostbitten face.

"I wanted you to see what I hold dear, I wanted you to understand what's at stake."

Now I was even more confused. I glanced at the servant, whose deliberately expressionless expression was of no help, then back out at the snowy landscape. Surely he didn't mean *that* icy hell. "Sire?"

"Come—let's retire to my library, get some warm mead into that belly of yours," he gave the aforementioned belly a pat, "and thaw you out." With that he started for the doorway as the servant stepped back, allowing us to pass.

I eagerly if clumsily followed, wanting to put space between myself and that room while dearly hoping my leg wouldn't give out on the way down—I wasn't sure he'd find it in his heart to forgive me if I stumbled and knocked him down a flight of stairs. That might be pushing his good graces just one step, as they say, too far.

Besides, Taskim's bodyguard might reasonably assume it wasn't an accident and react accordingly.

Fortunately I negotiated the stairs without mishap despite my feet having gone quite numb, albeit very slowly with Taskim and the servant forced to wait on me several times. Then, after trudging back across the courtyard, we reentered the main Keep by a different, ground level doorway. After another tiring and painful slog up several flights of stone stairs I found myself in a familiar hallway, and a few moments later, inside a very familiar, and I might add toasty warm library.

Some considerate soul had anticipated our arrival: a roaring fire filled the firebox and a large decanter, along with two mugs and a roll of ribbon tied vellum, sat on the table.

"Please, Centurion, seat yourself by the fire," Taskim urged as the servant helped me out of my snow-dusted cloak.

Taskim, who'd already shed his cloak and tossed the heavy garment over a nearby chair, picked up the rolled vellum and joined me in front of the fireplace as the servant filled the two mugs.

I waited until Taskim had seated himself, then I eased down in a chair and, following his lead, propped my frozen feet on the hearth, close but not too close to the source of the heat.

"Here, Centurion, this should help thaw your insides." He motioned to the servant, who handed me a mug.

I accepted it; Taskim accepted the other then cradling the vellum roll in his lap, settled back and stared at the blaze.

The servant retreated, presumably back to the doorway or some other inconspicuous station.

I took a sip of the warm mead, swallowed, took another, deeper gulp of the potent liquid, then sagged back in the chair, utterly worn out by the walk, not to mention the worry. I was, in a word, exhausted. But I also knew he was working his way up to something—I hoped it was a full explanation as to why I was taken prisoner in the first place as no one had yet bothered to tell me, despite repeatedly promising me they would. At that moment I was satisfied by the prospects of feeling warm, both from the mead and the fire.

In fact I was so satisfied I could have happily sat there for hours with not a word being exchanged, but just as with the trip to the tower, Taskim had brought me here for a reason—

"Feel up to some translating?"

—and there it was.

It wasn't like I could refuse; besides it was something familiar and I had a sneaking feeling I might soon be in need of a few simple reassurances, a few reminders of my past life to help diminish the vast uncertainties that lay ahead. "Of course, sire." I dropped my feet to the floor, straightened up in the chair then placed my mug on the hearth.

He handed me the roll of vellum.

I accepted it, managed, after a moment of struggle to tug the ribbon free, then carefully smoothed the manuscript across my lap. One half was filled with a beautifully illuminated and illustrated map—I instantly recognized many of the place names—it encompassed all of the Empire and beyond, *far* beyond, to places I'd never heard of before, to places I had a sneaking suspicion no Roman knew existed.

Perhaps, I thought, *it's in one of these far distant lands I now find myself, lands so distant they have their own pattern of seasons. Not exactly beyond the end of the Earth—or even the underside of that metaphorical table—but pretty damned close.*

The other half was filled with script. Greek—an unfamiliar dialect, but still readable: surely the very same manuscript he'd mentioned earlier, and it suddenly occurred to me that I might in fact be holding that fabled and long lost manuscript of Pytheas, or at least a copy—my heart began to thumb against my ribs as my breathing quickened. *Could it be true?*

I flashed him a nervous smile, then began to translate, at first aloud, shaping each word carefully, drawing out the subtle nuances of the writer's tongue and matching it with my own understanding of the base language, deciphering the signs and sounds, analyzing the resultant images—the words—that formed in my mind. It didn't take long for me to realize that it wasn't the tome of Pytheas. It was something equally unexpected. As I became more and more engrossed in what I was reading I stopped reading aloud—stopped simultaneously translating, totally unaware I had done so.

When I reached the end, I gathered my thoughts and lifted my thoroughly puzzled gaze to find Taskim watching me intently. "This is a peace treaty, my lord."

He smiled, a very pleased smile. "Indeed it is."

I stared at him—by his tone it was obvious he'd known what it was all along; so he'd lied to me.

My expression must've given me away because he quickly added, "A minor deception on my part, Centurion. A—"

"*Test?* To see if *I* was telling the truth?" I interrupted, punctuating my obvious annoyance by leaving off the requisite 'sire' and he had the good graces to look mildly sheepish.

He dipped his head. "My apologies."

I blew out my cheeks, looked back at the vellum and continued, "It's a treaty between two peoples, the…" I hesitated, eyes narrowing. The names were utterly unfamiliar to me, and therefore unworkable at least with any chance at accuracy and after having my veracity questioned, I was reluctant to make a hash of names so critical to the discussion.

Taskim offered helpfully: "Tuatha Dé Danann and Faoimhuir."

I looked up, repeated not quite as smoothly, "Too-ath-ah-day-dan-ann and… and Fay-ohm-oor." Feeling the latter form on my tongue, hearing it spoken aloud prompted the tickle of dim recollection.

Before I could remember exactly where I'd heard it before, Taskim replied, "Yes."

"Ending a war that lasted ten thousand years."

This time he only nodded.

I stared at him for a moment then looked back at the treaty—at the map itself, which suddenly didn't make sense. It accurately placed far-flung settlements that had only recently sprung into existence, the outgrowth of earlier frontier garrisons—I knew this for I'd visited many of them. Then there were the well-established towns and ports scattered across the map that bore their Romanized names, the surrounding territories having been absorbed into the Empire within the past century. The map also pinpointed mountain passes and islands discovered within my mother's lifetime.

As I stared down at the map, I found my gaze turning to Britannia and specifically to Lindum and has I started to reach out to touch the marker, the location of my garrison as if by some magic I could be instantly returned to where I belonged, I thought I saw something move, or more accurately, something *appear*… another marker for another settlement, one with a very Roman name: *Venta Belgarum*. I'd heard of the Belgares of course; they were Gallic kinsmen of the Atrebates and erstwhile allies of the Regni, whose client king, Togidubnus, had mentioned to Perus his Roman guests' fondness for stuffed boar. But the Belgares certainly had no settlement where the map now placed one, much less anything so grand as a capital—even going by the locals' definition of a 'capital', which was usually nothing more than a larger than normal pig-wallow.

Worse, the marker and place name hadn't been there a moment before, unless my eyes and the wavering firelight were playing tricks on me.

I gave my head a shake, looked again. Surely that was the case—a combination of shifting firelight and my vision—I was still experiencing the occasional bout of double vision; nothing worth mentioning to Mabog, just a mild annoyance. Maybe the cold, too. And the mead.

I peered more closely at the map. *Yes. That's it—has to be*, I assured myself. But in truth, the more I stared at it, the uneasier I became, and not just because it appeared to have changed, subtly, just in the brief time I held it. Rome ruled most of the known world and had done for centuries yet this treaty and the map plainly said otherwise—I mean, wouldn't I, a soldier of

Rome, have heard, somewhere along the line, of a war that encompassed the entire empire and beyond but didn't include it?

If this treaty was in fact authentic—and I'm not saying I believed it was—it suggested that there were forces even greater than Rome at work behind the scenes, possibly like Turan, manipulating people into doing their bidding while all the while thinking it was of their own free will.

That was a truly staggering thought: control the likes Turan possessed but on a massive scale. Then another thought came to me—one that caused my heart to flutter in dreadful anticipation. I slowly lifted my gaze. "Someone's broken the treaty."

"Yes."

"Who?"

He dismissed that with an impatient flick of his hand. "What matters is that it *was* broken."

As a soldier, as some often tasked with sorting out broken treaties in the most efficient, dare I say brutal ways, I've always found that when treaties are broken the offended party has absolutely no problem pointing fingers—in fact is more than eager to point fingers. So Taskim's reluctance to appoint blame suggested that whichever side he was allied to was the offend-*er*, not the offend-*ed*.

I looked back at the treaty, reread the last few lines, then again met Taskim's steady gaze. "It says if this treaty is ever *broken* by force of arms, then the matter must be *settled* by force of arms and whoever is victorious will determine the fate of humanity."

"Yes."

As I stared at him, Turan's voice echoed from the depths of my memory: *'To save humanity'*. That had been her cryptic, not to mention daunting explanation for capturing me in the first place. I heard a *click*, like a key in a mnemonic lock: *I* was to save humanity—even barbarians. Even people I'd never met. *Everyone.*

I fixed my gaze on the fire and chewed on my lip, not wanting to take the next step yet realizing there was also no retreat. I felt Taskim's intense gaze on me, prompting me to ask the logical question, take that step. I wouldn't give him that, not *yet*. A long-overdue explanation was owed to *me,* in full and without hesitation—I shouldn't have to ask.

Taskim abruptly rose from his chair, said, "It's time that you to meet the full Assemblage of the Sidhe, Centurion," and nodded to the awaiting servant.

Startled, I pushed myself unsteadily to my feet, placed the treaty on my chair then turned my back to the fire and clasped my suddenly very sweaty hands behind my back.

The servant walked over to the double doors, opened them and as I watched in startled silence, seven men and a woman—the blond I'd seen with Taskim—filed in and once formed up in a row, fixed their cold eyes on me. As I stared back I had to wonder how long they'd been standing outside, waiting—*listening.*

My heart began to beat faster.

"Centurion, over here if you will." Taskim motioned to the library's oblong table and its accompanying ring of high, hard-backed chairs.

I walked stiffly to the closest—nearest the fire and sat down as the others quickly found their own seats. Once everyone else was seated, Taskim lowered himself onto the chair next to me.

The servant, responding to some unseen cue, exited the library. As I heard the doors close and *lock* softly behind him, I glanced around at this new crop of faces, not sure what to expect. I had to wonder if Turan had known about this meeting. Her worried expression as we parted had certainly augured ill, maybe this was what she feared, not the tower—and I suddenly wanted her here, wanted *her* seated beside me, not Taskim. *I needed her—*

"Centurion Niger," Taskim began, drawing my wary gaze, "these are my fellow Lords—and Lady," he nodded to the woman, "of the Tuatha Dé Danann—we are in sum the Nine Chosen Lords, the full Assemblage of the Sidhe."

I met each set of coolly dispassionate eyes in turn, sensing that this was as far as the introductions were going to go—they all clearly knew who I was by name and reputation after all, so why bother to put me, a prisoner, a slave, on equal footing?

"I ask your indulgence, Centurion Niger," the woman said, "in answering some of our questions."

As if I really had a choice in the matter. I had a sneaking suspicion if I refused, and despite Taskim's fatherly approach—which I now realized was an act for my benefit—I'd find myself having the answers teased out of me by the most painful methods possible.

So I sat there, for how long I cannot tell you, and answered their questions—lots and lots of very specific questions about my military career, about the places I'd been, the battles I'd fought and against which foes, injuries I'd sustained—I was even ordered to strip down to my trousers and stand before the fire so each could take his or her turn examining me while asking questions about the origins of the old wounds, a lengthy ordeal eerily reminiscent of Turan's equally and deliberately degrading interrogation. Worse, the blond woman's reactions were disturbingly evocative of Turan's curiously delayed responses.

Once their morbid curiosity—what else could it be?—was thoroughly satisfied, I was allowed to redress and resume my seat. By now my legs were shaking, I had a fierce headache and a *very* sour stomach.

More questions followed—about Roman tactics, siege engines, armor—how much food and water a man would need to sustain him in top fighting form depending upon the conditions he faced. I was asked about allies and enemies alike—who could be trusted, who could be bought off— who were no more than mere nuisances, minor impediments to the empire's expansion and who truly posed a threat to Rome.

I answered until my throat was every bit as raw as my nerves, constantly on guard against revealing information that could be used *against* Rome— that I would not give *anyone* willingly. These people would have to hack that out of me—a pledge I made to myself knowing full well it might come to that.

Those questioners seated nearest, like the woman, like Taskim, showed me some small measure of respect, something akin to compassion, asking after every question answered to their particular liking if I needed anything—a sip of water perhaps?

I was never offered what I sorely wanted and richly deserved: an explanation for this harsh, protracted and unexpected interrogation.

Others, in particular a dark-haired man with a neatly trimmed beard seated at the far end of the table wore looks of poorly concealed contempt and an obvious desire to have done with the meeting as quickly as possible, as if they risked catching something if they stayed too long and in such close proximity, as if I were a disease, a plague rather than a man.

Finally, and I have to say, rather abruptly, the questioning was over. With a curt nod from the dark-haired man to Taskim, the group rose as one. No thank you, no acknowledgement that they'd utterly exhausted me. *Nothing.*

I made no effort to rise, to show proper deference. I was too tired, too angry, too... confused to do anything but stare after them as they filed out of the room. Once Taskim had closed the doors behind them, I dropped my gaze to the table and stared wearily at my own distorted reflection in its polished stone surface, hoping I too might see what they'd seen in my face which had left *them* so unsettled and at the same time, strangely so... confident. *Of me?*

Next thing I knew Taskim's hand was on my shoulder.

I dearly wanted to twitch it off—I didn't, but only because I was just too damned tired.

"Here." He offered me my forgotten and now replenished mug of mead that I'd left on the hearth.

I took it grudgingly and gulped down its fire-warmed contents, then fixed my exhausted but nevertheless wary gaze on him as he settled on the seat next to mine.

"Are you all right, son?" The fatherly Taskim was back—I would have none of it.

"I want my bed," I grumbled, still clutching the mug in my hands.

"Of course you do, of course—how 'bout a little more, first?" He refilled the mug from the decanter. He made no move to fill his own—thinking back, I didn't remember him taking any sips from his.

I was never one to drink alone, even more so with a sober audience, but my throat was still painfully raw and my mouth dry, so with an annoyed grunt, I brought the mug to my lips and emptied it in three loud, wincing swallows, scowling at him over the mug's rim as I did so.

"Another?" He filled the mug the instant my hand settled it back on the table.

Why the hell not. I licked the foam from my lips—vaguely aware of an odd, bitter taste to it then with a shrug, I again lifted the mug. Half way to my lips, my arm began to shake, threatening to spill the mug's contents.

He wrapped his fingers around my wrist, helped me bring the mug to my mouth.

I drank greedily, with much drizzling down my chin, my throat, staining the tunic. And before I realized what was happening, he'd refilled the mug as was again pressing it to my now oddly numb lips.

"No," I turned away, managed a slow, deliberate shake of my head. "No... no more—*bed*," I slurred. "I... I need my bed." I tried to rise.

He grabbed my arm—I thought at first to steady me then I realized he was keeping me pinned to my chair.

"Stay where you are," he said in a tone that suggested disapproval at my present state but with no guilt as to his own complicity. "You're far too drunk to walk and I cannot carry you."

It seemed like reasonable advice. In the time it took for him to speak, the room had begun to spin and my limbs had turned to mush. Only I wasn't drunk—I'd been drugged, *again*. I was sure of it as I felt an all too familiar, all too frighteningly muzziness wash over me, dragging me downwards into a yawning darkness. I couldn't keep my eyes open and my body, my bones felt as if they were melting and at any moment I'd turn completely to liquid and pour into that gaping, bottomless hole.

I slumped forward, towards that cold and unforgiving stone of the table, helpless to stop myself and I dearly wanted to panic, to brace myself for what was surely going to be a painful impact but my heart and muscles simply refused to react.

Then I felt Taskim's arms around me, catching me just before my face would have hit the tabletop.

He shoved me back into the chair, roughly enough my head snapped back, and groaning, I feebly tried to shake loose of his hold. *"Leeeegooooooffmeeee—"*

"Relax, Centurion… don't fight…"

Within his voice were other voices, whispered voices—Rasaben's, Kyrou's, Mabog's—others; I felt hands on me.

I was dragged, legless, from the chair and to my feet then none-too-carefully hoisted onto someone's shoulder, to be taken who knows where and I screamed soundlessly, *TURAN…!*

— ii —

I opened my eyes to find myself seated in a padded chair next to a crackling fire. My mouth tasted of strong drink mixed with bile and my legs were splayed, my feet rolled painfully inwards as if I'd been utterly limp when dumped in the chair with no concern as to the position of my limbs and left there without the ability to reposition myself—for how long a period was anyone's guess but I was still so groggy I couldn't muster up my usual outrage at time leaving me, literally, in the dark while it traveled on.

Then something else came to me, something even more worrisome, akin in many ways to the dull throb of an open wound—not in a literal sense mind you. I was physically intact, but at the same time I had this nagging awareness that something had been cut out of me, leaving a large, gaping hole, a soul-deep emptiness, along with an intense all over body ache, like I'd been severely roughed up.

I tried to lever myself up in the chair, to look around, and got as my reward a shooting pain up my spine. My head threatened to explode and I couldn't help but cry out.

Hands touched me; I flinched—or tried to, tried again to rise, to defend myself, even turn my head to see who it was, but my body simply refused. Arms and legs were still like jelly and now my back was aflame.

Warm fingers caressed my chin: Turan's faint voice spoke within the intense pounding in my mind, *Listen to me, Arri*—

Yes! I latched onto that, desperate for that small, familiar comfort as she stepped into my limited view.

—don't try move until you're more awake, it will hurt less that way.

What... what happened? Where am I?

You're with me, in my apartments—you're safe. That's all you need to know for now. Safe, understand?

I hurt, Turan, I hurt all over—

She wrapped her arms around me, drawing me into her embrace.

As the blinding pain ebbed, I found revealed a profound fear that something terrible had happened—that something truly terrible had been done to me.

What's hap—

"Shhhh," she soothed aloud, stroking my head. *"It's over, it's all over and you're safe now—"*

Over?

Instead of answering, she began to sob.

I struggled to free myself from her embrace, to embrace her, *comfort her*, but I was still unable to move and terribly, terribly muzzy-headed.

"I'm so sorry... I... I'd didn't realize you see." She drew me more tightly against her as she continued to weep softly. *"I thought we had more time... I'm so, so sorry..."*

Sorry? I waited for her reply. *Turan...?* I was instead answered by silence, a warm, dark, all-encompassing and solitary silence. *Turan... please! Don't leave me...*

When I next opened my eyes, I was no longer in a chair by a fire. Instead I was sprawled belly down on a bed and covered in blankets. In Turan's apartments? It seemed a reasonable guess, and what I could see matched my memory of the furnishings and the general layout. I had no memory of rising from the chair and walking, which suggested I hadn't done it by choice or under my own power. I felt nauseated with a fierce headache, and try as I might, I couldn't roll over, much less rise—more evidence that I'd been carried or dragged to my present location.

As I stared dully at the fire, a vague memory surfaced of whispered voices—Ainiaan's? Mabog's? Boian's?—of someone wiping my lips and chin, of fingers combing my hair out of my eyes, of warm hands gently massaging my back and shoulders—a blanket being drawn over me, followed by more urgent whispering, of retreating footsteps and the muffled thump of a door closing. I tried to lift my head and look around, but after a moment of struggle I gave up, realizing it just wasn't worth the added misery any attempt at moving would incur.

I did manage to shift my blurry gaze to the lead-paned balcony doors, only to find the glittering ice world beyond tinged in the forged warmth of twilight. Squinting, I made out a few bright stars suspended in a purple-pink sky beyond. Whether that meant evening or dawn, I couldn't tell. At best, I'd lost a day. At the worst... I had no idea. I didn't even want to think about it.

So I didn't. Instead I fell back asleep—or, more likely, passed out again.

Sometime later, I was again drawn out of a dreamless slumber by the distinct *'click'* of a latch. I opened one eye and slowly swiveled it towards the room's main door alcove. The door was indeed shut—at least I couldn't see a gap and the glow of the hallway torches beyond suggesting it had been left ajar. I also hadn't felt a draft of icy air, so I felt it safe to assume the *'click'* I'd heard hadn't come from the balcony door's latch. Someone had been here and left—to check on me?—or, I realized as my heart picked up speed, someone had just entered and had closed and *locked* the door behind them.

The only illumination was from the dying fire and scant little of that, so if my intruder sensed I was awake and remained stock still, he—or she— would be as good as invisible—perhaps whoever it was stood in the alcove, watching me from its dark recess. Just the thought sent my heart thumping faster. I was still on my stomach, one bare and decidedly chilled arm hanging limply off the edge of the bed—and still unable to move. In other words, totally defenseless. So I listened, straining to hear any noise to suggest I still had company.

Several minutes passed, and all I heard was the occasional faint crackle and sputter from the guttering coal bed.

Satisfied I was truly alone, I shifted my full concentration from listening to moving.

I focused on wiggling my toes, curling my fingers... pursing my lips. Slowly, ever so slowly, muscles began to respond to my mental commands, feebly at first, but then to my intense relief, with more coordination and strength.

Finally, with one tremendous heave I got my arms under me and pushed myself into a seated position. Dropping my feet to the floor and cradling my head in my hands, I dry heaved several times, my entire body painfully convulsing in response.

Once the spasms stopped, I very slowly lifted my head. Pushing my hair out of my eyes, I peered around. At first all was a muddle. It was pitch dark outside; it was close to pitch dark inside. My last coherent, albeit fragmentary memories were of looking out through those same lead-paned balcony doors and seeing the sun well up in the sky... of that icebox of a tower room... the library and drinking warm mead... and suddenly everything came rushing back: the treaty, the interrogation by Taskim and his fellow lords, the absolute certainty that I'd been drugged, then being carried... somewhere, of excruciating pain, feeling as if my head was being cracked open and screaming in agony as hands forced their way into my skull and began pulling out my brain, bit by bit... and finally, waking up sprawled in a chair...

My eyes darted to the chair by the fire—*that chair*. And Turan holding me, sobbing, while assuring me I was safe.

Safe... from what? Had it all been a dream?

Maybe I hadn't been drugged. Maybe I'd just imbibed too much mead while in Taskim's library—I clearly remembered him chiding me that I'd drunk far too much, so maybe I was experiencing nothing more sinister than one a hell of a hangover.

I'd drunk far too much before, plenty of times, but never had such binges been accompanied by such vivid and frightening imaginings—or such a *truly* ferocious headache.

I had two choices as I saw it. I could lay back down and hope I could sleep off the hangover, or I could get up and go in search of Mabog and one of his magic potions which I had no doubt would knock down the pounding in my skull and calm the nausea.

The throbbing behind my eyes was so fierce I doubted I could actually get back to sleep, so I really had only one choice: find Mabog. And hope he would in a sympathetic mood and wouldn't tell me my present suffering was just reward for my previous overindulgences and so therefore nothing he was willing to treat.

I gave my beard-stubbled face a vigorous rub, trying to stir some life into it then lurched unsteadily to my feet. I was still in my trousers, minus tunic and boots. I looked around for my missing clothing and finally spotted the tunic draped over the chair by the fire, the boots just below.

I somehow stumbled over to the chair, grabbing the high back with one hand and snatching up the tunic with the other. The leather was stiff and held the stale reek of regurgitated alcohol—*and something else.*

I very reluctantly held it close to my nose, hoping my rebellious stomach would cooperate and what I smelled wasn't just mead that had paid a return visit to the outside world. My nose picked up another scent within the musky odor of mead—the all too familiar and sickly sweet scent of that lozenge Hanni had insisted I swallow shortly before we disembarked the *Sulaviae*—a lozenge that had knocked me out cold for, at minimum, an entire day.

I grit my teeth as my fingers clenched tight around the tunic. So, I *had* been drugged—*again*, and for what purpose I could only speculate. *Safe*, Turan had said. *It's over, it's all over and you're safe now.* Her assurances hadn't left me feeling the least bit safe, then, and especially now. In fact the more I thought about being drugged into a stupor whenever the urge struck Turan or Taskim—meaning whenever they considered my willing cooperation in their labyrinthine schemes in doubt—the angrier and yes, more frightened I became.

I sat and somehow, don't ask me how, managed to pull the boots back on, then I sagged back into the chair as I fought down the almost overwhelming urge to vomit. I stayed like that for several moments, eyes squeezed shut, listening to my heart thump in my ears, waiting for the blinding pain and intense nausea to lessen, even a bit, as I confronted the awful fact that something truly terrible *had* happened. I had no doubts about that now. Something had been done to me—I just didn't know what that 'something' was.

Time to find out.

I rose slowly and very stiffly from the chair, gave my thoroughly chilled shoulders a rub then gathered up the tunic. The smell made my stomach turn anew, but since I hadn't been left a change of clothing and I wasn't about to challenge the frigidly cold halls bare-chested, I held my breath as I pulled it over my head. As I tugged it into place, I noted with perverse satisfaction that I'd puked all over Turan's coiled serpent. *Good!*

I took a deep, mind-clearing breath—I was owed a full and apologetic explanation for this latest insult, whatever it was, and this time I was going to get it!

Keeping that indignant thought foremost in my mind, I staggered over to the door. After some loud cursing and angry fumbling with fingers that didn't seem completely mine, I managed to lift the latch and yank the door open.

The hallway was deserted, but this time I knew which direction to go.

By the time I found myself standing at the top of the staircase leading down to the Great Hall, I was fully awake, the last vestige of my earlier muzziness gone. The near-blinding headache and nausea, along with my abused rage and unfocused fear remained, each in turn fueling the others.

I started down the stone stairs, slowly, *cautiously,* one hand keeping a loose grip on the railing just in case my legs suddenly gave out but I reached the main floor without mishap. As I'd hoped, I heard familiar voices coming from within the Great Hall.

I marshaled my anger and focused my unruly thoughts—I wanted to have ready exactly what I was going to say, to demand of my captors—not let them distract me this time—then I lurched towards the doorway, grabbing the frame just as my knees were about to go.

I stood there, trembling, watching as everyone seated at the massive table turned, warning by those facing me of my unexpected and clearly unwelcome arrival.

Turan was the first to her feet, quickly followed by Ainiaan and Hanni along with Jaro, Taskim, Kyrou and Perus—others I didn't recognize—not to mention at least a dozen soldiers who'd been seated at the far end of the table. Rasaben too lurched to his feet with such force his chair tipped over; servants who'd been moving about, refilling mugs or removing empty platters turned, only to stare at me, mouths agape.

For an instant everyone remained stock still, as if frozen in place, then they all rushed towards me. I stumbled back, panicked by the haunting similarity to the Iceni's charge that had begun this never-ending nightmare.

My heel clipped the bottom-most stair—I made a desperate grab for the railing, missed and unable to compensate, fell backwards, sprawling across the stone steps and striking the back of my head in the process. I thought I was going to black out—in fact I desperately, strangely, hoped I'd black out, find refuge in unconsciousness—let them do what they wanted with me while I was gone as they had a habit of doing—but the blow only made my vicious headache pound all the more.

"Don't move, Arri," Turan gasped, falling to her knees beside me. "Get Mabog!" She looked up at the circle of faces that now loomed over me as Ainiaan knelt beside her. *"Hurry!"*

"What... what happened...?" I mumbled over the sounds of feet pounding up the stairs past me.

"You fell, hit your head." Turan eeled an arm under me, carefully drew my head and shoulders onto her lap. I squeezed my eyes shut, slowly opened them again. The circle of faces remained the same, as did their anxious stares—even Rasaben looked anxious, which did nothing for me. Even worse were the stares of the soldiers—not the eerily emotionless stares I'd come to expect from them. Their eyes now held blatant concern, distress... and yes, alarm.

One even reached out, as if to touch my shoulder but I recoiled and Ainiaan grabbed his hand just short of making contact and jerked his armored fingers away.

I found it hard to breathe, surrounded as I was, and Turan's reassuring touch did nothing to ease the sense of being suffocated.

"What happened?" a new voice demanded, echoing my own; Mabog moved into my limited view, snarled, *"Get back, all of you!"* and motioned for everyone to step away, to give me much needed air as he knelt beside Ainiaan and looked me over.

"He fell, struck his head on the steps," Turan replied, her eyes darting between Mabog and me. Then she held up her blood-smeared palm, the palm that had been cradling the back of my head.

Mabog fixed me with a very unsympathetic stare as he reached behind me and fingered my skull. "Didn't I tell you to stay in bed?"

I grimaced at his deliberately painful prodding. "I... I don't remember."

"I don't doubt that, not with the whack you just gave your head."

That wasn't what I'd meant, but before I could say so, he rocked back on his heels and began running his hands over the rest of me—modesty be damned and not particularly gently, either. "Anything feel broken?"

"I... I don't think so."

"Then let's get you back to bed—where you'll *stay* this time until *I* say otherwise. Hear?"

I felt a flutter of panic—afraid he planned to tie me down to make good on the demand.

He leapt to his feet and motioned for the ogre to pick me up. Turan and Ainiaan reluctantly rose and stepped back as Hanni carefully eased his massive arms under my shoulders and knees while closely watching my face for any sign of startled pain. Then, in one smooth movement, he got back to his feet, taking me with him.

As we started up the stairs, Mabog leading the way, the rest presumably following, I looked up at Hanni, only to find him avoiding my pleading gaze.

"Hanni? What's happened? Tell me—I know something bad's happened—and I'm not talking about me tripping on the stairs," I added quickly, sensing he was going to try the same transparent diversion as Turan and Mabog.

"You shouldn't have gotten out of bed on your own—you're very weak."

I wanted to say, 'I was fine this morning', but with time playing its nasty tricks on me, I honestly had no idea of how much time had elapsed since I'd found myself slogging through the snow alongside Taskim. It *seemed* like this morning, but—

J. E. Bruce

"Hanni...?" I whispered, the slight catch in my voice making it clear he was my last hope.

"You need to ask Lady Turan, all right? Don't ask me, Arri. *Please.*"

So, something bad *had* happened—something very, *very* bad. I bit my lip, hunched down in his embrace and closed my eyes. If I could have folded myself up into nothingness, I would have—as it was the best I could do was shut everyone out—even Hanni.

A few minutes later, I felt myself being placed on a bed, felt the blankets being drawn up over me, heard whispered voices—someone calling for servants to rekindle the fire and draw the drapes—felt someone sit beside my hip. For some stupid reason I hoped it was Turan. I'd have even settled for Ainiaan—

"Now let's take a look at that head."

It was Mabog.

"Leave me alone." Without opening my eyes I tried to pull the blankets up over my head—finishing the job of shutting everyone out.

He roughly jerked the blanket back down. "You're being foolish—you might have cracked your skull. Now, stop acting like a child—"

My eyes flew open and I sat bolt upright, coming eyeball to eyeball with Mabog, who wisely froze. My head felt like it was going to burst, but it was worth the unadulterated agony to see the look of equally unadulterated terror in his eyes. "Leave. Me. *ALONE!*"

"But—"

"I don't want you to touch me," I hissed in my most menacing voice—my really, *really* pissed off, 'I'm going to eat your kidneys for supper' Centurion's Voice. "I don't want *anyone* to touch me—*hear?*"

He hastily rose from the bed, took several steps back, far enough he felt a little braver then he turned to Turan and said huffily, "Perhaps you can talk some sense into him, m'lady."

I fixed my slitted stare on her, daring her to try as I eased my legs from under the blanket and dropped my booted feet to the floor.

"Arri, *please*, don't try to get up."

I glared at her as I straightened up, looking as if I was about to stand. I wasn't—I knew if I did I'd fall flat on my face, but I was mad—damned mad—furious in fact, and scared stiff. I felt this odd, skin-crawling sensation of *things* wriggling around within me, blind, desperate to find their way out, struggling to surface, to break into the light, yet if I tried to reach out, to touch, they plunged back into the depths, only to quickly claw their way back.

I fought the urge to dig into my skin, my skull and tear open a hole so they could escape and be done with it. Instead I kept my forearms pressed against my thighs as my hands balled into white-knuckled fists.

Turan stared fixedly at my face, not at my fists—she was terrified, every bit as terrified as I was, but not of me striking her. She was terrified of how I'd react when whatever was struggling to free itself within my mind finally broke loose. She wanted to see it first in my eyes before the horror washed over the rest of me.

As I glared back at her I saw a sudden bleakness in her eyes, a cold realization of what she'd done—what they'd *all* done to me was beyond any hope of absolution.

Her expression alone sent a cold chill racing down my spine.

"What have you done?" I asked, my calm voice startling even me.

Then it hit me like a fist to the belly—*I knew.*

Turan let out a soft gasp, mirroring my own gut-wrenching reaction.

I somehow managed to get to my feet and stood there, swaying slightly. I flicked Hanni a sidelong look of utter betrayal—my one friend, my *only* friend, who, I now knew was in fact no friend at all—then fixed my furious eyes on Turan. "Bring one to me."

"But—"

"NOW!" I bellowed. Clutching my head, I staggered sideways, wincing as my voice ricocheted around inside my skull.

She instinctively stepped back. Looking past her, I saw Rasaben standing just inside the doorway. Ainiaan stood beside him, a horror-stricken look on her tear-streaked face. "Do as he says, Ras," Turan said. "Bring one. *Hurry!*"

He nodded then looked down as if just realizing Ainiaan was beside him. He wrapped his arm around her shoulders and hurried her from the room. She made no effort to stop him, never looked back.

Turan turned to me, hands outstretched, beseeching. "Arri, please, let us explain—"

"You had plenty of time to explain!" I was in a murderous mood. I knew it—she knew it and I had no desire to be in any way agreeable, to be the slightest bit reasonable with *anyone*. I *despised* being used. *I* used people, dammit, not the other way around! "You never had any intention of explaining beforehand, *did you?* If you did, you'd have run the risk of me refusing—not that my refusal would have stopped you, oh, no—but you would've known your thievery was being done against my will! This way you could rationalize to yourself that I hadn't actually refused, that I might actually agree. *Isn't that right?"*

She stared at me, eyes glistening.

"ISN'T THAT RIGHT?"

"Yes—"

I laughed, a short, sharp and bitter laugh. "And you said it was your hope I'd eventually *trust* you! I *stupidly* believed you—wanted *desperately* to believe you because I desperately wanted you—*NO!*" I shook my head and flicked her a look of pure venom, found myself intensely pleased by her flinching reaction and added harshly, "First you take my freedom, then my armor. You *lie* to me; you promise me what I want more than anything else and you tell me you're with child, *my* child—is that even true? *I doubt it!*

"Then you steal *my* memories to serve *your* purposes—this is how you go about gaining my trust? By cannibalizing *everything* that makes me who I am? *And for what? To feed your voracious needs?* What about *my* needs? Did you—did *any* of you," my furious eyes swept those who remained, Hanni, Jaro and Mabog—even two servants kneeling beside the fireplace, who'd been feeding the now roaring blaze but were now frozen in place, staring at me in naked terror, "*ever* once truly consider my needs, ever look upon me as something—*someone*—other than a means to an end?"

"Arri, please—"

"ANSWER ME!"

Tears spilled down Turan's face; her hand came up to cover her trembling lips—there was nothing she could say, no answer she could give that could even begin to make amends and she knew it.

I wanted her to hurt. I *abhorred* her, abhorred Hanni, abhorred them all, every bit as much as I abhorred Gracchus and Porsenna, and for the same reasons—*read my murderous thoughts Turan, read them right now, I dare you!* Had I had my sword I'd have killed them all before any could have reached the doorway and they all clearly knew it. "You should've wiped my mind clean once you were done with your pilfering—"

Overhearing the echo of footsteps I turned away from her in absolute dismissal and fixed my suddenly apprehensive gaze on the doorway. The living proof of my worst fears was approaching—I'd asked to meet one of them—no, *demanded* it and I briefly wondered if I hadn't been a bit hasty in that. Now it was too late.

One of Rasaben's soldiers very reluctantly appeared in the doorway. Behind him stood his grim-faced master, as if to block the man's retreat if he suddenly had a mind to bolt once he saw the homicidal look in my eyes.

The soldier was scared—every bit as scared as I. He wore the strange, luminescent ring-mail hauberk they all wore, but, I noticed, he was unarmed—a wise precaution on the part of Rasaben.

"Come here," I managed to say without my voice quavering.

The soldier's eyes darted to Turan, to Mabog, to Hanni and Jaro, even the servants, as he walked slowly and warily towards me, the haunted stare of a man convinced he was walking to his own execution.

He stopped in front of me and using both hands carefully pushed back his ring-mail hood, revealing an unruly mane of curly, light blond hair. For several moments we stared at each other and what I saw in his blue eyes sent another icy shiver racing down my spine—it was as if I was staring into a mirror.

"What... what are you?"

A faint smile—a very familiar, albeit nervous smile tugged at his lips. "I'm you."

I shook, starting with a fine tremor in my hands that quickly flowed up my arms and then down my body. As it reached my knees I staggered back a step, hoping to reach the bed before my legs gave out. He followed, reaching for me, but I viciously slapped his hand away. *"Don't you touch me!"*

He stepped back, his hand falling to his side as I carefully eased myself down on the bed.

He looked around again, confused, utterly lost. Unsure if this hostile audience was over with and he could take his leave, or if it was only just beginning of his ordeal.

"Out." I looked at Turan, Rasaben and the rest. The servants didn't need to be asked twice. They fled what they knew was a crazed man, a man about to commit murder. *"You!"* I again fixed my eyes on the soldier as he started to step back, clearly hoping to make good his escape, my tone clearly confirming his worst fears. *"You* stay. The rest of you—*OUT!"*

The others did as I demanded—Mabog and Jaro urging Turan towards the doorway with Hanni bringing up the rear, just in case I switched targets and went for Turan.

"And shut the damned door!"

The sound of the door latching was like a thunderclap in the ominous silence that now filled the room.

The soldier hadn't moved; his wide eyes were fixed on me. He swallowed, hard and loud, then said in a voice barely above a whisper, "I'd very much appreciate it if you'd kill me quickly." He risked a glance around, as if looking for something to do the job.

"Why would I want to kill myself?" I replied in an equally strained voice.

Another nervous smile darted across his mouth. "It would be rather counterproductive."

He looked absolutely nothing like me—a head taller and of lighter build, with curly blond hair with very fair skin, ruddy, clean-shaven cheeks and bright blue eyes—in the shifting light of the fire he actually looked a lot like Felix. But he sounded just like me, an uncanny echo of my own voice, my own inflections, my accent.

"How much do you know?"

"You mean how much do I know of our background, our life?"

"I'd rather you not speak of 'our' life," I snapped. "*My* life is *not* yours! I never agreed to share it."

"And *I* never agreed to accept it. None of us were given a choice."

"*Us?* You mean me and you."

"I meant the rest of us—*Kellesuf.*"

I felt a sudden chill gather around my shoulders as I recalled the no longer impassive eyes of the soldiers who had loomed over me when I'd fallen on the stairs. "*How many…?*" I asked, my voice catching in my throat.

"How many now have your memories? I was told three, including me—for now. We're what are called… *proto types*. At least I think that's what they said we're called—you'll have to ask Lord Mabog. He can tell you." He looked around again, saw the chair by the fire and motioned to it. "May I?"

I very reluctantly nodded. I had no desire to make this man in the least bit comfortable, but he had done me no harm. In fact if he was telling the truth, and something about his manner told me he was being truthful, he was every bit as much the victim in this horrendous larceny as I was.

He pulled it closer, sat down and fixed his gaze on the fire. "I frighten you."

"And I frighten you."

He laughed—an eerily familiar, easy laugh *and not mine*—then he looked back at me. "You absolutely *terrify* me."

I was no longer staring at a stranger who wore my mannerisms as one would wear a cloak. His face had *changed*, albeit subtly. I tried to tell myself it was a trick of the flickering firelight that caused his cheekbones to appear more prominent, his jaw more pointed and his eyes more deeply set. Then he smiled and his cheeks dimpled.

It was no trick of the light.

"*Oh, gods…*"

"You've missed me, haven't you? You missed all of us."

My heart began to hammer against my ribs; my throat tightened and I forced out, "*No—!*"

"You did everything you could to save us. None of us blame you, you know. Not even Rufinius—well, not now, although he was mad at the time. Damned mad. But not at you—at that cowardly bastard Cerialis."

"What... what are you?"

He lifted his brows. "First I was Kellesuf. Then I was you. Now... I'm me." He smiled again, again dimpling his ruddy cheeks. *"Felix."*

I squeezed my eyes shut, felt hot tears roll down my cheeks. *"No— you're... you're dead!"*

"I'm not a ghost. Not any more, thanks to you. I'm real. I'm alive."

I opened my eyes, stared at him. *"Why?"*

"Because you missed us."

"That's no answer!"

"Yes it is."

I rose, shakily. "This is some sort of trick, isn't it?"

He also got to his feet and with arms akimbo, slowly shook his head—a perfect mimic of Felix. "You missed us—you told Lady Turan so. You told Lady Ainiaan and Hanni. You dreamt of us—relived our deaths— tormenting yourself, endlessly. You even tried to kill yourself because of us."

I bit my lip as more tears streamed down my pain-contorted face. My mind was splitting at the seams and there wasn't a damned thing I could do about it. What memories they hadn't pulled from me by force now hemorrhaged from the gaping holes they'd left, a result of their awful butchery.

I was going insane; I was becoming one with my nightmares.

"You're not crazy—"

I glared sidelong at him.

"That's what you're thinking—I can tell."

"Either *I'm* crazy or *you're* not Felix," I replied hoarsely as I roughly wiped my face with the back of my hand. "*You* pick."

He sighed. "I know you're scared. I'm damned scared too, if that helps." He glanced around him, then looked back at me. "There isn't anything to drink is there? I wouldn't mind getting really drunk right about now."

I shook my head as I carefully lowered myself back down on the edge of the bed.

He blew out his cheeks—another perfect copy of one of Felix's more endearing habits. "Well, that's a damned nuisance."

I couldn't help it; I chuckled. Granted, a very anxious chuckle, but still a chuckle.

He grinned then in a conspiratorial whisper, said, "I bet they're all out in the hallway, ears pressed against the door, listening."

"Probably."

"Shall I scream in agony, just to see what happens?"

I shook my head. "Best not. Our hosts don't appear to have much of a sense of humor."

"Pity," he replied, then: "Lady Turan—*very* handsome. Hadn't noticed before—wasn't capable of noticing…"

That drew my curious gaze.

"…she's yours, I presume—no luck for the likes of me. Not with such a late start."

"Actually, I'm hers—bought and paid for, as she likes to remind me every chance she gets."

He arched a disdainful brow—again, another faultless mannerism. *"Do tell."*

"Rather not."

"It might help to talk about it." He grabbed the chair and at my unenthusiastic nod, drew it even closer.

"There's not much to tell—I was dragged off the battlefield, half-dead and sold into slavery, ended up here."

"I'm sure there's a lot more to it than that—"

"I thought you knew everything I know."

He shrugged as he reseated himself. "I *am* what you know. There's a difference."

"What do you remember?"

"What you remember."

I squinted at him as I massaged my temples; deliberately or not, he was making my fierce headache worse. "Do you remember dying?"

"No. And I strongly suspect that's a really good thing—you know me and pain. Not a good mix." He shook his head and a lock of flaxen hair fell across his eyes. He puffed it away—another Felix habit; he never wanted to risk getting his hair dirty if he could avoid it so he always blew his hair out of his eyes rather than use his fingers. "I do know *how* I died—through your memories—" He made a face, muttered, *"Ghastly business,"* and searched my blood-shot, watery eyes for a moment. "Were we all killed in that damnedable bog?"

"Yes."

"Everyone?"

I looked away, nodded and replied tightly, "Aside from me—and Cerialis… yes."

He shook his head. "Gods. I'm sorry. Truly I am. I can't even imagine the torture you've put yourself through on our behalf."

I dropped my gaze to my balled hands, blinked rapidly, hoping to clear my blurry vision.

"You're a good officer. You never failed us."

"I was a *damned* good centurion," I replied in an attempt to regain my composure, but my voice gave me away by cracking.

"Yes, you were, *damned* good. The best in fact—still are. You would've made Primus-Pilus for sure, if things hadn't... well, you know, turned out the way they did."

"When the real you said that, I took it for truth. As it is, it's just my memory of Felix saying it. Doesn't have quite the same heft—it's rather narcissistic in fact."

"Do you really doubt your abilities that much? Even now?"

"More so now—I'm the only one who survived, *remember?*"

"And you think that because you and you alone survived that somehow proves you're an incompetent officer?"

I scowled at him. *"What the hell do you think?"*

"You survived because Lady Turan intervened. Either you would have died in that bog with the rest of us or the Iceni would have discovered you and killed you on the spot, or worse, dragged you off for use in some gods-awful sacrifice." He paused. "Dead is *dead*—there's no shame in surviving. I certainly don't hold it against you."

"Why should you?" I snarled, banging my fists on my thighs, too late realizing that was a really dumb, not to mention painful, thing to do. *"You've been created from my memories! If it weren't for me you wouldn't exist!"*

He stared at me for a moment then turned his face to the fire and murmured, "You're right of course. You were always much smarter than me—always so much smarter than everyone else."

It was hard to tell by his sincere tone if he was being truly sincere. Of course the same had been true of the real Felix. He had a special knack for insulting people while sounding as if he'd just paid them a huge compliment. It was a skill I'd never mastered.

"I assume the other two are Aetius and Rufinius," I said, not bothering to hide the intense bitterness, the overwhelming rage I felt at having my memories, the memories of my closest friends—my *only* friends—so deeply violated.

He looked back at me. "They will be, once they meet you." At my guardedly quizzical stare he added, "We need to interact with you directly to take on the characteristics of the individuals you remember—don't ask me how or why, I don't understand it, but it's true. Did I sound like Felix when I arrived?"

I shook my head and suddenly recalled Turan telling me I had an extraordinary memory for details, facial tics, inflections—all the usually overlooked minutiae that made each person unique. While I'd doubted her at the time, as it turns out she'd been right. The corroboration was seated before me.

"So the same will be true for them. Shall I call them?" He started to rise. "They're dying—I mean they're very eager to meet you, as you can well... um, *imagine.*"

I wasn't sure I could handle that—I was barely handling the situation as it was. "No."

He sank back into the chair, looked sadly at me. "You may never accept us as who we are—I *am* Felix. Maybe not the original Felix, but I'm *still* Felix. And the more I'm around you, the more I will *become* Felix, the less I will be a... *copy.* A proto type. I'll think for myself, not as you would think I should think, or even want me to think—do you understand?"

I angrily wiped my eyes on my sleeve. "Where'd you come from? Where'd all of you come from?"

He looked thoughtful for a moment, shrugged. "I'm not sure. I must've been someone else, once, but who I was, or what I was, or where I came from or how I got to be here and how long I've been here I cannot tell you." He said it without regret, without anger, without resentment, as it was just his lot in life. Totally accepting.

I stared back at him and suddenly knew the full and appalling extent of what Turan and her accomplices had done and without thinking replied furiously, "You *were* someone else—you've had your mind, your memories wiped clean!"

He stared back at me, unblinking, then again fixing his eyes on the fire as if he too suddenly grasped the horror of what had been done to him, done to the others. A moment later he whispered, *"Who was I?"*

"I honestly don't know—I wish I did. Maybe you were Roman, maybe you were an enemy of Rome." *Maybe you were another Kyrou—another me— someone Turan grabbed for whatever reason and then, for whatever reason, just as easily discarded.* "But whoever you were is gone for good." It was a cruel thing to say, but it was the truth and he deserved that. "Turan warned me that once a man's mind is wiped clean, there's no going back, no second chance."

He took a deep, ragged breath and his luminescent ring-mail shimmered eerily in response, like quicksilver.

I gave him a few moments to digest what I'd said, then asked, "How many Kellesuf are there?"

He shrugged again, replied softly, *"Here?* Including me, two hundred and eight at last count. There were more, but I don't know what happened to them. Until now I never even thought about what might have happened to them. They just weren't... with us any longer. And I think there are more, a lot more, elsewhere."

I felt a shiver run up my spine, goose-pimpling my flesh. I had a damned good idea where the others were: housed in the Keeps of the other Lords of the Sidhe. "Do you know what they want of you—all of you—of me?"

"To fight this war of course, just like the last—"

"They started it—*let them finish it!"* I smacked my fist against the bed for emphasis, having learned not to strike my left thigh again unless of course I wanted it to throb like hell.

He looked back at me, appalled. "But... but that's why Kellesuf exist, why *I* exist."

That set me back. He and his fellows had been snatched, like me, from who-knows-where. Unlike me, and for some inexplicable reason, they'd had had their minds wiped clean so they would fight Taskim's war without question or complaint—it made my blood boil. They were worse off than slaves, naïve and trusting—utterly at the mercy of their masters' whims.

But I now realized why Taskim and his lords needed me, needed my knowledge, my skills: an army of soldiers incapable of thinking for themselves, soldiers who would follow orders blindly might seem like a really brillant idea, but anyone who'd actually fought would instantly recognize the glaring flaw in any such scheme. Rasaben had, I realized, recalling his bitter remarks to Turan when they thought I was unconscious and incapable of eavesdropping on their squabbling—that's why he'd been so opposed to the plan. He'd volunteered, he'd said—to have his memories transferred? Too risky, she'd countered. But not too risky for me... or for this man—no wonder Rasaben loathed me. I'd usurped him: me, a lowly Roman foot soldier and him a highborn Tuatha lord. If I'd been him, I'd have loathed me too.

Oblivious, the soldier continued. "You always wanted to be Primus-Pilus—how many times did you tell me such?"

I stared at his earnest and yet deceitful face. He *wasn't* Felix. He could never be Felix, despite someone—Turan? Ainiaan?—clearly going to great lengths to find a man among the ranks of Kellesuf who looked a great deal like him. Then another explanation came to mind: perhaps I only *thought* he looked like him, perhaps my perceptions were being manipulated, *again*. He certainly hadn't looked like Felix's perfect double when I first laid eyes on him. Now I'd be hard pressed to tell them apart, but whether I was being tricked into believing he looked like Felix, or fooled into believing Felix looked like him was anyone's guess.

So now I couldn't even trust my memories of what the real Felix looked like. My fury at this latest theft tainted my voice: "I told *my* Felix that—I *never* told you, and now you mock me with words spoken to a dead man?"

His chilling metamorphosis into the man I considered my closest friend left me feeling duped in the worst way and he reacted to my tone, my words, the look in my eye by flinching as if he'd taken a physical blow.

I dropped my slitted gaze to my balled hands. *Dammit!*

For several minutes neither of us spoke then he said calmly, quietly: "Fair enough. But you now have the chance to be even more than Primus-Pilus, more than any of us could have ever imagined—to lead not just a century, not a cohort, *but an entire legion*, to fight the ultimate battle—with me, Aetius, Rufinius at your side. If you asked, I'm sure they'd even give you Duccius, although why you'd want that half-crazed Marcomanni is beyond me."

I felt his pleading gaze on me but I refused to look at him. I *couldn't* look at him. "I don't want to fight their war," I replied bitterly. "I'm weary of fighting. They can do what they want with you—I'll take no willing part of it."

"That's your choice of course."

"I doubt it." I angrily wiped my nose on the back of my hand. "They've never once asked my opinion on anything, least of all if I wanted any part of you and the others."

"Again, fair enough."

I glared at him. "Stop being so damned agreeable!"

He held out his hands, palms up, a practice Felix had learned from his Greek mother—not a Roman gesture. "What would you have me do or say?"

I started to open my mouth, to tell him to be more like Felix then clamped my jaw shut. He *was* being like Felix—too damned much in fact.

"You don't have any idea of what it was like before, Arri—do you mind me calling you Arri? Would you prefer I call you Centurion?"

I shrugged, feigning indifference, when in fact hearing Felix's voice calling me by name and rank brought with it a tremendous amount of pain. "I'm not a centurion any longer, remember?"

He paused, shifted around then continued, "I watched you come ashore with the others that day you know. I was there; saw you. We'd heard the servants talking amongst themselves you see. Just because Kellesuf can only speak when directly spoken to—because no one cares to know what we think or what we might need, I suppose—everyone assumes we're deaf and dumb, don't ask me why, but we *aren't*.

"We knew Lady Turan had gone to fetch someone who was going to help us, make us... *whole*, make us more than we were, and somewhere deep inside I desperately hoped you'd be my deliverance, *our* deliverance from this terrible, protracted limbo we've found ourselves in, although in truth I didn't realize it at the time—"

He bit his lip and flicked me a sidelong look, as if he'd said too much, or perhaps worried that like everyone else I didn't care to hear what he had to say—what he desperately wanted to say.

"Go on," I murmured coolly.

He took a deep, shuddering breath then continued: "I remember being pulled off my scheduled duty, told to report to Lord Mabog, of him telling me to undress then lie down on a cot, and him sticking something in my arm and telling me I was being put to sleep—he'd done this sort of thing before, plenty of times. Tests, he said, but later, when I woke up, I felt... *cold.*"

He smiled, briefly. *"Cold.* I never woke up feeling cold before—it was frightening and strange and uncomfortable, yet at the same time... *wonderful.* To *feel* cold! I couldn't stop shivering, even after Lord Mabog gave me a blanket. And I *hurt.* All over—truthfully that didn't feel so wonderful, but Lord Mabog told me it was a good thing, just like feeling cold. At first I wasn't even sure what it meant as I never remember feeling pain before— even that time when my horse lost its footing and rolled on top of me and broke my leg—it didn't hurt, even when I tried to remount.

"Now Lord Mabog kept poking me with things which made me hurt more—to the point I wondered if it was possible to have too much of a good thing—while Lord Rasaben asked me all sorts of questions, most of which made no sense, although I did my best to answer him. And all of a sudden I realized I was really hungry, famished in fact and I asked if I could have something to eat—no one had offered me food or drink, no, *I just asked!* I never remember doing that before, either—in fact, now that I think about it, I don't remember feeling hungry before. I ate when I was told to eat, nothing more.

"But now I was so hungry I actually interrupted Lord Rasaben to ask. I feared he'd be angry, feared Lord Mabog would be angry, but they were...

well, pleased? Well, not pleased maybe, but they weren't angry either. At least Lord Mabog wasn't. Lord Rasaben said I was to get dressed then I would accompany him to supper and that I would sit with him and Lord Taskim and Lady Turan and the other lords—he said they wanted to meet me, talk to me and… and the other… proto types.

"After I got dressed, I met the other two—I vaguely remembered them from before, and they me. I wanted to ask them what was happening, but I was too scared—Lord Rasaben had ordered us not to speak privately with each other until he and the others had had a chance to speak with us.

"He brought us to the Great Hall and we were in fact seated with the lords and ladies, not with Kellesuf. I didn't want to sit with them—none of us did. We wanted to sit where we belonged, eat our suppers and go back to the barracks and pretend none of this had happened—but then a plate of food placed in front of me. It smelled wonderful. I never remember smelling food before and it made me even hungrier, almost the point I couldn't hold myself back.

"Only after everyone finished asking their questions and we answered them to what I have to assume was their satisfaction were we finally permitted to eat. I started wolfing it down… then realized I could *taste* it. It had a wonderful taste, so wonderful I forced myself to slow down and savor every bite. That's when Lady Ainiaan told us she'd personally selected us to be proto types. She said it was a great honor to have been picked—that we weren't to disappoint you.

"I didn't know what that meant—none of us did, I'm still not completely sure. All I knew was that I could now feel, I could taste, I could… *see*. It was overwhelming—I was no longer Kellesuf, and worse, no one told me why. I was so scared I desperately wanted to go back to the way I'd been; I even asked to go back, but Lady Ainiaan asked me why I'd want to do that—she even held my hand and told me not to be scared—next thing I knew—"

"I made my unexpected appearance."

He nodded.

"And when I fell, it was you who tried to touch me, wasn't it?"

He nodded again. "Lady Ainiaan told me never to do that again, that I'd greatly upset you, but I meant no harm, truly."

I exhaled and shook my head. No wonder he'd arrived looking like he was about to be executed—for simply offering his hand in support—

"When I was ordered to come here, to meet you, I was terrified out of my mind. Like being called to an audience with a god—

"You told me once you weren't sure you believed in gods."

He smiled, guardedly.

Then I realized what I'd said and grumbled irritably at my lapse, "I meant Felix told me that."

"No, what Felix told you was that he wasn't sure the gods *deserved* our belief in them."

I only scowled at him. He was right of course. That *was* what Felix had said, damn him—*damn them both!*

"I'm terribly sorry you feel I've stolen Felix from you. But I *want* this identity, Arri. I was scared at first, as I said, unprepared and overwhelmed, and while I'm still really scared, I like who I am, *now*—I really like who Felix was, to himself and to you. I want—" He bit his lip, looked away and fixed his now glistening eyes on the fire.

"You want... *what?*" I growled.

He shook his head and roughly wiped his eyes. "You wouldn't believe me if I told you."

"Try me."

He took a deep breath then looked back at me. "I want very much to be Felix for you—help *you* feel whole again."

I stared at him but said nothing. I couldn't.

He cleared his throat, looked around again, eyes still aglitter. "Are you sure there's nothing to drink?"

"I... I could call for something I suppose," I replied hoarsely.

"Please do. I don't know about you, but I feel like getting blind drunk right now."

"Sounds like an excellent idea." And it was an excellent idea to let him get blind drunk, so drunk in fact he wouldn't notice I'd made good my escape. I truly wanted no part of this war, in part because I was now convinced I'd fallen into the hands of an enemy who didn't give a damn about humanity.

Seeing this man, this eerie twin of Felix, hear the soul-deep pain in his voice, see the anguish over his missing identity, the sense of loss and being lost... I did *not* want to end up like that. And I had a sneaking suspicion, now that Turan and Rasaben and the lot had what they wanted from me, that I'd made it very clear to Turan that there was no hope of me ever trusting her, I'd just placed myself at the top of their to-do list when time came to create another Kellesuf. Hell, they'd probably wipe my mind clean then re-instill my memories and I'd never realize it. I'd be *grateful*, just as this man was grateful.

I reached for the rope pull on the wall next to the bed and gave it a hard yank.

He raised his brows.

"Room service," I replied, having seen Mabog use it. "Calls for a servant." I suddenly hoped he hadn't been pulling my leg along with the rope—otherwise I was going to look damned foolish.

"Why didn't we ever have that?"

"I never remember frequenting such rich accommodations." Then I glanced at him. The real Felix had been the bastard son of a senator after all; he'd grown up in a very wealthy household.

He grinned. "I did—as you well know. I still don't remember a contraption like that." When I didn't return his easy grin—if I had, I'd be acknowledging more than just his expression and he knew it—he again fixed his glittering stare on the fire.

I kept my eyes on him—the likeness was now truly uncanny—no, *not* likeness. There *were* physical differences. His mannerisms were what made him an absolute dead ringer for Felix. He'd even crossed his ankles and was wiggling his toes just as Felix did when he was deeply perturbed but didn't want anyone to know—the subtle movement visible through the tips of his boots. It was a nervous tic I'd become so habituated to that I'd stopped being consciously aware of it. But there it was, and I had to wonder how far down they had to dig into my memories to find it. Even more worrisome, what else had they stumbled across while plumbing the depths—could they produce Gracchus on a whim? *Porsenna?* My stomach turned anew at such prospects—

A knock at the door startled me and I jumped. So did the soldier.

I tried not to look as relieved as I felt that the rope trick had actually worked, said "Come," and the door opened.

"Boian," I smiled thinly as the woman cautiously entered the room as if fully expecting to be asked to clean up after a very messy if noiseless murder. "Would you bring us something to drink—mead, wine, anything that has a kick to it?"

She glanced at the soldier, clearly surprised to find him not only alive but apparently no worse for being left alone with me. "Of course, sire. Would you care for something to eat as well?"

I turned to my unwelcome and at that moment unhappy companion. "Hungry?"

"You did interrupt my supper if you recall," he replied softly.

I looked at her. "Whatever's prepared and convenient, Boian, don't go to any trouble—"

"But if there's any of that roast boar left...?" the soldier interrupted with a hopeful smile.

She fixed him with a very curious stare then nodding to me, withdrew.

The instant the door closed behind her, he whipped his face towards me and said, "I've never had sex."

"What?"

"I've never had sex—oh, yes, I know your Felix had, plenty of times. I haven't—at least not that I can recall. I hadn't realized it until just now."

"Oh."

"I think I'd very much like to have sex—" he grabbed himself, as if to check if he had the right equipment and by his expression was startled by what he found. He immediately let go and looked back at me. "See for myself if it's as fantastic as you think it is."

I couldn't help it—I laughed.

"What's so funny?"

"You."

He took offense at that, just as Felix would've.

So I said something to mollify his pride: "I suspect if you asked really nicely, Boian *might* oblige."

"Really?" He looked back at the door, then at me, pale eyebrows raised. "You think so? *Truly?"*

I *knew* so, but I felt it wouldn't help his vanity if I said so. Boian had made her proclivities known to me and it wasn't like I was foisting off some odious task as he was extremely good looking: tall and well-muscled with a handsome, albeit obviously naïve face. And in my experience women found inexperienced men to be... well, *very* attractive for some inexplicable reason. Just like dimples. Perhaps it was because of the sheer rarity of such individuals—outside of the priesthoods of some of the more masochistic cults that is. Even really, and I mean *really* ugly men—like Aetius—could truthfully claim some breadth of experience, even if it was all gained at some financial cost to them.

I seriously doubted this man would have any trouble finding a woman willing to deflower him. Sifrie, I'm sure, would be at the head of the line if the call went out for volunteers.

But his ingenuous face left me questioning if Sifrie would be the best first choice—knowing her she'd eat him alive, in *every* sense of the phrase. Boian, on the other hand, might be a better pick: kind, gentle... and forgiving. And since the decision did seem to fall on me, Boian it was—and it would guarantee me at least a minute or two head start. Nowhere near as much as getting him blind drunk, but...

Good to her word, Boian returned, a pitcher and two mugs gripped in one hand with a platter of sliced boar and some bread and cheese balanced in the crook of her arm. She set her burden down on the small table near the fire as she gave my companion a sidelong glance. He stared back at her—the boar all but forgotten—with such intense yearning that it almost made me laugh aloud.

She pulled her uneasy eyes off him and turned to me. "If you're in need of more, young sire, just call."

As she started for the door, he tore his eyes off her and looked at me in something akin to panic.

Realizing I was going to have to do the asking, I sighed, "Boian...?"

She stopped, looked at me. "Yes, sire?"

"My... friend here." I motioned 'up' with my hand and he rose obediently, if little unsteadily. "He's never... well, um, *known* a woman."

Her brows shot up, then she turned to him and gave him a very slow, head to toe appraisal as he swallowed convulsively, not once, but repeatedly.

"You're one of Lord Rasaben's men," she asked, "aren't you? *Kellesuf.*"

He glanced at me, clearly fearful if he admitted so, she would refuse him. It had been obvious to me that most of the servants, even some of Turan's men—certainly Hanni—harbored a strong dislike, almost a dread of the soldiers. Hanni, after all had warned me to stay well away from them. A case of collective guilt? Or perhaps a well-placed fear that one misstep would result in a new Kellesuf?

"He was, Boian," I said. "But now he's a friend of mine—name's *Felix.*"

She gave me a sidelong, startled look—as did he—then she turned back to him and gave him another good, long stare and by her expression found him... well, if not immediately appealing, then at least mildly intriguing. And why not? He *was* almost as good-looking as me. And utterly innocent. Let's not forget that. *With dimples.*

"I was wondering..." I continued, "if you might... uh, help him?"

Keeping her eyes on him, she walked back to where she'd left the pitcher and mugs, leaving him to stare at me in bewilderment, clearly suspecting this was her way of saying no and desperately hoping I'd intercede... again.

I didn't need to and knew it. I'd thrown out the line and she'd, *ahem*, swallowed the bait.

She filled both mugs, then walked over to me and as she handed me one, she winked at me and whispered so only I could hear her, *"Will it be the both of you, young sire, or just him?"*

I honestly hadn't seen that proposition coming. *"Just him... for now,"* I replied softly as I brought the mug to my lips.

She looked a little disappointed.

"Later," I added, sweetening the pot so to speak, and winking at her, took a deep gulp.

She grinned. *"Very good, young sire, very, very good."* Then she walked over to the soldier, swaying her hips suggestively the entire way. She pressed the other mug into his hands. "Here, young sire—you look quite parched."

He nodded vigorously, then obediently and loudly gulped down its contents while she walked around him, giving him another slow, head to toe exam as she loosened the ties of her bodice, then gave it a tug here and a yank there, exposing more of her abundant flesh.

He noticed. In fact his wide-eyed gaze was now stuck fast to her large breasts, the empty mug held loosely in his fingers, forgotten.

"You're *very* handsome, young sire," she murmured as she ran her hand over his shoulder and down his ring-mailed chest to his belt. *"Very handsome."* She gave the buckle a gentle tug as she ran her tongue over her lips.

His only response was to wet *his* lips; his eyes were still affixed to her breasts, her ample cleavage, utterly enthralled by the sight.

Smiling, she took the mug from his unresisting armored fingers while giving him another ogle then tugging at one of the loosened bodice ties, purred, "Would you like more?"

More? I could clearly see the word form on his lips. And I knew what he was thinking—*Oh, gods, yes, please!* But that wasn't what Boian had meant, at least not quite... yet.

"She wants to know if you want more to drink," I prompted.

He somehow managed to pry his eyes off her cleavage and looked at me, eyebrows raised, but whether he was asking my advice or was just confused, I can't say.

"I wouldn't—it'll dull your senses and lessen the full experience."

He turned back to her and shook his curly blond head.

"Very good," she breathed as she tucked a lock of that hair behind his ear, in the process pressing herself against him.

She *was* good, damned if she wasn't and watching her I suddenly began to seriously question my plan of using her as a distraction while I made good my escape—*Maybe I should show him how it's done, first and then—no.* I shook my head. *No!*

"Here." I rose from the bed before I could change my mind. "Be my guests."

Boian took his gauntleted hand in hers and guided him across the room to the bed. I made my way over to the door, opened it and glanced both ways down the corridor and was somewhat surprised to find it was deserted—perhaps Boian had assured everyone that I was behaving myself, that I hadn't bludgeoned my guest and they'd wisely decided to leave the two of us alone to sort things out over a late night repast?—then I made it sound as if I'd slipped outside when instead I firmly closed and locked the door, from the *inside.*

"Let's get you undressed, young sire."

I watched from the darkness of the door alcove, grinning at his expression, at the blatant mixture of sheer terror and intense anticipation on his face, at Boian's gentle hands, her purring flatteries and her well-practiced, and, I must say, impressively quick technique at separating a man from his clothing—in this man's case, his gauntlets, belt and baldric, ring-mail and heavy leather hauberk, boots and trousers. All came off in amazingly rapid order. I did say she was good, didn't I?

Within a very short time he stood there like a just-shorn sheep, Boian eagerly running her hands over his naked, milk-white skin which was now glistening with sweat, admiring his lithe body while he labored for breath.

"Lie down," she murmured, gently nudging him towards the bed.

He dumbly did as he was told and she quickly disrobed as he watched in rapt fascination. I'd been right about her backside—it *was* delectable. So was the rest of her.

I waited a few minutes longer, watching them—not as a voyeur, mind you. I wanted to make absolutely sure Boian had his undivided attention and satisfy myself that in arranging this tryst, I was paying this man, this replicate Felix, some small amends for what I was about to do, which was to abandon him, abandon the other Kellesuf to whatever the Fates—and the Tuatha—had in store for them.

This of course necessitated that I observe. I felt my resolve slipping yet again, not so much at the sight of a naked Boian astride Felix, but at the idea of abandoning him and the others to a people every bit as cruel as the Iceni and the ugly comparisons that raised.

I tore my eyes off them and crept over to the lead-paned door that opened onto the balcony.

It was snowing—of course. Large, wet snowflakes falling in large, wet clouds. I risked one last glance back at Felix only to find him on top now, going at her like a bull.

Finding some small satisfaction that I was leaving this man in a far better way than I had his progenitor, I bid him and Boian a silent farewell.

I cracked open the door, slipped onto the snow-covered balcony and into the falling snow, then closed the door softly behind me—considering how much noise the two were making I could have probably slammed it and neither would have noticed, but on that note I also realized my already very short head start was rapidly coming to an end. With luck, Boian would find other ways to keep him occupied, at least for a few minutes longer.

The icy chill took my breath away—I hadn't anticipated it being quite so damned cold. But I also had never planned to bring a cloak, even if I could have found one. My hastily planned escape was going to be temporary at best. Just long enough to find a place to hide… then settle down and wait for the cold to kill me, which in this climate wouldn't take long.

I sidled, tip-toe, along the stone wall, wanting to avoid any betraying footprints and peered over the balcony. The ground was a story below, so I eased myself over the balcony railing, said a silent prayer that the snow was deep enough to break my fall, that I wouldn't end up breaking an ankle or a leg, let go… and ended up waist deep in a snow bank. After a moment of struggle, I heaved myself free, only to have to ease my head and shoulders back into the hole I'd made and fish out my right boot.

That done, I sat down on the bank, tugged the boot back on and brushed myself off as I glanced around. I was still within the Keep complex, still behind its protective and, for me, imprisoning walls. I thought about the tower room as a place that might be overlooked, at least for an hour or so—then I just as quickly discounted it, realizing Taskim would think of it and find me before death did.

I shook my head at the irony that I so abhorred the cold and always had, and had now freely chosen it as my executioner—perhaps there had been a reason for such a life-long loathing. Perhaps I'd known all along that it would be cold that ultimately killed me, not a barbarian's pike or some cuckolded husband's dagger.

I scooted down the ice-crusted slope of the snow bank then lurched to my feet. I had to find my hiding place and quick—considering it was his first time, I knew it wouldn't take long for the soldier and Boian to finish, only to discover I was nowhere to be found, make the logical deduction and raise the alarm.

Keeping that worrying thought foremost, I slogged through the knee-high snow and over to the inner circuit wall, where the snow was a little less deep and the going a little easier. The main gateway with its portcullis was no more than a hundred feet away, its torch-lit, gridded maw barely visible through the falling snow. I'd been told that sometimes there was a small side door, or a door within the portcullis, as there was with the massive cedar doors that gave entrance to Lady Ilissia's villa—if I could just reach that, I might, just might be able to escape the Keep itself and disappear into the surrounding forest where I doubted I'd be found... until the spring thaw that is.

I trudged towards it, boots crunching through the frozen crust on the snow, all the while nervously glancing about, expecting detection at any moment. If there were guards about, they were patrolling somewhere else—probably someplace toasty warm, like the Keep's kitchens—and I reached the grilled gate without incident.

There *was* a door, barely noticeable, in a deep, narrow alcove to the right of the main gateway. I hurried over to it, looked back at the torch-lit courtyard and the massive Keep beyond, then cautiously lifted the metal-reinforced bar and opened the door. The flickering light from the courtyard torches caught glimpses of falling snow beyond, and little else.

I slipped around the door, gave one last glance back at the Keep, bid my bitter farewell to Turan—quickly clamped down on that thought in sudden fear she might sense it and realize what I was about—slowly closed the door and heard the muffled *thump* of the bar settling back into place. I then turned and faced what would be my tomb: a pitch dark, snow-bound forest. In order to reach it, I'd either have to cross the drawbridge and in the process, leave myself briefly exposed, or cross the moat, which was hopefully frozen solid. If it wasn't, if I happened to break through the ice, then my grand plan of walking until the cold killed me would be cut mercifully, but far from painlessly short. I couldn't help but swallow convulsively, suddenly wondering if I'd been a wee bit impulsive.

Then I remembered what had been done to me—with Turan's willing complicity—what they might do again, that it was likely I'd never get another chance. I remembered with intense bitterness the humiliation I felt when I couldn't force myself to jump overboard, of being handed over to Turan to degrade and demean further, to salve her own hurt. I could only imagine the punishment this time, if they caught me.

Besides, Turan had suggested I get some exercise, work off those unsightly ounces I'd somehow managed to gain back. Granted, I doubted this was what she'd had in mind, but... I took a deep breath, exhaled slowly and started off—not in the direction my soon to be pursuers might assume I'd gone, which was across the drawbridge then follow the road, or even to my right. No. I turned to the left and after a quick look-see to make sure no one was nearby and might spot me, I crept past the portcullis just beyond the warm, shifting glow of the torches. Once I was safely on the other side,

I neared the outer wall again and felt my way along for some distance, at least, by my figuring, a quarter of the way around the massive Keep. Satisfied I'd gone far enough, I found a spot thick with scrub to hide my point of descent then I carefully climbed down the steep slope to the moat, using the bushes to slow my sliding and stumbling passage. I took another steadying breath, then very carefully stepped out onto the moat's frozen, snow-covered surface.

Satisfied it would indeed take my weight, I glanced up at the Keep just to make sure no one had spotted me from the ramparts, then I started across, skidding, sliding and slipping—not to mention silently cursing—each step of the way.

Reaching the other side without actually falling, I scrambled up it then headed into the forest at an angle, a sweeping arc away from the road and away from the Keep and hopefully, in the exact opposite direction everyone else would take, searching for me.

There was no need to run, to exhaust myself by hurriedly trudging through the deep, wet snow. Death would come for me soon enough—no need to hasten it along. Besides, I had something to prove. Come spring, I wanted them to stumble across my thawing corpse miles and miles from where they'd expected to find it and be in awe of my resolve, that I'd actually managed to "get that far" before I collapsed and died. It would be a posthumous honor, but an honor nonetheless. Even better, some would rightfully attribute my doggedness to Roman discipline—and so one last thumb in the eye to Rasaben. *Hah.*

So I walked—slowly, almost casually, as if I was just going for a stroll and was soon surrounded by thick wood and pockets of dense underbrush which I deliberately eased myself through, rather than going around—all the harder to track me. It was a technique I'd picked up from some of Kyrou's equally uncouth cousins, the Suebi—while trying to hunt down some of their men who'd ambushed and wiped out one of our foraging parties. Never did find the buggars, and now I hoped the same tactic would produce the same results. Of course I must mention for accuracy's sake that the Suebi didn't entirely get away with their despicable deed: we ably demonstrated our pique by burning every Suebi village within a fifty mile radius to the ground. Ah, the good old days.

But I digress…

The snow softened everything—deadening sounds, leaving the forest eerily silent aside from the constant, muffled patter of falling snowflakes and the rhythmic crunch of my boots. And it was *dark*. So gods-damned dark I was as good as blind; I kept bumping into tree trunks and stumbling over fallen branches.

The sky above was invisible, lost within the dense canopy of snow-cloaked treetops and falling snow; soon even the fire-glow above the Keep vanished behind a dense palisade of trees and brush.

And something else: I was rapidly becoming oblivious to the bitter cold—*me!* Under other circumstances this would have been a very worrisome thing, and not just due to my usual anathema to all things icy cold. As it was, it just meant I wasn't uncomfortable—my cunning plan was working! My feet had gone numb, my face was numb. My hands, which I'd kept tucked in my armpits, were rapidly going numb. My only thought was to get as far away as possible before the rest of me succumbed to the intense chill.

Then I had another thought: what if they *don't* come looking? I stopped, glanced back in the general direction of the Keep. More than enough time had passed—they'd had plenty of time to realize I was missing, even search the Keep. Yet I'd heard nothing. Even in the depth of the forest, with the snow falling, I should have heard... something—*if* they were looking. But what if they weren't? And then: Why should they? They'd taken everything they wanted, had everything they needed.

So, having finally expended my usefulness, I'd been cast aside once more—the last time. And by my own hand.

Expecting to feel the now habitual bitterness, I realized with some surprise I felt nothing—*I was nothing.* Not even worth my own pity.

So, with a shrug I started off again.

Around me the snow continued to fall, its soft, wet patter keeping me company as I traveled deeper into the wood and at the same time covering my trail: death disguised as the consummate friend to the last.

Then, far behind me, I heard a deep lowing wail of horns—it took my sluggish mind a moment to grasp what that meant. Then it hit me: my absence had been discovered and now the hunt was on.

Run...!

I felt a flutter of panic, which I quickly tamped down by reminding myself that I had time and distance on my side, not to mention that I was one man and around me was a vast forest. I'd seen that for myself when I'd gone to the tower room with Taskim—it stretched as far as the eye could see and I had no reason to doubt it went even further than that. I did however pick up my pace—from a slow, determined walk to an easily sustainable lope in the rare spots where the fresh snow cover on top of frozen hardpack was only a foot or so deep, and a rather ungraceful, trundling slog where the snow had formed hip-deep drifts.

As I struggled through an especially deep drift, I cursed myself for not taking the time to make myself a pair of snowshoes from bundled twigs, as we'd used in Cisalpina to hunt game, a trick we'd picked up from some of the friendlier locals. Had I done so at the start I'd have covered a lot more ground by now. Too late—my fingers were too numb to manage the task. And besides, somewhere along the line, the desire to prove anything to anyone had simply... *gone.* I now had only one goal: succumb to the cold before I could be captured.

To that end I had to keep moving until my body could move no more. If I pushed myself to the point of exhaustion, once I collapsed I'd die that much faster, and relatively painlessly, too. That much of my survival training I remembered from my otherwise forgettable deployment to Germania and the bitterly cold and utterly miserable winter I'd spent there: build a snow cave, wait for rescue if you get separated—don't go wandering off alone, don't go looking for help from the natives as they were just as apt to murder you, and whatever you do, don't work up a sweat; that was the mantra of the reconnaissance and foraging squads and one that usually held us in good stead. Now I was using that very same knowledge—but for the exact opposite effect.

I hadn't heard the baying of dogs—which meant that I only had to evade human hunters and human eyes—always an advantage to the hunted, especially at night. Then suddenly I remembered Turan's shape-changing skills, her ability in her hound-guise to seek me out by scent, a scent she now knew *intimately.* For the first time since I'd escaped the Keep I was gripped by an overwhelming fear that I might be captured again, very much alive.

RUN!

This time I listened to my panic and ran, heedless to the deep snow and my numb feet, to the low branches that whipped and scratched my face and tore at my clothing, to rocks and roots underfoot I couldn't see until I tripped over them.

I fell, rose, ran some distance, tripped and fell again, lurched back to my feet and kept running, compelled by the distant voices of the hunters, the whicker of horses and the thumping echo of countless hooves and feet. Occasionally I even caught a glimpse of a torch bobbing along, briefly caught in an arrow-slit between trees.

My throat and lungs burned with each breath, my muscles ached and my joints hurt with each jolting step and still I kept running blindly, mindless now in utter panic… which is how I came to run smack into a tree—*THWACK!*

I stumbled back a step, stunned by the impact and sat down. *Hard.*

My head spun. My vision refused to focus and now my face was bleeding. I felt the warm trickle as it wormed its way down my frozen cheek to the corner of my mouth. I tasted the coppery tang, and tried to spit— couldn't. My lips were too numb. I felt the sting of blood in my right eye but I when I tried, I found I couldn't lift my arm to wipe it clean.

Ahead I saw a faint blur of light—*torchlight,* then realized… no. *Sunrise.* In a matter of minutes the forest would be flooded with sunlight—one of my staunchest allies deserting me, fleeing before it.

Then I heard the wail of horns all around me, of men yelling— desperately, hoarsely calling my name, others bellowing orders. They were getting closer.

I tried to get back to my feet but found my legs unwilling as the penetrating cold caught up with my sweat-drenched and exhausted body.

Yes, I thought and surrendered, my body falling back, onto a soft pillow of snow. I took a breath, another and strangely, I felt warm—suddenly, blessedly *warm.* And sleepy… *intensely*… sleepy…

I closed my eyes as the rest of my body relaxed, cradled in the powdery snow as more fell, knocked loose from the branches above me, slowly covering me. I could feel it settle on my eyelids.

Go to sleep, I urged my utterly spent body, my spent mind, *go to sleep and we'll never wake up…*

I took another breath, another, yet another, each shallower than the last. I felt death's fingers tug at me, whispering my name.

Arri…

I smiled, murmured, *Yes, I'm here…*

My shoulder was shaken, roughly. "Arri!"

I somehow managed to open my eyes.

"Arri, damn you!"

I squinted through the crust of snowflakes at the face that hovered over me and wanted to laugh at the irony that Death looked remarkably like the torch-lit face of Rasaben.

I grinned stupidly.

"What the hell do you think you're up to?" he snarled as he stabbed the butt of the torch into the snow beside me.

I thought how very odd Death would ask such a question when the answer was so damned obvious. Not wanting to piss him off as I had a sneaking suspicion that would be a *very* bad idea, I managed to part my frozen, blood- and snow-coated lips and mumble, *"Haaaavingaaaaahnap?"*

He exhaled forcefully, shook his head, then without further ado, grabbed a fistful of my tunic collar and hoisted me to my feet.

I stood there, swaying drunkenly as he held on to me.

"You're an idiot!"

Okay, so Death and I didn't get off on such good footing. You'd have thought he'd have given me a little leeway, considering how many I'd sent in his direction over the years. But no, of course not. I never catch a break from anyone.

He gave me a rough shake to emphasize the point and my body responded as if it was a rag doll, my head snapping this way and that.

"We've had the entire Keep out searching for you!"

Once my body stopped wobbling, I peered at him, suddenly not so sure I was staring Death in the face, but rather Rasaben himself. *Uh-oh.* I tried to ooze back down onto the snowy ground.

He tightened his hold and gave me yet another violent shake. *"Wake up, man!"*

That hurt. I mean really, it *really* hurt. It made my head pound, my vision blur and as my jaws slammed together, I bit my tongue. I spit out the blood, blinked, blinked again. *"Raaasaben…?"*

He scowled. "Who'd you think it was, *fool?"*

I decided he might not appreciate knowing, so I fibbed: "I… I waasssn't sssssure."

"Why I bother I don't know," he muttered, squinting furiously at me.

I didn't either. In fact if asked, I would have said so, but of course I wasn't asked.

"Stay right here," he growled, "don't you *dare* move." He let go of me and turned to yank the torch out of the snow.

I did try—honest I did. Can I help it if my legs refused to cooperate?

Down I went, like a felled tree, face-first into the snow. I was vaguely aware of a horse's startled, snorted whinny; of Rasaben's explosive curse then I was again grabbed by my tunic collar—only the back this time—and again hoisted back to my feet.

Now I was *sure* it was Rasaben. I glanced over my shoulder at his grim face. "Leave… leave me here—I promise I won't tell… tell anyone."

His eyes narrowed to slits, he tightened his fist-hold on my tunic, effectively making it a near-stranglehold, and gave me another violent shake—so much so I thought for sure this time my eyeballs would come flying out—I think they would've had they not been frozen to my eyelids.

"I didn't spent half the goddamned night chasing around the wood, freezing my ass off only to leave you here, you fucking Roman!"

Okay. Now I was angry. *Damned angry.*

I somehow found my legs, managed to shake off his hold, then I turned around, granted, none too steadily. More like wobbled around. But the result was the same. I was now facing him. "You... you have everything what you want from me—now let me be!" I started to back away. Stupid, really. Really, *really* stupid.

He crossed his arms, pointedly making no effort to stop my pathetic, back-stepping retreat, which in hindsight should have been a warning.

I backed right into a tree, promptly got my tunic snagged on the stub of a broken branch and tried to surreptitiously free myself, found I couldn't, then stood there, trying to act like I'd planned it all along.

Not that he was fooled. He shook his head, slowly and grumbled, "I do wish I could do as you ask but I can't."

"Why not? You've made it abundantly clear that you absolutely detest me and I've come to the unshakable conclusion that I feel the same about you."

He drew himself up and glaring balefully at me, replied, "Because for some inexplicable reason my sister loves you, and for some equally inexplicable reason I love my sister."

"Oh."

"You *do* know you made her pregnant."

"She mentioned it—I gather you're none too pleased."

"My sister, a highborn woman of the Sidhe, made pregnant by a goddamned piece of gutter filth like you?"

"Oh, and here I thought you'd be upset—what a *huge* relief." I managed to wipe my snow-crusted brow as I sagged against the tree. Granted, I hoped he'd take it for emphasis but in truth my legs had just given out. If it hadn't been for the snag, I'd have fallen again.

He eyed me as he furiously snatched up the reins of his horse, startling the animal, then the two started trudging towards me. "I would not see her hurt for anything, even if her hurt was due to grief over your death."

I waited until he was within grabbing range then I snorted, "That's nice, because I certainly don't give a damn about her. Not good in bed you see—not like Sifrie." I wiggled my snow-dusted eyebrows.

Rage flared in his eyes.

"Kill me," I goaded him further. "Go on, do us both that favor—"

"I'll do the next best thing," he snarled and I barely had a chance to wonder what he meant by that before his meaty fist connected with my jaw and everything instantly turned black.

— XVIII —

In the years that followed my departure from the Alexandria Garrison for Meroë and the Empire of Aksum, I found myself in the service of one officer after another. I saw many exotic lands, even more exotic people, learned their strange ways and in the process discovered quite by accident that I had a talent for languages and as a result became fluent in a number of foreign tongues.

I learned the intricacies of political guile. I learned to control my temper, to use my wits rather than my sword to settle disputes and perhaps most importantly of all, I learned to reckon slowly, carefully and on multiple levels, sizing up a situation from all possible angles before committing myself.

I became adept at anticipating my officers' needs; I learned their personal weaknesses, their vices and yes, I exploited them—if possible to our mutual satisfaction, if not, then to mine. Always mine. Officers took notice of my skills as an interpreter and negotiator and vied for my allegiance—some offered money, others a rise in rank. I took whichever suited me at the time and repaid their generosity, their belief in me a hundred-fold. I also made more than my share of mistakes—mistakes that came very close to killing me on several occasions. But unlike many, I learned lessons from each and never repeated my miscalculations.

While Rome churned in political turmoil, I marched with Tamphilus into Parthia—and right back out again, quickstep—followed Caecilius into Dacia and as a newly minted centurion, accompanied Vulso into Germania. Each step along the way was marked by personal glory and professional acclaim. My reputation grew. Men were eager to follow me while officers were just as eager to have me as their own.

By the time I found myself attached to the Ninth Legion Hispana, and anticipating deployment to Britannia and our legion's permanent base of Lindum, I'd attained the rank of Hastatus-Posterior. It seemed as if nothing was beyond my grasp—I had squarely met every obstacle placed before me and had come out triumphant.

I'd even allowed myself the private vanity of becoming Primus-Pilus, and not just any Primus-Pilus, but the youngest Primus-Pilus ever. I only had to succeed in my next post as centurion to Quintus Petillius Cerialis—if I did that, and there was no absolutely reason to believe I wouldn't, my life-long goal would be mine by the time I turned thirty. It would be an unheard of accomplishment, one that would make my name known across the empire and beyond—mother, would you be proud of me now?

I clearly remember my last day in Gaul, the day before we were to board the troop ships that would carry us across the narrow straight between Gaul and Britannia. It was a bright, sunny spring day: chill, but with the promise of warmer weather on the way. Everything was in bloom after a wet, cold and dreary winter and the air was thick with the heady fragrance of wild hyacinths and the wind-blown petals of apple blossoms.

I sat cross-legged on a low bluff overlooking Bononia, my back warmed by the sun, watching our ships bob at anchor while small boats scurried to and fro, carrying supplies to the galleys.

Felix sprawled beside me, staring up at the cloudless blue sky while chewing thoughtfully on a blade of grass. Aetius and Rufinius stretched out nearby, barely visible in the rippling green sea of grass and the fluttering heads of bright red poppies, lost in their own worlds, or, more likely fast asleep. We'd gotten ourselves pleasantly drunk and for once had nothing to do but soak up the sun and relax—an unheard of treat and one to be savored to the hilt.

I grabbed the wineskin I'd been cradling in my lap, brought the teat to my lips and squeezed, gulping down its contents as fast as I could fill my mouth.

It was a blustery spring day—we'd picked a spot that was somewhat sheltered, but the sea itself was extremely choppy, whipped into a frenzy by the north wind, with large waves crashing against the rocks below and making hard work for the boat crews tasked with ferrying supplies.

I lifted my gaze and shielded my eyes with my hand.

Along the horizon I could clearly make out a thin line of chalk-white cliffs: Britannia.

Rumors abounded that Britannia was going to be the last frontier, that Rome would push no further, that everything worth conquering had been conquered—with the exception of Parthia and besides, there was nothing Parthia had that Rome wanted, or so it was said—and once Britannia fell under the yoke there would be no more major military expeditions and the only chances to advance one's career would be through political channels.

I had no political connections. While in Dacia, I'd received word that Lady Ilissia had died—murdered in her bed by a slave. Silva, who'd risen to the rank of legate, had been killed in a skirmish in Judea a year before. Vallus too had died but not at the hand of an assassin or foe on the battlefield, but true to his mother's prediction just as his father had died, a victim of his own excesses. Anyone who might have helped me could not. So if the rumors were true, Britannia was my last chance to rise to a position that would, at the very least, guarantee me a comfortable retirement.

Retiring was an alien concept for someone like me who had fought my way through life, and for whom fighting was a way of life. Now, I had a good chance of reaching the end of my service well before I reached the end of my life, of actually settling down—but where? I had no desire to return to the land of my birth—it had remained poor and beset with tribal rivalries. Gaul and Germania, while wealthy, were far too cold in winter for my liking. Dacia was beautiful, with rich soil and abundant land, but it was still too uncivilized, meaning still too chock full of damned Dacians and would likely remain a very risky place to live, even if you were damned Dacian, for decades. No, I wanted to retire somewhere warm year round, somewhere where I could find the comforts I had fought so tirelessly to secure for others.

Somewhere where I didn't have to constantly watch my back.

Or, I could always reenlist; that had always been my fallback position—

The raucous cry of a gull wheeling high overhead drew me out of my daydreams and back to the reality at hand.

It was too soon to think of retirement, or reenlisting for that matter—too much to do, too much to gain and possibly everything to lose before I was faced with what to do with myself when that fateful day finally came. Britannia remained: the last frontier.

Its chalk cliffs beckoned to me.

From this vantage point they looked more like another line of whitecaps in a white-capped sea and I reached out as if to touch them, to see if they were indeed solid and not sea, then I quickly dropped my outstretched arm, fearful Felix would notice and laugh.

Lady Ilissia's tutors had told me that Britannia is an island—that damned, oft-quoted Greek Pytheas had said so—and beyond it Hibernia along with a scattering of smaller isles, like a broken necklace of pearls, and beyond them, endless sea—sea as far as the very edge of the Earth. I'd heard of the edge of the Earth before, many times and I'd always wondered why the water didn't flow over the edge, like a gigantic waterfall. It couldn't—otherwise the seas would have run dry long ago. But no one had ever explained to me why this was not so—even my tutors, the finest Alexandria had to offer, had told me I was foolish to think in such ways and when I persisted, even going so far as to suggest this phenomena might be proof of Pytheas' 'congested seas', they scoffed and challenged me to seek the answers for myself.

I told them I would, and clutching the star pendant, vowed that I would travel to the four corners of the Earth and see for myself what lay beyond. And so, as I stared at those distant chalk cliffs, I realized that I'd succeeded in that promise beyond my wildest dreams even though I'd never found the answer to the original dilemma.

I smiled, told Felix that it was there, in that distant Britannia, that I would finally make history, finally grasp what I had so long sought, finally seize what the Fates had tried for so long and so hard to deny me.

He grunted his agreement, lifted his head and snatched the skin from my hands and squeezed some of the wine into his mouth, then dropped his head back onto the warm pallet of grass with a soft thump.

Privately, I told myself that I would finally be legitimate—no longer the bastard son of a legionary and a prostitute, no longer a man who wore another's name as I wore his necklace, but truly Arrius Marcus Niger in every way, accepted as such even by the Emperor himself when news reached him that I had been nominated to the rank of Primus-Pilus and all that remained was his stamp of approval—

Beside me, Felix began to snore, loudly.

I stared at him, briefly annoyed he'd intruded on my lofty daydreams, then, as I stared at his relaxed face, I grinned and quietly snatched up a handful of blood-red poppies, then artfully stuck them in his breeze-ruffled curly blond hair—a crown of sorts, akin to a champion's wreath of laurel, but one that much better befitted this battle-weary conqueror of the meadow on this auspicious Eve of Florales.

I carefully freed the wine skin from his sleep-loosened fingers, filled my mouth with the sun-warmed fluid then as I swallowed, I turned my wincing gaze to the line of chalk cliffs and smiled.

Britannia, I give you fair warning. Prepare yourself—I'm coming.

"Hold still, damn you!"

I *was* holding perfectly still despite Turan angrily, and I must say, none-too-gently rubbing the frozen blood from my equally frozen face. She clutched my chin painfully in her fingers—but on the up side, I could feel her fingers now. I hadn't a few minutes before. And another plus: I no longer had the terrible headache that had dogged me ever since I'd first awakened in that chair by the fire. No thanks to Mabog or one of his magic elixirs, oh hell no. The bitter cold could take all the credit—clearly my mind was so preoccupied with my impending death by exposure it had totally forgotten about the headache, perhaps feeling that was all rather too much, or like the rest of me, it had been numbed by the intense cold.

But back to Turan: there was no comforting, *Listen to me,* this time. Oh, no. She was *pissed.*

Of course I'd been pissed at her too, murderously so, but that was *before* my invigorating stroll. Now I was just too damned chilled and bone-tired to be anything but chilled and bone-tired. I couldn't even muster up the bitter taste of utter defeat or fear that I was doomed to be Kellesuf.

Beside her, Mabog muttered about ungrateful patients, that I'd be lucky if I only lost a few toes and fingers to frostbite. He wiggled the little finger of my right hand with such vigor I had a sneaking suspicion he was actually trying to snap it off, just to prove his point.

I kept my eyes closed, tried manfully not to flinch each time Turan, using a rag, dabbed the cuts on my face with something that smelled simply awful and stung worse; I refused to acknowledge Mabog or his grumbled threats and I pointedly ignored the bleating from that gods-damned box above my head as I sat—naked of course—on a cold, hard table.

They kept telling me I was half-frozen—not that I needed any convincing—yet did either one think to offer me something warm to drink? *No.* All I'd been given was a thin blanket, which was now draped around my goose-pimpled shoulders—

"You are an idiot," Turan growled, for what I believe was the tenth time—I might be wrong though. It very well might have been the hundredth—one loses track after a while, you know? "You risk everyone's life searching for you and for what? To establish beyond doubt that you're an idiot?" Again grasping my chin, she jerked my head painfully upwards and to the left, running the cloth down my blood-smeared throat and onto my chest. Whatever foul concoction the rag was soaked in found every scratch, every abrasion, every twig-puncture and set them on fire. "Look at you! You're a damned mess!"

I didn't want to look at me. I didn't want to look at anyone. I just wanted to be put to bed so I could sleep—I'd worry about everything else, later. But was I? *No.* Mabog had already warned me I wasn't going anywhere until what he called my core temp—whatever the hell that is— was back to normal—whatever the hell *that* was—which necessitated him sticking something small and hard up my butt.

I felt *that* was utterly gratuitous and the force with which he did it held the taint of pure nastiness on his part.

But I was in no position to protest. Hanni stood nearby, and even he was pissed. I could tell by the regular, violent snorts of breath coming from his general direction. In fact, everyone was pissed at me, even Ainiaan.

Especially Ainiaan...

I'd returned to the Keep an hour before, arriving in a very heroic fashion, surrounded by my grim-eyed searchers and draped limply over the saddle of Rasaben's charger just like the moldy sack of grain I'd so long aspired to. Once within its imprisoning walls, and the portcullis firmly secured and everyone who'd been out looking for me accounted for, I was roughly dragged from the horse and back to my feet. I barely had a chance to look around, to grasp the sheer size of the search party—it looked to be most of the Keep—not one of whom looked in the slightest bit pleased I'd been found alive, when Ainiaan walked up to me, fixed me with a look that cut right to the bone, then she stalked off without even saying a word—

A hand alighted on my shoulder. I expected a rough shake—maybe Turan or Mabog had thought I'd somehow fallen asleep and were damned if they were going to let me escape their wrath so easily; instead the fingers gently tightened their grasp, followed by a softly spoken, *"Centurion?"*

I very reluctantly opened my eyes to find the soldier—all right, *Felix* if you must—standing beside Turan. He sported a lividly bruised and swollen shut right eye, along with another ugly bruise on his jaw and mouth and a freshly split lower lip.

I stared up at him, mouth agape. Then I recovered. "What... *what the hell happened to you?*"

"Nothing—I'm fine," he managed while trying to move his jaw and puffy lips as little as possible. "Are you all right?" The look in his left eye and the tone of his voice suggested the question was truly heartfelt.

"He will be," Mabog growled. "If he does exactly as I tell him—not that there's a fat chance of that."

Turan pointedly ignored everyone as she continued to dab at my face. So I pointedly ignored her, too.

"Someone hit you—*because of me?*"

That garnered a derisive snort from Turan; from the soldier: "No, Centurion. I fell."

"You must be really clumsy." I remembered Ainiaan's reaction to my own attempt at sidestepping the truth behind my battered face by a patently obvious lie.

He smiled, briefly. It clearly really hurt to smile and his awkward, shifting stance suggested the vicious pummeling extended well beyond his face. And suddenly I was angry—I'd never intended for him to suffer for my actions. Get a good verbal upbraiding for being so easily duped? *Fine.* Soldiers needed to learn, sometimes the hard way, not to be so gullible before it cost them, or their fellows, their lives—a humiliating lesson they would not soon forget. But beaten to a complete pulp? *No, damn it!* I shoved Turan's hand away and flicked Mabog a warning glance as he started to grab me.

"I ask again: who hit you?"

"No one, Centurion—I told you, I fell... from... *from my horse,*" he added hastily, in the process reopening his split lip, which promptly began to bleed profusely. "Yes," he nodded vigorously, "my horse."

"Like hell!"

"Please," he begged desperately while mopping his lip with a rag Turan had handed him, "Centurion—it's all right. I'm fine, really."

I'd had these discussions before—hundreds of times with my soldiers. Always the same response, "I'm fine, really," when clearly they'd had the snot pounded out of them and I'd been tasked with finding out exactly what had happened and punish whoever had been the snot-pounder—even if it turned out the person I was speaking to was the original instigator and had somehow ended up getting the worse for it. In this case I seriously doubted this man would have even thought to fight back. He had the thoroughly trampled look of someone who had obediently submitted to an extremely painful and prolonged thrashing as if it was his due.

J. E. Bruce

I looked furiously at Mabog. "Have you examined him?"

"He wouldn't let me—insisted on being part of the search party. An unfortunate but not entirely unexpected consequence of using your memories as a template is that he shares your truly astonishing mule-headedness."

I pursed my lips and made a note to have a private word with Mabog at a later date.

He seemed to sense what I was thinking and suddenly made himself busy elsewhere.

I turned back to the soldier. No one hit one of my men and got away with it—if punishment needed to be meted out, *I* did the honors, thank you all the same. "I ask *again*," I growled in my best Centurion's Voice, "*who punched you?*"

He flinched back as if expecting *me* to punch him—and I must say, I was sorely tempted. As a centurion I'd often had to prove to a soldier that I was an even bigger, nastier bully than the bully who beat him up in order for him to tell me who that bully was.

"Rasaben," Turan answered when he only stood there squirming under my ferocious stare.

I glanced sidelong at her.

"When he discovered how you'd managed to slip away."

I looked back at him to find him now staring at his feet, blood dripping from his lip and to the floor unabated. "You're to let Mabog examine you—*no argument!*" I snarled as I saw a protest start to form on his bruise-swollen and now very bloody lips.

I pushed myself off the examination table—barely noticing in my black mood that in doing so I'd accidentally pulled out whatever Mabog had stuck up my ass—a probe, he'd called it—then I motioned angrily for the soldier to strip down. "Off—all of it!"

He did so, slowly and carefully, occasionally flicking Turan a sidelong, deeply self-conscious glance.

Turan, for her part, stared at him, oblivious to his intense embarrassment while wincing in sympathy as more and more injuries were revealed.

It was worse than I'd thought—clearly far worse than either Mabog or Turan had assumed. He was covered, knees to neck, in angry welts and bright red and purple splotches, and by his grimacing, clearly in a serious lot of pain as Mabog helped him sit on the table. Seeing the look in his bruised eyes, seeing his jaw muscles bunch as Mabog felt for broken bones and clearly finding plenty, my blood boiled anew.

342

I snatched up my clothing—it was wet and ice cold but I didn't care—and quickly redressed. *"Where's Rasaben?"* I grabbed the soldier's hastily discarded ring-mail hauberk and pulled it over my head.

"Don't!" Turan grabbed my arm as my head immerged from the hauberk's neck slit. "Please, Arri—"

"You expect me to stand by and let him do this? *Like hell!*" I roughly shook off her grip, picked up his baldric, belt and broadsword and quickly outfitted myself in them. "If Rasaben wants to beat up someone let him try with me." I grabbed the mailed cowl then looked back at the soldier. "Did he hurt Boian?"

He gave his head a quick, emphatic shake. "But he made her watch." His eye began to glisten.

Okay, now I was *really* angry—murderously angry. Even Turan and Mabog had the decency to look truly appalled. I tugged the cowl over my head and settled it in place. "Hanni."

The ogre, who'd been standing next to the door, silently observing, lifted his shaggy head and met my gaze.

"Stay with him—make sure... Felix does *exactly* as he's told."

Out of the corner of my eye I saw the soldier lift his watery left eye and stare at me, clearly unsure if he'd heard what he thought he'd heard.

I winked at him and he responded with a faint, decidedly lopsided, puffy-lipped and yet very grateful smile.

"I think I should come with you," the ogre protested.

"This is between Rasaben and me—*just the two of us.*" In truth I no longer trusted Hanni—a realization that, like Ainiaan's look, cut deeper and hurt more than I'd expected. I turned to Turan. "Where is he?"

When she hesitated, I growled ominously, "I'll find him, sooner or later."

"I'd rather it be much later, when you've calmed down."

I motioned furiously at Felix. "You think I'm going to calm down after seeing what he did to him?"

"Not really, no. But you're in no shape to go up against him."

"You underestimate me."

"Quite the contrary—you *never* cease to amaze me..."

I flicked Felix another sidelong look, wondering if he had somewhere found the time to tutor Turan in the fine art of the gracious slur.

"...I just don't underestimate him, either—if you come at him armed, he won't hesitate to kill you."

"I'm counting on him to try. I won't have it be said I killed *him* in cold-blood." I'd done that once and found it had left a very bitter taste in my mouth. I spat on the floor for emphasis then wiped my lips with the back of my hand. With that I strode out of the room, down the length of hallway.

I stopped at the top of the stairs just long enough to pull the hood of the cowl up over my head to provide me with a little concealment, then I hurried down the stairs and over to the doorway that gave access to the Great Hall. I pressed myself up against the wall next to the door and listened for voices.

Sure enough, I heard Rasaben's deep, booming voice, along with Taskim's *and* Kyrou's. They were laughing loudly at something—maybe at me, maybe at what Rasaben had done to Felix. Maybe at the very concept that Felix had been so easily sidetracked, had been so naïve in so many ways; that as someone so long denied his own individuality that when he finally became someone his first desire had been something so basic as to feel a woman's warm, naked body against his.

My fingers reflexively tightened their stranglehold on the grip of the sheathed broadsword.

I knew what I was doing of course: I was winding myself up. Turan had been right—I *wasn't* in any fit shape to go up against Rasaben. I was still half-frozen for one thing and aside from my nighttime frolic through the snow, hadn't had any serious exercise in weeks. I wasn't familiar with a broadsword; I hadn't even thought to test the flexibility and strength of my left arm, having accepted Mabog's guarantee without question—which now seemed rather, *um*, questionable. And Rasaben wasn't alone. I'd have Kyrou and Taskim to deal with as well—and who knows who else. Jaro? Perus? *Kellesuf...?*

I told myself I'd been up against worse odds before—like in Thracia. Eight against one—and guess who alone survived to tell the tale? And then there was that ambush in Dacia—at least six to my one—all at the same time, and two were gods-damned Sarmatian armored cavalry. And the battle of the bog had not entirely gone in favor the Iceni and their bitch queen Boudicca. Before I'd been ordered to take the hillock, I'd personally seen at least thirty of the buggars—er, I mean her loyal subjects—off to a meet and greet with their gods, which, I suspect, is why their buddies were so damned keen to send me off to meet and greet mine—

"Need some help?"

I wheeled around—my heart in my throat—and came face to face with two Kellesuf. The nearest and shorter of the two, the one who'd whispered, grinned.

I didn't need to be told who they were—or, should I say, who they were supposed to be. The whisperer, a stocky, dirty blond, ruddy-faced and blue-eyed man was Aetius reborn. And behind him, a pale-skinned man with black hair and eyes to match: Rufinius. This version of Aetius had clearly benefited greatly from his reincarnation. While he wasn't exactly handsome, he wasn't exactly ugly either and I suddenly realized it might be best not to think about just how damned ugly the real Aetius had been. If I did it might go badly for his replacement.

Aside from similar coloring, this Rufinius didn't bear even a passing resemblance to his predecessor. This man was barrel-chested with powerful arms, thick, straight hair as blue-black as mine but with skin every bit as milk-white as Felix's, and strange, heavy-lidded eyes that lent him a perpetual squint. I'd never seen someone who looked anything like him— the closest was one of Lady Ilissia's domestic slaves, a small, shy girl I was told had come from somewhere beyond the Emodian Mountains. So perhaps he had, too.

Enough! I had a far meatier issue at hand: *revenge.* I'd worry about where these two men came from later—assuming there was a later.

That said, the odds were looking better. Of course I had no idea how good these two were. Their predecessors had been excellent, close-in fighters—not the sort you'd want to find yourself up against on a battlefield... or for that matter a dark alley. I also wasn't sure exactly where their loyalties lay—Felix, after all, had submitted to the truly awful beating without struggle. Perhaps it was a trick—make me think I had support, then once committed I'd find out it was actually all against one—

"I *know* what you're thinking," the replicate Aetius said. "Can you trust us not to, *um,* stab you in the back?"

"Well?"

"We *saw* Felix—helped him get dressed while Boian told us what happened."

I looked past him to this version of Rufinius. If I'd had any doubt as to their feelings in the matter, the homicidal glint in his black eyes snuffed it out.

"I want Rasaben."

"You can have him," Rufinius growled as he fingered the hilt of his broadsword. "I want that snot-nosed runt, Kyrou."

"Which leaves that skunking bastard Taskim *all* for me," Aetius said with a gleeful rubbing of hands.

It was *so* tempting to say, 'Be my guests.' Instead I said, "No. I don't want the others hurt."

"Why not?" they replied in unison.

I looked at one then the other, somewhat taken aback, although in truth there had been times when the original Aetius and Rufinius had defied my standing as their superior and needed some gentle reminding, usually requiring a whack or two from my vine-staff. "Because *I* say so. *I'm* the centurion. What *I* say goes."

Aetius scowled. "Meaning we get to distract everyone while you have all the fun."

I grinned. "It's good to be the centurion."

"Which means yes."

"Which means yes," I confirmed.

Aetius blew out his cheeks. He'd always been up for a fight—was, more often than not, the instigator in brawls, be it camp, garrison or tavern, and he was always far and away in the lead in any running charge, despite his short legs. Clearly those fond memories had found solid form in this man. He was itching to spit someone on his sword and I wasn't sure I could trust him, any more than I could have trusted the real Aetius, not to get carried away when things heated up. He was the only soldier I'd ever met who could—*literally*—scare the crap out of war elephants.

I looked past him to this new Rufinius for help and found myself suddenly and sorely missing Felix—even the replicate Felix. The original Felix was always able to keep better control of Aetius than Rufinius and I hoped the same would be true of this one. Rufinius had this irrepressible penchant to egg Aetius on then act utterly innocent afterwards. This one looked like he was seriously considering the possibilities.

"I'm not sure I want to kill Rasaben," I began, "I think—"

"Why not?" Aetius again. Big surprise, huh? "We do, don't we?" He looked at Rufinius, who nodded vigorously—a little too vigorously.

"Because I've had a chance to think about it and I'm not sure that's the most productive way to handle the situation."

They both looked mightily put out, but again, it was Aetius who said, "May I kill him?"

"No."

"May I stab him?—nothing instantly fatal, I assure you, but something that will cause a long, lingering and painful convalescence with the remote—I stress *remote* possibility of him dying in agony at the end?"

"No."

"Lop off his head?"

"I think that qualifies as killing him. No."

"A simple slash then, across his rather substantial gut—let some of the hot air out."

"Again, probably fatal. So again, no."

"How 'bout just a *teensy* poke, just enough to draw blood?"

"No."

"Why?" he demanded, arms akimbo.

"Because you won't know when or where to stop—he'll be mincemeat by the time you stop."

"And you have an issue with that."

"Haven't I made that sufficiently clear?"

He sighed heavily, leaned his mailed shoulder against the wall and unsheathing his broadsword, began to clean his fingernails with the tip. "This is no fun. No fun at all. And not damned fair. You arrange it so the first thing Felix gets to do is bed a woman. We get... what? *Shit,* that's what."

It was a favorite fallback position for Aetius whenever he felt slighted when it came to favors—that I liked Felix best. I'd known Aetius the longest, but Felix was without a doubt my closest friend, the closest friend I'd ever had. I never claimed otherwise, but these two were close seconds, despite their *very* glaring character flaws.

I looked around him at Rufinius.

Rufinius stared back, clearly every bit as disappointed, every bit as frustrated in every way imaginable, but true to his new-found personality, knowing better than to actually say so.

"I could arrange the same for you—"

"When?" they said in unison, Aetius straightening up, his impromptu manicure instantly forgotten, his sword suddenly re-sheathed.

"When we're done here," I replied slowly, realizing it was probably a mistake to put any ideas in their minds other than the idea of dealing with Rasaben. "One thing at a time, all right?"

They nodded, again, in perfect unison—a habit I was going to have to break as I found it a little unnerving.

"You two go in first—"

Aetius grinned, rubbing his hands together. *"Now* you're seeing sense—"

"To *distract* them."

He squinted wrathfully at me as his now balled fists fell back to his sides. "As I said, *shit."*

I pointedly ignored the testy remark—and the fists. "Act just like you used to—walk in, head for the far end of the table."

Aetius flicked Rufinius a sidelong, pout-lipped glance.

"We can do that," Rufinius said, jabbing Aetius with his elbow. "Can't we?"

Aetius muttered, "I suppose so."

"Good. I'll be right behind you—I don't want them to realize it's me until it's too late."

Rufinius and Aetius looked at each other, then at me and nodded, this time with grinning zeal. Their predecessors had had this shared obsession with springing unpleasant surprises on others—from elaborate practical jokes that victimized their hapless tent-mates to straightforward but astonishingly deadly ambushes that could take out an entire enemy foraging squad. I'd always found it to be one of their more endearing pastimes—as long as *I* was not the unwitting beneficiary of one of their intricate pranks.

I started for the door and had no sooner taken one step than Rufinius said, "If I might offer a helpful suggestion, sire?"

I looked back at him and nodded. "Always."

"When you engage Rasaben, come in low and from *his* right."

I raised a brow.

"He can't see so well out of the right eye. Old injury." He shrugged then added, "I'm his sparring partner, or should I say I *was*—"

"When he says sparring partner," Aetius interrupted with a sidelong look at his grim-faced companion, "he really means punching bag. Rasaben picked him because he didn't want it to look like he was beating the hell out of someone who couldn't defend himself—"

"Like you," Rufinius growled, glaring down his nose at him.

"*Couldn't* rather than *wouldn't*," I said, cutting off the angry retort forming on Aetius' lips; the last thing I needed was for these two to go for each other—I needed them to stay focused on the real villain here or we were all going to end up dead. "So he picked the biggest, brawniest Kellesuf he could find—"

"And regularly beat him to a pulp," Aetius replied. "With the rest of us unable to do a damned thing but watch."

I shifted my gaze to Rufinius as it occurred to me that he might be more of a concern than Aetius when it came to making mincemeat of Rasaben—he certainly had cause.

To add to my worries, Rufinius replied, "I doubt he'd want to fight me now with matters being more... *um*, equal?" and cracked his knuckles for emphasis. "But don't worry, sir. He's yours—he's all yours... *for now.*"

I gave myself a shake, then happened to remember that we were still standing just outside the Great Hall and in plain sight of anyone coming or going. If we didn't make our move and quickly, we risked discovery. "Low and from his right, huh?"

He nodded.

"I'll bear that in mind." And I would. While we'd been busy colluding, my anger had cooled somewhat and I'd begun to have serious doubts. Not about these two, but about my plan—plus, in delaying I'd given Turan time to get word to her brother. We could be walking into a trap—not that I could back out now.

Rufinius' suggestion had just provided me with much needed morale boost—and no matter what, I'd just reclaimed at least one element of surprise and maybe that would be enough.

I took a deep breath, exhaled. "Let's go."

Aetius was like a bull out of the gate and I had to grab him by his mailed cowl and jerk him back, then I whispered harshly in his ear: *"Remember the plan! Or you'll have me to deal with afterwards—assuming you don't get all of us killed!"*

"Yes, Centurion," he replied sullenly.

I let go.

He irritably tugged his cowl back into place, then he and Rufinius stepped forward and I fell in behind and the three of us walked into the Great Hall.

Kyrou and Perus were seated facing us and as Kyrou glanced up at the sound of our footsteps, I ducked my head and he returned to his meal, seeing no threat in our approach. Taskim was seated at the head of the table as usual. Thankfully Rasaben had his back to us, making it that more unlikely he'd spot his former sparring partner and get suspicious—and there was an unexpected windfall: two of the Sidhe Lords, the dark-haired man and the blond woman were seated at the table as well, the man to Taskim's right, next to Perus, and the woman to his left, next to Rasaben.

Servants with trays of food and drink unwittingly aided us by funneling us closer to the table as we made our way towards the far end, towards a group of soldiers already seated and silently eating their midday meal. In the process I had a taste of what life had been like for the soldiers. We were totally ignored, treated as if we weren't even there. *Invisible*. No one in fact seemed to notice—or perhaps care is closer to the mark—that two of the soldiers who approached were in fact two of the *proto types*, as Felix called them and that aside from the hauberk and cowl, I was not properly attired.

In this case the utter lack of regard served my purposes perfectly—unless they were all very good actors and just waiting for the right moment to spring their trap.

Aetius and Rufinius dutifully walked past Taskim and the woman, past Rasaben—Rufinius having placed himself closest to the table, just in case Aetius found himself just *too* tempted by an easy target.

My heart pounded as I followed. If anyone had cause to look up at that moment they would've recognized me instantly and just as quickly realized what I was about. But they didn't. They kept up their animated discussion about a recent stag hunt between mouthfuls of what looked to my eyes and smelled to my nose like my damned roast boar—*can you believe it?*

I abruptly stopped directly behind Rasaben. Rufinius and Aetius walked on, but slowed their pace, ready to come to my aide.

Perus at this moment did look up and his eyes got *very* round. I grinned and put my finger to my lips then used the same finger to tap Rasaben's shoulder.

He twisted around and looked up and his eyes got almost as round as Perus's.

The hall fell silent. No one moved, not even the servants, as Aetius and Rufinius unsheathed their broadswords: the echoing *schhhhinnnng* of the blades coming free of their scabbards a warning for the rest not to do anything stupid.

I stepped back, motioning for Rasaben to rise.

He did so, keeping his hands visible and making no sudden moves. Once standing, he straightened up, using his bulk in the hopes of intimidating me. He *was* a lot bigger than me, I'll grant him that—and taller than I remembered; bigger and taller than Rufinius, too, now that I could compare them almost side-by-side. But I wasn't impressed—I was too damned pissed to be impressed, having effectively reclaimed my earlier rage.

"You and I have a matter to discuss."

"Indeed?" he scoffed. "And what, pray tell, could that be, *boy?"*

Okay. If I hadn't been damned pissed before, I was now—calling me boy in front of audience? I was in fact mightily damned pissed. "The gross maltreatment of one of my men."

He chuckled, "Your men...? *Your men? Your* men were all *slaughtered*— led to their deaths by *you*, if I remember correctly."

I forced a smile. "True." Well, it was true, wasn't it? I could give him that.

"Then whose men are you speaking of? *These men?"* he sneered as he pointed to Rufinius and Aetius.

Aetius started towards him, eyes flashing; Rufinius grabbed him by the baldric and jerked him back, then held on—an impressive display of strength and supreme restraint on the part of Rufinius.

"Or those men?" Rasaben continued in the same baiting tone as he gestured to the group at the far end of the table. *"Kellesuf?"* He laughed. "Kellesuf have only one master—*me.*"

"Like fuck we do!" Aetius snarled, tugging against Rufinius's vice-like grip; I was duly impressed. If I'd been Rufinius, I'd have let go.

"Well," I replied quietly, "that's about to change. I speak of any who choose to join me, who choose to not to be your slaves, to do your bidding without any thought for themselves. For any who choose to be *men*—"

"Don't expect Boian to bed them all!" Rasaben's laugh was short-lived, cut off by a rustle of armor at the far end as the seated soldiers rose as one.

"SIT DOWN!" he bellowed. *"ALL OF YOU!"*

They remained standing and their unexpected defiance clearly unnerved Rasaben—must say I hadn't been expecting it either—not that I'm complaining.

I nodded to them and they nodded in return, again, in perfect unison, *damn it.* I then turned back to Rasaben, in the process noticing that Aetius was now grinning smugly at Rasaben.

Rasaben noticed too. "What are *you* grinning at, fool?"

"I guess Lord Mabog has been so busy he forgot to mention that he's running a wee bit ahead of schedule with the transfers." Aetius nodded to the soldiers before again meeting Rasaben's suddenly appalled stare. "Or maybe you were otherwise occupied—beating the hell out of Felix."

I made note to thank Mabog for his efficiency—then as I too turned back to Rasaben I happened to catch Taskim's equally disconcerted stare. "Ah, yes, *Lord* Taskim. We have much to discuss as well. But later, yes? I have more pressing issues at the moment." While I was speaking I saw, out of the corner of my eye, Rasaben's fingers slide towards the hilt of his sword. "Ah, ah, *ah!* I wouldn't do that."

He froze then looked around a bit stiffly for support.

None was forthcoming, not from Perus, not even from the normally hot-tempered Kyrou.

"So, you're not as stupid as you look—not likely, but I did have my doubts." My remark had actually been aimed at Kyrou, however Rasaben, not unreasonably, assumed I meant him and his expression turned from arrogantly incensed to downright murderous.

I replied with an impervious smile. "I must tell you that I'm an expert swordsman." Not with a broadsword, no, but I saw no reason to mention that.

"So am I," Rasaben growled, his eyes sparkling as if I'd just handed him my own death.

"I know. That's why we aren't going to use swords to settle this matter."

He looked briefly baffled by that. *Hah!*

"Disarm him." I motioned to Rufinius, having little choice but to trust him to do the honors, while Aetius also stepped close, his sword ready to do some serious persuading if need be.

I'll give both men credit. Rasaben remained perfectly still while Rufinius separated him from his broadsword and dagger with a tad more gusto than the task required then went on to very roughly pat him down for more, hidden weapons, despite Rasaben looking as if he was being groped by a lecherous leper. And Rufinius didn't use the opportunity to gut the man who had caused him so much grief—using Rasaben's own dagger to do the honors. I would've—count on it.

"So, you plan on killing a defenseless man?" He snorted as Rufinius stepped back, taking Rasaben's weapons with him. "I'm not surprised—it's not like you haven't done it before."

I didn't react. That's what he wanted.

So he continued, "All you Romans are gutless. Never met one who wasn't."

Okay, now this was something I could respond to: "Really? Then why on earth would you want to use a gutless Roman's memories to fight *your* war? *Hummmm?* Or lead *your* troops? Why aren't *you* doing the honors?" Oh, the look in his eye to that; it was so much better than hearing the gurgle of his dying gasp of breath, much, *much* better. "It couldn't possibly be due to *you* being unfit, could it?"

He didn't have a ready answer for that—he was far too busy staring daggers at me. *Hah.*

I tapped my ear, just to drive home my point. "Excellent hearing, along with an excellent memory—you might want to bear that in mind the next time you whisper around me after you think you've drugged me into a stupor." I grinned and as I politely waited for him to come up with a suitable rejoinder, I caught the furtive sliding of Aetius' blue eyes to something behind me, but he didn't change his loose-limbed stance. Whoever had just entered the hall was no threat. A servant perhaps. Then I realized it might be Turan and I felt a brief surge of panic that she might try to control me—Rasaben was her brother after all, and Aetius might be blithely unaware of her abilities and therefore wouldn't consider her anyone to be concerned about until it was too late.

I hesitated, waiting to feel her company in my mind but if she was there, she wasn't making her presence known.

"If you're going to kill me," Rasaben growled, taking my brief distraction has a serious case of cold feet, "then please *do* so. Otherwise I'm going return to my meal—it's getting cold." He actually started to turn his back on me!

"My *most* humble apologies, *Lord* Rasaben…"

He stopped, turned back to me, drawn by the sneer in my voice.

"… I did not mean to keep you waiting." And with that my right hand reached for my sheathed sword and as I saw his eyes go for the feint, I swung my left fist up and into his jaw—

—and he toppled like a felled tree.

"*Shit!*" I snarled and danced back, grimacing, as I gave my now bleeding knuckles and throbbing hand a quick shake—his jaw was a hell of a lot harder than I'd anticipated, *damn it*, but as I rotated my shoulder, working out the shock of the impact, I realized Mabog had been good to his word, it *was* almost as good as new, or it had been up until the instant my fist met Rasaben's jaw. Now it might need some serious tweaking.

Using my right hand, I withdrew the heavy and unfamiliar broadsword from its scabbard with a flourish and as the luminescent blade rose and caught the torchlight, I grasped it in both hands, swung it over my head then as I brought it down with the assumed intent of delivering a killing stroke, I heard a gasp from behind me. I stopped the blade a hair's-breadth from the back of Rasaben's neck and risked a quick glance over my shoulder.

I'd been right, it was Turan… *and* Ainiaan.

Damn! The demonstration of swordsmanship and with a strange weapon no less had been for Turan's benefit—and yes, Kyrou and Taskim's—in fact everyone in the Great Hall. I hadn't actually planned on killing Rasaben—I just wanted them to think I was going to, although after bringing up why my memories had been used rather than his and in public certainly upped the chance of me having to do just that to a dead certainty down the road. I certainly hadn't planned on frightening Ainiaan.

I met her horrified gaze, shrugged and smiled apologetically, then turned back to Rasaben and gently smacked the flat of the blade against his cheek, hoping to bring him around. When that failed to do the trick, Aetius happily stepped forward and grabbed Rasaben's full goblet of wine.

With a defiant grin at those seated at the table, he took a deep gulp, winced in surprise at its taste and wiped his full lips. "I taste fresh herbs… a hint of oak, an underlying smokiness… with an unexpectedly light, acidic aftertaste. All in all not a bad vintage, a tad precocious perhaps and might benefit from some aging." He then dumped what remained on Rasaben's head. "Oops." He looked around as if truly mortified by the slip of the hand.

Rasaben groaned, forcing Aetius into hastily stepping back; his eyes fluttered then he slowly turned his face towards me. His nose and lip were bleeding profusely and his eyes were smarting from the dousing of wine as he kept squeezing them shut and opening them, only to squeeze them shut again.

I leaned over him. "It's always a good idea to ask a man if he's right handed or left. I'm *left*, in case you were wondering." I flicked Rufinius a sidelong look to find him grinning from ear to ear.

"Go to hell," Rasaben mumbled through bloodied lips.

"Have you been outside lately? Oh, wait, that's right—you *were* forced to freeze your ass off searching for me outside for most of the night, weren't you? Then you simply have no excuse not to know we're already there."

He squinted up at me, muttered something that sounded remarkably like, "Fuck you."

"Thank you all the same, but I'll pass."

He grumbled something else, something that clearly called my preferences, or perhaps *lack* of preferences, into question. If he thought I'd take that as an insult, he was sadly mistaken—of course since he'd been directly involved in sorting through my memories, he should have known that.

"What was that?" I cupped my ear as if to hear better as I again smacked him on the head with the flat of the blade, this time not quite as gently. "You say you're very sorry for what you did to Felix? Well, I certainly can't speak for him and I'm not sure he has the heart to forgive you."

He tried to rise, but I jabbed the tip of the blade between his shoulders, puckering the soft leather of his tunic. "I'm *not* done yet." And I wasn't. I had quite an audience: servants, soldiers, Turan and Taskim. Ainiaan. Kyrou. Perus. Not to mention two of the Sidhe Lords. I even happened to spot Boian within the knot of soldiers—which, I noticed, had swelled to at least double their earlier number. Clearly word had gotten out—their numbers and expressions more evidence that Mabog was far ahead of schedule, which meant she was as safe as safe could be in their midst—as long as she stayed in their midst.

Suddenly I was afraid for her, afraid she would be the next target of Rasaben's temper. As if reading my thoughts, she nodded and smiled.

I smiled and nodded in return, then turned back to Rasaben.

He and his breed ruled by fear, by intimidation and humiliation—I wanted him to feel, if just for a moment, what he instilled in others—I wanted Taskim and his fellow lords to suffer the same by proxy.

"When you beat Felix, you beat someone who wouldn't fight back—of course you did, because to fight someone who would fight back might put you at risk of losing and then, oh, my, what would happen? People might start to talk. You beat *me* when I couldn't fight back, just as Kyrou did. You regularly beat this man—" I pointed to Rufinius, "—again, picking a Kellesuf who wouldn't, who *couldn't* fight back, you made damned sure of that. So I'm going to spare everyone precious time and say this to these witnesses so assembled: you and Kryou are the absolute worst sort of cowards—"

Rasaben either forgot I had the sword to his back, or was so enraged he didn't care and tried to push himself to his feet. All he succeeded in doing was forcing the blade into his flesh. He groaned, reached back and desperately tried to grab it, pull it from his back, cutting his hands on its razor sharp edges in the process.

"Arri..." Turan gasped, taking a step closer, her hands held out in supplication.

"Stop it!" Ainiaan cried and ran to me. *"Arri, please don't kill Lord Rasaben!"* She futilely jerked at my sword arm and looked up at me. *"Please!"*

I waited a moment longer, savoring his helplessness, his humiliation, fighting the intense urge to finish the job and full of bloodlust, then I glanced at Ainiaan. "As you wish, m'lady." I jerked the blade free and sheathing it, stepped back, suddenly breathing hard.

I licked my lips. "Saved by a sister who for some *inexplicable* reason loves you, Lord Rasaben... and a child's plea—no, not a child." I nodded to Ainiaan. "A young woman who is far braver than you'll ever be—you owe Lady Ainiaan and Lady Turan your life—I strongly suggest you make sure you do *nothing* to make them regret their interference." I kicked him viciously in the flank, snarled, *"Get up!"*

Rasaben, under the very watchful gaze of Rufinius and Aetius, staggered unsteadily to his feet and I was pleased to note that his back and hands were every bit as bloody as his face.

With Ainiaan's help he staggered back to his chair, dropped heavily into it and I turned to Taskim.

"These men," I motioned to the soldiers, "*all of them*, every Kellesuf who freely *chooses* to serve under me is now *mine*—"

A booming cheer went up from the soldiers, their voices echoing off the walls of the hall, magnifying and multiplying them, but the moment the tumult settled, I added, "And *we'll* decide our fate—humanity's fate—*not you.*"

Taskim rose, slowly, watchful of the nearby Rufinius. "You don't know the enemy, Centurion, what they're capable of—"

"I've already been forced to deal with those who broke the treaty—can the other side be worse?"

That gave him pause. Then the old Taskim was back, the fatherly, friendly Taskim. "May we please discuss this in more... amenable surroundings?" He motioned to the doorway, as if I'd follow him without question.

"Like your library, Lord Taskim? I think not. I think I've had my fill of your library and the likes of guests you entertain there." I flicked the two Sidhe lords a murderous look, just in case they didn't catch the hint.

"You can bring your men, Centurion—as many as it would take to ease your mind. But in the library are documents you need to see, to read in full, so you'll fully appreciate and understand the foe that you—that all of us— are up against."

"The Faoimhuir you mean."

He nodded, reluctantly.

"Who are rumored to be originally from Numidia—"

He started to open his mouth but I cut him off.

"—why else would anyone find my humble origins of any interest? You should've read that treaty more closely, my lord, grasped its nuances." I grinned as I mimicked the gesture of grabbing something out of midair and clutching it in my fist. "I did."

He looked helplessly at Turan—as if she could make me see reason— then back at me as I said, "Understand this, Lord Taskim: as a Massaesyli I have no love for the Massyli, and I certainly have no loyalty to the Massaesyli, who cast me out as a child younger than young Lady Ainiaan, to die. So if your dreaded Faoimhuir are in fact originally from Numidia, and if they are, like me, Mauri, then I care nothing for them either. Just as I care nothing for your petty squabbles—"

"*If the Faoimhuir were to come out victorious, they would enslave all of humanity— that's why we broke the treaty, Centurion!*" His voice had taken on a desperate edge. "They're taking your people elsewhere—*off world*—using them in the most unspeakable ways—"

"Off world…?" I looked around, baffled.

"To other worlds—*other* Earths," Taskim replied, with an impatient flick of his hand.

I stared at him as if he was mad, then I too brushed it aside the remark if it was nothing more than his attempt at distraction—just like his allusion to a table and its underside was a distraction—*it had to be.* "And you'd treat us better?"

"Of course!"

"You've given me little evidence of that, Lord Taskim. Quite the contrary." I pointedly stared at the gathered Kellesuf, then at him. "You believe what you've done to them is *not* unspeakable?—oh, wait, it *is*, because not only did you take away their memories, their identities, you took away their *ability* to speak without first being spoken to, isn't that right?"

"You don't know the whole story, Centurion, and sometimes the ends do justify the means, as awful as those means may appear."

"May appear? You mean there's some doubt?" I turned to Aetius. "Who are you? Tell everyone your *real* name, tell them where you came from, tell them how old you are if you have a wife and children—not the first Aetius', *yours*. Go on."

He blinked, taken aback, just as Felix had done when confronted with the truth, as if he hadn't considered it, hadn't wondered until it was pointed out to him, then he turned his now homicidal stare on Taskim. "I dearly wish I could."

I crossed my arms. "Need more proof? Ask any of them. They'll all answer the same. Every single one of them—"

"We saved your life—just as we saved their lives!"

"Again, to serve your purposes, willing or not!" I fired back with equal heat. "At every turn I was forced to bend to *your* will, to the will of Lady Turan—" my baleful eyes flicked to her, back to Taskim, "—humiliated, brutalized and terrorized when I resisted. I was never asked, never consulted—everything I had, everything I am—was taken from me by force or by the threat of force—and now you ask that I thank you for that?

"You've yet to prove to me—prove to any of these men whom you treated far worse than me—that you and your kind are even *capable* of kindness!" I paused, let some of the heat drain from my face, my voice, then I added quietly, "There's a belief—a widely held belief that the farther one travels from the center of the world, from the center of civilization, the more barbaric people become. You told me we're no longer even *on* Earth—*so what does that say about you?*"

With that he appeared to deflate. He slowly resumed his seat, as if conceding my point then after a moment he lifted his gaze, met mine and said softly, "We gave you your friends back."

"*You?*" I shook my head. "I think it is Lady Ainiaan I have to thank for returning my friends to me." I shifted my gaze to her and was pleased to notice that she now stood between Rufinius and Aetius, arm-in-arm with the two and looking not the least bit nervous about it despite them staring balefully at Taskim.

She replied with a slight tilt of her head. Like Boian, she was publicly announcing where her allegiances lay; but unlike Boian, as a child and a Tuatha, she was likely safe from reprisal.

"I thank you Lady Ainiaan. I owe you a debt I can never fully repay." Then I turned back to Taskim, my expression turning chill. "You went along with her well-intentioned plan, but *only* as a means to an end, which was, presumably, to win me over to your side, get me to willingly lead your army. You knew what you'd done to me was wrong, that you'd treated me horribly, that I'd likely refuse, so you magnanimously 'give' me my friends in hopes that this will undo all the wrongs you've done?

"I sincerely thank you as well for my friends—I thank you for all of the Kellesuf who have been patiently, *silently* waiting for their own identities and now will finally receive them. But I curse you and each of your fellow lords for what you did to me—" I spat on the floor, "—*and* especially what you've done to them!" I motioned to Aetius, to Rufinius, to the soldiers then I spun on my heel and stalked out of the Great Hall.

I didn't need to look back to know that the soldiers to a man followed—the clatter of armor, the rustle of ring-mail and the echo of footfalls was proof enough.

— ii —

Soon after my dramatic departure from the hall I discovered a very unpleasant truth: I had no place to go, or should I say I had no warm and comfy place to go to have a nap—and getting warm and having a nap were now of paramount importance to me. I'd been up all night if you remember, playing hide and seek in a blizzard, then deciding I hadn't had quite enough excitement, I topped it off picking a fight with a man almost twice my size. Now I was stiff and sore and incredibly bone-tired, not to mention still chilled to the marrow of those same said bones. Worse, I was still wearing my damp clothing, which had *really* begun to chafe.

I'd happily accompanied the soldiers back to their Spartan quarters, assuming I'd find myself a bunk near the fire... only to find there was no fire in the massive barracks' single firebox, in fact it looked like it had been years since there'd been a fire in the firebox, which meant the barracks was every bit as freezing inside as it was outside.

Cold had never bothered the soldiers while Kellesuf, just as pain and hunger had never bothered them. But cold *really* bothered me. I sent off several of the soldiers to find a servant who would fill the damned firebox with wood and get it burning, but it would take hours, if not days to heat the huge residence and right now I desperately needed to find a warm place to bed down before I fell down; yes, I was that exhausted and now that all the excitement was over, I was feeling decidedly wobbly.

Despite its obvious comforts I had absolutely no desire to return to Turan's apartments and the library was *definitely* off limits.

So, no place to go... but right back to the Great Hall.

Rufinius and Aetius accompanied me as there was a good chance Rasaben might still be there, nursing his wounds not to mention a serious grudge, as well as Taskim and Kyrou, and I was clearly in no shape to deal with any of them. And while Aetius and Rufinius's presence certainly increased the odds of me being allowed to nap undisturbed, I was reasonably concerned about what would happen if I did nod off, thus leaving my two bodyguards to their own devices. Things might prove a wee bit too tempting. Both still had their blood up after all.

I needn't have worried. This Rufinius, like his predecessor, had an air about him that discouraged extracurricular activities, even by his partner— even by himself—when he deemed it unacceptable or counterproductive. This did not preclude, I'm sure, any future practical jokes or elaborate ambushes that he did deem acceptable and productive.

The possibility that this matter of Kellesuf suddenly vowing their fealty to me and me *only* might be nothing more than an elaborate ruse was something I categorically refused to entertain. I was just too damned tired and besides, if it was, there wasn't a damned thing I could do about it.

When we arrived we found, to my immense relief, that Rasaben, Kyrou and Taskim were nowhere to be found; the hall was empty, save for a few servants. Presumably the three, along with the two Sidhe lords were off somewhere—my guess the library—planning my very ugly demise. Good for them.

So, I picked my spot, sat down and settled down for what I hoped would be a nice, long and toasty-warm nap. Servants came and went as they always did, ferrying food and drink to the table or gathering up empty platters and pitchers to be refilled but they did so as quietly as humanly possible while wisely avoiding the fireplace and its surrounds. They only dared approach when the fire needed feeding, which it did, regularly, then hastily withdrew. Anyone who came to the hall looking for a meal, as people had a habit of doing at all hours, found all the foodstuffs stacked at the far half of the table: a blatant hint, along with my two steely-eyed guardians, to stay the hell away from the fireplace and the person sprawled and apparently snoozing in the chair beside it.

Hanni came for a snack, as did Jaro and Perus. Even Ainiaan showed up, accompanied by her father and Sifrie: all had kept their distance. How did I know? I'd spent the first hour or so pretending to be asleep as my hoped for nap eluded me. Instead I observed the comings and goings through slitted eyes, observed Rufinius and Aetius and their muted but unambiguous responses to anyone who entered the hall.

Whereas my mind had accepted this version of Aetius, Rufinius's new guise was, I readily admit, taking some getting used to. Hearing Rufinus's voice, seeing Rufinius's mannerisms on someone so vastly different than Rufinius was jarring, which led me to wonder why Ainiaan had picked this man for the role. I'd noticed at least two others among the ranks of Kellesuf who in fact bore a closer resemblance, in complexion and build.

The more I surreptitiously scrutinized these two men, watched them guard me with the same fierce devotion I'd come to expect from their predecessors, I realized it didn't matter what they looked like or why Ainiaan had picked this man over the others. She had her reasons and that was enough.

I now trusted these two with my life which mean that, superficial differences aside, I indeed had my friends back.

I took a deep, relaxing breath, closed my eyes and drifted off... only to be awakened by approaching footfalls that stopped barely a few paces from me, followed by whispered voices. Rufinius and Aetius... *and Boian.*

I forced one eye open and peered muzzily up at the woman who now stood over me. She met my less than enthusiastic, sleepy-eyed squint with a nervous smile. And behind her were two more soldiers, presumably *her* bodyguards. These men, these former Kellesuf were clearly starting to think for themselves, and one of the first things they thought about, and reasonably so, was Boian's safety.

Boian edged a little closer. "I'm sorry to disturb you, young sire, but may I have a word?"

I slowly, painfully, levered myself up in the high-backed chair—yes, the same chair I'd sat in that first day, the one from which I had launched myself into a celebrated career as a master vomiter—raked my hair out of my eyes and in a raspy voice replied, "Of course, Boian, of course."

Aetius promptly delivered another chair and placed it next to me, then with an expansive wave of his hand, invited her to sit.

She did and smoothed out the folds in her skirts, then met my now fully awake and yes, increasingly apprehensive gaze.

"What's happened?" My first thought was there *had* been an attempt on her life, a warning of worse to come—maybe the bodyguards hadn't been their idea, but hers. I looked her over but saw no obvious signs of injury. Then again, the most obvious type of attack wouldn't be visible. "Has someone threatened or hurt you?"

"No, sire. I'm fine." She glanced at the two soldiers then turned back to me. "But thank you for being worried about me."

I started to say I hadn't been the one to order bodyguards—a serious oversight on my part, I admit—but before I could do so, she continued: "Are you truly going to fight the Faoimhuir as Lord Taskim hopes, young sire?"

I eyed her; her tone, her expression suggested *she* was hoping I would, too.

I'd never considered Boian had a stake in any of this; she was a servant, a human, like me. She did as she was told and if she was smart, and I had no reason to think otherwise, she lived her life largely out of the direct gaze of her Tuatha masters. Or did she? Suddenly her motives, her allegiances came into question. I'd foolishly considered Hanni an ally too.

"Why do you ask?" I tried to keep my suspicions from tainting my voice and failed, miserably.

She glanced around then scooted her chair a little closer—Rufinius reacted, subtly mind you, by adjusting his grip on his broadsword's hilt. She noticed and met my gaze. "I mean you no harm, young sire, I just didn't want others to overhear."

I motioned to Rufinius and he eased off his hold, just a bit, but kept his coal-black eyes on her hands, on the folds of her shirts, folds that could easily conceal a dagger—wary of someone who'd been too easily presumed a friend.

"Lord Taskim..." she paused, licked her lips. "He's not all bad, young sire."

Just mostly bad, I thought bitterly, *like ninety-nine percent bad.*

"I know he's treated you terribly, treated the rest of you," she looked up at the soldiers, "horribly, but he's telling you the truth about the Faoimhuir." She glanced around, assuring herself none of the servants were within hearing then lowering her voice to a whisper continued, "They're taking people away—hundreds and hundreds—"

"So I've been told—"

"—selling them into slavery or worse, far, far worse—" She bit her lip, wiped at her suddenly glistening eyes then added tightly, "My own family, my brothers—I told you about them…"

I nodded, guardedly.

"…my husband, and…" She abruptly looked away and fixed her now streaming eyes on the fire.

"And?" I prompted, drawing her gaze.

"My babies. All of them—*taken*, by the Faoimhuir."

I lifted my eyes to Rufinius and Aetius, to her two bodyguards as Boian used her apron to dab at her eyes and wipe her wet, ruddy cheeks. They stared back at me, clearly disturbed by Boian's distress but unsure how to respond. She had won herself a special place in the hearts of these men by publicly allying herself with them, and now four of those men were coming to grips with the possibility that her kindness towards them was nothing more than yet another deceit, a ruse.

Boian's distress was genuine: none of us doubted that—it was the cause of that distress that had us worried. Had she been threatened? Had Rasaben or Kyrou or even Taskim made threats against her, or possibly her children? Maybe the Faoimhuir hadn't grabbed them; maybe Rasaben had and was now holding them hostage.

"When?"

She looked me and managed a slight, knowing smile. "Does it matter? The loss of one's babies never lessens over the years, young sire, and I truly loved my husband just as I loved my brothers. I came from a big family—and when it was over, when the Faoimhuir finally left, I was all alone." More tears spilled down her cheeks; this time she made no effort to wipe them away.

I looked up at one of the soldiers, a gangly, flame-haired youth. "Bring Boian something to drink—and the rest of us as well." As he hurried off, I turned back to her. "And you're telling me this now… why?"

"You have to stop them, young sire." She suddenly reached out, grabbed my hands in hers and squeezed them tightly, adding, *"You have to.* Lord Rasaben tried, and Lord Vela, Lord Tistriya's father, before him, and others, but they keep coming back—getting bolder each time, raiding and taking whole villages, towns, even an entire city I've been told—terrible raids where nothing's left. My village was burnt to the ground—I alone survived and only because I'd gone to pick mushrooms in the nearby woods."

She sniffed, wiped her nose, her face, then continued. "I heard the ships of course—saw them drop out of the sky and knew what it meant. I hid, knowing my family would be doing the same—but when I realized they were attacking my small village, not the neighboring town... I started running, screaming and waving my arms... I... I didn't want to be left behind. I wanted to be with my family no matter our fate." She took several deep, ragged breaths, dabbed her eyes again then looked up to see the soldier offering her a mug, his own eyes glittering.

She reluctantly released her hold on me, took the mug, took several deep gulps then looked back me. "But I was too late—they were gone, everyone was *gone*. The village had been razed, the cattle dead—even the chickens, dead in their coops. They even set the fields and woods on fire as they left—they're like locusts, voraciously consuming everything in their path and utterly destroying what's left." She heaved a sigh, fixed her eyes on the mug she clutched tightly in both hands, staring down at her reflection in the quivering surface of its contents.

"I have no clear memories of the days after that. I must have wandered quite a distance, because the next thing I remember was finding myself standing in the middle of a wide road. Coming down that road was a group of horsemen escorting a wagon. There wasn't any cover, no trees, not even a hedgerow, just rolling fields of grass as far as the eye could see... I thought... I thought I was about to be attacked but I wasn't scared.

"In truth I didn't care what they did to me—I only hoped they'd kill me when they were done, but none laid a hand on me. It was Lord Rasaben and a group of his horsemen, along with a wagon-full of more men, ten or so—I thought maybe they were survivors from a raid, too, as they all looked dazed..." She shifted in the chair suddenly and intensely uncomfortable, her gaze now fixed on the flagstone floor at her feet.

I kept my eyes on her down-turned face, unable to meet the sidelong stares of my men.

"Lord Rasaben didn't ask what had happened to me," she said abruptly, breaking the awkward silence while keeping her eyes downcast. "He only asked from which village I'd come. I told him and he sent some of his horsemen to search for other survivors even though I told him there were none, and one of his men—Harne is was—he did what he could for me, wrapped me up in a blanket he did—I didn't realize until then that my clothing was in tatters and badly singed—" she reached up, touched her hair, "and gave me something warm to drink that he said would help.

"Lord Rasaben asked me where I wanted them to take me—did I have relatives nearby? All my kin had been taken, I told him, my village and everything in it destroyed so he suggested I go with them, with winter coming on and all; I'd be safe with them, he said. I don't remember if I agreed or not—I do remember finding myself seated atop the wagon, beside Harne. He was a good man, Harne was—and now he's been taken, too, and being he was a servant of Lord Taskim, one can only imagine what the Faoimhuir have done to him." She sniffed again and dabbed her nose, her eyes with the apron, then again met my steady gaze.

"That's how I came to be in Lord Taskim's service. And Harne—I later learned he was no more than a boy when his family was taken, Perus as well and Jaro... others too; they've all seen with their own eyes the evil of the Faoimhuir, and like me, were rescued by the Tuatha. In turn we've served them willingly, gratefully, hoping that one day we will see justice done."

She took another gulp from the mug then handed it back to the red-headed soldier and seeing his anxious, blue-eyed stare, she patted him on the hand, then she turned back to me. "You asked when. Twelve years ago—a lifetime ago. The Tuatha, they offered me a new life—they didn't have to. Lord Rasaben and his men could have ridden right by me that day and I wouldn't have thought twice about it. They could have done what I thought they were going to do. But they didn't—none laid a hand on me and what was left of my clothing might have been excuse enough for some." She grasped the front of her bodice, clutching the fabric tightly in her fingers, an equally eloquent and troubling gesture.

"Safe, Lord Rasaben told me. Go with them and I'd be safe. I'd never been a household servant to anyone, least of all a Lord; I never aspired to such a lofty position. I was a cowherd's daughter and a cowherd's wife, but I learned the ways of the Keep and while it's not the same as the village, I've never wanted for anything, except... except my family. *I do miss them, terribly.*"

The soldier she'd comforted returned the gesture, lightly gripping her shoulder and giving it a squeeze and she clutched his pale, freckled fingers, holding them tightly to her.

"What they did," Boian continued, "to you and these men is beyond forgiveness, indeed it is, young sire, but if you'll excuse me for saying so, you don't know the whole story. You don't know the Faoimhuir and what they're capable of, what they do to the people they capture. The Tuatha aren't truly bad people, not like the Faoimhuir, they just... well, they're terribly burdened by their responsibilities, desperate to protect us, protect Earth. Lord Rasaben for one... he wasn't like he is now. Something happened, something terrible to cause him to become so cruel." She dabbed her eyes, adding, "The Tuatha truly care about us—"

"They have a strange way of showing it," I couldn't help but grumble before I took a grimacing sip from my own mug—the Tuatha version of wine.

"Indeed," she murmured, wiping her nose again. "Indeed they do, but I owe them my life, young sire. We all do." She looked up at the two soldiers, at Aetius and lastly, pointedly, at Rufinius then back at me. "Some more than others."

I couldn't help but look at Rufinius too, not sure what she meant by that and still not quite ready to fully believe what she was telling me—still openly suspicious, and for damned good reason.

"I knew what you were when they brought you here—I knew what they had planned," she continued. "Lady Ainiaan told me you were a very brave and successful soldier and I knew you were a prisoner—I thought you'd been bought... like the others," she flicked Rufinius another sidelong look then Aetius before again fixing her eyes on me. "Unlike them, you had the precise skills the Tuatha desperately needed.

"We were all terribly worried when you fell so desperately ill. Lord Mabog said he'd done all he could, he said it was up to you now—and for the first few days it seemed a forgone conclusion that you would die—your life along with everyone's last hope dangling by a thread. Then, to everyone's relief, you began to improve, bit-by-bit, day-by-day.

"I helped, you know. Helped Lady Ainiaan tend to your needs while you slept, keeping a vigil of sorts as she refused to leave your side, talking to you, carefully massaging your arms and legs just as Lord Mabog showed me, turning you to keep you comfortable, alerting him when you were feverish, when you appeared to be in pain or were having trouble breathing, all the while hoping that in some small way I would aide in your recovery, and at the same time I'd be there, just in case, as no one wanted Lady Ainiaan to be the one to..."

"Realize I'd died?"

"Yes," she murmured. After a pause, she continued. "I thought you'd agreed, you see. Your memories of warcraft in trade for your freedom perhaps—or maybe I just hoped that was true, since unlike the others, you hadn't had your mind scrubbed clean."

This time she kept her glittering eyes firmly locked with mine as she suppressed a shiver. "I didn't know until... until afterwards that you'd never agreed, that you didn't even know what they had planned for you." She took a ragged breath and dabbed her eyes.

As I stared at her, I recalled her strange reaction, after my bath, to something I'd said, and me being left with the worry that I'd accidentally offended her, and then another memory, much later, of her washing my face, gently combing my hair with her fingers, then massaging my shoulders, my back as I lay, helpless and semiconscious on Turan's bed after the ordeal of having my memories torn from my mind; of her sniffing softly as she did her best to clean me up and make me comfortable—a thankless task akin to Hanni's guardianship.

"But even if I had known," she continued quietly, "I wouldn't have warned you."

I couldn't help but blink at her blunt admission.

"It wouldn't have stopped them," she replied almost defensively. "They'd have gone ahead, no matter if you were willing or not, so one might even argue that it was a kindness not to warn you. And one life... if it stopped the Faoimhuir, seemed a very small price to pay. I'm sorry, young sire, but it's true. And I'm not saying that because it was your life, not mine. I'd have volunteered—any of us who've seen the Faoimhuir in action would eagerly volunteer if it meant ending this horror. But I can't; Jaro and Perus can't—we don't have the knowledge, the skills. But *you* do; you can stop them, once and for all. And while I understand your hurt and your rage at what was done to you and you certainly owe me nothing, I ask that you consider what I've told you."

She gave the soldier's hand one last squeeze, then rose and smoothed out her skirts with her hands. She looked back at me. "It's too late for my babes, my family, young sire. But it's not too late to spare others the same terrible fate. Please listen to Lord Taskim and Lady Turan—hear what they're trying to tell you... and if you still don't believe them, if you still think I'm misleading you, then I beg you, speak with Lady Ainiaan—but not until *after* you've heard what Lord Taskim has to say."

I arched a brow, wondering what a little girl could say to me that would persuade me when the impassioned words—eloquent words—of adults could not, then: "I'll do as you ask, Boian, but I'll make no promises as to how I'll decide."

"Fair enough, young sire." She leaned close and kissed me on the forehead. Then she stepped back and walked away; her guards, at my approving nod, wordlessly followed.

— iii —

I sat, arms crossed as I listened disdainfully to Taskim's entreaties. While I'd agreed to Boian's request and finally accepted Taskim's invitation to "talk," I didn't have to act happy about it—in fact no acting needed. I *wasn't* happy about it, not one damned bit. Just being in the same room with this man gave me a very sour stomach—and in the damned library no less. I must admit I broke out in a cold sweat as I entered the now all-too-familiar chamber—yet another thing I could hold against him: my fond memories of libraries had been forever desecrated.

A week had passed since the confrontation in the Great Hall and in that time Mabog had successfully transferred my memories to all two hundred and five of the Keep's remaining Kellesuf. Surprisingly, neither Rasaben nor Taskim had put a stop to it as I reasonably feared they would. Of course I'd softened my approach, leaving both men with the distinct impression that Boian's eye-witness account of a Faoimhuir raid had caused me to revisit my views on fighting their war—I was a soldier after all, I'd said many times in a voice that would carry, my presumably drunken boasts overheard by the servants who brought us our meals, overheard by Perus and Jaro or anyone else who happened to find themselves in the Great Hall while I was there, sharing a meal with my men.

I was a good Roman and a damned good centurion. Like any decent and upstanding Roman legionary, I added for good measure, I knew no other trade but war and I'd never backed down from a fight and had no plans to start now—but only if I had enough soldiers to do the job. I just never let myself be pinned down to exactly what job that would be and being the considerate man that I am, I graciously allowed Rasaben and Taskim and the Sidhe Lords to think what they wanted.

Word also spread that I now commanded any soldier who *freely* offered his fealty and no sooner had each Kellesuf received my memories and had barely recovered from this horrendous ordeal than he immediately swore his allegiance to me—not to Taskim, not to Rasaben. *Me.* Of course the same could not be said for those who were *not* former Kellesuf: Perus, Jaro, Kyrou and the like, about fifty or so that made up the backbone of the Keep's male servants and men-at-arms, not to mention their womenfolk, like Boian. They remained steadfastly loyal to their Tuatha masters, which I grudgingly admit lent some credence to Boian's claims.

That said, I did have to wonder why this not wholly unexpected outcome with its associated complications and potential for serious reprisals hadn't occurred to Rasaben or Taskim—more likely it had but they, in their arrogance, assumed they could turn it to their advantage at any time, so why not humor me by letting me think I'd outsmarted them? That was one quirk I'd learned about the Tuatha—they loved toying with those unfortunate enough to fall into their clutches.

And me being me, I was more than happy to return the favor by humoring, or, more accurately infuriating my Tuatha 'hosts' at every opportunity. They might not be totally bad people, as Boian claimed, but they weren't damned nice either. And what better opportunity than this much anticipated meeting, a meeting where Taskim was to produce the 'proof' of his accusations against the Faoimhuir and my first face-to-face with him and Rasaben since the ugly matter in the Great Hall. Plus, I felt that by being utterly obnoxious, by challenging them and generally pissing them off, I was assuring myself—as much as one could assure oneself of anything while in the present of a Tuatha—that no one was controlling my thoughts, my actions.

Reason enough to want to be as insufferable as possible at every opportunity—if I was deluding myself, at least it was a thoroughly enjoyable delusion.

I arrived deliberately late, forcing them to wait upon me—and yes, fine, part of being late was that I had to screw up my courage in order to walk into that damned library. I admit it—just the thought unnerved me—but, if delaying served two purposes, then so much the better.

And as one more thumb in the eye to Taskim and his ilk I also arrived wearing full Roman kit—*my* kit: ring-mail shirt, greaves, phalerae, gladius, dagger... the lot. Granted, everything was fashioned of that strangely luminescent yet robust material from which Tuatha armor and weaponry was made, but aside from its eerie shimmer, it *was* a perfect match to mine—right down to the asymmetrical pattern of rivets on my beloved chest harness; even the *phalerae* had been replicated to the finest detail. And thankfully, the armor wasn't transparent as I'd feared. It was *translucent.* There's a big difference.

Only my helmet was dissimilar: I'd asked the armorer if he could recreate the scenes from that officer's amazing appliquéd brass and silvered helm from so long ago—admittedly a vanity on my part, but I felt after all I'd been through I'd earned it, dammit—and he'd far exceeded my expectations.

Not to be outdone, my soldiers to a man had demanded that my helmet be festooned with a high-arching sagittal crest of black alternating with white blocks of horsehair: the helm of a *legate*, or, more accurately, what they'd been led to believe was the helmet of a legate, with a lot of creative input from Ainiaan, who'd mistaken a fancy parade helmet for a true battle helmet. Legates in my experience—and I speak of the ones who didn't shirk their duties on the battlefield, the ones who'd earned their rank the hard way—rarely wore helmets. They would plunge into the fighting often as not bareheaded and to the roaring approval of their troops.

The result was one *damned* impressive, albeit not exactly an authentic or practical piece of battle headgear—which perhaps explained why most battle-hardened legates I'd known had elected to enter the fray sans-helmet, preferring to risk their life rather than laughter.

Now the armorer and his apprentices were hard at work creating more armor, enough to outfit each Kellesuf in full *Roman* kit and in their choice of ring-mail or band-armor; he'd started, of course, with Felix, Rufinius and Aetius—no Kellesuf hauberks bearing a Sidhe Lord's heraldic device of ownership for them again, *ever*.

And speaking of Felix, Rufinius and Aetius: while Mabog had the ability to instill my memories of these three in as many of the Kellesuf as I so chose, I decided that they were to be unique, just as their predecessors had been; besides, I wasn't sure I could control any more—these three were handful enough, again, just as the originals had been.

I'd known so many men over the years, good soldiers and each in their way undeniably brave, the embodiment of what it was to be Roman legionary—or a Roman auxiliary as the case may be—there would be plenty to choose from. Duccius for one, truly crazy as the Marcomanni was, then there was Caelius, Accius, Caepio, Atticus, Lupus, my partner in chariot-borrowing, Carbo, Baculus and Pictor—even Jotia, the centurion who was known to terrorize other centurions, tribunes and yes, even the occasional legate—especially the sort of legate who preferred to follow the battle from the protection—er, I mean the *perspective*—of a distant hillock, which meant *not* the sort of legate I planned to be, which in turn meant I was likely safe from Jotia's ire not to mention his vine-staff, and hundreds more, too many to recite each and every name.

But thanks to my extraordinary memory each had his place in my thoughts; each had left his indelible mark on my mind. My childhood memories and the soldiers who inhabited them, were, however, kept apart and private—that Mabog had promised me surreptitiously, as he too understood the perils, perhaps better than I did, so no risk of any Gracchuses or Porsennas appearing among the ranks—*absolutely none*.

Unlike Felix, Rufinius and Aetius, who Ainiaan had hand-picked and so had not been given a choice as to who they were to become, the remaining soldiers were, at my insistence, granted the opportunity to freely select his own template and grow from there, as Mabog said each would.

Felix, Rufinius and Aetius, when I informed each of them privately of my decision, did not object; each told me separately that while he hadn't been consulted as to who he would become, each felt that filling the roles of my closest friends was as good as good could be and wouldn't swap with someone else if given the option—a reaction, I must admit, that left a lump in my throat.

Some of the former Kellesuf chose to be amalgams of shadows distilled from scant reminiscence, eventually becoming someone who had never been. Others more sensibly took hold of one strong recollection. Mabog assured me that each man would build upon his new personality, eventually becoming a truly unique individual, not just a copy, just as Felix, Aetius and Rufinius would eventually become someone other than who the originals had been, or would have become, given time.

They would grow and change and mature, just as the first Felix, Aetius and Rufinius would have done, had they lived and I privately wondered what my old friends would think of their replicates. Would they approve? Be appalled?

Felix would probably find some twist of wry humor in it all. He was, after all, the most pragmatic of the three. Knowing Aetius, he'd probably pick a fistfight with his double, furious the man had somehow avoided his less than appealing looks. Rufinius would likely keep his opinion to himself but if pressed reply with a laconic, "It is what it is," then join forces with his close twin to urge Aetius on.

I'd taken up residence in the austere barracks alongside my soldiers—having solved the heating problem early on—eating and sleeping with my men, sharing both the depravations and the sorely missed camaraderie, not to mention helping each man adjust to his new individuality. So for me life had finally taken on a comforting, if not particularly comfortable familiarity; my sleep was rarely disturbed by nightmares—the Lemures had, like me, found some measure of peace and for that I was extremely grateful.

I had no desire to enjoy the comforts of the Keep denied the soldiers, nor did I have any urge to visit Turan's bed—in fact I deliberately avoided her, even refusing to hear messages she sent via the servants. Only when she began sending Boian did I listen—but only to spare Boian hurt. My reply was always the same: I was too occupied to spare Turan any time, which wasn't far from the truth. That said, I freely admit that her feelings, her needs were no longer a concern of mine.

I did reluctantly accept one surprising and at first baffling offering from Turan: several rolls of the finest vellum, *blank* vellum, a quill and a small pot of iron-gall ink. When Boian brought them, I thanked her then promptly put the gifts aside, refusing to be bought by such a strange yet appealing present, refusing to admit even to myself that Turan knew me this well. Soon, the temptation was too great.

At first I satisfied myself by jotting down notes. Before I realized it, this occasional habit it had become a nightly ritual: after a communal evening meal in the Great Hall, and as my exhausted soldiers staggered off to their bunks, I would sit on the raised hearth of the barracks' fireplace and commit my memories to the solidity of vellum.

Why, you ask? I have an extraordinary memory, after all. But Turan's gift, intentionally or not, had prompted me into acknowledging that I also have a mortal body. Just as part of me would live on through the child I'd sired, so would my experiences, in my own words—perhaps both serving a purpose I could not even begin to imagine.

While my nights were devoted to writing, my days were spent training these former Kellesuf in Roman discipline and tactics—a very satisfying balance of mind and muscle, I have to say. There'd be a cavalry unit too— I'd already chosen its commander, a wiry and dark-skinned man who'd taken to his heart the memory of Marcus Polycleitus, ironically a thickset and pale-skinned Gaul and one of the few cavalry officers I'd come to hold in high regard, not just for his bravery in battle, but for his fair treatment of the infantry.

It was a familiar role for me: turning raw recruits into a formidable fighting force. Only this time the men under my command weren't farm boys and sons of privilege unskilled in fighting—they were men and former Kellesuf, which presented me with some very unique challenges. I *relished* it. I relished each and every day, each and every lesson, every rigorous training session as I watched these lost men, bit by bit, find themselves anew; and yes, as I, bit by bit, found myself, again.

Just the evening before a fistfight had broken out between two soldiers which had quickly spread through the barracks. While that might not seem particularly remarkable, Kellesuf never fought amongst themselves. *Ever.* To get angry, much less throw a punch, never would have occurred to any of them; even more remarkable was that Aetius *hadn't* been the instigator. He'd been busy elsewhere, having somehow caught the eye of one of the Keep's cooks.

Despite the fact that seven needed Mabog's skills to patch up the damage and still more were left nursing bruised knuckles, black eyes and split lips and complaining bitterly about how much their injuries hurt, pain being a novel experience for them, I decided not to reprimand anyone—this time.

Privately I was incredibly pleased with the speed at which they were becoming individuals again—it was as if I'd poured water on parched soil, then had to hurriedly step back as long-dormant plants sprang forth and stretched for the sun. I'd seen it happen in the desert each spring—ground that was barely more than shifting sand and exposed rock one day would be transformed into a verdant garden within hours of the first hard rain. As a child I'd found it magical.

While it still might be the dead of winter, I thought, grinning to myself, *Kellesuf are now in full bloom.*

Then I recalled perhaps an even more precise analogy, one that had fascinated me as a youth: the Greek legend of Cadmus, who sowed dragon's teeth and reaped an army—*hum. Perhaps I need to nip this habit of fighting amongst them in the bud...*

I pulled my mind off that path and turned to the business at hand. And that business was, sadly, my chosen vocation: war.

I could've continued to ignore Taskim's polite but insistent summons just as I'd ignored Turan's, but I knew just how far push and still maintain the high ground. So here I was—but I hadn't come alone. Oh, hell no—you honestly think I'd put even one toe in that accursed library without a heavily armed escort?

I was not one who believed in half-measures, which meant Aetius, Rufinius and Felix had accompanied me, just as their predecessors had done when I'd been dispatched to parley with some petty tribal chieftain. We'd wanted to send a very clear message to said chieftain that my safe return could not be used to enhance his bargaining position and if he tried, he'd quickly find himself the hostage, not me.

While this Rufinius and Aetius were obvious choices for this odious task, Felix was still recovering from his terrible beating, still nursing broken bones and had spent the entire week in bed—at Mabog's firm direction, with Ainiaan and Boian acting as nurses, thus lessening the sting of his enforced convalescence. But when he got wind of this meeting—Aetius had let it slip, purely by accident, or so Aetius insisted—Felix insisted on coming too, and managed, somehow. He had something to prove, to himself, to me, and most of all, to Rasaben—always a huge motivator among men and making any injury, no matter how serious or painful nothing more than a minor hindrance.

Now all three were in full Roman kit, although at Ainiaan's urging they'd opted for the more impressive band-armor over my preference of ring-mail, and wearing *centurion* helmets—*oh, yes!* I forgot to mention that we'd held a small ceremony in the barracks four evenings before—as soon as Felix was strong enough he could stand unassisted for a few minutes— only my men and myself were invited, to award these ranks to the three and to the thunderous applause of their fellow troops. They now stood shoulder to armored shoulder behind me, with Felix centermost and bracketed in case he started to wobble, and clutching my elaborate helm to his armored chest. And six more soldiers stood behind them, also in Roman band-armor and helmets.

And we had impressive company: Hanni, despite his earlier reservations about the Kellesuf, and mine about him had openly allied himself with us— or, more accurately, he'd allied himself with me, much to Taskim and Rasaben's obvious displeasure. But what could they say? Hanni was an ogre after all, and no one in his right mind trifles with an ogre once his mind is set.

While it hadn't been an easy thing to do, I'd managed to put my bitterness at his earlier betrayal to rest; he was an impressive ally, and while not Tuatha he understood the inner workings of Tuatha society—I freely admitted I was largely ignorant on the subject, and that ignorance was a serious blind spot.

This display of overwhelming force, not to mention force in the guise of Roman armor had not set well with Rasaben. He was seated next to Taskim, his fierce eyes fixed on me as if willing me to keel over dead while pointedly ignoring the three men directly behind me. I noted with some glee that his jaw, like Felix's face, still bore the marbled coloring of a beating—in this case, my left fist.

Behind me I heard someone fidgeting, hobnail boots scuffing on flagstone—I didn't need to look to know who it was. Aetius could see Rasaben's challenging expression and desperately wanted to do something about it, to add some fresh color to Rasaben's fading, piebald complexion. He knew better than to act on that impulse—we were here under a flag of truce, so to speak, each side guaranteeing the safety of the other.

All manner of documents were now spread across the library table— documents Taskim had repeatedly assured me would back up his claims of the Faoimhuir's brutality, their enslavement of men they'd taken elsewhere—'off world' as he had a habit of stressing. He kept gesturing to the treaties and maps and the scores of personal accounts—written by those who'd sought protection from the other Sidhe Lords, or so he claimed—as if the words that flowed across their vellum and papyri surfaces would reach me as he clearly assumed Boian's story had, that they could make me see sense when his promises, his petitions had not.

Under other circumstances I might have been persuaded by his impassioned arguments, might have looked sympathetically upon the statements of those who'd somehow escaped the Faoimhuir—*if* I'd been told the truth from the very start; *if* I'd been treated as an equal I might have accepted his claims as factual, accepted what I'd read as truth. But I hadn't been told the truth at the start, I'd never been treated as an equal and I was only now being told the whole story—Taskim's side, the Tuatha's side and their loyal servants' side of the story—because this was their last hope in persuading me to their cause, and, oh, yes, I now had two hundred and eight armed and decidedly cheesed off men at my beck and call, and each one, like Aetius, were just itching for an excuse to turn the tables on Taskim and his fellow lords. And more were on their way, or would be, eventually, as each Lord was donating all of his or her Kellesuf to the cause—generous of them, no? I had no idea how many in total, but presumably enough to do what needed to be done.

"So," I said, "you and the Faoimhuir agreed that if either broke the treaty by arms, which you've admitted you've done—"

"Only because we discovered they were taking your people off world," Taskim interrupted, "and in vast numbers. Centurion, I keep—"

"You mean Legate," Aetius growled, drawing Taskim's annoyed stare, not to mention Rasaben's contemptuous snort, "unless you're speaking to me, Felix or Rufinius… *sire."* Aetius added that last bit of deference at the elbowing insistence of Felix. I could tell as I heard the slight *ooof* of wind from Aetius between 'Rufinius' and the grunted 'sire'. The original Felix too had been a stickler for protocol; he'd certainly saved me from a few political gaffes in when I was called upon to act as a diplomat—he'd grown up in the household of a Roman senator after all. Etiquette came as naturally to him as brawling came to Aetius—and yes, gaffes to me.

Taskim squinted at Aetius then dropped his gaze back to me. "I keep telling you this—"

"And I *heard* you the first time, and the second… and third and so on. I only *stopped* listening after the tenth time."

That shut him up, thank you.

"Now," I set my elbows on the table and steepled my hands in front of me, "as *I* was *saying*, the treaty says if it's broken by force of arms, it must be settled by force of arms and those arms must be wielded by humans, not by you or the Faoimhuir, correct?"

"Correct," Taskim replied in a clipped, decidedly aggrieved voice.

"Why? Since *you* started it, why don't *you* finish it?"

"Because a war between the Tuatha and the Faoimhuir would draw in other forces, forces that are far beyond your understanding, Centur—"

Aetius coughed.

"Legate," he amended unhappily.

I sat back, tapped my finger on my pursed lips and replied dubiously, *"Really?* It strikes me far more likely that you and the Faoimhuir believe human blood is far cheaper than yours—and therefore yours to squander at will."

"That's not true!" Taskim slammed his fists on the table for emphasis but I was unmoved—okay, I was a little moved. I hadn't expected him to do that, so I'd flinched. But in all fairness so did Rasaben. So did the men behind me. "The treaty was written such as it was to prevent any possible violation from causing an escalation that could spread far beyond Earth—"

"Meaning it might draw you in, force you to actually fight, a fight you might actually *lose?"*

That garnered a flare of rage in Rasaben's eyes. So I decided to add some more kindling and twisted around in my chair and fixed my sullen-faced companions with a questioning glance. "Why does this sound familiar?"

Rufinius, not Aetius, surprisingly, was the first to snap at the bait. "Perhaps because Lord Taskim, like Lord Rasaben, has amply proven himself to be a bully-coward?" He fixed Rasaben with a challenging smirk, well aware that Rasaben was every bit as constrained as he was and taking great delight in taunting him with the fact. Next time Rasaben needed being taken down a peg or two—or twenty, I was going to let Rufinius do the honors, for Rasaben's sake, not mine as it would be so much less humiliating for him to be soundly trounced by a former sparring partner rather than being knocked silly—again—by a veritable pipsqueak like me, right? See? I can be the bigger man… so to speak.

Taskim took a moment to collect himself then he settled back in his chair and plastered on an abettor's comfortable smile, as if we were true allies—true equals. "'Legate' sounds so formal. May I call you Arri?"

I replied with a comfortable smile of my own. "No, you may not."

He inhaled, his nostrils flaring then sitting up, continued, "I can fully understand why you believe what you're suggesting."

"How incredibly munificent of you—"

"But you are, to be kind, blissfully unaware of the larger forces at play here."

I shrugged, unoffended. "Probably." I was; I make no claim otherwise.

"There are beings out there," he waved his arm around, "beings with such incredible powers you would believe them gods—Si'aafu for one—who are just waiting for a reason to invade and conquer Earth—worlds such as yours are hard to come by and therefore highly prized. It's only this balancing act between Tuatha and Faoimhuir that has kept Earth safe from such a fate—"

"Are these... these *See-ah-foo* more cold-blooded and deceitful than you?" I asked sweetly.

Taskim immediately looked away and fixed his furious gaze on the far wall.

I took the opportunity to look utterly innocent of antagonizing him. Not that the others seated at the table were taken in. Rasaben looked just as enraged as Taskim. The dark-haired, neatly-bearded man—Lord Tistriya, yes, he'd finally introduced himself, or should I say Taskim let his name slip during a whispered conversation, then, realizing I'd overheard, made the introduction a formal matter—looked as if I'd just satisfactorily proven beyond doubt his opinion of Romans as being nothing better than stupid, stubborn beasts.

The blond woman—Boian had earlier informed me her name was Lady Urme—who, having spent the first few minutes sizing me up, clearly amused by my cheek, sizing up Rufinius and yes, even the bruise-faced Felix while she was at it as if debating which one she'd later take to her bed, had clearly lost interest by our continued churlish behavior. Turan just looked... immensely weary of it all, as if she knew I was playing them, tormenting them for the sheer joy of pissing them off and knowing there wasn't a damned thing any of them could do but go along with it until like Mugwort I grew weary and in my case agreed to fight their damned battle.

But I was far from weary of tormenting them. I still wasn't entirely convinced I wanted to help, wanted to commit my life, my soldiers' lives to their cause. Truly. I still needed a little... persuasion, not to mention more facts. So I tossed out a bone. "So, we're to fight your war?"

That drew Taskim's wary gaze, along with Tistriya's sidelong, condescending squint. "Presumably the Faoimhuir have their own human army?"

"Yes," Taskim answered flatly.

"Levied the same way? By kidnapping and force?"

"No. They have a large population of slaves to draw from."

"Separate and distinct from those they've been snatching of late?"

"Yes."

I tapped my forefinger on my chin. "But still a slave army."

"Yes."

"You mean they made the same foolishly short-sighted mistake you did?" I blinked in astonishment. "My, my. They aren't very smart, are they?"

Taskim scowled at me, but replied in a bland voice: "These aren't slaves as you would know them, Legate. They've grown up never knowing anything but servitude to the Faoimhuir—they've been conditioned to it; to them there is no other conceivable way of life, so never doubt that they will fight for their masters without question and ferociously."

"And die for them as well."

"Of course."

"Just as you expect us to do for you."

He hesitated then with a nod of the head, answered, "Yes."

I smiled. Not a nice smile, just a slow, drawing back of my lips to expose my teeth, then: "I do believe that's the first completely honest thing you've ever said to me."

Taskim responded by shifting around in his chair.

Morituri nolumus mori, I thought as I watched him squirm, which garnered a soft chuckle from Lady Urme and a pained look from Turan. Taskim, Rasaben and Lord Tistriya exchanged quizzical glances as if they weren't in on the joke. And perhaps they weren't; perhaps they believed they were too important, too superior to eavesdrop on my lowly thoughts, so I repeated aloud: "We who are about to die don't want to."

Well, it was true, wasn't it? Who truly wants to die, especially if there are more pleasant alternatives? I didn't, damned if I did; I certainly didn't want to die for some damned Sidhe lord—or lady for that matter. Let's not forget about the ladies. I turned my attention back to Taskim. "So, as I was saying, you have your human army, they have theirs. Same size?"

"Yes."

"How many in total?"

"Fifteen hundred on each side..."

That was more than I'd expected, but far from a full legion.

"...numbers enough to win a decisive victory, but not so many to waste—*to squander*, as you claim."

"But one too many if you're the one who dies."

He had no pat answer for that.

"So," I went on, all business-like, "where do we fight?"

"The terms of the treaty were very clear—you read it."

"You're right, I did. Admittedly I didn't quite understand all of it, but what I did grasp is that whoever breaks the treaty—*meaning you*—must yield to the choice of the one who didn't break the treaty—*meaning the Faoimhuir*—when it comes to exactly when and where the battle is fought. Correct?"

"Yes."

I crossed my arms and leaned back into my chair. "When?"

"Six months from now."

That was more time than I'd expected. "And as to the where?"

"A neutral planet—but very Earth-like, I assure you—I can show you on a star chart." He started to rise, suddenly eager for the distraction and clearly believing that I was actually warming to the idea. "It's in the constellation—"

"Not necessary."

He looked back at me and seeing my hard expression, slowly sank back into his chair.

Now, I readily admit that I had no idea what the hell he was talking about—what a neutral planet was, what he meant by 'very Earth-like' but I was damned if I was going to let on. "I also gathered from the treaty that once the location and time has been decided by the offended party, the offender does have one choice, and that's how the battle is to be fought."

"Yes," he replied warily, as if unwilling to again get caught with all his hopes on display.

"And so you decided...?"

"To fight the Roman way."

I feigned utter puzzlement—actually, I didn't need to feign it. I was utterly puzzled. "I had the very distinct impression that none of you thought very highly of Romans." I swept my gaze around the table, making eye contact with each of the Tuatha present. "In fact I got the distinct impression that you all consider us Romans worse than vermin."

Lady Urme smiled at that, not a pretty smile, while Rasaben snorted then looked away and vigorously rubbed his still-bruised and misshapen nose.

Taskim looked pained as he replied, "I confess that many of my fellow Tuatha hold a very low opinion of your Empire, Legate—"

"Meaning you don't?" I replied with what sounded like genuine surprise because it *was* genuine surprise.

"—in large part because its very existence has at times been a great inconvenience to us—"

"Then for every Roman who has ever breathed, I offer my most sincere and humble apologies," I sneered.

"—because by your constant expansion, your insatiable need to conquer, you have, unwittingly, served Faoimhuirian ambitions."

"Oh, I am *soooo* sorry." But I wasn't, not in the slightest, and everyone knew it. "Now, back to this forthcoming battle." I tapped the table top for emphasis. "It's to take place elsewhere, the time and place decided by the Faoimhuir, while you—"

"Choose the way in which the battle is fought, *yes*. The Faoimhuir assume we'll pick a technologically advanced—"

"A... *what?*"

"Technologically advanced," Rasaben growled, speaking for the first time. "Like long-range, heat-seeking missiles..."

I knew what that was—at least the missile part.

"Land mines... tanks..."

All right, I didn't have a clue what these were, but before I could ask, Rasaben continued.

"...hunter-bomber drones."

Okay, now he was being deliberately abstruse and I saw no reason not to call him on it and readily admitted my ignorance. "What the hell are they?"

He smiled, as if he finally had me. "Warships that fly."

I couldn't help but stare at him, agog. *"Fly?"* Then I started to laugh.

"Like a bird?" Aetius added, flapping his arms for emphasis, his band-armor clanking in response and the men behind him chuckled.

Rasaben grinned up at him, at them, then at me. "Yeah, *just* like a bird. Only these 'birds' can shit liquid fire all over your troops from a mile up in the sky."

That didn't sound good. Or fair. Definitely *not* fair. Aetius stopped flapping his arms and the soldiers fell deathly silent as I looked narrowly at Taskim. "You said the Faoimhuir assume you'd pick such fearsome weapons—but you haven't. *Why?*"

"We know the planet they've picked, even better, *we* know the battlefield far better than they. Such weapons as Lord Rasaben describes are undoubtedly fearsome, but they can also easily break down without constant maintenance and support—neither of which we would be able to supply. The treaty expressly forbids it—each side must be self-contained and self-sufficient.

"The Faoimhuir, who love their physical comforts and who have chosen a far different, superficially more sophisticated and, dare I say, *softer* lifestyle than Tuatha, a lifestyle dependent upon advanced technology, have not taken this into account… *but we have.* We considered all the possibles, all the technologies and all the warrior cultures of human history and realized the most effective, the best suited for the conditions and the most adaptable is the Roman legion."

"So we're going up against these fire birds?" Felix asked huskily, his voice, like the rest of him still not fully recovered, and clearly not liking the sound of this, not one damned bit. Neither did the men behind him; I could hear their feet shuffling nervously. Even Aetius, whose progenitor had single-handedly charged *and* routed Parthian war elephants and lived to brag about it, was unhappy.

"No, ah… *Centurion,*" Taskim said with a hint of contempt while meeting Felix's gaze for the first time. Whether his disdain stemmed from using Felix's rank or being forced to speak to a former Kellesuf and do it with some deference I cannot tell you. Plus, as I mentioned before, Felix's handsome face had yet to fully recover from Rasaben's fists: a visible reminder of just how much things had changed, just how much the power had shifted in little more than a week. "You see there's a clause in the treaty, one the Faoimhuir appear to have overlooked as it appears to be so inconsequential: whatever period of human history we pick from which to derive our army, they must also pick an adversary—"

"From the *same* period," I interrupted, suddenly remembering that clause and drawing Taskim's nodding stare in the process; it had seemed inconsequential to me, too—okay, in truth it didn't make sense to me. It still didn't.

"And as you yourself told me and my fellow Lords at this very table," he continued, nodding to Urme and Tistriya, "no other army on Earth is a legitimate challenger to Rome *at this moment in time*—your empire has very successfully eliminated all adversaries—yes, there are some who can still deal serious, but not fatal injuries to your empire. To utterly eliminate all possible threats, external *and* internal, would itself be the greatest threat, yes?"

I nodded, grudgingly.

"Rome and its legions are currently, how would you say it, Legate, *unrivaled?*—something that, for the most part, has never happened before in human history, and will never happen again."

It was true. Rome had conquered just about everything and everyone who had stood in her way. Mountain ranges and rivers were only minor hurdles to our engineers, oceans a brief impediment—apologies to the sadly misguided Sapor. Barbarian armies were an annoyance that were quickly brushed aside. Only obdurate Parthia, along with the equally mulish Britannia and parts of Germania remained but I had no doubt they too would fall, eventually, that they had only briefly slowed the inevitable. Rome could never be completely stopped, except by its own choice.

The most likely, and potentially the most worrisome adversary the Faoimhuir might choose would be those from Pontus—their king, Mithridates, had, after all, come very close to ending Rome's aspirations at becoming an empire, or even an internal foe, like Julius Caesar—civil war being as devastating if not worse than war against an outside threat. And then there was the likes of Spartacus—Rome hadn't seen that fucking rabble-rouser coming, that's for sure.

And let's not forget the Varian Disaster where the Cherusci—yes, Kyrou's folk—and their allies tidily dispatched three Roman legions without breaking a sweat. And of course one couldn't overlook those pesky Parthians, not to mention the equally vexing Carthaginians, who, under Hannibal, left a permanent scar on the Roman psyche...

And speaking of Parthians and Carthaginians, I made a mental note to order the armorer to start turning out caltrops as quickly as possible as I didn't want to be caught off guard if the Faoimhuir decided to up the ante by adding chariots and, gods forbid, *war elephants* to the mix, despite the original Aetius' formidable reputation in dealing with the heavy-footed beasts.

As part of my early training I'd studied the campaigns of the Civil War that birthed an empire; I'd been required to examine from every possible angle the long-ago battle that had cost Rome three of its legions and as a result knew well the battle tactics of the disparate Germanic tribes. I'd analyzed the armies of Mithridates and the Parthians, and fortunately while living in Roman Carthage I'd spent a good deal of time researching the great generals of Punic Carthage: Hamilcar, Mago, Bomilcar and Hasdrubal and of course the greatest of them all, possibly the greatest of all time barring Alexander, *Hannibal.*

I'd even picked up a humorously ironic—at least to me—link between my ancestors and Carthaginians in the process: Massyli had allied themselves with Carthage at the start of her second disastrous war with Rome—you'd have thought even the stupid-as-sand Massyli would have known better—whereas the Massaesyli, showing slightly more smarts, had thrown in their lot with Rome, but half way through the war the Massyli *and* the Massaesyli inexplicably switched sides—which, as anyone who knows their history knows, was not an advantageous move—for the clearly just as stupid-as-sand Massaesyli. See what I mean? Ironic.

But I digress. We in fact weren't talking about Hannibal, or Mithridates or Spartacus or Julius Caesar as potential adversaries. They were in the past—in some cases hundreds of years in the past. The treaty was *very* clear: both armies had to be drawn *from a particular moment in time.* Not a decade, not a century. *A moment.* And at this particular moment no one, not even the Parthians, posed a truly serious threat.

And suddenly I understood; I understood the clause *and* understood that I'd grossly underestimated Taskim. He'd carefully maneuvered his enemy into doing everything he wanted—had in fact maneuvered me with the same skill. But for the benefit of the others I said, "Answer me honestly—did you have this all planned out, knowing they'd pick the place, knowing you could then pick the method, and knowing if you picked the Roman army *at this moment in time,* they'd have no comparable adversary from which to choose *before* you broke the treaty?"

Taskim smiled, a straightforward and immensely pleased smile. "Of course... *Legate.* You *still* think me a fool?"

— iv —

I left the meeting in the library even more unsettled than I arrived—and that's saying something as I'd been pretty damned unsettled by the prospect of returning to the library and facing the many demons who'd taken up permanent residence there—not to mention facing Taskim and two of the Sidhe Lords, both of whom, I'd learned, had been present when my memories had been ripped from me, had observed, even participated in the horrendous act and therefore knew things about me, about my past that I'd never shared with anyone, not even my closest friends. In fact I'd feared they'd use this information against me, throwing my ugly past back at me, but they hadn't. They probably wanted to—I'd bet my entire pension Rasaben dearly wanted to—but realized that any chance of persuading me to their cause would have gone up in smoke if he had.

I was in fact so unsettled by Taskim's parting remark that I headed directly for the barracks, seeking the reassurance its austere surroundings provided. My escort wordlessly followed, Felix walking abreast of me, or, more accurately, limping abreast of me and so clearly hard-pressed to keep up and wheezing audibly that I finally forced myself to slow down, with Rufinius and Aetius on our heels and the six soldiers behind them.

I felt Felix's curious, bordering on anxious eyes constantly darting to me as we strode down the hallway. Aside from slowing my pace, I ignored him, just as I ignored the startled stares of passing servants, servants who at our clanking approach hurriedly sought door alcoves only to watch our passage in wide-eyed silence. Had I not been so damned preoccupied, I might have enjoyed their reactions at suddenly finding themselves in the path of a fully armed and armored group of Roman soldiers—very grim-faced soldiers to boot.

Had the Tuatha truly out-maneuvered the Faoimhuir so easily, thus handing me an almost certain victory? Either the Tuatha were far smarter than I'd given them credit, or the Faoimhuir were far stupider. Or maybe they suffered from the same affliction as the Tuatha: terminal arrogance. Maybe Taskim was telling me the truth, maybe the Faoimhuir, in embracing a far different, softer lifestyle as he called it, had failed to see the trap so neatly laid out before them.

As I headed down the stone staircase, bits and pieces suddenly began to fall into place, like a complex mosaic. The picture that formed was not a particularly pretty one—Boian had said something had happened to Rasaben to make him so cruel... Taskim admitted that the Tuatha had broken the treaty by force of arms. And then there were the remarks exchanged between Turan and Rasaben, when they thought I was still unconscious: that Rasaben had lost a battle, a battle he was *supposed* to lose—in order to break the treaty? He'd warned Lord Vela... of what? And hadn't Boian told me Lord Vela was Lord Tistriya's father, that Vela had tried to defeat the Faoimhuir and had failed, and that Tistriya hated Rasaben?

I was so involved in trying to sort out the tangled fragments and make sense of it all that I flinched violently when I was grabbed from behind and roughly jerked to a halt and my hand instinctively reached for my gladius. Then I realized it was Rufinius who'd grabbed me, grabbed my ring-mail yoke stopping me in my tracks—and why.

Ainiaan stood in the open doorway that gave access to the courtyard and the barracks beyond. Her arms were crossed, her jaw was set—and by her stance, she deliberately blocked our path—a small child against ten armed and armored men. From her expression, she was not at all worried that we would in fact yield. In truth had Rufinius not stopped me by his timely grab, I very well might have run right into her in my distraction.

I cleared my throat and tugged my ring-mail yoke back into place. "Yes... m'lady?"

"Have you forgotten your promise?"

"Promise...?" It took my troubled mind a moment to alight on what she was referring to—I'd assumed I'd be given a chance to digest what I'd just learned from Taskim before I was confronted by whatever Ainiaan had to tell me, but clearly that was not the—

"To meet Mugwort."

I tried to get my bearings. *Mugwort...?*

She eyed me with a look of such utter disappointment I couldn't help but feel my face flush and stamped her foot. "You did, didn't you? And *he's* been so patient, and so looking forward to finally meeting you. *Well,"* she huffed in her reedy, child's voice, "I'll just go tell him that now that you're a fancy legate and all you're just too important, too busy—I'm sure he'll understand, he's *just* a pony after all." With that she spun on her heel, strode through the doorway then started stomping her way down the main steps.

I looked at Felix, eyebrows raised.

He stared back.

I then glanced over my shoulder at the men behind me. They all gave me the same baffled yet mildly chiding look as Felix. Ainiaan was very popular among the soldiers—the only Tuatha who could claim such— helping her father and Boian tend to their injuries, making sure they all had enough to eat and plenty of warm blankets—she'd been instrumental in getting the long disused barracks chimney cleaned and keeping the firebox constantly fed; she'd kept vigil over Felix as he recuperated, making sure he ate; and of course adding her fanciful suggestions to our arms and armor, ideas my men, naïve as they were, took as fact.

To that end she'd become a mascot to them, while at the same time happily imparting her vast knowledge of all things furred and feathered to any who showed an interest—all did, soaking up her wisdom like sponges.

I turned to face them. "It would appear I have some serious fence-mending to do with a pony..."

My feeble attempt at humor garnered a round of requisite chuckles.

"...so I'll see you gentlemen back at the barracks in a little while."

The soldiers nodded, then slipped around us and then down the steps, leaving me with Felix, Rufinius and Aetius.

I no longer feared assassination by Taskim and his lot—who'd lead their army if I just suddenly turned up dead?—and what would these former Kellesuf do if I was harmed? My hosts had to have considered that and not liked what they came up with. That said, there remained other threats, ugly and not particularly smart threats... in other words, Kyrou. And Kyrou was known to spend a lot of his time lurking around the vast and dimly lit stables, clearly preferring the company of equally furry and foul-smelling creatures to his fellow man. Not that I could really blame him.

He carried a very bad odor with most people in the Keep as it turned out, and I'm not just referring to his rather pungent and pervasive body odor. So perhaps the horses *were* his only friends—and only because they didn't have a choice in the matter.

The three men clearly assumed they were accompanying me to this latest meeting. But Felix was just as clearly suffering and would be hard pressed to defend me, in fact might be more hindrance than help if things did indeed take a bad turn. And Aetius, while undeniably brave and fully capable of defending his legate single-handedly, might not know when to stop defending him.

"Felix," I said and he straightened up—or tried to, struggling not to wince in the process. "You're to return to the barracks—Aetius, see he gets there and to his bed."

Both opened their mouths to protest.

"I went against Mabog's direct orders by allowing you to attend the meeting with Taskim," I continued, snatching my helmet from his hands. "I will not extend it to a meeting with a damned pony! Now be off with you—Aetius, see he does as I say or you'll be the one answering for it."

The two nodded sullenly and Aetius offered Felix his hand for support, which Felix pointedly, angrily refused as they walked away. Once they started down the steps, I noted that Aetius had grabbed Felix's elbow to steady him and this time Felix didn't rebuff the offer as he was noticeably wobbling and at serious risk of taking a bad fall down the ice-slippery stone stairs.

I exhaled then shifted my worried gaze back to Rufinius.

He shrugged, sympathetic to Felix's plight, even Aetius's, but at the same time quite pleased he'd been chosen to accompany me, and not just for the singular honor of bodyguard to the legate, oh, no.

I'd spent the past week living, eating and sleeping with these men and in the process had discovered quite by accident some interesting quirks about them. Kellesuf had no memory of who they had once been, they did only as they were told to do, they never spoke unless directly spoken to and they took everything said and done to them literally. And a lot of very bad things had been done to them as it turned out, as they were the obvious go-to targets for anyone's frustrations, be it a Tuatha or one of their servants.

Perhaps Mabog, Taskim and the others believed that any brutality heaped upon them would be forgotten immediately after it happened—making Kellesuf the perfect victims. Perhaps they'd assumed, even if these experiences were retained, the process of implanting my memories into these men would wipe these ugly incidents from their minds.

Just as likely it never occurred to the Tuatha to wonder if this was true or not, just as the physical welfare of the Kellesuf beyond the most basic of needs never concerned them. As I soon learned, nothing could've been further from the truth. Granted, it always took something, usually something minor, something commonplace, something otherwise innocuous to prod these hidden memories loose, to gel them into something that could then be put into context, for the man in question to fully grasp what these memories meant and what was done to him. But when that happened, they *did* remember, sometimes in exquisite detail.

Case in point: Kyrou was one of the worst offenders and had a habit of choosing his victims from the bigger Kellesuf; presumably he took a great deal of perverted pleasure in beating the hell out of man twice his size— with of course absolutely no risk to himself. Strapping Rufinius, not surprisingly, had been a frequent target, just as he had been with Rasaben, but for the exact opposite reason. Now it was payback time. I honestly don't know what triggered these memories in Rufinius; he never said, perhaps he was concerned if I knew what he was about, I'd warn Kyrou.

Like hell.

Of course Kyrou was blissfully unaware of his peril… at first.

According to barracks hearsay, Rufinius had crossed paths with Kyrou twice in the past week. Neither of the seemingly by-chance meetings had gone well for the top-knotted Cherusci. The first must've come as a hell of a shock to Kyrou, an utterly unexpected and brutal pummeling in the barracks latrine—Kyrou had stupidly gone there looking for a Kellesuf to beat up—the latrines had been one of his favorite hunting grounds, or so I was told… and got far more than he bargained for when he was stuffed, head first, into a shit hole, but not without first having the shit, literally, beaten out of him; the second… I have it on good authority that the moment Rufinius spotted Kyrou from across the courtyard and Kyrou, warned by the clatter of hobnails on cobblestones and spotting a murder-minded Rufinius charging towards him, the chase was on.

Did I mention that Rufinius had quickly mastered a really vicious one-two kick with his proper Roman hobnailed boots?

No wonder Kyrou was now keeping a very low profile—I'd have done the same if I thought I was going to get my butt, not to mention my face, back, arms, legs and yes, groin roundly kicked each time I dared to show my face—and kicked with hobnails to—*ahem*—boot, which, if you haven't experienced it yourself, really, really hurts. But I also had to accept that this self-imposed exile to parts of the Keep off limits to the soldiers and unknown to me only added grist to Kyrou's burning desire to do me serious harm, given a chance, as I continued to be the source of all his woes, or so I'm sure he'd convinced himself.

"Mustn't keep Mugwort waiting, Centurion," I said. Rufinius nodded and together we headed down the snow-covered steps and onto the snow-covered courtyard. There I stopped, briefly, to don my very impressive if utterly impractical helmet. If I was on my way to an audience with the legendary Mugwort, I simply had to look my best. Then we began trudging through an ankle-deep muddy mix of icy slush towards the stables.

While it felt good to be back in Roman armor, even if the armor was a Tuatha copy, I did dearly miss my Tuatha boots. Socks and Roman boots—even thick woolen socks and hobnailed boots are not in the same league as knee-high, fur-lined boots when it comes to keeping the snow and slush at bay.

By the time we'd reached the stables the cold had seeped up my shins, up my thighs and was well on its way past my hips and I was reduced to rubbing my upper arms against the bitter chill, a chill that made my thigh and shoulder throb, painfully.

Rufinius, unfazed by the freezing cold, offered to enter first, but where horses were stabled there was dry straw—and stables, while decidedly smelly, were always warm—or at least they were marginally warmer than the outside. I had no desire to stand around in that bone chilling outside while Rufinius was inside, poking about in the warm dark with his sword, hoping to locate the whereabouts of Kyrou by a loud, startled squeak.

If there was poking to be done, especially if the poke-e was Kyrou, I wanted *in*. Plus, it meant getting out of the damned snow. So, Rufinius opened the heavy wooden door and slipped through and I followed and closed the door behind us—and instantly regretted my decision not to let Rufinius go first as the moment I closed the door we were plunged into total darkness.

Rufinius seemed unconcerned—at least he was breathing normally, which to me meant he wasn't concerned. So, I followed his lead and soon my eyes adjusted from the snow-glare outside to the torch lit inside of the stables.

Our arrival hadn't gone unnoticed by one of the grooms, an elderly man with a hunched back and a noticeable limp. He approached, asking what he could do for us. As it turned out, this man was on excellent terms with Rufinius and happily, dare I say gleefully informed us that he hadn't seen Kyrou for well over a day, that he'd heard from one of the cooks that Kyrou was ill and had taken to his bed—but quickly added with a sidelong wink to Rufinius that it was far more likely Kyrou was nursing the results of his latest run-in with 'someone'—news that brought a sly grin to Rufinius' lips.

"Where's Lady Ainiaan?" I asked.

The groom pointed to the far end of the massive stable. "With her pony, sire. If you'll follow me?"

"No need, Tev, I know the way," Rufinius said.

The groom, Tev, after patting Rufinius' broad shoulder and nodding to me, shuffled back the way he'd come, into the warm and horse poop-scented dimness.

"Friend of yours?" I glanced back to where I'd last seen the aged groom.

Rufinius shrugged, replied straight-faced, "More a fellow admirer of men with silly hairdos."

I bit my lip. Enough said.

"Legate? This way," he motioned, and I dutifully followed.

A few minutes later, after repeatedly tripping over clumps of straw—at least I hope they were clumps of straw—I found myself standing in yet another, smaller doorway. This one opened to a spacious and torch-lit box stall.

Ainiaan was inside; her back was to us and she was speaking softly to the presumed object of our quest, the legendary steed Mugwort—who was even shorter and fatter than I remembered. Close-up he looked less like a large dog and more like an overturned rain barrel on peg legs—in fact if he hadn't tossed his shaggy head and snorted, I would have sworn he *was* an overturned rain barrel on peg legs.

As if reading my less than complimentary thoughts he rolled his eyes towards us and stamped his tiny hoof and Ainiaan, sensing they were no longer alone, turned—and started in genuine surprise. Then she grinned. *"Arri!"*

I grinned in reply then motioned to her. "Permission to enter?"

"Please!" She eagerly beckoned to me, to Rufinius then turning to the pony, said, "Mugwort, this is Arri—see?"

Mugwort eyed me; he did not look any more impressed with me than I was with him.

"And you didn't believe me when I told you he'd come as soon as he could," Ainiaan added, either oblivious to his less than positive reaction or chalking it up to wounded feelings.

I cautiously approached Mugwort, not sure if I should kneel, bow, salute… or pet the astonishingly stout creature. I think I've mentioned that horses and I have never gotten along. Somewhere along the line I'd picked up the useless morsel of information that ponies are even more prone to biting and kicking than their taller, more svelte kin, possibly a result of bearing a grudge for being shorted in the leg and looks department.

Having been bitten and kicked by full-sized horses and not finding I enjoyed the experiences one bit, I'd made a point to avoid any horse if I could help it. Up to this moment I'd managed to stay well away from any horse that was substantially shorter than me—and Mugwort, I must mention, barely came up to my waist.

Ainiaan made my decision for me: she held out the brush she'd been using on the rotund beast. "I want you two to be best friends, so here, he loves to be groomed."

I looked sidelong at Rufinius as I reluctantly accepted the brush. Here I was, a damned legate, and in a legate's damned parade finery no less... and now I was stooping—literally—to groom a damned pony? I reached out, tentatively—all right, terrified in fact—and then at Ainiaan's guidance, I ran the brush down the length of his very broad and low-slung back, from withers to croup.

Mugwort pointedly ignored me, not to mention my display of deference, preferring instead to snatch the handful of grass Rufinius offered him—I felt Rufinius' blatant attempt at usurping this moment of budding friendship to be underhanded and rude and favored him with a glance that said so.

He whispered in my ear, "I was hoping to distract him—he was looking to nip your ass."

I looked down at the beast and damned if he didn't look like he was thinking about nipping me; I wisely backed up a step and handed the brush back to Ainiaan.

She gave me a look, clearly disappointed in what she perceived as a half-hearted effort on my part—never mind that Mugwort wasn't even trying, unless you mean trying to bite my butt—then she slipped around us and walked over to the doorway. She peered one way, then the other.

Satisfied we were alone, she withdrew back into the stall, closing and locking the door behind her. When she turned back to me the look in her eye left little doubt that this had all been a pretense to get me away from prying ears.

"So you didn't forget your promise."

"To Boian? No, m'lady."

"Did you listen to Lord Taskim and the others?" Suddenly her voice, her expression was no longer that of a young girl—and I had to wonder what she truly was. She was a Tuatha after all, and female, which meant—

"I'm not a shape-changer," she said, reacting to my unguarded reaction. "I mean at least not yet—Lady Turan says maybe in a few years if I work really hard at it, so this is what I really look like."

"A little girl."

"A young *Tuatha,*" she corrected.

And it was true, on so many levels. I dipped my helmeted head in acknowledgement. "Aye, m'lady."

She smiled, and the freckle-faced and pug-nosed Ainiaan I knew was back. "Let's make ourselves comfortable, shall we?" She gestured to the straw-covered floor.

It was clean straw, believe me I looked first. So I sat then removed my helmet.

Rufinius, taking on Felix's role of always being the gentleman, assisted Ainiaan to a seated position and then he sat, but with far more care—he was wearing band-armor after all, and band-armor, while far more flashy than ring-mail, has one huge drawback: it can grab you when and where you least expect it.

Once he'd gotten himself comfortable and cross-legged, and like me, removed his helmet and placed it in his lap, I met Ainiaan's gaze. "I've listened to Boian, I've listened to Taskim and I've read the accounts, the treaty—and I must be totally honest with you, m'lady, I'm still not entirely convinced."

"Of the threat the Faoimhuir pose or that we're telling you the truth."

"Both."

"Fair enough." She picked up a handful of straw and offered it to Mugwort.

He ambled over to her and lipped it from her hand, neat and gentle as you please—no biting or snatching. Then with a loud *whumph* of air he abruptly dropped down beside her and like a dog, tucked his stubby legs under him and placed his shaggy head in her lap. "The Kellesuf..." she began as she lifted her gaze back to me.

"What about them?"

"It didn't start as you think it did."

"You mean snatching them from all over for the sole purpose of turning them into mindless soldiers?" I replied more harshly than I'd intended. This was Ainiaan after all. And Rufinius was present—for an instant and in my anger, I'd totally forgotten about him.

I flicked him a sidelong glance. He stared back at me, all expression having left his face. And I'd come to know this man well enough in the past week to know that while his face might appear utterly expressionless, an eerie echo of his former Kellesuf expression, just behind those strange black eyes of his, his mind was churning and I suddenly regretted bringing him along and into Ainiaan's confidence. I should've told him to remain outside the stall, to guard against eavesdroppers. And being former Kellesuf, he would've put his full concentration into that, never once eavesdropping himself.

It was too late now—asking, even ordering him to leave now would only make the matter worse. Besides, he'd been present for everything else, heard everything else; it was only fair he be present—

"Boian told you about her village…"

I tore my eyes off Rufinius and fixed them on Ainiaan. "Yes."

"She told you that Jaro and Perus had had similar experiences."

"And Harne."

She nodded as she scratched Mugwort between his ears. "We tried stopping the Faoimhuir directly—first we tried negotiating with them, but when we found they'd repeatedly broken their word, Lord Vela argued that the only way to stop them was by force. The other lords knew what that meant, knew in doing so we risked breaking the treaty, but Lord Vela said it was the Faoimhuir who'd violated it, not once but repeatedly, badly bending if not breaking it by vastly increasing their… *their harvest* beyond the agreed upon limit." Ainiaan briefly shifted her gaze to Rufinius, as did I only to find him now staring fixedly at his helmet he now clutched in his hands, as if that absorbed his singular interest.

Ainiaan, despite clearly being distressed by his distress, pressed on: "Lord Rasaben argued that we didn't have enough freemen under arms to force them to do anything—each Keep had only a token force; there had never been a need for more."

"Which is when the Sidhe Lords hatched this idea of snatching men, turning them into Kellesuf—"

"*No!*" Ainiaan interrupted sharply; Rufinius looked up at that and Mugwort rolled his eyes towards me as if giving me fair warning to behave… or else. "You don't understand—I'm trying to explain, so will you please just *listen?*"

I clamped my mouth shut but I also glared briefly at Mugwort. I was damned if I was going to let a damned pony tell me to shut the hell up and think he got away with it.

"We'd done it before—wipe people's minds I mean," she said softly as she began toying with the pony's bristly mane. He immediately settled and with a soft *whuff* of breath, closed his eyes. "Lord Azraad, Lord Vela's physician, was the first to succeed in doing it, and my father perfected the method."

"Remind me to thank them," Rufinius grumbled, fingering the grip of his gladius.

Ainiaan glared at him and like me, he clamped his mouth shut, but he didn't release his hold on his sheathed sword.

"Are you two going to listen, or make snide remarks?"

When I hesitated, she started to get up, startling Mugwort in scrambling to his tiny hooves. "Please, m'lady, I give you my word, we will listen." I shot Rufinius a look. Granted, he had a far greater stake in the matter of wiping men's minds, but to my relief, he replied to my pointed stare with a curt nod and promptly let go of the sword's grip.

"My apologies, m'lady," he said tightly. "I meant no insult to your father. I beg you, continue."

She took a deep breath and angrily wiped the bits of straw from her skirts, giving all of us a moment to calm down, then she resumed her seat while Mugwort remained standing, unwilling to be as forgiving as Ainiaan. "Lord Azraad didn't develop the technique to be cruel, Rufi…"

I couldn't help but look covertly at the man seated beside me. *Rufi?* This truly fearsome man had a diminutive? One only Ainiaan dared to use, I'd hazard to say, and hopefully only within his earshot. Gods help us all if Aetius ever got wind of it.

"…quite the contrary and neither did my father. They felt it was the most humane response to some of those we came across who had somehow managed to escape the Faoimhuir—most were terribly traumatized, like Boian, but with time and proper care, recovered. But there were some who had been left insane by the experience, utterly unable to function and deemed incurable; they would have starved to death or been murdered by frightened passersby had we not interceded. Many were killed before we could rescue them—most of the men were, certainly.

"The women and girls, the very youngest boys…" she bit her lip and looked away for a moment, then added tightly, "…were horribly brutalized by those they had the misfortune of coming across in their mindless wanderings and then left for dead. Most were, in fact, dead when we found them, but it was obvious how and why they'd died."

I couldn't help but shift uneasily.

"You think we Tuatha are so terribly cruel? So are your people, Arri. Given the right circumstances, each one of us can commit the most heinous of crimes, especially on those least able to defend themselves."

I nodded, acknowledging my own experience and my own culpability in that regard—not that I needed to. Ainiaan, being a Tuatha, could read my thoughts after all.

"Lord Azraad truly believed if he could free these poor souls of these terrible memories and these memories *only*, they would recover. A handful did and went on to live a semblance of their former lives, albeit in a very protected environment—it was those few successes early on that kept Lord Azraad at his work and encouraged my father to build on it, but it was undeniably brutal, trying to sever certain memories from the rest, and most who underwent the procedure, I'm sad to say, died as a result, more often than not during the procedure itself—but to have left them as they were, well, one could argue that death, even death by such a means, was preferable."

I couldn't help but shudder. I vividly remembered the utter and prolonged agony I'd experienced when I'd undergone Mabog's 'perfected' technique; I didn't want to think about what these people had been forced to endure through trial and error—

"As Tuatha, we believed this was part and parcel of our duty of protecting humanity, and that was to protect and care for those who had suffered so terribly at the hands of the Faoimhuir and provide for them for as long as they lived. To that end," Ainiaan continued, "each household accepted responsibility for his or her share of those treated by Lord Azraad and my father—a few, here and there, a handful at most as they were capable of only the simplest of tasks, often requiring constant supervision. But as we soon learned, this was not a rare event—and with each subsequent illegal harvest, more and more of those left behind were left terribly incapacitated."

"Why? May I ask that?" I said.

"Why were those left behind left insane?"

I nodded; I'd had the misfortune of stumbling across with a few truly insane people during my travels. I'd grown up believing these individuals were inhabited by demons, or who had somehow garnered the ire of a god or goddess and had paid dearly for it—and if what Ainiaan said was true, then maybe the latter wasn't that far from the mark. Maybe this explained all of them. That said, they were no better than wild beasts, cowering and rambling nonsensically, prone to terrible fits, or worse—far, *far* worse. Emperor Caligula was rumored to have been insane—at least that was the rationale the Praetorian Guard used for removing him from office by the most expeditious of means. Perhaps the emperor himself had come face to face with the Faoimhuir.

This could also explain some of the razed villages we Romans had come across and had reasonably had chalked up to the locals burning everything before our advance, thus denying us any foodstuffs—it was a common tactic. Perhaps I *had* crossed paths with the Faoimhuir, not to mention the Tuatha, before, perhaps I'd had many close encounters and had been blissfully unaware of it.

Just the thought gave me a fresh case of the shivers.

Ainiaan, clearly reading my thoughts, my suddenly perturbed expression, broke into those thoughts with the answer to my question: "Lord Azraad and my father speculated it was as a direct result of what these individuals had witnessed during the Faoimhuirian raids. Lord Vela championed the view that the Faoimhuir could only take only so many at one time—so whoever they left behind, they left incapacitated, knowing we would be obligated to help, thus stretching our resources to the breaking point—more evidence as to just how truly brutal, how unimaginably cruel and calculating the Faoimhuirians are.

"Or maybe they assumed that we, rather than waste our resources, would just sell them to the Si'aafu—something we knew the Faoimhuir were doing with many they took and thus we'd be as guilty as they and therefore reluctant to press the issue with the Jaglavak."

She paused, gave me a moment—time enough for me to realize there was more to selling people to these *See-ah-foo*, something she wasn't going to expound on, possibly for Rufinius' sake—or mine—then she continued, "Most, as I've already mentioned, did not recover from having selected memories removed, many died as a direct result as it was a hugely complicated and lengthy process, and Lord Pateke argued that the best solution, the least risky and yes, most humane solution was to completely wipe their minds, which was a far quicker process—"

"And Kellesuf were born," I ended for her.

"Yes, but not right away, Arri—not as soldiers I mean. There weren't enough for one thing—"

"Meaning you had to find other sources because what the Faoimhuir left behind weren't enough." I couldn't help but keep the taint of disgust out of my voice, and Ainiaan reacted to it, defensively.

"Most were women, girls and young boys—hardly suitable for soldiers."

"And these *suitable* sources were...?"

Her eyes flicked to Rufinius, then back to me. "Slave markets, mostly."

"So, when *was* it decided to turn these slaves into Kellesuf and from there into soldiers?"

She fixed her eyes on me and took a deep, ragged breath. "When the Lords decided to break the treaty—"

"Using Kellesuf to attack the Faoimhuir."

She hesitated, then nodded and whispered, *"Yes."*

As I stared at her I suddenly recalled a fragment of the conversation—the argument—between Rasaben and Turan while I was in Mabog's surgery, still extremely groggy and presumably incapable of eavesdropping: Turan's peculiar remark, *'The purpose wasn't to win, as you well know,'* and Rasaben's angry rejoinder, *'We got what we wanted.'*

At the time the remarks made no sense to me; in fact most of the heated, albeit whispered quarrel had made no sense. *But now...*

My jaw dropped as the full import hit me. "Because the intention was never to win," I said slowly, "in fact the whole point was to lose and you didn't want to lose any precious Tuatha—but mindless Kellesuf? Now *that* was perfectly acceptable—you'd saved them, from insanity or from a life as a slave, and now it was your right to squander them."

She looked away, replied with a slight twitch of her shoulders, and a soft, "I suppose so."

"But the question remains, *why?* Why *want* to lose?"

"You read the terms of the treaty."

"And it didn't distinguish who won, who lost, only who broke the treaty by force of arms—which is exactly what the Tuatha did."

"And Lord Taskim suggested that the best way to break the treaty was to confront the Faoimhuir when they were in the act of raiding a town, so that even the Jaglavak couldn't argue—"

"And once broken," I interrupted, not wanting to be distracted by whoever or whatever the hell these oft-mentioned *Jag-la-vaks* were, "the treaty states that the *offended,* meaning the Faoimhuir, gets to choose where and when, while the *offender,* meaning the Tuatha, get to pick how it's to be fought—"

"No, that's not what it said, not... *exactly.*"

I arched an annoyed brow. I was sure that's what the treaty said. "What do you mean, not *exactly?*"

"The treaty only gives the right to pick *how* it's to be fought if the *offender,* as you refer to the Tuatha, *lose* the original fight. If whoever breaks the treaty by force of arms goes on to defeat the side that didn't initiate hostilities, then the *offended,* as you refer to the Faoimhuir, get to decide *everything.*"

Both brows shot up then I squinted at her. "You've *got* to be joking." I was used to Roman political guile that bordered on labyrinthine, where murdering your siblings, parents or children before they got a hankering to murder you was considered a laudable career move, where political one-upmanship was played for keeps and where powerful alliances were as ephemeral as raindrops. Up until to this moment, I thought the emperors and their kin had the market cornered on such deviousness—which begged the question, were the Roman emperors in fact closely related to the Tuatha? Or the Faoimhuir? Backstabbing brethren perhaps? It boggled the mind—

"I wish I was—would you like me to get the treaty so you can reread it?"

I swallowed the bile that had soured my mouth and puckered my lips and replied quietly, "So that's why you went into this confrontation with the intention of losing—so you could pick how the deciding battle would be fought. Meaning your precious Lords knowingly led Kellesuf to their deaths; they knew Kellesuf would never question what they were being told to do, even if that meant walking into an obvious deathtrap—they would follow blindly."

"Lord Vela died with them," Ainiaan said defensively.

"But purely by accident I'm sure, as I cannot imagine any Tuatha Lord doing anything heroic, least of all fighting to the death alongside his Kellesuf soldiers. He must've been struck a deathblow in the back as he fled the field."

"Don't judge every leader by the actions of Cerialis," she fired back.

I opened my mouth, thought better of it and biting my lip, settled for scowling furiously at her—it was a low blow after all. Very, *very* low—smack-dab to the testicles to be exact, made all the worse by who'd said it. It was something Turan would say, or Rasaben—a calculatingly brutal comeback. But Ainiaan? I hadn't thought her capable. Now I knew better.

She stared back at me, long and hard before replying stiffly, "As I started to say earlier, we decided the best way to break the treaty was to confront the Faoimhuir while they were raiding a village. We had spies—we knew what village and when and we set up an ambush..."

I couldn't help but snort.

"Yes, Arri, the plan was to lose Kellesuf, I admit that. It had to look real—a few lives in trade for thousands, perhaps Earth itself; the Faoimhuir needed to believe this was a serious but spur of the moment, and therefore poorly thought-out attack by us silly, technology-averse and 'noble-minded Tuatha'—"

That garnered another, far more derisive snort.

Snakestone and Sword

"—coming to the defense of a defenseless village, a blunt if clumsy warning to stop their unlawful harvesting—but serious enough they'd claim we'd broken the treaty.

"It was Lord Vela's idea to make it look as if we'd happened across the raid by accident while on our way to one of our own 'legal' harvestings—it would explain the troops, enough to keep a Sidhe Lord safe while abroad, but too few to pose a truly serious threat. That way if things didn't work out as we'd planned, if the Faoimhuir didn't protest, didn't claim we'd broken the treaty, which was a risk as they had to know that by lodging a protest, their own recent and very egregious behavior would come under scrutiny, Lord Vela would—"

"Would take the blame."

"Yes."

"How *very* noble of him."

Ainiaan's eyes flashed.

"So what happened," I replied coldly.

"The Faoimhuir had their own spies. They knew what we were about… and they, along with their Si'aafu allies, decided to take it one step further, up the ante so to speak."

I could help but arch a quizzical brow. *Up the what…?*

"The Faoimhuir decided that they were going to use this 'ambush' as an pretext to launch an all-out attack on the Tuatha, using their advanced weaponry—the fire birds Lord Rasaben told you about, as well as other weapons that are beyond your comprehension—in truth beyond mine. Their intention was to destroy us, once and for all, using the excuse that we'd started it, then divvy up Earth between themselves and the Si'aafu. You see, they'd been convinced by the Si'aafu that this alliance of theirs was strong enough that together they could even take on the Jaglavak—take on anyone who dared to question their actions."

She paused, took a deep, ragged breath then met my gaze. "Since the ambush had been Lord Vela's idea, he insisted that he be the one to challenge the Faoimhuir. Lord Rasaben was accompanying him on his—"

"Shopping trip abroad?" I offered helpfully.

She hesitated only a moment before continuing: "Lord Vela ordered Lord Rasaben to take command of the majority of the troops, a hundred or so—to stand back and to enter the fray only if the Faoimhuir on the ground tried to use the villagers as hostages, or escape with them—while Lord Vela took the remaining fifty with him to confront them.

"The Faoimhuir waited until he and his troops had engaged some of their men—they too wanted to make sure there was no question who'd started it, but then..." She suddenly looked away and swallowed, hard.

I risked a sidelong glance at Rufinius to see him watching her intently, his expression no longer that of an impassive Kellesuf, but rather a man confronting some inner horror—a sudden and terrible memory—then overhearing a sniff, I looked back at Ainiaan to see her angrily wipe her cheeks.

"Realizing the whole plan had gone terribly wrong," she said, "Lord Rasaben's first thought was to ride to the aid of Lord Vela, but by then it was too late, Lord Vela had been dragged from his horse—not by Faoimhuirian soldiers but by Faoimhuir *themselves*. Lord Rasaben never saw him after that... and Lord Vela's Kellesuf, leaderless, were now at the mercy of the Faoimhuir—he said the Faoimhuir made a hideous game out of killing them, like a cat with a frozen with fear mouse, playing with these soldiers, wounding them terribly but not killing them, not right away, and laughing as they did it."

She hugged herself tightly. "The Faoimhuir, emboldened and realizing our soldiers couldn't fight without direction, then turned on Lord Rasaben and his troops, who, up to that point, had not engaged, and in doing so made it clear their intention wasn't to stop until they'd butchered every last Tuatha.

"Lord Rasaben, rather than attacking, rather than letting his men suffer the same fate as Lord Vela's, ordered them to retreat and in quitting the field, he managed to save all but a handful but ever since he's had to live with the whispers that his were the actions of a coward..."

Which begged the question: did Cerialis face similar condemnations upon his return to Lindum—or was he somehow able to place the blame squarely on others, like his dead centurions, and go on to an illustrious career untainted by that accursed bog that had swallowed the lives of so many of his men? I doubted I would ever learn for certain, but if I was a betting man, I'd bet on the latter.

"Lord Tistriya maintains if Lord Rasaben had gone to his father's defense, if he'd thrown his troops at the Faoimhuir, Lord Vela might still be alive. He never wastes an opportunity to remind everyone of that, despite strong evidence to the contrary, that nothing, not even a full army could have saved Lord Vela—he says Lord Rasaben loved his Kellesuf more than he loves his fellow Tuatha—and I don't mean that in a purely figurative sense, *if* you follow me."

My lips formed a silent 'O'.

"Lord Rasaben is a cruel man, Arri, make no mistake about it, but he has cause—and sadly this cruelty, more often than not and with few other outlets, was heaped on Kellesuf. Until they were given your memories, they remained a constant reminder of his disgrace, a silent, always obedient... and worst of all, totally *forgiving* reminder of all that was done to them—and to him. He did what he thought was right—in fact he *did* what *was* right: he saved those Kellesuf he could..." she again looked at Rufinius. "Including *you*, Rufi." She leaned forward and wrapped her small hand around his thick, muscular fingers. "You were badly wounded—he risked his life to save you."

Rufinius blinked and as he stared down at her hand, tears rolled down his cheeks.

Then he made up for the slip of conscience by picking you as his 'sparring partner' so he could beat the hell out of you at every opportunity, I added to myself. Yes, Ainiaan could hear me—and clearly had, by her quickly concealed expression, but Rufinius could not, and at this moment it was his feelings, and what he'd endured that were of paramount importance to me. *Damn you, Rasaben—damn you all to hell!*

"Worse," she said in a carefully controlled voice, "Lord Rasaben had, from the start, repeatedly warned the Assemblage that Kellesuf would not make good soldiers—that they could not fight without direction, to which Lord Tistriya jokingly suggested that only meant that their Tuatha masters would have to yell orders to them from the safety of some distance—a joke even his father, Lord Vela, found offensive; Lord Rasaben begged them to wait, begged them to give him the funds along with the time to raise and train an army, not of Kellesuf, but of freemen.

"Lord Vela brushed his protests aside in his eagerness to engage the Faoimhuir—to finally teach them a lesson, saying his plan was foolproof and would be far less costly, the deaths of a few Kellesuf, a hundred or so, at most..."

I clenched my teeth.

"...and he paid dearly for his blind arrogance." She squeezed Rufinius' hand then let go. "But the price Lord Rasaben has paid has been even higher. He once told my father than if he was given the chance, he would choose this time to ride to Lord Vela's aid, taking his Kellesuf with him and thus die a hero just like Lord Vela—a selfish, arrogant hero.

"Lord Vela's death caused a terrible rift within the Assemblage as various Lords took sides and everyone was pointing fingers..." she shook her head, "...it came close to finishing what the Faoimhuir had started, but fortunately Lady Urme and Lord Taskim finally managed to get both sides to see reason by reminding everyone who the real enemy was—and that there was still the matter of the treaty—the Jaglavak had meanwhile determined we had in fact broken it—never mind the provocation—and that the Faoimhuir were therefore, as you say, the *offended* party."

"Which means you got exactly what you wanted."

She replied to that with a slight tilt of her head. "The Faoimhuir, reasonably wanting to take advantage of the disarray within the Assemblage, demanded that the battle be fought right then and there. But the Jaglavak said no—and gave both sides time to prepare. Lord Tistriya said he was willing to let bygones be bygones and to help with the preparations, but only *if* he was compensated for his terrible personal loss, and his price for losing his father? Lord Rasaben's ancestral lands, which also meant Lord Rasaben's place at the Table of the Assemblage, a position he'd only recently inherited from his father—and to be kind, Rasaben is not the skillful diplomat his father was—"

"I find that hard to believe," I grumbled.

"—which meant he had few allies," she added, ignoring my testy remark. "Lord Tistriya's demand was utterly outrageous and purely vindictive—but the Assemblage, fearing further internal strife would in fact tear the Assemblage apart and thus guarantee a victory for the Faoimhuir—which would mean losing Earth—agreed."

I wanted to feel sorry for Rasaben as he'd clearly gotten the proverbial shit end of the stick, truly I did, but Felix's horribly battered body kept coming to mind each time I thought that maybe I needed to revisit my opinion of this man. "So how'd Rasaben end up here?"

"As part of the settlement, Lord Taskim offered him and Lady Turan and their servants, along with their complement of Kellesuf sanctuary here, and here Lord Rasaben and Lady Turan remain, guests in perpetuity, Sidhe Lords who are landless and therefore largely powerless. To that end Lord Rasaben has tried repeatedly to marry off Lady Turan to one of the Lords' favorite chieftains, hoping in doing so he might be able to shift the balance within the Assemblage to one more sympathetic to his plight and thus regain his lands—"

"But then a lowly piece of Roman gutter filth got her pregnant…"

"Yes, which kinda put a crimp in his plans."

I took a deep, ragged breath, exhaled forcefully then turned to Rufinius. "And explains why he loathed me on sight." Of course there were other reasons, too, plenty of them.

Rufinius didn't appear to have heard me, or realized the remark was aimed at him; by his distracted expression he was still very disturbed by what he'd heard and trying to get his head around the idea that Rasaben had saved him, not once but twice—only to single him out for almost daily abuse. I lightly grasped his elbow; he flinched violently and looked at me.

I smiled, a worried, prodding smile. He replied with a slight twitch of his shoulders, just as the original Rufinius would have done, laconic as always, keeping his true feelings to himself.

Mugwort snorted and pawed the ground, as if reminding us that he, like Rufinius, had been temporarily forgotten.

"Yes, of course," Ainiaan murmured and patted him on the neck. "There still remained the matter of the battle. As I said, each Keep had only a token force of freemen-at-arms, and there wasn't time or in truth the funds to recruit and train more—"

"So naturally the Lords turned to Kellesuf," I interrupted, finding it impossible, without Felix's sharp elbow, to keep my promise to listen, furious at how much this discussion had disturbed Rufinius yet blindly unaware that I was making it worse, "which they happened to have in abundance, a veritable army... but with one *teensy* problem: Kellesuf make terrible soldiers... but you Tuatha are nothing if pragmatic, not to mention you're a real thrifty bunch, and here you'd spent all this money buying up these men, not to mention all the valuable Tuatha time you'd spent washing their minds clean, *so hey!*" I slapped my thighs for emphasis, *"let'em earn their keep and let's do something with 'em!"*

Ainiaan stared impassively at me. "That's basically what happened, yes. And that's when Lady Turan asked if was possible to instill someone *else's* memory into Kellesuf. Their original memories were gone for good, but could new memories be implanted, she asked? That idea intrigued the Assemblage—it intrigued my father and Lord Azraad as it had never been tried. Rasaben immediately volunteered to be the 'donor', but the Assemblage refused. Everyone knew or suspected it would be a dangerous procedure for all involved, and besides, it was deemed unseemly for a Tuatha to donate his memories to—"

"To mere men," I finished for her, mindful of Rufinius.

"Yes," she replied simply. "So Turan came up with another idea—"

"To kidnap a real soldier..."

"Not just any soldier but a Roman soldier as the Assemblage, now that this plan had been adopted—to implant someone's memories—had carefully studied every martial culture throughout human history and after prolonged debate, settled on Rome's legions as their choice, based in part on where the battle is to be fought and in part on the fact that your legions are—"

"At this moment in time," I interrupted coldly, "currently unrivaled."

"Exactly."

"Which is when I came into the story."

"It's far more complicated than that—Lady Turan spent quite some time observing, wanting to make sure she picked the best candidate, but yes, she eventually she settled on you." She reached over and patted me on the knee, as if this was a good thing, as if I should be proud.

"I'm not honored by this choice, Lady Ainiaan, far from it…"

She immediately and wisely withdrew her hand.

"…I worked tirelessly for *these* honors," I motioned to my replicate chest harness, to my replicate phalerae, "while serving *my* empire as a *free man*. Understand that. Given a choice, I would have nothing to do with you Tuatha or your plans. But like Rufinius here, and the other Kellesuf, I *wasn't* given a choice."

"Yes, of course, I'm sorry," she murmured.

I blew out my cheeks, squeezed my eyes shut and shook my head.

"There," Ainiaan continued and I reopened my eyes to see Mugwort nuzzling her hand, looking for treats. "You know the *whole* ugly truth, and now it's your turn to decide, Arri. Help us defeat the Faoimhuir or don't. It's up to you." She rose, walked over to the stall door and opened it—a less than subtle signal that the impromptu meeting was over.

I needed Rufinius' help to get back to my feet then I brushed myself off as best I could. Satisfied I'd knocked off most of the straw, I followed Rufinius over to the doorway but just short of stepping out of the stall, I hesitated.

"Yes?" she asked.

I turned back to her. "Why you, m'lady?"

She cocked her head to one side, looking genuinely perplexed. "Why me what?"

"Why were you the one picked to tell me 'the whole ugly truth'? And don't say you weren't picked."

She stepped close and gently plucked a piece of straw from my hair, another from my chest harness, then brushing my ring-mail with her small fingers and smiling up at me, replied, "Would you have willingly listened to Lady Turan?"

I started to say yes, but she pressed a finger to my lips.

"You refused her, Arri, each time she asked to see you—*true?*"

I hesitated then nodded, reluctantly.

"She wanted to tell you, desperately, but she knew your hurt, your sense of betrayal was so deep, even if she was given the chance to tell you, you wouldn't have listened and even if you *had* listened, you wouldn't have believed her."

"But I'm supposed to believe you."

"You're supposed to do the right thing, *silly*—"

Suddenly the little girl was back again, the one by the fire, the one who desperately wanted me to pet her pet fox... and meet Mugwort. I hadn't realized that up until that moment I'd been dealing with someone who was anything but childlike.

"—what that is though is entirely up to you."

I glanced over my shoulder to see Rufinius waiting for me, his now helmeted face in shadow and torchlight playing off his band-armor, flashing and glimmering as he breathed.

I turned back to her and kissed her lightly on the forehead. "Thank you, Lady Ainiaan." I then stepped back and saluted the pony in time-honored Roman-style, right fist to chest. "Sir Mugwort."

Ainiaan giggled; Mugwort snorted and shook his shaggy head.

I donned my helmet, tied the cheek pieces and once the helmet was secure, I dipped my head to both then pivoted smartly on my heel. I walked out of the stall and Rufinius fell in beside me but as we reached the main stable doors, an inner voice urged me glance over my shoulder and as I did so, I swear I caught a glimpse of Turan, or at least a woman who looked remarkably her, her back to me, talking to Ainiaan, both of them standing haloed in the doorway of the stall.

I stopped in my tracks but before I could turn around for a better look, Ainiaan saw me and hastily shut the stall door.

"Something wrong, sir?"

I jerked my eyes to Rufinius. "I thought I saw Turan..."

He glanced around. "Where?"

"In the stall."

"Impossible, sir. There was barely room for the three of us and Mugwort."

"Yeah," I replied slowly. "That's what I thought."

"The torchlight's playing tricks on you, Legate." With that, he threw open the main door, filling the stable with eye-dazzling wintry sunlight. "Maybe it was one of the milkmaids... or perhaps a cook who'd come to collect eggs and who stopped to speak with Lady Ainiaan." With that he stepped outside then turned back to me. "Coming?"

I eyed the now shuttered stall, then with a shrug and a shiver, strode into the sun and snow-filled courtyard. Ainiaan had given me plenty to think about... more than enough to make my decision. And as I pondered what she'd said, what Taskim and Boian said, Rufinius walked beside me in silence, his sharp eyes darting here and there, looking for trouble—giving me free rein to focus on the matter at hand, rather than possible threats to my person.

It all boiled down to trust, I realized, as most things in life did, *not* facts. Granted, the Tuatha had even me scant reason to trust them—they'd given me every reason not to. Still, everything I'd been told—and better, things I'd overheard when no one realized I was capable of eavesdropping—had fallen into place, not *too* neatly mind you, or I'd have reasonably suspected it was all a carefully arranged ruse. No. They'd fallen quite messily into place, as life had a tendency to do, and in the process painted a very unflattering portrait of my hosts—again, more evidence that what'd I'd been told was the unvarnished truth, or as close to it as the Tuatha could come.

What Taskim had said, what Boian and Ainiaan and yes, even Rasaben had said made sense, a whole lot of *very* ugly sense.

I'd spent my entire military career fighting for emperors I'd never seen, and had circumstances permitted me to continue down that path, I would likely never see, with an even greater likelihood that I'd die carrying out one of their decrees. Yet I never once questioned their legitimacy or the legitimacy of their intentions, much less if they really existed; I'd advanced their political agendas by brute force based on nothing more than orders from my commanding officers, in the process risking my life and those of my men, and sometimes on a minute-by-minute basis.

The vast majority of the time I had no idea what the end game was— what was in it for me, personally, aside from coming out alive at the other end and perhaps living to enjoy my hard-earned pension—as a soldier and later as a centurion, it wasn't my place to question anything beyond where exactly to place a camp latrine, and did that ditch *really* need to be dug that deep and wide, or why hardtack was on the menu three days in a row, or which barbarians was I supposed to slaughter on any particular day. My job was simple and straightforward: do as I was told, which meant shove aside or kill anyone who dared to stand in Rome's way and leave the thinking to my betters. Why? Because I *trusted* them, *trusted* they knew what the hell they were doing and because of that, I *trusted* it was the right thing to do.

Now I found myself in the very curious position of being been given a whole hell of a lot to think about—by my betters no less; of being brought into the fold, of being told not just what they expected of me, but *why*. Granted, it would have been nice had they done this *before* rather than *after* ripping my memories from my mind, but better late than never, I suppose.

Half way to the barracks I again stopped in my tracks.

Rufinius lurched to a halt and glanced around, one hand on his gladius, the other on his dagger, wondering what threat I'd seen that he hadn't. Seeing nothing amiss, he looked at me, thick black eyebrows raised.

"Get word to Lord Taskim…"

He stared at me, even more baffled.

"If I'm going to fight this battle for him and win, I need every last damned Kellesuf he can find—and I need them *yesterday.*"

He continued to stare at me as if not really believing what he'd just heard.

"What the hell are you waiting for? *Go!*" I gave him a rough shove and he staggered sideways then with one last bewildered look at me, took off, running across the courtyard and up the steps to the Keep.

— XIX —

The Lords of the Assemblage did as I demanded and quickly, without question or complaint—with the exception of Lord Tistriya who held out until the last moment, more another thumb in the eye to Rasaben than over concerns about me and my motives. Every day brought more Kellesuf to Taskim's Keep—until their numbers reached the promised fifteen hundred which conveniently, as it turned out, was in fact the full complement of men who were Kellesuf. While it perfectly matched the promised strength of each opposing army, it presented immediate logistical problems as the barracks, designed to hold one hundred men and required to house twice that many with the addition of Rasaben and Turan's displaced Kellesuf was unable to house them all.

So, we moved outdoors, outside the Keep in fact... and into tents, good, solid legionary-style goatskin tents to be precise. Yes, it was still winter, and yes, it was cold—fucking cold in fact—but what had started out as a singular massing of Kellesuf—quiet, docile Kellesuf who would sleep where ever they were told to sleep, even if that meant sleeping in a terribly crowded barracks or on bare, muddy or snow-covered ground—quickly took on the flavor of a legionary camp with all its noise and occasional disorder as each arrival underwent Mabog's 'treatment' and then stumbling and staggering, still reeling from the ordeal, was released into my care and the care of my centurions.

It was all too much for the inhabitants of the Keep, who now wisely remained within its stone and wooden walls, leaving the forest, open meadows and nearby river, not to mention every creature that dwelled in the surrounding wilds to the mercies of my inquisitive soldiers.

Foraging parties became a daily and for my men, an unloved ritual—blizzards be damned—every man was expected to take his rotation, no bribing of the centurions allowed, although in truth foraging was not completely necessary. Each of the Sidhe Lords had sent along more than enough rations of grain and cured meat to feed the soldiers well into summer, along with cooks to aid in keeping up with the voracious appetites of men who spent every minute of their waking hours in drills, grueling marches carrying full kit through knee-deep and in some cases hip-deep snow, or in mock combat so realistic it had its own share of casualties as they learned the Roman way of fighting—as a cohesive and rigidly disciplined force, unlike the unruly tactics of the Germanic tribes that were our presumed adversaries in this real life and death game of latruncŭli.

And as the soldiers practiced, as they skirmished and as their skills and confidence grew, as their newly planted personalities took root, I began to pick out men who, like Felix, Rufinius and yes, even Aetius, demonstrated they had what it took to be a centurion. All of them did, to some degree or another, as all had been drawn from who I was, but I soon realized that while their memories had been wiped clean, they retained some degree of their original personalities—some were braggarts, others high-strung and nervous; some were thoughtful and reserved while others were easily provoked to violence, *just as one would find in any legion. The most obvious choices of course were those men who'd readily adopted the personalities of centurions from my past, but in a few notable cases, the results were not what I would have expected—take for example Florianus. The Florianus I'd known, briefly, had been a damned scary centurion, scarier even than Jotia when it came to meting out punishment for what were usually fabricated infractions. Needless to say,* he *didn't meet a good or glorious end but instead was impaled on a pilum, hurled by an enraged subordinate. This Florianus had no desire to wield power— at least not as a centurion, perhaps having taken the ugly fate of his predecessor to heart. No. He wanted to be a cook... and once I'd granted his wish, he proved to be a* damned *fine cook by producing a meal of roast boar stuffed with eggs and onions that far surpassed that of the Keep's cooks, thus instantly endearing himself to his legate.*

Mabog, also with my blessing, had his pick as well: we were going to need trained surgeons after all, and he selected one from Rasaben's lot, two from Lady Urme's and one from Lord Pateke's compliment, four men whose unexpectedly rapid grasp of combat medicine, without Mabog's close guidance, suggested a previous exposure to the profession that no memory purge could completely obliterate.

I insisted on the foraging parties regardless of the weather and despite the loud grumbling of my troops—it was vital training—every bit as critical to a soldier's survival as learning to fight with a gladius, not the broadswords they were accustomed to wielding, hurl a pilum with great accuracy and construct from scratch and safely use a ballista, scorpio and onager. They also built and rebuilt the wooden fortifications around the camp each day in practice for the real thing. Had someone happened across the scene, they might have reasonably assumed the Keep itself was under siege by Roman forces.

While Taskim had assured me that I needn't worry about provisioning my men once we were deployed, I felt it prudent to teach each man the fine art of acquiring his own food, just in case the need arose. This was an ability that had always held me in good stead. And as winter finally loosened its grip on the surrounding forest it also had the added benefit of supplying the soldiers with a more varied diet—root vegetables, hare, venison, and yes, even the occasional wild boar once my gastronomic preferences became known—foodstuffs we all clearly appreciated, even if I did find myself having to explain on more than one occasion that just because something looked or smelled edible didn't mean it was *edible. A stubborn few ignored my advice and learned the painful truth for themselves.*

I also learned to ride—and yes, I mean ride a horse. *At first I'd adamantly refused, but Felix, damn him, put the matter to a vote and the soldiers unanimously agreed it was only fitting that as Legate, I should lead them into battle astride a horse. I agreed after forcing one grudging concession from my men: once we engaged the enemy, I would dismount and fight on foot.*

Somehow—I'm not pointing fingers mind you—Ainiaan got wind of this and when she insisted that she be my riding teacher I'd had visions of leading a cavalry charge atop

Mugwort. I even confessed my fears to Felix, fully recovered now, who couldn't stop laughing, so you can perhaps understand why I arrived at the Keep's stables at the appointed hour for my first lesson with much trepidation. It didn't help that Felix had insisted on accompanying me—to help me mount, he claimed, saying I couldn't possibly expect Lady Ainiaan to boost me up onto the back of Mugwort. That would be just plain unseemly he managed to say before he doubled over in another fit of laughter to which I answered with stony silence.

Ainiaan and Mugwort were in fact the first to walk out of the darkness of the stable and into the sun-filled courtyard and I felt my heart sink while Felix, who'd wisely sidestepped out of my reach, kept making these strangled noises. Then to my surprise, Turan immerged from the darkness accompanied by Tev leading her dapple-gray... and a stable boy leading two thickset warhorses, one a glossy black, the other, a truly spectacular example of the breed, white-faced and stockinged, with a coat the color of burnished copper.

I defiantly stuck my tongue out at Felix then turned back to what I suddenly realized were beasts as massive as the carthorses. Felix immediately went for the black, leaving me the copper one with a shaggy blond mane, feathered legs and a long, flaxen tail that simply refused to stay put. Of course the same was true of his huge hooves. He appeared to be dancing—whether it was just sheer exuberance at being out in the early spring sunshine, or in gleeful anticipation of killing me in some truly hideous manner I didn't want to hazard a guess, but if I was a betting man, I'd bet on the latter.

Ainiaan couldn't help but notice my convulsive swallow and sweat-beaded face despite the chilly breeze and quickly assured me that Wushah, as he was called, was a really, really nice horse.

I didn't feel it politic to dispute this, even when she placed several carrots in my equally sweaty palm and instructed me to offer them to the monster—to get our friendship off to a good start, she said. As I reluctantly held out my offering, I had to wonder what the horse was going to offer me in return. I could only hope it was all of my fingers and more or less intact and attached.

To my surprise, Wushah immediately stepped forward, carefully lipped the carrots from my shaking hand and once he'd finished this peace offering, he brought his large head close to mine and began sniffing me.

I kept perfectly still as he snorted and snuffled and examined every bit of me, then, seemingly satisfied, he nudged me with his muzzle, his intention clear: pet me.

I did—carefully mind you—just as Ainiaan had showed me, a scratch between the ears, a firm pat on his thickly muscled neck and a smooth, downward stroke over his withers. He turned his head, watching me as I edged my way closer to the saddle then he snorted again, loudly. I swear I almost soiled my underwear. He nudged me again, pushing me against his huge body, against the saddle. Again, his intention was evident: go on, fool, get up and let's get this murder over with.

With the stable boy's help—not Felix's—I managed to mount then somehow gathered up the reins. Felix was far too busy admiring his all-black horse, a gift from Lady Urme Ainiaan informed us. Before I could ponder exactly what *he'd done to earn such a gift, Ainiaan added that Wushah had also come from Lady Urme's stables and that Lady Urme had expressed her hope that Felix and I would find the horses to our liking. I'd done nothing to garner such a gift, aside from agreeing to fight their battle, so perhaps Felix was just as innocent. Perhaps.*

That said, Felix was behaving like a small boy on his birthday; he was so excited he giggled as he petted the creature, stroking its withers and combing its mane with his trembling fingers, his eyes constantly darted to me, to Turan, to Ainiaan as if desperately needing reassurance that this massive and yes, truly magnificent beast was in fact his.

Felix was, in two words, in love.

I was a little more... um, circumspect. My gift was a horse too, and you know my private feelings about horses—and more germane to the matter at hand, theirs about me. While Felix needed reassurance that the black was truly his, I was in equal need of reassurance that this copper-clad beast beneath me wasn't plotting my untimely murder.

Wushah continued to watch me out of the corner of his eye and once I was settled, he took a step, then another, the stable boy now discretely holding onto his bridle as we made a slow circuit of the courtyard with Ainiaan, now astride Mugwort, trotting alongside. I have to give Mugwort credit, he wasn't the slightest bit cowed by Wushah who was at least triple his height and easily ten times his weight.

By the time we returned to where Felix and Turan stood at our starting point, I was feeling marginally less terrified, having been taught the rudiments of controlling a horse by Ainiaan. Even better, Wushah had shown absolutely no inclination to scrape me off using the rough stone of the courtyard walls, neither had he tried to throw or bite me. He did swat my legs with his tail, but I quickly realized this was not his attempt at annoying me, but rather to keep the biting flies away from both of us.

I should have stopped while I was ahead—but no. Buoyed by this early success, pondering the truth of those long ago and increasingly frustrated assertions that as a Mauri I was a born horseman, and yes, finding myself privately pleased that Turan had accompanied Ainiaan to the stables, hoping she too might be looking for a face-saving way out of our prolonged estrangement, I found myself agreeing to join Ainiaan, Turan and Felix on what I was told would be a gentle ride through the spring countryside—no galloping. Not even a canter, absolutely not. *A slow, safe and relaxing walk, they assured me, to enjoy the wildflowers and songbirds and blustery sunshine.*

Wushah had other ideas.

No sooner had we passed through the main gate than he was off, me clinging on for dear life. A column of soldiers returning from their morning drills were sent scattering, their initial pleased grins replaced by wide-eyed panic as Wushah bore down on them with no intention of dodging any who failed to get out of his way. Behind me Felix yelled out helpful suggestions, as he, Turan and Ainiaan took up the chase, Felix also a gallop, Turan and Ainiaan at a more sedate pace: a nod to Mugwort's short legs and Turan's enlarging belly.

Wushah and I had quite a head start and we quickly lost them as the road took a sharp turn and then another through the dense wood. Despite my terror, I found myself falling into the regular pattern of the horse's powerful strides. I even managed to release my two-handed death-grip on the saddle horn to gather up the reins that Tev had thoughtfully tied together. And Wushah, sensing I was more at ease—that I'd survived an equine version of trial by fire and felt a celebratory snack was in order, abruptly left the road in preference for a sunlit and flower-filled meadow.

As he stopped to crop some grass, I gave him a pat on his neck, and he responded by snorting and tossing his shaggy head as if laughing at the sheer joy of being outside and allowed to stretch his legs after a long winter confined to the stables.

I managed to get him turned around—after he finished grabbing a few more mouthfuls of grass—something that pleased me immensely—and get him back onto the road just as Felix rounded the bend, clearly expecting to find my broken body sprawled in the dirt and Wushah nowhere to be seen.

I gave a gentle tug on the bit; Wushah obediently stopped and we both watched as Felix, agog to see me still in the saddle, reined in his own mount.

I grinned at his look of amazement, then I started to laugh, and Wushah responded by dancing sideways, tossing his head and whinnying in reply.

A few minutes later Turan and Ainiaan arrived. After a thorough chewing out by Ainiaan over my 'foolhardy stunt', we started back, Turan and Ainiaan leading the way this time, Felix and I taking up the rear. As we rounded the last bend, I was startled to find the road leading up to the Keep and our camp lined by my grim-faced troops. They watched our approach in silence—clearly expecting a funeral procession, but seeing I was not just alive, but still astride my warhorse and apparently no the worse for wear they began to bang their swords against their shields, the cadenced boom echoing off the trees.

Wushah seemed to understand and pranced as I grinned broadly at the soldiers' loud—and thoroughly Roman—display of approval.

Realizing this must have been what Caesar had felt as he returned triumphant to Rome after defeating the Gauls I began to seriously question why I had been so easily dissuaded from a career in the cavalry—

"Are you *listening?*"

I jerked my head up and fixed my distracted gaze on Ainiaan. "M'lady…?"

"Why I bother I don't know." She exhaled and shook her head, adding irritably, "Do you want to understand this or not? You said you did."

I glanced at Turan, who was seated across from me at the library table then I turned back to Ainiaan, who was at the head of the table. "Yes, I do, m'lady." I dipped my head and looked suitably contrite. "I just let my mind wander for a moment—my apologies."

Summer was almost upon us and preparations for the battle ahead had taken on an air of urgency. For me, everything now revolved around what had become a self-contained, fully Romanized military camp: there was a mess, a hospital and a stable for our cavalry, neat rows of tents in barrack blocks, a legate's tent—centrally located of course—and even a rudimentary bath and attached latrine, so I had absolutely no reason to venture into the Keep.

Yes, I saw Turan occasionally, but only at some distance when she, in the company of Sifrie, would walk to the end of the drawbridge but no further, to observe my men going through their drills, of the horsemen putting their mounts through their paces, of the archers and ballistarii honing their targeting skills. Sometimes servants would bring along chairs, along with a small table and foodstuffs, so the Ladies of the Keep could lunch on venison and hare in relative comfort while watching my soldiers beat the crap out of each other.

I would have discouraged the practice except it had an invigorating effect on my men, each and every one hoping he'd be the next to catch Sifrie's roving eye with his combat prowess, which in turn gave my physicians more practice in the healing arts. The proverbial win-win scenario, one could say. And yes, if camp scuttlebutt was to be believed, a goodly number of my men were rewarded for their efforts.

Rasaben and Taskim too kept to themselves, a wise move on their part, although every so often I'd catch a glimpse of their faces staring down at us from that damnedable tower—presumably Taskim "enjoying the view" while Rasaben gleefully plotted my murder. I never saw Kyrou—and neither had Rufinius. I know this because I asked Rufinius on a regular basis, not out of concern for Kyrou mind you, but so I'd have a current and ready-made alibi for my trusty centurion just in case Kyrou's body was found floating face down in the moat. Presumably he was just lying low until we left—or maybe he accompanied Lord Tistriya or Lady Urme back to their respective Keeps.

Ainiaan was another matter. I spotted her in camp on an almost daily basis, sometimes with her father when he came to see how his protégés were doing, and other times she'd come alone, to share her wisdom with the soldiers and check on the welfare of our cavalry horses—all two hundred and two of them. My interactions with her or her father rarely involved more than a quick hello or a passing wave.

It was on one of these regular visits that I happened to run into Ainiaan—literally. I'd been in my tent going over the next day's duty roster when I suddenly realized I had a serious need to visit the latrine. I was so preoccupied with the sudden urge to pee and also briefly sun-blinded as I stepped out of my tent, I didn't see her until I collided with her.

She stumbled one way, I went the other, then I whipped around to snarl, 'Watch where you're going!', realized it was Ainiaan and managed to grab her before I uttered a word or she actually fell.

It was an awkward encounter in more ways than one. I'd been avoiding her you see, just as I'd been avoiding Turan—life was so much simpler when I didn't have to constantly be on guard about my thoughts—and I still *really* had to pee. Not that I could tell her that. Granted, all she had to do was read my thoughts, but still… it didn't seem the sort of topic a grown man should discuss with a little girl.

Fortunately, she didn't give me the chance. She said she'd come to see how I was doing since *I* hadn't come to see her. I told her I was doing fine, just terribly, *terribly* busy… as I tried to slowly, unobtrusively sidle away, but she would have none of it. She looked me up and down and said that she was really glad I'd chosen not to regrow my beard and that I looked very dashing in my armor—even without the helmet.

I thanked her for her compliments, nodding hurriedly, as I continued to side step towards the latrine.

She followed and I wondered if she would actually accompany me into the latrine if it came to that; I'd say she was oblivious to my plight but I knew better. She was deliberately delaying me—I just didn't know why, so rather than end up peeing on myself, I decided to go for the direct approach and asked her what she wanted.

She said she'd waited for me to come back to her, to ask more questions, that our meeting in Mugwort's stall had been, as far as she was concerned, only the first in many lessons, assuming I truly wanted to understand the Tuatha—not to mention the Faoimhuir, adding that of all people, I should know that the more one knew about the enemy, the better.

It was a painfully transparent gambit, but I had to pee so badly I found myself agreeing to meet with her the very next morning… and in that cursed library no less. Strangely, when I finally reached the latrine—thankfully alone, Ainiaan having parted company with me once she had what she wanted—I found I didn't have to pee as much as I thought I did… which left me wondering if Ainiaan hadn't planted the sense of urgency in my mind only to get me to agree to something I might have otherwise refused.

So here we were, in the damned library of course, and I'd just let my mind wander… again.

Worse, Ainiaan knew it. She chewed furiously on her lip, clearly doubting I was capable of keeping my mind fixed on anything for more than a few minutes, and therefore debating whether she should continue or take a break and resume the lecture *after* we took our mid-day meal. It didn't help that in the silence that followed my stomach took the opportunity to make its preferences known.

Ainiaan glared at my belly and I clapped my hand over it, hoping to silence it then, I swear out of spite, she resumed her lecture. "All right, as I was *saying*, legend has it that the Faoimhuir first appeared in Numidia, hence everyone thinks that's where they're from, but in truth they can move through different dimensions at will—just as we, meaning Tuatha, can, but the Faoimhuir can go one step further: they can move through things like soil, but fortunately *not* solid rock. Their first recorded appearance was when they immerged from the sands of Numidia—"

"Is this why you always made camp on rock?" I interrupted, looking at Turan, rather than asking the question that I really wanted to ask, which was what a 'dimension' was.

"Of course," Ainiaan answered, as if I was very foolish indeed, drawing my eyes back to her. "And you'd be well-advised to follow this precaution when you set up camp. Faoimhuir aren't to be trusted, hear?"

Point taken. Of course there was a far simpler explanation. Perhaps they'd just immerged from a particularly strong sandstorm, appearing, to those uneducated in the capricious ways of the desert, that they'd immerged from the ground itself. But Ainiaan didn't look to be in a mood to hear such. Neither did Turan. "And what about these, um, *See-afoo* you've mentioned, these allies of the Faoimhuir?"

"*Si'aafu,*" Ainiaan corrected as she suppressed a shiver. "You best hope you never ever meet one."

"Nasty bastards?"

"Yeah, and really, *really* ugly—they're gigantic bugs."

I didn't like the sound of this and very reluctantly asked, "*How* gigantic?"

"Taller than you; taller *even* than Felix." And that *was* tall, according to Ainiaan, even though Felix was barely more than a head taller than me.

413

I looked, wide-eyed, to Turan for confirmation, not fully trusting a child when it came to proportions; she replied with a slight nod, and, "The closest to your ken would be scorpions—*huge* scorpions."

Okay, I *definitely* didn't like the sound of this.

"Plus they eat people," Ainiaan added.

"Remind me not to annoy one then."

"No one wants to annoy them, except the Jaglavak—no one annoys the Jaglavak, not even the Si'aafu, but you misunderstand—Si'aafu consider human flesh a delicacy."

"Oh." I couldn't help but swallow, hard. I also found myself reluctant to ask her who—or what—these *Jag-la-vaks* were—but I did remember them from our previous conversation, back in the stable, as something akin to arbiters in the dispute between the Faoimhuir and the Tuatha. And it was then that I recalled something else she'd said in the same conversation, something that at the time had tickled the back of my neck, warning me there was more to what she was telling me, far more: 'they assumed that we, rather than waste our resources, would just sell them to the Si'aafu."

"Is that why you refused to sell these incurably insane people to the Si'aafu? You knew they were going to use them as food?"

Ainiaan didn't answer but instead looked sidelong at Turan; so did I only to notice that Turan was shifting uncomfortably in her chair.

Boian had told me she was having a very difficult pregnancy and while Turan's eyes were shadowed and sunken and she'd certainly lost weight as her belly swelled, I couldn't help but wonder if this wasn't a ploy, a way of manipulating me, possibly getting me back into her bed and her back into my good graces—perhaps even making me believe she looked this way when in fact she was quite well.

"Of course," Turan answered, then added bitterly, "But I don't expect you to believe me," thus proving she hadn't lost her knack for eavesdropping on my thoughts.

Ainiaan had failed to tell me Turan was going to present when she offered—one might even say insisted, using *very* underhanded tactics—to fill me in on why the Tuatha and Faoimhuir were at odds so I could better understand 'the' enemy. Of course she had. Just as I knew it was a set-up from the get-go; I even suspected it was Ainiaan's way to get Turan and me in the same room, and maybe deep down I wanted an excuse to see her too, one that would provide each with some face-saving—just like the horseback ride several weeks before. In truth I had missed her, even caught myself wondering if I loved her—if I *could* love her after what she and her fellow Tuatha had done to me, even going so far as to make excuses for her, telling myself what she'd told me, that she'd tried to stop what happened.

So, I'd decked myself out in my full armor—minus only the helmet—for this meeting, I'd even skipped the morning meal in order to bathe and shave and oil my hair; I clearly wanted to look my very best, but for whom? Ainiaan? Ainiaan was one of the few people I'd met who, aside from telling me I looked so much nicer without the beard, seemed oblivious to such things—I hadn't thought to ask if she still harbored ideas of marrying me. Maybe I'd proven to her that even without the beard I was just as mean as Rasaben—and for similar reasons.

That said, now that I was here, now that I was facing Turan, I found the old angers, the old, unresolved hurts had rushed to the surface, shoving aside everything else.

I leaned back, crossed my arms and fixed her with a cold stare. "Try me."

She hesitated, just long enough to make me wonder if she was going to answer or not, then: "We caught the Faoimhuir taking large numbers of people off planet."

"That's old news," I grumbled with an annoyed flick of my hand, and so it was.

She shrugged, then continued coolly, "We'd long been aware that they were engaged in slavery—a very lucrative trade, sadly not just on your world, but throughout known space, and humans have long been a prized commodity due to your amazing adaptability and intelligence. The treaty did not explicitly forbid such commerce, in fact there is a clause which, depending upon how you interpret it, could be said to encourage it, and so, I am ashamed to admit, we looked the other way... for a time, fearful if we attempted to stop it, it might draw the unwanted interference of the Si'aafu, who have always viewed the Faoimhuir more favorably than us.

"But then their human trafficking became so egregious and was such a blatant breach of the spirit, if not the wording of the treaty and as a result put our continued protection of humanity at risk."

"Meaning you couldn't keep up with the terrible cost of caring for those they left behind—and I use the term 'caring' in the *loosest* possible sense." *Fine.* I'd already agreed to fight their damned war, which meant I'd come to terms with their side of the story—I'm not saying I totally believed it, no. I'm sure the Faoimhuir had an equally plausible and yes, truly admirable excuse for exploiting humans in such a horrendous fashion. But I was in the hands of the Tuatha, not the Faoimhuir, and therefore it was their truth I had to work with—see? I'm not naïve, just pragmatic. That said, it rankled that the Tuatha used the techniques they'd honed on these poor unfortunates to forge an army of mindless soldiers only to find out that wasn't such a prize-winning idea—

"So it was decided," Turan interrupted my thoughts, "that the only way to stop what was happening was to break the treaty—"

"But not without first figuring out a way to make it impossible for the Faoimhuir to win the battle—by the Tuatha losing the skirmish… at the cost of how many Kellesuf lives? And oh, yes, let's not forget Lord Vela because his death was the only one that mattered," I added sulkily.

Turan stared long and hard at me before replying, "While I am the last person to doubt your abilities, Arri, you'd be wise to temper your over-confidence of an easy victory. Yes, the lords created a situation where we would choose *how* the battle was fought, and in doing so, put the Faoimhuir at a distinct disadvantage, but as Ainiaan just said, the Faoimhuir are not to be trust—" She suddenly cupped her belly in one hand and wincing, struggled to rise from her chair.

I had to fight the urge to help her as I would have immediately done for any woman in her advanced condition, but in this case to do so might have suggested a concern I did not feel, or, should I say, I did not wish to express.

She managed to get to her feet unaided, and gripping the back of her chair, said, "The Faoimhuir were selling humans to the Si'aafu for *food.*"

"You mean the insane ones."

"No. Those they left behind for us to deal with. Si'aafu, as Ainiaan has already told you, find human flesh a delicacy—and the Faoimhuir elected to exploit this market in hopes of securing the Si'aafu's continued favor. As I said, there's a clause in the treaty that states that Faoimhuir and Tuatha may take up to two thousand humans apiece, every year to use for whatever purpose they wish—a payment of sorts for our protection—"

I snorted.

She took a deep, steadying breath, then continued, "Most are sold, off-world, as slaves, and I'm sorry to say the Faoimhuir were not alone in exploiting this clause in such a manner, we just didn't exploit it to the extent they did—"

"A point utterly lost on those snatched and enslaved," I replied icily.

Turan replied with a slight shrug. "Most probably."

"Most probably? I think I can speak for all who were taken against our will—given our druthers we'd have preferred to left the hell alone. But it does help explain your rationale for creating the Kellesuf—were they nothing more than part of your yearly harvest? Wiping their minds would

certainly make them less troublesome to handle and far less costly to care for."

She looked at me, a deeply pained look. "Arri, I know you hate me, hate what I am, hate *who* I am, hate all Tuatha for what we've done to you and the others. But can you set aside that hate just long enough to hear what I am trying to tell you? It might just save your life and the lives of your men—who, I might mention, are no longer Kellesuf and so *will* reasonably fear for their lives as they enter combat, feel the fatal stab to the gut… feel the agony of slowly bleeding to death."

I settled back in my chair, scowling at her because she was right, damn her and growled, "Go on, I'm listening."

"The Faoimhuir had in their greed agreed to supply the Si'aafu with more humans than they could possibly supply under the terms of the treaty and when they couldn't meet those demands, the Si'aafu ordered the Faoimhuir to turn over their own slaves—highly-trained slaves the Faoimhuir needed to crew their ships, farm their lands, mine their asteroids—"

"Fight their wars?"

"Yes," she exhaled wearily. "They had little choice but to hand over some to make up for the immediate shortfall, but—"

"But they also illicitly increased their 'harvest'."

"In vast numbers. We believe they took over twenty thousand just in the past year alone. At this rate their 'harvesting', in combination with your species' proclivity to kill each other with astonishing efficiency will lead, in a matter of a few decades, to the loss of entire cultures, and within a century to a population collapse so complete and wide-spread humanity will be unable to recover from it. In short, humans will cease to exist on Earth. We could not permit that to happen, because along with facing the very real threat of the extinction of humanity on its home planet, a terrible, irreplaceable loss—"

"Indeed—where else would you find such highly adaptable, intelligent and oh, yes, let's not forget free for the taking slaves?"

"—we would lose Earth itself."

I stared at her, blinked then slowly raised my brows. "I don't—"

"There is one universal law that even the Si'aafu must abide by or risk extermination: no planet can be claimed and colonized if it supports sentient life *unique* to that planet."

My brows remained firmly fixed in the baffled position.

"Sentient meaning *intelligent* life…"

My mouth formed a silent 'O'.

"...and humans, in spite of all your glaring flaws, are remarkably intelligent... and unique."

"Don't forget highly adaptable, free for the taking and oh, yes, *damned* tasty." I emphasized the testy remark by clicking my teeth together.

She only stared at me with eyes that looked bruised. So I dropped my gaze and plucked nonexistent bits of lint from my immaculate chest harness.

Ainiaan and Turan exchanged exasperated stares—I could tell even without looking—while giving me the time I needed to tend to this urgent task of personal tidiness, clearly hoping in the process I'd lose some of the attitude.

Finally satisfied my harness was lint-free, I gave it one last sweep with my hand as I lifted my eyes back to Turan. "Truth?"

"Yes, Arri, *truth*. Every bit of it. I dearly wish it wasn't so."

"Why didn't you tell me this at the very start?"

"Do you think you would've understood what an alien species was when we rescued you? What other planets were? I told you that I would tell you all, but only when you could fully understand. Just as Ainiaan told you 'the whole ugly truth', but only after you'd listened to Boian and heard what Taskim had to say."

And that *was* truth. Had she—had Ainiaan or Taskim for that matter told me all this when I was first brought here, much less when I was first captured, I wouldn't have understood. Now it seemed not just reasonable, but entirely plausible, which raised another specter: "Are you manipulating me, controlling my thoughts?"

"Give yourself some credit for once. You're beginning to fully comprehend because you are very, *very* smart." She tapped the side of her head. "*Brains*, Arri, remember?"

I thought about that for a while—until those thoughts shook loose another concern, a nagging unease. "What are you?" I looked first at Ainiaan, then Turan. "You look human, you say you are Tuatha."

"We *were* human," Turan replied, "just as the Faoimhuir *were* once fully human, tens of thousands of years ago. And we still *are* human... of a sort, otherwise I could not bear your child. We're just not... well, we're not *you*."

"And *you* didn't answer my question," I replied coldly, refusing to play into her hands—figuratively speaking.

"My ancestors," Turan replied, visibly rebuffed and in kind, "Ainiaan's and Sifrie's and Rasaben's and Taskim's ancestors were also taken against their will by Jaglavak, just as the ancestors of the Faoimhuir were taken, then manipulated in such a way that we have abilities you do not."

"Such as changing form and hearing others' thoughts?" I pointedly ignored the reference to them being 'taken', just as I was 'taken', just as the Kellesuf were 'taken', as if somehow that made us all victims in the same horrendous scheme—*hardly!*

"Among other skills, yes," she continued, her voice even chillier than before. "And while all Tuatha can shape-change—given the proper training—only our womenfolk can read minds."

I blinked. It hadn't occurred to me, up until that moment, that Taskim and Rasaben had never shown any indication of being able to read my thoughts; if they had it might have saved them a lot of headaches and despite my less than brotherly feelings towards them, they *were* men—of a sort, just as I was a man and this definitely gave women a decidedly unfair advantage.

"Legend has it that the Jaglavak offered the skill to men, too," Ainiaan said, eyeing me in a way that left little doubt she too had just put this female-only gift to practice, "but they said they had far more important things to occupy their time than to eavesdrop on the 'frivolous' thoughts of women."

"Oh." Hate as I do to admit it that did sound like something a thoughtless man would say.

Ainiaan snorted. *"Precisely."*

I massaged my forehead—a purely unintentional retort—then turned my pinched stare on Turan. "Are you slaves of these Jaglavak?"

"Slaves? No. Servants? Perhaps so. We were created to protect you, protect humanity—"

"By exploiting us—taking *us* as slaves, selling us for... *food.*"

"Everything has a price, Arri. You know that's true."

And it was, damned if it wasn't.

"So where have you been all this time?"

Suddenly the old Turan and her sphinx-like smile were back. "Hiding in plain sight."

I didn't like the implications of this, but I also wasn't sure I wanted to ask what she meant by that—maybe I *had* crossed paths with the Tuatha before, many times, maybe even Turan herself—she had, after all, studied me for some time before deciding I was the one she wanted to snatch. She'd admitted so. So had Sifrie. They just didn't mention for exactly how long—a few days? A week? A month? *My entire life?* Had the Tuatha imbued *me* with special abilities, just as the Jaglavak had done to them, such as my astonishing memory, early on? Had my fate been sealed from the start? Had my amazing career had less to do with my dogged determination and unique abilities and more to Tuatha meddling?

Or was my rise truly due to my own abilities, my *brains* as Turan liked to call it.

Which touched on another, equally unsettling and related matter: I'd come to appreciate that the Tuatha did not perceive the passage of time the way I did, as the perpetually forward rolling of minutes, hours, days—unstoppable. To them time was malleable—a tangible substance they could manipulate at will. It didn't make sense, and yet, at the same time it did—

"You did it again!" Ainiaan interrupted irritably.

I jerked my eyes to her. *Did what again?*

"Let your mind wander—in your case, more like darting here and there like a hound chasing hare."

I looked suitably insulted because I was—comparing me to an easily abstracted dog? That was just plain rude. And totally uncalled for. But this was Ainiaan, a child, so I answered civilly, "You Tuatha give me a lot to think about, m'lady—perhaps too much. It's hard to stay focused on one issue."

"You could at least *try.*"

My stomach took this instant to again make its wants known—*loudly*, which of course further soured Ainiaan's mood and, presumably, her opinion of me and my ability to control myself—and at the same time cemented my likeness to a dog in search of a meal. Granted, my belly had fair reason to complain; I hadn't eaten since the previous evening and I'd worked up quite an appetite preening—er, I mean *preparing* for this meeting.

"Perhaps the remainder of this discussion could wait until another time?" Turan said, her gaunt and shadowed face twisting into a wince. "You are clearly in need of a meal, Arri, and I need to retire to my bed—your son is kicking me."

Son...?

Turan nodded to my unspoken reaction.

A son! I slumped back into my chair, stunned. I'd never given the gender of my unborn child any thought; it wasn't like I could stipulate a boy over a girl after all—I'd take whatever I was given. Then I wondered if this wasn't another feint; Turan had to know that men, at least privately and especially those facing a very uncertain future as I was strongly desired a son and since she had known the actual moment she had conceived, then perhaps she *could* also decide what that child would be, or at least know what it was.

There was also a very good chance I'd be deployed before she gave birth and an equally good chance I'd never return—so an easy lie.

Ainiaan passed through my distracted gaze, favored me with a *very* angry stare and muttered, *"Maybe you should regrow your beard,"* as she slipped her arm around Turan then together they started for the door.

I hesitated, well aware that any action I took at this moment would have long-lasting consequences. Even doing nothing was an action of a sort.

I shook my head, rose and strode around them to reach the door, first. I opened it, stepped back to allow them to walk out, arm in arm then I followed, ready to grab Turan if she stumbled. Clearly she and Ainiaan expected my uneasy and yes, unhappy escort to end at the doorway to Turan's chambers but as Ainiaan let go of Turan's waist long enough to unlatch the door, I stepped forward and slipped my arm around her.

Turan stared up at me, startled, as did Ainiaan.

"Thank you, Lady Ainiaan, I will attend to Lady Turan from here."

She looked at Turan, eyebrows raised.

Turan nodded.

"If you need me…"

"I will call for you," Turan replied, her voice suddenly thin, strained.

Ainiaan, with one more warning look at me, stepped aside.

I gently scooped Turan up in my arms, mindful of the harness, the ring-mail and the pommel of my gladius, carried her into her chambers and over to the bed. I placed her carefully onto the pallet, Ainiaan softly closed the door behind us.

"I'll be all right now—I just need to rest a bit."

I knew a dismissal when I heard one and I knew I should heed her suggestion and my own better judgment and leave.

Of course I didn't.

I eased myself down, next to her hip and watching her face out of the corner of my eye, lightly ran my hand over her distended belly. She suddenly winced and I jerked my hand away then sat there, frozen.

"You didn't hurt me, Arri—just another kick. He's a strong boy—strong enough to survive the birth."

Her soft words hit my gut. "You fear you are not?"

She lifted her arm, her fingers outstretched, almost but not quite touching my face, my lips. "Yes."

Another blow that knocked the air out of me. "Then… *why?*"

She smiled and lightly caressed my chin and I forced myself not to pull away but she sensed my reaction, dropped her hand to her belly and fixed her watery gaze on what lay beyond the lead-paned windows. "Selfishness, Arri, plain and simple selfishness. I lied to you, not once, but repeatedly—something I know you'll have no problem believing."

"But...?"

"I wanted to conceive, wanted you as the sire to infuriate Ras, if you want the unvarnished truth—no—*absolute* truth: any Roman, any *human* would have done."

I almost rose from the bed in offended rage but something compelled me to stay, to hear her out—

"I knew it was only a matter of time before he forced me into a marriage—he was so terribly desperate to reclaim our lands, to recover what was rightfully his. Someone else could have been tasked with capturing a Roman suitable for our purposes, but it would've had to have been another high-born woman, Lady Urme for one, or Lady Holle—someone not only highly skilled at shape-changing, but extremely adept at listening in on others' thoughts at some distance, being able to weed out the background 'chatter' and hone in on what particular people—in this case, certain targeted soldiers and officers were thinking—and because it was my idea, I made the case that I had right to first refusal.

"Of course I had no intention of refusing—I wanted to go, to see for myself these exotic lands from which so many of our Kellesuf had come from, to see if your empire was as intriguing, as colorful as Ras had told me, as Jaro and Perus and said. But I also desperately wanted to find a soldier to fit our needs, to solve our 'Kellesuf problem' as the lords had begun to call it, in hopes that perhaps this alone might make the Assemblage rethink their hasty decision in agreeing to hand over our lands to Lord Tistriya and strip my brother of his rightful place at the table, but there was the added benefit of keeping Ras at bay a little longer—"

"Until you could get yourself pregnant by that soldier, thus making you unfit for such an arranged marriage, your womb tainted by the seed of a mere human."

"Yes. But by the time we returned with you, I realized that there was more to it than that. I'd actually fallen in love with you. Now another hard truth to dispel another lie: I *had* hoped a child would keep you bound to me, out of your strong sense of duty if nothing more, but deep down I knew that once you learned the awful truth of our intentions I'd lose you, that even a child would not be enough to hold you to me, which, as we both know, has come to pass."

She again stroked my cheek, caressed my chin in such tenderness I couldn't deny her. "I knew you'd never willing agree to the transfer of your memories—I know you won't believe me, you have no reason to believe anything I tell you, but I *tried* to stop it, Arri, I pleaded with Taskim and the other Sidhe Lords to find some other way but I was refused—in fact worse than refused: I had my idea thrown back in my face; I was reminded at every opportunity that this had been *my* plan all along... and so it was. I just never planned on falling deeply, madly in love with the man I'd selected." She stopped, closed her eyes and took a deep, ragged breath and as tears spilled out from under tightly closed lids and down her now hollow cheeks. "That morning, when Taskim commanded that you to go with him..."

She opened her eyes to stare up at me with the distant look of someone mortally wounded. "I *knew*. I *knew*, Arri. I wanted to warn you but I, in turn, had been warned if I gave you any hint as to what was about to happen, they'd take you away and once the transfer was over, they'd simply kill you."

"You should have let them," I whispered.

She blinked, roughly wiped her face. "They brought me to you—after you'd been drugged, just before they started the transfer. Mabog assured me that if he was careful, if he took his time, you would survive, and survive with your mind intact, so Rasaben gave me a choice: you could be left as you were, where you'd realize what was done to you, or Mabog could wipe your mind once they were done.

"The latter would mean I would have you as mine for as long as you lived, but as what? Kellesuf? That would mean you'd be the only Kellesuf now, while the others walked around with their heads full of your memories? I simply couldn't bear that—I couldn't bear to see your amazing intellect, your unique way of seeing the world destroyed, so I agreed to the former, knowing when you finally came to fully grasp what had happened, what we'd done, you'd hate me most of all and deservedly so."

She took another ragged breath, added, "I desperately wanted you, Arri—I was telling you the truth when I told you I loved you with all my heart—I still do, but I also knew that you could never forgive my betrayal. So I chose to continue the pregnancy despite the risks; I told myself, told Mabog I'd still have a part of you that I could love, have a child who would love me as I knew you could not and never would—and if we both died, well... better that than a life without you or the child."

I squeezed my eyes shut and exhaled, *"Damn..."*

"It's not totally unheard of for Tuatha to take humans as lovers," she continued, drawing my watery stare. "In fact it's a mark of status in some circles..."

I couldn't stop my visceral response as I recalled the look in Lady Urme's eyes as she sized me up, sized Felix and Rufinius up, deciding who she was going to take to her bed—it never happened, at least not with me as I'd adequately proved to be very tiresome; I couldn't speak for Felix or Rufinius as I'd never asked them, in truth because I didn't want to know. Fortunately Turan failed to notice.

"…and I knew Tuatha men could sire children by human women—Sifrie and Ainiaan are proof of this, or so I believed."

"Believed?"

"At the time I never thought to question Mabog about Marwe's untimely death—I was told she and the baby died as a complication of childbirth, a tragedy yes, but nothing more. I also never thought to ask if the reverse was true, if a human could father a child by a Tuatha—not until after I'd committed myself."

"Why didn't you end it once you knew?" Knew *what* exactly, I wasn't sure, except that Turan was dying. That I knew now—it was no ruse, no attempt at garnering sympathy.

"Would you believe me if I told you I love this child every bit as I still love you? I could no more kill him than I could kill you, or let you be killed."

"Even if it kills you."

"It's not the child's fault—he's every bit as blameless in this as you are."

I slowly, carefully eased myself down on the bed next to her then wrapped my arm around her. I would have tugged her against me, but I was wearing my armor and she was clearly very uncomfortable just as she was. She nestled her head against my ring-mailed shoulder and for several minutes neither of us spoke.

"I don't want you to die," I said, finally, and meant it.

"It's not a *certainty*—Mabog assures me there's a chance we'll both survive, but you see the iron in his blood is slowly poisoning me and my body's attempts to produce an antitoxin to it is risking the child. That's what killed Marwe, Sifrie and Ainiaan's mother—"

"But she safely gave birth to two children—"

"Only because she was *half*-Tuatha."

I raised my brows.

"I didn't know that—I thought she was fully human. No one knew but Mabog, Marwe and the Lords of the Sidhe—too complicated to explain now, but that's why Mabog and Marwe were granted permission to continue the pregnancies, a rare consent and one Taskim explained away by saying that Mabog had in fact made Marwe his legally recognized wife and

Mabog, to be kind, is from a undistinguished family—as I said, Tuatha do take human lovers, but resultant pregnancies are discouraged."

Discouraged—*not* terminated. Meaning the resulting offspring were likely treated no better than their human parents, as chattel, slaves to be bought and sold—gods forbid the Tuatha taint their *distinguished* bloodlines—

She lifted her head in order to look me in the eye; I bit my lip as if that could stop her from reading my thoughts.

"In a word, yes. At least that's we've been raised to believe—that in watering down our bloodlines with non-Tuatha blood, we will eventually lose our 'enhancements', and thus our ability to protect you."

"But if she was part-Tuatha…"

"She was from a disgraced family—exiled because they freely interbred with humans, that's why she hid the truth about herself, claimed to be fully human and only revealed the truth to Mabog, to the Lords when she realized she was with child. Which is why she and Mabog were granted permission to carry the child, Sifrie, to term and then later, Ainiaan.

"But as it turns out, like incest in many human cultures, there's actually a solid physiological rationale behind this cultural taboo. In the case of Marwe, because she was half-Tuatha, she was able to survive the birth of Sifrie, and later, Ainiaan, but with each pregnancy the resulting antitoxin became stronger, and with the third, it began to break down the components in her blood. Mabog said when he realized what was happening, he begged her to end the pregnancy but she refused, convinced she'd recover as she had after Sifrie and Ainiaan. Instead both she and the child died and he's never forgiven himself—"

"It explains why he's not the most attentive father, as he himself told me." Little did I know, when he told me that, that I might face a similar situation—or worse, the child I'd sired would be born an orphan—assuming he survived—never knowing either parent and left to the likes of Taskim and Rasaben to do with as they liked—an eerie echo of my own childhood. I forced those deeply troubling thoughts out my head, hoping Turan would be so preoccupied with her own she wouldn't have heard it.

"He'll have Boian and Ainiaan and Hanni to see to it that he's well-raised," she murmured.

I winced.

"I'm sorry—I shouldn't have thought that." I kissed the top of her head, at a loss to say more.

"Mabog did his best to convince me to end it, Arri, really he did. From the moment he learned I was with child, and every day since. I just—"

My stomach took that moment to growl again.

Turan chuckled then carefully eased herself out of my embrace and onto one elbow so she could stare down at me. "You sound as if you've swallowed an entire dog, Arri, and he's quite put out by it."

I lifted my head and kissed her on the lips. She kissed me back, then motioning to the door with her chin, said, "Go—feed your belly before it decides to feed on me." She then eased herself back down onto the bed.

I rose, offered her my hand. "Join me?"

She shook her head and as I stared at her—really stared at her I realized just how frail she looked—how frail she truly was.

"May I bring you something?"

She shook her head, whispered, "Go."

I grabbed the blanket that was folded at the foot of the bed and drew it over her then, as I tucked it around her I asked, "May... may I come back?"

That offer surprised her. "I would like that very much."

I leaned down, kissed her again on the lips then started for the door.

"Arri?"

I turned back to her.

"How do you like your armor? I never had the chance to ask."

I looked down at myself then back at her and forced a smile. "I'm very pleased."

She closed her eyes and murmured softly, "Then I'm pleased," as if it was suddenly almost too much effort to speak, as if breath itself was too much.

I started back for her then stopped as I realized she was still breathing, that she hadn't suddenly died as I'd first assumed, she'd just fallen asleep. With a shake of my head, I again walked back to the door, then opened it only to find Felix and Rufinius standing just outside, clearly waiting on me.

I stepped into the passageway, closing the door softly behind me as Rufinius tried to peer around me, into the room. "Something wrong?"

Rufinius' black eyes slid back to me as Felix answered, "We became concerned—you've been gone all morning."

I gestured irritably for them to follow then I hurried down the stairs, towards the Great Hall. There was always a rich and plentiful array of foodstuffs on its massive table—surely I'd find something to tempt my palate as well as provide a few minutes of distraction. Once within its stiflingly warm interior my two companions headed to the far end of the table where, as Kellesuf, they always sat, ignored by their masters.

We now had our own mess hall, granted it offered up far simpler fair but none of my men, now that they had their ability to decide for themselves restored to them had shown any desire to seek out this table's richer offerings.

I followed, oblivious until I heard Felix urging me to sit. I pulled out a chair, sat down then fixed my surprised gaze on him.

"Habit," he shrugged as he and Rufinius began helping themselves to the venison piled high on a nearby platter.

I took several pieces myself then looked around. It had been weeks since I'd set foot in the hall—there was no need, after all. "Where's Aetius?" I asked, suddenly noticing his absence.

"Last time I saw him, he was merrily bouncing off the buttocks of that cook of his," Rufinius muffled through a mouthful.

I nodded and took a loud gulp of wine as Felix said, "Want to talk about it?"

I swallowed with a wince. "About *what?*"

"Lady Turan."

I another took another deeper gulp from my mug, scowling at him over its rim as I swallowed then I angrily wiped my lips on my hand and grumbled, "What about her?"

"She's ill—everyone says so."

"Everyone?" I replied in a warning tone.

Rufinius became very busy eating. Felix, however, pressed on, just as the original Felix would have done.

"Boian says when she asked, Lady Ainiaan said she was pining for you—"

I banged my mug down on the table with such force wine splattered from it and everyone froze—even those at the far end of the table, along with the servants tending to their needs.

"She's dying," Felix continued, undeterred by the sudden silence that filled the hall or by my baleful stare. "That's what the servants say."

I looked away, fixed my slitted gaze on the far end of the table, saw Perus and Jaro sitting there along with three men I recognized as part of Turan's entourage, all watching me uneasily, almost accusingly, just as Rufinius was watching me uneasily, hands full of food and half-way to open mouths.

"Is it true?" Felix persisted.

"Yes," I hissed, *"it's true."* Realizing I had no appetite, I angrily pushed myself away from the table and to my feet.

Felix and Rufinius immediately followed suit, but I flicked each a look that warned not to follow me further, then I stormed out of the hall, leaving them, Jaro, Perus and their companions, and the servants to stare after me.

I started for the nearby main doors with the intention of returning to the Keep's now-abandoned barracks and hopefully lose myself within its silence—or find myself, knowing no one, not even Felix, would dare disturb me there, then I remembered my promise to Turan—that I'd come back. I stopped and looked over my shoulder.

I couldn't face her, I couldn't face what I'd done to her, both by accident and intent. *Besides, she's probably fast asleep—she needs her rest.* So keeping that feeble excuse topmost in my mind, I hurried to the doors, down the stairs and across the courtyard. I'd almost reached the barracks when I stopped again as Felix's voice echoed: *She's ill... everyone says so...*

No, not ill—she's dying and all because of you, you gods-damned selfish bastard—and now you don't even have the courage to make good on your promise?

I took a deep breath, then pivoted on my heel and walked determinedly back across the courtyard, up the stairs, down the hall and then up the stone steps, taking two at a time, but once I reached the second level, instead of turning to my right, towards Turan's apartments, I turned to my left—towards Mabog's quarters.

I hurried down the passageway and quickly found myself standing before his door. It was ajar, just a crack and from within I could hear the distinct scrape and click of tableware. I didn't knock, I didn't hesitate—I kicked the door open with such force it swung inwards and banged against the wall.

Mabog, who'd been seated at a small table eating his midday meal, leapt to his feet, startled, and seeing the look in my eye, seeing I was in full armor, including my gladius, whatever indignant protest had formed on his lips, died.

"Wha... wha-what d-d-do you w-w-want?" he stammered, backing away as I approached.

"I want you to save Turan!"

He instantly stopped his terrified retreat and gave me a strange look. "I *have* offered, Arri, she's refused every option."

"She *won't* refuse me."

Then he said something that genuinely surprised me: "Are you certain?"

And suddenly I wasn't certain—Turan was a very strong-willed woman. She'd proven that, time and time again.

"Please, Arri, sit down and let's discuss this." He motioned to another chair at the table. I very unhappily eased myself down as he cautiously resumed his seat and pushed his half-eaten meal aside. "Has she told you...?"

"That by me getting her with child I've poisoned her, poisoned them both?" I replied bitterly. *"Yes."*

"Arri—you didn't know. You had no way of knowing. Turan *should* have known; she chose *not* to know. You're not to blame—"

I smacked my fists on the table with enough force that all the color that had just returned to his cheeks, again drained out of his face. *"I came here not to accept or assign blame—I came here to tell you to save her!"*

"Or what? You'll kill me?"

I stared back at this puny man, jaw muscles working, enraged at his audacity, and at the same time overwhelmed by a sense of utter helplessness.

I swallowed, hard, and dropped my suddenly watery eyes to my white-knuckled fists. *"Do... something,"* I managed, my voice cracking as I forced my fingers to unfurl, *"I beg you!"*

He leaned back in his chair and studied my distraught face for what seemed like an eternity, until I could stand it no longer. Turan was dying—and he was sitting there, staring at me?

I pushed myself away from the table and to my feet. "We *must* hurry—"

"I just checked on her before you arrived," Mabog replied calmly, remaining where he was. "In fact I gave her something to make her more comfortable." Then his eyes looked past me and I wheeled around, hand reaching for my gladius, expecting... I don't know. Rasaben? Kyrou? Felix? But it was Ainiaan standing in the doorway.

I took a deep, convulsive breath, visibly shaking as I exhaled.

She stepped into the room, closing the door as she did so. "She's sleeping, Arri... and stable." She smiled and patted my hand—the one still clutching the pommel of my gladius. "Calm down." She turned to her father.

"Please, Arri, sit down," he said. "We need to talk."

I hesitated, angry and confused neither could see the urgency, but I also knew Mabog wasn't going to budge, figuratively or literally, that neither of them would do a damned thing until I did as he asked. So, I sat.

"Did she explain to you why this is happening?" Mabog asked. "It's critical you fully appreciate the situation.

While he spoke Ainiaan positioned herself behind me, her hands lightly grasping my shoulders—to offer comfort or to remind me to stay put I cannot tell you. Maybe both. The result was I felt confined, trapped.

I shrugged, irritably—only afterward realizing I'd dislodged Ainiaan's small hands in the process, but she got the hint and didn't resume her hold. Instead, she walked over to stand beside her father. "She did—but... but I didn't understand." It was a hard thing to admit, to Mabog, to Ainiaan, but it was true. All I knew was that she was dying—the baby was dying and only Mabog could save her. That was enough for me. But clearly not enough for Mabog or Ainiaan.

He settled back, crossed his arms and said, "Iron. That's what's killing her—"

"*I know*—that's why they took my armor from me—"

"It's what's called a fail-safe," Ainiaan interrupted.

I arched a brow as I jerked my eyes from him to her. "I don't—"

"The Jaglavak put a tremendous amount of time and energy into creating us and the Faoimhuir, you see," she continued. "They knew it was only a matter of time before other advanced species happened across Earth, species that are not as... shall we say, *beneficent* as the Jaglavak—"

"Like the Si'aafu."

"So you were listening," she replied, then, "Yes, exactly like the Si'aafu, among others. And the Jaglavak believed the best way to protect Earth was to create two equal but opposing forces levied from humans themselves, forces that would guard humanity from extermination or exploitation, and therefore protect Earth itself from external colonization—"

"Because as one cannot colonize a world that is already home to intelligent life," I interrupted, having this nagging desire to prove to her that I *had* listened and to Mabog that I really *did* understand, so we could skip over a lot of the details and speed up this 'talk'.

"Exactly so," Mabog picked up where Ainiaan left off. "But the Jaglavak also knew that by giving us—I mean the Faoimhuir and the Tuatha—powers and skills normal humans did not possess could also put humans at risk, that perhaps the temptation to exploit or interfere with the natural evolution of human culture would be too great for us—the Jaglavak, after all, hoped they wouldn't have to watch the watchers, so to speak, but instead could go about their affairs, only occasionally checking in to see how things were going."

"So?"

"Iron is common in your world—your weapons, your armor... even in everyday objects like harness, wagon hardware, cooking utensils, pots.

Ubiquitous. And better, you carry it in your blood, although in tiny amounts. So, the Jaglavak did some further tinkering with us—"

"By making iron poison to you."

"Exactly." he nodded. "By doing so, it meant we could not stay long in your world—we could not interfere, if we attempted to do so, we risked death, thereby protecting *you* from *us*. But there was an additional rationale for making iron a deadly poison to us—to protect *us* from *you*."

"How could we possibly threaten you?" I asked, genuinely baffled. "You yourself have acknowledged Tuatha and Faoimhuir possess powers, not to mention weapons we do not—"

"There's no risk to close physical proximity, no—unless one of you takes a hankering to stab or strangle one of us as we are every bit as mortal as you are..."

Don't tempt me...

"...the risk is in interbreeding—a direct exchange of bodily fluids, fluids that contain iron... or its antitoxin. But it's more than that. Each generation of interbreeding would dilute those very powers you speak of, thus slowly defeating the whole purpose of our existence.

"The Jaglavak," Mabog paused as he steepled his hands on the table, "in their wisdom, instilled in our distant ancestors strong taboos against such interbreeding, very strict rules, with equally strict punishments. But as you and I well know, rules are there to be broken, especially when it comes to sex and in truth, punishments, aside from what we brought upon ourselves, was rarely meted out. So, over the generations the rules became more lax as the very solid rationale behind these taboos was eventually lost, or perhaps deliberately hidden by those who had come to resent the Jaglavak's continued 'interference' and control.

"It's true," he continued, "that many Tuatha and Faoimhuir consider humans inferior, I'm sad to say, and therefore looked upon sex with a human as somehow..."

"Disgusting? Like being caught having sex with a sheep?"

Ainiaan blushed and Mabog blinked in shock—*fine*. Maybe I shouldn't have been so crude in front of Ainiaan, but Turan had told me Ainiaan had walked in on Sifrie and her constantly changing roster of paramours on a regular basis. So chances are, she'd walked in a sheepherder or two as well.

"I was going to say beneath us," Mabog replied. His lips quirked into a faint smile, "but that brings with it its own set of images. So another taboo of sorts, not that it was any more successful in stopping these assignations—some even considered human lovers a—"

"Mark of status?" I kept my voice calm and my eyes locked with his—Ainiaan had made it known she planned on marrying me when she was old enough after all. I'd chalked it up to nothing more than a child's infatuation, but maybe there was more too it.

"Yes," he replied. "Bottom line, people are people, no matter what else we are, and sex is a primal, driving force that often overrides all else, including common sense. The Jaglavak clearly felt there was a far greater chance that one of us would impregnate a human, rather than the reverse it, and designed it so that without proper care such a pregnancy would rarely reach term—childbirth is always risky, and so when a pregnant woman dies, or when the baby is born sickly, too weak to even suckle and succumbs, no one thinks twice about it. It's just the way it is.

"Yes, children of such pairing can and do survive," he nodded to Ainiaan. "But each birth is risky, as you now realize—as I realized too late—and subsequent births dramatically increase that risk." He heaved a sigh, said, "But fortunately for you, Turan and the baby, you realized it in time—and speaking of... it *is* time." He rose and started for the door and as I hastily followed suit, he turned back and grabbed my wrist. "Can you do exactly as I tell you without question?"

I glanced at the hold he had me then met his gaze.

He tightened his grip, gave my arm a shake for emphasis. "I ask again, Arri, will you do exactly as I say without question?"

I glanced sidelong at Ainiaan, then back at him. "If I do, can you save her?"

"Yes."

"Then I will do exactly as you say—"

"I'll hold you to it." He let go and opened the door. "Ainiaan, you know what to do." Then to me, "Come—it's not too late, but it will take both of us." He hurried down the passageway towards Turan's apartments; I followed on his heels, suddenly fearful of what, in my haste, I'd agreed to.

He cautiously opened the door, stepped inside, then turned and put his finger to his lips: Turan was indeed asleep and her face, reflecting the glow of the nearby fire, at first appeared relaxed but as we stood there, watching, I saw her mouth tighten, her hands, which had been held loosely across her belly, suddenly tightened, wrists arching in response and she groaned, softly.

I started around Mabog, but he grasped my arm, jerked me back, then again put his finger to his lips and motioned for me to remain exactly where I was.

I nodded, reluctantly.

He walked over to the bed, knelt beside it, and reaching out, lightly touched her arm. Turan stirred; her eyes opened.

"Turi?"

"Mabog...?"

"I've brought Arri."

She stared at him for a moment, as if not believing him. Then at his encouraging smile, looked past him as I stepped out of the door alcove, my armor glittering in the warm firelight that filled the room. She smiled, murmured, "You came back."

I knelt beside Mabog. "I told you I would."

"I thought I was dreaming."

I touched her cheek. Startled by how just clammy she felt, I couldn't help but glance worriedly at Mabog.

"It's time, Turi," he murmured. "The baby cannot wait any longer. Arri will carry you."

She fixed her suddenly frightened eyes on me and I forced what I hoped was a reassuring smile.

"Come." He rose, motioning for me to pick her up.

I carefully eeled my arms under her then got back to my feet, taking her with me.

She rested her head against my armored shoulder as we started out of the room, Mabog leading the way, back to his quarters, and then into another room, the one he had once told me was his surgery. There we found Ainiaan waiting for us, busily setting out wicked looking tools on a spindly-legged tray.

"Place her there." He motioned to the very same table upon which I'd sat after my asinine frolic in the snow—the same place, I now realized, that I'd overheard Turan tell Rasaben she was carrying my child, the same place I'd silently begged her to choose the child, to let *me* die. Now I fully understood why she could not make that choice.

I did as he asked and carefully, very carefully, lowered her onto the cold, hard slab.

She winced as her body came into full contact with it and I had to fight the urge to pick her up again, hold her in my arms.

She stared up at me and smiled tightly.

I clutched her hand, kissed her on the forehead, the lips, all the while painfully aware of Ainiaan and Mabog fussing around us, of him carefully slipping a small tube into her arm, of Turan's breathing becoming deeper, of her eyes taking on a dull cast.

"Save the child," she whispered thickly.

"Save both!" I snarled sidelong at Mabog.

"It's all right, Arri," she whispered in a voice so faint I could barely hear her.

I leaned close and stroking her hair whispered hoarsely in her ear, *"I love you—I do! Turi, please, please don't die! I simply could not bear it if you died."*

Her eyes flickered briefly back to life and she mumbled, "I love you too," and then her eyelids fluttered and closed and the breath seemed to come out of her.

I looked up at Mabog, horrified and reached for my gladius as Ainiaan hastily stepped between us. *"You—!"*

"I've only put her to sleep, Arri," he replied hastily. "She's all right… I swear to you! Now, come, assist us. We don't have much time." He leaned around me and pressed a small knob on the wall.

A moment later a disembodied male voice answered: "Yes, my lord?"

"Get Boian up here—*hurry!*"

I stared, wide-eyed at the wall, then at Mabog. Before I could ponder the idea of a talking wall, he said to me, "Boian's been a midwife often enough she knows exactly what to do—but we'll still need your help." He began to cut Turan's clothing from her, pulling the rich fabric away, exposing her distended belly. "I must surgically remove the child—do you understand me?"

I nodded, dumbly. I'd seen the procedure a few times—military surgeons performing the operation on women caught in the violence of battle, as a desperate grab to save lives, more often than not killing both woman and child. It was butchery; there was no other word for it and now Mabog was about to perform the same butchery on Turan, on *my* child.

"Remember your promise," Ainiaan said, drawing my gaze.

"What will you have me do?" I asked tightly.

"Prepare a place for the baby," she replied cryptically.

I looked around, at a complete loss as to what that could possibly mean.

The two seemed utterly unaware of my bewilderment as Mabog and Ainiaan carefully peeled away Turan's clothing, leaving her painfully naked on the table.

I couldn't help but shift uncomfortably, embarrassed for her—appalled at what I'd done to her once beautiful body. I'd never seen a naked woman this far along, never considered the price women paid to bring a new life into the world and I suddenly felt terribly guilty for all the lives I'd taken in such a careless fashion.

Next thing I knew Boian was at my side, gently pushing me away.

I stumbled back, just enough to give her room and stood there, helpless to do anything but watch.

Then I realized there was something I could do—beyond staying out of everyone's way.

I knelt next to Turan's shoulder and entwined my fingers with hers, and leaning close whispered in her ear: *"I love you, Turi... don't leave me, I beg you,"* then I pressed my forehead against her cheek and tightened my grip on her limp fingers, forcing myself to focus on her breathing rather than what Mabog, Ainiaan and Boian were about.

Once I heard Boian call my name, ask if I was all right—I somehow managed a slight nod, worried if I didn't answer she'd turn her full attention to me rather than keep it on Turan, and twice I felt Ainiaan's tiny fingers lightly grasp my arm before she returned to her grisly task—

A loud and decidedly irate outcry drew my startled gaze just in time for me to see Mabog hand Boian a squirming, blood-covered infant. He cried again, a feeble, yet incensed cry as Mabog cut the umbilical cord.

"Sire," Boian whispered, bumping me with her knee. "I need your assistance."

Whether she truly did or it was a way of distracting me I don't know. As she turned away from the table and Turan's gaping belly, I somehow managed to get back to my feet and follow as she hurried over to a basin someone—certainly not me—had prepared.

She placed the baby in the basin, then grabbed a nearby pitcher and poured warm water over him.

He continued to protest, loudly, as tiny fists pummeled the air.

I did as she bade me to do, mutely handing her cloths to wipe the blood from him as I kept glancing over my shoulder at Turan's seemingly lifeless body.

"Here, sire—you hold him while I help Lord Mabog and Lady Ainiaan." With that she pushed a wiggling bundle of cloth and baby into my armored chest then grabbed my hands and wrapped them around him. "Don't you be dropping him."

I reflexively tightened my hold.

"And don't be squeezing him to death either!"

I tried to push the baby back into her trained hands, but she refused; instead she readjusted my hold, placing one palm beneath the baby's head, the other cradling his backside. "There... see? Nothing to it."

She left me there, holding this crying infant—*my son*, red-faced and wrinkled and with a very irate look about him, as if he'd only just realized I was his father and he was not particularly pleased by this revelation.

I looked up, hoping Ainiaan, Mabog or Boian would notice I was utterly panicked by this tiny, delicate creature, only to see Mabog putting the finishing touches on a very neat line of stitches across Turan's still swollen and now hideously discolored belly, while Ainiaan and Boian busied themselves gathering up the scattered remains of her clothing and tossing them aside, out from underfoot.

I stepped closer, momentarily forgetting my fear of what I was holding. "Is she… going to be all right?" I asked, my voice having gone very thin.

Mabog looked up, briefly then his expression hardened. "Are you going to pass out?"

Boian wheeled around, expertly grabbed the baby from my hands just as my knees begin to buckle.

I didn't pass out—I swear I didn't. I did, however, somehow end up seated on the floor at Boian's feet.

She stared down at me, shook her head and sighed, "I can't carry you both, young sire, so get your butt up off the ground." With that she walked out of the small surgery and into an adjoining room—the very room in which I'd awakened, months before, to the sound of my heart beating from a box on the wall.

I no sooner managed to get myself back to my feet when Mabog said, "Arri?" He was still standing over Turan but she was now draped in a heavy blanket.

"We need to move her, just into the next room—she'll be more comfortable there."

I nodded, started for her, but he grabbed my arm. "I think it best if I call someone else to carry her—"

"I'll call for Hanni." Ainiaan reached for the mysterious knob on the wall.

"No," I said, my voice not sounding like mine at all. "I'll… I'll do it."

Mabog looked me up and down, doubtful. "You'd seriously injure her if you were to stumble, or worse, pass out again."

"I didn't—I mean," I amended, "I won't." With that I carefully drew her utterly limp body into my arms. I wanted to believe she was alive, wanted to believe I was feeling her faint breath on my face, but she was so limp, so deathly pale, so… seemingly lifeless I wasn't sure what to believe.

Mabog wrapped his hand around my elbow. "Come along." He guided me into the room, over to the bed Ainiaan had prepared some time before; I carefully placed Turan on the soft mattress then reluctantly stepped back—in fact was none too gently elbowed aside—to again watch helpless as Mabog, Ainiaan and Boian fussed over her.

The baby was safely ensconced in a wicker basket not far away; I could see him feebly kicking but at least he'd stopped crying. The same could not be said for me. My cheeks were wet, my throat was wet, my undertunic was soaked.

Dammit! I angrily wiped my hand across my face, smearing my cheeks with Turan's blood, but the tears kept flowing, unabated. I wanted to leave, to go someplace and collect myself, but I dared not. I'd promised Mabog I would do exactly as he said, and he had not said I could leave.

So I sat down beside the baby, borrowed a corner of his cloth wrappings to wipe my face and throat, then bracing my back against the wall, dropped my chin onto my chest and closed my eyes; I'd done nothing, absolutely nothing, yet I was utterly exhausted and still very, very shaky—

A hand gripped my shoulder. "Arri...?"

I flinched and jerked my head up. Mabog leaned over me, clearly very worried.

My heart quickened in panic. *Is she all right?* I tried to scramble to my feet, but he pushed me back down.

"She's sleeping."

That wasn't what I meant and he knew it.

"When did you last eat?"

I hesitated; in truth I couldn't remember.

"As I thought. My advice: go have something to eat and then get some sleep—use Turi's quarters, that way you'll be left undisturbed."

I glanced past him to the bed, to Turan. Her beautiful chestnut hair now clung to her skull and her skin was deathly, deathly pale, like alabaster. "Tell me truthfully—is she going to live?"

This time his hesitancy was answer enough. I pushed his restraining hand off my shoulder and lurched unsteadily to my feet. "I'll eat and sleep later." Then I noticed the baby and its wicker basket were gone. *What—?*

"Boian has him to wet nurse. He's a fine, healthy son, Arri—a little small, but that's to be expected for one birthed before he was fully ready."

I nodded dumbly as I walked over to Turan. I cautiously knelt beside her and gathered her cool hands in mine.

"I'd strongly advise you get some food into you, along with some rest—you fainted, you realize that?"

"I didn't faint—I don't faint at the sight of blood!"

He placed his hand on my shoulder, drawing my incensed stare. "I don't doubt that, not in your line of work. But you did pass out, which says to me you need to get some food into you."

Ainiaan added, "It's true, Arri—remember this morning? Your stomach was growling so loud—"

"I'm staying right here," I interrupted, shifting my gaze back to Turan's gaunt face. "I'll eat later."

"I assumed you'd say that." He gave me a pat on the shoulder. "I'll have the servants bring you something to eat, all right? Promise me you'll eat, sleep if you can—you won't be doing anyone any favors, least of all Turi if you don't."

I nodded, reluctantly, even though I wasn't the least bit hungry or sleepy.

"Good." He gave my shoulder a squeeze. "Ainiaan and I will be right next door—call us if you need us."

I nodded and he started to leave, started to follow Ainiaan back to his private quarters, then he abruptly turned back. "If she lives through the night, her chances greatly improve, with each passing hour her chances improve—"

"Why didn't she tell me…?" I asked as I reached out and ran my finger down her clammy cheek.

"Perhaps she didn't want you to know—"

"She believed I didn't care," I replied, then softer, "I didn't think I did, either—now… it's too late."

Mabog's hand again came to rest on my shoulder and he gave it a fatherly squeeze. "Talk to her, son. She knows you're here, with her. Turi's a lot stronger than you think. Give her a reason to live and she will. I've done all I can for now."

He let go and I listened to his retreating footfalls, then heard him and Ainiaan whispering, heard her tell him he needed to follow his own advice and him easing himself back down into a chair with an exhausted sigh. Until that instant it hadn't occurred to me that they'd done all the work—I'd done nothing but be worse than useless. I wanted to tell them I was sorry, I wanted to tell them I was grateful for what they'd done, but as I turned my head towards the open doorway, I felt Turan's fingers twitch.

I leaned close, stroked her clammy face, murmured, *"Turi?"* I kissed her on the forehead, on the cheek. *"Turi, I'm here."*

If she could hear me, I saw no sign. So I settled down, uncomfortable as I was, but I dared not move for fear if I let go of her, even for an instant, she'd let go too.

Arri...?

I jerked awake, jerked my head up then, realizing where I was, I glanced at Turan. She looked no different than she had, hours before: still deathly pale, still clammy to the touch. I decided I'd dreamt it; in my exhaustion I'd heard what I so desperately wanted to hear, her voice, calling to me.

Arri?

I stared at her, wide-eyed and replied voicelessly, *Turan?*

Arri... where are we?

Now I was sure; I wasn't dreaming. *In Mabog's surgery—*

Have you been hurt?

I could the feel the panic gathering behind her weak voice. *No—Turi, you're a mother—he's beautiful!*

Our son?

Yes.

I gave birth? But... I was still more than a month away—

He had other ideas.

She was silent for a moment. *Mule-headed, just like his father.*

I chuckled, softly, touched her face again, fearful that maybe I was still dreaming, but her eyes opened, slowly and at first unfocused. I glanced over my shoulder, intent on calling for Mabog.

"Arri...?"

Her voice drew my gaze.

"Are you really here?"

I kissed her then as I straightened up, wincing as my stiffened muscles rebelled, she looked at me. Her eyes narrowed. "Why are you sitting on the floor, and in your armor?"

"You were hogging the bed."

That seemed to confuse her. So she looked around and seemed to find herself. "How long have I been here?"

I shrugged, rubbing my bloodshot eyes. "Not sure. Mabog felt we couldn't wait—"

"And the baby—you've seen him?"

I grinned proudly. "I *held* him."

"And he survived?"

I stared at her, my pleased grin evaporating. Then seeing her faint smile, I responded with one of my own. "Boian showed me how to hold him."

She briefly lifted her head again, clearly an enormous effort. "Where is he?"

"With her—he needed to nurse. He's a healthy boy—Mabog says so."

She closed her eyes. For a moment I thought she'd lapsed back into sleep, but as I carefully eased my hand out from under her head she looked up at me again. "You're got blood on your face—have you been fighting?"

I touched my cheek, smiled. "It's yours."

Her lips opened, closed, then she said, "I'm cold—lie with me."

"Are you sure...?"

"I'm cold, truly. Keep me warm—or get me another blanket."

"Like hell." I disentangled my fingers from hers, rose and managed to shed my armor in record time and once naked I lifted the blanket and cautiously eased myself down beside her. The bed was never meant for two, but somehow we managed by me wrapping myself around her, avoiding her belly. She *was* cold—like ice.

She snuggled down against me and kissed my throat. "You're so warm..."

I kissed her on the forehead, murmured, "Go back to sleep."

It didn't take long, a few minutes at most, before I heard her breathing deepen and slow. I drew her a little more tightly against me as I heard someone enter the room—Mabog I assumed, possibly Ainiaan or Boian—and walk softly over to the bed only stand over us. I felt another heavy blanket settle over us—a welcome addition as my back was entirely exposed, my concern was for Turan's comfort, not mine.

A hand then lightly touched my shoulder and I looked up. It was Mabog and he didn't look like he'd slept. He smiled wearily, murmured, "It's morning," then gave my shoulder a squeeze and quietly withdrew.

— XX —

Our son, Neshoue, as Turan named him, choosing her father's name with my blessing, was surprisingly healthy for one of mixed parentage and born prematurely, with a very healthy set of lungs. While I'd moved back into Turan's chambers after his birth, I often found myself longing for the relative quiet of the camp. I'd long ago become habituated to the amazing repertoire of bodily sounds emitted by sleeping men—but a crying baby was a novel and not altogether happy experience for me, especially when I was awakened every few minutes—or so it seemed—by some new and unreasonable demand.

Turan was still too ill to attend to him, bed-bound on orders of Mabog; so the job fell upon Boian and Ainiaan during the day, and upon me—and a wet nurse—at night. After spending all day in the field with my soldiers, to return after dark, bone-weary and often too tired to eat, only to be repeatedly roused from my sleep by this creature was at times almost more than I could bear.

But daylight brought me no respite: my soldiers, in particular Aetius, never wasted an opportunity to poke fun at my new profession of nursemaid. I pretended to be angry, embarrassed, but in truth I valued the time I had with my son, even if those times fell in the middle of the night when everyone else was deep in their well-earned slumber. Time was short—all too soon I'd be leaving, with no guarantee I'd be coming back. While I knew he wouldn't remember me if I in fact failed to return, I'd remember him, remember these moments for as long as I breathed.

I also savored every minute I had with Turan, again, knowing all too well the dangers that lay ahead, fearful of leaving her while she was still so frail, even more concerned that the unspoken worries she carried about me might too much for her to bear.

I wanted her to know, for Neshoue to know, how I felt about them, what I'd say to my grown son if fate chose to make that conversation impossible. Most all I wanted my son to know me, even if he never remembered meeting me.

So one evening I retrieved the vellum and pot of gall-ink from my command tent and brought them to Turan's chambers. Late into the night, and every night from then on, while Turan slept and Neshoue was cradled in my lap, I added to what I'd already written, each passing day adding to a sense of urgency that forced me to stay up later, sometimes all night, fearful I'd run out of time before I ran out of what I needed to say.

At times I wrote to them as if I was speaking to them, telling Neshoue to obey Turan, to listen to Hanni and no matter what he chose to do with his life, to always make his mother proud. To Turan I wrote my true feelings for her, that I did love her, that if I had one wish it would be that this whole enterprise would be suddenly called off, that a lasting peace would be forged and I wouldn't have to leave her to fight another man's war, that I was weary of fighting, weary of killing and seeing my friends, my men die.

I also continued to commit to vellum my experiences, not as some vanity, but because I truly believed that perhaps some worth might be drawn from them, that by entrusting my life story, my memories to something more tangible, more permanent than flesh and blood, I too might derive some measure of peace by putting everything in order, and yes, finally allow myself a measure of pride in a life that while far from exemplary, was truly by anyone's standards, extraordinary...

"Arri?"

I looked up to find Felix standing in the open doorway of Turan's apartments.

"I knocked—"

"Is it time?" I asked, brushing aside his apology; I hadn't even heard the door turn on its hinges.

"Soon—still getting some last-minute gear loaded up." He smiled, nodded at what I held in my hands. "Finished?"

"Almost." I looked down at the vellum, at the words that flowed across its surface, at the sum of my life. But it was more than that. *A lot more.* "Think he'll learn from my mistakes?"

"Possibly, but he'll make his own. That's what makes us who we are."

I glanced back at the bed, at Turan and nestled in her arms, Neshoue. "I wish I could be here, see him grow up."

"If the gods favor us, so it will be."

That had been one of Felix's favorite comebacks when truth was too painful to voice.

"I want to warn him, Felix, I want to warn humanity—tell them we aren't alone, but will the Tuatha allow them to hear, and if they do, will humanity listen?" I asked, desperate for an answer I knew he could not give.

"We can hope, Arri. We can hope. And if anyone can make the Tuatha, make humanity see sense, it's you." With that he stepped back, into the torch-lit hallway. "I'll wait for you outside, but don't be too long. Sun's almost up."

I nodded, watched him turn and walk away, then I took a deep breath, dipped the quill into the inkpot and smoothing out the vellum, picked up where I'd left off: *But understand this: there are places we should not venture; there are peoples we should not confront with our military might... and most of all, there are beings we dare not offend if we, and our Empire, is to survive.*

To all who read this, I implore you—heed my warning.

I lifted the quill, watched the ink dry, then carefully rolling the vellum, I rose and placed it next to the others, on the table beside Turan's bed. It was all there, my life from beginning to... *end.* There was no more to be said.

Time to go.

I donned my armor, sheathed my gladius and gathered up my helmet, all in total silence as I didn't want to risk waking Neshoue. Turan too was fast asleep, her beautiful face completely relaxed. I thought about leaving them as they were, I even turned to the open door as I carefully arranged my chest harness, my phalerae—stalling the inevitable.

I'd never thought to ask Taskim how long my legion was expected to be gone—a year? A decade? *More?* I had no idea how far we'd travel, how long it would take, or even how we'd reach this neutral, Earth-like planet he'd spoken of—until this moment such questions had never seemed particularly relevant. Now these terrible uncertainties gnawed at me and I knew I couldn't leave without saying good-bye.

Steeling myself, I tucked my helmet under my arm and walked back to the bed, knelt and kissed Turan on the forehead.

She stirred, opened her eyes and smiled sleepily up at me.

I stroked her hair, whispered, *"It's time,"* and saw her eyes widen and instantly fill with tears. I kissed Neshoue on the head, lightly, touched his tiny fist with my finger and found myself marveling yet again at how small he was, how delicate he was, and how much I already missed him, how much I already missed Turan.

I tugged the snakestone from under my mailed tunic and seeing it, Turan managed a smile. I murmured, "I'll always be your faithful servant, m'lady." With that I brought it to my lips then slipped it back under my tunic.

"Come back to me."

"If it's in my power to do so, I will." I kissed her on the lips, the forehead, let my fingers have one last feel of Neshoue's downy head, then I rose. I turned and walked to the doorway, but there I hesitated and glanced back to find her watching me, eyes aglitter.

I donned my helmet and as I tied the cheek-pieces in place, I said, "While I'm gone, m'lady, I beg you, teach my son to read."

www.ingramcontent.com/pod-product-compliance
Lightning Source LLC
Chambersburg PA
CBHW050021030726
47506CB00001B/55